Stephen White is a clinical psychologist and the author of several *New York Times* bestsellers. He lives in Colorado with his wife and son.

Visit his website at www.authorstephenwhite.com

Also by Stephen White

The Best Revenge
Warning Signs
The Program
Cold Case
Manner of Death
Critical Conditions
Remote Control
Harm's Way
Higher Authority
Private Practices
Privileged Information

STEPHEN WHITE OMNIBUS

Blinded
Missing Persons

Stephen White

sphere

SPHERE

This omnibus edition first published in Great Britain in 2007 by Sphere

Previously published separately:
Blinded first published in the United States in 2004 by Bantam Dell, a division of Random House, Inc.
First published in Great Britain in 2004 by Time Warner Books
Published as a Time Warner Paperback in 2004
Copyright © Stephen White 2004
Missing Persons first published in the United States in 2005 by Dutton, a member of the Penguin Group (USA) Inc.
First published in Great Britain in 2005 by Time Warner Books
Paperback edition published by Warner Books in 2006
Copyright © Stephen White 2005

A CIP catalogue record for this book is available from the British Library.

ISBN: 978-0-7515-4017-8

Papers used by Sphere are natural, recyclable products made from wood grown in sustainable forests and certified in accordance with the rules of the Forest Stewardship Council.

Printed and bound in Great Britain by Mackays of Chatham Ltd.
Paper supplied by Hellefoss AS, Norway

Sphere
An imprint of
Little, Brown Book Group
Brettenham House
Lancaster Place
London WC2E 7EN

A Member of the Hachette Livre Group of Companies

www.littlebrown.co.uk

Blinded

to Kate Miciak
for your vision, and your friendship

ACKNOWLEDGMENTS

Thanks to Jane Davis, Sharon Stein, Stan Galansky, Chuck Lepley, Elyse Morgan, Al Silverman, Patricia and Jeffrey Limerick, and Nancy Hall.

Enduring gratitude goes to my editor, Kate Miciak, and to my agent, Lynn Nesbit.

Rose, Xan, and my mother, Sara White Kellas—after a dozen of these I'm running out of ways to say thank you. You leave my heart full.

Every love's the love before
in a duller dress

—Dorothy Parker

PROLOGUE

SAM

Every cop knows the taste and the odor that assault the senses when tenderness collides with evil. It's a baby coddled in a bassinet in a fume-filled meth shack. It's the fractured face of someone's grandma after a purse-snatcher has done his thing. It's a pregnant woman bloodied and dead on the floor.

I'd been a cop a long time. I knew the aroma. And I knew the taste.

I did.

It may sound goofy, but I also believed that on good days I could smell the spark before I smelled the fire and I could taste the poison before it reached my lips. On good days I could stand firm between tenderness and evil. On good days I could make a difference.

What the heck is it about a woman sleeping? Okay, a woman who isn't your wife of double-digit years.

A woman was sleeping right beside me, no more

than half a foot away. The spice of her perfume tickled the back of my throat, and the fire from inside her radiated right through my clothes. Yeah, I was paying attention to a thousand things I should have been ignoring. The intimacy of her breathing. The edginess of her eyes darting below their lids. The pure power of the rise and fall of her chest. The vulnerability of her slightly parted legs. They were all way too distracting to me.

Guilt about it all? A little maybe. Not that much. Not given what had happened already.

Still, I should have been looking in the other direction, out the window. I should have been watching for signs of the inevitable collision—for the arrival of the evil—because I knew that it was coming. I did. I could taste it in one tiny spot on the back of my tongue. Left side, all the way back where an oral surgeon having a very bad day had once hacked out one of my wisdom teeth.

I allowed myself a last greedy inhale of her tenderness—just one more taste—before I forced my attention outside. Had I missed something? Didn't look like it, no. But when I cracked open the window, I instantly detected tenderness in the air out there, too. Outside right on in, the tenderness was being swept along on the glorious aroma of a roasting Thanksgiving turkey.

I even thought I knew the bird. It was a big tom, twenty-two pounds. Traditional stuffing like my mom used to make.

Tenderness in here. Tenderness out there.

So where was the evil?

Where?

I could taste the turkey as though it were already

on my lips, and I could taste her spice as though her sleepy head were resting on my chest. But I could also taste that tiny spot of evil on the back of my tongue.

She moaned just a little.

Inside, I did, too.

ONE

ALAN

Nine-fifteen on Monday morning. My second patient of the day.

Gibbs Storey hadn't changed much in the ten years since I'd last seen her. If anything, she appeared to be even more of a model of physical perfection than she'd been in the mid-nineties. I guessed yoga, maybe Pilates. Her impeccable complexion hadn't suddenly become pocked with acne or ravaged by psoriasis, nor had her high cheekbones dropped to mortal levels. Her blond hair was shorter but no less radiant, and her eyes were the same sky blue I remembered. The absence of any wrinkles radiating around them caused me to wonder about a recent Botox poke, but I quickly surmised that Gibbs's fair skin would probably never be susceptible to the tracks of age. She'd be in possession of some magic gene, and she'd be immune.

She'd always had beauty karma. Along with popularity karma. And the ever-elusive charm karma.

She didn't have marriage karma, though.

I'd first met Gibbs and her husband, Sterling, when they came to see my clinical psychology partner, Diane Estevez, and me for therapy for their troubled relationship. Diane and I saw them conjointly—a quaint, almost anachronistic therapeutic modality that involved pairing a couple of patients with a couple of therapists in the same room at the same time—for only three sessions. Ironically, with therapy fees being what they are and managed care being what it is, Diane and I hadn't done a conjoint case together since that final session with Gibbs and Sterling Storey.

After they'd abruptly canceled their fourth session and departed Boulder—"Dr. Gregory, Sterling got that job he wanted in L.A.! Isn't that wonderful!" Gibbs informed me breathlessly in the voicemail she'd left along with her profound thanks for how helpful we'd been—neither Diane nor I had heard a word from either of them. That was true, at least, until Gibbs called, said she was back in town, and asked me for an individual appointment.

Gibbs's call requesting the individual appointment had come ten days before, on a Friday. My few free slots the following week didn't meet any of her needs, so we'd settled on the Monday morning time. At the time she had accepted the week-and-a-half delay graciously.

In the interim between her call and her first appointment, I'd pulled her thin file from a box in the storage area that was stuffed with the records of old, inactive cases and examined my sparse notes. The few lines of intake and progress reports that I'd scrawled after the conjoint sessions told me less than did my memory, but I didn't need copious notes to remind me that Diane and I hadn't been all that helpful to Gibbs and Sterling.

Couples therapy is not individual therapy with two people. It is a whole different animal, more closely akin to group therapy with a radioactive dyad. Issues within couples aren't subjected to the simple arithmetic of doubling; problems seem to be susceptible to the more severe forces of logarithmic multiplication. Therapeutic resistance in couples work, especially conjoint couples work, isn't just the familiar dance between therapist and patient. Instead, a well-choreographed routine between husband and wife takes place alongside every interaction between either client and either therapist. Each marital partner knows his or her steps like an experienced member of a ballroom dancing pair. She retreats as he aggresses. He surely demurs as she swoons.

A couples therapist needs to learn everyone's moves before he or she can be maximally effective.

My memory of the Storeys' conjoint treatment was that Diane and I had only just begun to recognize their peculiar tango when they terminated the therapy and moved to California.

The first conjoint session had been a typical "what brings you in for help" introductory. "Communication" was the buzzword of the day in the care and feeding of relationships, and that's the culprit the Storeys identified as the reason they had entered into our care. Each maintained that they desired assistance "communicating" more effectively with the other. He was, perhaps, a little less certain than she of his motivation.

Neither Diane nor I had believed either of them.

No, we didn't entertain the possibility that they were out-and-out lying to us—at least I didn't; I could never be a hundred percent certain about Diane—but rather we were waiting for them to approach the revelation that they might be lying to themselves, or to each other, about their reason for being in our offices. "Communication problems" was a socially acceptable entrée to treatment—an acceptable thing to tell their friends.

But Diane and I weren't at all convinced at the time that it was the reason we were seeing the Storeys.

"Hi, Dr. Gregory," Gibbs said as she settled on the chair in my office for her first individual appointment. Her greeting wasn't coy exactly, but it wasn't not-coy exactly, either. "Long time," she added.

Her fine hair was pulled back into a petite ponytail. She smiled in a way that almost dared me not to notice how together she looked.

I nodded noncommittally. My practiced chin dip could have been measured in millimeters.

"I'm sure you're wondering why I'm here," she said.

Another microscopic nod on my part. Most days while doing my work as a psychologist, if I were paid by the word I'd go home a pauper. But Gibbs was right, I was wondering why she'd come back to see me after so many years. I had a guess—I was wagering that she'd divorced Sterling and had moved back to Boulder to start a new life. It was a scary journey for most people. Me? I was going to be the tour guide.

That was my guess.

"You remember Sterling? My husband?"

Husband? Okay, I was wrong. The Storeys were separated then, not divorced.

I spoke, but since it was Monday morning I failed to assemble a complete sentence. "Yes, of course" was all I said.

Gibbs raised her fingertips to her lips and leaned forward as though she were whispering a profanity and was afraid her grandmother would overhear. She said, "I think he murdered a friend of ours in Laguna Beach."

Okay, I was wrong twice.

TWO

The previous weekend.

I decided that I couldn't stand watching her struggle with the damn halo.

It just wasn't natural.

She hated it. And even for something as unearthly as a halo, it didn't look right on her. Maybe it was the size—did the thing really have to be that big?—or maybe it was the way it seemed to block her off from the world. Was that the intent? And tight spaces? No way. If she could squeeze through a narrow pathway headfirst at all, she ended up making enough of a clanging racket that she emerged hanging her haloed head in shame. I wasn't sure exactly what she hated most about wearing the damn thing, but I was absolutely sure that she hated it.

Still, I'm a psychologist not only by training but also by demeanor, and I was determined to help her live with the halo. Taking it off wasn't an option.

We had our orders.

I wondered, why not transparent material instead of opaque? Wouldn't that be an improvement? Maybe a rearview mirror would be nice. Or . . . wouldn't the plastic cone be more tolerable if it were just smaller?

And there was always duct tape. Couldn't I create some alternative with duct tape?

The ultimate solution hit me at a quarter to three in the morning in the utter darkness that divides Saturday from Sunday as I was soothing my year-old daughter back to sleep on the upholstered rocker in her room.

A paw umbrella.

I had to figure out a way to make Emily a paw umbrella. If I could shield her paw from her mouth, then she wouldn't have to wear a bizarre plastic Elizabethan collar to shield her mouth from her paw. A little over a week before, her veterinarian had excised a basal cell carcinoma from the top of her front left paw. Now the dressing was off so that the excision could be exposed to the air. Emily's only job was to let the wound heal without the aid of her big tongue and her copious saliva, a state of affairs absolutely in contradiction to a Bouvier's instincts, which dictated that her drool was the finest salve on the planet.

The halo effectively prohibited her from licking the wound. But the bizarre collar was making our dog morose. A paw umbrella was the obvious alternative. How hard could that be?

I explained my project to my friend Sam Purdy, who'd come over for a late-morning bike ride. We were sitting at the kitchen table in my Spanish Hills home. The Thanksgiving decorations embellishing all the stores in Boulder and the naked trees below us in the valley at the foot of the Rockies screamed late autumn, but the day promised to read more like late spring. Bright sun, clear skies, gentle breezes, and the guarantee of an afternoon in the seventies.

"I decided—I think it was sometime around four o'clock this morning—that I needed to use rigid foam to make the doughnut piece," I said. Sam didn't answer me. I thought he was trying to swallow a belch. The surprising part was that he was trying to swallow it; Sam didn't usually allow social decorum to interfere in his digestive processes.

I proceeded to trace a circle about five inches in diameter and then began cutting a hole in the gardener's kneeling pad that I'd swiped from my neighbor's barn. "It has to hold its shape," I explained. "This foam will be perfect."

"Lauren won't care that you're cutting up her stuff?" Sam knew me well enough to know that if it had to do with gardening, it couldn't belong to me.

"It's not Lauren's. I stole it from Adrienne's shed. But even if it were Lauren's, she wouldn't care. It's for a good cause." Sam was a Boulder police detective, so I was demonstrating a modicum of trust by copping to a misdemeanor before lunch.

Adrienne was my urologist neighbor and the keeper of a sizable vegetable garden. Our unofficial deal was this: For the right to steal goodies from her plot at will, each August, using her tomatoes, I made a year's supply of fresh tomato sauce and roasted tomato salsa for her freezer.

Her tomatoes and basil and chiles, my kitchen labor. Communal living at its purest. I figured that the foam rubber I'd swiped would somehow become part of the annual accounting.

I cut a Bouvier-ankle-sized hole in the center of the disk of foam and then sliced from the center to the outside so I could close the contraption around Emily's lower leg like a handcuff or, more accurately, pawcuff. The thing I'd created was the size of a DVD, more or less, but the hole in the center was larger, more like the circle in the middle of an old 45 rpm record.

"Is Adrienne home?" Sam asked.

I was so distracted by my veterinary appliance manufacturing that I almost failed to notice his fingers pressing up under his rib cage. Almost.

"Why?" I asked. Adrienne was a good neighbor—she lived with her son in a big house across the dirt lane—and a great friend, but what I suspected was more germane to this discussion was the fact that she was also a fine urologist who had once treated Sam for a kidney stone.

"Nothing," he said. "I was just wondering."

I began laying out some rigid plastic craft strips that I'd swiped from Lauren's craft cupboard. Lauren wasn't particularly craft-y; supplies tended to age indefinitely once they made it into crafts storage. There was some Elmer's glue in there that I suspected dated back to Jimmy Carter's administration.

The plastic strips I chose were about two inches by four. To accomplish my design, I'd figured I would need to cover about 270 degrees of the foam circle with the plastic strips. With a pair of kitchen shears I began to turn my circle into a rough octagon to accommodate the attachment of the flat strips.

Sam rotated his neck. Up. Side to side. Back. His fingertips disappeared below his ribs again.

"Nothing?" I asked. "You sure?"

"I'm thinking I may be developing another damn stone."

I tried not to act obvious as I began using filament tape to attach the plastic strips to the octagon of foam, but I was watching Sam, too. Sam was usually stressed out, he was chronically overweight, he frequently ignored the diet that Adrienne had recommended after his first stone, and he didn't get enough exercise unless I dragged him along on an occasional bike ride somewhere. All in all, he was a prime candidate for a return trip down the river of agony that carried sharp little stones from the kidneys to the hellish port of *Oh my God*!

"I'm sorry. Does it feel like the last one?" I asked. I'm quite adept at keeping alarm out of my voice. I think I kept the alarm out of my voice.

"Not exactly. But then I've worked hard to repress the memory of the last one. Who knows?"

"Suppress. Not repress. If you have to work hard at it, you're suppressing. Repression is an unconscious act."

He snorted at me and shook his head. "Work on your damn paw umbrella. Don't insult me with your psychobabble."

I used a totally benign please-pass-the-salt voice to inquire, "How is it different this time?"

"I don't know."

He stood up but didn't go anywhere. He craned his chin upward, then side to side.

"Is your neck stiff?"

His face said it was. He added, "I must have slept on it funny."

"Adrienne's already gone for the day. She and Lauren took Jonas and Grace to the zoo in Denver. But I can probably reach her on her cell. Do you want me to give her a call?"

"Nah. I'll be fine. You almost done with that thing?"

I was taping the plastic strips together, sealing the gaps between them with filament tape. I figured any slender gap was a potential escape route for Emily's wily Houdini of a tongue. "Why don't you sit, Sam?"

To my surprise, he did. I noticed beads of sweat dotting his wide forehead like drizzle on a car windshield.

"You don't look too good. Let's bag the bike ride. Why don't I—I don't know, take you somewhere? Go see a doctor. If you're passing a stone, you're going to need some drugs. Given how bad you felt last time, some serious drugs."

"I'll be okay. If it doesn't go away in a minute, I'll take some Tylenol or something."

Yeah, that should help. And when you're done, I thought, *why don't you go put out a forest fire by pissing on it?*

He grimaced and twisted his neck some more. "Put that thing on her. I want to see how it works."

Taping the device to Emily's left front paw proved more challenging than manufacturing it had been. She didn't fight me; the halo was so humiliating to her that a multicolored Clydesdale-hoof-shaped paw umbrella was little additional insult to her doggie fashion sensibilities. I needed two different adhesive tapes from the first-aid kit and then had to reinforce the harness with an astonishing quantity of filament tape. But the thing ultimately held together and stayed where it was supposed to stay on her lower leg.

I told Emily to stand.

She didn't. She sighed.

I took the damn plastic halo off her collar and told her to stand.

She stood.

The umbrella hung over her wounded paw. The plastic strips stopped half an inch above the floor. Without delay her instincts emerged, and she leaned over to lick her open wound.

She couldn't.

She lay back down to lick her wound.

She couldn't.

She got back up and took a few tentative steps, offering a quick disciplinary nip at our other dog, a miniature poodle named Anvil. Anvil hadn't done anything to warrant the discipline. Emily attempted to discipline him at irregular intervals because she could and, she believed, she should.

Anvil, as always, was unfazed. I'd realized long ago that he didn't recognize discipline in any form.

"You know Jonas? Adrienne's son?" I asked.

Sam grunted in reply.

"He has trouble saying Anvil, so he renamed him, calls him Midgeto. I think it fits, don't you?"

Sam's eyes were shut tight. Apparently so were his ears.

Emily returned her attention to the multicolored umbrella on her paw. She walked in a circle as though she were trying to determine if the thing was really going to stay with her.

After a careful appraisal from multiple angles she

stared at me, gave a little flip of her bearded head, and uttered a familiar, guttural, all-purpose murmur of approval. To the untrained ear, the noise probably sounded like an insincere growl. But since I spoke a little Bouvier, I knew differently.

Rarely in history have members of two different species been so enamored of the same invention. I loved the paw umbrella. Emily, our big Bouvier des Flandres, loved her paw umbrella.

Sam's opinion of the paw umbrella was more difficult to discern.

When I turned back to him to share our joy, I finally realized that he was having a heart attack.

THREE

Not wanting to alarm Sam unnecessarily with my amateur diagnostic assessment, I excused myself, walked then ran to the bedroom phone, and called 911. When I got back to the kitchen, Sam said, "I'm a little better, I think."

I handed him a small handful of baby aspirin. "Chew these, and come lie down on the couch in the living room."

"What are they?"

"For once don't argue with me."

He chewed the aspirin and followed me the short distance from the kitchen table to the sofa in the living room. The hand that had been poking below his rib cage was now pressing firmly at his sternum.

"You called for an ambulance, didn't you?"

I considered lying. But I didn't. I simply nodded.

Anvil—Midgeto—jumped up on the couch and snaked under Sam's arm to spread his lithe body across Sam's lower abdomen. It appeared as though he was determined to be a little canine heating pad.

Emily rested her big head on Sam's thigh.

Sam absently stroked the dogs' fur and said, "You have good dogs."

Sam and I rarely agreed on anything. But we agreed on that.

"Am I having a heart attack?"

"I don't know. I'm afraid you are."

"I don't want to die, Alan."

We agreed on that, too. I didn't want him to die, either.

FOUR

"I think he murdered a friend of ours in Laguna Beach."

I kept my gaze locked on Gibbs. Her words were as provocative as anything I'd heard in a therapy session in quite some time, but I was having a hard time not thinking about Sam.

Less than twenty-four hours earlier the ambulance had taken him to Avista Hospital, which was closest to my house in the hills on the eastern side of the Boulder Valley, not Community Hospital, which was only blocks from his house in the shadow of the Rockies on Boulder's west side. The cardiologist who worked him up in the ER and busted his clot with some cardiac Drano had scheduled an angiogram for the precise hour on Monday morning that I was seeing Gibbs Storey. At the moment when Gibbs told me she suspected her husband of murder, Sam probably already had a puncture hole in his groin and a long catheter snaking up an artery to his heart.

What would Sam, an experienced homicide detective, do in response to Gibbs's revelation, were he sitting here with Gibbs and me? I wasn't sure. If I could have channeled his presence to assist in this interview, I certainly would have.

I could have said, *"Holy shit!"* in response to Gibbs's accusation of her husband, but I didn't.

Or I could've said, *"That doesn't really surprise me,"* because it didn't. Not totally, anyway. Sterling Storey was, like his wife, not only charmed but a charmer. I also suspected that he was a bully. Or more accurately, an intimidator. I'd seen his act up close and personal during one of our conjoint psychotherapy sessions.

As I exhaled, I reminded myself that the fact that Sterling had taken a few cheap verbal shots at Gibbs a decade before didn't mean he was capable of murder.

But I also recalled the razor edge of his glare. The fact that I remembered it at all told me something that I was certain was relevant. I'd witnessed the glare, I think, during the second of our three sessions. Gibbs had said something about . . . God, I couldn't remember what Gibbs had said something about, and Sterling had touched her knee to get her attention and had then frozen her with a look so menacing that I remembered it as though it had happened only yesterday.

Gibbs had backed down like a good hound ordered to heel.

And then she'd changed the subject.

What had the subject been?

I couldn't recall.

In reply to her accusation about Sterling, I could have asked Gibbs, *"Why are you telling me this? Why aren't you at the police station with this information?"* But I knew there would be a reason. Maybe not a good reason, one that might sway me. But there would be a reason, one that would teach me something important about the woman who sat across from me.

I bought time. I crossed my left leg over the right and said, "Why don't you tell me exactly what you're concerned about."

Announcing her suspicion of her husband hadn't robbed Gibbs of any of her composure. Her feet stayed side by side in their fashionable sandals, and the smooth inner surfaces of her knees still touched as though she were intent on keeping a slip of paper clenched between them without dimpling it. Her shoulders were straight enough to please a Marine drill sergeant, and her spine erect enough to parallel a flagpole. She held her hands as though she were waiting for a photographer to finish snapping a glamour shot of her God-knows-how-many-carat engagement ring.

"I don't really even know how to talk about this." She adjusted those lovely hands, moving them to a position as if in prayer, but her fingertips were pointed toward me, not the heavens. "Louise was our friend in California. In Laguna Beach. But . . . it's not just Louise."

It's not just Louise?

"Louise is the one who was murdered?"

"Yes, in 1997. While we were living in Corona Del Mar. She was killed at her apartment on Crescent Bay on Thanksgiving Day. Or nearby, anyway. We'd just finished redoing our cottage. Right from the start the police suspected that her assailant wasn't close to her. They thought the guy who killed her might have known her, you know, casually, but wasn't close to her. She wasn't from there; she was British. But no one has ever been arrested."

We'd just finished redoing our cottage?

"And you think Sterling was involved?"

"Involved? That's a funny word. Well, I think Sterling did it. Who am I kidding? Although I don't want to believe it, I guess I know he did. He had a thing . . . going with her."

"A sexual thing? An affair?"

"Of course."

The string of her earlier words that had initially caught my attention was still bouncing around my head like a Miller moth trapped behind a miniblind. I repeated the words aloud. "Gibbs, what did you mean when you said before, 'It's not just Louise'?"

"This is weird," she said.

Tell me about it, I thought.

"What did that mean, Gibbs? 'It's not just Louise.' What did you mean by that?"

"I don't even know why I said it."

My mind raced ahead of her, but I tried to keep my focus. I decided not to say what was on my mind. Why? What was on my mind was that I didn't believe her most recent denial. Inconsequential to the therapy perhaps, but an important point considering the circumstances.

Things that are unimportant to the progression of therapy may be crucial to the prosecution of a murder.

She clenched her teeth and tried to smile. Maybe she was fighting tears, but as incongruous as it was, I thought she was actually trying to smile.

She raised her hands to her face to cover her

mouth, then took them down again before she said, "You know Sterling, Dr. Gregory. I mean, yes, yes, yes, he has a temper. But could I really be married to a murderer? Or am I nuts?"

Two different questions, I thought.

Two different questions.

Before I conjured up a response, I remembered what it was that Gibbs had said a decade before that had earned her the memorable glare from Sterling.

Sex.

Gibbs had said something about sex.

FIVE

Louise had walked down the path to Crescent Bay from her flat on the cliff above the beach a hundred times. A thousand. She could have dodged the fat ropes of seaweed on the sand in her sleep. From where the shoreline started at the foot of the trail to the beginning of the rough rocks on the north end of the horseshoe cove wasn't more than a few dozen steps. Carrying her old trainers in her hands, she crossed the area in seconds, careful to stay above the high-tide line. The beach had already yielded the day's heat, and the sand that crept up between her toes was cool and dry.

She wondered what he had planned.

Something imaginative, she hoped. God, she needed a man to show some imagination.

That lad in Paris? The Australian? He hadn't been bad. But it was all about the shot for him, not about the setup.

She needed someone to care about the setup, too. The match wasn't just about the goal.

She'd checked her watch before she left her flat. He'd said seven-thirty. She hadn't walked out her door until a quarter to eight. She knew she was worth waiting for. Whatever he had planned, she was worth waiting for.

And she was game.

She checked the Walkman in her hand and adjusted the headphones on her ears, waiting for his next words. His first words had been "Leave it running, now. The silence is part of the mystery. Follow my commands. And trust me. Do what I say."

At the foot of the rocks she brushed the sand off her feet and pulled on her shoes, then scampered up the rocks toward the tide pools. Her favorite pool, the big one that was shaped like Maui, would be covered by the encroaching tide already. She hoped that in the recession between waves—she thought of it as the ocean's inhale—she could maybe steal a quick glance at the cluster of urchins in the southeast corner of the pool.

She loved those urchins, though she couldn't have said why.

"Up toward the pools. Do it without a flashlight, now. No peeking. Let yourself be surprised." The voice in her ears, electronically distorted, made her smile. It was a nice touch.

She wasn't carrying a torch; she didn't need one here any more than she'd need one to find the loo in her flat in the dark. The night wasn't totally black, but even if it were, she knew these rock paths like she knew the cabin of a 747. She could wander these cliffs at any tidal level without a map. She knew the path all the way from Crescent Bay to Emerald Bay. She could do it in a storm if she had to.

"Keep going, my lady. Don't be impatient. You'll

find your reward. Soon, soon, soon." The voice prodded her. "Look up. Look down. Look, look, look."

Finally, she spotted a basket. An old-fashioned picnic basket. High up on a rock shelf, almost above her reach.

She pulled it down, flipped open the lid, and her heart soared just a little.

Meursault. God, she loved Meursault. Fresh gherkins. Pâté. Well, *she thought,* I'm not a vegan tonight.

She was late. But where is he?

She removed the cork from the bottle, poured herself a glass of wine, and nibbled on a gherkin as she watched the fluorescence of the nighttime waves crash higher and higher on the rocks above the pools, closer and closer to her perch.

"Lovely," she said aloud. "Lovely."

"The night will surprise you. Prepare," the recorded voice murmured into her ears.

"It's a good start," she admitted out loud.

Sitting on the sharp edges of the jagged rocks was less than comfortable. She moved to a squatting position and began to wonder how on earth the goal was going to be scored without scarring one of them forever on the rock faces.

She smiled. It will be fun to find out.

"Open your blouse. Now!"

Ooooh. Urgency.

Okay, okay. *Button by button, she did.*

"Don't turn around."

Her chest pounded. She was having trouble catching her breath.

Less than a second later her feet were out from be-

neath her and something sharp and hard was surrounding her neck and her attempts at breathing were thwarted. Totally thwarted.

She struggled at the ligature. It didn't help.

Moments later she didn't even feel the cold chill of the Pacific as she spilled forward into the darkness.

SIX

Patients returning to see me after an extended absence from treatment, like Gibbs Storey, tend to labor under the suspicion that a decade does nothing to alter my recall of the facts of their lives. The truth is that that is not the truth. Since Gibbs and Sterling last left my office on their way to Capistrano or Corona or Laguna or Newport Beach or wherever they ended up, a few hundred new patients had crossed my threshold and told me their tales. That's too many stories for my brain to juggle. Way too many. Scores too many. Sometimes I got the details confused. I would assign faulty facts to a patient or misremember who had died in what year, who had what illness, and who had slept with whom.

So why didn't I just go back to my patient files and refresh my memory?

Because as a general rule I put few facts in my case notes. The more potentially private the fact, the less likely I was to put it on paper. Why? Because doctor-patient confidentiality is not a brick wall that forever separates my knowledge of my patient from the gaze of the judicial system. Confidentiality is actually a brick wall with a few conveniently spaced locked gates. And the courts, not I, hold the keys to those gates. Whatever I wrote down might therefore someday become public. In all my years in clinical practice I hadn't discovered a single reason to volunteer to be a conduit to making the private public.

Consequently, I didn't write much down.

I caught Diane Estevez in our little kitchen about an hour after Gibbs left my office. Diane would remember everything that I'd forgotten about our ancient conjoint treatment of the Storeys. I suspected sometimes when I queried her about such things that Diane made up whatever she didn't actually remember, but in any event, her recall would appear seamless and complete.

"Hey, Alan, how's Sam?"

Although I hadn't had a chance to tell her about Sam's heart attack, I wasn't surprised that she already knew. Diane had sources everywhere. If gossip was an art form, she was the Picasso of our generation.

"He had an angiogram this morning. I'll know more later today when I go visit him."

"Angioplasty, too? Stent?"

"I'm still waiting to hear."

"But it was an MI?"

"Enzymes say yes. They used clot busters."

"Keep me informed."

"Of course, but we both know that you'll probably know his prognosis before his cardiologist does. Guess who I saw this morning?"

Diane was scooping ground coffee into a filter basket. My question caused her to lose count of her tablespoons. She said, "Shit. Tell me."

Dr. Estevez and I had been friends since we'd interned together many years before. Although our practices were independent businesses, we shared the first floor, and the ownership, of a small century-plus-old Victorian that housed our clinical offices on Walnut Street on the edge of downtown Boulder.

"Guess."

"D. B. Cooper?"

An inside joke. "Close," I said. "How about Gibbs Storey?"

She looked at me. "The Dancing Queen?"

Diane had always called Gibbs "the Dancing Queen." I thought the moniker was some obscure reference to the old ABBA song, but I wasn't absolutely certain what the allusion was. I did know that Diane had never been fond of Gibbs. And I'd never been fond of ABBA. Not before the Broadway play.

Not since.

"That's the one."

"Where'd you see her? In town someplace?"

"No, right here. In my office."

She placed the carafe full of water in the sink and faced me.

"For therapy?"

"It's what I do."

"Why are you telling me this?" Diane wasn't being argumentative—although she was quite capable of it. She was querying me as to why I was breaching Gibbs's confidentiality so cavalierly.

"Because I have a signed release to talk to you." Before she'd left my office at the conclusion of her session, I'd asked Gibbs if I could consult with Diane, and she'd said I could.

"I'm not going to like this, am I?" Diane asked.

"Probably not."

"Is she still with Platinum? Or did she leave him? If she's still with him, don't even ask because I'm not doing conjoint again. Especially with them. With her. Count me out. I mean it."

"Platinum" was Diane's nickname for Sterling. Although I was never quite sure, I'd always operated under the assumption that she wasn't particularly fond of him, either. Regardless, I knew she'd liked him more than she'd liked Gibbs.

Hell, she liked bad cheese more than she liked Gibbs.

"She's still with him. At least temporarily. She doesn't feel she can leave him without him resorting to stalking her, or something worse."

Diane shot me an I-told-you-so glance. "Every battered woman feels that way. That's why God invented safe houses and restraining orders. The Dancing Queen will need a good kick in the butt to get out of that marriage. God knows Sterling will never leave her."

"Why's that?"

" 'Cause she's such a little dreamboat. You ever notice her fingers? She has perfect little fingers."

I didn't admit to Diane that I had, in fact, just noticed Gibbs's fingers. Instead, I said, "Anybody ever tell you that you have a propensity for sarcasm?"

"Don't worry; the tendency is soluble in caffeine. Let me finish making myself some coffee, and I'll be much nicer. I'm glad it's your job to help the Dancing Queen, not mine. Don't even think of recruiting me for this one. I'm out, Alan. Out. Out, out, out."

Diane was better at acting definitive than she was at being definitive. Despite her best efforts, compassion softened her steely heart. Still, I knew I had to get her on board before she convinced herself that she really was a taciturn bitch. I said, "Gibbs thinks Sterling murdered someone a few years ago."

Without missing a beat, Diane said, "Sometimes I pretend Raoul's on the FBI's most-wanted list. I play the special agent making the bust. If we don't run it into the ground, it's always kind of fun."

Diane's husband was an irascible Spaniard named Raoul Estevez. I knew nothing about their sex life and preferred it that way.

"I'm not kidding, Diane. Gibbs thinks he may have killed a friend of theirs. A woman he was involved with."

The pause that followed permitted Diane sufficient time to convince herself that the calendar indicated November, not April first.

"And you believe her?"

"A hundred percent? No, not that he did it. Not yet. But yes, I do believe that she believes what she told me."

"How does she know? What's her evidence against him?"

"It's a mix of things. Things he did. Things he said. Part circumstantial, part supposition, part confession."

"If Lauren heard it, would she be swayed?" Lauren, my wife, was a deputy district attorney for Boulder County. Where prosecutorial conclusions were concerned, she was a stickler for, well, facts.

I shrugged. "I asked myself the same question and

decided Lauren would be interested in what Gibbs has to say."

"But Sterling confessed?"

"So Gibbs says. Not an 'I did it' confession exactly, but he told her things that she thinks only the murderer would know."

"If—a big 'if'—what she says is real," Diane reminded me before she shifted her focus from the forensic to the psychological, "why now? Why is she talking about this now? The murder of the friend was when?"

"Nineteen ninety-seven. It's a good question, and I'm not sure about the answer. I assume it has something to do with them being back in Boulder. But that's a guess on my part. I asked, of course, but she didn't have an answer."

"Why you?"

The subtext was *Why not me?*

"I wish I knew the answer to that one, too. Maybe she's aware of your, um, countertransference issues."

I was certain Diane was going to argue that she didn't have any negative feelings about Gibbs. But she didn't go down that road.

"Other than murder, did you and Gibbs talk about anything else that was important during your . . . session?"

I explained that Gibbs wanted me to make a call to the police about the murder. Diane narrowed her eyes upon hearing that news. I continued. "And we talked about you, and what help you could be. I'd like your consultation about all this, and specifically your help setting up a meeting with Celeste what's-her-face over at Safe House. Make sure she's okay with this situation. Gibbs will need Safe House's services when the shit hits the fan."

"Clayton. Celeste Clayton. When?"

"Later today, if possible. I'm seeing Gibbs again tomorrow morning. I'd like to be confident that Safe House is comfortable having her by then so I can assure her it's safe to go to the police with what she knows about Sterling."

"She should be in Safe House right now, Alan. Not tomorrow."

"I know. I suggested. She refused. I strongly encouraged her to reconsider. She refused."

"Can I come to the meeting with Celeste? I'd really hate to miss this."

"I was hoping you would. The release lets me tell you whatever I think is appropriate."

"And Gibbs signed one for Safe House, too?"

"She did."

"She didn't argue with you?"

"No. She's not the arguing type. You know that. Maybe that's the source of your countertransference."

Diane considered my words for a heartbeat before she said, "I treat lots of wimpy women. That's not it. Do you find it odd that she dumped all this in your lap? The old murder, making the call."

"I find this whole thing odd."

"I know you don't want to hear it, but this isn't just about *my* countertransference, you know?" Her voice was now at least a half-octave lower. The change was intended to draw my attention.

I bit. "What do you mean?"

"Are you going to call the police for her?"

"I don't know. I guess."

"This is your countertransference, too, Alan. What you're doing for Gibbs you wouldn't do for a lot of patients. Making all these arrangements, making all these calls. She's pushing some button for you, too. Call me cynical, but I suspect it has something to do with the blond hair and the pert breasts."

Pert breasts? "I don't think so. The circumstances are unusual. If they were repeated with anyone else, I'd do the same thing."

"You would call the police in another state and report an old crime for any patient who asked?"

"Yes."

"Any old patient who wasn't cute and blond?"

I was grateful that the pert breasts had disappeared from the equation. I said, "Yes."

"Sure you would." Diane returned her attention to finishing the coffee-making process. With her back to me, she said, "Alan, why is it you who always gets cases like this? You have more dead bodies in your practice than a small-town undertaker. Do you ever think about that?"

I could have confessed that I thought about it all the time, but I didn't want to give her the satisfaction.

"I promise to think about it if you'll think about something for me, too. Way back, Gibbs brought up something during conjoint therapy. When she mentioned whatever it was, Sterling doused it like a Boy Scout putting out a campfire. Do you remember what it was? He glared at her. Really glared at her. That's what I remember most clearly. The glare."

"I don't have to think about it at all. I know what it was. I know exactly the incident that you're talking about."

"Yes?"

"Gibbs was saying that at some point she wanted to talk with us about their sex life."

"Yes, yes, okay," I agreed. "Maybe that was it. I remembered that, too, that it was something about sex."

Sort of.

Diane said, "Don't patronize me. That was it. And what she was about to tell us was that she and Sterling were swingers, or he was a cross-dresser, or something good and juicy like that. For a while I thought it might be bondage, but try as I might, I could never quite see the Dancing Queen in a black leather G-string and a studded bra. The whip? Maybe."

The mental image that Diane was painting was a little distracting to me. "And you think she wanted to talk about it?" I asked.

"Exactly. Something about their weird little sex life was starting to give her the heebie-jeebies. And Sterling didn't want her to let the cat out of the bag. He let her know he didn't want her to talk about it. That's what the look was about. You can take it to the bank."

"Come on, Diane. Seriously. Bondage? Cross-dressing?"

She stared me down. The glare was only minimally less effective than Sterling's glower at Gibbs had been.

"I am serious. But I told you, I ruled out bondage and S&M early on. My vote? I think they were swingers. Probably still are swingers. Gibbs wanted to talk about it with us; Sterling didn't. I'd guess he was pushing her to try something she didn't want to do, and he didn't want our votes counted."

"Swingers swingers? Like . . . you know?"

"Yeah, like having sex with other couples on a regular basis. That kind of swingers. Do you know another kind?" She giggled to herself. I assumed it was at the thought that I might possess more esoteric deviant sexual knowledge than she did.

I didn't admit that I had been actively considering the country-and-western dancing connotations of the word "swinger."

"Gibbs and Sterling, swingers? How exactly did you come to this conclusion? She never actually said anything about that, did she? Did she say something to you in private? God, you'd think I'd remember if she'd implied they were swingers."

"I just knew where she was going. You could tell."

"How come I didn't know where she was going?"

"What we do? Psychotherapy? People sometimes think we read minds. But what we do is more like seeing in the dark, you know? I knew where Gibbs was going. Sterling knew where she was going. You, sweetheart? You're such a prude. You don't like to go places like that. You're a very good therapist, but where sex is concerned, you can't see too well in the dark. Honestly, it's one of the things I love about you."

"You love that I'm a prude?"

She placed a mug beneath the dripping brew to catch the first, strongest cup of coffee. "I have to pick something to love, don't I?"

SEVEN

Sam's heart attack wasn't awful by heart attack standards. The cardiologist didn't think he'd suffered significant muscle damage.

During my visit to the hospital early Monday afternoon, Sam pointed out the location of the narrowing they'd discovered on a plastic model of the human heart that was about the size of a grapefruit. I'd had to hand him the model; he was flat on his back with some strange device that looked like a single-span suspension bridge straddling his groin. He'd explained that it was pressing on the incision in his artery with approximately the force that nature used to turn coal into diamonds.

All in all, not the precise degree of pressure that most men preferred in the vicinity of their groin.

"The one that got blocked up is called the diagonal artery. It's that one there." He pointed at a little red line on the model. "They put a stent in it to hold it open. You know what that is?"

I nodded. I rested my fingertip on the diagonal artery on the model in my hands and tried to visualize the blockage in Sam's heart and the small wire-mesh pipe propping open his fragile blood vessel.

"Doctor said it could've been much worse. My other arteries are open. Not wide open. But enough open."

"That's good news, right?"

"It's not bad news. But best case is you want them all wide open."

"Where's Sherry?" I asked. I sat and held the model heart in my hands. It seemed inappropriate to set it back down. Even though it was plastic, I felt like I should be extra careful with it.

"She's been here most of the day. Right now she's taking a walk or something. Getting some tea, I don't know. She said she needed a break from all this." He waved at the voluminous paraphernalia of the cardiac care unit. Monitors, pumps. Lots of plastic tubes and two- and three-digit LEDs telling those intelligent enough to understand them important things about Sam's condition. "It's okay."

I knew Sam's wife pretty well. I thought I knew her well enough to guess that her sympathy for her husband's condition would erode at some point and that her anger that Sam didn't do shit to take care of himself would emerge in a form that would cause him to cringe.

"Is she mad already?" I asked.

Sam nodded. "I fucked up. She told me this was coming. The heart attack. My father had one, you know. Same age I am right now. She's been bugging me to work out with her, eat better. Shit."

I couldn't see how regret and remorse were going to aid Sam's short-term recovery. I said, "That's neither here nor there. It's what you do from now on that matters, right?"

He snorted. "God, that's an intelligent thing to say, Alan. If I had my checkbook, I'd write you a check for your wisdom this very second. What is it these days, a hundred and something for fifty minutes? What a bargain! But they took my pants when the ambulance brought me in, sorry. My wallet was in it."

Sam fenced with me constantly about my profession; it was part of the fabric of our friendship. This particular jab was halfhearted at best. After dealing with Diane—who had been at the top of her game during our morning joust—I had no trouble absorbing Sam's feeble sarcasm. "Forty-five minutes, actually. You scared, Sam?"

He looked away from me before he nodded. "I'm glad I was with you yesterday. I never would have called for an ambulance if I was by myself. I would have convinced myself that it was a kidney stone. Or two stones. I'd probably be dead because I'm stubborn."

"I'm glad I guessed what was going on. It was lucky."

"How did you know?"

"I didn't know. The neck thing got me worried, though. Didn't see what it could have to do with your kidneys."

He sighed, or groaned. I wasn't sure.

"The doctor told me I need to develop some collaterals, whatever that means. In case there's a next time."

"Collateral what?"

"Blood vessels. Blood supply."

"How are you supposed to do that?"

"Exercise, apparently."

He spoke the word with an inflection usually reserved for a phrase like "root canal" or "prostate exam."

"I'll help," I said. "We'll start off walking, then we'll bicycle or run. Whatever they recommend."

"Thanks," he said. He hadn't wanted to ask for my help, but he'd hoped that I'd offer. "Want to know what's ironic?"

"Sure."

"Krispy Kreme is finally coming to Boulder. That's what I heard. I'm probably never going to get to eat another doughnut in my life, and the Taj Mahal of doughnut shops is finally coming to my town."

"There are worse things."

"Name three."

"I thought your cholesterol was okay."

"It's been going up for a while. It's kind of high. The truth is, I eat a lot of crap. So I've been wondering, how did that thing work on Emily's paw? The umbrella thing you were making?"

"It's working great; she loves it. Lauren thinks I should quit my job, patent it, and get rich."

"You don't want to be rich."

"I don't?"

He shook his head, but he didn't elaborate. In other circumstances I would have pressed him, but my mind had already darted back to the conundrum of the Dancing Queen and her husband the murderer.

I opened my mouth to ask Sam for advice about Gibbs and Sterling, but as my eyes flitted from one of the unpleasant accoutrements of acute cardiac care that were surrounding him to another, I kept quiet. I admit that I briefly entertained the notion that Sam would find my unsolved homicide problem a pleasant distraction from his health and family problems, but that rationalization left an immediate sour taste.

Discretion ruled. I decided that I would struggle with the Dancing Queen on my own.

A nurse bustled through the door to Sam's room as though she'd had a running start. She was all business, and her fresh white Reeboks told me she had a sprinter's soul. She checked me out while her eyes took in the readings on Sam's various monitors. She adjusted the pump on his IV and flicked at the spaghetti of plastic tubing leading to his forearm as though she were sending a malarial mosquito on its way to the afterlife.

"How's your pain, Detective?" For some reason she was touching his toes as she inquired.

"Hey, Snoopy," Sam said, as though he'd just recognized she was in the room. "It's still there. It's hard to stay in this position for so long, you know. I feel like Ray Bourque kicked me in the kidneys and he's been standing on my groin for most of the third period."

"Yeah, that's exactly what I hear it's like," she replied.

I stole a glance at the hospital ID hanging around her neck. It indeed read "Snoopy." Snoopy Lipner, R.N. I could tell she didn't have a clue who Ray Bourque was and was more than content to go to her grave without learning why Sam Purdy would have an image of the man standing on his groin. I could've explained to her about hockey's place in Sam's universe and his peculiar love of traditional defensemen, but I didn't think Snoopy really wanted to know that, either. I was tempted to ask her about her first name, but was guessing that just about everyone did and that she'd grown weary of the inquiries a long time before.

She pulled a syringe from the front pocket of her tunic, uncapped it with her teeth, and had the needle in a port in Sam's IV tube faster than Wyatt Earp could draw his six-shooter. She depressed the plunger and disposed of the empty in a sharps container in another blink of the eye. "This'll make it easier for you. Just another hour or so, and we can take that thing off your groin. Hang in there, and I'll be back to check on you soon."

"Can I have some more of those ice chips before you go?"

She lifted a paper cup off the table and placed the edge against his lips.

Sam tilted the cup and spilled a few slivers of ice into his mouth. Afterward he seemed to exhale for ten seconds as the medication from the syringe entered his bloodstream and the molecules started mating with the appropriate receptors in his brain.

"What did you give him?" I asked.

"Water, in the form of ice chips. Who are you?" Snoopy asked.

"A friend."

"He's the one who brought me in," Sam said. "He's a good guy, a doctor. Not a real doctor. You know, a Ph.D., a psychologist."

She eyed me as though she'd finally decided that she'd let me stay. She lofted the IV tubing. "That was fentanyl. For the pain. That position he's in is a killer." She returned Sam's water glass to the bedside table. "You did good work yesterday," she told me. "We got him early enough that we were able to bust his clot in the ER. Because of that he's going to walk out of here with most of the heart he came in with."

She was gone in a flash.

Sam mumbled, "Nurses are nice to cops. Don't know why that is."

Gingerly, I placed the plastic heart on his rolling bedside tray and watched his eyelids grow heavy as the fentanyl continued its work and the inevitable sedation went along for the ride.

His eyes suddenly popped open, and he said, "Marriage is a funny thing. Love isn't enough, you know? People think it is, but it isn't. Other things happen sometimes. They do."

"What do you mean?" I asked, honestly curious.

He didn't respond.

I sat beside him for a few moments more and watched his breathing get into the uniform rhythm of narcotic semisleep.

I was aware of an impulse to run home and make Sam an umbrella for his heart. Rigid foam rubber, plastic strips, some filament tape. That should do it. Something to shield his heart from whatever out there might want to bruise it. And to protect it from whatever he might be inclined to do to it, too.

I whispered, "Nurses are nice to cops because most of the time the cops deserve it, Sam. That's why."

I sat beside him for a few more minutes, silently rehashing what Gibbs Storey had told me that morning. In my mind I asked Sam what a cop like him would say to a story like hers. I asked him what the Boulder police were likely to do after the police in California informed them that they had a killer in their town.

Sam slept through it all.

EIGHT

In the dozen-plus years I'd been in practice in Boulder, I'd referred at least a dozen women—and one man—to Boulder Safe House. I helped Safe House raise money each year. I was an advocate for all they did.

But I didn't know where the actual sanctuary was located. None of my patients who used the services had ever told me. None of the Safe House staff had ever told me. My wife, the DA, had never told me.

Why? The more people who knew the location of the building, the less safe Safe House was.

So I wasn't surprised when Diane's message informed me that the five-thirty meeting with the Safe House director to discuss Gibbs Storey's situation would be at our offices on Walnut Street, not at Safe House.

Celeste Clayton—CeeCee to her friends—was a contemporary urban *balabosta*. She was all smiles and hugs, competence and compassion. If she couldn't tuck you in, feed you, or wipe away a tear, her day was ruined. Ten minutes late for our meeting, she bustled into my office with a big smile and with her arms spread wide to engulf Diane in an embrace.

My turn was next. I'd been perfunctorily introduced to Celeste at a couple of fund-raisers and had spoken with her on the phone a few times about mutual clients. Still, the hug she gave me was every bit as robust as the one she gave Diane.

She plopped onto the chair across from me, looked around my office, and said, "Nice digs."

Diane said, "Don't be fooled. The decorating panache is mine. He just wrote the checks."

It wasn't completely true, but Diane knew that I wouldn't contradict her in front of company. I said, "Celeste, thanks for doing this on such short notice."

" 'Notice' is a foreign concept in my business. People don't usually anticipate when they will need emergency shelter from abusers. So what's up? Diane said this one would raise my eyebrows. That'll take some doing. I've been in the battered spouse business for so many years that I know most of the stories before anybody tells me word one."

I handed Celeste a signed release from Gibbs Storey. She glanced at it and proceeded to stick it into a fat Day-Timer that screamed "black hole." I was confident there were papers stuffed in that book that were older than my Social Security card.

"Years ago, ten or so, Diane and I briefly treated a married couple. The wife's name is Gibbs Storey. They left—"

"Gibbs. That's *b-s*?"

Diane laughed. I said, "Yes. Well, two *b*s and an *s*."

"Go on."

"The Storeys left town after what, Diane, three or four sessions?" Diane nodded. "Neither of us heard from them again until ten days ago when Gibbs called me for an appointment that took place this morning. She told me they'd moved back to town a few months ago. Within a few minutes she went on to implicate her husband in an unsolved murder in California."

"Implicate?" Celeste asked.

"She accused him of murdering a friend of theirs with whom he was having an extramarital affair."

"Wow." My impression was that Celeste wasn't registering amazement at the facts. She was registering amazement that she was really hearing a new battered woman story.

"Gibbs feels that she will be in significant physical danger from her husband once he discovers that she has spoken with the police. I don't have any valid reason to question her conclusion."

"Is there a history of battering?"

Diane spoke up. "We're in a difficult position with you on that, CeeCee. Alan and I saw the Storeys as a couple. Virtually all of what we know about him comes from that couples treatment. That therapy is confidential—we can't talk about it without his permission."

"Even if she's in danger?"

"Danger's not enough," Diane replied. "He would have had to make a threat against her for us to breach privilege. Sterling"—she cleared her throat—"hasn't done that. At least not in our presence. Absent the overt threat, we can't talk about him without a release."

Celeste said, "Something tells me he's unlikely to grant the release, isn't he? How about I just assume that I wouldn't be here if his history in the bully department was untarnished? Is that an assumption that we all can live with?"

Neither Diane nor I contradicted her.

I thought, *And* that *is how the high hurdles of confidentiality are effortlessly cleared.*

"Well, good. Where is Ms. Storey right now?"

I said, "She went home after our session this morning. She feels certain that her husband doesn't suspect anything. She insists she'll be safe until the police show up to talk with him."

Celeste smiled ruefully. "I can name this song in three notes. In case you're wondering, it's a very sad song."

"I did my best to keep her from going home." I don't know why I felt the need to protest my innocence, but I did.

"I know how it goes. I've beaten my head on that wall a few hundred times myself, Alan. Kids? Please tell me there are no kids."

"None, thankfully."

"You'll talk to her again when?"

"Tomorrow morning. At that point I hope to get her permission to contact the police in Laguna Beach and pass along her suspicions about her husband. She prefers not to do it herself. Obviously, the moment that occurs—should they believe her—she'll need protection."

Celeste said, "Her suite at the palace is ready."

Diane said, "This could be high profile, CeeCee. You sure you're ready for the publicity?"

"There's no reason for anyone to know she's at Safe House. If someone does connect the dots and is irresponsible enough to go public with the information, we'll deal with it. That's what we do. We're here to protect women at risk. This sounds like a woman at risk."

"You're sure?" Diane asked. "The press will be all over this."

Celeste took a moment to move her gaze between Diane and me, then back to Diane.

"What don't you like about her?"

"Me?" Diane asked. "What do you mean?"

"Don't play with me, Diane. What is it about this woman you don't like? Something's bugging you."

Diane uncrossed her arms and crossed her legs instead. She started to speak and stopped. When she started again, her words came out as though she'd floored her tongue and her transmission was locked in first gear. "Gibbs Storey is an alpha bitch, CeeCee. She's everything I—I—I hate about every *über*-popular girl wrapped up into one too-cute, too-thin, too-precious, too"—Diane actually growled at this juncture—"too-perfect little package."

Without the slightest alteration in her tone, Celeste said, "You know I love you, right, Diane? Good. Then please take this the way I intend it: It's obvious your high school years left you with some unresolved issues, dear." She paused. "I suggest you get over them. I'm happy to refer you to someone who will be delighted to help you exorcise those demons."

Celeste's hand disappeared into the Day-Timer and miraculously emerged with a business card. She handed it to me. "That's my cell number. Call me when your lady's ready for our services. I'll have someone come over here and get her. I don't want her followed to the shelter. Anything else? You guys know about the

Christmas benefit? Good, I thought so. I'll see you there. Be sure to bring your checkbooks."

And she was gone.

I looked at Diane and said, "*Über*-popular alpha bitch?"

NINE

I was late getting home.

After the meeting with CeeCee ended I squeezed in a few minutes of decompression with Diane before I drove out to Louisville to visit Sam again. The torture contraption had been removed from his groin, and he'd been turfed from the coronary care facility to a telemetry unit. I found him propped up in bed staring at a muted TV screen. He'd already trashed the hospital gown and was wearing nothing but a pair of running shorts and a tangle of wires that snaked to an array of sensors plastered to shaved rectangles in the thick mat of hair on his chest.

Sherry plodded into the room a minute or two after I arrived. We hugged. I explained that Sam had just asked me a poignant question about his son Simon's reaction to the heart attack. Sherry stood with her arms folded across her chest while I finished telling Sam what I thought he might expect to see.

Sam's wife had lost weight since I'd last seen her. Her face was thin, almost gaunt. I wasn't totally convinced that the gauntness wasn't a side effect of the makeup that was liberally applied around her eyes. Saturday night makeup in the middle of the day, I wondered. *Stress,* I thought. *What's that about? Sam's health, probably.*

I excused myself moments later, kissing Sherry on the cheek. I implored her to call if she needed anything from Lauren or me. Anything. I told Sam I'd see him the next day.

Before I made it to the door he said, "Alan?"

I turned back toward him. He pinched a thick roll of skin at his waist—the roll of flesh had the heft of a healthy brisket—and asked me if I thought he was fat, adding, "I think my cardiologist thinks I'm fat. He hasn't said so exactly, but that's what he thinks."

I glanced at Sherry before I looked my friend in the eye and said, "Yes, Sam, I think you're kind of fat."

For a split second he looked injured, then he said, "Yeah, me too."

My laugh echoed in the room.

It sounded like a fart at the opera. The tension between Sam and his wife was as thick as plasma.

Ten minutes later I was home.

Grace was sick. Lauren had her hands full with a work problem that had followed her home from the office. She was short-tempered and fearful that our daughter had croup. I was determined not to join in the chorus of catastrophizing—rare things happen rarely, after all, and common things happen commonly—and I decided that I would act as though my daughter had a cold until her symptoms insisted otherwise. But it was clear that both of my girls required some immediate attention.

The dogs hadn't been out all day, and Emily in particular was restless. Her paw umbrella had fallen like a forty-year-old's butt so that it *clack-clacked* on the wood floors with every step she took. The noise, coupled with whatever was going on at work, was driving Lauren closer and closer to distraction, or worse.

"Do that first," she directed me as I went to relieve her of Grace. She was pointing at Emily's paw. "Fix that thing, please."

I did what I was told. It took me fifteen minutes to check Emily's paw wound—it looked terrific—to dress it with antiseptic, to retape the plastic umbrella into place, and to walk both the dogs down the lane and back.

Lauren tucked the portable phone between her ear and shoulder and carried Grace to the nursery while I threw together some pasta and bean soup. Experience told me that if I hurried I could make a passable version in twenty-five minutes.

During the half hour or so until I had dinner on the table, Grace finally fell asleep. Lauren came into the kitchen for dinner with her hair wet. She appeared much less harried after her quick shower, and with a smile she told me that the work problem was solved.

I poured her a glass of wine and filled her in on developments with Sam and Sherry.

She asked a few questions. I answered as best I could.

"Has Sherry said anything to you, Lauren? Is there any trouble brewing between them? She seems really angry at him."

"I haven't talked to her in a while, and the last couple of times we did talk she wasn't very open with me. But you know that Sam was a heart-attack-in-waiting. His weight, his stress, his diet. His family history. I'm not surprised she's furious. He should have been taking care of himself."

Not the level of compassion I'd expected to hear from her. "Tough day?" I finally asked. "You feeling all right?"

The second question was a back-door way of wondering out loud about the current status of her struggle with multiple sclerosis. New symptoms? Aggravated fatigue? Anything?

I hated asking. She hated answering. I think I hated asking because of how much she hated answering. She hated answering because she believed that her chronic illness and its myriad symptoms constituted the most grievously tedious subjects in the world.

"I just realized what I said about Sam and Sherry. Do you get angry with me, Alan? Because I'm sick? Do you think it's my fault when I'm not feeling well? That I do something to . . . or I don't do something that . . ."

I sat back. "I get angry that you're sick. But no, I don't get angry at you for having MS."

"I do," she said. "I get angry at me. I think it's okay if you do, too."

No, it's not, I thought. *It's not. You would like it to be okay, I know you would. But it's not.*

Lauren sipped some wine. "Grace isn't going to let us sleep tonight," she warned, having successfully ignored my question regarding the current state of her health. "We can't let her stay down too long."

"Let's leave her down long enough to have dinner.

We'll get her up after. Maybe she'll be in a better mood."

Lauren lifted a spoonful of soup. "Yeah, that's likely to happen. So, is there anything new at the office?" she asked in a playful, I'll-go-along-someplace-else-with-you voice.

I surprised her. I said, "Actually, there is something that came up. I could use your advice."

Without using any names or revealing in what state, let alone in what city, the events had taken place, I gave Lauren the broad outlines of the tale of Gibbs and Sterling Storey. I included my suspicions about the psychological and likely physical abuse that were part of the fabric of their relationship.

My indiscretion with Lauren was a gray area in confidentiality that I usually tried to avoid. These "I have a patient who . . ." conversations happen all too frequently between psychotherapists and colleagues or laypeople. Most mental health professionals engage in them with a rationalization that if they do not reveal sufficient details to allow the listener to identify the patient in question, then the letter of the patient's confidentiality has not been violated.

Lauren's soup bowl was empty when I completed my exposition. I ladled her some more.

"So what are you going to do?" she asked me.

"Exactly what she wants me to do, I guess. As soon as I'm sure she has a safe place to stay, I'll call the police in the town where she was living and tell them what she told me."

"Yeah?"

"What do you think will happen when I do?" I asked.

"Depends on whether or not the cops believe you."

"And what does that depend on?"

"On whether she's given you any information that coincides with what the local cops already know about the crime. If your client knows something that isn't in the public record, I would predict that they would take you quite seriously."

"And then what?"

"I'm speculating, okay? If they believe her story, they would either ask her to travel back there so they could talk to her, or they would send somebody out here to interview her. Maybe him, too—her husband—if he's stupid enough to be accommodating. It all depends on what they've been able to develop at their end and how it matches up with what she knows. But it's hard to predict. You know what these cold cases are like. Detectives lose interest. Evidence gets lost. Witnesses die or move away. People forget."

"She said she'd testify against him."

"Sorry," Lauren said. "It's not that simple."

"I don't understand."

"Spousal privilege."

"So?"

"Spousal privilege is a trickier thing than most people realize. Each spouse has a privilege not to disclose marital communications, and—this is the part that people don't know—they also have a privilege to prevent their spouse from disclosing marital communications."

"Really? I thought spousal privilege meant that spouses couldn't be compelled to testify against each other. Well, she's willing to testify. Eager even. Her testimony would be voluntary."

"Like I said, it's not that simple. He could assert his privilege and prevent her from testifying. But there are some circumstances that would allow his privilege to be overridden."

"Teach me."

"There are statutory exceptions to the spousal privilege evidence rules. Every state I'm aware of has a battering and child-abuse exception. If one spouse batters the other or injures a child, the injured spouse is free to testify about that against the batterer. But the case you're describing is the murder of a third party, not domestic violence. Take Colorado. If the homicide you're talking about had happened in Colorado, spousal privilege wouldn't apply at all, because the case that's in question involves a serious felony and in Colorado all spousal privilege is waived for serious felonies. Other states have different spousal privilege statutes, with different exceptions. Some have felony exceptions, like Colorado, some don't. Ultimately, a lot is going to depend on what state this homicide of yours happened in."

"Please go on."

"In many states, including ours, spouses can't testify against each other without the consent of the other spouse. But in some states there's no felony exception to that rule. If your client is from one of those states, unless her husband granted his consent—which I think we can agree is unlikely if she's about to accuse him of murder—she wouldn't be allowed to testify against him, even for an alleged homicide."

Emily walked over, wanting her ears scratched. I obliged. "Do you know how the law works in any other states?"

"Any one in particular?" Lauren teased.

"Sorry, I can't tell you which state this is about. I wish I could. What other ones do you know?"

"I passed the California bar, remember?"

Lauren and I were both on our second marriages. Her first had taken her briefly to California. We didn't talk about our exes much, so her reference to her time in California hung in the air like the scent of burnt garlic.

"Okay, what's California's spousal privilege statute? Do you remember that kind of detail?"

"It was a lot of years ago, but my memory is that it's one of the more conservative laws, or liberal laws, depending, I guess, on whether you're a prosecutor or a defense attorney. I think there's a mutual consent rule in California, but I don't believe that there's a felony exception."

"Which means that, hypothetically, if this old murder took place in California, my client couldn't testify against her husband without his consent."

"If I'm right, that's exactly what it means."

I figured she was right; my experience was that Lauren was usually correct about matters of the law. I thought about the complications that her facts presented and explained, "I was going to run it by Sam today. To see what this would be like from a police point of view—you know, to get a call like the one I'm about to make. But I decided that it wasn't a good idea."

"No, it wouldn't be a good idea for him. Not now, given his condition. I'm not sure it's even a good idea for you. You may not want to be in the middle of this, Alan. Think it through carefully."

"Why? What do you mean?"

"Let's say it turns out that your client is right about . . . everything that she believes her husband did. If that's the case, then you know three things about her husband. One, that he's a killer. Two, that he's a batterer."

She raised her spoon to her mouth.

"And number three?" I asked.

Lauren swallowed, sat back, and sipped some Riesling before she answered. "That he's not going to be happy with you for turning him in to the police." She reached across the table and took my hand. "And Emily and Grace and I don't know what we'd do without you."

"Anvil too," I said.

"Yeah, Anvil too."

"Why don't you rest a little bit? I'll go wake Grace."

Lauren stood up. She probably didn't know that I was checking her balance when she did. She probably didn't know that I would be examining her gait as she left the room.

I stopped her before she cleared the doorway. "Does spousal privilege restrict the police in any way? Does the mutual consent part of the spousal privilege law apply to their investigation? If she tells the police things now without her husband's consent, could it taint future evidence?"

"Why would you think that's a problem?"

"Fruit from a poisonous tree?"

"Doesn't apply. Spousal privilege is limited to testimony in court. During the investigation, the police can find out whatever they can find out. They can talk to either spouse about the other. But . . . keep in mind that

I haven't reviewed the case law or the precedents recently. You might want to talk to a defense attorney—someone like Cozy or Casey—before you decide what to do next."

Cozy Maitlin and Casey Sparrow were criminal defense attorneys whom Lauren and I knew well. Professionally speaking, too well.

"I thought I just did talk with an attorney."

"I told you the legal issues involved, Alan. I didn't give you any advice."

"Well, may I have some advice?"

She thrust out a hip. The move was erotically provocative, all in all very unlawyerlike. "A little more salt in the soup next time. But the Riesling"—she blew me a kiss—"was perfect."

"Thanks," I said.

Lauren smiled warmly. "This all happened in California, didn't it?"

I smiled back. My smile was kind of sick.

As if on cue, our daughter's throaty wail pierced the quiet.

Lauren was right in her prediction. Neither of us got much sleep that night.

TEN

The whole country had seen a single, grainy, black-and-white security photograph of my Tuesday eight o'-clock. Her likeness had been on TV, in the newspapers, in magazines, on the Internet—anywhere a picture could be plastered. But as far as I knew, I was the only person who could actually put a name to the infamous photo.

Who was she? My first patient was an overstressed sales executive named Sharon Lewis who worked out the Diagonal at a company called Micro Motion. A fortnight plus one day before, at almost the exact same hour when she and I were sitting down for her second psychotherapy session, Sharon had been hustling to recover from a blown tire on the Boulder Turnpike that had caused her to arrive much too late for her flight at Denver International Airport. Her tardy arrival meant that she had exactly thirty-three minutes to get from her car in the parking garage to the B Concourse to catch her plane to Houston for a sales meeting that she absolutely couldn't miss.

Denver's airport was always a mob scene on

Monday mornings, and Sharon jogged into the terminal to discover that the post–9/11 security station was already jammed with an army of impatient briefcase warriors charging out on their weekly business patrols.

Sharon was schlepping her rolling suitcase on board the plane and wasn't surprised that she was immediately jostled by federal security personnel into a cutback queue that was moving like the blood of a glutton after a meal at Morton's.

When she finally arrived at the front of that line, she was directed toward a shorter line at an X-ray machine, where she was once again forced to cool her heels. She found herself behind a family of six who were behaving as though they'd never confronted a magnetometer in their entire lives. Each of them had more metal secreted on their bodies than Edward Scissorhands at a piercing convention.

After a lifetime's worth of sighs and rolled eyes, Sharon finally cleared herself through the metal detector where she was—no surprise—selected for a secondary security screening by a large, taciturn woman armed with an electronic wand and an attitude.

By her own admission Sharon Lewis was the type of person who tailgated mercilessly, who counted items in the baskets of those in front of her in the supermarket express lane, and whose idea of a vacation was an uninterrupted bath. Her friends—and there were precious few of those—would call her intolerant.

While waiting impatiently for her turn to be wanded by the uniformed woman she was certain was an ex-Marine, Sharon saw from a fleeting glance at her watch that she had nine minutes remaining to get to her gate to catch her flight to Houston. That meant she had only nine minutes to accomplish all of the following: to get past this grizzly bear of a security officer, to hustle downstairs to board the train, to make it down the track two stops to B Concourse, and then to run like hell all the way to Gate 19, which, of course, was almost the farthest possible gate location from the concourse train station.

It was then—at the crucial moment of her morning endurance trial when she looked at her watch and did the calculations—that Sharon Lewis made a memorably bad decision.

The infamous photograph of her—that grainy one that just about everyone had seen and that anyone who had ever been inconvenienced at any airport anywhere in the world had cursed—had run in that week's *Time* magazine with the telling caption: THE MOST SELFISH WOMAN IN AMERICA.

How had Sharon earned the title?

Sharon had gazed around the bustling security area and concluded that no one was paying any particular attention to her, especially not the gruff woman with the wand, who at that moment was busy assisting an elderly Asian gentleman with an aluminum cane remove his wingtip shoes. The fact that Sharon was being totally ignored not only infuriated her but also permitted her an odd sense of freedom. She was tired of waiting for her turn to be wanded. She was tired of things going wrong that morning. She was, as she put it to me later, "tired of counting idiots."

Her flight to Houston was minutes away from leaving Denver without her.

What did Sharon do? She took things into her own hands. She proceeded to lift the black nylon band from the security corral in which she was penned, casually slipped through to the other side, replaced the band into its track, grabbed her rolling suitcase off the stainless steel table where it awaited her post-X ray, and strutted—unimpeded—toward the escalators.

Less than a minute later she pushed her way in front of yet another old man—this one was in a wheelchair—to squeeze onto a departing train that carried passengers from the terminal to the distant concourses.

News reports revealed that eight minutes passed after Sharon removed herself from the secondary screening queue before the security force in the terminal—tipped off by a passenger who had been waiting behind Sharon—ascertained that their security perimeter had been intentionally breached. Within two minutes all the airport's security checkpoints were closed. Four minutes after that the trains to the concourses were shut down. And a couple of minutes after that, planes at the gates were directed to stop boarding, planes that were taxiing were ordered to return to their gates, and procedures were initiated to sanitize the concourses and return everyone to the main terminal to once again pass through the interminable maze of security.

Later, when supervisors reviewed the security tape of the incident, the authorities were able to isolate a terribly grainy picture of Sharon Lewis strolling unhindered around the boundary of the secondary security screening area, her suitcase trailing behind her.

But the security personnel didn't know it was Sharon Lewis who had caused the entire system to grind to a halt. They didn't know that the person who was responsible for costing tens of thousands of passengers precious hours and the airline industry millions of dollars in delayed and canceled flights all across the nation was a Boulder business executive. All they knew was that the culprit was a thin woman with dirty blond hair, about five six or five seven, wearing a black suit with a white blouse and tugging a rolling suitcase.

Sharon? She didn't know what the fuss was all about because by the time DIA was shut down, her United Airlines flight to Houston had just gone nose up. She only learned about the repercussions of the incident later that day. The buyer from the company she was visiting in Texas told her the entire story, describing the woman who had skirted security as "that self-centered bitch who shut down DIA."

She'd smiled wanly at him through her nausea. But, she assured me later, she'd closed the sale.

For the two weeks since the breach at DIA federal law enforcement authorities had been searching desperately for the woman in the grainy security photograph. They wanted to arrest her, convict her, fine her, and imprison her, though not necessarily in that order. From the tone of the public discourse that followed the incident, drawing and quartering didn't seem to have been totally ruled out as a punitive option, either.

But no one knew who she was, or where she was.

Except for me. And my lips were sealed.

ELEVEN

After Sharon's visit at eight o'clock I had another patient at eight forty-five. And another at nine-thirty. Yet another at ten-fifteen. A scheduled break at eleven o'clock to catch my breath—and cram in a visit to the toilet—was sacrificed for a follow-up session with Gibbs. My bladder wasn't happy.

"Sterling thinks I'm at that mall in Broomfield. He thinks all I do is shop," she announced as she settled onto the sofa.

I waited for her to go on. With that opening, all she had told me was that she considered me to be her co-conspirator. But I already knew that. Apparently, I'd volunteered for the role during the previous morning's session.

Admittedly, I was having second thoughts about how quickly I'd raised my hand to enlist.

"If he knew I was here talking to you, he'd kill me."

"Kill you?"

"You know."

"No, I don't know."

"He wouldn't be happy. Let's leave it at that."

Right, I'll leave it at that. That sounds like a great idea.

The high-pressure ridge responsible for the warm air that had enveloped the Front Range since the morning of Sam's heart attack remained firmly in place, and this mid-November day had broken from the gate fair and mild. I'd led Gibbs from the waiting room at one minute past eleven o'clock, and a glance out the window suggested that a day that had started gloriously had only gotten better. A month-plus before Christmas, a mile high, and eighty degrees wasn't out of the question.

Gibbs was dressed as though she had stayed up the night before in order to catch the late weather report and plan her outfit accordingly. She wore capris that were almost too pink and that hugged her slender legs almost too snugly. Almost. Her shoes, as always, looked fresh from the box. Actually, my shoes never looked that good, even straight from the box. Her champagne sweater set—I was guessing silk but allowing for cashmere—displayed a wide swath of her smooth chest but only the barest hint of cleavage. I tried to conjure the image of another one of my female patients who would have dressed the same way Gibbs was dressed for a similar morning session. I couldn't.

But on Gibbs the look worked.

Diane, I figured, would have argued that Gibbs looked slutty.

Über-*popular alpha bitch* slutty.

As far as nicknames went, I'd already decided that I preferred "the Dancing Queen."

My impression of Gibbs during the earlier

treatment had always been that she liked to live her life near the line where classic style and fashionable trends collide, but that she rarely wandered across it. Her outfit was a good metaphor for all that.

Accusing her husband of murder, though—that had definitely taken her across the line.

"Did you talk to those people you were going to talk to?" she asked.

"Yes, I did. I spoke with Dr. Estevez, and then she and I met with the director of Safe House on your behalf. The admissions people at Safe House are waiting for your phone call. They are more than happy to provide you with a safe place to stay. As soon as you're ready, they will send somebody over here to pick you up. They want to be certain that you're not followed on your way to the residence."

She crossed her legs, flinched a little bit with her eyes, and said, "I don't think I want to go there after all. I've changed my mind." With the slightest shrug of her shoulders, she added, "Don't be mad at me."

Perhaps there had been a time in my career when I might have found her display of world-class denial the slightest bit endearing, but if there had been, I was definitely past it.

"Yes?" I said.

That's what I said out loud, anyway. Inside, I was screaming things like *"What the hell are you talking about? Are you crazy? You just said the man would kill you!"*

But was I surprised at her change of heart?

Hardly. A colleague who spent much of her time treating abused spouses once told me that battered women had to leave their husbands five times before they stopped being drawn back. In her world, the sixth separation was the magic one.

Usually, anyway. She'd reminded me that she'd once treated a woman who went back eleven times.

Eleven. And anyone who'd been in practice doing psychotherapy for a while had treated abused women who never considered leaving even once.

As far as I knew, Gibbs was one of those. She hadn't left Sterling even once. This morning's short trip to Boulder's Safe House was going to be their virgin marital separation.

"You're concerned that I'll be angry with you?" I kept my voice as mild as the shampoo that I used to bathe my daughter's silky hair. I was already past my reactive anger and back in the shallows of the sea of compassion for the constellation of psychology and circumstances that caused abused women like Gibbs to make decisions that would seem muddled even for a four-year-old faced with a decision about whether to be friends with a bully.

"You went to a lot of trouble for me. And I don't like to appear ungrateful. That was nice, what you did."

Nice?

"You're concerned about my reaction?"

"Yes."

"Does that tell you anything?" Experienced therapy patients ask questions like that one on their own, without prompting. I didn't expect that Gibbs was even close to being able to do it.

"That I don't like to disappoint people?" She was guessing at the answer. I had sat next to a kid in high school algebra who'd answered every question with that exact same inflection. For an entire year.

"Or . . . maybe . . . you feel the same way with me that you feel sometimes with Sterling."

"I don't know what you mean."

"You make your decisions based on fear of disappointing people, or concern about making them angry. If you're worried about making me angry, I can only guess how concerned you might be about Sterling's reaction to finding out what you've told me, or about his discovering that you've left him."

"I don't think that's it," she said.

How much consideration had she given it? Less than a second. Apparently we weren't at a point in the therapy where I was being granted any wisdom transference.

I punted. "So you've changed your mind?"

"Not about the murder thing. No, no. About not feeling safe at home. That's what I changed my mind about."

Had she just said "the murder thing"? She had.

"You no longer think your husband will be angry that you're turning him in to the police for murder?" There is a year-long seminar in clinical psychology graduate school on how to ask obvious questions with a straight face.

I'd aced it.

"Sterling really loves me. I think he'd want me to stay with him while this works out."

"Works out? And how is this going to work out?"

"I think he'll get arrested. That will solve my problems for a while. At least about the murder thing. After that I just don't know. With a good lawyer these days, anything is possible."

Gibbs's musings were at once both rational and

incredibly naïve. Although I knew what I wanted to say next, I paused through a couple of breathing cycles before I said it. I would have preferred for her to respond to the echoes of her own words, but she didn't.

"When you started today's session, you said that Sterling was going to kill you. Now you would like me to believe that you're convinced that you are safe living with him even though you're about to turn him in to the police for murdering your mutual friend?"

Her face brightened inexplicably. She blurted, "That's so great! I think that's almost exactly what Dr. Phil would say."

"Excuse me?"

"Dr. Phil—you know, on the—oh, you don't know, do you? The guy on TV?"

She could tell I was befuddled.

She quickly added, "Don't worry, it's not *that* important that you know who . . ." Her voice trailed away.

I actually had a vague idea who Dr. Phil was. What I was befuddled about was the question of whether it was a good thing or a potentially embarrassing thing that I was beginning to sound like a psychologist who plied his trade on daytime television.

I made a mental note to ask Diane how humiliated I should be. She had her finger on the pulse of things like that.

"Yesterday," I said, "you were frightened enough of Sterling that you asked me to solicit help for you from Safe House. Today you've convinced yourself that the danger isn't real. Which am I supposed to believe?"

"Sterling doesn't want to hurt me."

I thought it was an interesting statement. Wishful, but interesting.

"Can you hear your own confusion?" I asked her.

"I'm not confused. I changed my mind. People do that. People react impulsively sometimes."

Softly, I probed, "Gibbs, has Sterling not wanting to hurt you kept him from hurting you in the past?"

She sighed, gave me a little half-smile. I took it to mean that I'd asked another Dr. Phil question.

"If he hurt me now, wouldn't that be like proof of what he did to Louise? He wouldn't risk that. Sterling isn't stupid."

"And you are willing to run that risk? You're willing to believe that, despite his threats, despite his past behavior, despite the fact that you're accusing him of murdering a friend of yours, he won't hurt you now?" I allowed a tincture of incredulity to enter my voice.

"Yes, I am," she said definitively. "I am. I don't want to go to Safe House. I want to go back home. Will you call the police in California now? Right now? I want to get that over with."

"Why me? Why don't you make the call yourself, Gibbs?"

"I can't. Betraying Sterling to you is as far as I can go. It's been hard even going this far."

I sat silently, urging her to say more. She didn't. The quiet stretched over two minutes or more.

Finally, I said, "But you'll cooperate with the police and testify about what you know?"

"If they arrest him? Yes, I'll testify. And if the police ask to talk with me before that, I will talk with them. I already told you that. I'm trying to do the right thing, Dr. Gregory."

I recalled Lauren's caution about spousal immunity. I wondered if Gibbs knew what I knew on that topic, that she couldn't testify against Sterling in California, which meant that the police would have to develop substantial evidence on their own to support her allegations.

"If the police ask to talk with you right now? While I'm on the phone?"

"No. Not right now."

I considered the fact that I had an out. Gibbs wasn't keeping her end of the bargain we'd made the previous morning—seeking shelter at Safe House. I concluded that her change of heart abrogated my responsibility to keep my end of the bargain—calling the homicide detective in California.

In my own heart, however, I knew that I was still inclined to make the call to California, not solely because I'd told Gibbs that I would, or because of some absurd sense of responsibility I was feeling because of a hypothetical bargain I'd made with her.

I was inclined to make the call because it was the right thing to do. Why? Because of the murder thing. I could spend some unpredictable amount of time in therapy trying to influence her to make the phone call herself, but with an unsolved homicide hanging in the balance, it didn't seem like a prudent plan.

I had received information about an unsolved murder; I was in a position to help the police close the case and put the responsible party behind bars. That was a novel state of affairs for me. But what made things even more unique in my experience was the fact that the screwy circumstances allowed me a rare ethical sanctuary: I actually had my patient's permission to share information in my possession with the police.

That doesn't happen very often in my business. I couldn't think of another time it had happened in my career.

But sitting across from Gibbs, I wasn't feeling free to act. What I was feeling was hesitant. Maybe I should have heeded the caution I was feeling right then. The caution was saying: *Reconsider.*

But I didn't. Instead I stood, walked over to my desk phone, and lifted the receiver.

"I brought the number with me," Gibbs said.

I placed the receiver back down. "I'm not as comfortable proceeding with the call as I would be if you weren't planning to return to your home."

Her shoulders sank a little. "Sterling is what he is whether or not you make the call."

"True. And I'm afraid he's someone who may hurt you."

"I don't think so. He's protective of me. I'm not saying it's normal protectiveness, Dr. Gregory, whatever that is, but he's protective of me."

"Protective?"

"Yes. Very. Sterling is controlling. Very controlling. But he's only touched me once. In anger, I mean, and that was . . . years ago. Many years ago. Are you going to make the call?"

"I don't know." I didn't.

Gibbs shifted on her chair. She sat back, crossed one leg over the other, and rested one forearm on the other. Each hand grasped the opposing biceps. "Remember I said yesterday that it wasn't only Louise?"

"Yes." Goose bumps shot up my spine.

She looked away from me. "You can't tell this to the police, okay? What I'm about to tell you."

"Actually that's not my call to make, Gibbs. It's yours. You decide what leaves this room."

"Then what I tell you from now on doesn't leave the room. You can't tell this to Dr. Estevez or to the California police."

"Would you like to rescind your previous release in writing?"

I immediately wondered why I'd asked her that. I couldn't remember ever making that offer to a patient before.

She made eye contact again. "No, that's not necessary. I trust you."

Somehow her assurance that she trusted me wasn't the most comforting of news. I didn't say "okay" or "fine." I waited silently for what was going to come next.

It turned out that Gibbs didn't need much time to hurdle whatever obstacles she faced about continuing.

"It's not just about Louise. I wish it were. Although I think she was the first, it's not just about Louise. My husband has killed a number of women. All over the country."

With false confidence I'd set down the cards of my two-pair hand, and Gibbs had trumped me with the old serial killer royal flush.

TWELVE

Good advice.

"Do not wander from designated paths and trails." That's what the first sign said. It was a hundred yards back, where there was still some light from the visitors' center.

"Do not go near any water." That order was posted ten yards farther along the trail.

Now here she was breaking all the rules. She was off the trail. She was near the water. Beneath her bare feet she could feel the muddy ground begin to turn into something that was the consistency of wet, putrefied hay. The stench was sour. In the darkness the odor screamed at her.

Gritty moisture squished up between her toes.

She bathed twice a day. Every day. Morning and night. She detested filth.

And decay? Please! Shivers shot up her spine.

The night was moonless. Her eyes found streaks to focus on, but the streaks disappeared as soon as she tried to reel them in. She couldn't see. It was the smell, and the feel of the rotting life between her toes, that convinced her that the swamp water was near.

And there had been one more sign. It had read, "Do not smoke or litter."

She wasn't breaking that rule. Five minutes ago, maybe. No, *it had only been two or three. She'd been breaking that rule, sitting there in the car. Smoking, yes; not littering. Fantasizing. Had everything changed so much in two minutes?*

Yes. Everything had changed.

She shivered. And why am I naked?

Oh, yeah.

Sterling.

Damn Sterling.

Five minutes ago she was still loving it. Every bit of it. The headphones, the tape, the music, the voice, the whole thing. Disrobing in the car. Waiting for him there, naked. Waiting for him to . . .

She tried to think.

Truth? She was more frightened of the swamp than she was of the gun. She'd grown up around guns in Virginia, was a pretty good shot herself. She didn't have the gun this time, though. It was pointed at her. That was hard to ignore.

But not as hard to ignore as the swamp.

She hated swamps and everything that lived in them. She hated snakes. She hated alligators. She hated frogs. She even hated the damn harmless dragonflies. When she was thirteen, one had become tangled in her hair at school. She'd been so frightened by the flapping that she'd pulled the hallway fire alarm to get some help.

Her friends had never let her forget it.

She told herself not to panic in the swamp. There was a way out. She had to find the way out.

The voice from the Walkman had instructed her to duct-tape her mouth. Let that awful stuff even touch her hair? Yeah, right. *She'd thought he was kidding. He wasn't. She'd done it. Now the tape across her lips limited her to whimpers.*

Her wrists were bound in front of her with the same awful gray tape. The instructions had made sense at the time *is what she told herself.*

What was I thinking?

On an exhale, she thought of blue herons. Herons liked swamps. She'd loved watching them on that boat tour she'd taken that time in the Everglades. She liked herons. Okay, she didn't love them. Birds made her nervous. But she tried to imagine walking into a flock of blue herons. That would be okay. She could survive that.

She stopped.

Behind her the voice said, "Keep going." It was a hoarse whisper. The same strange voice that was on the Walkman. "Don't turn."

The voice said keep going. She kept going.

Her next step took her ankle-deep into the dank water. Two more steps, and her kneecaps sank below the surface.

She'd lived in Augusta for four years. During that time she'd never visited the Phinizy Swamp Nature Park. Not *once. She hated swamps. A girlfriend had once said something about there being bobcats out here.*

Bobcats? She shivered.

She preferred golf courses. That was all the nature she needed: the back nine at Augusta, across town. Midnight on the thirteenth green again? She didn't need to be a member for that round, did she? That night was . . . perfection.

She had no idea what was spread out in front of her. A pond-size swamp? An Everglades-size swamp? Are swamps deep? Shallow?

She heard a splash, then realized that she had made the noise herself. How far behind her was the gun? She didn't know, but she couldn't wait. She had to move. She decided to run. In her head she flipped a coin. Tails.

She would run right.

Before her first step, she heard another splash. She knew she hadn't made that one. She screamed into her gag.

"Keep going." The gun hadn't moved with her. "Don't turn." The gun was farther away, back a few steps. The odds said now.

Now!

She lifted her knees high and sprinted to her right, hoping, praying that her next few steps wouldn't be her last few steps.

She splashed. Can't run in knee-deep water without splashing.

Please don't shoot, please don't shoot.

She thought she spotted the glooming outline of a tree. Someplace to hide. Something to provide cover. How far away was it?

She heard more splashing. Her own? She didn't know. She tripped on something solid below the surface of the swamp and slipped right down as though she'd been slapped. Muck seeped into her nose and ears. She tasted decay as she tried to scream, "I'm sorry, Daddy," but despite the tape her mouth was full of the effluent of the Phinizy Swamp.

Have to get up. *She tried to stand.*

She felt a tug on her thigh.

It was insistent. And then it was crushing.

Suddenly, she was swimming backward involuntarily. Her last thought was I hate alligators.

THIRTEEN

"A serial killer?"

"I don't want to say any more than what I said, Dr. Gregory. I just needed you to realize what is at stake here."

"Sterling has killed women all over the country?"

"Yes. Please call the police. He needs to be behind bars. We can't wait."

We?

I digested the implications.

"Is anyone else in danger?" If Gibbs identified a future potential victim, it would launch me into a gray stratosphere where I might be required to breach her confidentiality.

"Not that I know of," she said.

Silently I counted to five. I spent the seconds trying to decide whether or not I believed her.

FOURTEEN

I had only fifteen minutes to begin to digest what I'd just learned.

The lunchtime appointment that followed my Tuesday morning session with Gibbs belonged to a member of the local bar. Jim Zebid was a defense attorney, a litigator who also did occasional plaintiff's work on malpractice claims. He had an interesting background, having been around the Boulder County criminal justice system working as a private investigator while putting himself through law school.

I'd been seeing him for a few months during the same Tuesday slot, and the therapeutic relationship continued to fascinate me. At times he was eager to spar with me over seeming inconsequentials; at other times I felt he would be content to curl up in my lap in parody of my foster poodle, Anvil. Not having a solid handle on one of my patients' psychological profiles was nothing novel for me, but I found Jim Zebid a particularly interesting and perplexing man.

Since our first session I'd been working under the assumption that Jim chose me as a psychotherapist because I was married to a prosecutor whom he knew. His underlying motivation for making that choice? I wasn't sure, but I felt confident that he and I would come around to it before too long. I suspected that it had to do with competition, or with secrets, or with some curious transference that would follow a serpentine trail back to his mother and his father.

Or maybe it had to do with all of the above.

Jim's presenting problem was anxiety. His anxiety manifested itself in traditional ways: through nervousness, irritability, trouble sleeping, rumination, and occasional self-medication with alcohol and marijuana. By history, the present symptoms weren't novel for him. Although only thirty-one, he'd suffered from anxiety problems since his days as an undergraduate at UCLA. Later, when the symptoms had aggravated during law school, he'd rationalized away the problems as stress-related. But the symptoms continued unabated, and Jim had recently, albeit reluctantly, come to the conclusion that something more intrinsic might be responsible for his chronic misery.

Early on I referred him to a psychiatrist for a medication consultation. The Xanax Jim was prescribed had succeeded not only in taking the edge off his symptoms but in making him more psychologically available for the insight work that he insisted he wanted to do with me. Occasionally, though, I thought that his anxiety still proved an impediment to psychotherapy, and I wasn't quite sure about the ultimate efficacy of the Xanax.

For a few weeks I'd been weighing asking the

prescribing psychiatrist to consider an anxiolytic antidepressant instead.

The session after Gibbs's second individual appointment was one of those days when I wasn't so sure about Jim Zebid's desire to work.

I admit that he didn't have one hundred percent of my attention. Although most days I prided myself on my ability to move from one patient to the next with the clarity of flipping channels on a TV remote, Gibbs's most recent revelations were still clouding my focus that morning. I was making a conscious effort to fight through the static of Gibbs's serial killer accusation so that I could make certain that Jim had a sufficient quantity of my concentration.

"Anyway, my client says he sold half an ounce of blow to Judge Heller's husband. My guy is only up for an aggravated burglary, and I'm not sure I want to complicate things by revealing he's dealing, so I'm not sure what the hell I'm going to do with the information. But you have to admit it's something. Too bad it's not Judge Heller's case."

Jara Heller was the youngest judge on the District Court bench. I knew her socially—in the sense that I could have picked her out in a crowded room. I wasn't sure I could say the same about her husband, although I felt it was likely that I had met him at some legal affair or reception or cocktail party over the years. For all I knew he and I may have commiserated or shared a look of mutually felt angst while fulfilling our spousal obligations by our attendance.

"Still . . ." Jim said, apparently continuing to muse

over the illusion of leverage that came with knowing that a young judge's husband used cocaine and purchased it in quantities large enough to suggest that he sold some, too.

The look on Jim's face reminded me of a guy who'd just witnessed a wallet crammed with bills spill from a woman's purse and was wondering how he could rationalize clipping a few fifties before he handed the billfold back to its owner.

Most days I don't hear a single fact during psychotherapy that would be meaningful to anyone other than my patient, me, and a limited circle of people who happen to share my patient's plot in the universe. But that day? I'd already heard an update from a wanted woman, a report about a serial killer, and news about a judge's husband possibly selling cocaine, and I hadn't even given a thought to my midday meal.

FIFTEEN

Gibbs's revelation that she feared her husband was a serial killer, and not merely a killer, had changed things for me. The shocking news that he'd left a string of victims across the country not only cemented my decision to make the call to the detectives in California but also subtly altered my resolve. As I drove across town to visit Sam after Jim Zebid's session, I turned down the radio and pondered the philosophical underpinnings of it all, ultimately concluding that John Donne wouldn't be pleased by the metamorphosis of my attitude. One death should have been as consequential as many. One death should have been sufficient.

Sam had one additional "should" for me: "You should've talked to me as soon as you knew" was how Sam admonished me after I gave him the headline about the California murder.

He was feeling better. Although he was still in the telemetry unit when I was with him during my late lunch break, he and his cardiologist had radically different opinions on how long he should remain tethered to heart-monitoring equipment.

"You've had a few other things to deal with," I said.

The automated blood pressure cuff encircling Sam's biceps chose that moment to inflate. Sam jumped. "Damn thing scares me so much that it probably sends my blood pressure right through the roof. Hey, maybe you can convince my cardiologist that my mental health requires that I return home immediately."

"Good one, Sam. But I don't think you really want me to go on record commenting on your mental health."

"Point."

After I'd heard the multiple murder accusation, I negotiated one final rider to my bargain with Gibbs Storey. I would go ahead and make the call to the homicide detectives in California only if she would permit me to consult with a friend of mine who was a local detective regarding the Louise/Sterling situation, and with an attorney, if I chose. I told her I wouldn't need to use any names, just the facts of her accusation. Gibbs had agreed to my request without protest.

Actually, what she said was "The whole world is going to know my family's dirty secrets in a few days, Dr. Gregory. What's to be lost by giving this detective friend of yours a head start? If it will help you better understand the legal process that's about to happen, please go right ahead. Talk to a lawyer, too. I don't care. But just about Louise. And no names until it's in the press."

I'd had her sign a release.

*

Once I'd explained the broad outlines of the Louise/Sterling situation to Sam, he asked me to clarify some facts about Gibbs's accusation before he said, "So when you called the detective in this other state, this mystery state? Did he hang up on you, or what?"

"She came close. It actually didn't come down the way I thought it would. When I called, there was nobody there who could talk to me. I left a message. Eventually a Detective Reynoso called back. We didn't stop playing phone tag until about an hour ago."

"Well? Is your lady's story for real?"

"Reynoso seemed interested enough in what I had to tell her, but she didn't reveal much to me. It was kind of like trying to get information out of you."

"Be nice. I just had a heart attack."

"What's going to happen next, Sam?"

"Hard to say without knowing how closely your client's story meshes with what the cops already know. That's the gold standard."

"If it meshes, then what?"

"If it were my case and I got the call? I'd go to my superiors and make a case that I should fly to wherever the woman is and interview her. Maybe talk with her husband, too."

"Would you make an appointment with her or just show up?"

"I'm a big proponent of just showing up."

"Why?"

"In my business, when you make appointments, you almost always end up talking with lawyers. As much as I adore your wife, she's a rare exception to the breed, you know? I'm trying to arrange my life so that I interact with as few lawyers as possible. It's a good stress-reduction strategy—you know, for my heart."

"So you show up. When you get to town, do you have to call the local cops?"

"Absolutely. My guess is that one of my colleagues has already spoken with your detective—what's her name?"

"Reynoso. Carmen Reynoso. Can you find out who?"

"Can I find out, or will I tell you? What's the question here?"

"Will you tell me?"

"No."

"Didn't think so. So this Detective Reynoso talks to one of you guys at the police department, and you do what?"

"We listen to her story, weigh what she wants to do, and decide whether we want to cooperate. Odds are that her requests are somewhere close to reasonable. We consent, maybe we tag along on the interviews, whatever."

"How long could all this take?"

"Depends how hot it all seems. Reynoso could get on a plane today if she wanted to. Politics might be tough on her end and that might slow her down, or she could spend a couple of weeks, maybe even longer, getting her ducks in a row before she comes out."

"And the whole time a murderer is just wandering around doing his thing."

Sam made a dismissive face. "Perps are like snakes, Alan. They're always out there, living in holes. They're always close by, doing their snake thing, whether you see them or not. The ones that end up scaring the shit out of us are the ones that slither across our backyard during a barbecue. Well, this one—this lady's husband—just slithered right across your yard. But the truth is he was out there for years before you knew about him. And he may be out there for years longer before anybody does anything about him. Fact is, he's just another sick snake."

Over my first cup of coffee early that morning, I would probably have been placated by Sam's assertion that Sterling was just another sick snake. But no longer. If Gibbs was right about Sterling, I knew he wasn't just another sick snake. He was a cobra with blood from some undetermined number of women dripping from his needlelike fangs.

I reminded myself that Gibbs hadn't given me permission to talk with Sam about the other women she believed her husband had killed, only about Louise. "Some guys are . . . more dangerous than others, Sam. Right?" was all I could think of to say.

"You mean this guy? I don't know. From what little you've told me, I'm thinking the murder was a heat-of-passion thing. What are the odds of a repeat? Higher than you and me—or at least me, anyway—but statistically not that high. Contrary to public opinion, most people don't develop a taste for it. For murder, I mean. What does he do, anyway? For a living?"

I wondered whether I could reveal that information based on the limited release I had from Gibbs. I decided I could. "He's involved in the production of sporting events for a national cable TV channel."

"ESPN? Does he do hockey?"

"I'm not going to tell you any more than I've told you."

"Have I heard of him?"

"I doubt it. Maybe if you read credits." If Sam read credits, I'd eat a hockey puck.

"It's not like . . . Barry Melrose or Don Cherry, is it?"

I didn't know who Barry Melrose was. Don Cherry? I knew I'd heard of him, but I couldn't have guessed who he was, either. Given that Sam was asking, I assumed that both of them had something to do with hockey, and neither was in the production end of the game.

I said, "Production, not talent."

"Cherry has a temper. Impulse problems, you know?"

"And that's unusual among hockey players?" I asked innocently.

"It's all relative."

"Don't worry; it's not Don Cherry, Sam."

He sipped water out of a cup with a straw. "She's going to stop by to see you, too, you know."

"Who is?"

He burped and lifted his hand to the center of his chest.

I almost screamed for a nurse.

"Reynoso. She won't make an appointment, or ask you to Starbucks for a latte. But she's going to show up to talk to you, too."

"That's okay. I'll tell her exactly what I told you. That's all I have permission to tell her."

He stuck the tip of his finger so far into his ear canal that I wondered whether he was missing some essential part of his aural anatomy. "That might not satisfy her. Some cops aren't as easygoing as I am."

"Now there's a scary thought."

"You know more, don't you? Your client didn't give you permission to tell me everything, did she?"

"I can't answer that, Sam. Confidentiality. I'm sorry."

He nodded. "I may get out of here today. Doc's coming by later. Says he may let me go home and get into an outpatient rehab program. You know: exercise, diet, stress reduction."

"That's great," I said. "Maybe Adrienne can get you doing some yoga. It'd be great for your stress."

"You're kidding, right?"

"Hockey players do yoga."

"Now you're giving me chest pain."

"Don't joke about that, Sam. What about work?"

"My captain came by, made reassuring noises about me going back. He says they want to make sure I'm in the best possible shape before I'm back on the job. A million docs will have to clear me. He said I shouldn't even think about working until after New Year's."

"A six-week vacation will do you good. Give you a chance to break in your new healthy lifestyle."

"Six weeks at home right now is not exactly my idea of a stress-reduction prescription. Sherry's already making noises about having to roast tofu instead of turkey next week. She's not going to be happy having me moping around the house until after New Year's."

I knew I didn't want to ask Sam what was going on in his marriage. I sensed he didn't want me to ask, either. I played along with his denial. I didn't feel good about it, but that's what I did.

"You'll have a great time with Simon, Sam."

"He's in school during the week, takes the bus up to the mountains to snowboard with his friends every weekend. Copper Choppers, you know about it? When Grace gets older, you will. Anyway, I don't think my cardiologist is going to endorse me doing a whole lot of snowboarding this winter." Sam asked, "Why did she stay with him so long? Your client? She's known he was a murderer for a while. Why did she stay with him for so long?"

"Fear. Loyalty. Denial. That's a tough question, Sam. Why do women stay in unhealthy marriages? We both see it all the time."

He turned away from me and from my question. He moved a tissue box on his bedside tray. "Why is she turning him in now?"

"Another tough question."

Sam picked that moment to adjust his bed. Once he had it right he said, "If it happens—if I get released from this place—would you maybe be around later to give me a ride home?"

I almost asked, "What about Sherry?" But I didn't. I said, "Of course."

SIXTEEN

"Although I don't really want to," Gibbs began, "I think maybe we should talk about sex."

I almost said what I was thinking. What I was thinking was that Gibbs and I should be talking about serial murder. Sex could wait.

Instead I stifled a yawn.

At my insistence Gibbs had come back in for a session on Thursday. My only free time was seven-fifteen. In the morning. As good a time as any to talk about sex, right?

There was a brief time in my career when a preamble like the one Gibbs offered would have caused my ears to perk up just a little. Part of the arousal of interest I'd have felt would have been prurient or voyeuristic, I'm sure, but mostly the increased interest on my part would have had to do with inexperience.

I would have mistaken an introduction like hers for a promise that I'd hear the titillating prelude to something new, something different, something intrinsically interesting.

But just as my first visit to a nude beach had taught

me that most people are more attractive—much more attractive—with their clothes on, my experience doing psychotherapy had taught me that most people's sex lives weren't particularly fascinating, and that the more details I knew, the less fascinating they turned out to be.

Where sex was concerned, a little mystery did indeed go a long way.

After well over a decade of clinical practice I tended to listen to tales of erotic encounters, or supposed erotic encounters, with the same detachment that I listened to the details of marital arrangements over housecleaning or the choice between individual and joint checking accounts.

"Just grist for the mill," one of my old supervisors would have said about sexual topics in psychotherapy. "It's all just grist for the mill." I would nod knowingly to her in response to her maxim, but the truth was that I didn't even know what grist meant. Still don't.

I found that I looked back and contemplated the professional road I had traveled more and more as the years passed. Maybe it was a function of age, maybe it was just the fact that I had a growing list of things to look back on. In graduate school I knew a guy who insisted that he never looked back and didn't even use his mirrors while driving. "Everything I need to see is out in front of me," he claimed.

Me? I lived believing that whatever I didn't spot creeping up behind me was likely to take a good-sized chunk out of my ass.

One of the items in my rearview mirror that early Thursday morning exactly a week before Thanksgiving was Diane's contention that during the prior conjoint therapy I'd suffered from night blindness and totally missed the sexual fuel that was simmering in Gibbs and Sterling Storey's relationship. I was determined not to make the same mistake twice.

Gibbs and I would talk about sex first.

Then serial murder.

"Okay," I said to Gibbs. *Let's talk about sex. Swinging, right?* "But first I'd like to take a moment to check on your safety. Are you all right, Gibbs?"

"Yes."

I waited for her to elaborate.

"I am," she insisted.

"You haven't told Sterling, though?"

"No. And I don't plan to until I have to."

"And the California police haven't contacted you?"

"No, they haven't."

"What if they suddenly show up at your door? And what if Sterling answers?"

"That will change things, won't it?"

"Are you as cavalier about this as you sound?"

"I'm really not. I'm serious about what I'm doing."

"Then I strongly recommend you reconsider your decision not to go to Safe House."

"I understand why you're concerned about me, but I don't think I can move out. I'm going to stay at home." She gazed down at her hands and said, "Now do you think we can talk about sex?"

Seven-twenty, and Gibbs looked like she'd been up for a couple of hours and had spent the time getting herself prepped for tea with some friends she was trying to impress. Her hair—perfect. Makeup—ditto. Outfit? A little too . . . something.

"Slutty," Diane would say, of course. But Gibbs's ensemble wasn't really slutty, just a shadow or two sexier than almost any other woman would assemble for an early-morning meeting to discuss her sex life with her therapist.

"Sex," she said, her voice suddenly crusty in a sultry Peggy Lee kind of way. "It's not just for procreation anymore."

Was it ever? Instantly, I was wide awake. Even at that hour I had the presence of mind to know that my sudden vigilance wasn't entirely a good thing.

"Sterling and I met in St. Tropez. Did we ever tell you that?"

I thought it was the kind of fact I'd have remembered from the earlier therapy. But I didn't recall previously musing with Gibbs, or any other patient for that matter, about any of the playgrounds of the privileged in the South of France. It was one of those things that didn't come up regularly in psychotherapy in Boulder, Colorado.

"I don't think so," I said.

"Sterling was working as crew on some rich guy's yacht—a big boat—and I was doing a summer-in-France-learn-a-language thing with a girlfriend after my freshman year in college. We all met at this big Saturday morning market in town in St. Tropez—Oh, you should go! The market was so much fun!—and he and his friends invited us onto the boat for a party later that day. It started with everybody swimming in the afternoon. We were anchored within sight of the beach, and Sterling put on this diving exhibition off the bow.

He was really good. Flips and pikes and God knows what else he was doing. He was the center of everybody's attention. I admit that I couldn't take my eyes off him.

"We hit it off; I mean, I really liked him right from the start. But you know, the party was going to be it as far as seeing him went; the yacht was sailing the next morning to Greece or Yugoslavia or somewhere. When my girlfriend and I left at the end of the evening—actually it was more like the middle of the night—I told Sterling where he could look me up in Palos Verdes if he wanted, but I never thought I'd see him again after that.

"Those summer things, they tug and tug, don't they? Did you ever have one, Dr. Gregory?"

Gibbs's breathing seemed to have grown deeper. Recalling her youthful memories had softened her persona just a little. My judgment was that she didn't really care whether or not I'd ever had a summer thing, but nonetheless my focus wavered for half a heartbeat with lusty reminiscences of an ancient August week with Nancy Lind when our families were both—

"Have you ever been to St. Tropez?" she asked, yanking me back to *her* summer thing.

I knew she didn't really want to know that, either. It was merely a way of stressing that *she* had.

"No," I said.

"It's not what you think. As a town, I mean. Well, it is, but then, you know, it isn't. It's not just the stereotype."

I was wondering why it was important what I thought of St. Tropez, a topic about which I never expected to have an opinion, let alone one firm enough to degrade into a stereotype. Asking her why it was important to her what I thought, I decided, would risk interfering with the direction of a journey I knew next to nothing about.

All I knew was that it was, directly or indirectly, about sex.

She didn't wait long to learn what misconceptions I might harbor about St. Tropez. "We didn't have sex that night," Gibbs said. "Other people did, almost everybody did. You know, it was that kind of party, but Sterling and I didn't do anything."

"Sex. It's not just for procreation anymore."

I started thinking that I'd never been to that kind of party. The kind of party where young beautiful people gather on a rich guy's yacht in St. Tropez and everybody has sex under the stars. A lost opportunity of my youth, perhaps. I didn't even recall the fork in the road with the sign marked WANTON SEX IN ST. TROPEZ, THIS WAY.

"We wanted to—I did anyway. I was a prude, and I wanted to, so I'm sure he did. For me, it was the most romantic night of my life. And not just romantic, but . . . erotic, sensual, you know? The Mediterranean, the yacht, the sky, the music, the wine, and these gorgeous people from all over the world. Sex was in the air. When you breathed, you inhaled it. It filled your nose like the flowers at the market that morning. You sipped some wine, and you could taste it. The sex, I mean. It was everywhere. Do you know what I'm talking about?"

Hardly. But I didn't say anything. I thought she had enough momentum to continue on her own.

"I'd never been to a party like that before. With

people so . . . uninhibited. Brazen. I mean, bold. And with strangers . . . So many languages . . . So much . . ." The final thought drifted away.

I admit that I was curious how her sentence would end, but any words on my part would have been distracting. I waited some more.

When she started up again, it was as though she were answering a question that I had never asked. Silence does that sometimes.

"What was it like to be there? I wanted to fall in love that night. I wanted to fall in love that night, and Sterling was there. He was handsome. He was charming. Oh, Sterling's not really tall enough to be my dream man, and I'd always fantasized that I'd end up with a guy with darker hair, but . . . that night he let me be there, but not be there. He let me dip a toe in the water—of, of that world—but he didn't throw me in the pool. He stayed with me almost the entire night while I tried to find out exactly where I might fit.

"That's not easy when you're nineteen and you're on a yacht in St. Tropez, right? Knowing where you fit?"

She found some affirmation somewhere in my impassive face, and she went on.

"There were other . . . you know, people for him on the boat. Plenty of them. Prettier than me. More adventurous than me, that's for sure. But . . . he didn't . . . go with them. He stayed with me. We danced. We kissed a little. Okay, we kissed a lot. And . . . you know. We watched a . . . little. But we didn't . . . So I guess that's why he was the one I . . ."

I was aware of the disconnect I was feeling. Despite the hour, despite my aversion to true sex adventures, the erotic escapade that Gibbs was spinning was actually interesting to me. I pushed myself hard against the cushion of my chair. It was a way of telling myself to take a step back. A way of reminding myself that whatever it was that was happening right then in my office, it was about Gibbs, not about her interlude in St. Tropez with Sterling.

My job was to ignore the fireworks and focus on the night sky.

To use my night vision. Not to be blinded.

"Anyway, he did call," she went on. "He actually called my parents' house the following Christmas Eve. I was home from school for the holidays. He came over, and we stayed out almost that whole night, just talking."

Instinctively, I guessed what was next. *No sex*, I thought. *He played it cool. It was just like St. Tropez, sans the yacht and the Mediterranean.*

"We didn't have sex then," she confirmed. "We just talked. But the whole night I felt like I was back on that yacht with him. It was that sensuous, that romantic, you know? I felt an anticipation, a sense of I-can't-wait, I-can't-wait, that I hadn't felt on Christmas Eve since I was eight years old. But of course it was different. And that's the charge I feel—still feel—when I see Sterling."

Mental note: She said "feel," not "felt."

The slope Gibbs was on suddenly changed. I experienced it as a physical sensation. Her momentum slowed as the gravitational forces eased. She pulled into herself, squeezing her biceps against her upper body. The effect was to force her breasts together, accentuating her previously modest cleavage.

Was that her intent? And was it conscious or unconscious? That was my call to make. It was why I was paid the big bucks.

But I didn't know.

"We had sex the first time a week later, on New Year's Eve," she said. "We were at a party, at a high-rise apartment on Wilshire Boulevard. You know, in L.A.? Some friends of his lived there. We ended up doing it on the balcony. The night wasn't that different from the party in St. Tropez. People were having sex all over the place. I could see another couple going at it in the bedroom next door while we were doing it outside."

She flicked a glance at me. If she could have read my mind, she would have known that I was musing that she and I had certainly spent our youths being invited to different parties.

What was she hoping? That I'd find her tale titillating? Scandalous? Mundane? I couldn't guess. I didn't like that I couldn't guess.

"That was the first time he said 'catch me.' "

" 'Catch me'?" I said.

"Yes," she said. " 'Catch me.' He said it again last night. It brought me back, reminded me."

I adopted a studied silence, waiting, wondering where Gibbs was going to go with her story of erotic adventure. It was clear that she wanted me to know that she'd made love to her husband the night before.

Was that it? Was that all?

What did the *catch me* story mean?

She matched my quiet. I set my sensors for defiance but wasn't sure exactly what I was detecting.

During the ensuing interim of silence I had a revelation—a slap-across-the-face kind of revelation.

My insight permitted me—hell, it compelled me—to finally ask the question I should have asked three days before, when Gibbs had first waltzed into my office and revealed that she believed her husband, Sterling, was a killer.

"Why did you come to see me, Gibbs?"

"What do you mean? We had an appointment."

My question had ambushed her, and her reply was more concrete than an interstate highway.

"Not this morning. I'm wondering why you came back into therapy with me."

She blinked twice in rapid succession. She parted her lips. But she didn't respond.

Finally I felt I knew something. Suddenly the therapy wasn't as amorphous as it had been.

What is it that I know?

I knew I had asked the right question. It wasn't much, but at that moment it felt pretty darn good.

So why had she come to see me?

SEVENTEEN

Twenty long seconds passed.

"I don't know what you mean. Why did I come to see you? I need your help to . . . get the situation with Sterling taken care of."

"Really?" I said. Her defenses had stiffened and become awkward as she tried to parry my thrust. My compassion for her swelled. With my simple question I was trying to sound dubious. It wasn't too difficult.

She dissembled. "What else could it be?" Gibbs asked. "I can't live with—what he's done. What else could it be?"

A tough question, one I was not prepared to answer.

I knew she wasn't, either.

I asked myself another tough question: *Well, Doctor, if this isn't all about sex and murder, what is it about?*

Something else.

Deep in my gut I believed that Gibbs Storey was

distracting me. First with her tale of murder. Then with the suggestion of serial murder. And now with sex in St. Tropez. I had to give her credit. As distractions, those were good hooks. Major league hooks. And yet I'd taken the bait for only three days.

Not too bad. For me, anyway. Skilled sociopaths had been known to suck me in and drag me along in their off-Broadway dramatics for months at a time. Diane liked to say that when sociopaths had me for lunch, they didn't spit out the bones until bedtime.

Diagnostically I didn't think Gibbs was a sociopath, but her diversion ammunition was as high quality as anything I'd run across recently.

The fact that I thought Gibbs was setting up psychological screens with me didn't mean I no longer believed her contention that Sterling was a murderer. And it didn't mean I no longer believed her tale about the summer thing on the yacht in St. Tropez. Nor did it mean I felt her efforts to dissemble were consciously driven.

My conclusion about her psychological deke—that's one of Sam's hockey words—wasn't even a hundred percent firm. From a therapy perspective, I wasn't prepared to put it to her in the form of an interpretation, or a confrontation. But it was my new working hypothesis: Gibbs was talking about murder and sex as a way of distracting me—and yes, possibly herself—from something that felt even more psychologically dangerous to her.

So what was more dangerous than extramarital sex and a husband who was a murderer?

Her final words of the session surprised me. She said, "It's as though you can read my mind."

I left her thought there, hanging. The truth was, I couldn't read minds.

On good days I could see a short ways into the dark, but that's as far as it ever went.

EIGHTEEN

I should have predicted it, of course, but I wasn't prepared for Sam's vulnerability. He had always been the tough guy. But that day, despite his size, he seemed frail and more than a little frightened.

A few hours after my appointment with Gibbs, Sam and I walked from his home near Community Hospital over to North Boulder Park. He met me outside by the curb. He was carrying a pedometer that he didn't understand how to use, and he futzed with it continually for a couple of blocks before he cursed at it and stuck it into the pocket of his sweatpants. It was apparent that he had about as much faith in the operation of the thing as he did in the diameter of the opening of his coronary arteries.

I was lugging lunch in a shopping bag that had originally been used to cart home a toaster from Peppercorn on the Mall. Lauren had packed hummus and roasted vegetable sandwiches on flatbread for Sam and me. Dessert was first-of-the-season Clementine tangerines. The beverage was caffeine-free green tea. I considered the homemade meal a special treat. Sam, I was afraid, would consider it evidence of all that was wrong with Boulder.

We did a lap around the park before we chose a place to sit and eat. Boulder was getting one of the latest extended Indian summer sojourns I could recall. The day was glorious.

Once we were seated, Sam didn't jump to unwrap his sandwich. He had two fingers on the underside of his wrist and his eyes on his wristwatch. "I think I'm okay," he said.

"That was convincing."

He chuckled, just a little. What was more interesting to me was that he started downing the hummus and vegetables without complaining about the absence of animal flesh in his meal.

"That Laguna Beach detective has been in touch with the department," he said between bites.

"What?"

"You know, that Carmen . . . something. The one you talked to. She reached out to us."

"And?"

"And nothing. I asked Lucy if any of the detectives had heard anything, she told me somebody had gotten the call. Maybe Danny, she thought. But that's all I know. I'm a little out of the loop."

Lucy was Sam's partner. I didn't know any detectives named Danny.

"So you don't know the next step for Detective Reynoso? If she's coming out here?"

"I don't know anything. I know less than nothing." He took another bite of his sandwich. "You make this? It's pretty good. There's no cheese in it, right? I'm trying to cut back on cheese. I used to eat a lot of cheese. The French eat a lot of cheese; they're not fat. I eat a lot of cheese, and I'm fat. I don't get it. One of life's mysteries, I guess. And how come so many of life's mysteries involve the French? Why is that?"

I didn't have an answer for his French puzzle. "You can thank Lauren for lunch. And no, no cheese. You want to know what's in it?" He didn't answer. I started to tell him anyway. "Garbanzo beans, tahini, a lot of garlic—"

"Did I tell you yes? Did I? I don't want to know what's in it. It tastes okay, that's all I care about right now. Tahini? Jeez. I can't believe I'm eating something called tahini."

"I'll tell Lauren you liked it."

"I'm ready to go back to work," he proclaimed.

"Yeah?"

"It's going to be a long time until January. I'm going to go stir-crazy. You know, I won't even be done with this stupid rehab program until Christmas. I only go for a couple of hours three times a week. Why don't they just let me go straight through for a couple of days, and then I'll be done with it? Wouldn't that be more efficient, less stressful? Isn't that the whole idea, to reduce my stress?"

"They give you any handouts on type A personality, Sam? If they did, you might want to take a minute and read them."

He grumbled.

I went on. "Attitude is half the battle. Give rehab a chance. And you can use your free time to get into the holidays this year. Make it fun. Decorate the house. Sing Christmas carols."

"Holidays mean food. Ham and prime rib and

pumpkin pie and Christmas cookies and all sorts of stuff I'm not supposed to eat anymore. I can't even sit around and watch Bowl games and eat crap in front of the TV."

"There are other things you can do." I finished peeling a tangerine and tossed it to him.

He missed it.

"You this banal when you're seeing people in your office, or you save most of your trite shit for your friends?"

I glanced at my watch. "I need to get back to the office. Come on, I'll walk you home."

"Maybe I'll stay here for a while."

I stood up before I asked, "Things tough with Sherry, Sam?"

"We've been here before. We'll muddle through." He stopped for a long pause and picked at some dead grass. Colorado's prolonged drought meant that there was a lot of dead grass to choose from. "She feels, I don't know, unfulfilled with me sometimes. I think I understand, kind of."

"It's not just the heart thing, though?"

"I don't know what it is."

"How do you feel? About things with Sherry?"

He didn't answer. He pulled himself slowly to his feet and walked beside me as I crossed the park. I matched his pace, wondering whether it was his wounded heart, literally, or his wounded heart, figuratively, that was slowing his progress across the wide lawn.

We spoke little until we got to his door. I went inside with him to use his bathroom before I drove the short way back to my office.

When I'd finished washing my hands, I stepped into his tiny kitchen to say good-bye. He was slumped over at the counter with his head in his hands.

"Sam? You okay?"

He didn't look up. With his elbow he slid a single sheet of floral paper in my direction. I could see it was covered in a tiny, neat script.

He said, "It looks like Sherry's gone. She took Simon to see his grandparents."

"For Thanksgiving? In Minnesota?"

He looked up, finally. His eyes were red. "I guess. I imagine I'll be alone for the holidays."

"What does it say? You guys haven't talked about this?"

"Talking's overrated. I think she's taking a break from me."

"Sherry's leaving you?"

He picked up the paper and shoved it into his pocket. "I don't know. Maybe."

The shock I felt was seismic. I couldn't imagine the effect of the quake on Sam's recovery.

"She loves me. That's not it, Alan. I'm not a hundred percent sure what it is, but it isn't that."

"Sam, I—"

"Go back to work. I think I want to be by myself for a while," he said.

My feet were stuck to the linoleum.

"Go on. I need the practice," he said.

He meant practice being by himself.

NINETEEN

I don't work most Fridays. No, that doesn't mean I do a short week. Even though I pack forty-plus hours into my four-day calendar, Puritan guilt occasionally interferes with my enjoyment of the break that I schedule every week. Still, most Fridays I treasure the extra hours I have to spend with Grace, or to do an uninterrupted bike ride on relatively uncongested roads.

That Friday wasn't destined to be one of the days off that I treasured, however.

I packed up Grace along with all her voluminous paraphernalia—once in college I went to Europe for a month with less stuff than Grace needed to go across town—and together we headed out of the house a few minutes after nine. We were going to do some errands. Not routine errands. Grace and I were skilled professionals at the grocery store and the dry cleaner. Returning videos? Getting gas? No problem. We could have a great time strolling the aisles at McGuckin Hardware or picking out a new pair of miniature tennis shoes at a shoe store. But the errands we had to do that Friday were errands I'd been putting off for weeks because they involved—gulp—public agencies and public utilities.

If doing errands was purgatory, doing that type of errand was hell.

Our first stop was the office that issues drivers' licenses for the state of Colorado. I was due for a renewal. Technically, because I hadn't been apprehended any of the times that I'd bent Colorado's traffic laws, the statute said that all that the renewal required was my right index fingerprint, my digital photograph, a few brief written questions, and fifteen dollars and sixty cents of my money. How long could that take?

How long?

Sixty-four minutes. I counted every one of them.

Next stop: the United States Postal Service. I had to mail a small package to Italy. Once the customs forms were filled out, Grace and I got in line. Maybe twenty people were ahead of us. Three clerks at the counter. I did the math and told Grace, "Fifteen minutes tops, baby."

Moments later, one by one, two of the clerks mysteriously closed their windows and disappeared into the back of the building. Someone asked, "What kind of business closes cashiers when they have this many customers?"

Nobody bothered to answer. The question was not only rhetorical, it was also supremely cynical. All of us in United States Postal Service suspended animation already knew we weren't in Kansas anymore.

There were still fifteen people in front of Grace and me in line. And at least that many had piled into the building behind us. Grace asked me how much longer. She did this by squealing and pulling at my ear.

"Another half hour, Boo," I explained. She asked again, and again.

How wrong was I? The total wait at the post office to mail our package turned out to be seventy-seven minutes.

On to Boulder's cable TV franchisee. The remote control to our cable box had died. I was on a simple mission to trade it in for a working model. In the parking lot of the cable company, I told Grace, "This is corporate America. This will be quick. Ten minutes, tops."

Times five, maybe. Fifty-three minutes later I had a fresh remote control unit and a splitting headache. Grace's patience, never exemplary, had evaporated totally.

My watch said ten minutes after one. Viv—our lovely, indispensable child-care-worker-nanny-person—had been waiting for us at the house since twelve-thirty.

I drove home, handed Grace off to Viv, downed an energy bar and a big glass of water, and went to change my clothes for a bike ride.

I'd finished stripping naked and was fishing in my closet for my cycling clothes when my pager started vibrating on the shelf.

I checked the screen.

It read "911" beside a Boulder phone number.

Before I had a chance to return the call, the phone rang. I jogged a few steps to the bedroom and answered. To my surprise, I heard Sam's voice.

"The shit came down," he said.

I thought he was talking about Sherry. I guessed he'd been served with dissolution papers or something similarly awful.

"God, I'm sorry, Sam. What happened?"

"They're executing a search warrant as we speak. Understand, you didn't hear it from me."

Why would they want a search warrant for Sam's house? And who else would I hear it from?

"What for? Who's searching your house?"

"Not here, you doofus. Don't be a jerk. At your client's house. That detective from California? The old murder? Getting warm yet? Need any more clues?"

"A search warrant? They haven't even talked to anyone. I didn't even know they were in town."

"I'm so sorry you didn't get copied on the memo. I promise to have someone look into that; it's inexcusable. Anyway, Lucy says Reynoso came into town with another detective, they met with the brass, and in no time they got a warrant from Judge Heller. They sure didn't waste any time exercising the thing. She said they have their game faces on. This one's serious, Alan. I gotta go."

He hung up.

My pager began to dance on the shelf again.

Same message as the previous one: "911" and the same local phone number that I didn't recognize.

I dialed the number and said, "This is Dr. Gregory returning a page."

"Can you come over?" Gibbs begged. "Please? They're searching our house. They're going through everything. They have our computers. They're even taking Sterling's *shoes*."

I was tongue-tied. Partly I was wondering why it was such an affront to Gibbs that the police were taking her husband's shoes. But mostly I was considering the curious strategy that Detective Carmen Reynoso had adopted for dealing with the accusation against Sterling Storey.

No talk, just action.

"Please?" Gibbs repeated.

"Give me your address, please, Gibbs. I don't recall where you live." She gave me directions to a new neighborhood I was almost totally unfamiliar with, somewhere west of Broadway and north of downtown. "Did you ever get in touch with a local lawyer?" I asked.

"Kind of."

Whatever that means, I wondered.

"Well, I suggest you give that person a call. I'll be over in a little while, although I'm not sure what I can do given the circumstances."

As I pulled on some boxer shorts and gazed longingly at my Lycra, I said aloud to myself, "I don't know why I'm coming over. But I'm coming over."

Sam had said that they "had their game faces on." That they were "serious." Which to me meant one thing: Detective Carmen Reynoso believed some aspect of Gibbs's story.

Suddenly Diane's caution about my therapeutic behavior flowed into my head the way water emerges from a cracked pipe: loudly, and with great insistence.

"What you're doing for Gibbs you wouldn't do for a lot of patients."

I stopped with one foot hovering above my trousers.

Diane was right.

Now what the hell had I gotten myself into?

TWENTY

Gibbs and Sterling lived in one of those big faux Victorians that had been all the rage in the build-out of the northwest and eastern expanses of Boulder in the 1980s when developers were finally beginning to believe that the city was serious about growth control. The architects had, I'm sure, been trying to pay respectful homage to the original Victorian heritage of the city's housing base in the 1880s, but the end result turned out more like Main Street in Disneyland than like Mapleton Hill in Boulder.

The Storeys' three-story house had to be five thousand square feet in size. As I approached the home from the corner—it was easy to tell which one it was by the convention of marked and unmarked police department vehicles clustered out front—I wondered what the Storeys did in there by themselves. A two-person game of hide-and-seek could go on for weeks without resolution.

Gibbs was sitting by herself in the driver's seat of a monstrous gold-colored SUV, the kind of motoring behemoth that I hated driving behind, next to, in front of, or on the same road with. It wasn't just that the latest-generation SUVs were big, it was that they tried so hard to be big. It was as though they thrust out their chests and puffed out their cheeks. Gibbs's colossus was a Cadillac. She was swallowed up behind the steering wheel of the thing like a five-year-old pretending to drive a fire truck. She was startled when I knocked on the passenger-side window, but waved me in after a moment.

She wasn't effervescent.

"Thanks for coming. I don't even know why I called."

I could have admitted that I didn't, either, but if I had, then I probably would also have had to consider aloud why I had responded by driving across town to be with her, and I wasn't eager to do that.

"What's going on?"

"They just showed up, shoved some papers in my face, and started rummaging through my house. God knows what they're doing in there. There are five of them."

"Are they from California? The ones I called for you?" I already knew the answer to the question, but I wasn't going to learn much about Gibbs if I didn't keep her talking.

"Yeah, um, yes. At least one of them is. Maybe two. There's a woman. She's really tall. She told me she's from Laguna. She said she was the one you spoke with on the phone."

"Detective Reynoso."

Gibbs shrugged.

"Any detectives from Boulder?"

"Yes."

"Did you get a name?"

"I've forgotten it already."

"Sterling? Is he here?"

"He left yesterday for Florida. The Seminoles, the Gators, the Hurricanes—I don't know. He's doing some game, a Florida team against some team not from Florida. Georgia, maybe. Or Alabama. Auburn? Where's Auburn? I'm sorry. I've tried and tried and tried, and I can't tell them all apart. I know it's important to some people, but for the life of me I can't tell them apart."

She actually seemed ready to break into tears over her college football dyslexia. In a more conventional psychotherapy, I would have figured that the marital repercussions of her gridiron ignorance—and her feelings about the same—were a topic we would get around to talking about in some more detail.

But now wasn't the time. "What city is he in?"

"Tallahassee."

"Have you tried to reach him?" I was aware that I was asking a lot of questions, not typical for me in psychotherapy and usually not a sign that things were going well. My database of therapy sessions in the front seats of Cadillac Escalades was, however, limited.

Gibbs lifted a cell phone from her lap. "He's not answering. He's always busy when he's setting up these broadcasts. Deadlines, deadlines. I left him a message."

"And your attorney?"

"There really isn't one."

"And you implied that there was one because . . ."

I allowed the thought to settle close by her like an unfriendly dog to see if she'd respond to it. I thought I noticed her jaw clenching, but that was the only reaction she displayed.

I finished my own sentence. ". . . because you thought I'd be angry or disappointed if you didn't have a lawyer."

She nodded. She wasn't looking at me. She was watching a very blond, very strong police officer carry an iMac out of her house. "That's not even Sterling's, it's mine. He hates Macs."

The strong blond officer placed the computer in the back of a gray Chevy Suburban.

"You didn't want to—what? Make me angry?"

She huffed. Just a little huff, but a huff nonetheless. "I don't like expectations in relationships."

Noted. "And you think that I had an expectation about you having a lawyer?"

Her nostrils flared. "From the beginning you've had an expectation about my doing this your way."

I reminded myself that my relationship with Gibbs was psychotherapy, a form of human interaction that often appears to have little in common with reality.

"My way?" is all I said, and I managed to say it in a measured voice, as though I were curious and not incredulous. I knew I could have pounced. Fortunately, I was also aware at some level that I wanted to pounce.

My way would have included Gibbs staying in Safe House, not sharing a bed with the man she was accusing of murder. My way would have included Gibbs calling the Laguna Beach Police Department on her own, not having me do it in her stead. My way would not ever, ever have included my sitting in the front seat of a Cadillac Escalade while a search warrant was being carried out.

But Gibbs wasn't talking about reality, she was talking about reality as she experienced it. Her real world. Not *the* real world. She was talking, especially, about the role that men assumed in her real world. My job was to help her make some sense out of that experience and perhaps ultimately help her see the extent of the divergence that existed between her real world and the place where most of us hung out, that universal theme park called "reality."

Just then a parade of three peace officers marched out the garage door of Gibbs's home. Each of the cops was carrying two large brown-paper bags that were folded once at the top. A tag was stapled at the fold of each bag.

Gibbs said, "I wonder what they're stealing. I have some nice things."

A little reality testing was in order. "I think they're trying to solve a murder, Gibbs. Your friend Louise? You called them, right? That's why they're here, isn't it?"

"I know," she said.

But she was much more annoyed than sympathetic.

"That's her," Gibbs said.

Carmen Reynoso *was* tall. From the distance where we were sitting, I guessed six feet tall. Like many visitors to our fine state, she was also unaccustomed to the vagaries of Colorado weather. The calendar said November, and many if not most outsiders figure that means blizzards followed by subzero temperatures followed by snowplows followed by commuters getting to work on cross-country skis until the mud season starts in May.

Reynoso was dressed perfectly according to the common lore. She was decked out in good leather boots, wool pants, and a thick turtleneck sweater that would have left me begging for a place to change into something more temperate. She carried a heavy navy jacket draped over her left arm.

The tail end of a little cold front had come through overnight, clipping the Front Range and dropping us from the high seventies into the mid-sixties. The sun was sharp, though—its rays filtered only by the thinnest ribbons of high clouds—and I thought I was a bit overdressed in cords and a cotton sweater.

"Nice boots," Gibbs said. "Though I wouldn't wear them with that coat. Nope."

Nice boots?

Detective Reynoso took two long strides down the serpentine herringbone brick walkway before she pirouetted to the sound of her name being called from inside the house and returned to the shadows.

"Did Detective Reynoso say anything to you about when she'd like to speak with you?" I asked.

"She asked me to stick around during the search. I assumed that meant she wanted to see me after."

"You should have an attorney present, Gibbs. For your protection." My wife had drilled into me that I should have an attorney present whenever anybody from law enforcement wanted to talk to me about anything. Yes, she would admit that there were exceptions, but she would insist that I first run them past my attorney.

Exasperated, Gibbs said, "I'm the one who called. I don't *need* protection. Don't you get that?"

I swallowed involuntarily. I didn't correct her and

remind her that technically it had been I who had called.

"Not from you, not from an attorney, not from Safe House, and not from *her*." Gibbs pointed in the general direction of Carmen Reynoso. "Got it?"

TWENTY-ONE

The last thing I did before I left Gibbs alone in her Escalade was set an appointment with her for the following Monday morning. Early. Seven A.M. early. It's all I had free.

I zipped down Ninth and stopped by my office to get some material for a report I planned to write over the weekend, then decided to run a couple of errands downtown.

I regret sometimes that the Downtown Boulder Mall is no longer a place where I can buy some brass Phillips-head screws or have a prescription refilled. Before the Mall was built—transforming a few blocks of Boulder's "Main" Street into an alluring brick and tree-lined promenade—downtown Boulder was like a thousand other Great Plains downtowns: a two-lane thoroughfare with a coffee shop, a hardware store, a drugstore, and maybe even a five-and-dime.

My old landlady—the kind woman who had given

me a lovely place to live during graduate school and had ultimately sold me the house that Lauren and I now live in—had regaled me over endless cups of jasmine tea and plates of fresh-baked cat's tongues about the Boulder she'd fallen in love with, the Boulder that existed before the gentrification of downtown in the seventies and eighties.

Lois had been a good friend of Fred, who'd owned Fred's Restaurant, and of Virginia, the matriarch behind the Printed Page. Lois didn't live much in the past, but she'd occasionally allowed herself some intense longing for a piece of Fred's apple pie, or for a copy of some unheralded book that Virginia would insist she just had to read. Neither the pie nor the literary recommendations had, apparently, ever disappointed Lois. Although she loved walking the new mall right up until the time she repatriated to Scandinavia, Lois never lost her affection for what Boulder had been for most of the century before.

Now? Fred's is gone. So is Fred. The Printed Page has moved away, and the Downtown Boulder Mall is lined with shops, not stores. There are lots of places to buy crafts. National chain stores seem to outnumber local retailers.

I was thinking about those kinds of changes as I rushed down Pearl Street in search of a DVD that Lauren wanted me to pick up for Grace. My daughter had developed an inexplicable fascination with trucks, and apparently there was no shortage of videos on the subject that were specifically intended for the toddler set. I had a list of acceptable titles from Lauren. What I didn't have was any confidence that the Downtown Boulder Mall contained a store that sold toddler-oriented DVDs about eighteen-wheelers and hooks and ladders.

I was approaching the pedestrian light at Broadway when I heard, "My God, would you slow down a little? Whose idea was it to put bricks down here, anyway? And whose idea was high heels? And is it 'was high heels' or 'were high heels'? I want to know that."

The fancy digital walk signal on the far side of Broadway counted down from six to zero while I waited for Diane to catch up. Traffic began to zoom by before she huffed up beside me. "You can probably find the answer to all your questions on the Internet," I said.

"Want to know the last thing I found out on the Internet? You'll love this. I decided that I wanted to be able to say 'My God' to my husband in Spanish—you know, so I could say 'My God, Raoul, aren't you lucky to be married to me?' in his native tongue—so I typed 'My God' and 'Spanish' into Google. What do you think I got? I got a website that told me how to say 'Oh my God, there's an axe in my head!' in one hundred and two different languages."

"Was one of them Spanish?"

"Yeah."

"There you go, then."

"*¡Dios mío, hay un hacha en mi cabeza!*"

"That will come in handy someday, I'm sure. How are you doing, Diane?"

"Good. My practice is full, my patients think I have a healing touch, my husband's a dream, I have money in the bank, and I don't have a *hacha* in my *cabeza*. What more can one ask? Oh, I know: What are you doing down here on Friday, and why the hell are you in such a hurry?"

"I'm on a mission." I explained about the DVD. I didn't explain about my front-row seat at the execution of the search warrant at Gibbs's house.

"Mind if I jog alongside? I have something important I've been meaning to ask you."

"I'd love some company. What do you want to know?"

The walk signal changed to green. The digital scoreboard said we had twenty seconds to cross Broadway. It seemed like a long enough time, in theory, but the numbers were descending so rapidly that I wanted to hurry even more.

"Were you popular in high school?" Diane asked.

"Excuse me?" I said, though I did not miss the irony that she had asked the question as we were approaching the display windows of the teenage clothing mecca, Abercrombie & Fitch.

"In high school, what group did you hang with? The geeks? The nerds? The jocks?" She took a moment to laugh at the thought of me hanging with the jocks. "Come on," she prodded. "What group? I'm testing a theory here. I won't tell anybody."

"I wasn't one of the popular kids, if that's what you're asking."

"Aha! I bet you were in the Freud Club or something."

"Your school had a Freud Club?"

"Never mind. Next question. This one's important. Did you ever have the hots for any of the popular girls?"

Oh. I watched the pieces begin to fall into place.

"You mean the *über*-popular alpha bitches?"

"Just answer me."

"Where is this going?"

"I'm trying to understand why you're being so precious with Gibbs. Like I said, I have a theory."

"And you've decided it has to do with some high school time warp I'm locked in to?"

"Just tell me, did you ever have a thing for any of the popular girls? You know who I'm talking about. *Them*. The ones who sat at *that* table at lunch, the ones who never said anything in a normal voice. The ones who were always whispering to each other or saying things loudly enough that the whole world knew what they were thinking."

Several steps passed before she repeated, "*Them*. You know exactly who they were."

"No," I said. But I immediately had a 70mm Technicolor image of Teri Reginelli flash onto the wide screen in my brain. Wavy hair, brown eyes, and a smile that could plaster me to Teflon.

"You're sure?"

"Yes."

"No, you're not. Be honest—who are you thinking about right now? Give her a name, come on."

I sighed. "Teri Reginelli."

"Cheerleader? Prom queen?"

"Neither. Mere goddess."

"She was above you socially?"

"It was crowded territory."

She punched me and said, "Still is." Her tone softened. "Isn't it strange how being an adolescent never really stops? Isn't it? Show me what someone was like during their high school psychosis, and I'll put together a damn good road map into their romantic future."

I didn't want to argue with her. Mostly because I knew that there was plenty of truth in her words. To deflect attention from myself I asked, "What was high school like for you?"

"I was fully occupied thinking up ways to kill the Teri Reginellis of the world. And *that* is the source of my transference to the Dancing Queen." She admitted her introspective success triumphantly.

"A question," I said. "Did you ever think about whacking a *hacha* into the *cabeza* of a Teri Reginelli or three at your school?"

"I was taking French—*Mon dieu, il y a une hache dans ma tête!* Otherwise, I'm sure I would have gotten there eventually. So, at what store down here do you think you're going to find your daughter a DVD about trucks?"

"I don't know." I'd totally forgotten about the DVD. Teri Reginelli had that effect on me.

We crossed Thirteenth. Diane leaned close to me, tugged my head down so my ear was closer to her level, and whispered, "It's called transference, Alan. It sneaks up on all of us. Don't ignore it just because I'm the one who brought it up."

Before I could reply, Diane peeled away from me like an F-18 dropping out of formation. She was making a beeline for the bank down Thirteenth, one of her favorite places downtown.

"*Dios mío,*" she said over her shoulder. "*Adiós.*"

Transference: treating, responding to, and/or having feelings about someone in the present as though they were someone important from the past.

Teri Reginelli.
Gibbs Storey.
Me.
Help.

TWENTY-TWO

DVD procured, the drive east was uneventful. I parked my car in the garage, got out, and took a moment to linger near my dark blue not-too-old Trek road bike. The bicycle was hanging securely on its pulley system from the rafters in the garage. I glanced outside even though I knew it was already too dark to make up for the ride that I hadn't taken that afternoon.

Lauren kissed me, Grace squealed, and the dogs seemed happy to have me home. Lauren got the DVD going for Grace while I made a couple of adjustments to Emily's paw umbrella. The thing was protecting the wound on her paw marvelously, but it required an abnormal amount of maintenance. I was no longer certain that a trip to the patent office and instant wealth were on the horizon for me.

Once we moved to the kitchen, Lauren sat down across from me while I sorted through a seriously uninspiring pile of mail. Neither of us had any fresh news to report from either Sam or Sherry. I filled her in on the morning adventures with the cable company, the post office, and the drivers' license office. Unmoved by my tales of institutional indolence, she moved into the business part of the kitchen to attend to the meal she'd been preparing.

Once she had her back turned to the stove, she said, "That's interesting. So who's Teri Reginelli?"

My breath caught in my throat.

Instinctively, I knew that my wife was facing away from me so that I couldn't see the I'm-sitting-in-the-catbird-seat grin that she had plastered across her cute mug. I said, "Oh God. I bet Diane called you right from the bank, didn't she? She was going straight to the bank."

"I heard the whole story while she was standing in the teller line. She said she left you befuddled on the Mall."

"Figures."

"Were you?"

"Was I what?"

"Befuddled on the Mall?"

"Most of the women in my life leave me feeling befuddled. I'm beginning to feel befuddled right now, for instance. Teri Reginelli was not an exception. Believe me, she was not an exception."

"So who was this mystery girl I've never even heard about? High school, right? Should I be worried?"

Lauren's tone was ninety-nine percent tease. "No," I said. "But Diane should be."

"Is this going to end up being like that Sawyer thing a few years ago? Is Teri Reginelli about to show up at our door with a suitcase and a few verses about how her life isn't complete without you? God, I hope not. I didn't like the Sawyer thing much at all."

"The Sawyer thing" was the one percent in Lauren's tone that wasn't tease. She wasn't kidding; she hadn't liked the Sawyer thing at all.

"I swear that Teri Reginelli wouldn't be able to tell you who I was if you held a gun to her head. Actually, get Diane to hold the gun to her head. Or a *hacha* to her *cabeza*. She'd relish the opportunity."

"What? What language are you speaking?"

"It's not important."

"Teri Reginelli is. At least to me. Go on. I want the details. Pretend you're talking to your therapist."

"Teri Reginelli was a high school crush I had. I never even went out with her. Not once."

"Then why are we talking about her?"

"Ask Diane."

"I did. She said you had the hots for her. For Teri, that is. She said after all these years Teri's still changing your oil. She told me to mention Teri's name, sit back, and watch you dance like your toes were on fire."

"That's Diane's phrase, isn't it? 'Changing your oil'? Diane said that, right? Am I right? Diane thinks I'm a prude. Do you know that? Do you think I'm a prude? A serious prude?"

"Don't change the subject."

"Part of it's true, I guess. In the high school era of my life Teri was the neighbor's wife whom I coveted."

Lauren looked puzzled.

"Figuratively speaking. Teri Reginelli was the head of the pack in high school. You know, the leader of the popular girls. The alpha chick? Senior year she dated a guy who slummed with me and my friends sometimes."

"Was he a hottie?"

"Yeah, Sean was a hottie."

"And?"

"This guy Sean treated her like shit. She would talk to me about it, ask me about things he did with other girls, what he said about her. You know how girls are when they're seventeen. She wanted to know what made him tick. I was a good listener—"

"Even then?"

"Yes, even then."

"And you fell in love with her, and she never even knew it. Right? It was unrequited love?"

I sighed. What had felt like a monumental event in my life was suddenly sounding like a carefully carved monument to banality. "Right, something like that."

Lauren was really getting into it. Me? I was losing interest, fast.

"She signed your yearbook 'Alan, you're the best!' or 'What a great friend!' or something like that, I bet. Yes? The 'XXX' was the closest you ever came to kissing her. Am I right?"

I sighed once more.

Lauren asked, "So what does all this have to do with Diane?"

"It has absolutely nothing to do with Diane. She's teasing me about an old conjoint case we did together."

I watched Lauren make connections, all the wrong ones.

"No, we didn't treat Teri Reginelli and her significant other. I don't even know where she's living, and I don't have a clue what guy is stuck with her. Teri Reginelli is just a metaphor for a point Diane was trying to make. Can we talk about something else? Please."

"Of course," she said.

Lauren leaned over to check something in the oven. I inhaled deeply but couldn't figure out what she was cooking in there. I was thinking chicken. I thought I captured the aroma of balsamic vinegar, too.

Her willingness to change the subject concerned me. It didn't take long for me to discover that I had good reason to be concerned.

She said, "There was an interesting thing at work today. Mitchell got called to oversee the execution of a search warrant on the home of a guy in town who's apparently become a fresh suspect in an old murder in southern California. A couple of detectives flew in from Laguna Beach and requested our assistance. The Boulder detective thought it would be better if somebody from our office was involved as an observer to the search."

I don't know whether I said "shit"—if I did, it certainly qualified as a mumbled profanity—or whether I merely thought *shit*.

Lauren said, "The whole case—a husband suspected of murder in another state, a loving wife who knows a little something—it reminded me of that question you asked me earlier in the week. Do you remember? The one about exclusions to the spousal privilege statute? Felony exceptions? Even as they might apply in some other state? Like California?"

"Yes," I said. "I remember."

She left the oven, walked over, and kissed me full on the mouth, tracing the outline of my lower lip with the tip of her tongue.

"Sometimes I love to watch you squirm. Mitchell saw you over at the house where they served the warrant today. So I think I know what spouse might be trying to exclude what testimony, and I think I know who the reincarnation of Teri Reginelli is, too."

She kissed me again. No tongue the second time.

There were days I had doubts that Boulder, Colorado, was still a small town.

Well, that day I had no doubts.

TWENTY-THREE

Saturday broke from the gates like a day that was intent on setting a new standard for late November. The morning was glorious. The air was crisp, clear, and dry, and the sunrise lit up the eastern horizon in shades of vaporizing gold.

I knew all about the beauty of the sunrise because I was heading east at the moment when the sun completed cresting the earth, my head up, my jersey zipped all the way to my Adam's apple, my spin well above a hundred, my padded butt barely on the saddle, my bike weightless between my legs. The back roads in Boulder County belonged to me alone.

I covered fifty miles of asphalt at a brisk pace and was back home sipping juice on my deck by nine o'clock.

The phone rang. Sam.

"You been outside yet?" he asked.

"I've done fifty miles already."

"Me, too," he countered. "Actually more like fifty yards. I walked out to get the paper. Who am I kidding? Given the size of my lot, that's more like fifty feet, isn't it? Astonishing day, huh?"

"Couldn't be better."

"We're going to get blasted, you know."

My living room deck faced the mountains. There wasn't a cloud in sight between my house and the Continental Divide, or from Pikes Peak down south to whatever peak that was past Longs Peak way up north. "Really? You think?" I said.

"It always happens. You get a run of unseasonably good weather like we've had lately, and then you get a day that's like, I don't know . . . perfect—like this one—and then five minutes later you're walking someplace and the wind is blowing hard enough to send you to Nebraska, and then five minutes after that you've got snow in your flip-flops."

He was right. That's just the way it usually happened. While I considered the image of Sam in flip-flops I took another glance toward the Divide.

Not a cloud. Not today—maybe tomorrow we'd get blasted.

I said, "How are you doing, Sam?"

He didn't exactly respond. He said, "There's somebody I have to talk to in Gold Hill. Want to come with? Bet it's pretty up there."

Lauren and Grace were at some weekly mother-child yoga event that Adrienne thought was the greatest thing going. I was tempted to go some Saturday morning just to watch. Grace had the not-so-svelte physique of a well-fed, chunky baby. My daughter could no more do yoga than I could fly. I left them a note about my plans and headed to Sam's house.

Depending on the weather, on a typical weekend

before Thanksgiving the ten-mile drive from Sam's house on the west side of Boulder up the Front Range to Gold Hill can take as little as twenty-five minutes or as long as—well, a long, long time. The road that curls up Sunshine Canyon into the mountains was paved for a while and then it isn't paved for a much longer while. In some places the dirt and gravel portion of the track is particularly steep and curvy, and in winter, with the sun low in the sky, some of the canyon stretches don't see the direct rays of the sun for months at a time. After a heavy snow and a deep cold snap, ice on the road can freeze as hard as a traffic cop's eyes.

The final descent into the valley that was home to the pioneer mining enclave of Gold Hill is a particularly spectacular section of trail. The road drops a few hundred feet in altitude—and about 150 years in time and attitude—in less than a minute.

Very few villages in the Rocky Mountains have managed to check the natural progression that leads from Old West town to Old West ghost town. Some of the ones that have managed to freeze themselves in time have become polished tourist magnets like Telluride and Georgetown, but only a precious few of the surviving nineteenth-century burgs have managed to remain invisible to the hordes of annual visitors who show up clutching tour books. Gold Hill was one of those few. Gold Hill was hard to get to, its fewer than two hundred full-time residents didn't exactly lay out a welcome mat for guests, and any attempt to find a location for a Golden Arches or Starbucks within the range of a .30-06 rifle from town would likely be met by a crowd of passionate locals prone to carelessness with torches.

The Gold Hill Inn, the town's enduring fine dining

destination, was open only during the summer months because too few Front Range residents could be counted on to make the drive up to nearly nine thousand feet in the inevitable springtime slush or the usually predictable autumn ice. Winter? For most people, casual travel to Gold Hill was too risky during an average snow year. I've always had the impression that four or five months of regular visits by curious flatlanders were about the maximum the residents of Gold Hill could tolerate anyway.

I hadn't asked Sam about his business in Gold Hill. The mountain enclave was in Boulder County, and Sam was a city cop, not a sheriff's deputy, so I suspected that his business was personal, not professional. But I also knew Sam well enough to know that if during the course of an investigation he wanted to talk with somebody who happened to reside a few steps outside the city limits, he would usually find a way to do so. The solution might be by-the-book legal, or it might be less-than-by-the-book creative. But the job would get done.

The fact that he was on medical leave from the police department? That would be no more of an impediment to him than the countless potholes we dodged in the dirt lane up to Gold Hill. Or the fact that I was certain he was under orders not to drive for a while after his heart attack.

Did I mention that to him? The driving restrictions? I didn't. When I arrived at his house, I had offered to drive. He had declined. That's as far as it went. I knew from experience that I could strongly encourage Sam's sense of self-preservation. But insisting on it only put my own at risk.

*

We parked on Gold Hill's main street across from the Gold Hill Inn. The street may actually have been called Main Street, but I didn't look for a sign. I was enjoying the gorgeous day and was reveling at being up in the mountains in a town that was so charmingly frontier yet didn't look as though it had been imagined by Disney set designers. As soon as I stepped out of the car onto the dusty dirt lane, I knew that, despite the fine autumn day, the air in Gold Hill—three thousand-plus feet above Boulder in altitude—held a chill that warned of imminent winter.

It should have felt ominous to me, but it didn't.

Sam led me across the road toward the ancient building I'll probably always think of as the home of the original Lick Skillet Café. My first wife and I had made frequent treks up the hill to the Lick Skillet for memorable meals in the late eighties before Dave Query packed up and trucked his culinary imagination down the mountain to Boulder and Denver.

The destination Sam had in mind was packed with locals. About half of the patrons seemed to make Sam for a cop before the cleft of his substantial butt cleared the jamb of the doorway. He pointed me toward an open deuce in a far corner. On the way we passed tables covered with platters that were plastered rim-to-rim with eggs and bacon and potatoes and flapjacks as big as hubcaps.

"Breakfast is hard for me," Sam said. "I miss meat that's been treated with nitrates. Outside of cheese, that's what I miss most. Brats, bacon, salami . . ."

I thought the waitress was just the slightest bit tentative as she approached our table. Sam waved off the menus and ordered an egg-white omelet, sans cheese, sliced tomatoes, and dry wheat toast. He asked her to be sure that the omelet was made with very little butter. Almost speechless, but eager to endorse his choices, I told her I'd have the same.

Although we both knew that we had just done the equivalent of going into a fine steak house and ordering steamed broccoli and brown rice, the waitress took the order with casual aplomb, as though the entire town of Gold Hill were already on the Ornish diet and our order was par for the course that morning.

"Wait here," Sam told me. "I have to go to the head. I won't be long." He stood and walked toward the bathrooms. Although I hadn't been back that way for most of a decade, I was guessing that the odds were about fifty-fifty that the plumbing Sam would find was still the kind that didn't involve copper pipes, or flushing.

I watched the choreography of turned heads that followed Sam's departure from the dining room. Just as the faces returned to their plates and their stained stoneware mugs of coffee, the waitress who had taken our order—a pleasant-faced young woman with close-set eyes and stringy brown hair—took the short walk toward the back of the house, too. She glanced over her shoulder before she turned the final corner.

Sam returned to the dining room first. He had been gone no more than ninety seconds total. The waitress followed him about ten seconds later and resumed her tasks behind the counter.

"Had to pee," he said as he sat down across from me. "Like to wash my hands before I eat."

"Yeah. You met with our waitress, too."

He nodded. "Wanted to remind her that the toast had to be dry. I'm off butter, you know."

"Yeah, I know. You want to tell me—"

"Maybe later."

Breakfast was bland, but then, we'd ordered it that way. Sam dug into his without complaint. I used the hot sauce on the table to add some zip to mine.

"Remember when we took the kids to Rocky Mountain National Park in September?" he asked.

"Sure," I said. Elk mate in the early autumn, and the beautiful dance concerts they produce at dusk prior to copulating draw hordes of human observers. Rocky Mountain National Park, northwest of Boulder, is prime territory for Front Range elk voyeurs. Sam, Sherry, Lauren, and I had taken the two kids, Simon and Grace, up the previous September for a cold picnic dinner and a visit to the annual elk show.

The elk had done their courting thing that night with philharmonic aplomb. Although the dance steps of the majestic bulls and their harems of cows were difficult to discern during the prime dusk time period, the acoustics that night were perfect. The bugling bulls sent their baritone calls bouncing off the granite faces in the park, and the eerie echoes quieted even the most restless *Homo sapiens* in the audience.

"That's when it hit me that Sherry was kind of unhappy. That night."

"Yeah?"

"Yeah."

He had wiped his plate clean and held up his mug for a refill of decaf before I realized he'd said all he planned to say about that night in the park. Me? I had a feeling there was more to discuss.

The waitress hustled over and topped off Sam's coffee mug. "There are a lot of rules after a heart attack. No caffeine for a while—that's one of them," he said. "As far as things I miss, it would be hard to choose between caffeine and nitrates."

"Sex?"

"I hope that's not an offer. If it is, you're a dead man."

I offered a grudging smile. Were I with a patient, clinical protocol would have had me waiting silently, feigning patience, for Sam to return to the topic of his troubled marriage. But with Sam I didn't have to follow any protocol. I said, "So that's it? That's all you're going to say about Sherry? That you knew she was unhappy?"

"She was showing me something. Maybe I wasn't able to see it. What more is there to say?"

"I don't know. That's why I'm asking."

"Did you notice anything?" he asked me.

"That night? No."

Sam caught the waitress's attention and pantomimed a request for the check. "Sherry said she was restless. That's the word she used. She was thinking of selling the flower shop. Maybe going back to school."

"I don't remember that."

"That's because she said it to me, not to you. You and Lauren and the kids were running ahead of us."

" 'Restless' for Sherry meant unhappy with you?"

"You know, you go back and look for clues. That's what I've been doing, anyway. I wonder what I missed. Whether I should have done something else."

"Like what?"

"I don't know. Something different. Maybe I let stuff slide that I shouldn't have let slide. Anyway, that's one of the things I'm thinking I did wrong. Other times

I think it's all her shit. I go back and forth. I have a lot of time on my hands."

"That night? What did you say to Sherry?"

"Probably not the right thing."

I sipped some water. "Why? What did you say?"

The waitress brought our check, sliding it to an empty spot on the table pretty much exactly halfway between us. She stacked all the plates and mugs in a careful cascade up one forearm. I watched closely; not even a glint of recognition flashed between her and Sam.

He said, "I don't remember exactly. I'm sure it wasn't what she wanted me to say."

I grabbed the check. Sam dropped a ten-dollar bill on the table.

"You're paying. That's the tip," he said.

"What about you, Sam? Are you happy?"

Did I get an answer?

Did Gold Hill have a Starbucks?

Almost halfway back to Boulder I asked, "What's the story with the waitress? Your meeting in the back of the café?"

A quarter of a mile of contemplation later he apparently decided that he was going to answer me.

"Four weeks ago last night she was with some girlfriends at a club downtown. One of those places on Walnut, not far from your office. I'm not going to say which one. You can probably guess. Maybe you read about it in the *Camera*. But she was on my turf. She got drunk—she admits that. She met some guys—she admits that—and she agreed to go to an after-party at some frat house by CU. She admits that. She decided to let them drive her over there in their car. She admits that. Crappy judgment after crappy judgment after crappy judgment, and she admits every bit of it."

His left hand snaked from the steering wheel to his upper abdomen, his thumb pressing on his sternum.

"On the way over to the Hill for the after-party, she was sexually assaulted in the back of a Chevy van."

"Raped?"

"Sexually assaulted."

The distinction was obviously important. I was curious why. Prurient interest? No. Just enduring curiosity about the perverse imagination of assholes on alcohol. But I didn't ask for any more details. Sam wouldn't have wanted me to know any intimate details of the waitress's horror. I liked that about him.

"And?"

"And it turns out that of all the people she's had to deal with about what happened that night, she trusts me the most. Go figure."

Sam paused. I think he was giving me the opportunity to make the mistake of saying something snide. I didn't.

"I've been concerned that if I wasn't around to hold her hand as this thing got closer to trial, she might get shy and drop the charges. The cops and the DA? We try real hard to make it okay, but the truth is that it's a bitch to be a sexual assault victim in the system we have. So I wanted to tell this girl personally about the heart attack and let her know that I'd be gone for a while but that I'd be back on the job to, you know, help her before this thing went to court."

I wasn't surprised at Sam's generosity, though his sensitivity sometimes snuck up on me.

That moment a sharp gust of wind exploded out of the west, which was behind us. The heavy car seemed to levitate like an amusement park ride about to careen down some ersatz mountainside. The sheer eighty-foot drop five feet from my window served as a reminder that this particular mountainside wasn't exactly ersatz.

I craned my neck to look behind us and saw that a thick bank of clouds had popped up and begun to shroud the highest peaks on the Divide.

Sam didn't turn around.

He said, "Told you. We're going to get blasted. Weather here is goofy."

We beat the approaching front down the mountain, though not by much. From our vantage on the street in front of Sam's house where he had parked his Cherokee, the army of clouds marching over the Divide had the determination of the Allies assaulting Normandy.

We were about to get blasted.

"You have rehab today?" I asked.

"Not until Monday. You know what they do there? These young kids in these dorky matching sweatsuits hook me up to all this heart monitor crap, and I do calisthenics with a bunch of old people, then they watch me walk on the treadmill, and then—then—they act like I'm lying when I tell them what I ate the day before. That's the entire drill. I don't see how that's supposed to help my heart, unless terminal aggravation is their frigging goal."

"You'll give it a chance, though? The rehab? I'm sure a big part of rehab is attitude."

"Don't talk to me about attitude. I'm feeling a little better every day. I think the medicine is helping. The beta-blockers. I'm more mellow, you know? That can't be all bad, right?"

I recognized that he hadn't answered my question about giving rehabilitation a chance.

"Of course not," I said.

He changed the subject once more. "I heard you made an unscheduled appearance at the execution of that search warrant yesterday." After he spoke, he punctuated his words by finally pounding the shift lever forward into park. I noted that he wasn't terribly kind to his transmission.

"Is anything a secret in this town? Jeez. I'm surprised my picture's not in this morning's *Camera*."

Sam laughed, first time all morning. I liked the sound of it, even if the joke was at my expense.

"I got a personal invitation from the search warrantee, Sam. Nobody knows that my friendly neighborhood cop gave me a heads-up. Did they find what they were looking for?"

He gazed at me over the top of his sunglasses. "You really think I'm going to tell you that?"

"Probably not. You wouldn't happen to know when she's going to, you know . . ."

"Accost you? No. But she will."

"Maybe not. I told her everything I know."

"No, you didn't. You told her everything you think it's okay for her to know. If Reynoso knows what she's doing, she knows damn well that you have more. And she's going to want to know what it is."

"What have you heard about her?"

He didn't answer that question, but he did answer

my earlier one. "The search at the house didn't go too well. There's still plenty of stuff to go over—couple of computers and file cabinets full of paper—but they didn't find anything damning. That can't have been too much of a surprise after all these years, though, right? You got to look."

"What about her—the detective? Do you know anything? Is she sharp?"

"I'm on medical leave, remember? Totally out of the loop. Trying to keep my stress level down."

"Okay, then tell me what you hear from Sherry."

"Simon's missing too much school. And I'm missing him way too much. That's all I know."

"Come on, pick, Sam. Carmen Reynoso or Sherry. Tell me something about somebody."

"Okay. Word is that Reynoso has a chip on her shoulder. Some incident in San Jose a few years back forced her to leave that department before she had her fifteen. She's about as happy chasing tourists around Laguna Beach as I would be chasing tourists around Aspen."

That wasn't very happy.

"What kind of incident in San Jose?"

"Won't tell you."

"Can't tell me?"

"Won't tell you."

"Do you even know?"

"No. But I wouldn't tell you if I did."

TWENTY-FOUR

By the time Detective Carmen Reynoso tracked me down for an interview, her outfit of wools and leathers was perfect for the weather.

The front that was carrying Pacific moisture over the mountains had collided with some supercold air that was blowing down from Saskatchewan, and together the two weather systems became a fast and furious snow machine along Colorado's Front Range. What had likely been the season's final Indian summer interlude was history before anyone had a chance to bid it adieu. I'd managed to drive only halfway from Sam's house to mine before the winds moderated below gale force and snow started falling in fat flakes that left melanoma rings in the dust on my car. I looked at the time.

Twelve-thirty.

I looked at the sky.

Winter.

At nine o'clock that morning, the day had been as splendid as any November day in memory. And now it was snowing like a son of a bitch.

We were getting blasted.

Carmen Reynoso was parked on the shoulder right where the pavement ended and the dirt lane started winding along the hillside toward my house. She was sitting in the front seat of a rented GM coupe reading an Avis road map. I knew the odds were good that the dirt lane that came to a blunt end in front of my home wasn't marked on the map she was reading.

At first I wasn't a hundred percent sure it was Reynoso behind the wheel, so I pulled alongside to get a better look. Once convinced, I lowered my passenger-side window.

"Detective Reynoso?"

"Dr. Gregory? You've been expecting me?"

I shrugged.

"Interesting weather you have around here. We don't get a whole lot of this in Laguna Beach."

What would the tourist board want me to say? "Well, I hope you enjoy the change. The storm will make the ski resorts very happy. They always love a good dump before Thanksgiving." The meteorological reality was that Front Range upslope snowstorms often left the big ski resorts on the west side of the Continental Divide basking in bright sunshine.

"Can we talk? I'm sure you know about what." Her words said invitation. Her eyes said something else.

I knew I could refuse. But what was the point? I wanted Reynoso to know what I knew. What I didn't want to do was fence with her about the things I didn't have permission to tell her, although that is precisely what I anticipated we would spend our time doing.

"Sure," I said. "Do you have a place in mind?" I didn't want to have the meeting at my house.

"We could have done it yesterday at your patient's house. You know, after the search. But I heard you only stayed for the first act."

Was that humor? I wasn't sure. A snowflake the size of a moth blew in the open window and landed on the tip of my nose. It melted instantly, and I wiped it away.

"Give me a few minutes with this"—she lifted the road map—"and I think I could get us back in the direction of the Boulder Police Department. That's—where? Thirty-third Street? Off, what—Arapahoe? Am I right? I'm sure they'd give us a room we could use. Everyone's been so nice."

I'd seen the interview rooms in the Public Safety Building on Thirty-third Street. Not my idea of a great place to spend a Saturday afternoon, blizzard or no blizzard.

I said, "You want to get some coffee somewhere?" I was thinking of leading her east into Louisville and finding some chain place like Village Inn. I didn't know as many people in Louisville as I did in Boulder.

She fixed her eyes on my face. A deep cleft had formed above the bridge of her nose, as though she were smelling something foul or facing directly into a bright sun. After a pause long enough that I would notice that she had delayed, she suggested, "What about your house? It's close by here, right?" She lifted the map again. "I bet I can find it."

The pace of the snow suddenly accelerated. The

lazy snowflakes that had been falling were replaced by millions of smaller, quicker reinforcements. A few super-frozen scouts started sticking to the windshield.

I was dressed in cotton cords and a light sweat-shirt. Home had its allure.

"Yeah, it is," I said. "Follow me."

I led Detective Reynoso down the lane and then into our house.

Lauren had scribbled a few words on the bottom of the note that I had left for her about heading out earlier in the day with Sam. She and Grace were home from yoga and gone again to a birthday party in Lafayette for one of Grace's friends. I use the word "friend" loosely. One-year-olds don't actually have buds; they have other one-year-olds that their parents make them hang out with.

I closed my eyes and cursed silently. Taking Grace to the birthday party had been my job: I was supposed to get Grace some lunch and then take her to her friend's party and bring her back home.

Two outings in a row taxed Lauren's multiple sclerosis–depleted energy reserves, which meant we would all pay a price later in the day, probably increased fatigue, for my oversight.

Damn.

During my interlude of silent self-flagellation, Reynoso stood patiently in the entryway. I finally remembered my manners. "Can I take your coat?"

"Sure. Nice place."

"Thanks."

She tried some small talk on me. "Do you know that Baseline Road is the fortieth parallel? I read that on the Boulder website."

"No, I didn't know that. You mean exactly? No minutes, no seconds?"

"Exactly. That's what it says. The road is exactly forty north."

"Well," I said as I led her into the living room and adjusted the thermostat to bring us some heat. To the west the usual glorious panorama of the Rocky Mountains was nothing but a screen of swirling white dots. "It's usually a nice view. In fact, on most days you get a pretty good look at the fortieth parallel."

"Your wife's a prosecutor," she replied, unamused.

Reynoso had moved on; we were apparently finished chatting longitude and latitude. But I didn't especially want to talk about my family, so I didn't respond.

She noticed that I didn't respond.

"I'll take that coffee," she said. "Actually tea, if you have it."

I didn't trust Reynoso alone in my house. What did I think she was going to do? Nothing specific, but at that moment I didn't even like the idea of her reading the titles that were lined up in my bookcase. "Of course. Come to the kitchen with me while I make it." I didn't say, *"If you're curious, you can check out the cookbooks."* But I thought it.

I made her a small pot of tea—Tension Tamer from Celestial Seasonings seemed an apropos choice. She sat on a stool and watched me. I could tell that she was enjoying our meeting more than I was.

When the tea was ready—she asked for milk, no sugar—I carried a mug back into the living room for her. She took a seat on the sofa, held the tea below her face—for the warmth, I decided, rather than the aroma—and took a tiny sip. After a moment she closed her eyes briefly and said, "Thank you."

I was settling firmly into the familiar security of therapist mode. I didn't say, "You're welcome."

Reynoso, I guessed, was a few years older than I. Her features were carved, and the ridge beneath her eyebrows was prominent and brooding. But what was most stunning about her appearance was the quality of her skin. Her complexion looked as soft and smooth as my almost-toddler daughter's.

"The other day on the phone? After your call? I wasn't cordial with you, Dr. Gregory. I'd like to begin by apologizing to you for that. The whole thing came out of the blue. I wasn't gracious."

"Accepted." My antennae were tuned for cynicism, and I immediately wondered whether she was disarming me or placating me or both with her apology. "You thought I was a crank, I bet."

"We get some crazy calls sometimes. You have a child?"

"A daughter." I still didn't want to talk about my family.

"This doesn't have to be difficult," she said.

"Although it's not a pleasant subject, I don't expect it has to be difficult, either, Detective Reynoso. I'm happy to tell you anything that I have permission to share with you."

"Ah," she said, and returned her attention to her mug. "That's the rub, though, isn't it?"

"The rub?"

"You deciding what you have the right to tell me. That's the complication for us, right?"

"Your profession has rules. My profession has

rules. I'm sure that we can respect each other's positions."

Actually I wasn't at all certain that we could respect each other's positions, but it seemed like a cordial thing to say, and it was apparent that we were both trying hard to be cordial.

The posted odds in Vegas were a hundred to one against things remaining cordial between us, however.

Reynoso said, "My profession's rules are geared toward discovering the truth. That's all."

I didn't want to joust with her. But I was willing to, if that's what she wanted. I said, "Mine aren't."

"Really?"

"Really."

"You don't have a goal of helping your . . . patients learn the truth about their lives?"

I figured it was a trick question. "Psychologically? Yes. Factually? No."

"I was in therapy once."

What would the American Psychological Association want me to say? "I hope you found it helpful."

"Very."

"Great."

"I don't have much leverage with you," she said with her eyes averted and her hand reaching for her purse.

I thought, *Good*. The fact was, I didn't think she had any leverage with me. But in the interest of extending the cordiality as far as possible, I said, "You don't need any leverage, Detective. I'm happy to do whatever I'm able to do to help you solve this crime."

She took a notepad and slender pen from her

shoulder bag along with a small tape recorder and a purse-size bottle of Tylenol. She set the recorder on the coffee table between us, threw a couple of pain relievers into her mouth, and washed them down with a gulp of tea. After flicking the recorder on, she pointed at the red light for my benefit, stated the date and time, and then touched the pause button. "Where are we right now? The address?"

I told her my address, adding, "You feeling okay?"

She touched her temple. "I've had a headache since I got here."

"It could be altitude sickness. Happens a lot. Drinking more water might help."

"Altitude sickness?"

I nodded.

"You have headaches all the time?" she asked.

"No, you get over it."

"Good." She returned her attention to the recorder, removed her finger from the pause button, repeated the address, explained the purpose of the interview, stated her name and mine, and asked me if I was participating voluntarily.

I had to think about my answer. Finally, I said I was.

"When did you first meet Gibbs and Sterling Storey?"

I considered that question carefully, too. "I'm sorry. I'm not at liberty to answer that one."

It was obvious that Detective Reynoso hadn't expected my response. She'd thought she was lobbing a softball my way.

She said, "What?"

"The circumstances of my meeting the Storeys—if,

indeed, I have met the Storeys—might be part of a therapeutic relationship, and any details about a therapeutic relationship, even simply whether or not there is a therapeutic relationship, and if there is, when it may have begun, are things that I'm not permitted to reveal under Colorado law."

"What?"

The second "What?" was born of incredulousness. "Dr. Gregory, I know you know her. You've already told me you're treating her. Come on. Don't be difficult just for the sake of being difficult."

"You didn't ask me whether I know Gibbs Storey, Detective. If that is the question, the answer is yes, I know Gibbs Storey. If you would like me to tell you when I first learned the information that brought you to Colorado, I can tell you that, too. It was last Monday. What you asked me was when I met Gibbs and Sterling Storey. That is a question that I'm not at liberty to answer."

"Why not?"

"I can only answer questions that are covered by an affirmative release of information. I have a limited release from Gibbs Storey. I do not have a release of any kind from Sterling Storey."

She sighed. "Have you ever met Sterling Storey?"

"Next question."

"Am I correct in assuming that if the answer was no, you would be free to tell me so?"

I didn't respond. I wasn't having very much fun.

"I'll assume that, then."

"Assume what you wish. Whether someone is in therapy, and thus whether I know them professionally, is privileged information. I can't discuss it without a release. We'll get a lot farther a lot faster if you just limit yourself to questions that I'm free to answer."

My frustration was showing. I'd expected that Detective Reynoso would know the rules as well as I did. If she did, she wasn't letting on, and her attempt to frustrate me was intentional.

And it was working.

She said, "And you are free to answer questions that . . ."

I swallowed a sigh. "I'm free to answer questions that relate to Gibbs Storey's accusation that her husband, Sterling, is responsible for murdering a woman named Louise Lake in Laguna Beach, California, back in nineteen . . ." I'd forgotten the year. "Whatever. That's it."

"Ninety-seven. What is Gibbs Storey's current diagnosis, Doctor?"

"I can't tell you that, Detective. I'm sorry, but it's not covered by the release."

"The release is that specific?"

"Yes, Ms. Storey has been quite specific about what she would like me to tell you and what she would prefer to remain privileged."

Carmen Reynoso sat back on the sofa, crossed her long legs, and smiled such a big engaging smile that I reflexively smiled in return.

"Twenty questions with you just isn't any fun," she said. "How about this? Why don't you tell me what you can tell me?"

So I did.

TWENTY-FIVE

I knew only what Gibbs wanted me to know.

Louise Lake was a British flight attendant who had shared two homes with two other flight attendants. One of the homes was an almost-derelict, two-bedroom, to-die-for maid's quarters attached to a ramshackle, early-twentieth-century shingled palace high on the rocky cliff above Crescent Bay in Laguna Beach in the southern L.A. metro area. The woman who owned the property and rented out the apartment was an elderly Australian who spent most of the year in Sydney.

The other home shared by the trio of flight attendants was a tiny one-bedroom flat in the fashionably tony Hyde Park section of London. Louise and another woman, named Helena, owned the London flat together. Their third roommate, Paulie, paid them a healthy rent for the privilege of crashing occasionally at one place or the other and, when circumstances dictated, didn't complain about sleeping on the sofa in the front room of the London flat.

All three close friends typically flew the busy Heathrow–LAX run for British Airways.

Sterling had met Louise in business class while he was on the long trip back from doing the coverage on the British Open in the summer of 1997. She told him that she was looking forward at the time to an almost full fortnight of holiday at her Laguna Beach hideaway. Sterling revealed to her that they were practically neighbors—that he and his wife were only weeks away from completing renovations on a cottage in Corona Del Mar, just a few miles up PCH from Crescent Bay.

Louise was seeing a guy in L.A. at the time. His name was Scott and he was the personal assistant to a young director who was a favorite of Steven Spielberg and David Geffen. Louise was a little embarrassed by the way Scott flashed his cell phone and beeper and BlackBerry PDA like a Boy Scout displaying his merit badges. She admitted to Sterling that she thought Scott was fun and pretty but was really just a "glorified freeway butler."

At the conclusion of the flight Sterling invited Louise and Scott to dinner. She accepted.

The meal was at a little French place that the Storeys loved on Balboa Island, and it went well. Scott turned out to be precisely as full of himself as Louise had suggested he was, and with precisely as little cause. Over the next few months as Gibbs, Louise, and Sterling became good friends, Scott was soon out of the picture. He disappeared to Europe with his boss, who was spending the late summer wooing a French actress in Brussels and scouting locations for "a period thing" he was about to start shooting in Budapest and Prague.

"The nature of the friendship, please. That's important," Carmen Reynoso prodded. "If you can, of course."

Louise was a working woman whose primary home was in Britain. When not in London she was usually traversing the North Atlantic doing her job, which left her mostly unavailable to accompany Gibbs on her frequent forays to her favorite haunts of Fashion Island or South Coast Plaza. Louise's unavailability didn't seem to matter; Gibbs adored Louise and almost immediately counted her among her closest friends. Gibbs especially loved Louise's cosmopolitan manners and her London accent. Although she didn't say so exactly, it was apparent that Gibbs thought Louise was a better accessory in the South Bay social scene than either Kate Spade or Manolo Blahnik.

"Louise Lake was a beautiful woman. Where did that fit in?" With the question, I noted that the cleft had reappeared between Reynoso's eyebrows. She wanted to know about Sterling and Louise, the couple. The thought apparently caused her to frown.

Gibbs didn't suspect that anything was going on between Sterling and Louise until a Halloween costume party that Gibbs had long planned to celebrate the completion of the renovation of the Corona Del Mar cottage. Louise wasn't even planning to attend the party; she had sent her regrets weeks before because she was scheduled to work the overnight from LAX to Heathrow on the thirty-first. Some combination of factors—Gibbs thought it was a mechanical problem and a crew overtime issue, but who ever knew with the airlines?—conspired to keep Louise in L.A. for another night.

She arrived at the Storeys' party in Corona after midnight, still dressed in her BA uniform. The party was already in its death throes, and the few guests still remaining on the patio were so inebriated that a couple of them even complimented Louise on the originality of her costume.

Gibbs was decked out as Grace Kelly. By self-report, she'd looked the part. Sterling came as Joe DiMaggio, and Gibbs remained troubled about his late change of heart about costumes. She had been counting on Prince Rainier or James Bond, her early suggestions. If she'd known he was going to be wearing pinstripe flannels as Joltin' Joe, she would have tried to talk him out of it.

Failing that dissuasion, she could have done Marilyn just as easily as Grace.

All he'd had to do was tell her. Was that too much to ask?

Louise was one of the last to leave the party, shutting down the new great room bar around three. Gibbs volunteered Sterling, who never drank when he was hosting a party, to drive Louise down the coast to her home in Laguna. After a tepid protest Louise agreed to give up her car keys and accept the ride.

Sterling pulled his car out of the garage in Corona at three-fifteen.

He didn't return home until the sun was beginning to crest the string of coastal hills in the South Bay the next morning.

"That was October. What about November? Can we get there soon?" Carmen Reynoso asked. I suspected that she lacked a therapist's natural respect for back-story, but didn't say so. It was something we could discuss at another time. Or not.

Sterling had blown off Gibbs's concerns about the lost hours before dawn on Crescent Bay on All Saints' Day morning. He told his wife that he and Louise had talked for a while. That was it.

Gibbs didn't trust Sterling much, from a fidelity point of view. And she didn't believe him often, at least where other women were concerned. But she'd let the issue go. She'd watch for signs. With Sterling and other women she did that a lot.

Louise didn't spend much time in Laguna during the first three weeks of November, and although she spoke with Gibbs a couple of times on the phone, they didn't see each other during that period. Louise had bid for, and received, a month flying routes into De Gaulle and JFK because she adored being in both New York and Paris over Christmas. She didn't want to be in either city for Thanksgiving, though. She had four days off, Tuesday through Friday of the holiday week, and she was planning to spend them alone in Laguna.

Helena was working, and Paulie and his latest partner were doing Ibiza.

Louise called Gibbs from her rental car on Tuesday afternoon to bitch about the traffic on the 405 and to gossip about an Australian tennis player she'd met while her actual date, an American lawyer, was in the WC at Les Deux Magots on the Left Bank in Paris. She reiterated her promise to come for Thanksgiving dinner on Thursday.

Gibbs reminded her that dinner would be early; the turkey would be carved at five.

And Louise reminded Gibbs that she didn't eat turkey and that she'd recently realized that she was only two minor obstacles away from being a true vegan.

Gibbs had asked what the obstacles were.

Louise had replied, "Paris, and meat."

"That was Tuesday?" Carmen Reynoso clarified. "Two days before Thanksgiving?"

"Yes," I said, recognizing that the calendar pages had flipped forward to almost the exact same spot in the current year. I went on. "Gibbs said Louise was killed that night, not the next day like the newspapers reported."

"Please go on with your story."

"Please remember, it's not my story. It's Gibbs's story. I'm just repeating what I was told. You can tell me one thing, though—is Gibbs correct about the time of death? Please tell me that."

"We'll get there, we'll get there," Reynoso said. When the issue was my ignorance and not her own, she was suddenly a very patient woman.

For some reason I thought of Sam.

The tape recorder snapped off. Carmen Reynoso fumbled in her bag for a spare tape. After she exchanged the tapes, she said, "Go on."

Sterling wasn't due home from New Orleans until Wednesday, late. Gibbs had completed the holiday shopping, supervised the house-cleaning, and done all the prep work she was planning to do in the kitchen before Thursday's meal. She had a Mexican woman whose name she didn't remember coming in to do most of the cooking on Thanksgiving morning.

By Tuesday afternoon Gibbs was bored. She decided to surprise Louise. She'd pick her up and welcome her home by taking her out to dinner somewhere in Laguna.

About a block from Crescent Bay, Gibbs spotted Sterling's car parked on the street.

She almost missed it. What caught her eye was the bright red hat with the network logo that he kept on the shelf behind the back-seat.

"A block away?"

"About a block away."

"She didn't tell you exactly where?"

"I don't know Laguna Beach, Detective. I wouldn't recognize any landmarks. I'm sure Gibbs will tell you."

"Did she say what kind of car?"

"I don't think so. She may have. If she did, I've forgotten."

"You forgot? Anything else you forgot, Doctor?"

*

Gibbs drove a few blocks away from Louise's home and phoned Sterling's office from her car. His secretary reminded her that he was still in New Orleans and suggested Gibbs try him on his cell phone.

To get to Louise's apartment, a visitor could use the public access path partway to the beach, then cut across an aging flagstone trail to the deck. Gibbs returned to Crescent Bay, parked near the top of the public path, descended a few yards, stopped, and listened.

She heard Sterling and Louise arguing. She couldn't tell about what. But she heard her name.

Gibbs.

Sterling had yelled, "I don't fucking care about Gibbs."

Gibbs headed back up the path in tears. Up near her car she heard a scream. She wasn't sure if it was Louise or not. At the time she thought it couldn't be. Why would it be? When she heard the news later, on Thanksgiving afternoon, she wasn't so sure.

Back at her car, she grabbed her phone and punched in the number of Sterling's cell. The distinctive sound of her husband's ringing phone traveled up the slope to where she was standing.

She killed the call.

"I think you know the rest," I said.

"I'd like to hear about his reaction when the body was discovered. Can you talk about that?"

"Yes. Yes, I can."

Sterling was home, as scheduled, late in the evening on

Wednesday. Gibbs never said anything to him about what she had witnessed the previous afternoon.

On Thanksgiving Day, as was his practice, Sterling had all the TVs in the house tuned to football games. But he wasn't watching football; he was watching coverage, production. The competition. At three-thirty a local news update reported that a partially clothed female body had been discovered facedown in a tide pool at Emerald Bay in Laguna Beach. Stay tuned, more after the game.

Gibbs hadn't paid much attention. Sterling didn't stray more than a few feet from the television.

A few minutes later Sterling asked Gibbs what time Louise was due for dinner. Gibbs said any time.

He said he hoped Louise was okay.

" 'Okay'? That's the word he used?" Reynoso asked, frowning.

"That's the word Gibbs said he used."

The news report from Laguna Beach was repeated about a half hour later. This time there was a news crew live at the scene, and they were showing videotape of a wide shot of a body sprawled on the rocks on the north end of the horseshoe that was Crescent Bay. The tide was coming back in, and waves were lifting plumes of spray into the air as they crashed onto the rocks. The earlier report about Emerald Bay had been in error.

The body by the tide pool was draped with a sheet striped in pastels.

"I'm going down there," Sterling said to his wife.

"Why?"

"I have a bad feeling about Louise."

" 'A bad feeling'?"

"Yes, a bad feeling."

"Huh."

When Sterling got home, dinner was cold. As he ate a turkey and stuffing sandwich with cranberry sauce and lots of black pepper, he told Gibbs that he thought Louise had been strangled.

" 'Strangled'?"

"Yes."

"He said that?"

"According to Gibbs."

"That would have been when—six o'clock, seven?"

"You'll have to ask Gibbs."

"Anything else?"

"Sterling told her that he thought that somebody must have broken into Louise's apartment. He bet that the killer had broken a window and just gone in that rickety back door."

TWENTY-SIX

Carmen Reynoso sat back and crossed her arms.

"Why did you make the call? Why didn't Gibbs call us herself?"

"I'm not quite sure about the answer to that one, Detective. It has something to do with the nature of the betrayal she feels she's engaged in. Turning her husband in is one thing. Making the actual call is something else."

"You think it's psychology, then?"

"Isn't everything?"

"No. Some things are just criminal."

The distinction was obviously clearer to her than it was to me.

"Are we done?" I asked. I was tired, and the clock told me my girls were due home any minute. I really didn't want Detective Reynoso here when they walked in the door.

She stood. "Except for your earlier question. Time of death? Remember? You still interested?"

"I didn't think you were actually going to answer me."

The snow was coming down in waves. A curtain of white, thick enough to obscure the entire valley, would blow by over the course of a few minutes, and then suddenly a sparser fall would reveal the dark geometry of the fence posts and dirt tracks in the greenbelt below our house. After a brief interlude of visibility the curtain would shut, the angularity would disappear, and the world would again become white.

A couple inches of snow were already piled on the grasses and in places on the ground that spent the late autumn in shadows.

Carmen Reynoso stared at the winter spectacle, her lips parted. "I've only seen snow a few times in my life. I'm an Oakland girl. Didn't ever get to Lake Tahoe much. It's mesmerizing."

The sardonic quality of her Lake Tahoe comment was oddly alluring. I said, "There's a moment during every storm when I'm overcome by the beauty of it all. And a moment, usually a little later on, when I'm almost—almost—overcome by the aggravation of it all."

She turned back toward me, puzzlement in her eyes.

I explained. "Driving in it. Shoveling it. Walking through the slush of it. It gets old."

Her next words surprised me.

She said, "You're not a romantic, are you? I took you for a romantic. A knight-in-shining-armor-type guy."

"Wrong conclusion, I think. I am a romantic. I'll be romantic about this storm all day today and all night. Then tomorrow morning, sometime around five A.M., my neighbor will fire up her little green John

Deere and start plowing our lane. That's when the romance will begin to disintegrate, with the sound of my neighbor singing Christmas carols on her John Deere at five o'clock in the morning."

"And that's so bad because . . ."

"You'd have to know Adrienne. She makes up her own words to the carols, and she can't sing to save her life."

Reynoso stepped away from the windows. "At least you get your driveway plowed."

"You have a little Pollyanna in you, don't you, Detective?"

"Very little, Doctor. Tomorrow's Sunday. Maybe your neighbor will take the Lord's day off."

"Maybe," I agreed. "That would be nice." I didn't bother to clarify that if Adrienne was anything religiously, she was Jewish, and that affiliation would make her Sabbath Saturday, not Sunday.

"The time of Louise Lake's death has never been made public." Reynoso's change of direction was abrupt. Sam did the same thing to me sometimes. I was beginning to suspect that cops in general have an underappreciation of the value of segue in conversation. "The press has always reported it was Wednesday, and we've never contradicted them in any of our public statements. Gibbs's contention that it was Tuesday, not Wednesday, is what hooked us—hooked me, anyway—that her story might be . . . real. Because the coroner says it was indeed late afternoon, early evening on Tuesday, and not late Wednesday, that Louise Lake was murdered."

I tried to keep my face impassive.

"But what really hooked me was something Gibbs

didn't say, that she only implied. We've left the public with the impression that Louise was murdered on the beach and her body was pulled out into the water. Numerous reports from neighbors indicated that she walked the cove and the tide pools at least twice a day when she was staying in town, often at dawn or dusk. The public version of the crime is that someone followed her to the beach, or waited and accosted her there, and killed her. Maybe a crime of opportunity, maybe not."

"But she didn't die on the beach?"

"No. She died on the rocks. Her body had premorbid wounds from the rocks. And the broken window in her back door? It's not public information, either. Therefore Sterling knew something he shouldn't know."

"Why was the window broken? Is there evidence of a struggle in the house?"

"No comment."

"You haven't talked with Sterling yet?"

"No. He's in Florida. Something tells me he's going to lawyer up anyway. I'm proceeding as though we're not going to have an opportunity to interview him."

"Do you have enough to arrest him?"

"If we did, he'd be in custody."

I tried a segue-free transition of my own. "Why a tide pool? The killer must have known the body would be discovered soon enough."

"Louise Lake's body was not placed in the tide pool. It was dumped into the Pacific, we think it got caught on something, and was in the water for almost thirty-six hours before it floated free and back into the tide pool during high tide."

We walked to the entryway, and I helped her with her coat.

"You can't repeat any of this," she said.

"Of course," I said. I was already wondering why she had told me what she'd told me. I wasn't considering the possibility that her volubility on the subject of Louise's murder was evidence of indiscretion. Rather, I assumed that Reynoso had another motive for talking with me. What? I wasn't smart enough to know.

She went on. "I heard from a couple of local cops that over the years you've demonstrated some wisdom about forensic things—you know, from a psychological perspective—so let me ask you something. From what you know about him—I'm talking Sterling Storey, obviously—could he have done it? Could he have killed Louise Lake?"

I considered the flattery—the spoonful of sugar—and the question—the bitter pill—that she wanted me to swallow. I said, "I'm sorry, but answering that would take me places that I'm not permitted to go, confidentialitywise. I wish I could respond, although I'm not sure of the value of what I might have to offer. Opinions are opinions, you know."

That little crease reappeared above her nose. She said, "I think I'll just take that as a yes."

Changing the subject seemed like a good idea. "Are you okay driving in this? In snow?"

"How would I know?"

"If you don't know, then you're not okay."

"Any tips for a virgin?"

"Take it slow. Don't be afraid to use second gear. Ignore the assholes plowing by you in four-wheel-drive pickups and SUVs."

"And if I skid on the ice?"
"Don't. It's better if you don't skid."
"Thanks. I'll try to remember that."

TWENTY-SEVEN

Lauren and Grace arrived home less than ten minutes after Detective Reynoso departed.

Their arrival wasn't a pretty sight. They had both left the house dressed for a warm fall day, and both were wet from the storm and chilled to the bone. Lauren's violet eyes had taken on the gray-purple pall of extreme fatigue; whatever she and Grace had been doing since I'd left to meet Sam that morning had worn her beyond whatever limits she possessed that day.

How guilty was I feeling?

With Grace in my arms, I cranked up the heat in the master bathroom and began running a bath for Lauren. Then I took Grace into her room, and got her dry and clean and into fresh warm clothes. My daughter, sometimes a tough kid to put down for a nap, found the sanctuary of sleep moments after her head hit the mattress in her crib. I promised her, silently, that because of her compliance during this crucial moment in our lives, I would overlook at least one moderate-to-severe teenage indiscretion that was certain to occur in her future. She seemed to smile back at me from her sleep, as though she were already planning whatever it was I would need to forgive her for.

I shuddered at the thought.

When I got back to the bathroom with a steaming mug of tea, I found Lauren in the tub.

"No caffeine?" she asked.

"Mint. No caffeine. I'm sorry, I screwed up today."

"I know you're sorry."

"Sam—"

She shook her head, just a little, and asked, "He's okay?"

I nodded. She forced a smile in reply.

"You didn't look too good when you came in," I said.

She lowered herself farther into the soapy water. She was covered all the way to her chin. Her toes and colored toenails, painted a shade of coral that I was sure Grace had selected, popped out of the water at the far end of the tub. "Something's cooking, Alan. I have brain mud. I'm more tired than Bill Gates is rich, and in case you haven't noticed, my eyelids aren't blinking at the same time."

I tried hard to look her in the eyes but not stare at her eyelids. "So what can I do?"

"Let's give it a few hours, see what develops. The pin is definitely out of the grenade. We'll see what's going to blow up."

"Maybe it's a dud. Can I get you something to eat?"

"No, I'm not hungry. Some quiet, okay? Take the dogs, and don't let me sleep past five. I love you."

*

Multiple sclerosis roughly translates as "many scars."

When a new wound forms on the protective covering of a nerve in the brain or spinal column—apparently caused by the body mistaking its own neural insulation for a gremlin of some kind—symptoms develop. What symptoms? It depends on what nerve is involved. As the wound heals and scar tissue grows to replace nature's myelin, the symptoms either disappear totally, or they don't diminish at all, or—and this is most likely—something happens in between.

It's a total crapshoot.

Lauren and I didn't often use the word "exacerbation." To use it had the ugliness of a profanity. But as I left her toweling off after her quick bath—I stayed until then because I feared sleep would take her right there in the bathtub—we both knew that an exacerbation, a fresh wound on some previously unaffected nerve, was what we feared was happening.

If we were right? I didn't want to think about it. But I knew the list of potential consequences was as long as the list of the body's miraculous capabilities. Numbness, blindness, paralysis, weakness, bladder problems, GI problems—I stopped myself before the list grew any longer. And it could have grown much longer.

But repeating the litany of potential disabilities wasn't helpful.

Did I cause Lauren to have an exacerbation by not taking my daughter to her friend's birthday party?

No. Of course not.

I didn't. Really.

Really.

TWENTY-EIGHT

Sunday was full of surprises. None of them good.

Lauren never really woke up from her Saturday "nap." She opened her eyes for a while, but whatever was going on with her neurologically and immunologically was consuming enough of her energy that she didn't venture farther from the bed than the bathroom.

She declined dinner. Grace and I ate alone.

As was typical, I was the first in the family out of bed on Sunday morning. Instead of pulling on Lycra and Gore-Tex and heading to my bicycle—the pre-Thanksgiving snowstorm made my typical weekend morning ride impractical—I tugged on some fleece sweats and thick socks and carried the local paper and a cup of coffee to the living room.

The sky above the Front Range of the Rockies was the color of deep tropical water, the soaring granite slabs of the Flatirons were bearded with snow, and the earth was carpeted white as far as my eyes could see.

It was absolutely enchanting. I hoped Carmen Reynoso was someplace she could enjoy this view.

I listened for the sound of Adrienne mangling Christmas carols or the rumble of her John Deere. Nothing. Lauren had left some Debussy in the CD changer. I flicked it on, turned down the volume, and lifted the hefty Sunday paper to my lap, fearing that the tale of Sterling and Gibbs Storey might have finally made it from the police files to the newspaper.

Below the fold, bottom right, some bold type caught my eye. But it wasn't an exposé about the Storeys. The headline read, JUDGE'S SPOUSE ARRESTED FOR POSSESSION OF COCAINE.

Huh, I thought, *I know about that.*

Jim Zebid had told me about it. I hadn't given his revelations about Jara Heller's husband's criminal activities a moment's thought since I'd heard them during Jim's regular session the previous Tuesday.

What was Judge Heller's husband's name?

I started to read the article. Jara Heller's husband's name, it turned out, was Penn Heller. I allowed myself to be distracted for a moment trying to figure out how someone ended up with the name Penn. Pennington? Pennsylvania? Penncroft? Couldn't. Nor did I recall any legal cocktail party chatter with a male spouse named Penn.

The article didn't have much information. Police, acting on a tip, arrested Mr. Heller, an investment banker with some firm I'd never heard of, early Saturday evening in a brewpub downtown, and they'd confiscated a "significant quantity" of white powder and an unspecified quantity of cash. The reporter apparently attempted to reach Judge Heller for a comment, but his calls were not returned by press time.

Huh.

I felt a pang of sympathy for Jara Heller. She had a decent reputation on the bench and was known as a hard worker who knew the law and played fair. I'd always thought she was personable and that she couched her ambition better than many of her colleagues did. Whatever her husband was involved in wasn't going to do much for her reputation. I wasn't smart enough to know what it would do to her future on the bench. I'd ask Lauren when she got up.

A distant humming sound intruded on my reverie about the Hellers. Within seconds the hum became an insistent rumble. Adrienne wasn't singing, but she had indeed fired up the Deere and was preparing to plow the lane. Sunday or not, she loved the damn tractor too much to allow a decent snowfall to melt of its own volition.

Solar energy was her sworn enemy.

The roar of the Deere awakened Grace, and within a minute I was called to my daughter's room by her surprisingly mature lungs.

Diaper change for Grace. Take the dogs out, feed them. Waffles. Sunday almost always meant waffles—from-scratch waffles—and lots of chatter. Debussy ended, and the next disk in the changer fired up. Tony Bennett and k.d. lang doing Louis Armstrong. Perfect.

The weekend morning routine was soothing but surreal. After breakfast Grace played in her high chair. I tried to focus on the paper. But below the surface calm lurked, I knew, the monster that lived in the depths: the closed bedroom door and the precarious state of my wife's health. I waited for the sound of the toilet flushing, or water pinging against the tile in the shower, anything to indicate that Lauren's day had started in a fashion that resembled normal. But eight o'clock came and went without a hint of her condition.

The phone rang at 8:05.

I pounced on it.

"It's me," Sam said.

"Another field trip?" I asked. "I think I'm busy."

"I'm calling from the pay phone outside Moe's. The place is crowded even after a blizzard."

Moe's Bagels was in a little shopping center on North Broadway not far from Sam's house. I made an assumption that he was out for his prescribed morning rehab walk and was seeking moral support from me much the way that an alcoholic might call his sponsor from outside a saloon. I said, "It's okay, Sam. But get something with whole grain. And nonfat cream cheese. Not the good stuff. But lox is okay. Omega-three oils."

"I'm not asking for help with the menu. I'm calling from a pay phone outside of Moe's so that if somebody ever subpoenas your phone records, they won't show that I talked to you at eight o'clock on this Sunday morning." His tone was gruff.

I sat down. "Yeah? Why?"

"Because Sterling Storey is dead. And I'd rather people not know that I'm the one who told you. Just in case that becomes important."

"What?" My exclamation had to do with surprise at the news of Sterling's death. But I was also wondering how it could become important from whom I'd heard the news. Paranoia wasn't part of my friend's character, so I assumed that Sam was a step or two ahead of me. Although all the chess pieces appeared blurred on the board to me, Sam was plotting moves farther down the line.

"Lucy came by to see me last night, kind of late. You know, to check on me. She told me about it."

"Why is Lucy worried about you?"

"That's not why I called, either, Alan. Focus."

I considered pressing it; after all, he'd offered the opening. But I didn't. "Okay, then what happened to Sterling?"

"I don't know what happened to Sterling Storey. All I know is what I'm hearing."

Another one of those critical distinctions that Sam liked to make. I asked, "And the Storey story is what?"

His voice changed. It became a little louder, a little less patient. "Hold on. I'm waiting for a woman to stop staring at me thinking I'll get off the damn phone any second if she's rude enough. I hate that. Don't you hate that? Now she's like five feet away. She's staring right at me. I'm staring right back at her.

"Hey, lady, I'm going to be a while, do you mind? Get over it."

"Did she go away?"

"She's like sixty or something—she looks exactly like my aunt Esther—and she just flipped me off behind her back as she was walking away. What is that? I don't think I want to live in a society where old people are pricks."

"She's an exception, Sam. Tell me about Sterling."

"You know he was in Florida, producing coverage for some football game? Yeah, of course you know that. After his damn football game was over yesterday, he was driving from Tallahassee to visit an old college friend in Albany, Georgia. You know where that is?

Me, neither. Personally, I think he was avoiding coming back here to face the music, but it's a free country, right? Until the cuffs are on, hey—he can do what he pleases. Lots of people want to talk to him, but nobody was ready to arrest him.

"Anyway, there was some freak rainstorm all across southern Georgia yesterday. Flash floods, the whole thing. A biblical-type storm. Witnesses say a car went off the highway and was about to slide into the Ochlockonee River. If I said that name right, I deserve a prize. I thought Minnesota had goofy names for places, but the South? It's like they had a goofy name contest and there were a thousand winners. No, ten thousand winners.

"Anyway, Sterling, being the sweet guy we all know he is, stopped his rental car and went to help this woman whose car was about to go in the river. He slipped on the bank, fell in, and went underwater almost immediately. His body hasn't been found."

"Wow."

"That's it? 'Wow'?"

"Sam, the man's about to be picked up for questioning for a homicide and instead he dies a damn hero trying to rescue a stranger from a car wreck? That's world-class irony."

"Warms your heart, doesn't it? Three witnesses to the whole thing, too. One of them is a damn preacher. The others are twin sisters. A social worker and a pediatrician."

"I take it you don't believe what you're hearing?" Sam often didn't believe what he was hearing. It wasn't evidence of a character defect so much as it was the foundation that made him a good detective.

"What do the lawyers say? Render up the body? Do I got that right? Well, when they render up the body, then I'll believe it. It's all too convenient as far as I'm concerned."

"How do you fake a rainstorm and a biblical flood, Sam? Sterling Storey isn't Moses."

"Moses? What Bible do you read? Moses doesn't fake any floods in the Bible I read. Forget my question—I don't want to know what Bible you read. No. All I'm saying about Sterling Storey is that maybe . . . maybe the guy thinks on his feet, that's all."

"I assume that the Georgia cops are looking for his remains."

"They are. The river he went into—I'm not going to try to say the name again—is pretty wild, apparently. Lots of things underwater—trees and shit—where a body could get caught up."

"Sam, why do you care about this case so much? You have plenty more important things to worry about."

He was silent for ten seconds before he replied, "I'm not sure. I think I'm going to go back home."

"Wait, Sam. Hold on. Do you know anything about Jara Heller's husband? Judge Heller?"

"I saw the paper. Nothing more than that."

"Will you do something for me? Will you check and see how they became suspicious of him? How they knew he was involved?"

"Why?"

"It's important."

"Somebody fingered him. You can count on it. Maybe he walked into a sting, but odds are somebody gave him up. You hang around with people who do drugs, especially people who buy and sell drugs, you come to realize that it's not the most honorable segment of our society."

"Just check for me, please. If somebody turned him in, I'd love to know that. I promise I won't ask who did it."

"You promise?"

"Yes, Sam."

"That means you already know who turned him in. You just want me to confirm it for you. Am I right?"

I stammered.

He said, "You should be seeing a higher quality of clientele. You hang out with a lot of scum." Then he hung up.

Across the room Grace—bless her—continued to entertain herself. She was absolutely captivated by the wrong end of a spoon.

I called my office phone and checked for a call from Gibbs. I wondered if she even knew what had happened to her husband the previous night, whether anyone had called her.

The only messages on my voicemail were from other patients. One was a cancellation; another was from a patient requesting an additional session. And one was a confirmation from a paranoid-obsessive guy I was treating named Craig Adamson. Craig always required confirmation that I hadn't forgotten his next appointment. Always. It was sad.

All in all, the messages on my voicemail were a zero-sum game and included no frantic calls from Gibbs Storey.

I was trying to decipher what that meant when,

behind me, Lauren said, "Who was that who called?"

A big smile exploded across Grace's face, and she said, "Mom Mom."

I pivoted.

TWENTY-NINE

SAM

My eyes stayed glued on the cranky old lady until she was all the way down by the wine store. I didn't want her to think I was getting off the line for her. When she hopped from the curb to jaywalk over toward Ideal Market, I hung up the phone.

Sherry would tell me I was being petty. Maybe she would be right. I can be petty sometimes. Especially with people who flip me the bird when I'm not doing anything but talking on the phone.

A little bubble of gas erupted down in my gut and began a sudden northern migration that would take it directly into belch territory. I could feel it rise. As the capsule crossed the midtorso territory that I now knew—*knew*—to be my heart's domain, my hand rose involuntarily to my chest. I placed my knuckles on my sternum and pressed gently. It took no more than a second for the gas to rise the entire length of my esophagus.

I did burp, kind of loudly actually. After, I left my

hand in place below and between the boobs on my chest that looked just like my dad's, the man-boobs I'd promised myself I'd never have.

Never.

Well, I had them now.

I inhaled deeply and exhaled slowly. No pain rose in my chest. It was okay to move my hand away, to slide my big feet.

I stepped away from the phone and got into the long snaking line that led to the counter at Moe's. What had Alan said I could order? Whole grain? Nonfat cream cheese? Lox?

Damn.

I had man-boobs, a heart artery that looked like a muck-filled galvanized pipe, a wife who hadn't smiled in my general direction since the summer monsoons had passed us by, and a kid I adored who was a thousand miles away from my hug.

What had Alan asked me?

"*Why do you care about this case so much?*"

The woman in front of me was ordering nineteen different things nineteen different ways. She wanted an "everything" bagel without sesame seeds. Jalapeño this with white meat turkey that. "You mean you don't have veggie cream cheese without those orange things in it? . . . Oh, those are carrots? Ooh, red onions? You don't have white? Are they bitter?"

She asked for a spelt bagel. What the hell is spelt?

The girl waiting on her had an oblong ring the size of a carabiner through her right eyebrow. She didn't care a hoot about the woman she was waiting on, or her act. The clerk's eyes didn't frown. Her lips didn't smile. She was going to get minimum wage for the next hour of her life no matter what the hell the idiots on our side of the counter wanted her to do.

I could relate.

The girl shook her head at the spelt question.

I was glad Moe's didn't have spelt. I would have been seriously dismayed if Moe's had spelt.

"Why do you care about this case so much?"

I realized that my left hand was in my parka pocket, and I was twirling something round between my fingers.

The little brown bottle of nitroglycerin.

"Why do you care about this case so much?"

In my life I've known maybe five people who could make me think. Alan Gregory is one of them. I've grown to appreciate it—his ability to get me going—but I've also grown to recognize that it isn't an altogether comfortable state of affairs for me. Introspection, I mean. I don't much like Indy racing, but I love NASCAR. Why? Traffic is traffic, but most of the time NASCAR is all left turns. You just drive fast, control your speed, hit the pit, react to the other guys. You don't always have to prepare for a hairpin, you're not always slamming on the brakes.

Having Alan as a friend is like driving the damn Grand Prix. Left turn, right turn. Brake, downshift, gas, brake *hard*. It isn't always fun. Sometimes I just want to drive I-80 through Nebraska. The road goes straight, the car goes straight. And me?

I go straight. No doubt about it, life is best for me when I go straight.

Why do I care about the case so much?

Because she loved the asshole so much, that's why. Because this Gibbs Storey lady lived all these years with a guy she knew had murdered her friend, and she stayed living with him even after she knew the police were coming after him to throw him in jail.

I wanted to know about love like that. I wanted to know about a marriage like that. I wanted to know about a woman like that. Was it him, or was it her? What made her tick? Was it strength or weakness? Was it confidence or desperation? I had a guess, sure, but I wanted to know.

My Sherry? After my heart attack she couldn't wait to get the hell out of our house. Out of town. Screw Thanksgiving, screw my rehab, screw whatever this whole thing was doing to Simon. Screw our marriage.

Screw me.

I didn't understand any of it. I was thinking that Gibbs and Sterling Storey could teach me something.

My turn finally came at the counter at Moe's. The girl with the piercing raised her eyebrow. The metal ring levitated ominously. It was her way of telling me I was next. Speaking was an inconvenience for her.

"Whole wheat toasted, please. Low-fat cream cheese, lox, and whatever vegetables you got. Lots of them."

Her eyes didn't frown. Her lips didn't smile. She made me my breakfast, wrapped it in white paper, and dropped it in a brown-paper bag as though she'd done it a few thousand times before, thrust it over the counter at me, and looked for the next person in line.

Poppyseed toasted with butter. Smelt on spelt with a schmear. It didn't make any difference to her.

With one last glance at the girl with the heavy metal in her brow, I paid for my bagel and crammed a buck into the tip jar.

The girl didn't know it, I thought, but she was auditioning to play the role of somebody's wife after sixteen years of marriage.

Later, after I picked up a couple of things at Ideal and stopped back for a cup of decaf at Vic's, I started walking home. I wasn't ready to go home, really, but I couldn't think of anything else I could do to avoid it. It was Sunday morning, and I'd gone every place but 7-Eleven that I could think of that was open. Except for church. But I couldn't do that. Not that the spiritual solace of an hour at church wouldn't have been welcome. I didn't go because I didn't want to see all the familiar faces and hear the litanies of "How're you feeling?" and "Hey, where's the family?" And I really, really didn't want to hear another story about somebody's relative's heart attack and how they were dead in a week.

I didn't want to hear how, oh, lucky I am.

I wasn't feeling too damn lucky.

The walk wouldn't take long—it was only a few blocks from North Broadway to the thousand square feet of siding-covered box that we called home—and I could feel the heave-and-ho of my chest as I made the gentle climb. Not chest pain; no pain exploding below my sternum. Not even a little twinge. The heave-ho was just the rise and fall of excess skin and the sway of my fat.

My man-boobs.

In sight of my house I stopped and watched a teenage girl shovel her sidewalk. Her outfit was more appropriate for an early summer day at Boulder

Reservoir than the first real day of winter. Shorts. Sweatshirt that said—what? I couldn't read her sweatshirt from thirty yards.

What was it with kids and clothes? I had to figure that out, had to. Simon was on his way. I had to get there first.

I made the decision to spend my forced medical leave of absence doing two things. I was going to begin to get rid of my man-boobs, and I was going to go looking for Sterling Storey.

I stopped and checked my pulse.

Eighty-four. That was good. Walking up the hill, holding an eighty-four? That was good. My cardiologist would be pleased. Those perfectly svelte physical medicine specialists who ran the rehab program would be pleased.

Or maybe they wouldn't be pleased. Their mantra seemed to be "I think you can do better, Sam." I had the sense that if you told them they'd won Powerball, they'd complain that the jackpot was only thirty million.

Sherry would like them. She thought I could do better, too.

What had Alan said to me? "*You have plenty of more important things to worry about.*"

He was right. And finding Sterling Storey was going to be my way of worrying about them.

My man-boobs? I'd never laid eyes on the guy, but I was betting that Sterling Storey didn't have any.

THIRTY

ALAN

"I'm having some trouble with my leg," Lauren said.

I'd deduced that already. The walking stick in her right hand was a dead giveaway. I tried to remember the last time I'd seen the thing emerge from the closet, but I couldn't. I guessed that it had been years. I purchased it for her at a mountain equipment store in Ouray, on the Western Slope, during another health crisis. Or was it Telluride? I couldn't remember.

I did remember that the circumstances were similar to these and that I'd seen the decline coming. It seemed disease exacerbations always arrived after a drumbeat of warning.

"Come, sit," I said. I took her by the elbow and led her to a kitchen chair next to Grace's high chair.

"It feels like it weighs a ton. I'm just dragging it around." She was talking about her leg.

"Yeah."

She bowed her head toward Grace and was

immediately lost in the vernacular of baby talk that allowed her to reconnect with her daughter and forget about whatever was going on with her myelin sheath. Grace was oblivious to her mother's malaise, but she was pretty interested in the walking stick. Were she developmentally able to stagger a few steps and simultaneously hold on to an object, I assumed I would see our daughter playing with a toddler-size version of the walking stick before the day was out.

I was examining Lauren for indications of other peripheral neuropathy. Her facial muscles were still unable to coordinate her blinks. Beyond that, my unskilled eyes found nothing anomalous.

"Any other weakness?" I asked. I wanted to hear her talk again, to taste the cadence for evidence of impairment in her speech.

She shook her head.

"Is that the same leg as before? You remember, that trip to help Teresa in Utah?"

"That was the other leg," she said.

She sounded okay. "Should I call the neurologist?" Lauren's neurologist, Larry Arbuthnot, liked to be aggressive with steroid treatment in the face of a fresh exacerbation that threatened serious consequences.

"I don't want to start steroids," she said.

Yeah, okay. "I know."

She actually smiled. "I'm due for interferon today. I'll take that and see how things develop."

Ah, yes, interferon.

Lauren's weekly interferon injection was preventive medicine; it was intended to protect her from waking up to mornings like this one. The IM injection that she plunged into her thigh once a week wasn't intended as a treatment in the event that a morning like this one occurred anyway. Interferon was a toxic prophylaxis against a rare event, akin, I sometimes mused, to lighting particularly noxious incense in an effort to keep elephants out of the living room.

In the case of interferon, burning the incense usually seemed to be effective, but it was inherently hard to tell. Last time I checked, the living room was devoid of elephants. But then again, it usually was.

Was it the incense?

Answering that question was the rub.

Regardless, interferon wasn't intended to deal with a rogue elephant that had snuck into our living room anyway. And that's what we had right now: a rogue elephant in the living room.

"You sure that's wise?" I tried hard not to say it in a tone that communicated that I thought her strategy unwise. I probably failed.

Lauren was almost totally focused on Grace. If it weren't for the walking stick she had clamped between her knees, I could have convinced myself that it was any other Sunday morning.

She finally answered me. "No, not at all. I'm not at all sure. Will you bring me half a cup of coffee, please? Maybe some juice."

I wanted to scream. I wanted to take the damn disease she had by the throat and tighten my grip on it until it died.

"Lauren, we're talking ambulation. It's a big risk."

She snapped back, "Don't you think I know that? I hate steroids. I want to give it a few hours, okay?"

I retrieved her coffee and juice. Her request for a few hours was reasonable. But then, so was my alarm.

Her voice was much, much softer when she said, "Was that Sam before? On the phone?"

"Yeah, there's a lot that's going on." I filled Lauren in on the events that had taken place outside Albany, Georgia, and Sterling Storey's ironic demise on the Ochlockonee River.

"That's convenient," she said, almost devoid of sympathy. Death a time zone away was so much easier on the soul.

"That's what Sam thinks, too. He said he wants them to render the body."

She laughed. "I think you mean render *up* the body. Rendering has something to do with separating out fat, doesn't it? It's a cooking thing, I think. Adrienne does it to chickens sometimes around the Jewish holidays. Is Sam okay?"

Her laugh warmed my heart. "He's doing the best he can. He's so off-balance. The heart attack. His family gone. I don't think he can really believe that Sherry took Simon away at a time like this."

Grace seized the moment to toss her spoon across the table. I caught it before it hit the floor. She thought the whole thing was hilarious. If I gave it back to her, I was sure the game would get repeated. Piaget would have given it back. I kept it.

Lauren said, "I can't either." Panic crossed her violet eyes in a flash, like the reflection of a lightning bolt in a pane of glass at midnight.

"Nor can I," I said. I didn't know if my wife wanted me to say that I wouldn't leave her, to reassure her that the latest permutation of her illness hadn't changed a single facet on the surface of my heart, but I feared that the very mention of her vulnerability might make the circumstances too real for her. So all I added was "I can't believe what's happened with them."

I slid the newspaper across the table to her, pointing at the article about Penn Heller's arrest for possession of cocaine.

She read the headline, gazed up at me, and said, "Really?"

I could have lied and said, *"I don't know anything more than I just read in the paper."* But I didn't. I said, "Apparently."

She scanned the article quickly. "It sounds like they have him for intent to distribute. That's not good."

"What's this going to do to Jara's position on the bench? How damaging is it?"

She shrugged.

"Do you know her husband?"

"A little," Lauren said. "Just a little."

It was apparent that Lauren wasn't eager to talk about Jara and Penn Heller.

A few minutes later Lauren hobbled back toward the bedroom with her non–walking stick hand full of the supplies necessary to inject a milliliter of interferon into her thigh. I glanced at the clock. I added two hours. That was when she'd start getting sick from the medicine. I added twenty-four hours more to that. That was when she would stop being sick from the medicine.

A day, every week, deducted from her life in a valiant effort to repel rogue elephants.

I waited until Lauren closed the door behind her

before I turned to Grace and said, "It's too late this time, I'm afraid, Gracie. The elephants are already here."

Grace tried to say "elephants." Anyway, I think what she tried to say was "elephants."

She pointed at the dogs.

Close enough.

I realized that Emily's paw umbrella needed my attention.

THIRTY-ONE

SAM

The list of people who were going to be pissed at me was longer than usual.

Alan? Absolutely. Top of the list. My captain? He'd kill me if he got half a chance—save my insurance company a lot of money and my doctor a lot of work. My cardiologist? I think he was coming around to the reality that I wasn't his normal post-MI patient. Still, he wasn't going to be happy about my extracurricular activities. I was pretty sure about that. And Carmen Reynoso? Eh, so? It'd just give her another reason to look down her nose at us mountain cops.

Who else?

I wondered what Sherry would think, but I finally decided that I couldn't really guess. I hadn't thought she was the type of person who could walk out the door with my kid less than a week after I had a heart attack.

Who am I kidding? Sherry wouldn't be surprised. When she heard what I was up to, she'd make that noise that I hated that came from someplace far back in her sinuses, but she wouldn't be surprised.

The noise was her marital shorthand for "See what an asshole he is."

Or maybe it was "What can I do with him?"

I didn't know anymore.

But at that moment I was coming to the conclusion that being on medical leave from the department wasn't all bad. My check was still coming in. The mortgage was going to get paid. I even liked not carrying my badge. And not having a gun on my hip or strapped below my armpit? It was fine, good even, at least for a while.

Two phone calls, and I had her address. If I was smarter, I could have figured it out in one, but I used one of the calls to get an answer to Alan's question about how the cops were tipped about Jara Heller's husband's cocaine problems. I admit I frittered away a minute or two trying to figure out why Alan wanted to know, too.

Gibbs Storey's house wasn't that far from mine, geographically speaking. Ten blocks? Twelve? I could have walked over there easily, but I didn't. Too much slush on the sidewalks, too little motivation to fight the muck on my part. I took the Cherokee and parked half a block down from her place. Why not in front?

I was on the lookout for media, especially media with cameras.

The whole connection between current Boulder residents Sterling and Gibbs Storey and the old murder in Laguna Beach hadn't yet hit the papers, but I knew it would. Any minute, probably.

And Sterling's disappearance in Georgia?

That was prime tabloid bait. The frosting on the cake. When that news hit the wires, we were talking nonstop cable TV chatter and lots of reporters making their first trips ever to southern Georgia so they could do their pompous stand-ups on some obscure bridge over the Ochlockonee River. There'd probably be good footage of gorgeous old bloodhounds on long leashes snuffling along the riverbank and maybe even some shots of gruff rescue guys in wet suits searching eddies. And of course, there'd be plenty of on-camera interviews with fat cops like me saying they're doing the best they can, ferreting out every lead, examining every possibility.

So I checked the street in front of the house as carefully as I knew how. I didn't want to get ambushed by some reporter.

Not yet.

Gibbs Storey was home. To my surprise, she answered her door. To my greater surprise, she invited me inside as soon as I told her I was a friend of her psychologist. That's what got me inside her door: Alan. Whatever. I was grateful to be off the porch; I'd felt like I had a spotlight on me when I was standing outside like some Jehovah's Witness or some almost-homeless guy walking across lawns going house to house spreading doorspam.

The entryway of the Storeys' home was all rose-hued marble tile. Nothing was out of place in the part of the house that I could see from where I was standing. No dust, no dirt. No kids' shoes. No crappy tennis balls the dog dragged in. If my crazy grandmother had had a ton of money and a totally different sense of what was tasteful—actually the dear old woman didn't have any sense at all of what was tasteful—this is what her house would have looked like.

"You're Dr. Gregory's detective friend? The one he wanted to talk to about . . . my situation?"

That part couldn't have gone better if I had written her lines myself. I'd never said I was a cop—technically since I was on leave, I wasn't a functioning cop—but she'd generously gone ahead and granted me detective status. Alan had once told me that status was a simple thing, psychologically speaking. One person assigned it, and as soon as someone else agreed, the status became real. That's all it took. Well, Gibbs had assigned me detective status. And me?

I didn't contradict her. Thus, my status was real.

"Yeah. I'm Dr. Gregory's friend. The one he talked to" was all I said.

"How did you find me? He said he wouldn't tell you my name."

"He didn't. He kept his word; he's big on that. But there's a lot of other stuff going on—you must know that. Things that I'm in a position to hear about without any assistance from him. The search warrant here the other day? The cops visiting from the West Coast? It wasn't hard to put numbers on the players' backs, if you know what I mean. I sort of put two and two together on my own."

She stared at me as though I were some kind of bizarre math whiz, and she feared I was about to do some jujitsu calculus on her.

I smiled back at her like a teddy bear. A big teddy bear with man-boobs.

I was wearing a coat, a nylon parka that had once had enough goose down in it to keep me warm in a blizzard. She wouldn't know about the man-boobs. Hell, maybe she would. Didn't matter. I wasn't planning on taking the coat off in front of her.

Why? I just wasn't going to do it.

Gibbs Storey was gorgeous, okay? I mean make-me-nervous, shift-my-weight, avert-my-eyes kind of gorgeous. The girls-guys-like-me-don't-even-get-to-talk-to kind of gorgeous.

Not pretty.

Gibbs was movie-star stuff.

If she hadn't been so pretty, or maybe if I had just been constitutionally more adept at being around someone so pretty, I might not have blurted out what I blurted out next. But she was, and I wasn't.

I said, "And of course, I heard about your husband. That's kind of why I'm here. Well, that is why I'm here."

Her face decomposed into tears. For a moment I thought she was going to run into my arms. Fantasy? Maybe. But she didn't turn to me; she turned and sprinted down the hall.

I decided that her rapid departure constituted an invitation, so I followed her.

It took about five minutes before things calmed down again.

We'd ended up in a long room that faced the greenbelt below the hogbacks on the western edge of town. Right where the Storeys' carefully manicured backyard stopped, the scrub of the greenbelt began. The previous owners of this place must have had a scary, scary night in July 2002 when the Wonderland Lake fire erupted and looked as though it were planning on turning this particular section of Boulder into raw material for Kingsford.

A quick calculation told me that the room we were in was almost exactly the size of my house. This family room/breakfast nook/kitchen combo was as spotless as the entryway, but it wasn't done in marble. This doesn't-it-look-like-a-ski-lodge? haven was all dark wood floors and wood-beam ceilings and plaid sofas and furniture converted from farm implements and a chandelier made out of a heck of a lot of deer antlers. A moss rock fireplace divided the view of the sharp hogback to the west almost exactly in half. If the fireplace had ever had an actual fire in it, somebody with a serious aversion to ash—I'm talking phobia—had taken on the responsibility of cleaning up after the blaze.

It crossed my mind that maybe that's why Gibbs Storey was seeing Alan. She was a neat freak, a pathological neat freak of some kind. He was trying to get her to loosen up, not dust for a day.

But who was I to say what was deviant, right?

While I was encouraging Gibbs Storey to stop crying—I do a surprising amount of that in my job day to day, and I'm pretty good at it—I was thinking that if somebody came and chopped off the rest of this house and just left this room standing, Sherry and I still couldn't afford to live here.

Why did we fight so hard to stay in Boulder? Why? We worked our asses off, together we made a decent amount of money, or what should have been a decent amount of money, and what did we get for it? A barely insulated frame box with a crappy furnace, a twenty-year-old roof, and wall-to-wall carpeting that smelled like a colony of prairie dogs used it for a few years before donating it to the Goodwill. If you're a cop, or a teacher, or a lady selling flowers in a little shop just off the Downtown Mall, that's what working your ass off gets you, if you want the privilege of living a dozen blocks away from Gibbs and Sterling Storey in beautiful, beautiful Boulder.

It gets you shit.

Maybe Sherry was right. Maybe it was time for a change. Back to Minnesota? I didn't know.

Gibbs was curled up in the corner of a big sofa. I was across from her on a chair made out of twigs and branches. Her sniffles seemed to be slowing. Finally, she whimpered, "I'm a private person. Soon everybody is going to know everything, right?"

Well, that gave me pause. I'm thinking I have a grieving widow on my hands, and that I'm going to be ladling out the comfort and tugging the tissues if I want to get anything out of her, but instead I'm wondering whether she's upset just because her family secrets aren't likely to remain secrets for too long.

That was a whole different state of affairs.

" 'Everything' being what exactly, ma'am?" I said. It was as innocuous as I could make the question sound. I hoped it was innocuous enough, because if Gibbs heard any semblance of the echo of what she'd just said to me—assuming she was one tenth as smart as she was pretty—I figured that my forward progress was going to be severely hampered.

She swallowed, opened her eyes a tad wider, and inhaled slowly. Yep, she'd caught wind of the echo.

"What is it that you want, Detective?"

"Please call me Sam. Sam Purdy."

She dabbed at her eyes with one of the tissues I'd handed her. It wasn't wadded; it was folded neatly. She used one of the sharp corners to do the dabbing. "But you are that detective friend of Dr. Gregory's, right? The one who works with the Boulder Police Department?"

Tricky question. "That is how I make my living, ma'am."

"Why are you here? Why did you come to see me this morning?"

"Something's been troubling me, I mean wake-up-in-the-middle-of-the-night troubling me about . . . your situation, and I'm hoping you can help me make some of my confusion go away."

She narrowed her eyes. "What?"

"You've lived with your husband a long time since you knew he had killed your old friend, right?"

"Yes."

It was a reluctant yes. Not reluctant because the facts didn't ring true to her, reluctant because she could spot the danger looming ahead if she accepted my premise.

"Well, I'd like to know how you could stay with him. It's important. To me, really important. I don't understand how you could go through the routines, you know, the daily . . . stuff that makes up marriage, knowing what you knew."

"He's my husband, Detective."

Yeah, yeah. But I heard the present tense. And knew she'd wanted me to hear the present tense.

"But wives leave husbands all the time, ma'am. All the time. They leave husbands over goofy things, over things that are much less consequential than murder.

Money, booze, other women. Snoring, halitosis, sex—too much, not enough—you name it. But you didn't, and I'm trying to understand that."

What I didn't say was *"My God, woman, your options are limitless. I know twenty men who would bow down and lick clean the ground you walk on."*

"I love Sterling."

I wanted to touch my chest right then, press on my sternum with at least three fingers to see if the tightness I was feeling had to do with my heart or with my *heart,* but I was afraid it might freak her out to see me caressing myself, so I didn't. Instead, I reached into my coat pocket and fingered the bottle of nitro the way I used to stroke the velvety rabbit's foot I carried around in my pants pocket as a kid.

I said, "And that's enough?"

"It was for me," she said.

Past tense now.

I took a moment to look away from her and give myself a pep talk. I told myself that I could look her in the eye and not be weakened by her beauty. That my resolve wouldn't dissolve in her loveliness.

When I looked back up at her, I was pretty sure that I'd been wrong.

"Can I admit what I've been wondering about you?" I said.

In an endearing way that ambushed me, she said, "Please."

"I've been wondering whether you've been threatened, you know? Or maybe you've feared what your life would be like if you turned him in, what would happen to you. Is that what kept you from calling us?"

My mother collects Lladro angels. The smile Gibbs

offered reminded me of the face of one of the angels, only prettier. "That wasn't it, Detective. I've gone over all this with that woman detective. With Miss Reynoso."

I waved off her objection. "Different departments. California, Colorado. It's a left hand, right hand thing. I don't mean to be repetitive—to force you to be repetitive—but in my business it truly helps sometimes to hear things yourself." I glanced away from her, then right back. Gibbs Storey was still gorgeous; that hadn't changed. "I'd understand those reasons. You know, if you were scared. If that's the reason it took you so long to—"

"But you don't understand that I love him. And that love made every choice difficult. Every option . . . complicated."

Is that what love did? Would Sherry say the same thing? I didn't know. I'd like to have asked her.

Maybe I would. Probably I wouldn't.

I said, "I'm having a little trouble with that, I'll admit."

Gibbs stood up and crossed the space between us. She leaned over, placing her hands on her knees so that the flawless skin of her face was only about a foot from my eyes. She said, "Would you like something to drink, Detective? Some coffee, maybe? It'll just take a minute."

She made me some decaf in a little glass coffeepot with a spring thing in the middle. It looked like something from a high school chemistry lab. The results were pretty good. I bet Alan had a pot just like it. Probably most of Boulder had a pot just like it. Sherry and I would be last. More likely, everybody would move on to another kind of coffee-making appliance before we got around to getting the one with the little spring thing in the middle.

We'd get ours on the sale table at Target.

She served the coffee in a cup with a saucer and a little platter of cookies. Often when I go into people's houses to talk, they offer me coffee, or a Coke, or even a beer, but I know it's fake polite, not real polite. They're seeking to grab some of my advantage; they don't really want me there. I didn't get that feeling from Gibbs. She seemed sincere with her coffee and cookies.

"About your husband's disappearance, ma'am? If you can bring yourself to discuss it—I'm sure it's painful—I'd very much like to hear your thoughts about what happened."

Her eyes filled with tears again. Was that grief? If it wasn't, it was a close approximation.

"I got a call just last night around bedtime. After eleven. It was from someone in Georgia, a policeman, I think. Maybe a firefighter. I don't recall. They're still looking for him, you know. I haven't given up hope."

"Yes, I know. That's why I called it a disappearance. I'm sure they're doing extraordinary things to find him."

"Thank you."

"You're welcome. Was last night like him? Like your husband? To stop and help someone like that? That was a courageous, selfless thing he did. An act of true heroics."

"What do you mean?"

"Maybe it's the work I do, maybe it's just some inborn cynicism—I admit that's a fault of mine—but I've come to believe that some of us are born with more of the Good Samaritan gene in us than others. I'm curious where Sterling fell on that spectrum."

She thought about it for a moment.

"It wasn't like him at all. Stopping to help someone like he did. Usually Sterling put his own self-interest first. It's not one of his best traits. Love doesn't require perfection, does it?" Her eyes found the small plate in front of me. "You don't like the cookies. Some fruit, maybe, instead? I think I have grapes."

I almost got stuck on that question. Not the cookies-and-fruit one. The one about perfection. Sherry hadn't done what she did because I wasn't perfect. No, that's not why she left. That had to be true. The day I said "I do," I knew I wasn't perfect. I went to bed every night knowing I wasn't perfect. I knew it the same way I knew that the stars felt like snowflakes under God's feet. I just knew it.

She knew it, too. Sherry left me for some other reason then, something more.

Or something less.

"No, ma'am. No thank you on the fruit, and no, love doesn't require perfection. So what evidently happened last night at the Ochlockonee River?" The name of the Georgia river rolled magically off my tongue. "Him stopping to rescue somebody. That would have been an exception then, what we might consider an anomaly?"

She nodded. "I've been comforting myself with the possibility that it was an act of . . . you know, contrition? Atonement?"

"Because he heard about the investigation that was going on? He was making up for what he had done?"

"Yes, I'd like to think so. I'd been keeping him informed of what was going on here, you know, legally. Sterling knew what kind of trouble he was in."

I lowered my eyes and allowed my expression to soften before I looked back up. "My understanding is that at the time of the . . . tragedy, he was traveling to visit a friend?"

"Yes, an old college friend. A man named Brian Miles. Brian lives just outside Albany, Georgia. He's a tech guy. An electronics genius of some kind. I don't know him that well. He and Sterling used to chase girls together in school—he's that kind of friend. They stayed in touch. We never socialized much together, though. I always thought Brian was kind of, you know, gay. Sterling says not."

Relevance? Got me; I filed it.

"And this visit? It was typical for Sterling to look up old friends during business trips?"

"No. Not male friends anyway, not just for the hell of it. Sterling likes women for company. He prefers women for company. Always has. He always will."

She managed to state it as though it were a simple fact, as though he preferred Hilton to Hyatt or Pepsi to Coke. But there had to be something more, didn't there? When people do unexpected things at unexpected times, it's important.

"Has that been a problem for the two of you? That Sterling prefers women for company?"

She stared at me again. She had quite a repertoire of stares. This one was an it's-none-of-your-business stare.

"All couples have issues, Detective. We have ours." She glanced at my stubby left hand and spotted the thin gold band almost disappearing in the lard on my finger. "You're married, aren't you?"

I was tempted to get lost with her. Tell her about Sherry and Simon and having Thanksgiving alone. But I don't tell stuff to strangers. Certainly not to strangers treading in homicide soup like Gibbs Storey. So I didn't tell her. But I knew I'd come close.

I came close because she's so pretty.

That was an ugly realization.

I moved my right hand so that the gold ring was no longer in view. What did I want to ask? I wanted to know how in the world a man could prefer the bed of another woman when he was married to the one who was sitting in front of me. I opened my mouth to ask at least twice, but each time I chickened out. Even rehearsing the words in my head, they sounded wrong.

I ended up asking a safer question. "So this whole sojourn from Tallahassee was unusual? The trip to see an old friend, a man? Then stopping to aid a stranger. Were you aware that Sterling was going to visit Mr. Miles?"

"Yes. Yes, I was. Sterling called me during the football game in Tallahassee. He knew about the search of our home, about the detective waiting here from Laguna Beach. He knew what was facing him here. He really wanted to talk it out—you know, his situation—with someone he trusts. Sterling doesn't have too many male friends, but Brian is someone he trusts. As much as he trusts anyone."

"Mr. Miles?"

"Yes."

"The one he chased girls with?"

"Yes."

"Was Sterling angry with you for your role in exposing him to the police?"

She maintained her balance and matched my steps as though she was accustomed to following bad dancers.

"He was, and he wasn't. I've been so torn—my loyalty to him, my love for him. An impossible choice. He understands that I've been placed in a difficult position by all this."

"And you have, haven't you?" I said. I meant two or three things with the question but figured she only heard one.

After a little sinus upshift she started to whimper again.

My decision-making process was abrupt, almost instinctive. I didn't plan to say what I said next. I just said it.

"I have some time off from work. Personal time. I'd like to help you find your husband. Try to find out what happened that night. At least go . . . to Georgia and do what I can to make sure everything possible is being done to . . ." I didn't know how to end the sentence.

Gibbs did. She said, "Find him."

"Yes."

She melted me with those eyes. "Please do that. Will you do that? Find him." I didn't know what to make of the stare she offered up next. But Gibbs Storey skipped third gear and went right into sniffle overdrive.

In seconds I had an arm around her, and she was

leaning into my man-boobs. Want to know what it was like? Having her in my arms, having her delicate beauty against my fat flesh?

Comfort. Solace. Succor.

Giving, getting.

I felt like goddamned Shrek with the goddamned princess.

It felt like heaven.

Didn't feel right, though. I can tell you that.

And it didn't answer that question about why Sterling chose the bed of another woman. Or the question about why I'd volunteered to go ask him.

Nope, it didn't do any of that.

THIRTY-TWO

ALAN

The storm had departed and left the Colorado plains in bright sunshine, which was typically what happened after a fierce snowstorm along the Front Range. But our seventy-degree Saturday had become a high-thirties, low-forties Sunday. Less than a full day had passed, and we were in a whole different season.

Lauren slept most of Sunday, a bad sign. Grace and I ran some errands, played some toddler games for which neither of us understood the rules, built a snowman out of snow that was the consistency of a Slurpy, and the whole time I pretended that the big bad wolf wasn't really at our door getting ready to huff and to puff and to blow our house down.

Once I succeeded in getting Grace into her crib for her midday nap, I checked my messages at the office. I was anticipating that I would be receiving a call from Gibbs seeking my compassion about her husband's disappearance in Georgia. But the only voicemail wasn't from Gibbs; it was a long message from Jim Zebid.

"Hey, Alan. It's Jim. I assume you saw the *Camera* this morning. I have to admit I'm a little concerned about it . . . um . . . you see, my guy—I'm sure you remember the one I'm talking about—swears he hasn't told anybody about his, you know, his thing with the guy, the one in the paper. And I certainly haven't told anybody about it but you. And now the cops know, obviously, and it's in the news. So it's a concern, obviously, and I'm left wondering whether—this is hard to say—you might have been a little indiscreet after we talked earlier in the week."

His tone wasn't belligerent. It wasn't even heated.

"I'm not accusing you, believe me, but the position my guy is in right now is really precarious. I mean, if her husband talks, you know—about, you know, it could be real bad for my guy. Anyway, if you have any thoughts about all this, I'd love to hear them. I'm on my cell all day. I think you have the number."

He's not accusing me? What else would I call it?

I dialed his cell number. He answered after three rings. "This is Jim."

"Alan Gregory, Jim."

"Alan, hold on. I need to get someplace I can talk. It'll take a minute, I'm downtown." I heard the sounds of a soulful saxophone. I knew exactly where he was on the Mall. He was at the corner of Pearl and Thirteenth. Some cold air wouldn't keep throngs away from the Mall on a sunny autumn Sunday when the number of shopping days until Christmas was dwindling away like Girl Scout cookies in a firehouse.

"Okay, this is better. Thanks for holding. So what do you think about what I was saying before?"

"What do I think?" I wasn't about to start this conversation. That was going to be up to him.

"The article?" he said.

"Yes?"

"Were you, maybe, a little indiscreet?"

"No, Jim. Not even a little. Until I saw the paper this morning, I'd totally forgotten about that part of our conversation. I'm almost embarrassed to admit that before this morning I hadn't given what happened with your client a thought since you left my office."

"Yeah?"

"Totally." I was determined not to sound defensive. I wasn't sure I was pulling it off. Instead I feared I sounded callous.

Jim was quiet. From the change in the background sounds, I guessed he was walking around on Thirteenth Street, down from the corner where the old black guy played the saxophone weekends on the Mall. There wouldn't be as many pedestrians on Thirteenth as there were on the Mall.

"Well," he said, "my guy had no reason to talk. And he assures me that he's told nobody but me what happened."

"Cops have other ways of finding out things, Jim. I assure you that nobody heard it from me. Directly or indirectly."

"What about your notes?"

"I don't put things like this in my notes. Ever." So much for not sounding defensive. Should I have told him that I wasn't even certain I'd written any notes about the session? Nothing was to be gained by going down that road. "I think there might be something else going on here, Jim."

"Good, I'd love an explanation. I'm planning on talking with my guy later on today."

"I think it's something we should talk about on Tuesday during our regular appointment."

"This can't wait until Tuesday. What do you have Monday?"

"I have a cancellation at eleven-fifteen. You want that?"

"Fine."

"Jim, I suspect this has more to do with you and me—issues in the therapy; I suspect that trust is high on that list—than with whatever you told me during our last session."

"You're kidding, right?"

"No."

"Jesus."

He hung up. Or the signal died. Either way, the deadness in my ear let me know I wasn't talking with him any longer.

The bedroom was dimly lit, blinds tilted to filter the western sun. The air had already taken on the stuffiness and stillness of an infirmary. Lauren didn't lift her head from the pillow as I entered. But she said, "Hi, baby. How's Grace doing?"

"Good. She's down for her nap. She ate a good lunch."

For a long moment I listened to her breathing, watched the bedding rise and fall above her chest.

She said, "Would you call the neurologist for me? Set up the steroids? I'm ready to start."

"You're sure?"

"Yeah."

"Here, or at the hospital?"

"Here."

"He may want to see you. That's cool?"

"Of course. And call somebody at work, tell them I won't be in for—God, I don't know—a few days."

"Sure. Is Elliot okay?" Elliot was one of Lauren's favorite people at the office.

"Elliot's good."

I touched her through the bedding. "I love you. Know that."

"I know. I love you, too. And I'm sorry."

I sat on the edge of the bed and placed my hand against her cheek. I said, "Don't be."

"I just am."

The home care nurse the neurologist sent over to our house arrived at dinnertime. She was a young woman named Petra, and I tried to engage her a little as she was gathering supplies. It didn't work. My clinical antennae said she was battling chronic depression. For some reason—maybe it was the barely restrained scowl she shot my way when she learned my profession—I guessed that she had already suffered through a bad stint or two of psychotherapy and had been the unfortunate victim of multiple antidepressant failures—a couple of tricyclics, some SSRIs, and maybe even an MAOI or two.

The good news is that what Petra gave up in gregariousness, she made up in efficiency. The IV was running and taped in place within ten minutes of her initial knock on our door. Moments after that she loaded the first gram of Solumedrol into a fat syringe and began pushing the liquid in it hard into the tube that led to Lauren's purple vein.

How much is a gram of steroids? If a healthy person were to injure a shoulder, say, or a hip, and a physician determined that major anti-inflammatory drugs were required, the doctor might prescribe oral steroids. Over five days of treatment the dose would decrease from a high of maybe thirty milligrams a day down to zero.

Lauren had just received over thirty times that maximum dose, and she'd had it forced directly into her bloodstream all at once. And the exact same procedure—with the same megadose—would be repeated on each of the next three days.

As I watched the blood pressure cuff inflate on her arm, Lauren managed a smile. She mounted the smile, I knew, for me. The syringe had just relinquished its final drops of steroids into the IV tube. She said, "The first twenty-four hours aren't all bad, you know."

I touched her hair. *And after that?* I thought. After the first day became the second and the first gram of steroids was followed by another, and another, and then, damn it, another?

After that, well, after that we'll just jump off that damn bridge when we get to it, won't we?

It wasn't until after Petra had departed—she'd left a buffalo cap behind affixed to the indwelling IV in Lauren's forearm—that I realized that Gibbs had never called me about Sterling's disappearance and possible demise in Georgia.

I usually didn't waste even a solitary calorie of effort worrying about patients who *didn't* call me after hours. My consistent message as therapist to my patients was that I expected they could handle life's stresses without checking in with me. I expected them not to call me after hours.

But emergencies are emergencies. And missing husbands who are feared drowned are usually considered emergencies.

As I prepared Grace's dinner, I couldn't help thinking that Gibbs *should* have called. Since I left her at her house during the search warrant execution on Friday, she'd had to endure an uncomfortable interview by Carmen Reynoso. Her husband had disappeared and was feared dead in some river I'd never heard of in Georgia. That had to be stressful.

I couldn't help wondering why she didn't call.

I thought of calling her, checking on her. I really did. The very fact that I was considering it was so unusual that it caused me to recall Diane's admonition that I was treating Gibbs differently than I would treat some other patient, which for some reason caused me to jump to a very disconcerting association to Teri Reginelli and *hachas en cabezas*.

I had an appointment with Gibbs Monday morning near dawn. If she could wait until then, I could wait until then.

THIRTY-THREE

My best guess is that Lauren hobbled out of bed after a few fitful hours of sleep somewhere around three A.M. The primary short-term side effect of high-dose steroids is agitation, and she was agitated. Not wide awake, but agitated. I followed her out to the living room to check on her but never looked at the clock. She got herself settled on the sofa with the remote control and sent me back to bed. Did I sleep after that? I don't know. I do know that the alarm jangled at five forty-five.

Grace started squealing at five forty-seven. She was my snooze alarm.

Viv, our daytime nanny, arrived at six thirty-five. I filled her in before I kissed Lauren and Grace and ran to my car at full speed.

Emily's paw umbrella *clack-clacked* on the floor as she chased me to the door. I apologized to her because I didn't have time to make repairs.

Gibbs looked much better put together for our seven o'clock appointment than I did. The morning was brisk, and she was modeling her fall things. The autumn forecast, fashionably speaking, apparently called for snug black jeans, tight sweaters, and large beads of silver and gold. Gibbs wore it all well, no surprise.

I'd brought coffee from home. Gibbs had stopped at Starbucks. Every time she sipped, she left a slightly wider lipstick stain on the plastic cover of the paper cup.

"Whew, interesting weekend" was her opener.

I suppose. I tried to read her face for signs of what she might be feeling, but no clues jumped at me.

I did, however, check "distressed" from my list.

"Tell me," I said. I could just as easily have chosen silence or said "go on" or "yes," but "tell me" is what I chose.

"I talked with that detective, finally."

She lifted her latte and took a baby sip. I expected her to continue with her tale of her meeting with Reynoso, but she returned the cup to the small table between us and looked at me expectantly.

I sat holding my mug just below my chin with both hands, and I waited. Gibbs had apparently decided that this appointment was going to be more dental than psychological and that it was going to be my job to pull the teeth. In turn, I decided that it wasn't going to happen. In therapy, when things go according to plan, the patient sets the pace.

On good days in the therapist's chair, I could outwait Job. And I felt like having a good day.

I needed a good day.

Two minutes, maybe three, later, Gibbs blinked. "Oh, and I met that friend of yours. Detective Purdy?

He stopped by my house yesterday for a visit. He's so nice. Don't you think he's nice?"

I thought, *You have to be kidding.*

But I kept my face impassive and said, "Tell me." Steam blossomed up from the mug below my chin.

I allowed Gibbs to go on uninterrupted. She sensed, I think, that her story was causing me consternation, but I doubted that she understood why I was feeling almost cataplectic at what she was telling me.

If Gibbs was to be believed—and I admitted to myself that I was experiencing more than a few instances of severe doubt about the veracity of her story—Sam was probably well over halfway, or more, to Georgia as she and I were speaking. I'd been on road trips with Sam before. The image in my head needed no further developing. He was crammed behind the wheel of his Jeep Cherokee, listening to some music that was as full of lament as was his current life. He was hungry. He was cranky. Road maps were spread out on the passenger seat beside him. Maybe they had already crumpled into heaps on the floor. He'd marked his preferred route with a pastel highlight pen, then marked an alternative in a different color. Something you could count on when traveling with Sam was that every time he stopped for gas, he would decide that there was a better way to get from where he was to wherever he wanted to be.

If it was more than an hour from his last fuel stop, he probably needed to visit a bathroom. But he wouldn't pull over again until he needed gasoline. Highway rest stops were for wusses. Sam was a velocity traveler, not a comfort traveler. Bladder be damned, full speed ahead.

I was willing to make a guess that he was someplace in Arkansas or, if he was making particularly good time, had already crossed the border into Louisiana.

I had a fleeting wish that I was beside him, riding shotgun. Sam grows reflective on long trips. The monotony of the road or the infinity of the sky or something about the miles passing below his feet causes him to consider opening windows into his life that were otherwise nailed shut and hung with blackout curtains.

There was so much for Sam and me to discuss right then: Sherry. Simon. Heart disease. Rehab. Cop work. Lauren's exacerbation. The future.

God, the future.

And of course, Gibbs and Sterling Storey.

But the real reason I had a yearning to be sharing the Jeep with him was that I wanted to be a fly on the wall, a silent spectator, as the inevitable collision occurred between the recalcitrant Iron Ranger and the southern good old boy. I wanted to watch as Northern Minnesota, personified by Sam, said hello to Southern Georgia, personified by any number of unwitting volunteers. I would have paid good money for a chance to witness what happened as Sam Purdy tried to reconnoiter Dixie.

I blinked myself back to the present. Gibbs was still talking, oblivious to the extended holiday my attention had just taken.

"He said he'd call when he got to Albany, but I don't expect that will be before tonight. I'm thinking thirty hours minimum."

"Tonight," I repeated for no other reason than to get my bearings. I didn't bother telling her that Sam would be doing the trip nonstop; that his head wouldn't see a motel pillow between here and there. I didn't know the mileage, but Gibbs should be dividing by seventy-five-plus miles per hour, not any pedestrian fifty-five.

"You think sooner? You know better than I do, I'm sure. Cops don't have to drive the speed limit, do they? He could just flash his badge and make the ticket go away, couldn't he?"

With those words she grew silent.

I used the interlude to consider the obvious. What was it Sam hoped to accomplish in Georgia? I knew him well enough to suspect that his motive had nothing to do with what he had told Gibbs: that he wanted to help her find her husband in the Ochlockonee River.

In usual circumstances Sam wouldn't have driven to Denver to look for Sterling Storey in the shallows of the South Platte.

So then, why?

The silence spread between us like a little pond of fetid water. We each sat on an opposing shore.

Gibbs finally said, "He used to think he was falling. Sterling did. That's when he used to say 'catch me.' Isn't it ironic? Isn't it? And now he goes and . . . disappears trying to catch somebody else. He really was falling, and there was nobody there to catch him."

The abrupt change in direction threw me, once again, off balance. The invisibility of the silent associations that had helped Gibbs traverse the undoubtedly rich affective territory between Sam's arrival time in Albany, Georgia, and her husband's beseeching her for support while he fantasized himself falling perplexed and frustrated me.

Catch me. Yes. Gibbs had once told me something about Sterling saying "catch me."

But what?

Sex. Was it sex? It was probably sex. But I couldn't remember. My brain was on full overload. I felt as though I had *un hacha en mi cabeza.*

It probably had been sex. An awful lot of what Gibbs ended up talking about seemed to ultimately be about sex. Maybe Diane was right: Maybe I just had a difficult time hearing it.

I asked, "Literally falling? Or figuratively falling?"

"Gosh, that's an interesting question," Gibbs said. "I never really thought about that. I always thought he meant falling like that first time on the balcony. Do you remember?"

Do I remember? Do I remember what?

"He was leaning against the side railing, and I was in front of him, you know. . . . I was wearing a skirt. But I wasn't wearing any . . ."

She blushed a little. I finished her sentence in my head. The next word was going to be "underwear."

Diane would have corrected me. She would have maintained that Gibbs's next word was going to be "panties."

"Well, I don't have to paint a picture for you, do I?" she said.

I considered whether the comment was flirtatious or seductive. Although it probably was, a conclusion escaped me. This was not my morning for clarity. I could blame it on the early hour, but that wasn't the cause.

No, of course not, I said to myself, *you don't have to paint a picture for me. I already have one:* New

Year's Eve party, Wilshire Boulevard. The balcony of a friend's condo. You and Sterling, the first time you had sex. You weren't wearing any . . .

"That was the first time Sterling said 'catch me,' " I said. My words sounded insincere, even to me. I knew I was saying them to offer proof that I remembered what she had told me.

"Yes," she murmured, reflecting on something I couldn't fathom, perhaps my insincerity.

"He said it again last week," I pointed out.

She nodded. "When we were . . ."

She stopped herself, searching for the correct verb. For that particular activity there were a lot of choices.

Then I remembered. Gibbs had already told me that she could see another couple in the bedroom that night. They were . . . doing that verb, too. I said, "There was another couple, too. That night in L.A. In the bedroom next door."

"Yes. Yes, there was."

She seemed surprised that I knew. Had she actually forgotten telling me? Had she?

"Sterling was so afraid he'd lose control. Lose his balance. That he'd fall, somehow. We were ten stories up, at least. That's when he said 'catch me.' He said it like he meant it."

In my head I was playing with the geometry and the anatomy and the physics and the possible erotic acrobatics. I didn't see how Sterling could have been at much risk of actually going over the railing backward—he wasn't that tall, and Gibbs had the body mass index of a large butterfly—but then my personal experience in such matters was limited. Diane would be able to explain it to me: She'd be the kid in the back row with her hand in the air, yelling, "I know that one. I know that one."

I said, "Really? He was really frightened of falling? Or was it, perhaps, something else?"

"That day, really. Later, I think it was something else. Afraid of falling, you know, metaphorically. He'd say 'catch me' when he was feeling down. Lost. He was asking for my help. To save him, I think."

"Was it always sexual?" I asked. Immediately—I mean instantaneously—I knew I'd asked the wrong question. At the very least I'd asked a question when I should have sat as mute as a bronze Buddha.

"Was what sexual?" she asked in return.

I tried to recover. "Sterling's concern about falling. Did he only say 'catch me' in sexual situations?"

She lifted the Starbucks cup, popped off the lid, and drained whatever remained of her morning coffee. Mocha-stained foam coated her upper lip like sea froth on a glossy red shore. She used her tongue to wipe her lip clean. She did it slowly, deliberately. Out first, then side to side.

Seductively? I just didn't know. I wanted to see the replay. Sometimes I just needed to see the replay.

She said, "We're back there again, aren't we?"

"Back where?"

"I told you once we needed to talk about sex, didn't I?"

I remembered that. "Yes, you did."

"Well," she said. "The truth is, I enjoyed it."

"Excuse me."

"I enjoyed it. It turned me on."

Talking with me about sex turned Gibbs on? Uh-oh. It's too early in the morning for this.

"And it has ever since that night on the balcony," she said.

I was grateful for the clarification. But her words, I thought, carried a hint of defiance. Or maybe it was provocation. Did the difference make a difference?

"Sterling saying 'catch me' while you two were having sex turned you on? That's what you're saying?"

She shook her head.

Damn.

"No, no. God, no. Watching the other couple that night. That's what turned me on. I told you about the night on the yacht in St. Tropez, didn't I? When we met? I did, right?"

"Yes." She knew she had.

"That was the first time I'd ever seen anybody else . . . do it." She laughed. "Everybody else do it, actually. The feeling that I had that night was . . . indescribable. It was so unexpected. Then came New Year's Eve on the balcony and the couple in the bedroom, and I . . . I was watching him and he was watching me and . . ."

Her words drifted away. She was breathing through her mouth, and her chest was rising and falling visibly.

The coffee in the mug in my hand had gone tepid. The light in the room had transformed from dawn to day, and stringy shadows from the naked branches of the leafless trees were streaking across the floor. Gibbs's perfume marked the air.

I was thinking, *Weren't we talking about Sam? I'm pretty sure we had started off talking about Sam.*

"Yes," I said. "Go on." Two heartbeats later, before she'd responded, my train of thought skipped back, then forward once more, and I added, "Gibbs?

You said Sterling was asking for your help when he said 'catch me.' Help with what?"

"I think he wanted me to help him stop killing the women."

Ah, yes. That.

THIRTY-FOUR

As strange as it may sound, the fact that Gibbs was confident that Sterling Storey had killed a number of women had to remain my secret.

Legally, I not only didn't have a responsibility to tell anyone—for instance, the police—about the other women whom Gibbs suspected her husband had murdered, but I also didn't have the right to tell anyone about them. If Gibbs had informed me that her husband was about to kill yet another woman, well, then that would have left me sailing in murkier waters. But even in those circumstances I probably couldn't breach Gibbs's confidentiality without her permission.

That's right. The only circumstance that would have allowed me freedom to spread the word about the other murders was if Sterling himself came into my office and told me that he was about to kill yet another woman, then proceeded to conveniently identify that woman.

Given the events on the Ochlockonee River on Saturday night, that didn't seem too likely.

But morally?

In the field of mental health, ethics and morals are an odd couple. Despite their differences, though, they get along most of the time. Sure there are occasional quarrels, but most controversies eventually get ironed out because their goals are so similar. Sometimes there occurs, however, a set of circumstances that creates a chasm between ethics and morals that is the size of the Mariana Trench.

This was one of those.

Morally, I knew I had to tell somebody that Sterling Storey had killed other women.

But ethically, it was just as clear that I couldn't.

Look up "quandary" in the dictionary. In the margin beside the definition there will be a picture of me sitting across from Gibbs Storey wondering what the hell to do next.

THIRTY-FIVE

SAM

I used my cell phone to call Simon from a truck stop outside Montgomery. While I talked to my son, I was strolling along the border of the property, kicking at weeds I didn't recognize and swatting at insects I didn't know lived on the planet with me. I didn't tell Simon I was calling from the South. It wouldn't have bothered me at all that he knew I was in Alabama—with his limited worldview he'd have figured I was at the U of A for a football game, and he'd have a question or two about the Crimson Tide—but I didn't want him to start conspiring with me to keep secrets from his mom, so I kept the news about my travels to myself.

Sherry didn't want to talk to me. Her father, a gruff, kind, barrel of a man whom I'd always liked, was the one she'd tapped to tell me she didn't want to talk to me. Angus had always been fond of me, and after I'd bulldogged my way a few years back into a position to help my niece—his granddaughter—get some medical care she desperately needed, he thought I was the son-in-law from heaven. I'd always tried hard to do nothing to dissuade him.

"She's still being a bitch, Sam, what can I say?" was the way Angus described the situation to me. Angus was never one to mince words about his progeny. When one of his girls acted heroic, he called her a hero. When one of them acted bitchy, he called her a bitch. Angus taught me good things about being a dad.

"How about you and I cut her a little slack, Angus? How about that? She's working stuff out." Sherry and I had our problems, but gang-tackling her with her father didn't seem like a fair way to confront them.

He harrumphed. "You okay? Your ticker?"

"It's ticking fine. I'm following all the rules, and the docs think I'm a star. Simon sounds good."

I didn't like lying to Angus, but there it was. Not the part about Simon, the part about following all the recovering-from-a-heart-attack rules. Buried somewhere in the fine print there had to be a rule about no nonstop road trips to the land of deep-fried everything.

Yep, that was probably prohibited. That's the one I'd broken. That one and maybe a few others.

"Simon's good. He's a great kid. A little on the wild side, but a great kid. Though he should be in school. You and I both know that."

"Stay cool, Angus. This will all work out."

"Ask me, it's goofy. They should both be in Boulder with you. But nobody asks me. You get to be seventy-five, and everybody thinks you're an idiot. You wait until you get old."

"You know I agree with you," I said. "And I don't think you're an idiot."

"Now there's an endorsement." He laughed. "There's something I got to ask you, Sammy."

"Yeah."

He laughed again, a deep roar. "Are those Avalanche of yours ever going to score more than one goal in the same game? I mean ever? The point of the game is to put the puck in the net, isn't it?" Angus's laugh exploded into a guffaw.

All I said in reply was "Let's see whose team is still playing in June, Angus, what do you say?"

He was laughing so loudly, I'm pretty sure he didn't hear me.

The bathrooms in the truck stop were surprisingly clean. The restaurant seemed to be run by a group of women my mother's age—two black, two white—who were suspicious about a guy my size ordering egg whites and grapefruit and decaf coffee. As soon as my order made it over to the kitchen, one of the waitresses came by and asked me where was I from, honey. When I told her Colorado, she nodded knowingly.

I didn't even have to say "Boulder."

She'd seen my kind before, apparently.

The matrons kept a careful eye on me after that. I figured they were waiting for me to call them over to the table and order some tofu, or a kiwi smoothie, or maybe a grande cappuccino.

Despite their suspicions they were kind women, all in all. Even brought me a side of grits I didn't order. There was a big fat orb of butter melting like a setting sun right in the center of the grits. I ate around the circle of butter so that what was left on the plate when I was done looked like a cool caricature of a sunny-side-up egg that my kid might have drawn at school.

I dropped enough money on the table to leave the ladies a hundred-percent tip on the meal, filled the tank out at the pumps, checked my maps, and pointed the Cherokee toward Georgia.

I hadn't looked in my rearview mirrors—not intentionally, not once—since I'd headed east on I-70 out of Denver. I didn't look at the mirrors when I pulled away from that Alabama truck stop. Nor did I bother to wave good-bye to the matrons who'd made and served my meal.

I'd told myself from the beginning of my trip that I would only know that I'd really finished leaving someplace when I passed a sign that was promising me that I'd arrived at someplace new. That was the way my life seemed lately, so that was how I was going to travel.

My current plan, always subject to revision, was to cross the border into Georgia right about where Phenix City, Alabama, ended and a highway sign said that Columbus, Georgia, was beginning. Then I would drift southeast toward Albany. Farther south than that, the Rand McNally road atlas said I'd find the legendary wilds of the Ochlockonee River.

When I got there?

The answer to that question eluded me, I must admit. For well over a thousand miles I'd been trying hard not to think about it. Instinct had rarely failed me in life, and I was counting on a visit from the instinct fairy sometime after I crossed the border into Georgia.

*

On the short stretch of frontage road between the truck stop and the highway I drove over some railroad tracks that were protruding high above the roadbed. I felt the sharp jolt from the rails as a punch below my sternum, and my pulse immediately popped up a good twenty percent.

Since I'd left the hospital, it seemed that I felt almost everything that happened to my body right in the center of my chest. It was as though any physical sensation was amplified and focused right below my ribs, centered a couple of inches down from my man-boobs.

A belch? Heart attack.

Indigestion? Heart attack.

Roll over in bed? Heart attack.

I knew that the next time I stubbed my toe, I was going to finger that damn brown bottle of nitro.

I thought about my injured heart, and about my broken heart, until I saw the sign for Phenix City. What I was close to deciding was that neither assault on my heart was going to kill me.

I was thinking maybe I was going to be okay after all.

THIRTY-SIX

ALAN

I didn't know where Gibbs had grown up. I didn't know what her family of origin was like.

Siblings? Dog? Cat?

Didn't know, didn't know, didn't know.

Had her parents loved each other? What did her dad do? Had her mother worked? What was school like for her? Did she wear braces? Had she lived in the same house her whole life or had she moved a dozen times? Did she play the piano or enjoy playing any sports?

Did she yearn for children?

Or a career?

Had her heart been broken? Had she endured wrenching losses?

I didn't know.

Typically, after a handful of conjoint sessions and a few individual appointments, I would be able to construct a pretty reliable social history of any one of my patients. But not with Gibbs.

With Gibbs, I didn't know much at all that didn't have to do with St. Tropez yachts and Wilshire Boulevard balconies.

I gave that state of affairs some thought.

What did I know?

I knew about an old murder that purportedly involved her husband, and I knew that voyeuristic sex turned her on. I knew that her husband sometimes said "catch me" during lovemaking. I knew about a magical night in St. Tropez.

And oh yes, I knew about Louise Lake and the other dead women. Gibbs kept reminding me about them.

Did I actually forget about the victims in between her reminders? Hardly. I just kept telling myself that when the chaos quieted, Gibbs and I would get back to it.

The chaos? Yes.

Murder, sex, multiple murder, sex, search warrants, sex, coffee with my friend the detective, sex.

In psychotherapy that kind of progression constitutes chaos.

And now she'd moved us again back to multiple murder.

Damn.

Psychotherapy rule number six: If you want to understand the motivation behind an act, first examine its consequences.

The consequences of Gibbs's chaos-creation proclivities? Her therapist—me—would end up way too off balance to focus on the big picture, whatever the big picture was.

Was that Gibbs's intent?

I didn't know.

But I suspected that my not knowing *was* her intent.

"Gibbs?" I waited until she focused her eyes on me.

"Yes?" she said pleasantly.

"Why don't you tell me about the other murders?"

She fingered her wedding ring. "Just between us?"

An interesting response. I replied, "Of course."

"What difference does it make now? If Sterling is really gone, what difference does it make?"

"I could answer that question for you, but I think it's better if you answer it for yourself. You keep bringing up the other women whom you think Sterling killed. You brought them up again just now. It apparently makes a difference for you that he killed more than one woman. That's what difference it makes."

Psychotherapy rule number eleven: Follow, don't lead.

Had I just broken it?

"They are all women he was involved with at one time or another. At least that's what he told me. I'm not sure I believe him."

I waited. I couldn't follow if she didn't take another step forward.

"You don't believe what? That he was involved with them?"

"I don't know. Sterling lies a lot. He . . . betrayed me. You know?"

"No," I said. "I don't know. The reality is that I don't know anything that you don't tell me, Gibbs. But

I don't understand why he would admit to affairs that he didn't have."

"He probably had them." She glanced at her hands before she continued. "The first one he told me about was at Augusta."

"Augusta, Georgia?"

"Yes. He met her at the Masters."

I waited, wondering why it was important that he met her at the Masters. "She was the first one he . . . killed?"

"She was the first one he told me about. But there was another one at West Point, too."

"The military academy?"

"She was a hostess he met. At the Army-Navy game."

I was still following her, but now I was on my tiptoes, trying to look over her shoulder.

"And then Indianapolis," she added.

I thought I was getting the swing of it. Sterling met women while he was producing the broadcast of sporting events. "The Indianapolis 500? The car race?"

She shook her head. "No, the College Combine. The NFL draft? She worked for the arena people."

I took a few steps back to give Gibbs room to lead. "Why just between us? Why not share this information with the authorities?"

"I don't want people to think he was that kind of man."

"Even though he was?"

She glowered. "He has demons, Dr. Gregory. Women make him crazy sometimes. Crazy. He's been fighting it his whole life. He really has. I don't think people will understand."

I couldn't argue with that. Gibbs was absolutely right: People wouldn't understand.

"Women make him crazy?" I asked. It wasn't much of a question. I could just as easily have said, *"I'm going to skip my turn, why don't you just keep going?"* But instead I said, "Women make him crazy?"

"He was afraid that they wouldn't let him go, that they would ruin what he had. All the good things he'd accomplished . . ." Her voice trailed away.

I was confused about the good things. I asked, "His career?"

"Yes, but . . . no. I was talking about his marriage to me."

"So he killed these women because . . . they threatened your marriage? I'm not sure I follow."

"I don't know very much about any of it." She wriggled and tugged on her sleeves, finally looking back my way as though I were a vanity mirror and she was checking her reflection. "It's not like we talked about this all the time."

I had a thousand questions. I asked none of them.

Her voice was pressured when she resumed. "Just once. We only talked about all this once, okay? Right before we moved back here to Boulder. He admitted the affairs with all the women—there were others, too, many others. I don't know the details. Ones he didn't . . . you know, kill, but I think felt an impulse to . . . There was one in South Bend, a sports information something"—she shivered—"and a girl in Flushing Meadows—she was a publicity something with the women's tour, I think. And Daytona Beach, maybe. I forget. I try to forget."

South Bend was Notre Dame University, probably

football. Flushing Meadows was tennis, the U.S. Open. Daytona Beach was NASCAR, I thought. Some car race. Sam would know.

She exhaled deeply. "That wasn't a surprise to me. The affairs. I knew he was . . . seeing other women. I just did. It's who he was. But he promised me that he was done. He told me he had changed, that moving back here would be a new start for us. That he valued our marriage too much to ever cheat on me again."

A tear moved a centimeter down her cheek, paused, and then tracked at an angle toward her nose. She touched it with the tip of her finger. Another tear soon followed the same track. Her chest heaved a little.

"Take your time," I said.

"He said he was going to prove his love for me all over again by putting his life in my hands. That's when he told me that the women were gone. The ones who were a threat . . . to us."

"Gone?"

"That's what I asked. He said they wouldn't bother us ever again. I asked him what he meant."

The tears on her cheeks were leaving silky tracks in the powder on her skin.

" 'Louise is at peace. They are, too.' That's what he said. Those were his exact words. What do you think he meant?" Gibbs's hands were rolled into fists.

I slid the box of tissues closer to her. She appeared not to notice.

I didn't have a prayer of knowing exactly what Sterling had meant with his words. But every one of my guesses chilled me.

Gibbs continued. "We made love that night. And he said 'catch me' again. He was trusting me with his secret, begging me to keep him from falling." She paused for a good hunk of a minute before she confessed, "His life was in my hands for a few weeks. That's how long it took me to betray him."

THIRTY-SEVEN

SAM

The bridge over the river where Sterling Storey disappeared wasn't much to look at.

I'd been working under the assumption that it was a major highway bridge on the stretch of Highway 19 that connects Thomasville and Albany, but it wasn't. For some reason, when Sterling had cut off the main road out of Tallahassee, which was Highway 319, he'd ended up on a smaller road, a two-laner that I guessed was a county road, marked Georgia 3, heading northwest just about parallel to Highway 19. The bridge on the smaller road was a concrete structure that had been doing its job for a lot of years, almost too many. The local cops figured Sterling had gotten lost in the storm and had taken the wrong turn out of Thomasville and ended up on the county road instead of 19.

It was a reasonable assumption, but assumptions trouble me.

The details of the accident weren't what I expected. The minivan that had gone off the highway and that had been in danger of sliding into the swollen river was traveling southeast, not northwest, before it went off the road. I couldn't figure out how Sterling had even seen it down there. It was on the opposite side of the road, on the opposite side of the bridge.

That wasn't all that I couldn't figure. After living in the high desert for as long as I had, it was a constant revelation to me how lush everything was in southern Georgia, even the week before Thanksgiving. With the accident having taken place at nearly eight o'clock at night, with all the woods and vegetation camouflaging everything, and with torrential rains obscuring anything that wasn't camouflaged, I didn't know how Sterling could have seen a damn thing out the windshield of his damn rented Camry.

Standing near the top of the bridge abutment, I stared at the placid river below my feet. The water in the Ochlockonee was more yellow than gray, and I suspected that with global warming and all, there were glaciers that moved faster than that river was flowing at that moment. It took every bit of my imagination to conjure up a picture of the biblical flood that had recently coursed down that channel.

Before I left the riverbank, I reread the police report that my partner Lucy had smuggled to me. The report was okay. Better than many I'd read. Written clearly, decent chronology, good descriptions. In most circumstances it would have sufficed. These weren't most circumstances, though, and standing on the bridge, I realized what wasn't spelled out in the report.

Who had arrived at the scene first? Was it the Baptist preacher, the twin sisters, or Sterling Storey?

*

According to the police report, the preacher who had witnessed Sterling's disappearance into the river was Reverend Nathaniel Prior, who served the faithful at a church in Meigs, a little town a short stretch northeast on Georgia 3 from the accident scene.

That's where I would start.

The drive from the river to Meigs passed through thick woods that alternated with fields harvested clear—I was guessing—of cotton. I didn't see much else that would support the local economy. I assumed I was in a poor county.

I drove up to a recently whitewashed church and asked a young man who was out in front raking leaves on the ragged lawn if he knew where I could find Nathaniel Prior.

"You've already found him. I'm Nathaniel Prior," he told me. "I'm pleased to meet you."

Nathaniel Prior was no more than twenty-five years old. He was smaller than me by a few inches but matched my weight pound for pound and then raised me a few for good measure. He had a voice that resonated like a diesel in a tunnel. The pile of leaves at his feet covered him up to midcalf.

He had big ears.

He tugged off a canvas glove, and we shook hands. I said, "Sam Purdy. Shall I call you Reverend?"

"That's fine, or Nate's fine, too. There are moments when I'm convinced I'm called worse things behind my back, but you've barely met me, so what reason would you have to insult me? What can I do for you this fine day?"

It was a fine day. The afternoon sun was shining, and the moisture in the southern air had already softened up my cuticles and the tender skin inside my nose. Those are the first parts that turn to papyrus after even a few days in the Colorado high desert.

"Do you have a minute to answer some questions about last Saturday? The accident at the bridge?"

Prior looked over my shoulder at the Cherokee. He said, "Mr. Purdy? Do I have that right? Why don't we sit a spell and get a glass of tea? I have a feeling you've come a long way to ask me these questions, and these leaves are probably more than content to wait to be imprisoned in Hefty bags."

"Sam," I said. "Some tea sounds great." I sat on the wooden porch of the church while the reverend retrieved the tea from inside. At least three people walking down the quiet lane waved hello to me while he was gone. I waved back to every one of them.

The tea was sweet, flavored with mint, and was delivered in painted glasses fat enough to hold a Big Gulp with room to spare.

"Thanks," I said after a long draw.

"Colorado, huh? You ski?"

"Snowboard, actually, if you can believe it. I have a kid I try to chase around as much as I can. The snowboarding is his idea. He thinks skis are dorky. For his benefit, I try not to be any dorkier than comes naturally."

"Copper? Winter Park?"

I didn't expect somebody in Meigs, Georgia, to be asking me about ski resorts on Colorado's Front Range. "Winter Park and Breck, mostly. You know—"

"I did a semester in Denver. At the Denver

Seminary. Went up skiing whenever I could afford it, which wasn't very often. A bunch of us got those cheap Buddy Passes at Copper. That was a good winter."

I almost said, "*No shit.*" But I didn't; I was on God's front lawn. "How long you been in Meigs?"

"A couple of years. I'm loving it. I have a wonderful congregation. My family's in Atlanta, close by. I'm doing what I've always wanted to do. Life is as sweet as this tea." He placed his glass between his feet. "So what caused you to drive all this way to ask me what happened at the bridge?"

"The man who disappeared? I'm assisting his wife. I told her I'd try to figure out exactly what happened to him."

"You an investigator of some kind?"

I considered lying to him but didn't want to lie to a preacher. I don't know why, exactly; in most circumstances I'd be happy to lie to the pope to advance an investigation. "Yeah, I am. I'm actually a police detective in Boulder. But I had a heart attack a while back and I'm on medical leave. So technically, at the moment, I'm nobody. Just somebody trying to help a friend."

This was the moment in conversations with strangers—the moment they learned I was a cop from Boulder—when they asked the did-you-work-on-the-JonBenet-case? question. I steeled myself for it.

"You don't look like Boulder."

I smiled at him, grateful that we'd skipped right past the Ramseys. I replied, "You don't look like Meigs."

"Touché," he said. "Fire away. What can I tell you?"

I took a battered notepad out of my pocket,

flipped it to the next empty page, and clicked open my pen. "When did you arrive at the accident?"

"I was the last car to stop before Mr. Storey disappeared in the water. When I arrived, he was already there, the two sisters from Ochlockonee were already there, and of course, Mrs. Turnbull's minivan was already down the bank."

"Pretty dark that night?"

"As Satan's heart."

"Raining?"

"Buckets."

"And you saw Mr. Storey go into the river? Personally?"

"I'd parked my car so my headlights were pointing toward Mrs. Turnbull's minivan, so even with the rain there was some light down there. Though most of the beam went above her car. She was hung up on a tree branch on a steep section of the bank. It was leaning—at least thirty or forty degrees would be my guess—"

"Mine, too. I saw the river this morning. That bank is like a slide. The other side, where the tree was, there was more vegetation over there."

"Exactly. Well, Mr. Storey was already easing his way down toward Mrs. Turnbull when I first saw him. He was only a couple of yards away from the minivan when his feet went out from under him and he slid down the bank."

"You saw that?"

"Sure. The whole thing happened in the blink of an eye. I didn't see him go into the river. There was no light down that far."

"But he slipped, and then he slid? That's definite?"

"Absolutely."

"He was on the mud side of the car, not the tree side?"

"Correct."

"Did he call for help?"

"He did not. We—the Wolf sisters and me—guessed he was in the water before he knew what happened. He could've been downstream a hundred yards by the time he inhaled. Or tried to inhale. It's awfully easy to hit your head in raging water like that."

"You think he's dead, Reverend?"

"In my heart? Yes, I do. I prayed for his soul that night before I left the riverbank. I felt death around me while I prayed." He gritted his teeth as though a fleck of ice cube had come to rest right on top of a cavity. "You don't, do you? Think he's dead."

"I'm not convinced, no." What I didn't add was that if Sterling Storey was dead, my whole trip to Georgia would dissolve into futility. I wasn't in the South seeking justice; I was in the South seeking understanding. Sterling was going to be my unlikely professor.

I placed my empty tea glass two steps below my fat butt.

"Anything else?" I asked.

"I pray for Mr. Storey daily. Please tell his wife that. He sacrificed himself doing a Christian act of mercy."

"I will pass that along. She'll be comforted, I'm sure."

"Thank you."

I think he could tell I didn't mean the part about Gibbs being comforted. I sat silently for most of a minute reviewing my questions and the reverend's answers, looking for omissions. I couldn't find any.

"If your church has a bathroom, I'd love to make a pit stop. Then I'll be on my way. I'm grateful for your generous help. And for the fine tea. Meigs looks like a pleasant town; the people are friendly."

"It is and they are. You're going to go see the Wolf twins now, aren't you?"

"Yes, I am. I like to hear everyone's stories."

"They won't be home before supper. Go then. They'll feed you well. Your patience will be rewarded."

"I appreciate the tip."

"You're a Christian, Mr. Purdy?"

"I am."

"Doing Christian deeds?"

"I try."

"That's all the Lord asks."

"Is it?" Usually my faith in God was strong enough that such a question would never have occurred to me. But I was in Georgia on a wild-goose chase, and the question appeared on my lips and escaped before I could trap it.

The reverend looked at me in a kindly manner as though he could read the doubt in my eyes, as though he could tell that my faith was suffering.

I didn't ask him why, if I was doing all the Lord asked, I'd just had a heart attack and how come my wife had left me and taken my son away from me a week before Thanksgiving. Why didn't I ask the reverend? I supposed I didn't want to hear him speak about faith and about God acting in mysterious ways. And I didn't know whether or not I would have felt any better when we were done.

But my faith was weak right then, and I doubted it.

Reverend Prior must have sensed that misgivings

were clouding my vision. He said, "Don't make the mistake of measuring God's love by the yardstick of your own life, Mr. Purdy."

"What else do I have?" I asked.

He was busy pulling his canvas gloves back onto his hands. I wondered if he was planning to answer me.

"If you question God's plan when life is spitting in your face, you must be willing to accept Him without question when He blesses you with a child who snowboards and doesn't want you to be a dork." Prior bent down and lifted the leaf rake. "Come by for services if you stay in the area. You're welcome here, Mr. Purdy. There is abundant love here."

"Thank you."

"It's nothing. The bathroom is right through there."

THIRTY-EIGHT

Julie Franconia didn't usually get to set these things up the way she wanted. Far from it. She didn't have that much experience, but the few times she'd tried something like this, it had seemed that her fantasies usually got lost in the jungle of some man's choosing. That's the way it was the first time with him, too.

But this time his message said that she got to pick the time, the place, the setup. He just wanted to "control the mood." The last time with him was the best ever. He'd taken her over the moon. The mood? He could have the mood.

That's not all he could have. From the moment she'd spotted him at the RCA Dome, she'd been dying to make him hers. It had turned out better than she could have hoped.

She fit the headphones on her head and snapped the tape into the Walkman.

Beethoven.

An otherworldly voice-over said, "You have twenty minutes to get to the campsite. That's all. Go, baby."

Her heart was swollen. Anticipation. Pure anticipation.

Beneath her hiking clothes she was all silk. Everywhere.

Everywhere.

She knew the spot; she'd picked it carefully. Morgan Monroe State Park, north of Bloomington. A favorite trail. She wouldn't have any trouble getting there in the dusk light. Getting the tent up? She could do it in three minutes.

The piano concerto ended, and some old rock 'n' roll filled her ears. She thought maybe it was the Animals, but she wasn't sure. That was before her time.

Before his, too.

"Okay, babe, get the tent up. Hurry. I can't wait. I'm close by; can you feel me? Can you? I'm watching."

She threaded the fiberglass poles. One, two, three. The tent was up.

"Into the woods, to the west, ten steps. Go on now."

Her hiking boots sank half an inch into the marshy soil. She smiled as she saw the picnic basket.

"Now set everything up in the tent. Everything."

She did.

Wine and chocolate. Two cans of whipped cream. A disposable camera. It didn't take too long to set things up.

The music changed. The Doors.

Jim Morrison sang, This is the end, my friend, the end.

And it was.

*

When the police found Julie's body, they concluded that she was a hiker who had been pulled off the trail and shot by a madman.

Her body wasn't in a tent.

And she wasn't surrounded by a picnic of wine and sweets.

THIRTY-NINE

SAM

The twins.

Identical, by my reckoning. One padded around their house in the little town of Ochlockonee in Acorns ancient enough that all the dye had worn off the leather soles, the other in tattered Reeboks. The footwear choices made any height differential between the sisters difficult to determine, but the one in the Acorns looked me right in the eye when she greeted me at the front door. She was tall. Real tall. They were light-skinned African American women, each had a highlight of gray hair above her left ear, both wore baggy jeans and bulky sweaters knitted from the same skein of yarn, and each was as skinny as a hose, with fewer curves on their bodies than any two women I'd ever seen in my life.

But they were friendly and kind and generous the way my aunt Josie was friendly and kind and generous. I was in the twins' home for less than two minutes, and I was already sitting in their best chair eating sliced carrots from their root cellar. They served them ice cold with lime juice and more salt than my cardiologist would have liked, but the treat was tart and fresh, and I was enjoying it immensely.

The twin in the Reeboks said, "We picked that idea up in a bar in Jalisco a few years ago. So simple, so good."

I assumed Jalisco wasn't a suburb of Thomasville or Valdosta. I didn't know what it was a suburb of. Alan would probably know, though I wasn't always sure that was one of the things I liked about him. He wouldn't shove the fact that he knew it down my throat, though, which was one of the things I did like about him.

To my untrained eye, Ochlockonee appeared to be a smaller town than Meigs, if that was possible. Poorer, too. But the Wolf sisters' home wasn't particularly modest, at least not inside.

From the street the house appeared to be similar to the few others that were close by—a lot of weathered wood yearning for more paint than most people had the inclination to apply—but inside it was an ethnic showplace for artifacts that I quickly deduced the twins had collected on frequent travels abroad. I guessed that Africa, Central America, the South Pacific, and Mexico were among their favorite places for holidays. The bookcase closest to me contained cookbooks from cuisines I couldn't identify, and on a lower shelf were tattered guidebooks alongside titles from Naipaul, Forster, Theroux, and Darwin. This was the home of world-wise women.

CNN was on somewhere in the house, but I couldn't exactly tell where the TV was located.

It was about the time a glass of wine arrived in my hand that I came to the conclusion that Mary Ellen Wolf was the pediatrician in the Acorns. Her sister, Mary Pat Wolf, was the social worker in the Reeboks. I said a silent prayer that they didn't change footwear during my visit.

The wine was offered by Mary Ellen, who informed me that it was from Chile and seemed to be waiting for me to be surprised. I couldn't have distinguished a Chilean wine from a French wine and could barely tell either from Manischewitz, but living in Boulder, I was way past being surprised by food I didn't understand. Half the people in Boulder ate food I didn't understand.

Truth was, I probably ate food that half the people in Boulder didn't understand. Or at least I used to, before the heart attack.

I said, "Really? Chile?"

She could tell I was just being polite, but she didn't call me on it. That, by itself, was different from Boulder.

Mary Pat led me from the comfy chair toward their dining room table and delivered a platter of toasted bread that was covered with chopped tomatoes, some dark, woody mushrooms I didn't think grew in my neighborhood, and some kind of fat white beans I'd never seen before, and she handed me a napkin. "That's bamboo," she said.

"The bread? Really?" I thought only panda bears ate bamboo. Or was that eucalyptus and koala bears? I couldn't remember.

I worried that the heart attack had made me stupid, or stupider. I worried a lot those days about what the heart attack had done. Or would do.

"No, silly, the platter."

Her reply made it sound as though my gaffe had been an intentional stab at humor. Her gesture was a small kindness but much appreciated at that moment. Sherry wouldn't have done it. Few people I knew in Boulder would have done it.

I asked, "Do you always have this kind of greeting ready and waiting for unexpected guests?"

They smiled identical smiles. I found it disconcerting.

"Reverend Prior phoned and said you would be by," Mary Ellen admitted. "He explained about your quest to assist Mrs. Storey. What can we help you with, Mr. Purdy? Please."

"I only have a few questions, really." That was my cue to take out my notepad and pen. I could take notes without my reading glasses, though I couldn't read what I'd written.

"Let's have them then." They were both sitting at the table with me, and I could no longer see their footwear, so I wasn't a hundred-percent sure which one of them actually said that. It was the twin on my right.

"It's about Saturday night and the accident at the river."

"Of course it is." That was the sister on the left. She handled my next few questions, too.

"You were traveling together?"

"Yes."

"What direction?"

"We were coming home from seeing a movie in Thomasville. Denzel's new one? Have you seen it? I swear I'd pay to watch that man cut kudzu."

"I don't get to the movies much," I said. "Videos sometimes. But I agree Denzel is something special."

"Well, we both work in Thomasville. Ochlockonee doesn't have much commerce."

I didn't know what to say in reply that might not be interpreted as inadvertently insulting to Ochlockonee, so I returned my attention to the Storeys and asked, "Were you the first to stop at the bridge?"

"Well, poor Mrs. Turnbull stopped first, if you wish to split hairs. And I have a feeling you are the type who wishes to split hairs, Mr. Purdy. Though she didn't exactly stop the way she might have wanted to stop."

The other twin spoke. "We saw her car leave the road. Her headlights went, swoosh, right down the side."

"Of course, we stopped," said her sister.

"Of course. And Mr. Storey was right behind us."

"Right behind us. He'd been following too closely, if you know what I mean. Especially in that kind of storm, on wet roads. With that visibility. His driving left a lot to be desired."

I wasn't there to give Sterling Storey a traffic ticket. I said, "But he stopped, too? Right behind you?"

The twin on my right stood and went to the kitchen to retrieve the wine bottle. I glanced down at her feet. She was Reeboks. I told myself *right = Reeboks, left = Acorns.* I repeated the mantra so that I had a prayer of committing it to memory. On my notepad, for insurance, I wrote "R-R, L-A" in large letters.

Mary Ellen, on my left wearing Acorns, answered, "Well, not exactly. He drove right on past us at first."

"He did?"

"That surprises you?"

"Yes, it does," I admitted. I don't think I could have lied to these two women if I'd wanted to. Fortunately, I didn't want to. "That's not in any of the police reports I read."

"He drove at least a hundred yards—"

"At least," Mary Pat agreed.

"—before he stopped, did a three-point turn, and came right back and parked beside us."

"What? As though he'd had second thoughts about driving by?" I said.

"That's exactly what we thought. That he found some generosity in his heart over that hundred yards. I'd like to think that's what happened."

"And then?"

Dr. Wolf—that was Mary Ellen in the Acorns—said, "I was already on my cell phone by then, calling nine-one-one, trying to get us some help. We were terrified that the minivan was going to slide the rest of the way into the river."

Mary Pat said, "I jumped out and ran to the riverbank. But I couldn't see a thing, not a thing. The accident had caused Mrs. Turnbull's headlights to go out, and it was totally black down that bank. And after I'd taken two steps from the car, I felt like I'd fallen into a swimming pool with all my clothes on. Drenched to the bone. I actually had to throw away my shoes when I got home. They were hopeless.

"Anyway, Mr. Storey appeared beside me on the bank. He said, 'Can you see it? Is that where it went down?' I said I thought so. And that's when Mrs. Turnbull started screaming for help for her baby."

"And?" I said.

"We just stood there, for"—she turned to her sister—"what would you say? A minute? A full minute?" Her sister nodded. "We were just standing there, wondering what to do. It was dark and wet and none of us had ropes, but we knew the fire department rescue people wouldn't get there for too long a time. Finally Mr. Storey leaned over to me, and he said he was going down."

"Those words? 'Going down'?"

She grinned at me. "I knew you were a splitting-hairs type of man, Mr. Purdy. I knew it. I can't honestly say that he used those exact words. But something very close to 'I'm going down.' "

"And then?"

"He did. He started down the bank."

"Not over on the other side, by the tree, where the bushes are?"

"No, down the bank. That's when Reverend Prior drove up. He moved his car so that it gave us some light."

It took me a minute to catch my notes up to the story. When I looked back up, I made sure that both sisters were looking at me before I continued.

"You saw Mr. Storey go into the river?"

Mary Pat said, "No. I saw him go into the dark. The river was just part of the dark."

Mary Ellen smiled approvingly at her sister's description. "Mary Pat puts it well, Mr. Purdy. We saw him go into the dark. Have you been out there? To that spot on the river?"

"Yes, I have."

"Then you know that from the spot where Mr. Storey slipped and fell, it's a straight shot into the water. And that night, the Ochlockonee was quite swollen. I mean it was as high—"

"It was way high, as the kids say," added Mary Pat, the social worker. "Where he fell on that bank, it was just like being on an amusement park mud-slide ride straight into the river."

"So you both believe that's what happened? That he lost his footing and slid into that river?"

They looked at each other and nodded. Simultaneously, they said, "We do."

"But you didn't actually see it happen?"

This time, when they looked at each other, they both shook their heads, but they said nothing.

Mary Ellen said, "You don't think he drowned? Is that what you're saying? He never went into the river?"

I said, "The odds are high that he slid right on down the bank into the river. Just like you both believe. But so far I can't find anyone who actually saw it occur. I'm thinking that maybe it didn't happen that way. His wife is certainly hoping that maybe it didn't happen that way."

"Then where is he? The rescue people were at the bridge about ten minutes after he disappeared down that slope. He never called out for help. We never heard him. The rescuers had lights and boats, and they looked everywhere for him. They searched downstream for miles with dogs. They even had scuba divers out the next morning after the storm passed." Mary Pat's tone was slightly conspiratorial.

"And no one found anything, right? Not a trace?"

"Nothing," Mary Ellen agreed.

I said, "It's been my experience that occasionally people have a reason to want to disappear."

Mary Ellen dropped her voice most of an octave. "Are you suggesting that Mr. Storey was one of those people who had a reason? Why on earth would a man like that want to disappear? An important job like he has, a wife who cares enough to send someone like you all this way."

"Just between you and me?" I said. They nodded vigorously. "Mr. Storey is wanted for questioning about a murder."

"Oh my," said Mary Pat.

"So you think . . . ?" asked her sister.

"He might have . . . ?" Mary Pat again.

"Well," I said, "you have to wonder."

You do. Sometimes you have to wonder.

FORTY

ALAN

Viv, our Hmong immigrant nanny, worked part time, squeezing care of our daughter and us into her crowded school schedule. She saved our parental asses on most normal days. On crisis days, and those days were crisis days, her presence in our home was an undeserved gift from the parenting gods.

It was Viv who answered the phone when I called home after Gibbs's appointment. Lauren was busy cleaning the master bathroom. I had to picture it in my mind: One hand was on her walking stick and one hand was in a vinyl glove, clutching a rag. She was scrubbing surfaces that an obsessive microbiologist would probably have already deemed surgically sterile. By the end of the day, I knew, the motor on the vacuum cleaner would need new bearings, our entire supply of cleaning fluids would be depleted, and virtually every square inch of our home would be a whole new category of clean.

I'd seen it before in the wake of previous exacerbations. I had a name for it. I called it *steroid clean*.

Steroids don't provide virgin energy; they aren't some gentle supercaffeine. No, steroids, especially megadose steroids, provide agitation with all the negative consequences of the word. Impatience? In spades. Irritability? God, yes. Steroids are pure rocket fuel. I knew from experience that Lauren's management of the extra horsepower that was coursing through her veins would be relatively adaptive for about twenty-four hours—thus the steroid clean house—but after that the agitation and the resulting sleeplessness would overwhelm her coping ability, and she would take on a few of the assorted characteristics of the Seven Dwarfs on amphetamines.

Grumpy on Speed would be the dominant Dwarf. He—or in this case, she—would be around virtually the whole time, only reluctantly sharing the stage with Sleepy on Speed and with Dopey on Speed. If Sneezy on Speed showed up, we were all in a fresh mess of trouble; during a previous steroid treatment his arrival had caused my poor wife to sneeze something like thirty-seven times in a row with hardly time for an inhale in between. Emily, our Bouvier, hated human sneezing and had barked in concert with Lauren's honking for the last dozen sneezes or so. It was a memorable duet.

Sadly, Happy on Speed would make only the briefest of cameo appearances. If history were a guide, the cameo would take place during a narrow window in the first act.

I felt a stab of self-pity. For the next couple of weeks I'd be married to a most distasteful subset of the Seven Dwarfs on methamphetamine. Fortunately, my corrosive self-pity was swiftly dissolved by the solvent of compassion: Lauren not only had to live with the meth Dwarfs for a fortnight; she had the misfortune to be possessed by them.

She broke from scrubbing the beleaguered bathroom germs long enough to tell me what time she was seeing her neurologist later in the day, then gave the phone back to Viv, who informed me that Grace's cold was almost all better and that she'd even managed to add enough filament tape to Emily's paw to keep the clacking sound from driving Lauren even closer to distraction.

Viv also told me not to worry; she would take good care of us.

I told her she was great. And I started plotting ways to thank her.

Since I'd seen Gibbs so early that morning, Sharon Lewis was my second appointment of the week, not my first. The continued media attention that her breach of security at Denver's airport was generating still haunted her. As did the fear of imminent arrest.

"Am I really the most selfish person in America?" she demanded.

Needless to say, I didn't cast my vote on the question.

Obsessing was one of Sharon's things, so she obsessed. Should she turn herself in? Should she get a lawyer? Was what she did so wrong? Really? Wouldn't other people have done the same thing? Wouldn't they?

Would I?

I didn't answer that one, either.

Once the legal part of the crisis was resolved whatever way it was going to be resolved, Sharon had a long stint in therapy ahead of her. I was responding to her in the short term so that I would be prepared for what the future would inevitably bring.

Jim Zebid was late for his rescheduled appointment. He didn't arrive until half our allotted time had vaporized into the therapeutic ether.

"Damn prosecutors" was how he started. "I swear they argue things just to waste my time."

I tried not to allow my face to reveal anything back to Jim. My wife was one of those "damn prosecutors." I knew it and he knew it.

After that prelude he dove right into the topic of the day. "I need to tell you that it's hard for me to believe that you weren't indiscreet with that little tidbit I told you last week. My guy's firm that he didn't tell anybody about selling blow to the judge's hubby. I tend to believe him; he has no reason to be shooting his mouth off. I certainly didn't tell anybody other than you. So that leaves you."

The pointed implication was that I did have a good reason to be shooting my mouth off: to gossip with my wife. "Are you asking me something, Jim? Or is that just a flat-out accusation?"

He shrugged.

I registered some surprise at the fact that he didn't seem particularly angry. Although his words were sharp, his tone was the same one he might have used to order take-out Chinese.

What did I do? I took the bait.

"I will repeat my earlier assurance. I told no one—no one—about our conversation last week. And I will repeat my earlier suspicion, Jim, that your accusation about the incident has to do with something between us—something in the therapeutic relationship."

"Like what might that be?" These words were delivered in a tone that was totally dismissive. Litigators, in my experience, are more skilled at being dismissive than most people on the planet. They are able to imbue layers of nuance into their dismissiveness that most of us can only dream of. A law school trick of some kind, I suspected.

"Trust, maybe?" I tried to keep sardonic echoes from my own voice, but I wasn't totally successful.

"Trust?" He slumped back and crossed his ankles. His wingtip shoes were the size of river kayaks.

I waited.

"Yeah, well. Like my client trusts me right now? That kind of trust? Sure, sure, we can talk about trust, Alan—after I somehow end up convinced that you're not just covering your ass. How's that?"

The remainder of my Monday was more or less routine from a patient point of view.

Midafternoon I reached Lauren again. Her neurologist was hopeful that the steroids would arrest the exacerbation and felt confident that her good history of recovering from previous flare-ups boded well for her this time, too. To boost prophylaxis even more he started her on a statin, something she'd been discussing with him for a while, and he gave her some Ambien samples to help her try to get some sleep until the Solumedrol loosened its grip on her psyche.

She said, "I hope it works."

"The Ambien?"

"Everything. The steroids, the statin, everything."

"You scared, babe?"

"Yes. I'm afraid you're getting tired of this."

"Don't worry about that. Worry about getting better."

"Sam wasn't worried."

"I'm not Sherry, Lauren."

"You must have second thoughts about marrying me. Everybody has limits," she said.

I felt my pulse jump. I wanted to bark, *"Of course I have limits. Of course I hate this. Of course I feel sorry for myself."*

I didn't.

"Be honest," she pleaded.

¡Dios mío. Hay un hacha en mi cabeza!

Lauren didn't want my honesty. She wanted my reassurance. In all my years in clinical practice treating couples, I'd seen honesty wielded much more often as a *hacha* than as a caress. There was a time in the eighties when the relationship mantra from the women's magazine gurus was *"All honesty, all the time."* What a disastrous few years of misguided advice that was. Since then, whenever I heard a romantic partner whine for unabashed honesty in my office, I tested the waters for one of two things. First I listened for the call of insecurity begging for reassurance. Alternately, I listened for the diseased call of someone begging to be hurt or begging for the license to inflict pain.

With her earnest "be honest" I decided that

Lauren was seeking the former and not the latter, and I prayed that I was right.

I wished I could touch her or kiss her nose. I couldn't. So I said, "I'm not even close to my limit." I didn't say *"I'm full of doubt,"* or *"I wish I were as good and generous a person as I'd like to be."* I didn't say *"I don't know my limit, but I think it's within range of my vision."* I didn't.

No, I reassured her. Why? Because the reassurance was at least as true as my doubts and a whole lot truer than my fears.

She made a noise in response. Disappointment? Dismissal? Relief? I wished I knew.

The cream of reassurance that I was whipping was already in stiff peaks. I added more sugar until it tasted just right. "I'm not going anywhere, sweetie. I love you."

It was all true. A little less than totally honest, but all true. Imperfect honesty in an imperfect world. Nobody, least of all Lauren, would have to spend the day removing any *hachas* from their *cabezas*.

But the telephone was a terrible instrument for gauging the effectiveness of comfort, and I feared that my words were barely palliative.

I was packing up to go home when my pager vibrated on my hip. No message, but I recognized the number. I threw my briefcase and jacket back down on top of the desk and dialed deliberately, giving myself time to pull my thoughts together.

I wondered whether the state of Georgia was in the Central or Eastern Time zone. I guessed Eastern. It took me most of a minute to find a place where I could balance my current annoyance with my compassion and my friendship.

Sam answered. "Hey, Alan."

I said, "Hi, Sam. What's up?"

"I'm in Georgia."

"Yeah." I wanted to say I knew that already, but confidentiality rules. "What time is it there?"

"A little after eight. How pissed off are you?"

"Lauren's sick. I don't have enough energy to waste any of it being pissed off at you."

"What's going on with Lauren?"

I explained Lauren's predicament as though I were talking to a friend, and Sam said all the right things in return. I felt better. Then I asked, "What about you. You feeling okay?"

"This—this road trip—has been kind of good for me, I think. Takes my mind off things. No chest pains so far. I'm watching my diet. Taking all my damn pills."

"Exercise?"

"I walk when I can."

"It's important, Sam."

"Yeah."

The "yeah" was his way of indicating to me that it was time to move on.

"Nothing from Sherry?"

"Nothing. Simon's okay, though; I talked to Angus."

He paused long enough for me to respond. When I didn't, he said, "She loves me. I love her."

"You still worried that it's not enough?"

"Things are complicated, you know? Life,

marriage, relationships—it's all complicated. Listen, I thought you might want to know that I think he might be alive. Sterling."

"What? Really?"

"The whole accident/rescue thing is too goofy for words. Nothing came down in a way that gives me any confidence in a scenario of him rushing to help someone and accidentally ending up drowning in a raging river."

"Like?"

"I'll tell you later when I have more time. A for-instance, though—on one side of the car he was trying to reach was all this brush and trees and crap—you know, stuff to hold on to—on the other side was a muddy riverbank, real steep. Which one do you think he chose?"

"The mud."

"Yeah. Like I said, goofy. I think if your IQ is anywhere near your golf score, you choose the side with the bushes on it. I keep trying to come up with excuses for him, but I'm failing."

"You think he planned it so he went into the river, or maybe just found himself swimming and took advantage of serendipity?"

"Good question, Alan. I'm impressed. Turns out that he hesitated at the top long enough to think it all through. Actually drove past the accident scene once and then came back. So yeah, I'm thinking premeditation. I got Lucy checking to see what kind of swimmer he was."

"I bet she finds out he was pretty good." I was thinking that anybody who crewed on a big expensive yacht and gave diving demos had to be more than a little comfortable in the water.

"What do you mean?" Sam asked.

I realized how close I'd come to an unwitting disclosure. "Nothing. I just think Lucy might find something."

"You could save her some work."

"Maybe, but I won't."

He let it go. "In case you're wondering, I'm planning on keeping my suspicions to myself until I have a little more evidence."

He was telling me he wasn't going to tell Gibbs he thought Sterling was alive. "Does that mean you're coming back home now?"

"No, I'm not done looking."

I allowed the buzz on the line to dominate for a few seconds before I asked, "Why, Sam? Why are you doing this?"

"This'll sound goofy, but I figure Sterling can teach me something about marriage. Sterling and Gibbs both, actually."

"What?" My "what?" was undiluted incredulity.

"Yeah."

He was serious. I could tell. "That's the craziest thing I think I've ever heard. And considering what I do for a living, that's wild indeed."

"Maybe it is crazy," he said. "But it feels okay to me."

"Sam, what if you're right about Sterling? What if he's not dead? What if he comes after her?"

"Gibbs?"

"Yeah."

"I didn't think about that." He was silent for a moment. "No, I don't think he will."

"I do."

"Why?"

"He has reasons," I said.

"Things I don't know?" Sam asked.

"I don't know what you know."

"You know exactly what I don't know. Just tell me, there are reasons?"

"Yes, for sure there are reasons," I said. I counted the dead women on the fingers of my right hand. *At least four reasons*, I said to myself.

"Then I'll call her and tell her that I'm not convinced he's dead. And she should be careful. Can you get her someplace safe to stay?"

"Let's say that offer is on the table."

Again he grew quiet for a few seconds before he said, "I hate situations like this. I hate 'em. The exact same woman who wouldn't let her kid walk out the front door to ride a bike without a damn bicycle helmet won't take the simplest step—the simplest step—to keep her own head from getting bashed in by some guy she's sure loves her. I hate those situations."

"Yeah. Thanks." I didn't know what else to say. Silently and involuntarily my brain was busy translating "to keep her own head from getting bashed in" to a pidgin Spanish version containing *cabezas* and *hachas*. Silently but totally voluntarily, I cursed Diane.

"By the way," Sam added, "I forgot to tell you: The tip the police got on that judge's husband? About the cocaine? It came from inside the DA's office. That's all I could find out. Hope it helps."

Helps? No, not exactly. All that meant to me was that Jim Zebid, if he learned the same facts that Sam had just disclosed to me—which he most likely would—would have more reason than he already did to believe that it was indeed I who had leaked the information about Jara Heller's husband's cocaine problems to Lauren, who had in turn acted on it through some colleague in the DA's office.

Great.

My second attempt to get out of the office ended almost the exact same way the first had ended: My vibrating pager interfered just before I made it to the door. Once again I dumped my things on the desk. Once again I recognized the phone number on the pager screen.

Gibbs was breathless. She answered before I was certain her phone had even rung. "She just left. Just now! Two minutes ago! How could you? How *could* you? I trusted you!"

"Gibbs," I pleaded. "Slow down, slow down. I don't know what you're talking about."

"She just left. I can't believe you told her!"

"Who is 'she,' Gibbs?"

"Reynoso. That—that—"

"What is it you think I told her? I haven't spoken with her since Saturday. I didn't even know she was still in town." My defensiveness was too reflexive; I was getting frustrated about the repeated accusations from my patients about my indiscretions with their secrets. And it was showing.

Half a beat passed. Hesitation? A pause to reload? I wasn't sure. But Gibbs's fury was turned down a notch when she resumed. "You're saying you didn't tell her about the other women? You didn't tell her what I told you this morning?"

It was apparent from her voice that she wasn't particularly predisposed to believing that I hadn't spilled the beans.

I, too, hesitated. The "other women" could have been the ones that Gibbs told me Sterling had slept with during their marriage, or they could have been the ones she told me he had killed. But a quick review convinced me that I hadn't told Carmen Reynoso about either group of other women. I replayed the events in my head thoroughly enough to convince myself that I hadn't even known about either group before that morning's session with Gibbs.

Then I remembered that wasn't exactly true. I had known about Gibbs's concern about other murder victims for most of a week; I just hadn't known details until that morning. But the reality was that I hadn't revealed the facts of Gibbs's concern to anyone. I was certain of it.

I said, "No, not a word."

"You didn't talk with her today?"

"No, Gibbs. I've been here at the office since this morning's appointment with you. I haven't shared the information you told me this morning with anyone. I wish you would give me permission, but until you do, I won't share that information with anyone."

"Well, I've never told anyone but you about these other women. How does she know?"

Damn good question.

Damn good.

Gibbs said good-bye after she asked me to change her regular appointment time on Tuesday. I offered her a slot that had just opened up on Wednesday.

*

I left my things on the desk and wandered around my office.

It wasn't a small room, nor was it palatial. Fifteen by twenty-two feet, maybe. Space enough for a chunky desk, a file cabinet, a seating area, and a couple of bookcases. Three windows and a solitary French door brought in abundant light. Double doors—not side by side, but back to back—one opening in, one opening out, provided security and soundproofing to the interior hallway that Diane and I shared. We'd spent a bundle during remodeling constructing the interior walls of offset studs and had even set the extra-sound-retardant Sheetrock in channels, all in an effort to reduce noise transmission from the office to the hallway and from office to office. The entire back hallway was separated from the waiting area by a door with a deadbolt lock. After an intrusion years before, Diane's husband had installed a sophisticated alarm system in the building, too.

I assured myself that there was no way someone could eavesdrop on a psychotherapy session in my office.

What about someone in Diane's office? Could they have eavesdropped? No, that wasn't possible. During the course of an average day the only sound I heard through our acoustically deadened adjoining wall was an occasional burst of Diane's sharp laughter. I couldn't recall a single instance of overhearing one of her patient's words. The tones of normal conversation just didn't make it through the walls.

I plopped down on the sofa and reviewed my day.

No matter from what angle I examined it, I couldn't remember a solitary indiscretion on my part regarding Gibbs's admissions to me about the other women. I hadn't written any of the data in my case notes. And I hadn't spoken a word about it to anyone.

Not even Sam? No, not even Sam.

Which meant one thing: The cops were developing the same information on their own.

What other conclusion was possible?

The answer to that question would come, unfortunately, soon enough.

FORTY-ONE

SAM

Before I left their home, the Wolf sisters invited me to come back in a few days for Thanksgiving supper. They explained that they usually deep-fried a turkey for the large group of family and friends that gathered in their home, but this year they were planning to slow-roast something they called a turducken for the first time, and thought that I would be a perfect addition to their holiday table.

"You deep-fry your turkey?" I said. When I'd first heard about people preparing their birds that way, I thought it was an urban myth, like jackalopes. Then the Boulder Fire Department started answering calls for turkey-fryer fires, and I accepted that it was a real thing, though I still couldn't figure out what people did with all the leftover oil.

Mary Ellen said, "It's the best way to do it, absolutely. Moist? Oh, Mr. Purdy. But we're going to try something new and finally do a turducken this year. Mr. Prudhomme, Mr. Paul Prudhomme from New

Orleans"—when she spoke the name of the Louisiana city, it was only one word, and it was absent the *w,* and when she spoke Mr. Prudhomme's name, it was with a reverence customarily reserved for heroes or saints—"recommends a very slow oven, so we'll actually have to start roasting that delight before we go to bed on Wednesday evening. The house should smell like the Lord's own grandmother's kitchen when we awaken Thursday morning."

Mary Pat was the one who recognized the ignorance in my eyes. "A turducken is a Cajun treat, Mr. Purdy. Oyster dressing and andouille sausage and a few other goodies are stuffed into a chicken that is then stuffed into a duck that is then stuffed into a turkey. More dressing is added between each bird during the assembly. It's all boneless. It's all delicious."

I tried to imagine the cascade of flavors that Mary Pat was describing, and I was momentarily lost in the fantasy. My hand crept up the contours of my tummy until my thumb found the lower edge of my sternum. Sculpted in place, my hand could have been a monument to my ambivalence: Part of my hand—the part caressing my gut—honored my usually indulgent appetite, part of it—the thumb on my sternum—honored my cardiologist's admonitions.

"And you roast this . . . thing for how long?" I asked. "It must weigh most of a ton."

"We are doing a large one. Fourteen hours should bring it close to perfection. Then it will need to rest a while to stitch the flavors together before we carry it to the table."

With a smile as warm as apple pie, Mary Pat said, "And you haven't had a real Thanksgiving supper until you've tasted my sister's gravy, or her cornbread."

Mary Ellen savored the compliment. "Red pepper," she explained. "Our mother's secret. Abundant red pepper."

"Can I let you know?" I asked them. "My plans for Thursday are still a little up in the air."

"No need to call. You just come by if you can. We'll have a place all set at the adult table for you, and you can be certain that the good Lord willing there will be no shortage of food beneath this roof on the day we give thanks. Mary Ellen will start carving right around two."

Less than a mile from the twins' home I stopped on the shoulder of a fallow field of what I was still guessing had been cotton and called Alan Gregory to catch him up on what I was up to in Georgia, and then I called Gibbs Storey to tell her that I thought it was premature to assume her husband was dead.

"He's alive?" she replied, of course. What else would she say?

I'd told her I thought that was a premature conclusion, too. But I suggested prudence might be warranted, and counseled her to temporarily move someplace where her husband couldn't easily find her.

"Sterling won't hurt me," she said.

"If I had a dollar for every time a woman's told me that in the past twenty years, I'd be driving a Lincoln."

She sighed at me and told me she'd think about it.

"Trust me, Gibbs. You're not thinking straight. After what you've been through . . ."

"I'm fine."

It's what I expected. I'd done what I could do. I folded up my phone and started driving again.

An hour later I was on the outskirts of Albany, Georgia, trying to decide between two adjacent motels for a place to spend the night when Lucy paged me using our personal code that indicated an emergency. At full arm's length I could barely read the code: 911 followed by the phone number. Imaginative, no. But it worked for us.

I picked the motel that wasn't a national chain and finished checking in before I used my cell to return Lucy's call. The motel room was full of my grandmother's oldest chenille, the air was musty, and the background smells in the shadowy room were born of burnt tobacco and constant humidity and were as unfamiliar to me as the accents of all the people I was meeting in Georgia.

Lucy had left me her own cell number, not her office number. I figured that was important.

"Hey," I said. "It's me."

"Hi, Sammy. I really miss you. You okay?"

"Later, what's up?" She didn't 911 me to ask me how I was doing.

"Listen, you're not going to believe this, but Crime Stoppers—yeah, I'm serious: Crime Stoppers—got a tip, anonymous, of course, that Sterling Storey may be responsible for as many as four murders. All women, all in towns where he's worked over the years. He travels around producing sporting events on cable."

"I know about his job. Does the story check out?"

"At least one piece of it seems to. There's a woman in Indianapolis who went missing in the same circumstances that the tipster reported. She's the same general description as Louise Lake—single, attractive, late twenties—and she worked where the guy said she worked. Donald and I have just started putting it together. There are other teams tracking down all the other women, but I haven't heard anything about their progress."

"You have a name?"

"Julie Franconia. She worked in PR or marketing or something for the Indiana Dome or—"

"It's the RCA Dome now, I think. The Colts play there. Peyton Manning. Good kid."

"Whatever. She disappeared in 2000. Late March, I think. Just a sec . . . yeah, March twenty-third, 2000."

"Remains?"

"We just got on this."

"Circumstances?"

"She told her co-workers she was going to meet some girlfriends for a drink after work. Disappeared."

"No body?"

"That's what we're trying to confirm. It was dumped on us as a typical without-a-trace, but a local cop told me he doesn't know what all the fuss is about, that they have it as a cleared homicide. We're waiting to hear back from the homicide guy. You know what it's like with the holidays coming."

"Is the press on this?"

"Nobody's called me personally, but I think yes, probably."

"Four? You said four?"

"Four total, including the California murder."

"Where are the other two?"

"Augusta, Georgia, and West Point, New York."

"That would be, what, the Masters and . . . I don't know, the Army–Navy game?"

"I guess," Lucy said. Other than occasional Broncos football, she didn't pay much attention to sports she didn't participate in, and she didn't apologize for it.

I asked, "Any progress on the river search down here? Did Storey's body show up today? Tell me yes. If you tell me yes, maybe I'll come home."

"I wish I could tell you yes, Sam. They're still looking, but nobody seems hopeful about finding the body. The search is winding down. Oh, and in case it matters, you were right about Storey. He is, or was, a swimmer—a star on his college water polo team."

"Water polo? Didn't play that a lot when I was growing up in Minnesota."

Lucy knew me well enough not to respond to my sarcasm. She asked, "You're not in touch with the local authorities down there?"

"I made a courtesy call when I first got here. They're looking for a body. I'm looking for something else."

"You think he's alive?"

"I'm not ready to think out loud. I assume someone interviewed Sterling's friend Brian Miles."

"Georgia State Police talked to him. Miles said Sterling called from Tallahassee and said he was coming to visit but never showed up. The story checks out." Through the phone I heard an overhead page in the background.

"Where are you right now, Luce?"

"Whole Foods, getting something for dinner. Why?"

"You going back to the department?"

"I'll be eating at my desk. For now, this case is all computer and phone work."

"I'll keep my pager on. Enjoy your dinner."

"You okay, Sam?"

"I'm meeting some nice people down here. Luce? Send some patrols past Gibbs Storey's house. Can you do that?"

"Sure. You do think he's alive?"

"I forgot, one more thing. Is Reynoso still in Boulder, or did she go back to California?"

"Her? None of the above. I heard she was leaving for Georgia to look for Sterling. You haven't run across her yet?"

"I think I'd recall that."

She laughed. "I imagine she'll be trying to find you."

"We'll see how good a detective she is. Thanks, Luce. Talk to you."

I leaned back against the headboard of the motel bed. My mass caused it to crack hard against the wall, and I imagined what a percussive racket an energetic couple could make on this bed. The thought froze me for a moment, as I wondered when the last time was that Sherry and I had rocked a bed. I mean really rocked it.

I couldn't recall.

Lucy had said that there were suspected victims of Sterling Storey in Augusta and Indianapolis.

Augusta was closer, but I'd be flying blind if I went there. Indianapolis was farther, but at least Lucy would have facts to feed me. What did I hope to find?

I didn't know. Maybe when I tripped over it, I'd know.

The guy at the desk didn't use a wheelchair as much as he wore one. It was hard to imagine him without the aged, rusting contraption that was pressing hard against his fleshy hips as he rolled back and forth behind the motel's counter. A tiny color TV—maybe three inches across—hung upside down on a braided nylon rope around his neck. He was watching a game show, occasionally tipping the little television toward the ceiling and staring down in the general direction of his navel.

Wheel of Fortune? I wasn't sure.

I tipped him ten bucks when he let me check out without paying for the few minutes I'd actually used the room.

"The way I see it, you're not checking out. What you're doing is unchecking in" was how he put it. "Where you off to in such a hurry?"

"Indianapolis, I think. Got a call, so I gotta go."

"Never been there."

"Me, neither," I said. I turned to leave but had a thought, so I stopped and asked him, "You ever had a turducken?"

"Sure, sure." He smiled so fast, his cheeks shook and his triple chin momentarily became one. "I have, I sure have. Three years ago. Thanksgiving supper. My aunt Totsy's—she's my daddy's little sister—her place on the Delta. It's a meal not to be missed, not to be missed."

"This trip I have to take up north means I'm going

to lose what may be my one and only chance to savor a turducken. And I'm beginning to think that's a minor tragedy. Well, I do hope you have a good Thanksgiving, sir," I said.

"I'll be right here," he said, as a way of letting me know he didn't expect to enjoy his holiday much or get anywhere close either to a turducken or to a family gathering at his aunt Totsy's on the Mississippi Delta. When he said "here," he didn't point at the office he was in or at his wheelchair.

What he did was, he touched his TV-on-a-rope.

A minute or two communing with Rand McNally left me with the impression that I could get to Indianapolis in ten to twelve hours of hard road time. I planned to drive for six, sleep for six, drive for six more, and then find someplace for lunch close to the RCA Dome.

By then Lucy should know something new.

And I might have a clue what I was doing.

FORTY-TWO

ALAN

Tuesday morning found Lauren solidly in hyper-energized zombie mode—think the Energizer Bunny meets *Night of the Living Dead*.

Her affected leg was no worse, maybe a little better. Less weakness. That was the good news.

But there wasn't enough good news. Worry about Lauren and the future—hers, Grace's, ours—stabbed at me incessantly, but she and I didn't talk about it during the duration of the extended steroid fog. Neither of us once mentioned the bull elephant that had pitched a tent in our living room.

We'd made it through the night—me with little sleep, her with less than that—and thanks to Viv's early-morning assistance with Grace, I managed to get to the office in time for my first appointment.

Tuesday's workday was remarkable only for its normalcy. I spent an entire day at work feeling almost effective. Going home that evening, I faced the more daunting task of trying to be an effective husband and father in a home that was quaking from the aftershocks of illness and treatment.

Together—Grace and Lauren and I, with a full assist from Viv and the puppies—we made it. Wednesday morning came. The respite of a four-day holiday weekend was only one workday away.

How hard could that be?

The local media had begun feasting on the Storeys' troubles. The morning TV news shows and the Boulder and Denver papers had pieced together most of the details of Gibbs's and Sterling's ties to Louise Lake. Now they were busy fleshing out the more lurid parts of the tale, including the details of the fruitless search of the Ochlockonee River and the revelation that authorities suspected that Sterling Storey might be involved in the deaths of three other women.

I anticipated that Gibbs would be overwhelmed by the public revelations. Reactive hibernation wasn't out of the question, and I wasn't a hundred percent sure she would show up for her early-morning appointment.

But she did.

"Not Safe House. I don't want to go there, I just don't think I'd fit in."

That was actually Gibbs's opening gambit, her first words after a perfunctory "good morning."

Had I expected it? No, not really. Was I surprised? No, not at all. The insidious nature of battering caused the pendulum of hope to swing from reality to denial and back again. This was Gibbs's denial talking. The way she introduced it told me that she had been busy having a conversation with me in her head and had just then decided to allow me to mouth my own lines. I was more than content to let her go on without me for a while, if she would.

"They followed me here. I'm sure they did. They were waiting outside this morning when I opened the garage."

"They?"

"Those newspeople."

I nodded. I could have encouraged her to go off on a rant about those newspeople, but I chose to look down the other path she'd offered. "You don't think you would fit in at Safe House, Gibbs?"

"I'm not a battered woman."

Arguing the point was a tempting option, but I made a quick judgment that it was neither the right issue nor the right time. Gibbs, I suspected, was protesting a different kind of "fitting in." And the truth was that her rationalization wasn't the real issue; her denial was.

Gently, I tried to draw her back. "But you are in need of a safe place to stay—you accept that?"

"I'm trying to be . . . cautious. Detective Purdy suggested it. Just in case there's a chance that"—she took a moment to decide how she wanted to complete her thought—"that I might be in some danger. He said he talked to you, too. Right?"

I nodded. I reminded myself that it had been I who had invited Sam into this conundrum; I shouldn't be too surprised that he was complicating it. At least his advice to Gibbs was sound.

"And now, with all the cameras, I can't stay at home anyway. I can't. I'm not even going to go back. I have some things in the car, and I have to find someplace else to stay."

"What are you considering?"

"I was hoping you would have an alternative . . . for me." She lifted her eyebrows. "Someplace besides Safe House."

Were there other options? Of course. Many women in vulnerable circumstances turned to friends or family for shelter. I usually didn't think that it was a good idea. "I think Safe House is where you belong. They know what they're doing. It's not just the shelter that they offer. It's the support, the counseling, and their experience. Everything. They work well with the police. They're the pros. When the stakes are this high, I think you go with the best."

Watching her face as I made my speech, I realized that it was as though I hadn't been speaking at all. She waited until the aggravating noise of my voice subsided before she said, "I'm actually thinking about going to a hotel. I'd be more comfortable there, I think. You know, more privacy?"

Not to mention a private bath, maid service, nice linens, room service, and maybe a chocolate on her pillow.

I stated the obvious: "Isn't that the first place Sterling would look for you?"

"He's dead, Dr. Gregory. Dead."

I softened my tone a little. "Is that what you believe, Gibbs?"

"No, not really," she said without any contemplation. "But it would be so much easier, wouldn't it? For everybody?"

I didn't respond. It wasn't a tactical silence. I just didn't know what to say. She leaned over and touched the handle on her purse. For a moment I thought she was going to grab it, stand up, and go. She didn't.

She settled back, crossed her legs, and said, "He went back to kill them, you know."

No, I didn't know. "I don't think I understand."

"Sterling met them one year. Had his little flings with them. And he went back to see them again the next time."

"The next time?"

"The next time he was covering the event, whatever it was. The golf tournament, or game, or race, or whatever it was. A lot of this stuff he produces is annual, you know? He goes back to some of the same places, and he does basically the same thing every year."

"And . . . he continued his affairs? He saw the same women each year in each city?"

To me, it sounded exhausting.

"If he . . . liked them. If their first encounter was . . . you know. Then, yes, he saw the same women again."

I tried to gauge her discomfort at our discussion of Sterling's serial infidelity. I thought it was high. Or maybe I just thought it should be high.

"And then he killed them?" I asked. I knew the beginning of the story, and a lot of the middle, and the very end, but it felt as though somebody had ripped out a chunk of pages just before the conclusion.

"Not usually. Just sometimes."

Great, I thought, allowing myself the luxury of some irony. *Maybe he can be rehabilitated.*

"Go on, please, Gibbs. Was there a method to his . . . a way to understand the motivation he used to . . . I mean, how did he, um—"

"Decide? Some of them wanted more from him. That wasn't the arrangement. That's why I think he . . ."

Killed them.

"They were the ones who wouldn't let go, who insisted. That's what put them at risk."

The arrangement?

Was Gibbs implying that the women were responsible for their own murders by violating some agreement they had with Sterling? Reaching such a conclusion would not have been that atypical for a battered woman.

Damn, I said to myself. Gibbs had once again distracted me. I'd been confronting her about her decision to stay in a hotel, not Safe House, and she'd managed to change the subject to murder. A compelling change, I had to admit: This misdirection was not the work of an amateur.

I prepared to point out the process when her face displayed sudden alarm. "You're not going to tell anyone what I just told you, right? Not the police? If anybody learns this, Dr. Gregory, they will have learned it from you. No one else knows about it. I couldn't bear it if any of this got out. I couldn't."

I'd been expecting Gibbs to revisit her distrust of the reliability of my silence from the moment she'd walked in the door, but the timing surprised me, and an undertow of accusation sucked at me. I said, "I haven't broken your trust, Gibbs. And I won't."

"Good." She smiled at me. "No matter where we go—you and I—we end up talking about sex, don't we?"

Were we just talking about sex? Or had I just been witness to yet another one of the greatest illusions since Penn and Teller?

"Sex. It's not just for procreation anymore."

*

In the ensuing minutes, in case I required it, I received a refresher course in the resilience of denial and the elasticity of resistance. Gibbs and I covered no new ground. The topic of Sterling's affairs? It was of no apparent interest to her. "Old news," she declared. "I prefer to look forward."

Sterling's being alive, or dead? "I think Detective Purdy is right. He's alive. I would know if he were dead. I would. That changes things. It does. I have decisions to make. Different ones."

The danger she was in? "He wouldn't hurt me. He did it once and he apologized. He won't do it again. I just need to get away from all the media."

I prodded her resistance directly. I went after the soft flanks of her denial. Nothing seemed to work.

Sometimes that was the nature of psychotherapy.

After Gibbs left her session—her exit was marked by a promise to call me once she was settled into a hotel—I ran into Diane in the hallway as we were both on the way to the bathroom. She was wearing jeans and a sweater: not office garb.

"I just came in to get my appointment book," she explained. "I have jury duty. Have to be at the courthouse in ten minutes. God, I hope I get sequestered. It would be so great to get sequestered."

"No lawyer in this town is going to let you sit on a jury."

"Why not?"

With the frequency with which Diane testified on custody and child abuse issues, she knew the county's judges and clerks, and the law, better than half the members of the bar. Every attorney wanted to believe that at the conclusion of a trial what ruled in the jury room were the echoes of the lawyer's own words of wisdom. But any lawyer who had ever crossed paths with Diane Estevez knew that she wouldn't think of allowing that to occur. Were she seated on a jury, what would rule in the jury room was what Diane wanted to rule in the jury room—which meant that the odds of Diane being chosen as a juror in Boulder County were about the same as Al Gore spending Christmas on a ranch in Crawford, Texas.

She tilted her head back toward my office, sniffed the air, and said, "Do I smell the Dancing Queen?"

I flared my nostrils and tested the air but didn't detect anything. Was I immune to my client's perfume? As a way of changing the subject, I asked, "You can't hear anything in your office, can you? When I'm in my office doing therapy, you don't overhear my sessions?"

"With your voice? You speak so quietly, I'm surprised sometimes that your own patients can hear you. Why, did I miss something good?"

"Nothing? You can't hear a thing?"

"No. Why? Can you hear me?"

"I hear you laugh."

She laughed. "Why are you asking?"

"I've had a few accusations from patients in the last few days that I'm divulging information that I heard during therapy. They're . . . concerning; they're accusations about serious things."

"Accusations? Not just worries?"

"Accusations."

"Oh, the Dancing Queen? Are you the anonymous

tipster? You're the one who called Crime Stoppers on Platinum?"

"Diane."

She had really perked up. "Well, are you?"

"No. Of course not."

"Nothing inadvertent?"

"No."

She squeezed past me and slipped into the bathroom. As she shut the door, she said, "Maybe your office is bugged."

I said, "Ha. Very funny."

But I'd barely shifted my weight from one foot to the other before I thought: *Sam.*

Rhymes with *damn.*

FORTY-THREE

It was surprisingly easy to find someone to sweep my office for bugs. I called a couple of lawyers I knew through Lauren, who put me in touch with the private investigators they used, and the two investigators both pointed me toward the same company: West Security.

The electronic security specialist I talked to at West was a woman named Tayisha Rosenthal. She explained that I had my choice between a cursory sweep of my office for about half of my practice's daily earnings, and a thorough sweep, which would cost me twice what my practice typically generated in a day. If I chose the thorough examination, she would give me a 99.99 percent assurance that my office was not being monitored by listening devices.

I said I would take the deluxe package.

She asked when.

"As soon as possible."

"Can you do noon?" she said. "I can squeeze you in at noon."

I looked at my calendar. It would mean canceling a

patient, maybe two. I said yes and I gave her the address.

I'd made a bad error in judgment when I'd asked Gibbs for freedom to consult with Sam about her suspicions about Sterling. That was certain. And it was clear that Sam had gone too far when he'd approached Gibbs himself and decided to take off on some ill-thought-out quest in Georgia.

But bugging my office?

He'd gone too far.

Way too far.

I picked up my address book and began looking for the phone numbers of the two patients whose appointments would have to be rescheduled.

Like neighbors everywhere, Diane and I kept keys to each other's office. Highly doubtful that what might be said in my own office would ultimately remain confidential, I took advantage of Diane's tour in jury duty limbo and saw the rest of my morning's appointments in her hopefully uncorrupted space. When my patients asked me about the change, I explained that my office was being fumigated. It was as close to the truth as I was willing to get.

Right at twelve o'clock I paced out to my waiting room where I spied an unfamiliar woman reading a copy of *Sports Illustrated*. She was a young African American with close-cropped hair and soft features. When she looked up, I saw that her dark eyes were brilliant, like fire and onyx.

"Tayisha Rosenthal?" I said. "Alan Gregory."

I invited her back to my office. She grabbed a fat

metal aluminum briefcase, and I allowed her to precede me down the hall. "It's not this whole place, right?"

"No, not unless you find something in my office. Then I suppose you'll have to search the whole building."

She tapped her watch. "Won't be today."

"I understand."

She stood in my office for a moment reconnoitering the place, then took long strides across the room to my desk, opened her case like a giant clamshell, and started fishing out equipment.

I waved her back into the hallway and pulled the door closed. "Let's talk out here. Just in case."

"You sticking around? You want to watch me work?" she asked.

"Why? Is that extra?" It was a lame attempt on my part to find humor in the experience.

She laughed. "Nah. I'll give you a running commentary of what I'm doing if you want."

"That would be great."

"Good. But the commentary is extra. Make it fifty, cash." She held out her hand. "Up front."

"Excuse me?"

She laughed again. "Kidding. You're a shrink, right? I thought you people were supposed to treat paranoids, not become one yourself. And here you are thinking that people are listening to your every word, just like some nutcase. Aren't you supposed to be the healthy one?"

"Yeah, that's the way it's supposed to be."

"There's some irony there, don't you think?"

"Yes," I admitted, "there is." I was eager to

change the subject. "How does someone end up doing this—what you do—for a living? Sweeping buildings for bugs?"

"Army intelligence. I did this same kind of thing for Uncle Sam's Army of One for four years."

She looked too young to have completed four years in the army. Apparently, she could tell that's what I was thinking.

"I'm twenty-four," she said. "Old enough. Do the math."

She stepped back inside the office and went to work.

The equipment she'd pulled out of foam rubber compartments in her metal case seemed to have been cobbled together from the detritus of a few visits to Radio Shack. Microphones, earphones, and a little machine that looked like what I thought a modern Geiger counter would look like. Gauges with long, jumpy needles. Digital scoreboards. A few knobs and switches that required some fiddling.

After about ten minutes of poking around and setting and resetting her electronics, opening drawers, and moving my furniture around, she said, "Hot-cha!"

By then I'd settled into a place on the floor by the office door, leaning against the wall reading the same *Sports Illustrated* Tayisha had been perusing in the waiting room. Tiger Woods was apparently still winning golf tournaments.

Tayisha's exclamation startled me. I looked up at the mess she'd made of my office and said, "What?"

She pointed toward the hallway, but she didn't look my way; she was totally focused on one of her little digital gadgets.

We stepped out of the office.

"Yo, Doctor? You paying attention? Good. On these private gigs, like this—by private, I mean I'm not out doing one of my routine sweeps for corporate security purposes, just a one-time for somebody who thinks somebody's listening in on him—on these private gigs I meet some of the craziest human beings ever. Nutsos. People with tin-foil all over their apartments. Husbands sure their wives are listening to them over the radio in their cars. Those guys always have mistresses, by the way. They're always getting something on the side. It's the guilt that makes them whacked; that's what I think. But crazy? You bet. I do a couple, three of those a month. Most of the time I feel like I should keep a syringe of Thorazine in my briefcase, you know, just in case?" She smiled. "And—and—you want to know what? I've never found a device on one of those jobs. Not one."

"Good, I'm glad to hear that." Maybe Tayisha's track record of ubiquitous failure boded well for me. Right at that moment I would rather have been judged crazy than discover that I'd been right about the bug.

"Until today," she said.

"What?"

She pointed at the equipment she held in her left hand. "This says that there's a device in there sending out a signal. Mmm-hmmm. Something's generating a fairly healthy signal that's going out of that room. It appears to be voice activated."

"What?"

"Don't worry, now that I've detected it, I'll locate it in a minute or two. You be real quiet while I finish up, okay? I'm concentrating."

Although in my fantasies I was already raising Sam by his thumbs, via pulleys, to some very high ceiling, the truth was that I had thought that I was being overly paranoid, too. I really hadn't expected that Tayisha Rosenthal would discover any devices in my office.

Locating the bug took another five minutes. Ninety-nine-plus percent of the device was inside one of the throw pillows on the sofa where my patients often sat. The electronics were buried deep in the batting.

"That's the transmitter. I just turned it off." Zipping open the pillow, she pointed at a tiny box about the size of a pack of gum. "And this here"—she pulled the batting apart and revealed a braided wire—"is the antenna. Like little strands of hair.

"And this little baby—can you see that, right there?" She used the tip of a pencil as a pointer. "See how tiny that is? That's the microphone. Good stuff. Quality equipment."

The lead of the pencil was pointing directly at a small gray dot about the size of a lentil that extended out at the edge of the pillow, near the zipper. If you weren't looking for it, you would never notice it.

"Really, that's the microphone? What's the range? How far can . . . a device like this transmit?"

"We could test it if you want, but I'd say not too far. I would guess that whoever's listening has a car parked nearby with a good receiving antenna and a digital recorder for the output."

The "output" was my therapy sessions. I waved at the pillow. "Who has stuff like this?"

"Lots of people. You can buy listening devices over the Internet these days. Easy. Equipment this good is pricey, though. Somebody invested some serious money going after whatever it is you have to say in here. The battery in the transmitter alone costs some serious bucks."

"What do I do now?" I asked.

"How about what do I do now? What I do is I document this—what I found and where—and I take some good pictures of the equipment in place. You'll get a fair-size stack of glossies for your photo album. Here's your part: Then you authorize me to remove the device. After I do, I screen one more time to be absolutely positively certain that there isn't a second device. Don't worry, there isn't. I'm ninety-eight percent sure already. Then you call the police to report the intrusion. There've been some laws broken in this room. Mmmm-hmm."

"Yes," I agreed.

"Then you sit down and have a long, hard conversation with yourself about who might do this to you."

"And why," I added.

"Yeah. That, too." She glanced at her watch. "I'll be out of here in ten minutes max. But hey, we're going to have to find a time to do a sweep of the rest of the building now, too."

She watched me swallow. The act was involuntary.

Tayisha was reassuring. "I'll give you a good rate, don't worry. This has been fun."

I wasn't having such a good time.

After punching in Sam's pager number, I listened for the beep before I dialed 911 and my cell phone number. Then I sat on Diane's desk and waited for my phone to vibrate. I used the dead time to try to compute the number of secrets from the number of patients that might have been intercepted by the jumble of sophisticated electronics that was stuffed in my sofa pillow. I quickly realized that I was missing an essential variable: I didn't know how long the bug had been in place.

The earliest accusation I'd received from one of my patients was the one from my attorney client, Jim Zebid, the previous Sunday accusing me of leaking the story about Judge Heller's husband selling cocaine. He'd told me that story the previous Tuesday, so the bug had been in place for at least eight days. Maybe longer.

I was seeing thirty-six patients a week. Which meant thirty-six unique sets of secrets were at risk of having been revealed.

After cursing silently for half a minute, I took Tayisha Rosenthal's advice and began to have that long, hard conversation with myself about who might do this to me.

And why.

FORTY-FOUR

SAM

Nashville was one of those legendary American cities that I'd always wanted to visit, but when I finally got there at a quarter after one in the morning on a dark, misty night a couple of days before Thanksgiving, all I wanted to see was the lumpy synthetic pillow waiting for me on a Nashville motel room bed. I begged a Mountain Dew–distracted clerk for a five-thirty wake-up call and was in bed three minutes after I slid the plastic card into the lock on the door.

DO NOT DISTURB sign on the door. Strip, pee, meds, bed.

I slept like a dead man.

By the time five-thirty came, my car was chilly, Dixie dew coated the windshield, and preholiday Nashville was still as sleepy as I was. I walked a couple of blocks to a little convenience store to try to scrape together some breakfast. Satisfaction wasn't in the cards. I was learning that one of the places where post–heart attack patients can't conveniently dine is a convenience store. Breakfast choices at the gas station were limited to doughnuts—a pretty good variety, actually—or Danish, or a sad-looking egg-and-sausage thing on a croissant. I settled for a dry bagel, burnt decaf, yogurt, and a carton of orange juice and walked back to the motel with every intention of eating my ascetic meal, climbing into the Jeep, and pointing it vaguely north toward Indianapolis.

It didn't happen.

I woke up later on only because I had to pee. The light outside my room said dusk. I used the bathroom, took off my clothes, killed my cell phone and pager, and fell back into bed. "Tired" didn't come close to describing my fatigue. "Exhausted" wasn't enough of a superlative.

The next change in light that registered in my consciousness was the wink of dawn. After a long shower I felt quasi-alive. In a fashion that reminded me, sadly, of Bill Murray in *Groundhog Day,* I retraced my steps to the convenience store of the morning before, bought the same food, and returned to the motel with the same intentions.

Practice makes perfect. The second time I pulled it off. Before Nashville was awake, and certainly before I'd had a chance to taste any of her charms, I was on my way out of town in the Cherokee.

Later on I stopped for some real food at a roadside café near someplace called Orlinda and lingered there for a while considering whether I was driving to Indianapolis, Indiana, to be a detective or to Rochester, Minnesota, to be a father. I climbed back in my car unaware that I ever quite reached a decision.

After my late breakfast some truckers and I

convoyed together up into Kentucky. I figured that the long-haul drivers were hurrying to get home to their families for Thanksgiving supper, so they were maintaining a speed that was far enough over the speed limit to make me reasonably content.

The countryside south of Louisville was as pretty as a calendar. The whole thing was much better than rehab for me and my injured heart. A day asleep, peaceful landscape, uncrowded roads, strange accents on funny radio stations, and problems that seemed a thousand miles away.

Or at least five hundred.

If you look at a road map of Indiana, Indianapolis looks like the spot where an award-winning sharpshooter left his first and only pop at an imaginary bull's-eye that had been pinned on top of the map. The state's largest city is almost perfectly centered north to south and east to west. As you approach Indiana from any direction, you feel a sublime confidence that you couldn't miss Indianapolis even if you fell sound asleep at the wheel. All roads may not actually lead to Rome, but in this part of the United States it sure seemed like they all led to Indianapolis.

The convoy of truckers and I were making good time as we cleared the northern boundary of Columbus. Out in front of us, Highway 65 was gleaming in the November sun like the Yellow Brick Road that was going to carry us nowhere but to Oz.

A while later my beeper vibrated on my hip, and I fumbled to find my Kmart reading glasses so I could read the little screen. I saw the 911 before the phone number and felt my heart rate jump. I reached down and shushed the volume on Faith Hill's lament, and signaled to pull the Jeep into a rest stop. Two of the truckers blasted a good-bye with their air horns, and I honked my reply. After I exited the highway, I settled into a parking place beside a big recreational vehicle full of gray-haired women. For some reason they made me think about Sherry, which caused a twang in my heart over Simon, and I let my mind wander in that neighborhood while I allowed myself a minute or two to decide whether to return the call.

I punched in the number.

Lucy said, "Is that you?"

"Yeah, what's up?"

"Where are you? Don't you ever answer your phone?"

"Just south of Indianapolis somewhere. A rest stop full of strangers."

"Don't bother going any farther, Sammy. Get back on 70 and keep an eye out for the mountains. Just before you run into them, that's home. The Julie Franconia mystery is solved. We got that one cold, I think. There's nothing for you to do in Indiana."

"Yeah?"

"A body was found in some woods outside Martinsville—that's just south of Indianapolis—three or four days after our Ms. Franconia disappeared. It was hers. The local police had originally cleared the thing by attaching the homicide to a serial killer who was traveling about that time from Chicago to Texas. He was one of those guys who maintained he'd killed scores of people since he was, like, eleven. You know the ones. Cops and reporters from *Dateline* follow him around the country with shovels and backhoes as he points out all the places he left bodies. I have his name somewhere; you want it?"

"Not unless it's relevant."

"It's not. A close comparison of the VICAP reports on the serial killer's known victims—there are six or seven; the guy was a killer for real even if he's a little boastful about the numbers—shows that our girl doesn't belong in his group. MO of her death wasn't really anywhere close to his known MO. Circumstances of her disappearance aren't right, either. Personally I think somebody around Martinsville was looking for a cheap clear. They got it. Anyway, that body was found. They're going to reopen now."

"Cause?"

"Single gunshot to the base of the skull."

"Front or back?"

"Back. They think a nine-millimeter."

"Mutilation?"

"No."

I grumbled at the news. That wasn't the work of any garden-variety serial killer. The feds would be working overtime to tie the case back to Sterling Storey. I had been hoping to do something useful in Indianapolis. As soon as I heard Lucy's news, I knew that wasn't going to happen.

Lucy said, "You can come home, Sammy. Start now, and you'll be here in time for Thanksgiving dinner."

"What about Augusta?"

"No body discovered down there yet. But it turns out that some clothing that might belong to that victim—the locals have soft ID on a shoe from a girlfriend of hers—was found dumped outside town in a place called the Phinizy Swamp around the time of her disappearance. Police still have the clothing, fortunately. They're revisiting the forensics."

"Revisiting" was a Lucy word. "This swamp—a good place to dump a body?"

"That's what I hear. Alligators live there."

"Yuck. What about West Point?"

"Progress there, too. Previously unsolved murder. But the pieces are fitting the Sterling Storey puzzle."

"Nothing actually ties any of this to Storey, does it, Luce?"

"Opportunity, opportunity, opportunity. Records from his network show that he was in the right place the day each woman disappeared. What are the odds of that, Sam? The same guy being in each town when the vics go missing? Those are bad facts, come on."

"Yeah? What else?"

"Means is easy. I bet we can end up proving he knew these women, you know, carnally. And motive? As far as I'm concerned, the motive for serial killers is always just smoke."

"Evidence, though? Back when I was a real cop, convictions tended to take evidence."

"Everybody's only been on this for a little more than a day. It'll develop. You're not going to be of any help to anybody in Indiana, Sammy. The local cops and the feds are all over these cases. You're not going to get anywhere close to the principals. Come on home."

"Georgia cops find Sterling's body?"

"No. In fact, they called off the search yesterday afternoon. A searcher found a hat with his network logo about a mile downstream. For all intents, he's presumed dead."

"That's convenient. Cops all over the country get to close old cases and blame it all on a Good Samaritan who disappears in a river in Georgia. No trials, no appeals. Everybody ends up looking good. This is fairytale stuff. I smell a documentary cooking on this one."

"Don't be snide. It's not good for your heart. One more interesting thing, though. Brian Miles—remember him? Sterling's friend in Albany, Georgia? The one he was on his way to visit? FBI went by to interview him again. Gone. Neighbors are baby-sitting his dogs. He apparently didn't tell anybody where he was going."

"What are you thinking?"

"Coincidence?"

"Yeah, right."

"Sammy, come home."

"I'll consider it."

What I was really thinking was that Rochester, Minnesota—which was where my son and his grandfather were hanging with my sullen wife—was closer to Indianapolis than Boulder was. Sherry wouldn't be thrilled to see me, but Simon would. We could watch the Lions' Thanksgiving game together on TV.

"Heard anything from Reynoso? Is she bagging it and going home to California or what?"

"I haven't heard anything since I heard she was going to Georgia. But I don't think I would, necessarily. I'll ask a few questions and let you know next time we talk."

"Yeah."

"You feeling okay, Sam?"

"Like a million bucks, Lucy."

"That means what—I shouldn't ask? I'm worried about you. You should be home resting, watching football, getting ready for your turkey dinner. You shouldn't be out there alone."

"It's true, I'm fine. Maybe a little tired. But I got another call coming in, so I have to go."

"Call me when you know what you're going to do."

"Yeah."

"I'm serious. Promise me."

"Okay."

"Sam—"

I killed the call. Lucy was sweet, and her heart was in the right place, but nobody knew what I should do next. Not her. Not me. Nobody. Anyway, the truth was, my pager was going off again. Another 911: Alan.

I was really tempted just to get right back on the highway and find my way to Rochester and ignore his call. But if I did, I'd ruin Angus's Thanksgiving for sure. And Simon would have to watch his mom use all her willpower not to kill me for showing up uninvited.

So I didn't. Although I doubted that whatever Alan wanted warranted a 911, there was always the possibility that Lauren had gotten worse, or something bad had happened to somebody, you know? So I called. Within seconds I wished I hadn't.

"Sam?" he said.

"Yeah. What's up?"

"I'm at work, and, uh . . . I'm here with a woman—she's a security specialist—who just swept my office for listening devices . . ."

I thought *That's pretty goofy*. Alan had paused at

that point like he was thinking that I was supposed to take over from there or something. I wasn't feeling terribly cooperative, so I just waited him out.

"... and it turns out she found one."

He paused again once he'd succeeded in getting the entire sentence out of his mouth. It was becoming apparent that he was planning on telling his story in fits and starts. Me? I was standing in a highway rest area next to a bunch of old ladies who had set up a card table outside their motor home to play bridge. At that moment they were finding something hilarious about diamonds and the women's rest room across the way.

Although I was mildly curious about the odd fact that my friend had a bug in his office, I wasn't feeling particularly patient with his storytelling pace. I didn't know what help he wanted from me, but I hoped he got around to asking for it before moms and grandmoms all over America started taking turkeys out of their ovens.

"Sam, did you put that bug in my office?" he asked.

I screamed, "What?"

The old ladies scattered away from the little card table. They were moving so fast, I was afraid one of them was going to fall down and break a hip.

"What the hell are you accusing me of?" I yelled, even louder.

The women reacted to my outburst by scrambling back into their Winnebago clone as though they were thirty years younger.

"I just asked a question," Alan said, smug as shit.

Yeah, right. "You're lucky you're a thousand miles away from my fist."

"I take it that's a no."

"I don't believe you, Alan."

"I guess the feeling's contagious," he said.

I hung up on him.

The old ladies were peering at me through the windows of the motor home. They had fear in their eyes. One of them had tossed her cards in the air before she ran for the safety of the RV. I picked the cards up, dusted them off, scanned them, and placed them back on the card table. She'd had a damn good hand. I smiled up at the women and mouthed, "Four spades."

Then I took my pulse. One-twenty. Too high.

I reminded myself that I had choices.

I considered heading to Albany, Georgia, to have a chat with Brian Miles, but that felt like a dead end. And I admit I was briefly tempted to find my way back to Ochlockonee for a holiday date with a pair of twins and a turducken. I even thought about a long drive to Colorado to be with Gibbs. But the strongest pull? The due north on my emotional compass?

Simon.

I climbed back into the Cherokee.

FORTY-FIVE

ALAN

Maybe I didn't handle things well with Sam.

When I heard the yeah-whaddya-want tone in his voice on the phone, I immediately figured I'd tracked him down in one of his infamous constipated moods. The way I was feeling I just didn't have the patience for it. In retrospect, I immediately topped that miscalculation with another serious mistake: When he returned my call, I wasn't allowing for the possibility that Sam was not the person responsible for planting the bug in my office.

The truth is that I actually didn't get around to seriously entertaining that likelihood until long after I'd talked to him. In fact, I was halfway through my one-thirty appointment, later that afternoon.

My one-thirty was an elderly woman with severe posttraumatic stress syndrome from the unlikeliest of causes. She was perhaps the sweetest, kindest, most genteel person who had ever come to see me for treatment. Ironically, both she and I were currently obsessed with bugs. Hers were the microscopic kind that make people sick. By her account, she had barely lived to be able to tell me the tale of her atrocious treatment on board a bug-infested Caribbean cruise the previous fall.

Her story, which she insisted on recounting in excruciating detail, was now in its fifth weekly installment. The ship she was on the previous November had aborted its scheduled island-hopping itinerary and rushed back to Miami after suffering its second sailing in a row plagued with an epidemic of Norwalk virus, a severe gastrointestinal malady not uncommon in North America. According to my patient, the cruise line had known about the epidemic—which had also infected a huge percentage of passengers and crew on the previous sailing of the same ship—for over a week and had made a corporate decision, despite the severity of the outbreak, to disinfect the ship and immediately sail again. That decision had put a whole new group of twelve hundred passengers, including my patient, at risk of exposure. She maintained that none of the passengers on board the second doomed sailing had been forewarned about the ongoing epidemic until moments before boarding. Certainly my patient hadn't been forewarned before she'd made the thousand-mile-plus trip to the dock in Miami.

"Why?" she kept asking me. "Why? What did I do to them that they would risk putting an eighty-year-old woman in the toilet for most of a week? Why? Don't they know what they did to me? Why?"

She answered her own question. "Greed," she said. "They made me sick as a rabid dog and they almost killed me because they're greedy bastards. They care about money, not about people. That's what I think."

If I had to guess, I would have guessed that she hadn't actually used the word "bastards" before in her eighty-two years.

My poor patient was at the part of her story where a fellow passenger threw up on her in the elevator—"and I was at least five feet away from him."

Her seagoing tales of explosive emesis, institutional rudeness, and Olympic-size lack of compassion by cruise line employees had just begun, I knew. The excruciating story had thus far only progressed to cover day three of her voyage; she and I had three additional long, long days at sea ahead of us. Covering them at our current pace would take us a month of weekly appointments.

"I don't blame them for the virus," she said. "I blame them for just about everything else they did." She'd said that before. I was certain she would say it again. And again.

"Greedy bastards," she repeated. "Do you know what they offered me for compensation? Do you?"

I did. But I also knew she'd tell me again anyway.

"They'd let me do the same darn death cruise a second time, and then they'd let me do another one at twenty-five percent off. That's it. That's the going rate for almost killing an old woman."

It was at that interlude in her session that I had the wisdom to cut Sam some slack. The thought I was allowing to ferment was: *Maybe he didn't do it. Maybe he was telling the truth about the bug.*

But if Sam didn't plant the damn device in my office in order to find out what Gibbs knew about her husband's murderous tendencies, who did? And why?

My dear patient, I knew, would have gladly blamed the whole fiasco on the greedy bastards from the cruise line.

The truth, I guessed, was not going to be so simple. Who had planted the device in my couch pillow? I didn't know and probably wouldn't know until I figured out why it had been placed. Knowing why meant discerning exactly what one of my patients might have had to say in the confines of therapy that was worth committing a felony to overhear.

I spent some time mentally reviewing my roster of patients, imagining which of their secrets, mostly mundane to me, was so prized by someone else. Although Jim Zebid's accusation about Judge Heller's husband selling cocaine was intriguing, and Sharon Lewis's identity would have certainly caused a tabloidish stir, Gibbs's story was the one that definitely had the most universal allure.

That's what led me to thinking that the culprit was the cops, and to Sam. The police would certainly have some interest in what Gibbs said to me.

So, I imagined, would Sterling. Had he somehow gained access to my office and planted the device before he left for Florida to cover the football game in Tallahassee? If he had—considering the likelihood that his corpse was caught on some debris beneath the surface of the Ochlockonee River—I'd probably never know. But at least everyone's secrets would be safe.

But I was overlooking something important: a possibility that I had to rule out. I phoned home. Lauren answered. I checked in on her battle with Solumedrol and commiserated as she reluctantly shared the details of her travails.

Then I asked, "Do you have time for a work question?"

"Sure, sure," she said.

Her voice was pressured, as though her vocal cords were too taut. I asked, "Is there any way the police could get a warrant to put a listening device in my office?"

"What?"

"Is there any way—"

"I heard you. You're serious?"

"Yes."

"No."

"No? No way?"

"No, no way."

"I just had one removed. A listening device was hidden inside a pillow on my sofa."

"If this isn't your idea of a joke, I can assure you that it wasn't the Boulder police who put it there."

"Thanks, I needed to hear that. I have to go."

"You'll fill me in on all this later?"

"Yeah. Love you."

If I could have answered the who and why questions, I might have been able to predict the complications that were to develop over the next few hours.

But I couldn't, and I didn't.

FORTY-SIX

SAM

Sometimes momentum rules. I'd been pointing toward Indiana's bull's-eye, so I kept going that way. I had some lunch in a Shoney's by a gas station, went and saw the Speedway just for the hell of it, and then backtracked downtown so I could be near the RCA Dome. I parked the car in a motel lot a few blocks away, checked in for one night, and started strolling over toward the immense sports stadium, waiting for some inspiration from the dead woman who had worked there. What was her name? Julie Franconia. Yeah.

But I got no inspiration.

Nothing. Julie wasn't talking.

My pager vibrated once again against my hip.

I knew it was him. I walked another hundred yards or so before I bothered to look at the screen.

It was him. Another faux 911.

First I kept my promise to Lucy, called her, and

told her where I was spending the night. She didn't have anything new for me. Then I called Alan.

The second the phone started ringing, I was already regretting phoning him back. "What?" I said.

"I'm sorry," he said.

I was still walking. It turned out that the Dome butted right up against downtown Indianapolis. I liked that. Sports should be part of things, part of a city's life, not some suburban reverse-doughnut thing where the arena is surrounded by acres of open space that are used to park a gazillion cars twenty times a year. There was even a nice green park with a big fountain outside the front door of the RCA Dome.

Cool.

"I'm sorry," Alan said again.

By then I'd walked around the corner, ducked under a sky bridge that linked the stadium with a garage, and stopped in front of a nice old church with twin copper steeples. I sat on the steps.

"I'm in a church," I said to Alan, lying. "I'm hoping it will make me be nice to you."

"I'm sorry, Sam."

"You said that. Next."

"If that was being nice to me because you're sitting in a church, I'm glad you're not sitting in a topless bar."

I laughed. It was a good comeback. "A titty bar would be way too much stress on my heart. Truth is, I'm actually on the stoop of the church. Not inside. God may be occupied with the folks who made it all the way inside, so be careful."

"I shouldn't have accused you."

"Accused me? You shouldn't have even considered

me. I play hard, but I don't play dirty. I might be tricky, but I don't cheat."

"I know. I was wrong."

"Is that it? I got to go."

"Where?"

It was actually another good comeback, although Alan probably didn't realize it.

"I don't know. I'm thinking of going up north and seeing Simon."

"Is that a good idea?"

"Seeing my kid? It's always a good idea. Always."

He didn't skip a beat. He asked, "You want to tell me what's going on with Sherry?"

"Nope."

My pager vibrated again. I was about to turn the damn thing off. I lifted it off my hip and held it at full arm's length from my eyes. Even that far away I could barely read it. I said, "Gibbs is paging me. Now I do have to go."

"What does she want? Call me back."

"Right."

"Detective Purdy? I'm scared."

Her voice did something to me.

It was something unfamiliar. I stood and moved two steps higher on the church stoop. That didn't feel quite right, so I moved back down and settled my fat ass one step lower than when I had started. I wasn't sure precisely what I wanted God's help doing at that moment, but I was aware that it might be something He wouldn't be eager to assist me with.

"Yeah?"

"I think he's alive. I do."

I assumed we were chatting about Sterling. "You think he'd come after you?"

She said, "No, not really. But maybe, I guess. God, what a thing to say."

As she implored the deity, I craned my neck upward toward the pointy ends of the steeples.

"Where are you, Gibbs? Are you at home?"

"No, I checked into a hotel."

I guessed she would be at the Boulderado. I saw her standing near one of the tall windows in the new wing of the downtown hotel, her body softer than soft behind the gauzy curtains. "Which one?"

"The Boulderado," she said.

Arguably Boulder's finest, and the first place Sterling would look for her after he determined she wasn't at home. The very first. Gibbs's judgment was impaired. That wasn't news. A lot of experience had convinced me that all battered spouses have impaired judgment.

Just like all squares have corners.

"Maybe not the best choice," I suggested.

"Do you think he's coming?" she asked.

"What do you think?"

"Over these years he hasn't hurt me, he's hurt them."

"Them?"

"The women he was . . . you know."

"Screwing?" I felt my pulse jump as though my heart had a turbocharger. Seventy to one-seventy in three seconds flat.

I thought she mumbled, "Mmm-hmmm," or something like it.

"The women he killed . . . he was . . . having affairs with them?"

"I don't want to . . ."

I found a fleece-lined version of my don't-fuck-with-me voice and used it like an exposed blade against her throat. I said, "This isn't the time to get coy with me, Gibbs."

"Yes," she blurted. "Yes."

"Do you know of others? Other women? Besides the ones who are in the news already?"

"No one else."

She had hesitated. Damn it. The pause was subtle, but it felt like a stomp on the foot to me. She was lying.

I didn't want her to be lying to me.

Her next words seemed to come out of her like a tabby's purr, all soft and comforting. She said, "I don't want anyone to get hurt. Do you think he's out there? Do you?"

I inhaled slowly, as though I could somehow detect the scent of Gibbs's perfume in Indianapolis's air. All I got was a lungful of bus exhaust. "Until someone finds his body, you can't be sure he isn't. I always tell people to trust their fear. It's usually pretty good advice."

"The FBI called and asked me about Brian Miles."

Gibbs's change of direction was abrupt. I felt like I'd just tripped over something. I regained my balance and asked, "Yeah? What did you tell them?"

"What I told you already. That Brian and Sterling had whored around together. And that I didn't like Brian."

"You didn't tell me that. That you didn't like Brian."

"He wasn't nice to women."

"No?"

"No."

"How wasn't he nice to women?"

"Maybe I should go to Denver instead of staying here. Or go up into the mountains."

Way out in front of my eyes I spied a couple of dots that needed connecting. I asked Gibbs, "What business is he in? Brian Miles?"

"Electronics."

"Huh? Like TVs? Stereos?"

"No, microelectronics. Stuff I don't understand. Do you like the mountains?"

I stumbled again trying to keep up with her. Gibbs was clearly accustomed to having men follow her wherever the hell she decided to go. So what did I do? I followed her, too. I asked, "Have you considered Safe House?" but I was still pondering Brian Miles and microelectronics.

"Actually, I was thinking Vail. Or maybe going back to Corona Del Mar and staying with friends."

Gibbs was definitely Vail. Not Aspen, Vail. Not the mountain, the village. She'd be right at home in Vail Village.

Through the phone I heard a horn honk loudly.

"You have a room on the Broadway side?" I asked.

She hesitated. "Close. I'm on the alley."

A siren blared by.

"That ambulance was really moving," I said. "They usually don't go that fast on Broadway."

Gibbs said, "I wish you were here, Detective. I'd feel safer."

It was the tabby's purr again, vibrating gently

against my fragile heart. I stood and stepped down the church steps. My feet felt like they were disappearing into sand. Lifting them—left, right—took extraordinary effort.

I made her feel safer. I made her feel something good.

I made her feel.

"Call me Sam" was what I said. Or just call me glib. Was I tempted? Yeah. Heading back to Colorado's high country to play bodyguard to Gibbs's princess sounded just fine to me. The impulse to go felt wrong. It did. But the sense that it was wrong came and went fast, like the roar of a passing stock car.

A homeless guy was sitting hunched over in the recessed doorway of a building just a few yards from the church steps. *That,* I thought, *is what hope looks like as it's dying.*

I tried, but I couldn't pry my eyes off him.

As a way to break free from the suction of his gravity, I pulled out my wallet and fished out ten bucks. I dumped the bill into the hat that sat upside down between his antique Air Jordans. He didn't even look up to check the identity of his benefactor, but a remarkable sleight of hand allowed him to suck the bill up into the sleeve of his ratty corduroy coat so fast that my eye lost track of the money.

I realized that quick-as-a-burp he'd replaced the ten with a single and that I'd been had. I hadn't contributed some needed charity to a homeless man, I'd made an unwitting payment to a skilled urban busker.

Gibbs broke into my reverie. "Detective?" she said. "Sam?"

She called me Sam.

"Yeah," I replied.

"If I decide to move somewhere else, I'll call you from Vail or wherever I am. I hope you have something for me when we talk again."

Me too. Me too. "Me too," I mumbled.

"I can pay you, you know, to protect me. I can. I'd like you . . . here."

"That's not it," I said. "I'm working on something here that might help."

She sighed. " 'Bye, Sam."

" 'Bye."

Where was I planning on finding whatever information it was that I planned on giving to Gibbs? That I didn't know.

I found myself again distracted by the costumed magician who had my hard-earned money up his sleeve. An elegant, elderly woman wearing a fox stole walked by, slowed, and threw a handful of coins into his hat. For a brief moment his hand hovered above the money. But her contribution apparently didn't equal the price of admission; this guy granted no magic show for a mere handful of change.

Then I remembered: Alan wanted me to call him back. It was just as well that I'd forgotten. If I'd remembered, I would have had to make a conscious decision not to do it. Then I would have ended up feeling guilty. And that would have been bad for my heart.

I pulled a five out of my wallet, folded it the long way into a V, and slid it into the magician's hat. Faster than my eyes could follow, the bill was gone and replaced in the hat by a solitary buck.

The surrogate bill wasn't folded down the middle.

I took a step back and applauded quietly and

politely, as I might if I attended the symphony, which I don't.

The homeless impersonator lifted his head an inch or two and mimed a tip of the hat for me.

All in all, it hadn't been a bad way to spend fifteen dollars.

FORTY-SEVEN

ALAN

Despite Tayisha's reassurance that my office was clean, I made the stroll to the waiting room to retrieve my four o'clock without feeling a whole lot of confidence in the sanctity of my workspace.

My four o'clock was the twenty-three-year-old named Craig Adamson who had called earlier in the week to confirm his appointment. Craig was one of those patients who kept me up late trying to find ways to help him. He was a terrific human being who spent every waking moment battling a whammy of mixed character pathologies—a moderate obsessive/compulsive disorder alongside a severely paranoid character. In his unfortunate circumstances the two problems coexisted about as well as quarreling neighbors. The DSM diagnostic code that I'd cobbled together to describe his condition looked like a European phone number—way too many digits—because it required that I tack on additional numerals to account not only for his depression but also for his occasional psychotic interludes.

A surprise greeted me as I opened the door to the waiting room. Craig was right where I expected to find him: in the corner chair, which was the location farthest from any other seat in the room. But sitting closest to the door was another patient of mine, one who didn't even have an appointment that afternoon. It actually took me a moment to recognize her. She'd dyed her hair so that it was a shade of red that nature tended to reserve for flowers and fruits, and she'd cut it short enough that she wasn't going to need a blow dryer for a while.

Sharon Lewis.

She shot to her feet, glanced at the hypervigilant man in the corner—apparently concluding that he wasn't much of an adversary—and with enough pressure in her voice to power a hydraulic lift, she announced, "I need a minute. I'm sorry, I'm sorry, but I just do." Then she squared and faced Craig. "May I have five minutes with him? I know it's rude, but this is an emergency. You don't mind, do you?"

Without waiting for either of us to reply, she squeezed past me into the hallway that led back to my office and disappeared from view.

Craig was having a difficult time comprehending what had just happened. I couldn't blame him for that. Finally, he said, "It's okay. Really." But his eyes were jumping with incipient panic.

"It's not okay," I told him. "This time is yours."

Despite a daily cocktail of psychotropic medications prescribed by a psychiatrist who knew what she was doing, and despite twice-weekly psychotherapy with me, Craig remained one of the most disturbed patients I'd ever tried to manage in outpatient therapy. I'd begun seeing him as a favor to my neighbor Adrienne, who worked with Craig's parents, both local anesthesiologists. They thought I would be the ideal therapist to treat their son, one, because I wasn't a colleague of theirs, and two, because my office was only a little more than a block from the town house they rented for Craig on West Pearl Street. Craig's pathology severely limited the geographic territory in which he felt comfortable traveling.

Sharon Lewis could not have picked a more vulnerable person to intrude upon if she had plotted her assault on my waiting room for weeks.

"No, no," he said. "It's okay. I'll wait. She needs . . . it . . . you . . . more than I do. I'll wait—wait here." He didn't look at me as he spoke. Not even a glance.

"I'll take care of this as quickly as I can."

"Fine. Fine." Exhale. "Fine, fine, fine."

"I'll be right back out," I said. A blind person could have read his body language. Craig was anything but fine.

He stuck his face closer to his magazine. I noticed that he was reading *Popular Mechanics*. It wasn't a title that Diane and I supplied to the waiting room, which meant that he had brought it along with him. It could have been, of course, that he wasn't fond of any of the magazines we provided for the waiting room. But I suspected the reality was that Craig wasn't comfortable picking up a magazine not knowing who might have touched it before him.

Would he admit that to me? Not yet. But we'd been making progress on the trust issue lately. Progress that I was afraid this event might annihilate.

*

Sharon Lewis was waiting on my sofa. She appeared as though she'd been hooked up to a Starbucks IV for most of the day. Her acute agitation made me think of Lauren's recent Solumedrol jolt.

"I should just go back to Ontario and hide."

"Ontario? California?" I felt an imperative to adjust my therapeutic gyroscope. Asking an inane question or two would buy me a few seconds of calibration time.

"I'm from Canada," she explained.

"I didn't know." I didn't.

"Well, they know," she said. "God damn it. They know. They know everything."

I took a slow, deep breath trying to find words that would challenge her without being accusatory. "What you just did out there in the waiting room, Sharon, is the same thing that got you into such a mess at the airport a couple of weeks ago. It's what we've been talking about. You impulsively decided that your needs were more important than anyone else's, in this case the other person in the waiting room. You once again allowed a sense of urgency"—I could have added, but didn't, "and a sense of grandiosity"—"to cause you to decide that the rules"—I omitted "of decency and compassion"—"don't apply to you."

"I said I knew it was rude. And I apologized to him."

"The problem is that knowing that the behavior is rude doesn't serve to deter you at all. And your apology sounded about as sincere as—as a campaign commercial."

Her jaws were clenched. Despite my bluntness my words hadn't dented her Kevlar facade. I hadn't expected they would.

"They know who I am. Today on the noon news, Colorado's fucking News Channel reported that the mystery woman who inconvenienced a million airline passengers—you know, *the most selfish woman in America*—they're reporting that her name is Sharon, that she lives in Boulder, and—get this—they said she's getting mental health treatment for her 'condition.' My 'condition'! Jesus."

The blood drained from my face. I guessed what was coming next. And I wasn't disappointed.

Or I was.

"Did you tell someone?" She almost spat the words at me. "Did you tell someone about me?"

"You would like to blame me for the situation you're in?" I thought I managed to ask the question evenly, with just the slightest hint of confrontation.

"Who else?" The subtext of her retort was *You imbecile! Nobody else knows but you!*

Yogi Berra once said that he couldn't think and hit a baseball simultaneously. His point? Some things happen so fast that they must be done by instinct.

My reply to Sharon should have been one of those instinctive things. But it wasn't. Why? Because I was absolutely frozen in place by the fact that one of my options was admitting to Sharon that I'd just had a listening device removed from the office in which we were sitting, and that it was likely that the little microphone and transmitter had carried her secrets out my windows or through my walls out into the world.

The fact that one of the local television news channels knew only her first name convinced me that the leak had been from one of our sessions. Rarely did I ever use a last name during treatment. But if I made the admission to Sharon about the listening device, I was certain that she would, rightly, accuse me of destroying her hope of confidentiality. Were she to accuse me in public, the notoriety of the case would bring me almost as much misery as she was about to suffer.

I sputtered to find words. Although I knew I'd eventually have to tell Sharon and all my other patients what I'd found in my cushion, I wasn't ready to start right at that moment.

In ten quick seconds of therapeutic silence I saw my precious career vaporizing before my eyes.

What did I end up saying? I said, "I don't know, Sharon."

She actually started to cry. "I was going to turn myself in. I was. Now? It will look like I did it because they found out it was me. Hell, I'm screwed. Screwed! I'm leaving—I have to talk to a lawyer."

A minute later I was on my way back out to the waiting room to retrieve Craig. I opened the door to discover that he was gone. I wasn't surprised, and I began considering the words I'd use that evening when I called Craig's home trying to repair some of the damage. I actually felt some hope that if he and I could deal with what had happened in the waiting room that day, it might ultimately be helpful in his psychotherapy. Nevertheless, I didn't take much comfort in being the unwitting foil in the provocation he had suffered.

I spent the dead time before my final appointment of the day making a list of all my patients and all their recent secrets, big and small. I couldn't keep myself from making tortuous detours as I imagined the admissions that I would have to make to each one about the possibility that their revelations to me were soon going to be in the public domain.

A few minutes before five Diane tapped on my open door. She was mugging a pouty face. "None of them wanted me. I got voir-dired to death on an arson case, but nobody wanted me. I'm crushed."

"Hi," I said. "It turns out you were right."

"Of course I was. About what?"

"The bug in my office."

"That? Right. Anyway, there was this one guy in the jury pool—"

"I'm not kidding."

She snapped her mouth shut, and I explained about Tayisha and the listening device and about the continued revelations about my patients' lives that were finding their way into public view.

She couldn't tell whether to believe me. Finally, she asked, "How many is that total?"

In my head, I counted. Jim Zebid and his story about Judge Heller's husband's cocaine. That was one. Gibbs Storey and her accusations about Sterling. That was two. Sharon Lewis and her ignominious behavior at Denver International Airport. That was three.

"Three that I know of," I said.

"That doesn't make sense."

Why it didn't make sense escaped me. "What, Diane? You don't like odd numbers?"

"Why would somebody plant a bug to discover something about one of your patients and proceed to broadcast information about three of them? It doesn't make any sense."

"I don't follow."

"One person walks into a park and paints a statue pink, you think there's something wrong with the painter, right? A wacko?"

"Yeah." Although I replied in the affirmative, my tone conveyed more doubt than assurance.

"But if three different people walk into the park at different times, and they each paint part of the statue pink, you have to begin to think that there's either a conspiracy going on—"

"Yeah." Less doubt that time.

"Or . . . there's something weird about that statue. Does anything—anything at all—tie those three patients of yours together?"

The possibility of a conspiracy was novel to me. "I can't see anything. As far as I know they don't know each other. They're all in different professions. Different social circles. They've never mentioned each other to me, that's for sure."

"Well, then take a look at the statue."

"Me? I'm the pink statue?"

"Exactly."

"What are you saying?"

"Somebody's out to get you."

"Me? What are they planning to do, Diane? Humiliate me publicly by revealing what I say to patients in therapy? I may not always be pithy, but I don't think what I say is *that* bad."

"Pithy? Did you say pithy? God, you're something. Whoever planted that bug didn't expect you to find it, Alan. Right? So why was it there? Not to embarrass you. A simple tape recording of your clinical wisdom would have embarrassed you. And I don't think it was to learn some deep dark secret that one of your patients might be telling you. Don't you see? Not with three different stories leaked already. Why would somebody do that?"

I'm sure I looked confused.

She went on. "If it was just one patient whose story was revealed, you could say that patient's secrets were the target, but if there are three—with maybe more to come—you have to assume that you, and not your patients, are the target."

"Then what? I don't get it." I was hoping we weren't on our way back to the pink statue.

"What was it you once told me in one of your rare fits of perspicacity? You said that if I want to understand someone's motivation for an act, then I should take a look at the consequences. Well, what are the consequences of all these leaks going public?"

"It's going to ruin me."

She walked close enough to me that she could rest a hand on my shoulder. "Exactly. Somebody's been trying to set you up as a therapist who can't keep secrets. You have an enemy, dear."

I tried to inhale. I failed. "Diane, if somebody did that, it—"

"It sure would. Once people in town think you can't keep secrets, you're dead meat."

"Hell."

"Just a guess on my part," she said. "But I would think that we've discerned the motivation. All you need to do is figure out who might want to destroy you."

FORTY-EIGHT

SAM

Want to know dead? Dead is the downtown of any major midwestern American city on the eve of Thanksgiving Day.

If the whole center of Indianapolis erupted in a spontaneous conflagration and burned to the ground that night, it would have to be considered a cremation, not a fire; that's how dead it was downtown.

If there were twenty people in downtown Indianapolis that evening, I somehow managed to miss fifteen of them. Even the faux-homeless guy with my money up his sleeve had packed up and gone somewhere for the night. Probably a suite in a fine hotel.

The clerk manning the desk at the motel where I was staying was a Sikh with a turban and an accent that made me smile. He suggested I try to find something to eat at the Marriott over by the RCA Dome. "Go there. They have to be open" was the precise nature of his melodic culinary recommendation. If he ever decided to change careers and shun all the opportunities available in the motel desk clerk business, I thought he had a promising future with Zagat.

I walked over to the Marriott, found an open restaurant inside, and got a table and a menu. A waitress wasted no time in ambling over and smiling a sincere midwestern smile. She asked, "You from out of town?"

I looked up and made good eye contact with her. "What, you get locals here? Like ever?"

She laughed.

"Didn't think so."

"Let me guess," she said. "I'm bored, okay. It's a slow day. Do you mind? I'm pretty good at this. Not as good as Wendy. She's like a champion, but she's off through Sunday. I'd say you're from Wisconsin. Maybe . . . Michigan—but northern Michigan, like Traverse City."

"Not bad, Christy." Her name was written in capital letters on a plastic tag above her ample left breast. "Born and raised in Minnesota. But I've been in Colorado for a while now."

She snapped her fingers. "That's what threw me. The Colorado part." She said "ColoRADo," emphasizing the penultimate syllable in a way that made me want to grate my teeth.

Behind her a woman stood in the restaurant's entrance craning her neck this way and that. I figured she was checking the room for her husband, or her date, or her girlfriend. I nodded in the direction of the foyer. "There's somebody over there who needs your help. I'll be ready to order in a minute, I promise. I'd love a beer when you get a second."

"What kind?"

"Surprise me." I'd already managed to forget that alcohol was on my post-MI do-not-consume list. Truth is, it wouldn't have made any difference had I remembered.

"You're nice," she told me.

"Nah, I'm not really," I said.

I could tell she didn't believe me. A bad judgment on her part. I had no doubt that if I had a beer with Christy, the first thing I'd learn from her was that all her boyfriends had been assholes.

Growing up, my family always had soup the night before Thanksgiving. It was part of our tradition. My mother, bless her heart, could throw together a big pot of soup faster than I could say, "What's for supper?" She considered soup a light meal that was appropriate in anticipation of the richness of the coming holiday feast. But Mom's soups were never really light—she wasn't a consommé kind of gal. Her soup was always something thick and chunky, hearty with sausage and white beans or kidney beans and plenty of rich cheese.

I endured a moment of sadness as I realized that all the love she'd put in her soups was now coating my arteries like spackling on a wall.

I'd returned my attention to the menu, looking for some soup not too much like my mom's, when I felt the waitress approach again.

"Almost ready," I said. "How's the minestrone? Come from a can?"

She didn't reply. I looked up.

The woman from the doorway stood with a hand on the top of the other chair at my table.

"May I?" she asked.

She was pretty. Well dressed. Polite. And tall. I was bumping into a run of tall women on my road trip. I thought of the Wolf sisters and the turducken that was about to begin roasting in their slow Georgia oven, and I lamented that not a single bite would cross my lips the next day.

I opened and closed my mouth a couple of times like I was some old fool who just realized he hadn't remembered to replace his dentures, before I said, "Actually, I'm fine all by myself, thanks."

She pulled back the chair and sat down.

Christy the waitress had a fresh place setting in front of her within seconds.

I stared. The pieces of the puzzle floated in front of my eyes. But they didn't come together.

My uninvited guest said, "You're having the minestrone?"

Two weeks ago I would have sent her packing. Two weeks ago I thought I had a healthy heart and a marriage that would survive until Christmas. Two weeks ago I wasn't sitting alone in a restaurant in a faceless Marriott in Indianapolis. Two weeks ago I hadn't met Gibbs Storey, and I'd never heard of a turducken.

"Have a seat, why don't you?"

"You don't know who I am, do you?" she said.

I hated questions like that—questions that taunted with I-know-something-you-don't-know. I reconsidered my decision not to send the woman packing. To buy some time to contemplate, I answered her first question. It had been more civil than the second. I said, "I like minestrone."

She held out her hand. "I'm Carmen Reynoso."

I made a little *ptttt* sound with my lips. The sound was part of my recognition that I hadn't made her as a cop. That troubled me. I thought I could make a cop in the fog with plugs in my ears and my hands tied behind my back. I didn't shake Reynoso's outstretched hand. Nothing personal to her; it wasn't one of my things.

The waitress brought my beer.

Detective Reynoso said, "I'll have one of those, too, please."

"You here looking for Julie Franconia?" It wasn't so much a question as it was my way of letting Reynoso know that I wasn't a complete dummy. I added, "The case is closed. Body was found south of here near Martinsville. Looks like your boy Sterling did it. If you get up and hurry over to the airport, I bet you can be home in sunny southern California in time for your turkey."

She nodded, so I thought she was going to agree with me. But she didn't. She said, "Actually, I'm here looking for you."

"Did I do something . . . particular . . . to interest the Laguna Beach PD?" I was thinking maybe surfing without a permit, or illegally parking my Range Rover, but I didn't say it out loud.

Once, after Alan observed me talking to a citizen about a crime I thought she might have committed, he complimented me on my interrogation technique. I said something to change the subject, which he ignored. He ended up going on and on the way he does sometimes, and told me that where conversation was concerned, I was good at making repetitive move ones, not falling into the trap of making reactive move twos. He said it served me well.

I didn't know what the hell he was talking about.

He, of course, explained it all to me. His lecture boiled down to this: In order to maintain control of a conversation, psychologically speaking, a person needs to make repeated assertive moves, not merely reactive moves. If someone says, "How are you?" the other person doesn't need to respond, "Fine," the other person can say, "Where were you last night at eleven?" He said I was good at that, at keeping control of conversations, at not making move twos.

I'd never thought about the linguistic structure of it all before. But he was right. I am good at that. It isn't tactical on my part. I just don't like feeling that somebody else is running the show.

It turned out that Carmen Reynoso was good at that, too. She ignored my sarcastic question about why the Laguna Beach Police Department might be interested in finding me. Instead she chose a fresh move one. She said, "I came looking for you because people say you're good."

I shrugged. "Doesn't happen too often, but sometimes people are right." That, by the way, was a classic move two on my part, which meant that Reynoso was firmly in control of this conversation.

It was okay with me for the moment. I was confident I could take back the wheel whenever I felt like it.

She said, "We're the only two people I know who believe that Sterling Storey is actually still alive."

"How do you know what I believe?"

"I'm a detective."

She didn't yield an inch of territory. I smelled Lucy. "My partner told you I was here?"

She smiled for the first time. Her lips were sealed during the entire grin. I was thinking she didn't like her teeth. Yellow or crooked? I guessed crooked, then instantly reconsidered my conclusion. Maybe she was a smoker. I sniffed at the air, didn't detect anything foul that wasn't coming from the kitchen. Still, she struck me as someone who'd maybe once smoked.

She said, "I'm picky about revealing my sources."

"You mean your snitches? What do you want with me, Detective Reynoso?"

"You Catholic?"

"I thought you were a detective. You should already know the answer to that." I wasn't sure whether my response had been a move one or a move two. But I thought it was pretty clever.

"I am. I'm Catholic. My father considers St. Peter's—you know, in Rome—the holiest place in the world. Notre Dame—the university, not the cathedral in Paris—comes in a close second. In my family Saturday afternoons in the fall are just as holy as Sunday mornings. Fighting Irish football? Anyway, this is a roundabout way of wondering if you'll accompany me up to South Bend."

I'm not Catholic. To the contrary, I hate Notre Dame University with the same kind of passion that heretics despised the Inquisition. Why? Lots of reasons. But mostly because Notre Dame stole Lou Holtz from the University of Minnesota.

Some things aren't forgivable. But I'd learned over the years that it wasn't a safe area of discourse with

Notre Dame fanatics, who tend to be about as rational about their beloved Fighting Irish as the real fighting Irish are about the British, so I kept my enmity to myself.

"Why?" I asked. My resolve about not revisiting the Coach Lou hijacking was weakening already; I was sorely tempted to go into my well-practiced Notre Dame harangue.

"If Sterling's alive, I think that's where we'll find him."

I left half my beer on the table. She left slightly less of hers. I never got a chance to taste the minestrone, but I suspected that it wouldn't have satisfied like my mom's bratwurst and cheese soup with ale. As Reynoso and I were walking out of the Marriott, I said, "There are three, by the way."

"Three what?"

"People who think Sterling's alive. His wife does, too."

I had to hustle to keep up with her long strides. "Actually," she said, "that would make four."

"Four?"

"I'm thinking Brian Miles."

Sterling's pal in Georgia. Smart lady. I said, "Gotcha."

Two more steps. "Gibbs is a piece of work," she added.

To that, I thought, *Amen.*

I was going to South Bend. That was the bad news.

The good news? Carmen Reynoso had rescued me from my impulse to drive even farther north to Minnesota. Every objective part of my brain was telling me that the trip to see my family would have been a bad thing to do.

How did Reynoso convince me that going to Notre Dame with her on Thanksgiving was the right thing to do?

The Crime Stoppers tipster in Colorado had called again. People who listened to both tapes thought it was the same guy as the first call. This time he'd told the volunteer who'd answered the phone that if Sterling Storey had happened to survive his swim in the swollen Ochlockonee River, he might be going after another victim, a woman he may have been planning to kill all along. The tipster suggested that the next victim would be found in one of three towns: South Bend, Indiana, Flushing Meadows, New York, or Daytona Beach, Florida. The tip also revealed that the South Bend woman worked in the Sports Information Office at Notre Dame. Reynoso had already done the footwork necessary to identify her. There was only one woman on the Sports Information Office staff who fit the correct profile: twenty-five to thirty-five, pretty enough to turn heads, a widow.

"Why you focused on that one? She's the only one at risk?" I asked.

"There're two other women on the list. The one in New York does advance work for the women's tennis tour. But we think she's in Australia at the moment setting up a tournament, so we're not as concerned about her. The other woman has something to do with Daytona Beach, Florida—maybe the car race—but so far we don't know enough to figure out who she is. So I'm here."

"The South Bend woman, what's her name?"

"Holly Malone. Good Irish girl."

I asked the obvious. "Isn't it likely the tipster's a crank?"

"He got the others right, didn't he? The other three homicides after the one in Laguna?"

"Still."

"Let's be real. You doing anything else for the holiday, Sam?"

It was the first time she'd called me by my first name.

"Not really," I admitted.

"Me, neither," she said.

"Why," I asked, "doesn't the South Bend PD take care of this?"

Reynoso was in the passenger seat of my Cherokee. We'd backtracked and dumped her rental car back at some no-name agency at the airport and had started driving north. Unless we got seriously distracted, we'd be in the hometown of the Fighting Irish just before we arrived at the Michigan state line.

Reynoso answered my question. "I called the local cops when I was still in Georgia, explained the situation real politely, and I requested some assistance. Hold on—let me try and get this next part exactly right."

She took a moment to collect her thoughts, and then she adopted an accent that was part something and part something else. I wasn't good with accents. It was one of my few liabilities as a peace officer.

" 'Ma'am,' " she said in character, then went back to her everyday voice and explained that "the detective I spoke with in South Bend called me 'ma'am.' I always find that improves my mood considerably, being called 'ma'am.' " She resumed her soliloquy with " 'Ma'am, you want us to go out and protect a woman from a killer who's already been declared dead by the Georgia authorities? You actually do that sort of thing regularly in southern California? Up here we don't get a whole lot of spirit homicides. We actually haven't had a good ghost killing in, dear Lord, aeons. And my memory is that the last one we did have got the death penalty. Well, we hanged him. Recall we had the darnedest time finding a good place for the rope. It got all tangled up in the sheets. But we managed.' "

"I bet he thought he was pretty funny," I said.

"The man thought he was hilarious. One of his buddies was cracking up, too. I could hear him. I hope we get a chance to meet both of them when we get to South Bend. That would please me."

While she was talking, she'd started fiddling with my radio, which wasn't pleasing me too much at all. The fine country station with the clear signal that I'd found south of Indianapolis disappeared in a sharp crackle, and suddenly I found myself listening to late seventies pap. I couldn't imagine a worse choice—I didn't like to be reminded that I'd actually been in the prime of my life during disco. It was a source of long-term humiliation for me. I worried how I would explain it to Simon when the time came to discuss the music of my youth. If rap hung around long enough, that would help; rap was at least as hard to defend as disco. Maybe harder.

I asked, "Who do you think the tipster is, the guy who's calling Crime Stoppers?"

"Don't know."

"Who'd know what he knows? Can't be too many people."

"It's a fair question."

"You're not curious?" I asked.

" 'Course I'm curious. I just don't know. Do you?"

I was thinking that I had a pretty good idea, but I didn't feel much like sharing right then. It was probably a side effect of the toxic music that was being forced into my ears like a watermelon suppository. So I said, "Sure don't."

We were skirting Kokomo when she asked me about my heart.

"You feeling okay? You want me to drive, I will."

"I'm cool," I said, trying to be cool.

"Hear you had a heart attack."

"Just a little one."

"Still," she said.

"Yeah," I admitted.

The tires hummed along on the highway.

Carmen Reynoso knew when conversations were over. I was already liking that about her.

Half a mile or so later I asked, "What have you been able to learn about Holly Malone?"

"Not much. She's an assistant director in the Sports Information Office at Notre Dame. Started in the office as an intern when she was just out of school. She's twenty-nine, attractive. People like her."

"You said she's single?"

"No, widowed. She has a four-year-old son."

"How did her husband die?"

"Cancer."

"Can't blame that on Sterling, can we?" I said. "Have you spoken with her?"

"I called. She was relatively pleasant until I mentioned Sterling. That's apparently a sore spot for her."

"Sore?"

"She wanted to know how I knew about him. My take was that she knew he was married when she did whatever it was she did with him. I thought she was embarrassed that I'd found out about their . . . history."

Kind of like having people know you lived through disco and didn't do anything to stop it, I thought. *Felonious stuff.*

"Got a photo?"

She retrieved a folded eight-and-a-half-by-eleven from her purse. "Pulled this off the Web. That's her on the left. First row."

I put my glasses on the end of my nose. It was a crappy picture of a group of people standing in front of a building. Holly Malone stood out as though she were Technicolor and everybody else was black-and-white. "She's cute. Has a nice smile."

"Yeah."

"You wouldn't happen to have a picture of Brian Miles, would you?"

Carmen pulled another crappy picture out of her bag and handed it to me.

One glance, and I knew there were no man-boobs on Miles. Nope. I kept that thought to myself while I stuffed my glasses back in my pocket. "We going to find Holly in town for the holiday?"

"We are. She's cooking for her two sisters and two brothers-in-law. They're all coming down from Chicago with their kids."

"Yeah?"

"She told me all that before I mentioned Sterling. Holly's chatty. If you're interested, she's doing a traditional bird and is poaching some salmon for her sister, who doesn't eat meat."

"Given the circumstances, I bet the salmon would consider itself meat."

Carmen chuckled. After her laughter quieted, I let the whine of the road fill my ears for a minute or two. I was thinking, *This is okay.*

I asked, "For argument's sake, why would he risk it? I mean Sterling. Let's say he survived the river. Why put himself in a position to be caught? Why not just run for it?"

"Odds are he'll do just that, Sam. Odds are we're wasting our time. Five years from now he'll get picked up on a Driving Under the Influence charge in Idaho, and his prints will get flagged by the Automated Fingerprint Identification System. That's the only way we'll know where's he's been since he crawled out of the Ochlockonee."

"I can tell you don't really believe that."

"Serial killers—and maybe especially serial killers who don't choose strangers as their victims—they don't think like you and me. They just don't. Why would Sterling go back and kill Holly? I don't know. Why did he kill the other four women? We don't know that yet, either. But I don't want the fact that I'm slow to the draw to cost some young widow in South Bend her life."

Slow to the draw? I wondered what she meant. I felt regret hanging on to her words like an anchor.

FORTY-NINE

ALAN

I bumbled my way through my last session of the afternoon. Diane, bless her heart, was in my office seconds after my patient departed. "So who wants to destroy you?"

I knew Diane loved me, but I also thought I detected a troubling touch of glee in her tone, a rub-your-hands-together, muted Wicked-Witch-of-the-West-type cackle.

"I can't think of anyone."

"God, I can."

"You can?"

She went into a staccato litany of some of my more public cases of the past ten years, eventually, and probably accurately, identifying a long roster of people who might be prone to seeking some redress for wrongs they could have been convinced they suffered because of me. It wasn't a pleasant list for me to contemplate. As Diane's soliloquy began to take on Elizabethan dimensions, I found myself wishing I'd walked out to my car and gone right home.

"You done?" I asked when she paused to come up for oxygen.

"I think so," she said. "Are you going to be able to remember all that, or do you want me take some notes for you?"

"Oh, I'll remember."

It turned out the pause was only Diane's version of a pit stop. Within seconds she was gaining speed again. Unfortunately for me, my seat belt wasn't fastened. She asked, "What about your current patients? You really pissed any of them off? Any of them want your, you know?"

I didn't know. Nor did I want to know, particularly. I said, "Not that I know of. Other than the leaks over the last few days. The three people whose information leaked aren't too thrilled with me. Other than that, my caseload is reasonably content with my efforts."

"Then what about nuts? You treating anybody really crazy right now? Any psychotic transferences creeping up on you? Ooooh, or any really hot erotic transference? Those can get wild. That might do it."

Despite the irreverent tone, her questions were reasonable. I thought seriously about my answers before I said, "No, nothing."

"Damn."

She seemed disappointed. I wasn't sure what to make of that.

"I have to get home. I have baking to do for tomorrow. Raoul has developed this thing for pumpkin pie. Who would have guessed? You sure you don't want to come over for Thanksgiving?"

"Thanks, but Lauren doesn't feel up to being with people. She's a little . . . irritable."

"Which we know is the Anglo-Saxon word for 'bitchy.'"

"Yes."

"Alan?"

She was in the doorway to my office, staring right at me.

"Yeah?"

"Stop feeling sorry for yourself. Jump this hurdle. Move on."

I wished her a happy Thanksgiving before I retraced my steps to my office and called Craig Adamson to discuss our fractured appointment that afternoon. His machine picked up. I left a message, packed up my things, and headed home.

The weather was pure Front Range autumn. Sweater-cold, hands-in-pockets, gusty-wind weather that came along with a promise of snow that is fulfilled less often than you'd think along the eastern face of the Rockies in October and November. I usually found the fall totally exhilarating, swollen with provocation.

But not that day.

The next day would be Thanksgiving. As I drove away from downtown Boulder, I reminded myself to count my blessings. It wasn't a short list—and Grace was firmly ensconced at numero uno—but I found myself distracted somewhere near number two or three by some of life's recent challenges.

My wife's feet were so full of edema, they wouldn't fit into Bozo's shoes, let alone her own. Somebody had bugged my office. My career was hanging by a thread. My best friend was alone somewhere in the Midwest, trying to find a way to recover from a troubled marriage and an angry heart. I had a patient whose husband might be trying to kill her.

And I had an enemy I couldn't identify.

I stopped on the way home to finish up the last of the holiday shopping. Bakery, groceries, wine. Everything took twice as long as it should have, of course. The butcher had our turkey listed under Allen, not Gregory, and I wasted almost half an hour trying to help him track down the bird while at least a dozen other joyous citizens waited behind me for their turkeys.

They expressed their holiday cheer to me via a well-rehearsed melody of sighs, nasal snorts, and whispers of "dear Lord" and "Jesus."

They weren't praying.

Sam once warned me that I would rue the day my parents decided to burden me with two first names. Maybe he was right. It wouldn't be the first time Sam had been right.

I wondered how he would spend the holiday.

The buffalo cap was out of Lauren's arm when I got home. That was her holiday gift, although the steroid misery wasn't completely over. She'd go from getting a gram a day of Solumedrol directly into her veins to getting eighty milligrams of prednisone into her mouth. Gradually eighty would become sixty and sixty would become forty and forty would become . . . and two or three weeks from now—I hoped by Christmas, for sure—she'd be completely finished with the steroidal assault on her metabolism. A few weeks later the side effects would dissipate to zero, and she and I would begin the familiar low-grade worry about the next time the elephant would camp out in our living room.

We had a light dinner as a family—actually I had a light dinner; Lauren was suffering the kind of munchies usually associated with chronic cannabis use but also common among steroid users, so she put down an unusual quantity of food—and then I read stories and got Grace down for the night. Lauren spent the whole time playing pool—the repetitive, endless nature of the game was one of the few things that seemed to help her outlast the Solumedrol.

After Grace was asleep, I joined Lauren in the dining room, where her pool table took up the space that an architect once envisaged for a dining room table. She didn't invite me to join her game. Lauren was once a highly rated amateur pool player. Let's just say that I wasn't. My opposing her in pool was as ludicrous a match-up as my lining up against Lance Armstrong for a quick sprint up Coal Creek Canyon to Wondervu on bikes.

Her strokes economical, Lauren dropped ball after ball into the leather pockets.

Through the steroid clatter in her brain she listened as attentively as she could to my story about Tayisha and the surreptitious device that was discovered in my sofa cushion. Other than offering empathy and wondering why I hadn't already involved the police, Lauren didn't have much to say in reply.

She was still playing pool when I retired to bed around ten.

I missed her.

The phone rang minutes after I flicked off the lights. I pounced on it so the ringing wouldn't stir Grace. As I lifted the receiver, I could still hear the *thwop-crack* of the pool balls coming from the dining room.

My "hello" earned me a "hey, buddy" from Sam.

"You okay?" I asked a little too urgently. I'd already convinced myself he was calling from some emergency room in some hospital. I was in a state of mind where I didn't have any confidence that anyone I cared about was okay.

"Yeah, fine, considering. Guess where I am?"

Given the mood I was in, I didn't want to play along, but Sam sounded happier than I'd heard him sound since his MI, so I tried to remember where he'd been the last time we talked. I thought Georgia, so I guessed, "Atlanta."

"South Bend."

My pulse jumped, just like that.

I was tired, but not so tired that my brain was unable to make the associations necessary to take me back to Gibbs's psychotherapy session the day before and to her revelation that Sterling had once been involved with a woman who lived in South Bend, Indiana.

Notre Dame University. The Sports Information Office.

Sam went on, filling the void. "Carmen Reynoso tracked me down. Remember her? It was her idea to come to South Bend."

Sam was telling me something. Given the hour, I

had to believe it was something important. Maybe because of how close I'd been to REM time when he phoned, I wasn't getting it. Not quite.

"Yeah? How's South Bend?"

"I'm not a big Notre Dame fan. I liked Indianapolis, though. I didn't expect to, but I did."

"I'm not a Notre Dame fan, either. It's like the Yankees, I think. You either love the Irish or you hate 'em." I was still drawing a blank. I wished I weren't so tired. God, I was tired.

Sam said, "There's a woman here that Carmen thinks we should go see."

Carmen? Sam called her Carmen. That's when I got it.

Carmen Reynoso knew what I knew about South Bend. My next line in the script? "I guess I'm wondering how Carmen heard about the woman in South Bend."

"Tip from Crime Stoppers. A guy."

"Anonymous?"

"You know how people are; they don't like to get involved. Listen, I don't need any details or anything, but—you know me—I'm curious whether you've had any conversations at work lately about any women in South Bend."

"Turns out I have, Sam. Just yesterday, as a matter of fact, I had a conversation about a young woman who lives in South Bend. Can't say any more, because of how I heard it, but yeah."

"Any reason to believe she might be in some danger?" Sam asked.

"The woman in South Bend or the woman who told me about the woman in South Bend?"

Damn! I'd just exceeded the parameters of the game I was playing. I'd told Sam that I'd heard about South Bend from a woman. He could have guessed it on his own. He probably had, of course. That would have been okay. What wasn't okay was that I'd told him.

"Either. Both," he said. "Listen, you ever heard of a guy named Brian Miles?"

"Don't think so. Why?"

"He's some old friend of Sterling Storey's. And it turns out his background is in microelectronics. Given your conundrum, that might be important."

Yeah, it might be. "An awful lot depends on what really happened in that river in Georgia, doesn't it?"

"The Ochlockonee," Sam said. "Funny, but it's gotten to the point where I like saying it. Och-lock-onee. Ochlockonee. You know it's yellow? The river?"

"No, I didn't know that."

"It is. Anyway, I figure it about the same way you do. It's all going to come down to Sterling and the Ochlockonee." He paused. "How's Lauren feeling? Any change?"

"Her leg's a little better. The medicine's making her nuts, though. Thanks for asking."

"Tell her I'm thinking about her."

"I will. Sam, it was Crime Stoppers, huh? That's how you knew about South Bend?"

"Yeah."

"Hard to trace, those Crime Stoppers calls?"

"We don't trace them. Did I say it was a guy who called?"

"Yeah, you did. And you said that this Brian Miles guy is in microelectronics. I'm grateful."

"Well, I hope it helps you with your puzzle."

"The fact that it's a guy cuts the number of suspects in half, roughly."

"There you go. Process of elimination. Just like a real cop."

Did I fall back to sleep right away? Hardly. I was consumed with thoughts of Gibbs and Sterling and St. Tropez and a balcony on Wilshire Boulevard and women in Augusta and Indianapolis and Laguna Beach and West Point and a guy named Brian Miles in microelectronics and mostly—mostly—Sterling saying "catch me."

"Sex. It's not just for procreation anymore."

Maybe Sam would catch him after all.

Maybe in South Bend.

Maybe.

I listened to the muted *thwop-crack* of the pool balls for a while and toyed with counting sheep.

Instead, recalling Diane's admonishment, I conjured images of me jumping hurdles, and I numbered each one as it passed beneath my feet.

FIFTY

SAM

Carmen Reynoso had an address for Holly Malone and a little map to the Malone house that she'd printed off the Internet. Although we didn't get into South Bend until after eleven, we decided to drive by Holly's residence just to make ourselves familiar with the area. We found the bungalow on a corner in a neighborhood more upscale than I thought that a university sports information officer could afford.

Carmen said, "Craftsman style. Nice."

I think I surprised her by saying, "This is the territory for it. Stickley worked around here someplace, didn't he?" The truth was that I knew damn well that Gustav Stickley's furniture company had been just up the road in Grand Rapids, but I didn't want to come across as a smart-ass. I figured Reynoso took me for a fat, dumb cop—most people did. Partly I cultivate that impression for strategic purposes: I like the advantage that comes with being underestimated. But partly I do it because I'm most comfortable hanging with people that fat, dumb cops get to hang with. Talking Stickley and Frank Lloyd Wright and Elbert Hubbard doesn't go over too well in most areas of my life.

That's okay with me. The point of knowing stuff isn't so you can let other people know you know it. Occasionally feigning ignorance is a small sacrifice for the companionship of good people. And in my life I got to hang with more than my share of good people.

Carmen smiled at me after my comment about Stickley's furniture company. She didn't just smile; she smiled at me. Her lips stayed smoothly together, though, so I still didn't get a chance to see her teeth. But I wondered if the quick smile was her way of telling me that she cultivated the angry Hispanic persona the way I cultivated the fat doofus persona. We would see.

The Malone bungalow was an Arts and Crafts classic. It had a shingled roof, a wide front porch supported by small clusters of efficient pillars, elegantly grouped windows, and a solitary second-story dormer that faced the street. The lights were all off downstairs, but the flickering glow of a TV screen was playing shadow games on the curtains in the dormer.

I circled the block once, hoping Sterling was stupid enough to be waiting in a car parked on the street watching Holly through binoculars. No such luck. I ended up parking on the corner opposite the house beneath a big tree that was totally naked of its leaves. After a second or two I killed the headlights and the engine on the Cherokee. The valves clattered loudly as they tried to find someplace comfortable to rest. I shifted my ass and did the same.

"She's still up," Carmen said. I could see Carmen's

breath in the dark car. South Bend was colder than Indianapolis. I inhaled a little more deeply than usual to try to taste Carmen's scent. Failed.

"Watching Leno," I said.

"Letterman," she corrected.

I smiled, turning my head and parting my lips, letting Carmen see my teeth. It was an effort at modeling. "Yeah, you're right, probably Letterman. He's from Indiana, too, right? What do you think, should we go over, pound on her door, tell her about Sterling, ruin her evening?"

"She's not going to be happy to see us, Sam."

"Nope," I said. "I don't know about you, but I find most people aren't happy to see me at times like this."

"It is pretty late."

"Murderers work all kinds of hours."

"You really think he's going to kill her tonight?" she asked.

" 'Course not. But are you a hundred percent sure he isn't? This could be one of those times when being a little wrong has serious consequences."

Carmen yawned. "Why do I get the impression that you go through partners the way I go through panty hose?"

"Lucy's been my partner as long as I can remember."

"Is she a saint?"

"No. Lucy has issues, too, just like me. The rocks in her head fit the holes in mine almost perfectly."

Across the street Holly Malone killed the TV, and the light in the dormer died along with it.

Carmen noticed the change in scenery the same

second I did. She said, "I guess we have a decision to make."

"Coming here was your idea, Carmen. It was a good idea, or I wouldn't be here with you. I think whether we ruin Holly's holiday tonight or tomorrow morning is up to you. I'll back you up either way you want to go."

She gave the puzzle fifteen, twenty seconds of thought. "We passed a motel a few blocks back. I vote that you and I go get some sleep, and we talk to her tomorrow morning when she's chopping celery and onions to stuff into her turkey."

"Okay, that's what we'll do." I started the car. "Tell me something, Carmen. Are you a Raiders fan?"

"What?"

I pulled a U-turn in the intersection before I switched on the headlights.

"Football? You a Raiders fan?"

"As I matter of fact, I am. How did you know?"

"Intuition. Did you have tickets when you lived up north?" What was I guessing? I was guessing that she had season tickets and that she owned a good-sized wardrobe of Silver and Black.

"Yes, I did."

"Thought you might."

"What else do you know about me?"

You like disco and the Oakland Raiders. That's about it. Don't necessarily like what I know, but I don't know as much as I'd like. That's what I was thinking.

I decided to circle Holly Malone's block one more time, slowly, searching for any sign of Sterling Storey. Why? Criminals almost always end up proving themselves to be a lot smarter or a lot dumber than people give them credit for. I was still hoping that Sterling was a lot dumber. That was why.

Halfway around the block I finally responded to Carmen's question. "Nothing," I said. "I don't know anything else about you. You have kids?"

"One. She's a freshman at UC Santa Cruz. She's spending Thanksgiving with her boyfriend's family."

I did the math, figured Carmen was maybe a little older than me. "I have one, too. He's a sophomore in grammar school. He's spending Thanksgiving with his grandparents."

She laughed before she said, "I know."

She knew.

"You married?" I asked. I didn't think about asking, I just asked. I don't like it when my mouth gets ahead of my brain. It doesn't happen often. Usually my mouth is pretty slow, my brain a little faster.

"No," she said, without explanation.

She didn't ask me if I was married.

She knew.

Or did she?

I sucked in my gut, knowing damn well the act did nothing to disguise my man-boobs.

What did I spend the next few blocks wondering? I spent the next few blocks wondering what it would be like to get one room at the Days Inn instead of two.

FIFTY-ONE

We got two.

I hoped I hadn't been obvious when the woman at the desk had asked, "One room or two?" I'd hesitated a beat too long—I knew I had. I was waiting for Carmen to say "two," but she didn't. Or hoping she'd say "one" or something. It might have been my imagination, but I thought she was waiting to hear what I was going to say.

After that beat-too-long passed, we both blurted, "Two."

My room had little NO SMOKING signs just about everywhere I looked, but it had recently been occupied by a smoker, no doubt about it. The fetid air caught in the back of my throat with each slow breath I took.

I took a minute to call Alan on my cell to let him know that Carmen, and therefore the Boulder Police Department, knew about the woman in South Bend and that they seemed to have a conduit that ran straight into his office by way of the Crime Stoppers program.

He sounded dismayed at the news. I felt bad for him. The guy's plate was pretty full.

Carmen and I had been assigned rooms right next to each other; they even had a pair of those odd connecting doors between them, as though the desk clerk thought it might be fun to tempt me with trespassing all night long.

She sang soulful songs as she prepared to sleep. Except for my shoes I was still fully dressed, and I lay on the bed as motionless as I could so that the bed wouldn't squeal and I wouldn't miss a muted note. I was almost certain that I'd never heard any of the songs she was singing before in my life.

That, I thought, was fitting. It seemed that all the melodies I'd heard since she sat down opposite me in the Marriott were composed of fresh notes.

Except for the disco.

She sang three songs, paused, I guessed, to brush her teeth, and then sang one more tune, something so full of lament that it brought tears to my eyes about Simon and Sherry and the holidays and my heart. I thought of Lauren and the fears that enveloped her, and even of Gibbs and what her life was going to be like when the dust settled, and I shed a tear for her as well.

I fell asleep right like that with my clothes on and woke at one-thirty, stripped in the dark, brushed my teeth, and fell back into bed. I listened for a while to the silence, pretended I could hear the soft percussion of Carmen's breathing through the walls, and replayed the songs I'd heard only once a short while before, and they worked for me once again like lullabies. I was back to sleep before two and stayed that way until she pounded on my door at a quarter to eight.

*

When Carmen busted me awake, she'd torn me from a dream about the Wolf sisters and their mostly cooked turducken. The details of the dream evaporated instantly, but I woke thinking that if I inhaled deeply enough, I would be able to smell the intertwined birds roasting in an Ochlockonee, Georgia, oven. A deep breath and a quick look around the room brought me back to the reality that all I was smelling was the stale smoke of some inconsiderate fool's Marlboros.

I chided myself for my juvenile romantic fantasies all through breakfast. What had I been thinking?

Whatever intimacies I had imagined the night before had disappeared with the darkness. If we'd been flirting at midnight, we weren't flirting anymore. Carmen played nothing but business at breakfast, and I ran along next to her, trying hard just to keep up. I returned to the buffet line in the motel's little breakfast room a couple of times, not just to get more food, but also to get a break from her intensity. The meal wasn't bad; I ate yogurt and fruit and Cheerios with nonfat milk. After two cups of decaf I switched to regular coffee. If the morning was any indication what our day was going to be like, I was going to need some rocket fuel to match her pace.

My cardiologist would just have to understand.

"What do you know about Sterling and Holly? Their relationship?" Carmen asked me when I indicated I was done eating by pushing the plastic cereal bowl and the plastic spoon away from me. I thought that her saying "Sterling and Holly" was particularly ironic; it managed to make the two of them sound like they were the cute couple that'd been crowned king and queen at the Homecoming Dance.

But Carmen's question caused me take a sharp breath, too. Or maybe it wasn't the question; it was the answer I was about to give. "They were having an affair," I said. Which was exactly what I'd been thinking about doing the night before. I tasted hypocrisy with my next sip of coffee.

I don't like hypocrisy in others. I hate it in myself. Hate it.

"Yeah, but that's not enough. When I talked to her yesterday, she was obviously upset that I knew about her and Sterling. If all the two of them did was mess around a couple of times, why would she be so upset? She's not married, so what did she do that was so wrong, other than show some bad judgment by sleeping with a married guy? That particular sin is committed about a million times a day in this country."

It couldn't have been clearer if she'd been shouting at me. Carmen was announcing to me that she'd almost made the exact same mistake eight hours or so before and that she wasn't feeling particularly good about how close she'd come to yielding to the temptation.

But I didn't see the issue she was describing with Holly Malone. "I don't know that it's that confusing. She's Catholic. She's Irish. She has a young kid. She lives in a small town. Maybe she's the guilty type, or maybe she's just afraid of scandals. Most people don't like to be reminded of their indiscretions. Or—wait, better—she met him through her work, right? Maybe there's a Fighting Irish Sports Information Office prohibition against sleeping with people they're doing business with. She's scared of losing her job."

"That's possible. It sounds Catholic enough. But I think there's something more than that going on."

"Why does there have to be something more than that?"

"There doesn't have to be, Sam. There just is. I feel it. Who did you call last night?"

"What?"

"The second you stepped into your room, you made a phone call. Why? What was so important? Who was it?"

I sat back and felt my man-boobs jiggle beneath my shirt. It was clear that I wasn't making much progress on the man-boobs segment of my self-improvement program. I tried to look her in the eyes, but I couldn't quite corral her gaze. "Are we on those kinds of terms, Carmen? Where you can ask me who I call on the phone?"

She sat back, and her boobs jiggled beneath her shirt a little bit, too—although it was an altogether different phenomenon. "You're right, you're right. I'm sorry. I don't know what I was thinking. I'm sorry."

She had been asking me something, but she had been telling me something, too. What did I conclude? I concluded that she was telling me that her songs the night before had been a private concert just for me. I chewed on that. "The shrink who called you about the Storeys? The one you met in Boulder? He's a friend of mine."

"I know," she said.

She knew a lot about me.

She hadn't looked back at me since her intrusive question about the phone call. I said, "I called him. He has a . . . problem. I had an idea that I thought might help him with it. So how do you want to play this with Holly later this morning?"

She finally looked back up at me. She smiled. "If you're up to it, I'd like you to talk to her. Yesterday didn't go too well on the phone with me and her. You can start fresh. Is that okay?" My eyes were locked on her smile. There was nothing wrong with her teeth. They weren't crooked. They weren't yellow. They were just fine.

"That's okay," I said.

FIFTY-TWO

She was talking to herself more than she was talking to me.

"Twenty-two pounds. Dinner's at four. I'd like the bird out of the oven by three, maybe a little after. Eighteen to twenty minutes a pound—that's because it's stuffed, otherwise it would be only fifteen. That means five hours, give or take, so I need to get this in the oven—oh my God!—in the next few minutes. Aaaagh."

Holly Malone was kind of cute. She would be the darling kid in the sitcom—the one you really liked, the one with the charm. Pretty, but not the kind of drop-dead-beautiful that made me nervous. Like Gibbs.

I was enjoying watching her flit around her little linoleum-tiled kitchen searching for utensils and roasting pans and ingredients that it was apparent she hadn't laid a hand on in months. Or longer. But she possessed enough enthusiasm for an entire cheerleading squad, and her positive energy was better for my heart than anything I'd run across recently.

I was also enjoying being in a kitchen on Thanksgiving morning, getting the opportunity to be a spectator at an event that I'd been privileged to witness almost every year of my life since I was old enough to remember. I was surrounded by tradition; the countertops in Holly's kitchen were upholstered with celery and onions and broth and butter and parsley and dried bread crumbs and a big fat naked turkey, and for a moment all was right in my world.

I looked at the clock that hung on the wall by the door that led from the kitchen to the living room, which was where Carmen Reynoso was waiting while I was doing my best to bond with Holly. The clock read ten-fifty. I did some arithmetic, considered for a moment the consequences of keeping my mouth shut, and said, "Relax, Holly. Dinner won't be until six-thirty or seven. Maybe later. You have all day."

"What are you talking about?" she said playfully. She thought I was teasing. "Everyone's coming shortly after two. Dinner's at four, promptly. My sister's husband Artie would have a fit if he thought his meal would be even a minute tardy." Holly had a trace of an accent of some kind that caused her to elevate the last syllables of her words as though she really, really liked them. The accent was cute, too.

I was having a very good time.

Reluctantly, I explained the turkey dilemma. "Twenty-two pounds at twenty minutes a pound is exactly seven hours and twenty minutes of cooking time, not five hours give or take. That sounds like a long time to me, but what do I know about turkeys? If you stick it in the oven right this second—and you and I know that's not going to happen—then that bird won't be coming back out of the oven until almost six o'clock this evening."

She froze and stared at me as though I had screamed at her not to move, she had a tarantula on her nose. I could tell she was using the interlude to check my facility with numbers.

"Oh my God," she whispered. "Oh my God!"

"What can I do to help, Holly?" I asked. "Chop something?"

Her shoulders dropped. She put a devilish look on her face and said, "Can you go and arrest Artie for something or other? Throw him in the slammer for a while? That'd slow him down."

* * *

Half an hour later the bird was finally in the oven, and Holly and I were sipping fresh coffee at her linoleum-topped, chrome-framed kitchen table.

"This is going to be the kids' table later on," she told me. "This and an old card table from the basement."

"I like the kids' table," I said. "Conversation's usually better."

She sighed and looked at the clock. "I was a math major at Williams. I swear I was," she said.

I assumed that Williams was one of those eastern colleges that I was supposed to recognize by reputation. I didn't. I'd gone to St. Cloud State and didn't hang a whole lot with kids who didn't.

I said, "Thanksgiving meals never happen on time. It's part of the whole tradition. Don't worry. If Artie gives you any trouble about it, he's a jerk. Dinner will be wonderful."

"Artie is a jerk. I don't know what the heck my sister was thinking. She has this thing for anal men."

I saw my opening. "Don't be so hard on her. We all make decisions in relationships that we'd like to do over. I know I've made a few. I bet you have, too."

She was staring into her mug. "Yeah," she said, "I have." She stood, walked over to the oven, and peered in on the bird. She and I both knew it was just as pale as it had been ten minutes before. And she and I both knew that she was getting some distance from me. We were getting a little too close for Holly's comfort.

I pulled the photo of Brian Miles from my pocket. "You know this guy?"

She took a serious look at it before she said no.

My first reaction was that I believed her. I reminded myself that that didn't mean she was telling the truth.

"Sure? He hasn't been around?"

"I'm sure. Who is he?"

"Not important."

She moved some things around on the counter. Finally, she said, "This is where we talk about Sterling, isn't it?"

"Stuffing's made, turkey's in the oven, the first round of dishes is done. Coffee's hot. Guests won't be here for hours. It's probably as good a time as any."

"I should check on my son."

"He's fine. Detective Reynoso loves kids." Or she hates kids. Or she can take or leave kids. I didn't know. All I knew was that she'd managed to keep one alive until the kid was in college.

"You're sure?"

"I am."

"Is Sterling dead? The papers say he's dead."

"I was down in Georgia a couple of days ago. They think he's dead. Me? I'm not convinced." I went into a long explanation about the Reverend Prior and the Wolf sisters, the precise order they all arrived at the bridge over the Ochlockonee during that terrible storm, and I even slid into a little digression about the turducken that had already been in the Wolf sisters' oven for over half a day.

I could almost taste it right that second.

Holly was much more curious about the construction of the turducken than she was in the logistics involved in Sterling's fall into the Ochlockonee River. At her behest I did my best to explain the precise way a creative butcher nested the birds together like a set of those weird little Russian dolls that fit inside one another.

"Artie wouldn't like it," she said. "All those meats in the same meal? He likes to keep his foods completely separate on his plate." The thought of disappointing Artie made her smile.

"Do you know about the other women?" I asked. Enough about poultry, enough about Artie. If I was still around when Artie showed up, he and I were going to have a chat.

She gestured at the morning newspaper. "I don't believe it. I don't believe what I've been reading. It's just—it just can't be true. Not Sterling." She'd been waiting for me to ask the question about Sterling and didn't spare a second in answering it.

"You don't believe it?"

She looked at me, which was good. Her eyes were

tight with something; I wasn't sure what. She said, "Sterling is . . . pretty, I mean—God, who am I kidding—he's really gorgeous and . . . he's . . . smooth. You know, he's not the Sylvester Stallone macho-type guy, he's more like a short—God, I probably shouldn't say that. Oh, what the hell—he's like a short version of George Clooney. Sterling's really charming, not the kind of guy I usually meet through the—" She stopped herself.

"Yeah?"

She went on firmly. "He wouldn't kill anybody. No, no. Sterling is just not that type of guy. I know men. I do."

I whispered a prayer of gratitude for the opening. "So what type of guy is he, Holly?"

I'd been traveling for four days plus through I'd-lost-count-of-how-many-states hoping to get the answer to that question. And now here it was. I was about to hear what kind of guy Sterling Storey was, what kind of guy could cheat on a woman like Gibbs over and over again.

Holly's phone rang. It was her sister, Artie's wife.

"You got my message?" Holly said, stepping away from me across the kitchen. "Is Artie going crazy with the delay?" She raised a finger to warn me that she was going to need a minute.

I stood and poked my head into the living room. Carmen had Holly's son in her lap. She was reading him Christmas stories. I recognized a funny little book that I always read to Simon over the holidays called *Bialosky's Christmas*. Simon thought Bialosky was one terrific bear, which was something I never really understood.

Carmen's storytelling style was full of melody, and she imbued each character with a distinct voice. She was making it sound as if one of Bialosky's friends was from the barrio. Carmen was good. I listened for half a minute, but only with the periphery of my awareness. Front and center? I was replaying the last few moments with Holly.

Behind me I heard her place the phone receiver back on the cradle.

"Sorry," she said. "My sister."

Before I stepped back into the kitchen, I killed the power on my cell phone so we wouldn't be disturbed, and I changed the weight of my voice, reducing it the way my mom used to reduce the gravy before bringing it to the table. The act was pure instinct, like a big cat flexing her muscles before she pounces. I was about to pounce.

My prey was a cute blond widow who was cooking Thanksgiving supper for her extended family.

"Sterling Storey's not the kind of guy you usually meet through . . . what?" I asked Holly.

She took a step back, literally, and bumped against the stove. "I hoped you hadn't heard that. I've been wishing I hadn't said that."

"Maybe. Or maybe you hoped I did. Regardless, here we are. I heard it. You said it."

"I'm a widow," she said.

"Got that. I'm sorry."

"People talk. You know what it's like. My . . . options are limited. In my personal life."

"Are we talking about sex, Holly?" I managed to ask the question with a certain panache, as though I talked about sex with cute young widows all the time.

Yeah.

My question amused her. "Yes, Sam, we are indeed talking about sex. Hello."

I said what, to me, felt obvious. "You're a lovely girl, Holly. Bright, funny. I don't see how your options are limited." I didn't say, "*You could have any guy you might want, any guy at all.*" I didn't say, "*A guy would be lucky to be with you. A guy like me would . . .*"

I didn't allow myself to finish the thought.

"Before he died, my husband and I had an . . . imaginative sex life. We enjoyed a variety . . ."

Holly turned away from me.

Holly wasn't bashful about sex. That's not why she turned away. She turned away because she instinctively knew I was bashful about sex.

I tried to focus. *A variety of what?*

"We were careful. Always careful, especially after Zach was born. We didn't take unnecessary risks."

At the moment she said that she was talking directly to the turkey. Unlike me the turkey didn't blush.

"That's good," I replied. "You and your husband, what you did together in your private time is . . . was . . ."

"Our business. Yes. Is this important? I'm not really comfortable talking about all this with you."

Neither am I. Trust me, neither am I.

"Your husband's name was?"

"Mark."

"Thank you. Detective Reynoso and I are trying to determine what kind of danger you might be in from Sterling Storey. How you know him and how you met him are important parts of that determination. We'd like to leave here today able to assure you that you're safe."

She considered my argument. She looked in her hand, pulled out a card, and held it up for me to see. "I don't have to talk to you, though, do I? Legally, you don't have any authority here, do you?"

The card she'd chosen from her imaginary hand was a good one. I acknowledged that she held it. I said, "Nope, I don't."

"But then," she said, "you don't have to be here at all, do you?"

"Nope, I certainly don't. I'm a volunteer in this fire department."

She turned back toward me. The fact that I was there on my own time and on my own dime carried a lot of weight. She said, "Who will know about this? I mean, if I decide to tell you?"

I sipped at some coffee. It was cold. "This is where I could lie to you and tell you nobody but us, me and Detective Reynoso, but the truth is I don't know who'll end up knowing. Secrets are like puppies. Once you let them out, they tend to be pretty hard to control."

"South Bend's a small town. Notre Dame's a Catholic university. A very Catholic university. I'm a mom. Some of the things I do in my private life aren't acceptable here. I have no illusions about that."

"I understand," I said. "I know about small towns and secrets. In case you've never been, Boulder is more small town than big city. I grew up in a much smaller town in Minnesota. So how did you meet him?"

Instantly, she entered a little time warp. I recognized it. It was a little Jules Verne moment where time stopped and she tried to decide whether to tell me the truth. Ten seconds later she exited the warp with what sounded to me like honest words. "I have personal ads on the Web. Adult personal ads. I try to meet men with . . . similar interests . . . who are traveling, you know, who are in town on business. Mostly I end up going to Chicago to . . ."

Part of me was grateful that she left the sentence unfinished, part of me was just the smallest bit curious about what happened when she went to Chicago. "But Sterling came here to South Bend?"

"Yes, he did. His work brought him here—brings him here. You know about that, don't you? His work?"

"I do. You didn't meet him through his job, though?"

"No, we met, if you can call it that, over the Internet. We never ran into each other on our jobs. Even after. My job concerns primarily women's sports. I don't deal much with the men's teams."

"See, I didn't know any of that. You have a copy of the ad you run? May I take a look at it?"

"*What?*"

Holly had heard me just fine. Her exclamation was understandable, about what I would have expected had I asked if I could fish through her underwear drawer. I softened the request. "I'd like to know what exactly Sterling responded to. It will help me . . . understand him a little better."

She exhaled, her eyes wide. She dropped her arms to her sides and spread her legs a couple of inches farther apart. "He responded to a revealing picture of an attractive woman who said she likes sex with strangers. It's not that complicated, Detective. Getting people to respond to my ad wasn't difficult—isn't difficult. Finding someone I can feel safe with . . . that's a whole different problem."

I blushed. "How do you—"

"E-mail. I set up temporary Hotmail accounts, and then I e-mail back and forth with the guy until I'm comfortable. If I don't get comfortable with him, I close the account and start all over with somebody else."

I didn't know what a Hotmail account was. Hell. I'd ask Simon when I talked to him later in the day. My kid would probably know. "How long did the process take with Sterling?"

Carmen chose that moment to step into the room. "Smells great in here. You guys making progress?"

"We're doing great, Carmen. Maybe a few more minutes?" I said. The expression on my face was intended to shout "bad timing." *Real bad timing.*

She backed out.

Holly said, "I don't like her."

"Yeah, well. She's great with your kid. That's good, right? You were saying how long it took to—"

"Not long."

"So you met him . . . where?"

"On campus."

"And you . . . ?"

"Jesus, Detective. Do you really need to know? Really?"

I said yes. I didn't feel yes, but I said yes. Some things you want to know even if you don't want to know them.

This was one of those.

Holly stepped over next to me, lowered her mouth

to my ear, and whispered what it was she'd done with Sterling Storey.

Maybe it was the moist heat of her breath, maybe it was what she told me, but I blushed all over again.

FIFTY-THREE

This was going to be a first. Holly and her husband had talked about doing something like it a couple of times, but the discussions were always more joke than anything else. But this guy from California? He was serious. Right from the start, she could tell.

Totally serious.

She thought about his proposal overnight. Excitement overcame fear, fear became excitement, and she e-mailed a simple lowercased yes.

It had been a Saturday afternoon in September a year before. Notre Dame was playing Michigan in Ann Arbor. The date for the date was Holly's idea. The university campus would be empty. The students and faculty and staff who weren't in Michigan for the football game would be holed up watching the annual tussle anyplace that had a big screen and plenty of beer.

One-thirty to two-fifteen. That was the window she'd given him. She'd be there by one-thirty. She'd leave by two-fifteen. They had to be gone before Saturday afternoon confessions began.

In between? For Holly, the sweetest of all aphrodisiacs: anticipation.

"What are you going to do while you're waiting for me?" he asked in one of his e-mails.

He knew all about anticipation. She'd figured he would.

"Pray," she'd responded.

Some secular universities have chapels; some Catholic universities have elaborate churches. Notre Dame University has a basilica.

Holly was waiting for Sterling opposite the Chapel of the Reliquaries in the vaulting nave of the Basilica of the Sacred Heart.

Ten minutes before two o'clock he knelt in the pew that was right behind her. She hadn't heard him approach. He was the church mouse.

"Don't turn around," he whispered. "No, don't."

Her lungs felt bottomless. She was breathing so deeply that she had to open her mouth to get enough air.

She already knew from experience that the fire of anticipation consumed immense quantities of oxygen.

She hadn't spent the time praying. No, she'd been counting the other people in the church. Currently, there were thirteen. One lovely woman in a dreadful purple suit was only a few feet from her in the Chapel of the Reliquaries. Thirteen was just right. Not too many, not too few. Just right.

"Sex in churches shouldn't be reserved for priests," he whispered to her in an over-the-top Irish brogue. "Should it, now?"

She'd been thinking that they'd use the confined space of the confessional for their tryst, but she wasn't so sure she wanted to be in the dark with him.

Fear? No. *That wasn't it.* Not *at all.*

She wanted to be able to see him.

Without a word Holly stood, walked down the length of the nave, and climbed the stairs toward the pipe organ. Her idea.

A few minutes later he followed.

She knew he would. They always did.

As his footfalls brushed the stairs, one by one, she knew that what she'd been thinking about, fantasizing about, since she was a thirteen-year-old schoolgirl was about to happen.

Holly didn't actually see his face until they were finished. Until anticipation was nothing but sweat on the cold church floor. When she finally turned toward him and saw the white slash of his Roman collar and the ruby light from the stained glass that limned his profile, his physical beauty almost took her breath away again. She thought, Mark would have vetoed him for sure.

For sure.

FIFTY-FOUR

Carmen and I left Holly's house before I had a chance to meet Artie. That disappointed me.

We were out the door and all the way down the porch steps when I thought of something else, told Carmen to go ahead and get in the car, and returned to the screen door. Zach was playing with a pile of those oversized fat Legos in the living room, making something that looked like Frankenstein's dog.

"Holly," I said, calling her back to the door. "I'm sorry, one more thing." I lowered my voice to a whisper. "You're not frightened of him? Of Sterling?"

"No, I'm not."

"The other women he's suspected of murdering? They don't—"

"I'm not convinced. Far from it."

Her expression changed just enough that I guessed that whatever came next was going to be at a different level of intimacy than what had come before. I found myself struggling to tune my antennae.

"Listen," she told me, "I e-mailed him again a couple of weeks ago. I asked him if he was interested in going to church with me again sometime. That's how not-frightened of him I am."

"You would see him again?"

"Before this week and all the news in the papers? Before you and Detective Loves-Kids-Lacks-Social-Graces started trying to scare the bejesus out of me? I would have seen him, yes. We had a great time together."

Sometimes people ask me why I'm a cop. I don't usually answer with the public service/public welfare refrain. I answer with the truth: People are endlessly interesting.

Holly Malone was a damn good example.

"Did Sterling respond to your e-mail?"

She shook her head convincingly. Even a little ruefully, I thought.

"I gave you my cell phone number, right? Just in case? You'll call if you see him around here, or even if you get a feeling?"

"Yes, Detective. You did. And I will."

I reached into my pocket and handed Holly the crappy photo of Brian Miles. "Him too. Keep it. Call if you see him."

"You're not going to tell me who he is, are you?"

"His name is Brian Miles. He's somebody you should avoid."

She held the picture loosely in her hand. "I told you, I'm careful. No matter what you think about my lifestyle, I don't take chances with my safety. You haven't convinced me that Sterling's a killer, but you've convinced me that seeing him might involve taking an unnecessary risk."

"Might?"

She smiled at me in a way that seemed full of understanding and wisdom. The wisdom was bearded with just the slightest tease. I found it all quite disarming. Me and women? What a frigging mess.

With my thumb and index finger I spread my mustache away from the center of my lip. Holly was watching me carefully, waiting to see where I was heading next; I thought she knew that I hadn't come back to her door to ask her about Sterling and Brian Miles and to make sure she had my phone number.

Holly probably knew things about men that I wouldn't know for the rest of my life.

In the grand scheme that was probably an okay thing.

I said, "You and your husband, you and Mark? Did your, what did you call it before, your 'imaginative' sex life—that's right? I got that? Did it include, you know, other people, other couples? Sexually, I mean. I don't know if I'm asking that exactly right. But what I'm wanting to know is . . . well . . ."

My voice disappeared like stormwater down an open manhole. *Swooosh*.

"Is this a professional inquiry?"

"Actually, no, no, it's not. It's, um, . . . it's personal. It's something I'm struggling with . . . myself."

I watched muscles change in her face. Her mouth softened, and the tendons along her jaw slackened. Fine lines erupted alongside her eyes. She said, "Yes, it did. It included other people sometimes. We were active swingers long before we were married."

"And it didn't . . ." Some questions are harder to ask than others. Those seemed to be the only kind I was asking. Or trying to ask. I wasn't doing a bang-up job.

"Didn't what?"

"Cause problems? For the two of you? In your marriage? Fidelity, and trust, you know? Feelings weren't hurt?"

She shook her head. "Far from it. This may sound funny, but it was all about trust for us. Mark knew every man I was involved with sexually, and vice versa. We each had total veto power over the other's partners. What we did enriched us." She glanced back to make sure Zach was still engaged with his Legos. "This is a hard thing to explain. Sex with other people brought us closer."

"It did?"

"Yes."

"It helped with trust?"

"No. We had trust going in. Honesty. Respect. That never wavered."

I was perplexed the way I'm perplexed by Stephen Hawking. The words he uses are English, but after one or two paragraphs I feel like I'm reading Armenian. Same thing right then with Holly. The arithmetic of the coupling was simple enough. Two plus two equals four. I shouldn't have been so mystified by the equation. But I was.

"Trust?" I said again, and then I sighed away some of my exasperation. "I wish I understood it better. I really do. It seems that . . . with you being . . . and him . . . I just don't quite get it. I'll think about it some more, though. I will."

"I appreciate that. I appreciate that you try to understand. Some people don't. Most people don't."

"Artie?" I said.

She laughed. "Artie, indeed. Have a happy

Thanksgiving, Detective. I'd invite you to join us for supper, but under the circumstances . . ."

"Of course, of course. Artie wouldn't be happy I was there. You, too, Holly, you have a good holiday, too. Don't let Artie ruin it for everybody."

I pivoted to leave but stopped and looked over my shoulder. She was still at the door.

"Would Mark have been okay with Sterling? As a sexual partner for you? Just curious."

The face she made was rueful. "No. No, he wouldn't. Sterling is . . . firmly on the wrong side of the Brad Pitt line. That's where Mark's comfort level stopped. At the Brad Pitt line."

She leaned out the door, took a step toward me, and touched her lips to my cheek. That was good-bye.

Carmen waited for me to get settled, pull my seat belt on, and start the engine before she said, "Holly seems like a nice girl. I'm sorry I got off on the wrong foot with her."

I smiled at the irony. "She is a nice girl. My mother maybe wouldn't think so, but she is. She's nice."

Carmen didn't want anything to do with my comment about my mother. Wise on her part. "Did you get what we needed?" she asked.

"To decide if Holly's in danger? I don't know. How about we'll decide that together? Let's go someplace, and I'll tell you what she said, and we'll put our heads together and decide if we should spend Thanksgiving hanging around South Bend waiting for Sterling or whether we should spend it doing something else."

"Do you want to go back to the Days Inn? We can

talk there. There's some kind of coffee shop on the corner."

"Nah. I don't think so. Where's the campus from here? I'd like to see that. That way you can tell your dad you've been there, and . . . anyway, I've heard some interesting things about the basilica."

FIFTY-FIVE

ALAN

Dawn broke on Thanksgiving with a cold front blowing furiously over the Divide. The pressure change was preceded by winds that caused the big panes of glass in the living room to hum ominously. I wasted a few minutes standing on the warm side of the humming glass watching the morning sun light up the sky and reflect off the quartz crystals embedded in the granite planes of the Flatirons.

Special.

I'd awakened with a plan. My plan was to make a plan. I tracked down an index card, no lines, and listed all the things I had to do that morning. Most of the items on the list were domestic—*Grace, bath! Dogs, walk*—or culinary—*Turkey, clean & dry.* One was fantasy—*Bike ride??* And one was business—*Gibbs?*

Although I wasn't usually a list-making guy, I felt better knowing that I had a battle plan for the day, which promised to be convoluted, and enjoyed a flash of empathy for my old college roommate, who had always carried an index card with a to-do list in his shirt pocket. When each list's tasks were completed, he would immediately grab a fresh card and scrawl a single line at the bottom: *Start a new list.*

With Diane's admonition about hurdling in my head, I began to leap over the items on my list one by one. I'd made a good head start on the day's complicated kitchen preparations before Grace announced, loudly, that she was ready for her holiday to begin.

Midmorning Lauren joined Grace and me in the kitchen. Lauren had managed a few hours of sleep after her pool-playing marathon, and her mood was softer than I'd seen since the previous weekend. I could see my wife reemerging from the nefarious cocoon of Solumedrol in which she'd been imprisoned. It felt great. She sipped some juice and coffee and offered a couple of gentle suggestions about my cooking techniques, and our little core-family-size turkey found its way into the oven just about on time.

That's when my pager informed me that someone had left me a message at the office. I picked up the phone and checked my voicemail.

Gibbs. The number she'd left was for her cell.

I excused myself from my girls and called Gibbs back from the living room, adopting an office demeanor before I spoke my first words. The wind had quieted to less than gale force, and the glass had ceased humming. The sky was as clear as my daughter's conscience, and the mountains were close enough to touch. I said, "This is Dr. Gregory."

"Hi, it's me. Gibbs. Thanks for calling back. I'm up in Vail."

At that moment I was gazing vaguely southwest toward Vail. Fifty miles of mountains and one imposing Continental Divide stood in the way, but I was pretty sure I was looking almost exactly in the right direction. Between here and there, cake-batter clouds seemed to be shadowing all the high valleys. "You're safe?" I asked. It wasn't a great question, but it was better than my first impulse, which had been to ask "Was it windy up there this morning, too?"

"I wanted someone to know where I was. In case something happens. You know, in case Sterling shows up."

That thought gave me a chill.

"Safe House is open on holidays, Gibbs. I'm happy to make a call for you."

"The nice hotels were all sold out. I'm in a crappy place by the highway. Do you hear the noise? The trucks going by? Sterling would never look for me here." She giggled. "Never."

Just for the record, I thought it was important to remind myself that crappy hotels in Vail aren't exactly like crappy hotels in Baltimore or Detroit. I told myself to imagine a cheap cabin on an expensive cruise ship.

"You're okay?" I said.

"Yes, I am."

"I appreciate that you checked in with me. We're set for Monday morning, right? Same time?"

"Sure, yes. I'll be there. Do you know where Detective Purdy is? Is he coming home for the holiday? I haven't heard from him. I'd feel much better knowing he was close by."

The purpose of a psychotherapist is not—is not—to provide information to a patient that is unrelated to her care. The fact that Sam was in South Bend was definitely unrelated to Gibbs's care.

"I can't help you with that," I said.

"If you hear from him, would you ask him to call me? His cell phone isn't working. I can't reach him."

"It's not an appropriate role for me. To deliver messages to people for you. If I'm going to prove helpful, it's important to recognize the unique nature of our relationship." My voice was even, but I was thinking, *I'm not your damned errand boy.*

I caught myself. Why was I so annoyed? Was this high school revisited? Was Gibbs playing Teri Reginelli, wondering if I knew where she could find my friend Sean?

And was I reacting now the way I reacted then, by being a spurned fool?

If that's what was happening, that was countertransference. Textbook countertransference. It was not a pretty picture.

She huffed, "I'm not asking for a big favor, Alan. Just pass along the message, please."

"I'm sorry, but I can't do that."

Clinically, I was standing on solid ground. Communicating with a patient about the location of one of my friends was not an appropriate therapeutic role. But experience had taught me that when countertransference melded perfectly with what appeared to be appropriate treatment, danger often ensued.

"You *won't* do that," she corrected.

"Okay, I won't do that. It's not an appropriate role for me. That you're asking me to do it might be important in terms of understanding some of the issues we've been discussing in your therapy. We can talk about it more during your appointment on Monday."

"Am I being dismissed? Is that your way of telling me that you and I are done talking for now?"

"Gibbs, I'm glad you're safe. But I think anything that is not an emergency can wait until we meet on Monday morning."

"If Sterling shows up and knocks on my door, I'll call you. That would be an emergency, right? My murderous husband at my door? You'll be able to find a couple of minutes to chat about that, right?"

She hung up.

I thought, *That went well.*

Forty minutes passed before I realized what I'd missed. I'd completed one basting cycle with the turkey and was about to go back for the second when it hit me out of the blue, even though I hadn't spent the interim consciously thinking about either Gibbs or her phone call.

The important clinical issue wasn't that Gibbs wanted my help tracking down Sam, that she apparently wanted to alter the nature of the therapeutic relationship so that my status devolved from helper to mere errand-runner.

No, the issue was that she was so desperate to find Sam at all.

Why?

"Are you going to baste that thing or just stand there letting all the heat out of the oven?"

I turned. Lauren had bathed and put on some makeup, and what was much more important was that she'd put on a smile. She was limping, but she wasn't carrying the walking stick.

I closed the oven door and said, "Hi."

FIFTY-SIX

SAM

The Basilica of the Sacred Heart was a monument to something. Had to be. I spent ten minutes walking around inside the giant church like a tourist at some midwestern Vatican, but I couldn't decide precisely what the pompous shrine was intended to honor. God? I came from a tradition of simple prairie churches with inadequate heat in the winter and nonexistent air-conditioning in the summer. I wasn't raised to pray to a God who sat around in heaven with His saints counting His cathedrals and basilicas like Midas counting his gold; a God who cared whether the glass in His windows was stained or the bronze on His altars was gilded.

Certainly not a God who gave a hoot whether Notre Dame beat Michigan. My old man once told me that if God cares who wins a football game while people are starving in Africa, we can all just give up. That hell on earth is just around the corner. My old man was not a genius, far from it, but he got that right.

Carmen was an observant lady. Being observant, she didn't waste any time before she asked why I seemed so interested in the massive pipe organ inside the basilica. I told her it was a thing I had, a fascination with organs and organ music. The truth was, I didn't know a division from a manual or a pipe from a stop. But it didn't make a whole lot of difference what I knew or didn't know: Carmen liked disco. I figured arguing musical taste with the woman would be about as fruitful as trying to teach a dog to gargle.

All that mattered to me at that moment was that the precise location where Holly and Sterling had had their profane tryst was going to remain their secret, and mine, and maybe God's—that is, if during their coupling He hadn't been too occupied watching the Notre Dame–Michigan game or hadn't been totally blinded by the quasi-Gothic glitz of His Indiana basilica.

Memory told me that one of God's commandments to Moses had to do with coveting thy neighbor's wife, so I was assuming that He maintained some interest in marital fidelity and duly noted the fact that Sterling and Holly had fornicated in front of His fancy pipe organ.

Carmen and I moved back outside and stood for a moment beneath the vaulting spire that dominated the front of the basilica. I said, "I hope God cares what happened to those four women, and I hope He cares what happens to Holly Malone and to Gibbs."

She touched my hand. "Feeling philosophical, Sam?"

I couldn't tell whether my hand was cold and she was all heat or vice versa. But the thermal contrast between her flesh and mine had all my attention. I said, "Kind of, I guess."

Carmen had listened carefully to my edited version of Holly's story—I transformed it from an X-rated melodrama to a suggestive PG-13 and totally omitted any reference to the Basilica of the Sacred Heart—on the way over to the Notre Dame campus. I was ready to hear her thoughts on how we were going to spend the rest of our day.

"Is she in danger?" I asked. "What do you think?"

"Maybe."

I laughed. The campus, deserted for the holiday, chewed on my guffaw and spit it back at me in fractured echoes.

"Well," I said, "that settles it."

Carmen laughed, too.

Our hands were still touching. The top of my hand rested against the side of hers. It was either an accident, or it wasn't. I figured that was just the way we had planned it. Total deniability. Know this: Cops are better at deniability than just about anybody but politicians and corporate executives.

Carmen grabbed two of my fingers and tugged me away from the church. When I chanced to return the pressure, she pulled away and stuffed her hands into the pockets of her coat. I did the same.

Didn't mean a thing.

She yanked us back to the work we were doing. "Let's assume that the way Sterling met Holly is similar to the way he met the other women. Can we do that?"

"Not Louise, the stewardess."

"Flight attendant."

"Don't get me started. I liked stewardesses. I liked waitresses. Turns out I'm not so fond of flight attendants and servers. Why is that? Sterling met Louise on a flight she was working, right? Isn't that the story? And he met Holly on the Internet, right? But I don't think it really matters. I don't think the meeting-them part is as important as the sex-with-them part."

"You're probably right. He met them. By chance, socially, at work, on the Internet—whatever. He met them. He made a point of meeting them. And he had sex with them."

"I don't think it's that simple," I said. "The sex with Holly wasn't . . . pedestrian. She made it clear that that was important. Not only to her but to him, too. He wasn't just into infidelity, he was into . . . sexual adventure. He was into women who might be as adventurous as he was."

"This another interest of yours, Sam? Like pipe organs?"

With the tease, her voice tingled a little.

"Don't make this more difficult than it already is for me."

"Holly's that adventurous?"

"Mmm-hmm," I said. Not only did I not want to violate Holly's confidence, I didn't want to have to repeat her story out loud to another human being. Especially not another human being of Holly's gender.

Carmen could tell. She Cliff-Noted the thing for us. "He met them, he gauged their interest, and he joined them on some sexual adventure. So why are four of them dead?"

"We know some things about Louise and Holly, right? We know they both survived their first sexual encounters with Sterling. Can we assume that the other women did, too? That there was an initial encounter—mutually satisfying—and that he went back a second time, or a third or fourth, and that's when he killed them?"

We covered a good chunk of dormant Notre Dame turf before Carmen answered. "Yes, for now we can assume that. We almost have to."

"That means that Holly's now in danger. Pure and simple."

"Maybe," she said.

"Maybe?"

"Sam, nobody was looking for Sterling when he killed these other women. He had the cover of anonymity. Now? He has to assume that we're after him."

"Is this devil's advocate time?"

"The risk factor has changed. He has to think that some cop—somebody like you and me—doesn't believe he drowned. If I'm him, I'm lying low."

"Why? The Georgia cops think he's dead. My guess is that your superiors have already suggested you go home, too. Or even ordered you back to work." Her eyes confirmed my supposition. "I bet you're using vacation days right now, aren't you?"

"Yes, I am."

She could have lied to me. Would've been easy. I said, "Sterling might think he's home free, Carmen. That this is like a free play in football, you know? After an offsides call?"

"We still don't know his motive, Sam. And we don't know where Brian Miles fits."

She was right about that. We certainly didn't know

where Brian Miles fit. But the possibilities concerned me. I said, "Half the collars I get I never understand what the idiots were thinking, Carmen. Criminals are goofy."

"Goofy? Is that a Colorado word?"

"Nope. Minnesota." Intentionally, I said Minnesota the natural northern way, accentuating the "so" syllable so that it became "soooo."

"That's what that accent is? Minnesota? That's where you're from?"

"The Iron Range. That's up north."

"Interesting," she said.

"Not really."

I wasn't sure she was going to let it rest there.

She did. I was impressed.

Ten more steps. I asked, "Do you think they call this the Quad?"

"Don't know," she said.

On the way back over to Holly Malone's neighborhood, Carmen said, "Since I left San Jose, this is the most time I've spent with another cop without being asked why I left town without my pension."

"Some things are personal." I was thinking about Sherry and me, but I was also thinking about Alan and that bug in his office, and about Sterling and Holly and their time down near the pedals of the pipe organ. Secrets? They don't mean shit. "You want to tell me what happened before you changed jobs, that's cool. You don't, I understand completely. I'm sure you had your reasons."

Traffic was light on the streets of South Bend.

Everybody was either watching football or cooking a turkey or taking a nap or playing with nieces or nephews or grandkids that they hadn't seen in way too long. In a perfect world I wouldn't be spending my holiday driving through the streets of some strange midwestern town with a California cop who liked disco.

In a perfect world Simon and I would be cuddled up in front of the TV making fun of the Detroit Lions.

But in the imperfect world where I spent most of my time, being with Carmen wasn't the worst of alternatives.

Carmen seemed to read my thoughts, sort of. "This your first holiday by yourself?"

"My wife took our kid to see her parents."

"Yeah, right, that's the reason you're alone. And I left San Jose because I like the beach."

It was a good comeback. The traffic light changed to red over the intersection in front of me. I thought of running it—mine was the only car in sight—but I braked instead. I tried to think of something smart to say back to Carmen, but nothing came to mind.

"It's mine," Carmen confessed after we'd been sitting at the light for a while. "My first holiday without my daughter. And it's not going to be the last, either."

I admitted something to her that I hadn't even admitted to myself. "Probably won't be my last, either."

She touched my knee. A quick little fingertip thing. There, and then gone.

"It's easier to be working," I said.

"Yes," she agreed.

I pulled into the parking lot of a gas station so we could both use the john. As we walked inside, I was thinking that Carmen and I had covered a lot of important emotional ground in that one block of West Angela Boulevard Road in South Bend, Indiana, and we'd done it without using too many words.

If damn Alan had been in the backseat, he would have made us jaw on and on until we reached the Canadian border and probably wanted to kill each other.

Until we definitely wanted to kill him.

I wondered how he was doing with his problems. The office thing. How Lauren was feeling. Whether that thing he'd made for his big dog was still keeping her tongue off her paw.

I'd call him later on, after I called Simon, probably just about the time they were sitting down to their turkey dinner.

FIFTY-SEVEN

ALAN

Lauren was trying. She was really, really trying. As I cleaned up the kitchen counters and readied Grace for her afternoon nap, I knew that behind my wife's beautiful closed lips her white teeth were busy biting down on the tip of her soft tongue over my various venial sins of omission or commission in the kitchen or the nursery.

I could tell that she was grateful for the way I was picking up the domestic load. And I was grateful for her diligent effort at smoothing out the speed bumps that figurative boatloads of Solumedrol had injected into her mood.

While Grace slept, Lauren and I snuck in a quickie. The urge surprised both of us, I think.

An embrace became a kiss became hands beneath shirts became a jog to the bedroom.

It was amazing to me how tentative two married people could be with each other while they were rushing headlong into compressing a familiar, intimate act into an unfamiliar window of time after an extended period of tension. While we were stripping each other naked we were simultaneously sprinting across a field of eggshells. Thankfully, we reached the finish line before the time limit, which, of course, was Grace's awakening.

In the naked moments after—naked both literally and figuratively—Lauren said, "You know Dennis, right? He's one of our paralegals."

"Sure." Dennis Lopes was happily gay, buff enough to be selected Mr. January on a firefighters' calendar and, as far as I could tell, solely responsible for the fiscal well-being of Ralph Lauren's clothing empire. In a field that's replete with professionals who have more agendas than a cut diamond has facets, Dennis was a hell of a nice guy who said what was on his mind.

Nonetheless, I couldn't fathom what he was doing making an appearance in our bed at that particular moment.

While I considered the destination of Lauren's segue, I couldn't help but notice that her diet of IV steroids was beginning to turn her usually svelte frame more Rubenesque.

"He was walking between the Justice Center and the Court House earlier in the week, and he went down Walnut."

Dennis was a fitness nut. That he walked, rather than drove, between the two county buildings was no surprise. "He went right past my office," I said.

"Yes." She paused. "He was on the opposite

sidewalk, and he saw Jim Zebid park his car and walk into your building. He mentioned it to me yesterday."

Instinctively, I pulled the sheet up to my waist. But I didn't reply.

She went on, her tone full of caution. "I hope you're not seeing him for therapy, babe."

"You do? Why?"

From the way she blinked—she held her eyes closed for a split second too long—I could tell that she had been hoping that Jim had been in the building to see Diane, or even to visit the funny Pakistani man who ran his software empire out of our tiny upstairs, and that she no longer had the luxury of that illusion.

"Jim and I have a history."

Reflexively, I teased. "Like Muhammad Ali and Joe Frazier?"

"What?"

I stopped teasing. "Yes, I know you have a history. I know you've beat him up a few times in court. That assault thing at Crossroads comes to mind. The one where his client was claiming self-defense after he threw a hot dog at the counter girl at Orange Julius."

"That's not what I mean," she said softly.

"What do you mean?"

"Lots of things happen at your office that you don't tell me about. Your work, your patients, right? Confidential things?"

"Of course."

"Me too. There are lots of things that go on at the Justice Center that I don't tell you. Things I know because of my position that I shouldn't, or can't, share with you. You know that?"

"Yes."

"Well, one of them involves Jim." She stood and began to pull on some clothes. "I wish you weren't seeing him."

From my earlier reaction, she knew that I was.

"You sound serious."

She opened her purple eyes wide and forced a sick smile. "I am. I wish you knew what I knew."

I stood, too, and began to pull on some boxers. While I did, I worked out the choreography to a little two-step that would allow me to tell Lauren something important without telling Lauren anything at all. All I said was "That problem I told you about at my office? With the bug?"

She was in the process of pulling a camisole over her head. "No?" she said into the silk. "He's not . . . Don't tell me he's . . ."

Ethically, I couldn't respond to her question. Practically, we both knew I didn't have to.

She turned her back to me while she tugged a thick cotton sweater over her head. I admit I was having trouble staying focused on the topic at hand. Steroids or no steroids, I still liked her ass.

"Alan, you need to call Jon Younger. Today, at home."

Jon Younger was an attorney friend. He handled civil matters. Like, say, malpractice.

I said, "On Thanksgiving?"

She sat on the edge of the bed and began to slide her legs into some fleece tights. "Yes."

"Why?"

"Because I don't know what Jim might have planned."

"Planned?"

"Look at me," she said.

I did.

"Your first appointment with Jim? Was it after the Fourth of July?"

I blinked.

"That's exactly what I was afraid of."

Okay, Jim had come to see me for therapy after some confrontation with Lauren in the DA's office that occurred around Independence Day.

"Lauren, your history with Jim? He has reason to be . . . I don't know . . . angry at you?"

"Call Jon. He knows the background. Give him a heads-up. I'll feel better."

From down the hall came the not-so-soothing trill of a tear-laced "Mom Mom Mom." Grace tended to throw the few words in her repertoire together in unfettered strings, oblivious—or disdainful—of punctuation.

Emily stood at the sound of Grace's call, and her paw umbrella immediately *clack-clacked* on the wood floors.

Lauren said, "I got Grace."

I said, "I'll get some tape. I got Emily."

Lauren and I and the two dogs all ran into one another in the doorway on the way out of the bedroom. Lauren hugged me and said, "I'm really sorry."

She took off for the nursery.

The gravitas of Lauren's alarm about Jim Zebid wasn't quite registering with me. I didn't see anything about the mess I was in that couldn't wait until Monday. Interrupting Jon Younger's Thanksgiving to warn him that I had a pissed-off patient didn't make much sense to me at all.

*

While Lauren played with Grace, I made a different call, to a different attorney. I called Casey Sparrow.

Casey was a criminal defense attorney. She was smart, brazen, and fearless. She had a head of red hair that she'd had no more luck taming than most prosecutors had had taming her.

As I punched in the long string of numbers, I knew that an even longer rope of electron activity would be carrying my voice up thirty-five hundred feet of the Front Range to Casey's rustic home on the Peak-to-Peak Highway below the Continental Divide.

"Casey? It's Alan Gregory."

"Oh, no. Not tonight. Who is it this time? You or Lauren?" Casey had once defended Lauren against murder charges. That chain of events had started with an after-hours call not too unlike this one.

"Don't worry, neither of us has been arrested. Listen, I'm sorry to call on Thanksgiving, Casey."

"But?"

"Do you have a minute to gossip with me?"

"Gossip?" Her voice went suddenly girly. I imagined that she curled her legs beneath her and stripped an earring from her ear to get more comfortable with the telephone.

I stepped out onto the deck and closed the door behind me. "Yes."

"My partner's family is due for dinner any minute. You can have me until they arrive. After that I'm going to be the best damn hostess in the high country."

I didn't waste any time. "You know Jim Zebid?"

Hesitation. Then, "Yes." The yes wasn't the least bit girly. The yes was almost totally "oh shit."

"Something happened with him and Lauren last summer."

"We're gossiping, right?" she asked.

"That's right. That's all this is, just gossip."

"Lauren won't tell you, right?"

"Right."

"I shouldn't, either."

I knew she probably shouldn't, but I shut my mouth while she did whatever carnival act she felt she needed to do to juggle the moral aspects of her dilemma. Given her role with the defense bar, I figured whatever Casey knew about Jim and Lauren she knew because of courthouse gossip. Thus, her hands weren't tied with the same ethical twine that bound Lauren's.

Gossip is gossip.

Casey said, "Okay. I heard . . . I heard she turned him in to the Supreme Court last summer for disciplinary action."

"For?"

"Serious stuff."

I said, "He's still practicing law."

"These things take time."

"What did he do?"

"Do I have to?" Just a little girly.

"Unfortunately."

"He had a client who was accused of forgery, a petty thing. I don't know the details, but I don't think the facts are important. Lauren was prosecuting."

"Yes."

"Leave me out of this, Alan."

"You know I will, Casey."

"The rumor is that . . . hell. In lieu of legal fees, Jim was *schtupping* the guy's wife."

I was speechless.

I heard a doorbell ring in the background. Casey said, "Oops, got to go pull on my hostess's apron. Jim's defense, by the way, is that it was her idea. His client's wife's. She proposed the bargain. Have a good Thanksgiving. Best to Lauren."

"Casey?"

"Yes."

"Thanks, and good luck with Brenda's parents."

She laughed. "I'll need it. Domestic, I'm not."

I clicked the phone off and stared out toward the mountains south of town. The sky that enveloped the mountains near Eldorado was the color of an old quarter. The wondrous rich colors of autumn were almost gone; the beiges and grays and blacks and whites of winter filled the entire landscape from mountains to plains.

Jim Zebid's first appointment with me had taken place during the beginning of August. In the intervening weeks he'd never mentioned anything about an investigation into his conduct. He'd certainly never mentioned a conflict with my wife.

Why had he come to see me? I hadn't been sure before, but I'd been working under a clinical assumption that it was because his chronic anxiety was becoming increasingly dysphoric.

That old assumption was mutating into something new. I was guessing that Jim had been hoping to trap me into doing something that could be construed as malpractice so he could get even with Lauren.

Now he had me by the balls. And I didn't see a way to free them from his grasp.

FIFTY-EIGHT

SAM

"Somebody's going to see us sitting here and call the cops."

Carmen and I had pushed the seats all the way back on the Cherokee. We were parked on the same block as the night before, diagonally across from Holly Malone's house. But this time we were a couple of houses farther away. It wasn't a neighborhood where people sat in cars parked on the street. Inconspicuous we weren't.

"That's always a risk on this kind of stakeout, Sam."

"This is different, though. Usually you and me, we're the cops. Here we're persona non grata."

"Okay, you're a Craftsman-style expert, and you speak Latin. What do I have on my hands here?"

I went through the list in my head: Fat-ass cop. Iron Ranger with man-boobs. Schlub whose family dumped him for the holidays. Post-MI jerkface who's running around the country like he has the heart of a teenager.

Don't know why, but right then I reminded myself that Gibbs liked me. It helped a little, as sad as that fact was.

"I am what I am." Until the words were out of my mouth, I didn't realize I was quoting Popeye.

Carmen tried hard to swallow a laugh.

I laughed first. She followed immediately. "Go ahead," I said. "Say I'm a complete idiot."

"A cop who's a Renaissance man. Quick as a wink from Frank Lloyd Wright to Popeye—I'm impressed."

"You done?"

She was wiping tears from her eyes. "Yeah, I'm done. Almost. So what are we looking for exactly?"

My neck was as far out as I was planning on sticking it. "This was your idea, Carmen. Remember?"

She reached into her bag and took a reprinted five-by-seven from her purse and stuck it to the center of my dashboard with some gum I didn't even realize she was chewing.

The photo was of Sterling. He and his buddy Brian looked like a couple of male models.

"Who names her kid Sterling?" Carmen mused.

I didn't know the answer to that question. "He's pretty, right?" I asked. "Holly called him pretty."

Carmen gazed at the picture as though she'd never really looked at it before. "Yeah. He's pretty-boy pretty."

"Not your type?"

"No, unfortunately, he is my type. My type—historically speaking—could best be described as 'assholes.' And from everything I hear about his life until the moment his rental car crossed that bridge over the Ochlockonee River, Sterling Storey was an asshole. Is an asshole."

"Assholes?" It wasn't much of a response, but it was the best I could do.

"Sad as it sounds, that about covers it. If I'm into a guy, he's going to turn out to be a bona fide asshole."

"Assholes have bona fides? Like diplomats?"

She found that pretty funny. "The ones I fall for do. I only take them in if they're credentialed." Her laughter stopped as fast as it started. "That's what happened in San Jose. My asshole that time was a judge. He had credentials up his wazoo."

Carmen had pushed open the front door. I walked in. "Yeah? What did he do to you?"

"My daughter and I had just moved in with him, were just getting settled in his house. I was in love." She spread out the lone syllable of "love" so that it sounded like a crowd. "She called me from school, said she'd forgotten her calculator—it was one of those fancy ones with all those buttons, you know? I gave her a hard time about her irresponsibility and then I went home to get it for her. I'm a softy."

"He was there?" I asked. The fact that he was there was necessary to the story, but it wasn't sufficient to explain walking away from a pension. I knew there would be more.

"With my daughter's best friend's mother. I'd introduced the two of them at a volleyball game a couple weeks before."

Nasty situation. But it still wasn't sufficient.

"On the stairs of all places," she added. "He was doing her from behind."

Interesting detail, though it didn't compare with what I'd heard about Holly and the basilica. But that wasn't it, either. "It got ugly?" I asked.

"You could say that. I went berserk—I could take what he was doing to me, but what he was doing to my daughter and her friend? Shit! I screamed the woman's naked ass right out of the house, but that was just a warm-up for what I wanted to lay on him. I started yelling and cursing—did I tell you I have a temper? Well, I do. And he took one step forward and . . . the asshole hit me. A hard slap right across the face. It was such a shock, it took me a second to recover, but then I started up again, and he slapped me again, harder still. I couldn't fucking believe it."

"That's when you should've left, huh?"

"Would have been better, yeah. But I didn't, I wasn't ready to walk yet. So I started yelling all over again. He made a fist, showed it to me—shook it at me, really—and came at me again."

"You shot him?"

"You already know this story?"

"No. But I know if you just beat the crap out of him, you'd still have your pension, and you wouldn't be living in Orange County."

"I shot him."

"Nuts?"

"Foot. Nuts was tempting, though. Real tempting. Think I might've gotten time for shooting him in the nuts."

"He's still on the bench?"

"Of course." She sighed, the exhale carrying a full cargo of cynicism. "He was indifferent to hurting me, Sam. He didn't care. About the affair, about the slaps, about the pension. None of it. He didn't care."

"How's his foot?"

She smiled just a tiny bit. "He doesn't play squash anymore."

Across the way a car pulled to a stop in front of the Malone house. An SUV, one of those little stubby Lexus SUVs that were scampering all over Boulder like Japanese roaches. I hated them less than I hated the really big ones, the Fords and the Cadillacs and the Lincolns, but I hated them nonetheless.

No particular reason. I just did. Actually, it was one of the few things that my friend Alan and I agreed upon.

"I bet that's Artie."

"Who's Artie?"

"The brother-in-law I told you about. He's an asshole."

Carmen perked up. "Really?"

"Not your kind of asshole, I'm afraid. No bona fides, and I suspect that Artie's the kind of asshole who doesn't like his women to be packing heat."

She sat back again. "Ahhh. One of those."

While we chatted, I was checking the parade of clowns climbing out of the little silver Lexus. Artie had been driving, no surprise there. A slightly older, severely less perky version of Holly climbed out of the front passenger seat, and three way-too-well-behaved, way-too-well-dressed children exited the rear.

Carmen said, "No Sterling in that bunch."

"Afraid not. We wait." I touched her hand. "Sorry about San Jose."

"Yeah."

Twenty minutes later I said, "Shit."

We'd been silent the whole time, and Carmen was startled by my exclamation.

"What?" she asked. She was staring out the windshield as though she figured she'd missed something important at the Malone house.

"I forgot to turn my phone back on. Damn." I hit the little on button, and the phone came alive and immediately started probing the atmosphere for a cell tower to mate with. Once the slutty little thing had finished getting intimate with some new anonymous electronic partner, I checked my voicemail.

The first message was from Simon.

"Hey, Carmen," I said. "Give me a minute? I want to call my kid."

"Sure, be good to stretch my legs. I'll walk around the block again, see what I can see."

Simon and I talked football and relatives and hockey and snowmobiles—that part was new for us; he'd never ridden one before this trip—for about three minutes, which was about all the conversation he could ever manage on the phone. But the contact with him eased something inside me that desperately needed easing. When he was saying his version of good-bye, he asked if I was going to be at his grandpa's in time for turkey, and the question almost sliced me in two. In my heart I felt that awful sucking thing you hear when the cranberry sauce is sliding reluctantly out of the can.

To distract myself from the reality of the fact that I was in South Bend and Simon was up in Minnesota, I went back to my cell phone and scrolled through the other messages.

Lucy, just wishing me a happy Thanksgiving.

Yeah, you too.

And Gibbs. Sounding a little frantic, letting me know she was in Vail. I tried her back but didn't get an answer.

No call from Alan. That surprised me.

Carmen climbed back in the car. She was shivering just a little. She should have worn her coat.

"Anything?" I asked.

"Nothing. No Sterling, no Brian."

I said, "Gibbs called, left me a message. She's anxious. One of us should be watching her, you know."

I expected Carmen to disagree with me. She didn't. "Probably. She's as much at risk as Holly is, but she wasn't as cooperative about being watched as Holly is. Gibbs should be in Safe House."

"Yeah, she should. Maybe Holly should be, too." I liked that idea. Hell, if we could talk Holly into going to South Bend's version of Safe House, I could drop off Carmen at O'Hare and maybe—just maybe—get to Minnesota before Simon crawled into bed. I could read him a Bialosky or two, and he could explain to me what he found so fetching about that little bear.

But Holly wasn't about to go to Safe House. Part of me knew that a part of Holly was enjoying the current situation. Where sex was concerned, she was a roller-coaster, bungee-jumping freak. In this situation there was more than enough danger to get her sexual heart really pumping. Add in a heavy dose of anticipation—it was clear that anticipation stirred something in her that had been dormant in me for a long, long time—and for her this could be almost as big a rush as sneaking into the pope's bed in the Vatican.

Carmen and I cooling our heels out here on the curb meant that there were strangers watching Holly's every move and, even better for her, the possibility of judgmental Artie walking around any corner. Yep, the setup was almost as good as that afternoon in the Basilica of the Sacred Heart.

All that, and a turkey in the oven, too.

No Native Americans. No Pilgrims. But nonetheless, for Holly it had the makings of a Thanksgiving to remember.

The dashboard clock informed me that it was exactly three minutes after four o'clock.

Why was that important? Sometime in the last couple of hours, a world or two away from South Bend, Mary Ellen Wolf had carved a long slender knife through the crisp skin on the outside of a beautiful Georgia turducken. After a little downward pressure—it would take just a little because after eighteen hours in a slow oven those nested birds would be as tender as a grandmother's whisper—the sequential beauty would be revealed. Turkey, duck, chicken, followed by some dark andouille, and then all the glorious components of oyster stuffing.

There are times in life when you just know that the train has left the station without you and that it's not coming back around, ever. A county fair and a girl you could have kissed. A job and a promotion you might have had. Some friends in a beat-up old car and a trip you might have taken.

Twins, and a meal you might have eaten.

The Wolf sisters and that turducken were going to haunt me for a while. I was 110 percent sure about that.

A foot away from me Carmen was doing something with her fingernails and a sharp wooden stick. Sherry did the same thing occasionally, but Sherry doing it never captured much of my attention. Carmen doing it did. She distracted me even more when she started humming the melody of one of those tunes she'd sung the night before at bedtime in the Days Inn.

FIFTY-NINE

ALAN

While the turkey was resting on the cutting board prior to carving, Lauren asked me if I'd spoken with Jon Younger.

"Maybe after dinner," I said. "But I'm still not convinced this can't wait until Monday."

She kissed me. "Call him. Please."

Dinner? The turkey was dry, the gravy a little salty, and the cranberries overcooked, but the caramelized Brussels sprouts were perfection, and the merlot that Lauren had picked was as supple as a young dancer. Jonas, our neighbor Adrienne's son, and his nanny joined us for the meal because Adrienne was taking call at the hospital. Grace made it through the entire affair without a meltdown, and Lauren fought her steroid malaise with a determination that was inspiring.

The dogs slept like dogs.

It was a pretty damn good Thanksgiving.

Lauren and I cleaned up the kitchen together. I grabbed my pager off my hip a moment after I started the dishwasher and promptly excused myself to make a couple of phone calls. Five minutes later I tracked Lauren down at the pool table in time to watch her rerack the balls and begin to fondle the white cue ball in a way that made me just the slightest bit jealous.

I said, "Our guests are gone?"

She nodded. "Jonas was approaching a cliff at high speed. We thought he should have a mattress under him when he went over it."

I pointed at my pager and said, "Emergency, unfortunately. I have to go into the office for a couple of hours."

She narrowed her eyes. "Yeah?"

I said, "Yeah."

She didn't believe me.

She leaned over the table and with a single powerful stroke turned the triangle of pool balls into a physics lesson in vectors.

I didn't make the third phone call, the crucial phone call, until I was in my car on the way downtown to my office.

"Jim? Alan Gregory."

"Alan. This is a surprise."

"Are you out somewhere, Jim? Am I disturbing your dinner?" The truth was that I didn't really care whether I was intruding, but feigning politeness was called for, and I was feigning politeness.

"I'm with some friends. We just finished. What's up?"

"It's about the problem with . . . your client's secrets. I have some information that you should know."

"I'm listening."

"I'm not comfortable going into it on the phone. Could you drop by my office later on? Maybe five o'clock?"

"On Thanksgiving? This is necessary?"

"I think you should know what's going on. Some of what I want to talk with you about other people already know, so I'd like to bring you up to speed as soon as possible in case some of it becomes public, Jim."

"Really. Five o'clock?"

"I'm heading into the office now, and I have an emergency—something with another patient—that I need to take care of first. She and I should be done by five at the latest."

"See you then," he said.

When I arrived in downtown Boulder, I detoured into the parking lot of one of the banks on Walnut near Fourteenth and withdrew the maximum amount that was permitted from an ATM. My plan required cash. Quite a bit of it, actually.

A few blocks farther west I pulled down the driveway of the building that held my office. She was waiting for me on the steps that led up to the French doors at the rear of the building.

"You got the money?"

I flashed the thick pile of twenties.

"Let's go, then, get this done. They're holding dessert until I get back. My sister makes a sweet potato pie that . . ."

Tayisha's words just faded into the night.

"Shouldn't take long?" I asked.

"Nope." She smiled at me in a way that made her sparkling white teeth jump out of the darkness. "My boss never hears about this, right?"

"That's right," I said.

"Then we're on. Where's my baby?"

SIXTY

SAM

Only one other house on Holly Malone's block seemed to be having people over for the holiday celebration. As far as Thanksgiving was concerned, this was a neighborhood of guests, not hosts.

Carmen and I took turns dozing off for the next couple of hours. On one of my turns awake I walked around the block, not so much because I expected to find anything going on as because everybody had been telling me that it was good for my heart to get my pulse up every once in a while.

I was beginning to suspect that Carmen was good for my heart, too, though the fact that she was sleeping right beside me in the car was distracting me in ways that left me uneasy. The minutes passed especially slowly as she napped, but it was okay. I spent a portion of the silent hours lost in a familiar cop reverie about evil, an evil that I felt was hovering over that South Bend neighborhood like a dark cloud in still winds.

Somewhere around six o'clock Carmen and I got

confused about whose turn it was to nap. The second I opened my eyes I knew something didn't feel exactly right. It took me longer than it should have taken to realize that she, too, was snoozing.

"Activity," I said.

Carmen's eyes popped open. "What, what?"

"Activity."

The activity was the arrival of a minivan, an older Plymouth that had those tacky fake wood panels on the sides. It hadn't been washed since water was invented. The minivan had parked right behind the little Lexus, so our view of the ensuing disembarkation was partially obscured. Still, I could tell that a small crowd was forming on the sidewalk.

"The other sister," I said.

With some wonder in her voice, Carmen said, "My, she's fertile. Look at the size of . . ."

I counted five kids congregating on the sidewalk, but anyone who was shorter than three feet or so in height probably remained invisible to me because of the angle and the intervening Lexus.

"Two adults?" I asked.

Carmen said, "Yes. One mom and one dad. One, two . . . five kids. Or six? What do you get?"

I counted again. "I get six. How old is Holly's sister? She tell you that when you talked to her yesterday?"

"If this is the one I think, she's five years older than Holly. Jeez, Sam, think—that poor woman has been pregnant almost every other day of her life since her eighteenth birthday."

The members of Holly's oldest sister's brood were dressed like kids, in sharp distinction to Artie's offspring, who were dressed as though they expected a relative to die during dinner and Artie wanted to be certain they were prepared to attend an immediate funeral.

The newly arrived posse broke ranks as they moved toward Holly's front door. Running. Laughter. Teasing.

"Wait," Carmen said. "I get three adults now."

"Yep, me too. The blonde is Holly's sister?"

"I guess," Carmen replied. "Who's the other one, then, the woman with the dark hair?"

I didn't answer. Holly answered the door, and the passel of nieces and nephews funneled inside, followed by the blond woman and then the rotund brother-in-law with the big smile. Everybody got either a hug or a kiss or both. The woman with the dark hair stood patiently on that classic Craftsman-style porch holding a covered dish, waiting for her turn to arrive. Once her relatives were safely inside the house, Holly stepped out to speak with the woman. Holly's head was tilted to one side the whole time.

After listening for about thirty seconds, Holly took the woman by the elbow and guided her farther from the door. They talked for another minute or so, their faces only a foot apart.

"A friend? Neighbor?" Carmen conjectured.

"Maybe." I didn't want to come to any conclusions at that point. I wanted to observe.

The covered dish finally changed hands, some final words were spoken, and the woman stepped down from the porch without a hug or kiss from Holly. She walked down the sidewalk away from the house, which was also away from me and Carmen. Holly hesitated a second at the door before she stepped back into the house. Had she looked our way before she went inside? I wasn't sure.

I figured she figured I was close by.

I checked my cell phone to make sure it was on. It was.

"Want me to follow her?" Carmen asked.

She was talking about the covered dish lady. That didn't surprise me. She was asking me what I wanted her to do. That did. "Don't think so. You're probably right. Just a neighbor."

Carmen said, "I'm getting hungry. You?"

"Always. You think maybe we could get Holly to bring us a plate? Her turkey will come out of the oven soon. I bet they end up eating around seven, maybe a little after."

She reached into her purse and offered me an energy bar. "You might get a plate, Sam. Not me."

I shocked myself; I took the bar. "If I get any turkey and stuffing, I'll share," I said. "Promise."

Six forty-five. Night had arrived under slate gray skies.

I said, "Turkey's coming out of the oven right about now. I'm going to do a stroll around the block again, see if I can work up an appetite."

It had been a joke, but Carmen missed it. She put a hand on my arm. "We wasting our time?" she asked.

"Probably."

"How long can we last? Just the two of us, I mean? Tomorrow morning? What then?"

I'd thought about that, too. "I'm hoping something new develops with the investigation, something we can use to get the local police willing to help keep an eye on Holly. If that doesn't happen, I'll go talk to Holly again, see if I can get her to go stay with one of her sisters in Chicago for the weekend."

"I know which sister I'd choose."

"Yeah. Artie doesn't seem likely to have a dominant good-host gene, does he?"

"I'm sorry about your holiday, Sam."

"Company's good, Carmen. That helps."

She didn't miss that I said that. Her hand was still on my arm. The pressure changed. "Sam? Before you go, call Gibbs. Do you mind?"

"I didn't think you were that attached to Gibbs's well-being."

"I'm not. I was just thinking that if Gibbs has seen Sterling in Colorado, then we're all done here, right? You and me, we can pack up and go someplace together and, you know . . . eat."

My heart hiccoughed during the hesitation at the end of Carmen's sentence. Missed a beat? Double beat? I couldn't tell. "I can do that." I pulled out my cell phone, fit my reading glasses on my nose, checked for Gibbs's number in the memory, and dialed. She answered after three rings.

"Hello," she said.

The sound of Gibbs's voice moved me like the refrain of an old song. I knew it wasn't right that it happened that way. But it did.

"It's Sam. Hey, how you doing?"

"Did Alan Gregory tell you to call?"

What was that about? "Nah. Just wanted to be sure you're safe. We haven't talked. Where are you?"

"Vail. A motel."

"Is it pretty?"

"Low clouds. It's okay."

"Here, too. Low clouds. Gray."

"I hear the South is like that sometimes."

She sounded cryptic. Maybe she was aggravated to be alone on the holiday in a motel. I could relate to that.

"I'm not in Georgia anymore. I drove north. I'm up in Indiana."

"You are? Why on earth would you go to Indiana? Where?"

"Currently, South Bend."

"Really? Do you have family there? Is that it?"

"No, my family's up in Minnesota for the holiday. I'm following up a long shot. A tip we got. Probably a waste of time. You're okay? You haven't heard from Sterling? Seen him anywhere?"

"I guess I'm okay. I feel terrible that my problems have kept you away from your loved ones on Thanksgiving. You shouldn't have to do that. I wish you'd just go get on a plane and go be with your family. I'll pay. That would make me feel better. Will you do that? Just go to the airport right this minute?"

"No Sterling?"

"No."

"Well, I'm fine, Gibbs. Don't concern yourself with me. You try to make the best of your holiday, but stay vigilant, okay? You'll do that? Keep an eye out for Sterling. Give me a call if anything makes you nervous?"

"I promise. Good-bye, Sam."

I closed the phone. "He's not there."

Carmen said, "Thanks for trying."

I'd stiffened up. Let's say pulling myself from behind the wheel to get out of the car wasn't one of the most graceful things I'd ever done.

Holly's house had a three-foot chain-link fence around the backyard. Since the house was on a corner, it was possible to get a real good look around the entire property by strolling the sidewalk. With ten kids inside I could hear noise and laughter from the house half a block away. I turned around at that point and retraced my steps toward the house.

On my first pass around the corner nothing had seemed amiss. On the way back, though, the latch on the backyard gate had been moved to a different position. The gate hook was one of those horseshoe latches that raise up to allow the gate to swing open and then slide back down to horizontal to lock everything into place. I was sure it was down during my first pass.

It was up during the second.

I crossed the street and phoned Carmen.

"It's me. The latch on the back gate. You know the one?"

"The chain link?"

"That's the one."

"Yeah, I know it."

"Was it up or down when you last came by?"

"Couldn't tell you. Why?"

"It's up now. I thought I remembered it being down."

"There's a houseful of kids in there, Sam. One of them must have run outside for something."

"I guess. Can you see it from where you are?"

She hesitated. "No, I don't have a good view of the gate from here."

"I'll get back to you."

I crossed back across the street, waiting in the dark shadows of a big tree I thought might be an oak, and I watched the rear of the house. Laughter, chatter, kitchen activity. An occasional child's yell. Just what you'd expect.

Nothing more, nothing less.

It took me a few minutes of watching to recognize that something was missing.

Holly.

Holly was missing. Her two sisters were making frequent appearances at the sink that was under the kitchen window. But Holly hadn't made a single appearance since my first pass around the corner.

Not one.

I felt a sharp tug just below my rib cage and reflexively reached into my pocket to find the little brown bottle of nitro.

As I rolled it back and forth between my fingers, I continued to stare at the kitchen window. It had been dark for a while. Now it wasn't.

I saw one blond sister. Then the other blond sister.

No Holly.

I listened to the cacophony of voices.

No Holly.

That wasn't right.

I checked my watch. Four minutes after seven. I figured it was just about time to carve the turkey. I was guessing the brother-in-law who wasn't Artie would be doing the honors.

I strolled closer to the house and leaned against the

corner of the detached garage that was about ten yards away across the little backyard. *Come on, Holly. Come on. Show your face.*

Talk to me.

I called Carmen again. "Holly go out the front door for any reason in the last few minutes?"

"No. What's up?"

"Maybe nothing. I've lost track of her."

"Sam, she's inside with her family."

"Yeah, I know that."

I flicked my reading glasses down, hung up, and searched for another number in my cell phone's memory. Found it.

Holly's number.

Four rings. Finally, a kid answered.

"May I speak to Holly, please?"

"Hold on," the child said. He or she threw the phone onto something hard. The resulting explosion in my ear was painful.

Come on, Holly. Come on.

A minute, a dozen different voices. A loud call of "Aunt Holly?" Another. Then, "Anybody seen Aunt Holly?"

Holly's voice anywhere in the mix? I didn't think so.

The child came back on the line, finally. "I can't find her. Can you call back, please?"

"Sure."

Just then someone shoved a dull knife up under my rib cage. Rotated it side to side. Did it again. Deep.

That's what it felt like, anyway. The pain took my breath away, literally. I did an inventory.

Pain in my neck or jaw? No.

Down my arm? No.

Sweaty? Yes, a little. Okay, quite a bit.

I unscrewed the top of the little brown bottle, popped a nitro under my tongue, and braced myself for the inevitable flush.

Here we go, I was thinking. *Here we go.*

SIXTY-ONE

ALAN

Tayisha was finished in five minutes.

She joined me where I was waiting for her in Diane's office.

"Don't be looking like your hemorrhoids are acting up," she said. "I won't charge you the whole thing. Tell you what, we'll make it . . . we'll make it two-fifty. How's that?"

For five minutes? I should have been grateful. Tayisha had cut her original price in half. It still seemed like a lot of money for five minutes of anything.

I started unpeeling bills. "I only have twenties. You know, the cash machine."

"We'll make it two-sixty, then. That'll work."

I finished counting to thirteen and held out a thick stack of bills. She snapped them from my hand, folded them once, and stuffed the wad into the back pocket of her jeans.

"The thing is going to work? You're sure?" Any enterprise that required me to turn over a large quantity of cash in total secrecy tended to leave me feeling a little bit anxious.

"I tested it; it's all good." She eyed me the way people eye a friend after he insists he can drive just fine after a night out drinking. "You know what you're doing, right? You're not planning something stupid?"

I shrugged.

"Figures. I'll be back next week to sweep the rest of your building. Just save the equipment for me. Don't rough it up; it's fine stuff."

"Sure," I said. "Thanks. I appreciate your doing this on Thanksgiving."

She patted the back pocket on her jeans. "That's a car payment. It's a pleasure doing business with you."

Diane's office, like mine, has a solitary French door leading out to the backyard. That's the way Tayisha left the building.

Five minutes later it was also the way that Adrienne arrived.

Adrienne was my neighbor, she was Sam's urologist, and she was, most important, my friend. I'd chosen her to assist me that night for two reasons. One, she was a conspirator by character. Her life as a respectable, and respected, physician was a cover for her true calling as an anarchist. Second, she was on call for Thanksgiving anyway and had spent a good chunk of the day at Community Hospital, which was only ten or so blocks away. Since I'd already fed her son, I knew I wouldn't be pulling her away from a holiday dinner with him.

She was dressed as though she'd awakened in

Boulder that morning and discovered the whole town had been moved to the Arctic. Scarf, hat, gloves. A down parka that made her look like the Michelin Man's little sister.

"This sort of thing doesn't happen to normal people, you know."

That was Adrienne's version of hello.

"I never claimed to be normal people."

"A bug? Somebody planted a bug in your office?"

"I'm afraid so."

"Do you know who?"

"I do. A lawyer."

She perked right up. "A lawyer? We're trapping a lawyer? Hell, I'll get naked with you for that."

"That won't be necessary, Adrienne." She would have. I had no doubt. I was more curious about the associative stream that led her to make the offer than I was about the prospect of seeing her *au naturel*.

She sat down on Diane's sofa and said, "What do you want me to do? If I get a page from the hospital, though, I'm out of here. Just so you know. Today I'm the catheter queen. Who knew? If the nurses can't thread the needle, they call me. Sometimes I don't do a single emergency Foley in six months of call. Today I've inserted three Foleys in five hours. Must be a turkey thing. Whatever it is, one more and I'm calling Guinness."

I didn't want to hear about any dubious urological records. Foley catheters made me squirm.

"You're going to play a doctor," I said.

"It's a bit of a stretch, but I can do that. What kind of doctor am I?"

"A shitty doctor who just screwed up a procedure."

"Hardly," she said. "Who's my patient?"

"You'll see."

Her face lit up. She'd started playing along with me in earnest. That was when I knew I had her cooperation. "Am I a urologist? Precisely what did this mystery patient come to me to have examined?"

"You're a Denver urologist, but you live here in Boulder."

"Which means I'm a Denver urologist with taste."

"You screwed up a vasectomy. You cut a nerve or something, made a guy impotent."

She shook her head at my ignorance. "Sorry, hon, but that's not exactly how the anatomy works. To make a guy impotent during a vasectomy, I'd have to use a tomahawk instead of a scalpel." She proceeded to explain the complex physiology of erections and the precise surgical maneuvers involved in completing a vasectomy in much more detail than I ever wanted to know. Erotic it wasn't.

"Once we get started in there, could you simplify it a bit, Adrienne? This is for a lay audience."

"Don't worry, even though your way is pure science fiction, I'll play along. But you'd better hope there are no doctors in the front row of the theater."

We rehearsed for a few minutes. I checked my watch. It was fifteen minutes after four o'clock.

I'd told Jim Zebid that I would be handling an emergency prior to our Thanksgiving evening appointment. If he was planning to eavesdrop on the emergency session, he'd be in place outside already. I imagined him sitting in a darkened car on Walnut Street with his receiving unit finely tuned and a pair of good headphones over his ears.

"You feel ready?" I asked Adrienne.

"Just show me the stage."

"This way, madame. Break a leg."

Adrienne whispered, "You know this would never happen in real life? Me screwing up a procedure like this?"

"I know. Goes without saying."

SIXTY-TWO

SAM

The rules of nitroglycerin are simple. If one tiny tab under your tongue doesn't make your chest pain go away in a few minutes, you throw another little white pebble into your mouth. The instructions don't tell you to pray, but if you're still caressing that minuscule brown bottle after those first few minutes of center-of-your-world, center-of-your-chest agony, then it's likely you've already made contact with whatever version of God that you consider might be the most influential.

I was sitting, leaning up against Holly's garage, when I popped the second nitro. As a general rule, standing and nitroglycerin go together about like beer and chocolate. Not too well. That's why I was sitting.

I started thinking about Simon. That freaked me out.

As a way of distracting myself while I waited for the second nitro to kick in and the pain under my ribs to ease, I refocused on Holly's house. Artie was at the kitchen sink. I didn't take him for a roll-up-his-sleeves, get-his-hands-dirty kind of guy.

But no Holly. Still no Holly.

My head was pounding. After the flush and the disorientation, the next side effect of nitro is the headache. An ice-cream brain freeze and a big bass drum. It's that kind of thing, and it comes on instantly.

Artie walked away from the window. One of Holly's sisters took his place at the sink.

Holly?

I phoned Carmen.

"Any sign of her yet?"

"Sam, where the hell are you?"

"Behind the house."

"You don't sound too good."

"A little indigestion."

"How can you have indigestion? You haven't eaten anything."

"It was probably that energy bar thing you gave me. My body's not accustomed to healthy crap like that. Any sign of Holly?"

I heard a car door open, then slam shut. I turned my head and spied the Cherokee, but I could only see the front end from where I was sitting.

"No," she said. "Nobody's gone in or out of that house." Her tone announced that she was pissed off.

I could hear her walking. First the sounds came through the earpiece of the phone, then gradually I could hear her footfalls through my other ear, the one that was uncovered. The steps grew louder, more determined. Finally, Carmen emerged above me. God, she was tall.

"I'm calling an ambulance," she said.

"No, no. It's getting better. I swear. The nitro's working. It is."

Was it? I couldn't tell. The pain wasn't gone. But I could almost breathe without gasping. That had to be a good sign.

I didn't want to get into another ambulance. Not on Thanksgiving. Not in South Bend.

She squatted beside me, adopting a posture that I knew I couldn't have managed after a year of dieting and daily yoga sessions.

She touched my face. "You're clammy."

"No, I'm Sammy."

She slapped me. A true little love pat.

"If you die out here after you talk me out of calling an ambulance, I swear I'll come to your funeral and piss on your grave."

"I'd love to see the surveillance tape on that."

She slapped me again.

The pain was easing. It was. The knife was out from below my ribs.

"I'm good," I said. "Just a little angina. Doc said I might have some angina every once in a while. That's what the nitro's for." The doc hadn't said that, but it sounded like something a doc might say.

She stared at me as though she didn't believe a word out of my mouth.

"I have a feeling Holly's not alone," I said.

"Don't change the subject."

"I'm serious. I think he might be in there. Sterling."

"Why?" Her solitary word was a simple question, but given its inflection, it was also a statement. The statement was *"Don't be an asshole. Not with me."*

Not now.

I explained about watching the kitchen window and about my phone call to the house.

"Okay, how would he have gotten in?" she asked. Her inflection? I recognized it. It was the one I used to employ with Simon when he was younger and he blamed mishaps around the house on his imaginary friend, Tank.

"Maybe he went in when everybody arrived, you know? He snuck in the back door when the family was at the front. Isn't that possible?"

"Anything's possible."

Carmen was staring at me, not at the house. She thought my sneaking-in-the-back-door scenario was about as likely as Gibbs going to Wal-Mart to buy her winter wardrobe.

"Or Holly might have let him in," I added.

"What?" she said. The tenor had changed. It was more like: Now you're saying something interesting. Tell me.

"She likes danger—risk might be a better word. We know that, right? Sexually speaking, Holly Malone likes risk. That was the whole thing with Sterling in the first place."

Carmen nodded. She completed my thought as though we'd been partnering for years, not hours. "And doing it with an accused murderer while her family is gathering for Thanksgiving . . ."

I visualized Artie's disapproving eyes. "Yeah, that sounds risky enough. That would qualify."

"How long since you've seen her?"

"Ten, twelve minutes."

We were both staring at the house. My eyes were

plastered on the window wells that led to the basement. That's where I figured they'd be, Holly and Sterling. In some room down there. For some reason I decided that it was the laundry room. An image of Holly propped up on the dryer began to develop in my consciousness until I shooed it away like some aggravating insect.

But like a yellowjacket in late summer, it came right back.

I was ready to move, to go inside the house, but I wanted Carmen to arrive at the same conclusion herself. While I waited for her to come around, I hit a speed-dial number on my phone. Lucy. "Hey, Luce. I just have a second. The feds ever find Brian Miles? . . . No? . . . Thanks. . . . Yeah, fine. Seriously. I'll call you in a bit." I hung up. "Miles is still missing."

Carmen nodded as though she expected the news. "You think they're together? Sterling and Miles?"

"Can't rule it out."

She said, "What about the car? Maybe they're doing it in the car. Have you checked the garage?" She nodded at the wall I was leaning against.

I felt stupid. I was so focused on the basement that I hadn't even considered the detached garage. And no, I hadn't checked the garage. I shook my head in response to Carmen's question, suddenly not wanting to risk having my voice carry through the bricks.

"Shall we?" she whispered.

I stood. My balance problems were gone. My headache wasn't.

Carmen hopped the three-foot fence as though it were the height of a curb. I stepped over using a more conventional scissors maneuver. Carmen's revolver was in her hand when she got to the side door of the garage. I pulled my gun, too.

I don't like my handgun. Some cops do. Some don't. I've never felt right with the damn thing in my hand. I'm a pretty good shot; that's not it. It's something more intrinsic that I've never understood. I'm more comfortable with a rifle or a shotgun pressed against my shoulder.

Carmen, on the other hand, held her Smith & Wesson with the comfort of a good cook holding her favorite knife over an onion. No ambivalence there at all.

Holly's vehicle was a late-nineties GM sedan. Through the hazy glass pane in the side door, I couldn't have identified whether it was a Pontiac or a Chevy or an Olds if my life depended on it. I could tell that it didn't seem to be moving—moving, as in rocking side to side.

Carmen turned the doorknob and entered the narrow garage in a single fluid motion that reminded me of a ballroom dance move. I was right behind her. Despite my adrenaline surge, I was thinking that I wouldn't want to be screwing in that car and have us burst into the garage with our guns drawn.

It could change a person's view of sex forever.

We covered the perimeter of the little rectangular space and the interior of the car in seconds and came to the same conclusion at the exact same time: The garage wasn't Holly's love nest.

"Okay," Carmen said. "I'm convinced. Let's go ruin a lot of people's Thanksgiving supper."

SIXTY-THREE

ALAN

As an actress Adrienne was a little over the top. I shouldn't have been surprised.

"Thanks for coming in to see me on Thanksgiving," she began. "I know it's a terrible inconvenience. The reason I needed to see you is that . . . I did something last week that . . . well . . . I can't get off my mind."

"I assumed it was important for you to have come all the way in from Denver." I realized my role in this drama was going to be entirely ad-libbed. And with Adrienne as the person responsible for hitting the ball over the net for me to return, I knew I was going to need to stay on my toes.

"I'm having trouble living with it, with what I did. And I don't know exactly what I should do next."

"Yes?"

If Jim Zebid was sitting outside listening, he was—thus far—hearing a pretty convincing presentation. If he was somehow watching, however, he wouldn't believe a word of it. When she wasn't choking down some laughter, Adrienne was leaning over, talking into the couch pillow like Maxwell Smart with his shoe phone.

"I was doing a vasectomy on Tuesday in my Cherry Creek office—I do a thousand of them, they're no big deal. First a little poke, a little cut, snip-snip, burn-burn—"

Burn-burn?

"—stitch-stitch."

"Stitch-stitch" I understood just fine. I was still stuck on "burn-burn."

"Burn-burn?" I asked. I shouldn't have asked—it wasn't germane to the trap I was setting—but I really wanted to know.

"Cautery," she explained with a frown.

"Cautery," I repeated. A rapid personal inventory didn't reveal any pieces in that vicinity that I would be eager to have fried during the "burn-burn" segment of her operation.

Adrienne went on. "During the procedure I cut one of the guy's nerves."

"You cut a nerve?"

"By accident, just after the first little cut. One of my snips? My hand slipped a little."

"Your hand slipped during a snip?"

"Are you just going to repeat everything I say? Is that all you're planning to do? I say 'my hand slipped,' and you add a question mark? I could go talk into a tape recorder and just play it back and add my own question marks, save myself a lot of money."

I glared at her. My nonverbal admonishment didn't faze her, though; she was having a great time.

"What did he say?" I asked.

"He doesn't know. I didn't tell him. How the hell would he know? You think guys watch while I do vasectomies on them? There are some things a guy likes to see done to his genitals, but that isn't one of them. You're going to have to trust me on this."

I almost said, "*You didn't tell him?*" but thought that another repetition might be too much provocation for Adrienne to ignore. Instead, I said, "It was an important nerve?"

That question cracked her up. She took five seconds to compose herself before she was able to say "Down there? They're all pretty important. That's what I hear, anyway."

It was my turn to swallow laughter.

"Is he going to be . . . impotent?"

"It's possible."

"Likely?"

"Maybe likely." She rolled her eyes.

"Won't he know you did it?"

"I'm sure he'll suspect I had something to do with it. But it'll be hard for him to prove. He's had trouble raising the flag before. And he knew the risks going in."

Raising the flag?

She ruffled a piece of paper. "You know what this is?"

I did, of course, but I said, "No."

"His phone number. I know I should call him. That's what I should do. That would be the right thing. To let him know what happened. But then the next thing I know I'll be getting served some stack of incomprehensible papers by some damn bloodsucking lawyer who'll make one little mistake seem like the assassination of King Ferdinand."

That last line—the World War I allusion—was pure ad lib. It was definitely not in the script. Not even close. I was tempted to ask Adrienne to defend Francis Ferdinand's posthumous promotion from archduke to king, but restraint was indicated and discretion ruled.

She leaned directly over the pillow and made a great show of ripping the paper into shreds.

"So you've decided not to call him?" I asked. That line was in the script.

"I've been staring at that number for two days. I have it memorized." That's when she recited the phone number in a lovely, melodic little singsong. She couldn't have delivered the line any better if she'd rehearsed it for days.

I mimed some silent applause for her benefit.

A beeper chirped. It wasn't mine, which was set to vibrate.

Adrienne responded to the interruption by diving at the little backpack/purse she carried and said, "Shit, that's my pager. I have to go, sorry. You've been . . . I don't know . . . 'helpful' isn't exactly the right word, is it?"

I sat openmouthed.

She grabbed her things and skipped toward the door. The skipping part wasn't in the script, either.

SIXTY-FOUR

SAM

"Back or front?"

I was standing with Carmen beside the gate in the chain-link fence in Holly Malone's backyard. Carmen had stopped my forward progress by placing her palm against my chest. To be more specific, her hand had come to rest on top of my left man-boob. A couple of inches below her hand my upper abdomen still ached from the angina or whatever it was. But the ache was dull, not sharp. I could live with it, I thought.

Figuratively, if not literally.

"The adults are all in the kitchen," I said. "We should probably just knock on the back door. We'll spook 'em a little bit, which is a good thing. And that way we don't have to fight through the whole bushel of kids at the front of the house." While I was speaking, I was also involuntarily sucking in my gut and tightening my chest muscles.

Carmen removed her hand from my chest. "You want the honors?"

"No, no. You go right ahead."

She pulled back the screen door and knocked. Artie opened the door with a carving knife in his right hand and a stern expression plastered on his face, as though he suspected that he'd just discovered that one of his dressed-for-church kids had snuck outside for something sinister, like fun, and he was planning to Jack-the-Ripper the child into submission as a lesson for the surviving siblings.

Through the open door I spotted Holly's two sisters lined up behind Artie. The other brother-in-law? Elsewhere.

Carmen said, "I'm Detective Reynoso. This is Detective Purdy. We'd like to speak with Holly Malone, please."

"I don't see any badges." For a moment I thought Artie might be a lawyer but quickly decided that he had merely watched a lot of TV. I was having more than a little trouble getting past the dancing-teapots apron he was wearing and the fact that he had his hands on his hips in some semblance of indignation. With the knife at the ready, he looked a lot like an angry, aging transvestite on a day that he forgot to put on his wig.

Carmen and I both flashed our badge wallets for Artie's benefit. All we offered was a bored, quick little flip/close. Nobody ever reads the damn things. I had forgotten mine one day in Boulder and just flipped open my regular wallet instead at someone's house. It turned out that my driver's license and a school picture of Simon worked just fine to get me in that door.

"Holly Malone, please." Carmen's voice was suddenly clipped into a no-bullshit tone that caused Artie to take a step back from her. "It's important. We spoke with her earlier; we know she's home."

The older of the two sisters appeared appropriately sobered by our presence at the door. She said, "A few minutes ago she went to take a quick bath and get dressed. I'll go find her."

With a what-did-she-do-now tone the younger sister, Artie's wife, asked, "Is she in trouble?"

Poor thing, she was actually asking Artie.

Before he could make a total fool of himself by pretending he knew how to answer her question, I intervened. "For something she did? No, ma'am. We just want to ask her a few questions."

Carmen leaned back toward me and whispered, "She's taking a bath, Sammy. I'm feeling kind of stupid."

"Yeah, well," I said.

I'd noticed that she'd called me Sammy.

But I wasn't feeling stupid. Not yet. There would be plenty of time for that later. The bath? What was I thinking about that? I was thinking, *What else was Holly going to tell her sisters? To please excuse her so that she could go down to the basement for a quick poke with a stranger who's probably a serial killer?* Tugging along immediately behind the locomotive of that thought came the unedited laundry room image of Holly on the dryer, followed by a cabooselike graphic still of what happened up in the organ loft after Holly and then Sterling climbed the stairs from the Chapel of the Reliquaries in the Basilica of the Sacred Heart.

Fortunately, all it took to make the prurient images vanish again was a quick glance at Artie in the dancing-teapots apron.

"Sir?" I said to him. "Feel free to go finish carving

your turkey. This shouldn't take long, shouldn't interfere with your meal." I smiled. "We came to the back door so we wouldn't alarm the children."

My suggestion about returning his attention to the turkey served as a reminder to Artie that he was holding a long thin knife in a provocative manner while speaking with a pair of police officers. He glanced at the blade, then at us. His face at that moment was priceless—he was the guy going through security at the airport who'd just remembered he'd forgotten to take his Mac-10 out of his carry-on.

Oops.

Artie slowly moved the knife behind his back, as though Carmen and I wouldn't notice he was still holding the thing.

Good move, Artie.

Sometimes I really love my job. Put them under enough stress, and most people are endlessly entertaining.

Big sister returned ten seconds later, breathless. For the first few moments after she reentered the kitchen, she couldn't make her mouth work. I had already started looking around for the basement stairs when she finally cried out, "I couldn't find her. And the bathtub was dry."

Carmen was halfway through the door. She demanded, "The basement stairs? Where are they?"

My cell phone rang. I should've been following after Carmen and grabbing my handgun in order to mount a search-and-rescue mission to the basement, but I grabbed the phone instead.

The caller ID? I held it at full arm's length from my aging eyes. What did it read?

To Carmen, I said, "It's Gibbs."

Carmen instantly recognized the possible implications. She stopped in her tracks and stared at me. Her big gun dropped from the ready position until it was pointing vaguely at my feet.

Artie's wife asked, "Who is Gibbs?"

"Yeah," I said into the phone.

"He's here, Sam! Sterling is here. Oh my God. Oh my God. Help me!" Gibbs was frantic.

I pulled the phone away from my ear, covered the microphone, and said to Carmen. "Sterling's in Vail."

Artie's wife asked, "Who is Sterling?"

Carmen said, "So where's Holly?"

The big sister said, "She didn't take a bath. The tub's dry."

I lifted the phone back beside my ear just in time to hear Gibbs's frenetic whisper, "Help me!"

SIXTY-FIVE

ALAN

The house was calm when I got home from the two-act farce I'd produced at my office.

The meeting with Jim Zebid had been brief and relatively cordial. He seemed surprised by my revelation that some of the same lapses in confidentiality that had been plaguing my practice were also plaguing my partner's practice next door. I went into a long explanation about the design of the soundproofing of the interior walls of the offices and why we had ruled out the possibility of eavesdroppers. I then revealed that my partner and I were planning to interview the couple who cleaned the offices for us the next day, and that we suspected that one or both of them may have found a way to get into our locked filing cabinets.

I promised to let him know the results of our inquiries.

He thanked me as he left. Truthfully? I didn't see a

sign that he was playing along with me. He was a better actor than I was.

I helped Grace into her pajamas and told Lauren to keep playing pool, that I would happily read stories to Grace before bed. I checked the charge on my cell phone battery, stuffed the phone into the pocket of my corduroys, and settled into the big chair in Grace's room to read. She picked the same books that she picked every night—she was in a phase where she liked the idea of cardboard characters popping up at her as she turned the pages. Her current favorite was a tall skinny book full of multicolored, pop-up monsters. We read it twice—I admit that I did most of the reading—and her delight was no more muted the second time through than it had been the first.

That's when the phone rang in my pocket.

I kissed Grace, lowered her into her crib, opened the phone, wrapped it hastily in one of my daughter's lilliputian T-shirts, dropped my voice an octave, took a deep breath, and said, "Yeah?"

"You don't know me, but . . . but don't hang up."

"What?"

"How's your sc-scrotum feeling? Your . . . balls?"

"What the— Who's this?"

"Just listen to me. The doctor who did your vasectomy? She—"

"What the— How do you—"

"No, no, listen to me. She screwed up when she did it. She clipped a nerve. No, snipped, snipped a nerve. You may be . . . impotent. You need to get a lawyer, sue her ass. She's . . . out to get you."

"Who are you?"

"A friend. You can . . . trust me."

My friend hung up.

I did, too.

While I tried to still my pulse, I kissed Grace again, told her I loved her, and made sure her favorite stuffed toys were within her sight.

I walked back out to the pool table, told Lauren that Grace was tucked in and waiting for a good-night kiss, and then plopped down on the sofa in the living room.

The lights of Boulder twinkled in the dark at my feet.

Emily waddled in, her stubby tail darting around on her butt in a parody of wagging, her paw umbrella clacking on the wood floor with each fourth step. She stood in front of me for a moment, looked me right in the eyes, and then lowered her head onto my lap. Prior to joining me in the living room she'd apparently just completed a visit to her water dish, and her long beard was dripping with enough water to wash a small car.

She was telling me that things were going to be all right.

Her instincts about such matters were usually infallible, but this time I couldn't figure out how it was all going to turn out okay.

SIXTY-SIX

SAM

"Calm, Gibbs. Calm. Did you call nine-one-one?"

"Yes."

"What did you see?"

"In the parking lot—he—he got out of his car. I saw him."

"Sterling's outside? Is he alone?" I said, repeating some of what Gibbs told me so that Carmen would know what I was hearing. Carmen was standing three feet away. I watched her eyebrows jump up at the news about Sterling. "You're not sure. The lights in your room, are they on or off?"

"On."

"Turn them off. The TV, too. Shhhh. Quiet now."

"I'm scared."

"The door's locked, right? The chain, too?"

"Yes. Help me, Sam. Help me."

"Do you hear sirens yet?"

"No, no!"

Carmen's eyes told me she was puzzled, the kind of

puzzled usually reserved for those times when you think you just heard your cat ask you for a beer.

"Shhhh," I told Gibbs. "Quiet voice. What floor are you on?"

"Um, uh. Third. Third story."

"Third story. Get on the floor, okay? On the far side of the bed, away from the door. Can you do that?" As soon as I told her to get on the floor, I remembered that she was on her cell phone and wished I'd sent her into the bathroom.

"Yes, yes. Help me."

"Sirens yet?"

"Uh, no. No."

The commercial section of Vail is a few blocks wide, a few dozen blocks long. That's it. A cruiser in a hurry could get from one end to the other in seconds. Where were they?

"You're on the floor, right, Gibbs?"

"Yes."

"You're doing good."

"Come help me."

"I'm in Indiana, Gibbs."

"I know. Come help me."

"Someone will be there any second."

I heard pounding. Gibbs said, "He's here, Sam. He's here. Oh no, oh no."

"Someone's there?" I mimed the act of knocking so that Carmen would know what Gibbs was saying. "It might be the police, Gibbs. Stay still. If you know it's him, run for the bathroom."

More pounding.

This time Carmen mimed the act of knocking. Then, inexplicably, she pointed down toward the floor.

For a long moment I was confused by Carmen's charade and then, suddenly, I got it.

Holy shit.

I lowered the phone from my ear, and my pulse rocketed as though my heart had a turbocharger on it.

I moved the phone back to my face and said, "Gibbs? Stay quiet until you're sure who it is. Don't open the door. Shhhh."

With the pad of my thumb firmly over the phone's microphone, I leaned over to Holly's oldest sister and whispered, "Get the kids and get out of the house. Now! Front door, everybody. Got a cell?"

She nodded.

"Call nine-one-one when you get outside. Tell them cops are in the basement and guns are drawn."

I looked at Artie.

His mouth was open. His brain wasn't.

He was staring at the big gun that was filling my hand.

"Artie?" I said, careful not to raise the hand with the pistol. "Put the knife down on the counter and follow your sister-in-law. Go on, get out of here."

Artie followed my directions robotically. I raised the phone back to my face.

"Gibbs, are you there?" I asked.

Nothing.

Shit.

SIXTY-SEVEN

ALAN

Maybe it was something she saw in my eyes, maybe it was something else entirely, but Lauren didn't even flinch when I told her I had to go back out on Thanksgiving night to see someone. She caressed my neck for a moment, kissed me in the lingering manner that more often than not constitutes an invitation, pulled away only an inch, and said, "Be careful. Please." Both dogs stayed by her side as I headed out the door.

Since my errand required that I pick something up at my office, I parked the car there before I strolled the short distance over to Pearl Street. I didn't take my usual pedestrian route, which would have led a block or more northeast in the direction of the Mall, but instead ambled westward toward the sleepy part of Pearl, the part that's on the side of Ninth nearest the mountains. The wind was gusting from Wyoming that evening, the collar on my coat was up, and my hands were stuffed in my pockets to thwart the chill.

I walked slowly, trying to find a reason not to do what I was about to do. Whatever that reason might have been, though, I wasn't able to walk slowly enough to find it.

My destination was a cluster of condos on the north side of Pearl that had been designed to mimic a grouping of Victorian row houses. Wedding cake trim, different on every home, was painted in colors that had aged to a palate that resembled the range of hues of an Easter basket. Lights from the waning moments of holiday celebrations brightened windows in about half of the units that I could see from the sidewalk on the far side of Pearl. From the way the numbers were running, I figured I would find the town house I was looking for at the west end of the front row.

The lights in that unit were on.

Each week, when Lauren injects a long needle full of interferon into her thigh to protect herself from a double-cross from her own immune system, she uncaps the needle and plunges it straight into her thigh. "Every second of delay makes it harder to do," she says. "No delay."

So I didn't delay at the door. I didn't want this to be any harder to do than it felt like it was already. I took my left hand out of my pocket, extended a finger, and touched the doorbell.

He came to the door quickly, within seconds. I could see the shadow of his eyeball as it darkened the peephole. He didn't open the door quickly, though. He stood behind the closed door and watched me, and watched me, and watched me through the tiny lens embedded in the door.

I checked my wristwatch after a while and began timing our little standoff. In other circumstances, with another person, I might have chosen a strategy other than dawdling, perhaps peppering the doorbell with repeated pushes, or maybe calling out, "Come on, open the door."

But not then. Not with him. With him I stood back a step and allowed him to see me clearly. Every couple of minutes I pulled my hands from my pockets and turned completely around so that he could be confident that I wasn't hiding anything behind my back.

Six minutes and ten seconds passed before he finally relented to some internal pressure I probably couldn't fathom and opened the door. When the time came, he didn't open it just a crack. He flung it wide open as though that had been his plan all along.

His physical appearance was a bit of a shock to me. He was wearing gray cotton sweats on top of a nylon running suit, had dark glasses over his eyes, and had a bandanna tied over his mouth and chin like he was Jesse James preparing to knock over a bank.

"Hello, Craig," I said. "I think I have something of yours. Can we talk?"

"You're the one," he said. "You're the one."

Craig didn't invite me inside, which didn't surprise me. I sat on the steps leading up to his town house while we talked. The whole time he stood a few feet from me with his back to the front door. He was more wary of me than he was during our office visits, but I'd anticipated that he might be. The therapy session that Sharon Lewis had busted in on and aborted late the previous afternoon was certain to take a considerable toll on someone like Craig, especially in the trust-your-therapist department.

Within minutes of sitting down on Craig's porch I reached a clinical decision about what I needed to do, but I didn't decide exactly how to go about doing it until another fifteen minutes passed. When I explained my thinking to him, Craig was so agreeable with my plan that I guessed he'd arrived at some version of it himself long before I'd arrived at his door. I'd hoped he would be cooperative, but I was prepared to do it the hard way if I had to.

His anesthesiologist parents lived in a lavish house they'd recently built a few blocks away on Third Street. To their credit, they both rushed to their son's home within minutes when I phoned and told them what I had in mind.

Craig chose to take an ambulance to the psychiatric hospital across town, not to ride over with his parents. Although I didn't understand his reasons, I supported his decision. Reluctantly, his parents did, too. When I phoned for the ambulance, I requested that a police patrol car come by, as well. I hadn't placed a person on a seventy-two-hour mental health hold for a while, and I had to ask the patrol officer for remedial instruction on how to go about it. Despite the fact that Craig was agreeable to being admitted to the hospital, I didn't want him changing his mind and discharging himself before he was stabilized by the combination of medicine and a safe, controlled environment.

I didn't accompany the Adamson family to the hospital. As the ambulance drove off, I turned my collar back up, stuffed my hands back into my pockets, and commenced the short stroll back to my office. I had a few calls to make to assure medical backup for Craig's admission and to get initial orders to the nurses on the unit.

I'd see Craig again the next day as an inpatient. I thought I knew where the psychotherapy session with him would begin. Craig had already admitted calling me that night about Adrienne's fake malpractice case. He'd denied, however, that the listening equipment that had been planted in my office belonged to him.

That troubled me. That's where I thought we'd start.

SIXTY-EIGHT

SAM

Carmen and I could have lost some important seconds by engaging in a how-could-I-be-so-stupid contest, but we mutually decided not to bother. We both knew it would have ended up a draw.

If the Malone home was a good example of the breed, whatever elegance and purity of design the Craftsman-era architects had built into the floor plans of their bungalows did not extend into basement layout. Holly's basement was a dark, confusing warren of tiny rooms with low ceilings. The aroma in the cellar was of moist concrete, standing water, and air freshener. I thought it was the same flowers-in-a-can Glade that Sherry liked to make such a show of spraying after I used the bathroom.

On our way down to the basement I was a few risers above Carmen. The stairs didn't squeak as we descended. Not a peep, which I thought was evidence of rather impressive construction.

Rooms opened up onto each side of the postage-stamp-size landing at the bottom of the stairs. We paused at the landing, our bodies touching at our hips. The phone was still at my ear. Once again I whispered, "Gibbs?"

Nothing came back into the earpiece. I shook my head at Carmen. She nodded and tilted her head to the left, so that's the direction we headed first.

She was still walking point.

Cellar noises? Nothing I didn't expect. Furnace sighs, plumbing burps, old-house creaks. But no more pounding. Above us the scampering of feet as children and parents rushed from the house had stopped.

The first room to our left was a furnace room with an alcove that had a workbench built in under a window well.

In the dark basement my eyes found shapes but no details. As I followed Carmen toward the door that would take us to the next surprise space in the maze, my foot brushed something on the floor that I hadn't seen. Carmen heard the noise I made. She stopped.

I crouched down and felt along the cold concrete surface with my hand.

I lifted a woman's shoe. A clog. Not really a clog; Sherry used another name for shoes like it, but I couldn't remember what. Why? I really didn't care.

Had Holly been wearing clogs in the kitchen that morning? I should have remembered, but the picture in my head of Holly preparing the turkey didn't go all the way down to the floor.

Carmen leaned over to touch the shoe. Feeling

what it was, she took it from me and set it aside. With her head close enough that I could feel her breath on my cheek, she said, "Let's go."

The next room was small and seemed to be full of stuff. Holly probably called it her storage room. But I could tell from the haphazard pattern of shadows that it was the place she stashed the junk she didn't know what else to do with. Storage is one thing. Sticking stuff in a room is another thing entirely. There's a big difference. Sherry did storage. I stuck stuff in rooms.

Carmen's eyes must have adjusted to the dark better than mine. She found a path through the stuff, and we were across that room and through another door in seconds.

The next room we entered was a bathroom. A window well provided enough light that I realized that "bathroom" was a generous description for the space. It was a tiny concrete room with inelegant plumbing and a couple of fixtures that existed in the time warp between modern and antique. Despite the shadows I could see streaks of rust on the porcelain surfaces of both the sink and the toilet.

Carmen reached behind her and held out her hand to stop my progress. Her fingers found me just below my belt.

It certainly stopped my progress.

Through the open door in front of Carmen I could see a square shape emerging from the darkness.

A washing machine. Maybe a dryer.

Here we go, I thought. *Here we go.*

*

I retraced all my steps to the landing at the foot of the stairs and opened the door that Carmen and I hadn't taken the first time. The room I entered was the largest room in the basement and was furnished with somebody else's things. A night-light spread a shadowy brilliance across its lowest reaches. From the looks of the bases of the pieces, I guessed that these were Holly's grandmother's things. Every one—sofa, chest, chair, table—was ornate, heavy, grandmothery.

Four long strides, and I was across the room and standing at the door that I was almost certain led into the laundry room. Carmen was waiting at the other door on the far side of the basement.

My role was straightforward. I was to keep anyone from exiting through this door until I went in on Carmen's signal. That was the plan.

From then on we would improvise. And hopefully try not to shoot each other in the process.

The phone call with Gibbs was over. I'd stuffed the cell back in my pocket.

My handgun was ready.

I was wondering precisely what the signal was going to be when I heard Carmen yell, "Police! Freeze!" and figured that was probably it.

I pulled open the door and stepped inside the laundry room in a flash, though it turned out there was little cause for hurry.

SIXTY-NINE

ALAN

It was a night of front porches.

Diane and I have an ancient oak swing on the porch of our building, and from half a block away I could see that it was moving to and fro in a tight arc. A solitary person sat smack in the middle of the seat.

I was guessing it was a homeless man. I pulled five bucks from my wallet, remembered what day it was, and replaced the five with a twenty. I held the bill folded in my hand. In my Thanksgiving fantasy the man would use the money to sit at a nice table in a nice restaurant and treat himself to a bountiful plate of turkey and stuffing.

The porch was in shadows. From the end of the driveway I couldn't make out the age or gender of the visitor.

Nor did I recognize the voice when he said, "I didn't expect to see you here tonight. You should be home with your family. I know I wish I was."

I stopped walking. "Excuse me. Who are you? Do I know you?"

The swing stopped moving, and the man stood. He was still in the shadows, but I could tell that he wasn't tall. "I brought you something. An explanation." He waved some paper at me. An envelope, maybe. "I thought it might help save somebody. I was just going to stuff it through the mail slot when I saw your car. Felt the engine; it was warm. I thought I'd take a chance that you'd be coming back."

"I still don't know who you are." I hadn't moved. I remained right where I'd been on the narrow driveway. Ten yards of drought-starved lawn and a border of unhappy euonymus separated me from the stranger on the porch.

He moved forward inch by inch, and with each inch the light from the streetlamps seemed to crawl up his body like water rising in a flood.

As the light moved up from his shoulders and began to paint his face, I said, "Oh my God."

"Hi," Sterling Storey said. "What a week it's been, huh?"

What did I think?

I thought, *Catch me.*

SEVENTY

At first, Holly didn't even notice the woman with the covered dish. The chaos associated with the arrival of her oldest sister's family for Thanksgiving dinner was demanding all of her attention. The woman with the dark hair and the perfect skin and the casserole waited patiently through a procession of hugs and kisses, waited until no one remained on the porch but the two of them.

"Holly?" she said.

"Yes."

"Remember your friend from church? From the basilica?"

Holly hesitated. Could she mean . . . ?

"He said to mention the organ."

She could. *"Uh, yes. I remember."*

"He's around the corner. Right this minute. He'd like to see you again."

She stammered, "I have guests."

"He knows. He wants to see you while they're here. In your house. He thinks it will be fun. Especially fun."

Holly took the woman's elbow and guided her a little farther from the door.

"Who are you? What do you want?" Holly emphasized "you."

"I want to watch. That's what I want."

"Watch?"

"At Notre Dame I was the woman in the purple suit. Remember me?"

Holly remembered. "My family . . . what—"

"Move them into the living room for a picture. Everybody. He and I will come in the back, go down into the basement. We'll know when, because you'll turn off the kitchen lights."

"And then . . . what?"

"Before dinner you excuse yourself, say you're going to take a bath. He'll be waiting downstairs. Me too."

At that moment Holly felt an explosion of anticipation. She felt it as she might feel the wind, or an ocean wave. It washed over her, covered her completely, engulfed her.

"Take this," the woman said, handing over the casserole.

"What is it?"

"Some music. Some directions. Put it on, and turn it on as soon as you get to the basement. I should go. Someone may be watching us."

Holly could barely breathe through the moist heat of expectation. She watched the woman go down the sidewalk and chanced a glance at the Cherokee with Colorado plates on the next block.

She went back inside. Fear?

Hardly.

Anticipation.

She peeked inside the casserole and saw the Walkman.

Her pulse shot way north of normal.

Once again she was off on an adventure. She was about to dash across the Brad Pitt line, again.

The family picture was a fiasco. Holly turned off the kitchen lights and herded everyone into the living room. Getting the ten children in place was like trying to get a bunch of houseflies to soar in formation.

Photos taken, Holly pulled the turkey from the oven, asked her oldest sister to remove the stuffing, and excused herself for a quick bath.

Instead of going into the bathroom, though, she scurried down the stairs, stopping halfway down to pull the headphones on and to hit the button on the Walkman marked "play."

Her voice, not his. The music in the background? Chant. Gregorian chant.

Nice.

"Bottom step? See the duct tape? Wrap a long strip around your head, covering your mouth. Good. Now do another. We're in the laundry room. Before you join us, take another strip of tape and bind your wrists. It's not easy to do, but I've done it. You can do it, too." Pause. "It's what he wants. What do you want?"

A few moments of silence, then:

"Are you ready, Holly? When you're ready, open the door to the laundry room. And come on in."

SEVENTY-ONE

SAM

I expected worse.

I was prepared for a whole mess of blood. I expected to find Holly's head bashed in—for some reason, that's how I thought she would be killed—but I was wrong. Holly's wrist and ankles were bound, and she was gagged. Duct tape. She was sitting on top of the washing machine, not the dryer, and her pose was absurdly proper, significantly less erotic than the laundry room loop that had been playing relentlessly in my brain.

A Walkman hung from the waistband of her skirt, earphones in place on her head.

Gibbs? She sat across the room in an alcove barely large enough for an orange plastic chair that would have been labeled for a buck at a yard sale and would probably have gone unsold at the end of the day. Her legs were crossed, left over right. She was gripping a kitchen knife with a five-inch blade—a good knife, she'd probably brought it from home—in her right hand. A cell phone rested on her lap.

She looked as lovely as she had the first time I met her. But that didn't matter to me at all this time. Not a lick.

Right.

"Let me go, Sam," she said. It was as though Carmen and Holly weren't even in the room.

Gibbs had two handguns pointed at her chest—mine and Carmen's—and yet she'd managed to make her request sound perfectly mundane, like she and I were out on a date and she was wondering if I'd mind getting her a beer.

"Drop the knife, Gibbs," I said. I'd like to say I barked the order. Or yelled it. But I didn't. I merely said it.

"If you don't let me go, Sam, I'll kill myself. I will. I'll plunge this right into my chest."

Where did my head go at that moment? For some reason I thought about those crazy people who destroyed art treasures in museums. Like the guy who took a hammer to Michelangelo's *Pietà*. I thought, *Gibbs, no! You can't!* But I also knew—instantly—that my silent protest wasn't about Gibbs, the person. It was about Gibbs, the lovely art.

Crazy.

"Drop the knife, Gibbs," I said.

She purred, "Come on, Sam. Hey . . ."

Carmen joined the discussion. She crowed, "Jesus H. Christ," took a little skip-step into the fray, and swatted the knife out of Gibbs's hand. The blade clanked against the wall and tumbled to the floor. "Cut herself? Shit! This princess? She wouldn't even use the wrong eyeliner on herself."

I kicked the knife even farther from Gibbs. I was feeling kind of stupid.

"So she gets to live," Gibbs said.

I assumed she meant Holly but didn't say anything at first. I thought it might be wise to leave the next move to Carmen.

Carmen immediately started the you're-under-arrest process with Gibbs, cuffing her and searching her and reciting the Miranda Rights to her like a bored schoolgirl spitting out the Gettysburg Address to a class full of kids who didn't really care.

I began the process of gingerly removing the tape from Holly's mouth. It wasn't coming off easily.

Miranda complete, I asked, "Why, Gibbs? Why does she get to live?" Part of me cared about the answer, part of me was trying to cover my embarrassment over the knife thing. All of me knew that whatever Gibbs said in reply would just be noise.

"Because you got here first. That's the only reason. If I had called you five minutes sooner, you would have rushed back to Colorado to save me. You know you would have, Sam. But you came in the house, you came down here . . . Timing. It was just a problem with timing." Her voice trailed away. "She wanted Sterling, you know? They all did. That wasn't the deal. One time only, that was the deal."

Suddenly I got it. I faced her. "Were you in the basilica that day, Gibbs? At Notre Dame? Up in the choir loft?"

Carmen stopped what she was doing.

I glanced at Holly. Above the duct tape, her eyes were wide.

Gibbs smiled. She actually smiled. "Of course I

was." She looked right at Holly. "Chanel suit? Purple? You remember me? She wanted him to come back again. She e-mailed him *again*. That wasn't the deal. She knew the deal. She'd agreed to it."

I got it all. Every bit of it.

"The deal?"

"Yes. The deal."

That's what I meant about the noise. My phone rang.

I checked the caller ID. Alan.

"Yeah," I said.

Alan's voice was full of rookie-cop wonder. "I'm at my office with Sterling Storey, Sam. You're not going to believe this: He says he thinks Gibbs has been killing all those women."

"Just a sec." I turned to Gibbs. "Guess what? Your husband survived the Ochlockonee. He's in Boulder, and he just gave you up to your doctor. Is that romantic or what?"

An army of footsteps erupted above my head. The locals had arrived to take over.

SEVENTY-TWO

The question of which jurisdiction was going to get first dibs on Gibbs would keep a whole lot of county attorneys across the country busy for a while. Other than hoping that Boulder didn't win that particular lottery, I wasn't invested in the outcome.

I spent a couple of hours answering questions for the South Bend police, who seemed to have suffered amnesia about their decision not to keep an eye on Holly Malone, and then I prepared to leave Indiana.

First I kept my promise and called Lucy, letting her know what had transpired in South Bend. She was astonished at the developments. She had some news for me, too, though: The feds had finally tracked down Brian Miles. They'd found him in a big suite at a fancy hotel in the Bahamas where he was on vacation.

Not surprisingly, Carmen had learned more about what had really happened than I had.

When I found her after my interview, she told me that it had indeed been Gibbs, in disguise, who had delivered the Walkman and the duct tape to Holly in the covered dish on the front porch of the Craftsman bungalow. Gibbs's pitch? She had promised Holly a visit by Sterling, who was offering a carnal encounter in the basement while the turkey was resting on the kitchen counter upstairs. Gibbs instructed Holly to wear the Walkman and follow all the instructions she heard to the letter, which included directions on binding and gagging herself with the tape.

Wow.

I told Carmen I was leaving town and offered her a ride as far as O'Hare in Chicago. She declined. She was determined to stay in South Bend in case there were any loose ends to tie up. What else? She didn't say so, but I think she still wanted to find that South Bend detective who had called her "ma'am" and then blown her off about Holly's peril. She wanted to help Orange County win the Gibbs Storey lottery. And she made me promise to tell her what really happened that day between Gibbs and Sterling in the Basilica of the Sacred Heart at Notre Dame.

Carmen and I ended up saying good-bye on the sidewalk outside the South Bend PD in one of those poignant moments that I haven't had many of in my life since I left college. I admit it crossed my mind that had I lingered a little longer in South Bend, Carmen and I might have had only one room that night at the Days Inn, not two.

That was the main reason for staying.

It was also one of the two main reasons for leaving.

The other?

Simon.

*

I filled the tank in the Cherokee and pointed it toward Minnesota.

I napped away most of the next morning in Angus's den, and then Simon and I spent a wonderful Friday afternoon arguing whether having turkey and cranberry sandwiches while watching college football the day after Thanksgiving was almost as good as having turkey and stuffing while watching the Lions lose on Thanksgiving.

I lost the argument. I didn't care.

Sherry and I talked after Simon was in bed for the night. We said what we had to say to each other in about five minutes. I gave Angus a big hug, declined his offer of a bed, and headed south on Interstate 35. I ended up spending the night in a Super 8 in Mason City, Iowa.

Things were feeling a whole lot clearer.

SEVENTY-THREE

ALAN

It was my first trip to Omaha, ever. Given that it was the Sunday of Thanksgiving weekend and given that I was flying standby, I felt lucky to get there at all.

A taxi took me to Sam, who was flat on his back in the University of Nebraska Medical Center. A Puerto Rican nurse named Yashira was being much nicer to him than he deserved. She was refusing to even try to find his "lost" car keys unless he arranged for somebody to drive him back to Colorado.

The somebody was me.

"It felt just like the heart attack. Maybe worse."

"That's what I've heard."

The day before, around lunchtime, Sam had started passing a gallstone he didn't even know he possessed and had driven himself to the emergency room in Omaha thinking he was having another MI. Two hours of agony in the ER provided enough time for the stone to move on, a one-night stay in the hospital for observation convinced the docs that Sam's heart was stable, and my presence in Nebraska motivated Yashira to search a little bit harder for his missing car keys.

While I was still trying to find my way out of Omaha, I summed up the obvious. "Kidney stones, gallstones, and heart disease. You're a picture of health, my friend."

"Stress might have something to do with it," he said.

"You think?" I replied.

"That, and the fact I'm fat. Though I might have lost a few pounds. Can you tell?"

Before I found the westbound entrance to I-80, we'd talked a little about Sam's day-after-Thanksgiving trip up to Minnesota, and I'd answered all his questions about Lauren's health and the long-term efficacy of Emily's paw umbrella. The Gibbs and Sterling Storey saga was a little more complicated, though; covering that ground took us almost all the way to Lincoln.

Sterling's story didn't surprise Sam. I'd started, of course, at the river in Georgia with Sterling's contention that he was washed downstream maybe a quarter of a mile before he pulled himself out.

"The Ochlockonee," Sam had said. "Tell me something. Did he really go down there to help that woman in the minivan?"

"He says he did, but who knows? I don't think Sterling exactly found God over the past week, Sam. He's still the same guy he was when he was flying around the country having extramarital sex with strange women."

"Not just extramarital: recreational. Hell, not just recreational: extreme."

"Yeah?" I was curious but decided to proceed without the details. "Anyway, an old man with a semi full of chickens gave Sterling a ride as far as Montgomery. He had enough cash with him to make his way back to Colorado to talk to Gibbs."

"He knew she was setting him up?"

"By then, yes. She basically told him when he was in Tallahassee. He says Gibbs is smart, and he figured she'd done a great job of pinning the murders on him. He came back to Boulder to talk with her, try to straighten things out, see if he could get her to admit what she'd done before your colleagues found him. When he couldn't find her, he came by my office to give me his side of the story, hoping I could help influence her to give herself up. Then he was going to see a lawyer on Friday, turn himself in, and try to get her picked up. That was his plan, anyway. What a mess."

"Did he know?" Sam asked. "What she'd been doing?"

"He says he didn't. In fact, with the exception of Louise—the woman in California—he didn't even know that any of the women he'd . . . you know, had these things with . . . were dead. When the women recontacted him to arrange a follow-up sexual encounter, Gibbs took the message. She was always the liaison anyway. That was her role."

"Her role?"

"She set everything up for him with the other women. And then she watched. She liked to watch."

Sam sighed deeply, as though he were trying to get something toxic out of his lungs. "She watched? She told you this?"

"I can't tell you what she told me. What I'm able to talk about I got from Sterling."

"There's something I don't understand," Sam said. "After all these years, why did this bust open now?"

"After their move back to Boulder a few months ago, Sterling decided he didn't want to be married to Gibbs anymore."

"Ah," Sam said. "So she was going to lose him anyway. All her efforts at eliminating the competition were for naught."

"Exactly. She was determined to make sure she didn't lose him to another woman, though."

"What was your part?" Sam asked me. "Why'd she bring you in?"

"I've been wondering about that. Clinically, I can't comment. But criminally? I think she needed somebody to help her play the battered wife card. She figured I'd do it." I sighed. "She figured right. And she wanted someone she could tell things to, somebody who couldn't tell the cops. And let's face it, indirectly she used me to get you involved."

"She needed a channel to the police. I obliged. Gibbs fooled you about where she was the whole time, too, didn't she?"

"She fooled me about a lot of things, Sam. I was in a better position than anybody to figure out what she was up to, and I didn't see this coming. I thought she was the victim in that relationship. I was blind to it."

"Me too," he said. "She's good at smoke screens, Gibbs is. She's so pretty, that's part of it." From Sam that constituted quite a confession. I waited, but he didn't elaborate. He repeated his earlier question. "But she fooled you about where she was?"

"Yeah, I thought she was in Vail."

"That's what she told me. You know something? Before cell phones? She never could have pulled it off. Flying to the Midwest while we thought she was in the Colorado mountains? Used to be a phone number meant a place. Doesn't anymore. Doesn't mean shit."

Sam seemed to need a moment to lament some loss of societal innocence. After a mile or so of silence I filled him in on what had really happened with the listening device in my office.

"So it was the lawyer who did it?" was Sam's reply to my story, as though he'd known it all along.

"Yeah. With his bug in place he'd overheard this other patient of mine—he's a really vulnerable guy—and then he talked him into doing some of the dirty work, but it was the lawyer who planted the bug and set it all up. He wanted to get even with Lauren for something that happened in court last summer. Figured he had a foolproof scheme."

"You turn him in?"

"I gave it all to Lucy. She's been great. I have some fences to mend with my patients, but . . ."

"You won't tell me the lawyer's name, but I'll see it in the paper, right?"

"Something like that."

"Will I be surprised?"

I thought about that for a moment. "No, not really."

"The other guy, the vulnerable one—how's he?"

I'd visited Craig in the hospital the day before. I said, "He's not doing too well."

"I'm sorry."

He sounded sorry. It made me think about the waitress in Gold Hill, the one whose hand Sam had been holding since her sexual assault in the back of the van on the way to the frat house on the Hill. Maybe Sam was thinking about her, too.

We made it all the way across Nebraska—it's a wide state—and were paralleling the Platte River on the stretch of Interstate 76 between Ogallala, Nebraska, and Julesburg, Colorado, before we got around to talking about Sherry. The conversation was a little cryptic at first.

"You want to talk about Sherry?" I asked.

"No," Sam said. "Not really."

That was the first installment in its entirety.

A hundred and twenty-five miles or so later I cut off I-76 at Hudson for the final westward push into Boulder. I could've spent the whole drive beating my head against the wall of Sam's stubbornness, but all I would have learned is how good it felt when I stopped.

Sam said, "In case you're wondering, I don't believe that talking helps."

I hadn't been wondering. But I was eager to hear his thoughts on the matter. "Yeah?"

"Sherry thinks talking about things makes them better. Round and round we go. Me? I don't think so. Words don't heal. Time? Maybe. Words? No."

I thought he was making a veiled editorial comment on my chosen profession, but rather than taking the bait, I waited to see where he'd go next.

I had to wait a while—about twenty miles—until

we crossed I-25 at Dacono. We were getting close to home.

Sam said, "Sherry and I are done. I'm moving out."

"You are?" I didn't have any trouble keeping the surprise out of my voice.

"Yeah. She's been seeing somebody."

"She has?" This time my voice was nothing but surprise.

"I've known about it. The affair. A guy came in to buy flowers for his wife, that's how she met him. He's a psych professor at the university. I followed him to work one day, that's how I know."

He'd emphasized the guy's profession, as though he wanted to spoil the air with the innuendo that the field of psychology had something to do with his problems. I wondered if I knew the man responsible for making Sam a cuckold. I hoped not.

"Did she know you knew?" I asked.

"No. I thought it was a thing. That it would pass. I still think it will pass. The affair's not the reason the marriage is over."

"What is?"

"Ask her? I'm a difficult guy. Ask me? I put up with a lot. Too much. She'd probably say the same, of course. That she put up with a lot from me. But I put up with a ton from her over the last few years. I did."

I recalled the tense visits I'd witnessed in the hospital. "What are you talking about? Criticism? What?"

His answer took a moment to compose. "There's a point where criticism stops and something else starts. Something more serious. More demeaning, damaging, you know? Somewhere near there was . . . us."

"Are you talking about . . . abuse, Sam? Sherry . . . did what?"

"Next topic, Alan. I said what I'm going to say."

Sometimes friendship means inquisitiveness, sometimes it means silent respect. I had a thousand questions. I asked none of them.

But Sam answered one that wasn't even on my list. "I almost had an affair, too. Over Thanksgiving."

I quickly catalogued the likely suspects. "Detective Reynoso?"

"Turns out we get along."

I glanced over at him. I was checking to see if he was joking. He wasn't. "Why didn't you?"

"Hadn't talked to Sherry yet. But . . . I've talked to her now, so who knows? California's not that far away. I like the beach."

I didn't know Sam had ever seen a beach.

"And you like Carmen?"

"Yeah, I do. Don't know how much that means. I loved Sherry. What good did it do?"

I hit the brakes to avoid running up on an old primer-covered Dodge truck that was pulling a long trailer piled high with hay.

"I'm sorry, Sam. About Sherry."

"Ever feel like you're playing the same music you were playing as a kid? When girls first became real? Where women are concerned, I don't know that I've progressed much in thirty years."

Sam's words transported me back to Teri Reginelli and *¡Dios mío, hay un hacha en mi cabeza!* I knew that the Gibbs Storeys of the world were still capable of capturing my feet in the quicksand of my adolescence, but I desperately wanted to believe that I had developed the maturity to pull myself back out. Before I had a chance to get lost any further in that old swamp, Sam yanked me back to the present.

"You know what? Sherry and me? We had a good thing. And then one day we didn't. It's been bad now almost as long as it was good."

"Simon?"

"We'll do okay with him. We will. We're not idiots."

"You want to run anything by me about his reaction to all this, I'm happy to listen."

"Yeah, thanks. If the phone doesn't ring, that's me."

I laughed.

"Marriage is a weird thing. Gibbs and Sterling—what was that? All the screwing around they did. And Holly Malone? The good Catholic girl from South Bend? Her and her husband? What were they up to with their shenanigans? You and Lauren seem like you're rock solid, but I know you're not. God only knows what sexual perversity the two of you are into."

I opened my mouth.

He held up his hand. "God knows, Alan—I don't want to."

The car lurched and hopped as we crossed two sets of railroad tracks. "You're allowed to hit the brakes, you know, before you hit the bumps," Sam said.

Metaphor? With Sam, I could never be quite sure. "I'll remember that," I said.

"I know you're not," he repeated. "Rock solid, I mean."

"It's a challenge, Sam. For us, for everybody."

"I'm glad we agree on that. Because I don't really want to talk about it after this."

I said I was sorry again about him and Sherry. He pretended to ignore it.

He said, "You see the papers? They found that woman who shut down DIA. She's from Boulder. Figures. I wouldn't want to be her."

Thanks to a brilliant moon the mountains were looming large against the night sky. The delta shapes of the Flatirons remained indistinct. It didn't matter. I could feel Boulder long before I could see it.

Missing Persons

for Lynn Nesbit

. . . *Peace is poor reading.*
– Thomas Hardy

A girl was missing.
In any other town it would have been local news.
Even here, on any other day, it might have been just local news.
But it wasn't any other town.
It was Boulder.
It wasn't any other day.
It was Christmas.
And a girl was missing.
Again.
God.

1

The fact that I was sitting with Diane behind Hannah Grant's office at 6:30 on a mid-December Thursday evening meant that I'd already lost the argument we'd been having since she yanked me out from behind my desk five minutes earlier. She killed the ignition on her Saab and summed things up for me anyway. 'We can't leave in the morning if we can't reach Hannah. It's that simple.'

She was right.

With only nine shopping days until Christmas, Diane Estevez and I were scheduled to make the short flight over the Rockies to Las Vegas for a weekend professional workshop – Diane, I suspected, was pretending to be much more enamored of EMDR than she really was – and Hannah was generously providing coverage for our clinical psychology practices while we were away. Without coverage, we couldn't go.

Diane had switched our Frontier flight the next day from noon to the cusp of dawn so that she could cram in a few additional hours getting intimate with some dice, and Hannah needed to consent to the slight change in plans. But Hannah – whose adaptive lassoing of her myriad OCD symptoms typically dictated that an unreturned phone call caused her a degree of psychological discomfort equivalent to the physical distress of a sharp stone in her shoe – had failed to return three different messages from Diane since breakfast.

'Is that her car? Do you know what she drives?' I asked. The only other car in the tiny lot was a silver Volkswagen Passat.

'Looks like hers.' Diane offered the comment with a slightly sardonic lilt, and I assumed that she was referring more to the car's pristine condition than to either its make or model. In stark contrast to the spotless Passat, Diane's Saab was covered in the gray-beige film that adheres to virtually every moving vehicle in Colorado after any slushy late fall snowstorm, like the one we'd had the previous weekend.

I stepped out of Diane's car and peered into Hannah's. No clutter on the console. No errant French fries on the floor. No empty Diet Coke can in the cup holder. In fact, the only indication that the vehicle hadn't just been hijacked from a dealer's showroom was a copy of *Elle,* still in its plastic sleeve, on the backseat.

The mailing label on the magazine read 'H. Grant,' and was addressed to the Broadway office. The code in the corner indicated that the subscription would terminate the following April. 'It's hers,' I said.

Diane had joined me beside the Passat. 'Hannah reads *Elle*?'

My own reaction was a little different; I was thinking, *Hannah leaves magazines in her car? Shame!* I said, 'I think you're missing the point. It means she's inside with a patient. She'll return your call when she gets a minute.'

'I don't know about that. I'm getting a feeling,' she said. 'And not a good one.'

'About Hannah?'

'A little, but more about Vegas.' Diane's tone was somber. She took her craps seriously. 'Let's go inside,' she said.

Hannah was a clinical social worker and her therapy practice was in one of the old houses aligned on the side of Broadway closest to the mountains, only a few blocks from the Pearl Street Mall. The cumulative force of more than a decade of migration by psychotherapists had allowed mental-health types to usurp most of that particular urban habitat from sundry lawyers and accountants who had previously set up shop in the houses – some grand, some not – in the row. The uprooted professionals had moved to less charming but eminently more practical spaces in the modern buildings recently erected to fill parking lots a few blocks away on Canyon Boulevard.

The back door of the single-story house was locked. Diane and I followed a flagstone path down the side past a hedge of miniature lilacs that stood naked for winter. We made our way to the front of the building and strolled up a few stairs into a waiting room that had probably been the home's original parlor. On the far side of the lamp-lit room a thirties-something woman with an astonishing quantity of frizzy hair was sitting on a green velvet settee reading a copy of *Yoga Journal* while munching from a bag of Cheetos. I noted that she checked her wristwatch after she glanced up at us.

I also noted that her fingertips were almost the exact same color as her hair.

'Which office is Hannah's?' I whispered to Diane. I'd never been in the building before. Hannah was one of Diane's close friends; I had no doubt that Diane knew which office she occupied.

'Down that hall on the left. The one on the right is Mary's.'

'Mary' was Mary Black, M.D., a psychiatrist who without benefit of fertility concoctions had given birth to triplet boys only a few weeks before, on Thanksgiving eve. Both Mary's extended maternal adventure and her extended maternity leave were in their earliest stages, which meant that Hannah was without doubt going to be working alone in the building for a while.

Diane stepped down the hall toward the offices. 'Look,' she said.

Stuck into the jamb of Hannah's office door were four folded notes. Two were addressed to 'Hannah,' one was addressed to 'H. Grant,' and one was intended for 'H. G.' Diane picked the one addressed to 'H. Grant.' It appeared to have been written on the back of a page from a daily calendar of unintentionally humorous quotations by the second President Bush.

'What are you doing, Diane?' I blurted. 'Those are probably from patients. You can't read them.'

Without even a microsecond of indecision Diane rejected my protest. 'Of course they're from patients. That's the point,' she said. She glanced at the first note, handed it to me, and said, 'Look, Hannah missed her one o'clock.' Next, she grabbed the paper that was addressed to 'H. G.' 'And see? She missed her four-thirty, too. How come she's missing all her appointments if her car's here? Huh? How the hell do you explain that?'

I didn't know how to explain that.

The other two notes were from patients whose therapist had stood them up earlier in the day. Hannah had apparently been missing her clinical appointments since at least nine o'clock that morning.

The woman with the orange Roseanne Roseannadanna hair appeared behind us in the narrow hallway. Despite the fact that she was balancing on tall, chunky heels, she still had to gaze up at an acute angle to look Diane in the eyes. 'Are you here to see Hannah?' she asked. 'I have a six-fifteen appointment. Every Thursday. She's never late.'

The woman's voice was part annoyed, and part something else. Concern? Fear? I wasn't sure. But her point about Hannah's reliability was well taken. Hannah's obsessiveness was legendary among her friends and colleagues. She was never late.

Never.

I'd begun tasting acid in my throat; I had a bad feeling, too. Though, unlike Diane's, mine had absolutely nothing to do with dice. I tapped lightly on Hannah's office door with my knuckles. My cautious incursion was apparently way too timid for Diane; with an NHL-quality hip-check she moved me aside and grabbed the knob.

The door slid right open.

2

Hannah's classic black patent-leather purse, as un-scuffed as the day it had been crafted, rested on the floor in the middle of the room. It stood up neatly, its arched handles perfectly vertical. But the bag was on the floor.

It shouldn't have been on the floor.

Diane apparently had the exact same reaction I had to the presence of the purse in the middle of the room. But since the distance between her cortex and her mouth was much shorter than mine, she verbalized her conclusion first: 'Hannah would never put her purse there.'

Diane meant on the floor. *Nope.*

In the middle of the room. *Never.*

What was certain was that Hannah had a place for her purse. A specific place. A correct place. I didn't know where she kept it. Probably in a drawer in her desk. Maybe someplace more esoteric, in her filing cabinet under 'P.' But in any circumstance that approached ordinary, she absolutely wouldn't put it on the floor in the middle of the room.

The rest of the office was neat. OCD neat, with one exception: Hannah's coat was tossed carelessly over the top of the desk. I noted the swirled torn paper from an open roll of LifeSavers licking out of one of the coat pockets.

Hannah's 6:15, the woman with the Cheddar-colored locks, was trying to peer past us into the office, but she was too short to manage a look over our shoulders. I felt her hand on my back and turned toward her.

I said, 'Hello, I'm Dr. Alan Gregory, one of Ms. Grant's colleagues. Why don't you have a seat in the waiting area while we try to figure out what's going on?' Not over-confident about her emotional stability, I'd adopted a voice that was as comforting as a hot-water bottle wrapped in fleece.

Neither my words nor my tone had the desired effect, though. 'This is *my* time,' the woman protested, tapping the crystal of a garish purple Swatch on her wrist. I detected more than a little pout in her retort, considered the bag of Cheetos, and gave a momentary thought to the clinical regression that Hannah was confronting in her therapy with this woman.

'I know,' I said even more gently. 'I know. But the circumstances today are a little unusual. If you want to leave your name I'll make sure that Ms. Grant gives you a call as soon as we straighten all this out. I'll tell her you were here. I promise.'

She wanted none of it. 'I'll just wait,' she said. 'It is my time. Though I do hope I'm not being charged.'

I sighed, pausing a moment as the woman retraced her steps and resumed her perch on the velvet settee in the waiting room. As she lowered herself to the sofa her fingertips left bright orange imprints on the forest-green velvet upholstery. Once I was sure she was settled, I joined Diane inside the doorway to Hannah's office.

I said, 'I think you should go check the bathroom, Diane. Maybe Hannah fell or something.'

'Oh God!' she said. 'Of course. Why didn't I think of that?' She rushed past me and down the hall.

I'm not sure why I did what I did next. Maybe it was because I was standing by myself in the hallway feeling lost and stupid. Maybe it was intuition. Maybe it was because I thought the Cheetos lady might be back and I was looking for a place to hide. I don't really know.

What I did was that I took half a step across the narrow hall and tried the knob on Mary Black's office door. To my surprise I discovered it unlocked. Immediately after I let go of the knob the door began to swing open on its own, as though the old building was listing just the slightest bit in that direction.

One look inside and I knew Hannah was dead.

I knew it because living people's flesh is never that shade of gray and living people can't, or don't, hold the posture that Hannah was in. Her body was splayed backward over a leather cube ottoman, her head only a yard from the edge of the open door. Her legs were spread immodestly, her torso twisted forty-five degrees at her waist. A dark pool stained an area the size of a basketball on the dhurrie rug below her legs. My gut reaction was blood. But my nose said urine.

Hannah's right arm was bent at the elbow and the thumb of her right hand was hooked in the fabric of the silk blouse near her armpit, as though she'd been thinking about hitchhiking someplace when she died.

Oddly, the left front tail of Hannah's blouse was tucked up under the front of her bra, exposing a few inches of pale abdomen. Why a woman would tuck her blouse up under her bra, I couldn't begin to guess.

Hannah's mouth was open, as were her eyes, and her fine dark hair spilled down, perfectly filling the eight- or nine-inch space that existed between the back of her head and the worn finish of the old pine floor.

I dropped to one knee and touched the smoothly

stretched skin on Hannah's neck with the tips of three fingers. I tried not to look into her dark brown eyes but they drew me in like pools of still water. Despite shifting my fingertips a few times I couldn't find a carotid pulse. It didn't matter; the chill of Hannah's flesh on my own had already confirmed to me that I wouldn't.

Hannah had been dead a while. I recalled the four notes that had been stuck in the jamb of her office door, and figured that she had fallen into her current posture sometime that morning. The arithmetic was simple. My watch said 6:45 P.M. Hannah's first known missed appointment had been almost ten hours earlier, at 9 A.M. A brief stint as a coroner's investigator earlier in my career had taught me the usually trivial fact that, after death, human bodies at room temperature yield core temperature at the rate of about one degree an hour. Ten hours meant ten degrees. I guessed that the flesh that my fingers had just touched was probably a good ten degrees cooler than my own.

But I knew it could have been cooler than that, or warmer than that. My experience touching the flesh of dead people was, admittedly, limited. I allowed for the possibility that Hannah had been dead since the night before and I tried to recall how long a body needed to be dead before the stench of death became apparent. Couldn't.

I began inhaling slowly and self-consciously, as though I hadn't already been breathing the air in the room. I thought it tasted stale and sour, but the only foreign odor I detected was that spill of urine.

I knew that medical examiners working to determine time of death also did calculations about flying insects and their eggs and the life cycle of maggots, but I quickly decided that I would leave that entomological arithmetic to them.

I was also self-aware enough to know that I was doing all the distracting contemplating so that I wouldn't be forced to confront the fact that I was unexpectedly alone in an office with a friend's dead body.

Behind me I noted the sound of a toilet flushing, followed by the timbre of water running, the click of a door opening, and the cadence of familiar footsteps down the hall. Diane, apparently forgetting that she and I were not alone, called out, 'Hannah's not there, but I really had to pee.'

I backed out of the room and saw Diane retracing her steps down the hallway from the bathroom. Her eyes caught mine, registering wariness that quickly disintegrated into shock as she digested my expression. I blocked her path and took her into my arms before she could reach the entrance to Mary Black's office. I whispered into her hair, 'Your friend is dead. I'm so, so sorry.'

The sound that came from Diane's throat as she processed my words was plaintive and poignant. Resignation and denial and the first disbelieving chords of grief were all mixed into one long, sad wail.

When I looked up I saw the Cheetos lady standing at the other entrance to the hallway, tears streaming down her face. A bright orange smudge across her cheeks marked the spot where she'd tried to wipe away her grief.

And failed.

3

Neither Diane nor I was going to get home in time for dinner.

It had taken all of my physical strength to keep Diane away from her friend's inert body – I was far from being able to consider it a corpse – and it had taken all my powers of persuasion to get both Diane and the Cheetos lady out of the house while we waited for the police to arrive.

I was staggered by Hannah's death, but my loss was nothing compared to the loss that either Diane or Hannah's patient was feeling. I kept telling myself that I could freak out later.

Diane needed to freak out now.

Outside the house, after I'd called 911 on my cell, I was standing helplessly with Diane on the front walk when she said, 'I don't want to leave Hannah alone. She shouldn't be alone. Let me go in and wait with her. Please. What can it hurt?'

My arm was firmly around her shoulders and I know I whispered replies to her pleadings, but I don't recall exactly what I said. My tight grasp on Diane reinforced my words: I didn't think she should go back inside.

Had Hannah died at home after an illness I would have led Diane to her friend's bedside, not held her back. But

Hannah had apparently died in strange circumstances in her colleague's office. Until those circumstances became clear, I knew from my coroner's experience that the environment around Hannah's body should stay uncontaminated.

Three things kept replaying in my brain.

Hannah had been in Mary Black's office, not in her own.

Hannah's purse had been in the middle of her office floor.

Her shirt was pulled up and tucked under her bra.

Why, why, and why?

The lady with the frizzy hair had moved away from Diane and me and taken off her shoes. She was sitting, almost immobile, her chin in her hands, on one of the steps leading up to the wooden porch at the front of the house. Her tears had stopped flowing, her expression a blank mask of shock.

'Are you sure she's dead?' Diane demanded more than once in those first few moments. I explained that I'd felt for a pulse and told her that Hannah's skin was already cold. And then I explained it again.

I didn't say anything about the dark stain of urine.

'She hates being cold,' Diane protested. 'Hannah shouldn't be cold. She doesn't like winter. Maybe a blanket. I could find a blanket. I have one in the car. Raoul makes me keep one in the car in case . . .'

It wasn't easy but I was able to get Diane settled on a kidney-shaped concrete bench that sat amidst some wild grasses beside the front walk about halfway to the street. I stepped a yard away from her, pulled out my cell phone, hit the speed dial and reached Lauren, my wife, who had probably just walked in the door from her job as a prosecutor for Boulder County.

'Hey, it's me. I'm glad you're home.'

'What's wrong?'

She could tell something was.

'Hannah Grant?' I said. 'You remember her?'

'Diane's friend.'

'She was going to cover for us while we were in Vegas. She's dead. We just found her body in her office. We're waiting for the cops.'

'My God. Are you all right?'

'We're okay. Call Raoul, okay? Tell him Diane's going to be late. I don't know how late, but you know how these things go. It's probably going to be a while.' Raoul Estevez was Diane's husband. 'Diane's very upset. They were close friends.'

Lauren set her empathy aside for a moment and got down to business. Her business. Cops and courts and lawyers and bad guys. 'Do you and Diane need lawyers?'

'No, nothing like that. Hannah wasn't returning Diane's messages about coverage for our trip. We were concerned. We just walked in and . . . found her body. That's all.'

'You're sure? Don't just say yes. I want you to think before you answer me.'

I thought. 'Yeah, that's all.'

'How did she die?'

'No idea. There was no blood I could see. Could be natural causes, but my gut says not. Her body's in a funny position.' I was still thinking, too, about that black patent-leather purse in the middle of the floor and about the blouse tucked up under the front of her bra. 'Is there any reason a woman would tuck her shirttail up under the front of her bra?' I asked.

'What? The front tail?'

'Yes.'

'No, not that I can think of.'

From the south side of the Pearl Street Mall I heard the piercing intrusion of a siren approaching, fast.

I said, 'The cops are here, babe. I should go.'

'I'll make some calls. Stay in touch. I love you.'

'Me, too,' I said. Diane walked up next to me. I said, 'Lauren's going to call Raoul and let him know what's going on.'

'What is going on?' she asked me. 'Do we know?'

The first of what would become four squad cars rolled up over the curb and then slowly powered up onto the sidewalk, blocking the path. A couple of patrol cops I didn't know jumped out of the car. The look on their faces was either that they didn't believe whatever the dispatcher had told them about why they were rolling to the Broadway address, or that they were hoping the dispatcher had gotten the story wrong. I stepped forward, introduced myself, told them I had called 911, and I explained what we had found inside.

One cop marched to the front door to check out my story. The other one stayed outside with his three witnesses. A minute later a couple of EMTs arrived in their bright, boxy wagon. They too went inside to confirm what I already knew. Everything everyone did, it seemed, was preceded and followed by whispers into radios.

To me it all felt like slow motion. I was thinking: *Somebody is dead. We should hurry.* The reality was, of course, different. The reality was: Somebody was dead. What was the point of hurrying?

More patrol cops arrived in the next few minutes, and after a brief consultation with the two first responders a couple of them strung a perimeter of crime-scene tape that reached all the way to the big trees along the front curb and included the larger houses and yards on each side. Gawking drivers quickly brought traffic to a virtual standstill.

Call it bad luck, call it a side effect of being married to a prosecutor, or of being best friends with a cop, but I'd been around enough crime scenes to know what to expect and wasn't at all surprised that Diane and the Cheetos lady and I were soon separated from one another.

The women were each offered a seat in the back of different squad cars while I was shuttled to the front porch of the elegantly restored Victorian next door. From there I watched the cluster of uniformed cops disperse. Two headed to the back of the house clutching a fat wheel of crime-scene tape. The ones who'd stayed in front were trying to look like they had something important to do, something besides wait. The EMTs waited for something, too.

We were all doing indeterminate time in the wake of unexplained death, a sentence that would endure until the arrival of an unmarked car bringing detectives to the scene.

Part of me wanted to see my friend, Sam Purdy, step out of the detectives' sedan.

That was the selfish part.

The generous part of me hoped that he had the evening off.

4

Sam had the evening off.

As soon as the two detectives who were catching new felony cases on that shift climbed out of their car, I recognized them. One was a buff, square-jawed, tight-eyed man named Jaris Slocum. Over a year before, while I'd been visiting Sam in the detective bureau in the Public Safety Building on 33rd Street, he had introduced me to Slocum as we passed each other in a long hallway. Once we'd paced out of eavesdropping range on our way to lunch somewhere, Sam had added, 'Slocum's kind of an asshole.'

I recognized Slocum's partner, too, though until that moment I hadn't known he was a cop. He was, like me, an avid recreational bicyclist. We ran into each other a few times a year on Boulder's back roads or in the nearby mountain canyons. The previous September we had ended up in an impromptu posse that had done a couple of memorable training climbs together up Four Mile. He was a pleasant, not-too-competitive guy who had legs and lungs that were designed for steep inclines. He was younger than me, stronger than me, and better looking than me. I knew him simply as Darrell.

The two detectives ambled across the sidewalk and

checked in with the patrol cop who was manning the log. I watched him point at me seconds before the detectives climbed the slope of the front lawn toward my solitary aerie on the neighboring building's front porch.

Remembering Sam's caution about Slocum, I greeted the bicyclist detective first. 'Hi, Darrell. What a night.' I held out my hand. 'Alan, Alan Gregory. Remember me?' He didn't. 'We climbed Four Mile together a few months back? I see you occasionally when you ride.'

It took Darrell a second but he finally recognized my face. 'Alan? Yeah, hi. You're, um, part of this?' He waved his left arm in the general direction of Hannah Grant's dead body.

'Unfortunately. I was the one who found her. Hannah. She's a colleague. Was. I'm a psychologist.' The last sentence felt like a complete non sequitur to me. I imagined that it did to Darrell, too. I added, 'Hannah was a social worker.'

'You're the RP?' He caught himself using cop vernacular and added, 'The one who called this in?'

RP. Reporting party. 'Yes.'

Slocum stepped up and took charge. His intrusion had all the subtlety of a belch during grace at Thanksgiving dinner. 'Sit right there, sir. Yes, on those steps behind you. Don't speak with anyone until we're ready to interview you. Do you understand my instructions, sir?'

For some reason – possibly the vice-principal tone in his voice – I found myself questioning the sincerity of his repeated use of 'sir.'

Jaris Slocum either didn't recognize me, which wouldn't have been surprising, or – and this was a more worrisome possibility – had recalled our prior introduction and decided that any friend of Sam Purdy's deserved an additional bolus of hard-ass attitude.

Fifty feet or so away from me a damn good woman lay dead. During traffic lulls I could hear Diane weeping from the backseat of the patrol car where she had been stashed. The Cheetos lady was still looking like she'd just lost her only friend in the world. The sum of those parts? I was in absolutely no mood for any I'm-the-boss-and-you'll-do-what-I-say cop crap from Detective Jaris Slocum.

'And you are?' I said. My tone wasn't exactly a model of I'd-love-to-cooperate-Detective.

Detective Darrell's badge wallet was hanging on his belt for all to see. Slocum's wasn't. Wisely, Darrell chose to answer my question even though it had been addressed to his partner. He was busily trying to douse the lit matches that Slocum and I were slinging at the kindling in each other's pants. To me, he said, 'This is Detective Jaris Slocum. And this is Alan . . . ?'

'Gregory,' I said.

'He and I ride together sometimes,' Darrell explained to Slocum.

'That's nice. Now sit, Alan Gregory. We'll be back to talk to you. Wait for us, understand?'

'I still haven't seen a badge,' I said. I shouldn't have said it. But I did.

Slocum couldn't find his badge wallet. He checked all his pockets, and then he patted them all a second time. Finally, after an exasperated exhale he barked, 'It must be in the car.'

If Slocum had wanted to transport the annoyance that he packed into those few words he would have needed a wheelbarrow, or a tractor-trailer.

'I can wait,' I said. 'Go ahead and get it. I'd like to see some ID. I think that's my right.'

Slocum and I both knew he wasn't about to slink back to his big Ford and fish around for his detective shield at my behest. He gave me an icy blue-eyed stare. 'I said to have a seat.'

I said, 'I'm fine standing.'

He took a step toward me. 'And I said to sit.'

I came so close to saying 'fuck you' that my lower lip actually came together with my bottom teeth.

Darrell sensed what was developing as though he knew either Slocum or me real well. I knew the person he knew real well wasn't me.

'Enough,' he said.

He was talking to both of us.

I had to cool my heels for almost an hour before the detectives got back to me. From what I could see, they'd spent most of the time either singly or together with the Cheetos lady and with Diane. For a while I was perplexed why they didn't go inside the offices and start detecting in there where Hannah and the evidence were, but then I realized they were probably waiting for a search warrant to arrive at the scene.

In the meantime, I was cold and exhausted and hungry and sad and angry and impatient and would have been much more comfortable sitting on the stoop than walking in circles on the front porch.

But I stood. It was a point of honor. Or a badge of stubbornness. One of those things.

The story I had to tell about discovering Hannah's body wasn't complicated and once things had calmed down a little bit between Slocum and me, it was simple to discern from the detectives' questions that Slocum and Olson – his cop ID had revealed not only bicyclist Darrell's last name, but also a double dose of middle initials, C. and R. – were primarily interested in two specific areas of my narrative.

The first? Why had I decided to reach across the hall and try to open the door to Mary Black's office? I stuck with the truth on that one – I didn't know. I just didn't know. It was one of those things that I had just done.

The truth, however, didn't set me free. One of the detectives – either Darrell Olson playing good cop, or Slocum naturally taking on the role of bad – revisited the question of me opening Mary Black's door at least five times during our relatively brief discussion. They seemed as dissatisfied with my fifth reply as they had been with the first. I told them I wished that I had a better explanation, but I didn't.

The second focus of the detectives' interest was more concerning to me. They wanted to know what I had been doing the rest of the day – minute-by-minute, hour-by-hour – up until the moment Diane dragged me from my office to her Saab to drive to Hannah's office.

'What? You mean from the moment I got out of bed? That early?' I asked in a futile attempt at levity when Slocum pressed me on my day's itinerary for the second or third time.

'Sure,' he replied. 'Assuming you have a witness for that part of your day, too.' His cold eyes weren't smiling at all but his cheekbones had elevated just enough to let me know that he was enjoying whatever temporary advantage he thought he had.

Not for the first time that evening I thought, *God, Sam, you're right. Slocum is an asshole.*

'As a matter of fact, I do have a witness. I want you to be sure to write this name down. Are you ready?'

He glared at me as though he'd rather beat me with a long stick than do what I suggested, but he brought his pen down so that the nib hovered just above the page in his notebook.

Stressing each syllable for his benefit, I said, 'My witness, for this morning's events, is Deputy DA Lauren Crowder of the Boulder County District Attorney's office.' I slowly dictated the ten digits of our home phone number, and then added Lauren's office number for emphasis. 'Give her a call. Please. I'm sure she'll be thrilled to tell you what time her husband crawled out of bed this morning.'

Slocum stopped writing.

Darrell Olson took a step back so that his partner wouldn't spot the smile that was forming on his face.

I said, 'I'm going home now, Detective. I think you know how to reach me if you have any more questions.'

Slocum made a quick move toward me – or at me – but Darrell stepped forward and spoke before his partner could do something he would regret. 'Warrant's here, Jaris. Come on, let's go inside and see what we have.'

I didn't go right home. I found Raoul, Diane's husband, pacing outside the crime-scene tape and filled him in on all that had happened late that afternoon. He was almost too agitated to attend to my words. Raoul Estevez had a roster of relatives who had not survived Franco's reign in Spain, and the sight of his wife squeezed into the back of a squad car being peppered with questions from law enforcement authorities wasn't sitting particularly well with him.

'She is not under arrest?' he demanded, his words causing little cartoonish puffs of steam in the cold air. Although it's his second language – actually, his fourth or fifth – Raoul's English is better than Prince Charles's, but the American legal system still perplexed him at times. English is my only language, isn't in Prince Charles's league, and the American legal system still perplexed me at times, too. Still, since I was the natural-born citizen, I assumed the responsibility of translating the proceedings for Raoul.

'No, they're just questioning her about what happened, what she saw, that's all. She'll be done soon. She didn't see much; I found Hannah's body.'

As if on cue, Slocum, who had not taken his partner's advice about going inside and looking around, hopped out of the cruiser and, I thought, reached in to help Diane from the backseat.

'See?' I turned to Raoul. 'It looks like she's done.'

Diane suddenly yelled, 'Get your goddamn hands off me!'

Raoul's voice grew hard. 'It doesn't look that way to me.'

I turned back to the cruiser. Slocum had Diane completely out of the car and was twisting her ninety degrees so he could shove her face-first up against the rear fender of the black-and-white. Instantly he had her legs spread past shoulder width and in seconds he had her arms behind her back and handcuffs on both her wrists.

I was shocked. 'Don't, Raoul.' I had to stand in my friend's path to keep him from crossing the yellow tape and joining the fray. I planted my feet on the ground and both my hands on Raoul's hard chest. Finally, he stepped back.

Ten seconds later I had Lauren on the phone. 'Get Cozy down here fast. I think Jaris Slocum just arrested Diane for something.'

Lauren said, 'Slocum? God help us, he's such an asshole lately.'

The verdict, it appeared, was unanimous.

5

Cozier Maitlin lived, literally, around the corner.

From my sentry position just outside the crime-scene tape, I spotted Cozy on the sidewalk as he was descending the final steep section of hill that drops down from Maxwell toward Broadway. Despite the crowd of gawkers gathered around the yellow police tape, he wasn't that hard to spot. Cozy stood six-feet-nine.

I checked my watch – no more than seven or eight minutes could have passed since Jaris Slocum had cuffed Diane and shoved her rudely back into the rear seat of the black-and-white.

Pointing toward the corner, I said to Raoul, 'That's the defense attorney Lauren called.'

'That was fast. He's tall.'

'He's good. He helped Lauren with that thing, you know, a few years ago. Hey, Cozy!'

Cozy didn't break stride as he approached, or wave. Maybe he elevated his chin an additional millimeter or two, but that was the only indication that he'd heard me calling his name. He was wearing the same suit I imagined he'd worn to his downtown office that morning – the blue was a navy that shared a lot of DNA with black, and it was lined with the palest of gray pinstripes. His white shirt appeared freshly starched and his black shoes were the shiniest things on the block.

A nice, full-length umbrella or a walking stick would not have been out of place accessorizing his outfit.

We shook hands. 'Good evening, Alan. At least the location is convenient this time. And the weather is delightful for December. No blizzard. I can't tell you how grateful I am for that.'

'Thanks for coming so quickly, Cozy. This is Raoul Estevez. Raoul, Cozier Maitlin.'

'A pleasure, Mr. Estevez. I'm aware of your work.' That was Cozy's way of communicating that he wasn't worried about his fee. 'It is your wife who is being detained?'

'In that car.' Raoul pointed at the squad that was parked at an angle on the lawn in front of the building where Hannah lay dead.

'Do you want to know what happened?' I asked.

'I understand someone died here under suspicious circumstances. Beyond that, not really. If either of you was an intimate of the deceased, please let me offer my condolences,' Cozy said, insincerely. He lifted one of his long legs, stepped over the crime-scene tape, and somehow managed to adopt an even more imperial deportment as he moved out onto the lawn. He paused, turned back to Raoul, and said, 'Give me a moment or two to sort this out. Everything will be fine. It will.' After one more step, Cozy looked back over his shoulder at me. 'Lauren said I'd be speaking with Jaris Slocum. That's true?'

I nodded. I considered the wisdom of editorializing about Detective Slocum's apparent personality flaws, but decided that I didn't need to do anything to inflame the situation any further.

'Slocum is . . . difficult,' Cozy said. He said it in such a way that it sounded more damning than Sam Purdy informing me that Slocum was an asshole, or than Lauren concurring.

'That's been my experience so far this evening,' I replied.

I was feeling a million things. Grief, anger, frustration, fear, even some relief, now that Cozy was there. Still, my anticipation of what was to come next was so sharp that I would have yanked out my wallet and maxed out all my credit cards for a ticket to the production I was about to get to witness for free.

Cozy immediately marched over to the cruiser and confronted the patrol cop assigned to keep watch on Diane, who was continuing to fume in the backseat. Cozy's approach wasn't tentative, and didn't have any excuse-me-please in it. He moved in until he stood toe-to-toe with the cop, a young black man who was about six-two, 210.

Cozy dwarfed him.

Cozy's introductory gambit to the officer consisted of a few words that caused the man to react by trying to step back to create some breathing room. But since the cop was already leaning against the car there was no place for him to go and he had to crane his neck upward to even see Cozy's face. I imagined that the view was like gazing up from below Mt. Rushmore.

The patrol cop listened to Cozy for only another beat or two before he raised his voice and barked, 'Step back, sir! Step *back*! Now! That's a warning!'

The cop's hand gravitated ominously toward his holster.

I held my breath and instinctively grabbed Raoul's arm so he wouldn't do something valiant, and stupid. I'd known him a long time, and knew that Raoul was capable of both.

Cozy, of course, didn't step back an inch. He was daring the cop to get physical with him. And if the young cop preferred to do loud, Cozy could do loud just fine. With volume that matched the patrol cop's do-what-I-say voice and then raised a few decibels for good measure, Cozy announced, 'I am her attorney and I would like to speak with my client, Officer. Officer' – Cozy leaned back at his waist so that he could read the cop's name tag – 'Leamer. It's a pleasure to meet you. My client – that is she, by the way, that you are *protecting* – won't, will not, be answering any more of the detectives' questions tonight.'

The volume of that soliloquy drew virtually everyone's attention to the cruiser, including Jaris Slocum's. He was up on the front porch and immediately began a march toward the car with long strides, his hands tightened into fists. Cozy must have felt him coming. He spun away from the patrol cop and greeted Slocum with, 'A pleasure seeing you, as always. Is my client actually in custody, Detective?'

Slocum stopped five feet from Cozy. I don't know why he kept his distance – maybe so that he wasn't close enough to shake Cozy's outstretched hand. Slocum's mouth opened and closed about a centimeter as he tried to process the latest developments: A large, imperial criminal defense attorney had penetrated the perimeter and he seemed to be making speeches for the benefit of the dozens of gathered citizens.

Not good.

'Haven't decided? Is that it? Perhaps I can help,' Cozy taunted. His words were polite, his tone was even doing a clever masquerade as respectful. But everyone, especially Slocum, knew it was a taunt.

Slocum opened his mouth again, but still no words came out. Finally he was able to mutter, 'I'm trying to investigate a suspicious death here.'

Cozy's reply was immediate. 'Good for you. As a taxpayer, I applaud your . . . conscientiousness. But that is neither here nor there at the moment, is it? The question at hand is, you see, quite simple.' Cozy leaned over and smiled at Diane in the backseat of the cruiser before returning his attention to Slocum. 'Is my client in custody? Yes or no?'

Cozy's voice carried through the heavy December air as though he were a thespian center stage at the Globe.

'She is not under arrest.'

'Ah, but I didn't ask you that, did I?' He was doing his best to sound like Olivier doing Henry IV. 'I asked you if my client was in your custody – yes, or no.'

I could barely discern Slocum's response. I thought he said, 'For now, she is . . . um, being detained for questioning.'

'I appreciate that clarification. As of now she is officially declining your invitation for further questioning, so I assume, then, that she is free to go.' Cozy leaned over and made quite a show of staring into the backseat of the cruiser. With mock horror he added, 'Has she been handcuffed, Detective Slocum?' He included Jaris's name so that the assembled citizenry would know who was responsible for the travesty. Had he next recited Slocum's badge number – had Slocum been wearing a badge – I would not have been surprised. 'Is that possible? Is she really handcuffed and locked in the backseat of a police cruiser? Are you planning on taking her to the jail and *booking* her?'

'She was not being cooperative.'

Cozy held out his own wrists and used the full power of his baritone. 'Was she? Like my client, I too am planning to be uncooperative if this is the way the Boulder Police Department is choosing to behave toward its law-abiding citizens.'

'Mr. Maitlin,' Slocum implored.

At that moment I actually had just the slightest sympathy for Jaris Slocum. Cozy's performance had gone more than a little over the top.

Cozy ignored Slocum's plea and made a great show of holding out his French-cuffed wrists to see if Slocum would dare put a slightly less elegant pair of cuffs on them. 'Would you like to handcuff me, as well? Is that the current policy of the department when citizens exercise their constitutional prerogatives to grieve silently?'

I could tell that Jaris Slocum would have loved nothing better at that moment than to handcuff Cozier Maitlin, but the presence of fifty or so civilian witnesses served to deter his more primitive impulses.

Darrell Olson's primary role in his detective partnership was, apparently, to sense what was about to go wrong between Slocum and one of Boulder's citizens. Once again, Darrell did his job with aplomb. He rushed up, grabbed Slocum's arm, pulled him closer to the house – and much farther from Cozy – and went nose to nose with him for about half a minute. I couldn't hear a word of their argument but my respect for Darrell C. R. Olson expanded exponentially as he barked whatever he was barking. When the tête-à-tête between the two detectives was over, Slocum climbed the porch and marched into the old house where Hannah lay dead.

Olson returned to Cozy. He used a low voice to address him, modeling for him, hoping to reduce the inflammation. As he spoke he spread his hands in conciliation, palms up, like a don trying to pacify a peer. I couldn't tell what he was saying, but it took him a minute or more to get through it.

Cozy's reply wasn't a whisper; his tone remained floridly oratorical. 'No, Detective. Not in a few minutes.

Right now. I want the cuffs off my client and I want her released. Now. There is no point whatsoever in prolonging her agony. She is despairing over her friend's death. I guarantee you that this interview is over for tonight.'

Olson dipped his head a little and spoke again. It was apparent that he was still determined to try to be deferential, to try to lower the temperature of the conflict a little, but that he was also trying not to roll over to Cozy's demands.

Cozy listened to Darrell's continued plea, thought for a moment, and decided that he wanted none of it. He said, 'Now, Detective.' Cozy gestured toward the old house and Jaris Slocum, and in a much lower, tempered voice added, 'That man is your problem, not mine. You have my sympathy, but nothing more. Now, please.'

Olson shook his head, scratched his ear, stuffed his hands in his pockets, and mumbled something to Officer Leamer. Without so much as a nod, the detective walked away from Cozy and the patrol car.

Leamer opened the back door of the cruiser, helped Diane to her feet, and removed the handcuffs from behind her back. The fire in her eyes, if focused, could have ignited candles across the street.

Cozy introduced himself to his client and said something to her so quietly I couldn't discern a word. Diane had fresh tears on her face. She said, 'Thank you, thank you.' Then, as though she'd somehow forgotten, she cried, 'My God, Hannah's dead.'

Raoul said, 'That's it?' Actually, what he said was, '*C'est finis?*'

I said, 'For now.'

6

Diane and I didn't make it to Vegas.

Hannah Grant's ashes were interred the following Tuesday after a sentimental service in one of the downtown churches. I had never before seen so much of Boulder's mental health community present in one place.

I was in a pretty good position to know that the police were flummoxed by the case. The local media was already reporting that the cops had no active leads. Lauren confirmed to me that after a week the investigation was spinning its wheels. My friend Sam Purdy, the Boulder police detective, usually wouldn't talk out of school about important cases with me, but he did roll his eyes when I mentioned Hannah.

That told me a lot.

During one late-night phone conversation he went way out on a limb. 'We got crap,' was what he said.

Lauren swore me to secrecy but revealed that Slocum and Olson had located no witnesses to anything that supported a finding of homicide. No one had seen Hannah leave her south Boulder condo the morning of her death, but she'd arrived at Rallysport Health Club early enough to work out before driving away just before 8:30. The time was almost certain. Two different witnesses recalled an incident in the locker room – Hannah had tripped over another woman's gym bag on the way back from the shower and both women had fallen hard to the floor. The witnesses were confident that they knew what time Hannah had dressed after her workout before heading to her car.

They were confident about one other thing, too. As she fell, Hannah had definitely hit her head on the tile floor. Someone had offered to go get ice. Hannah had declined; she said she was fine and had to get to work.

No one reported seeing her arrive at her office building. The few of Hannah's patients who had shown up for appointments on the day she died and who had voluntarily come forward to speak with the police reported nothing that provided any direction for the investigation.

The detectives weren't able to develop any motive for an assault. Hannah's personal life revealed no promising leads. Her finances were pristine. Her professional record was free of formal complaints.

The cops had no physical evidence that a crime had been committed. Actually, the truth was that they had way too much physical evidence. The little office building was chock-full of fingerprints and trace evidence. Dozens of different patients made their way through the space every week.

Hair, fibers? All the police could want, and more. Apparently Hannah's obsessive-compulsive tendencies had lacunae in the terrain where 'neat' stopped and 'clean' began. For investigators, Hannah's housekeeping weakness created a problem. To use trace evidence to rule in the presence of an intruder in the building, Jaris Slocum and Darrell Olson had to rule out the presence of any and all routine visitors to the building, which meant – minimally – obtaining exemplar prints and DNA samples from all of Hannah's patients and all of Mary Black's patients and from any other routine visitors to the building, including the woman who delivered the mail, the guys from UPS and FedEx, and the various tat-ted and pierced kids who delivered takeout from restaurants on the nearby Pearl Street Mall.

Mary Black, the psychiatrist and mother of three who shared office space with Hannah, declined to make her patient roster available to the police, citing doctor-patient confidentiality. Diane, whom Hannah had entrusted with the clinical responsibility of closing her practice in the event of her death, also declined to make Hannah's patient roster available to the police, citing the same doctor-patient confidentiality issues. When the police pressed the issue, she'd enlisted Cozy Maitlin to run interference for her.

Diane was ambivalent about keeping the information to herself. After what Jaris Slocum had done to her the evening Hannah's body was discovered, Diane wasn't, of course, particularly inclined to cooperate with him. But she was eager to do anything she could to help identify anyone who might have had anything to do with Hannah's death. As far as Hannah's patient roster was concerned, though, Diane had decided that was information to which Slocum wasn't entitled.

Hannah's death officially remained 'suspicious' until the Boulder County coroner issued his report eight days after her death. The medical examiner had identified two discrete blows to Hannah's head, and he identified her cause of death as traumatic head injury resulting in cerebral hemorrhage. He specified the manner of her death as 'undetermined.' The ME's opinion was that the damage inflicted by a flat surface, possibly the tile floor at Rallysport, had not been sufficient to cause Hannah's death. Hannah's death was directly attributable to the second head trauma, origin unknown.

The dual traumas either had been unintentional blows suffered during the fall in the gym the morning she died – one impact caused by the tile floor, one by something else – or had been the result of two blows to her head intentionally inflicted by an assailant. Sam pointedly reminded me that a third possibility existed: One blow had been suffered during the fall at the health club, and the second blow, the fatal one, had been inflicted by an assailant at Hannah's office.

Diane heard the coroner's findings first. Diane always tended to hear gossip first. What source she might have in the medical examiner's office eluded me, but she found me on Friday morning at the office at a moment when we were both between patients and stunned me with the news.

'Somebody may have killed her, Alan. My God, somebody may have killed her. Why would somebody want to kill Hannah?'

I held her while she wept. I'd lost count of how many times I'd held Diane while she wept since Hannah's death. The tears weren't endless, but they were frequent. Diane's grief arrived in short, intense bursts, like the August monsoons. Clear skies before, clear skies after.

I asked myself the same question Diane was asking a dozen times a day for a while after that. *Why would somebody want to kill Hannah?*

I couldn't provide an answer. I used the fact that I couldn't answer it to console myself with the likelihood that Hannah's death had been accidental. Nothing more than a freak reaction to a silly accident in a health club locker room.

But the police were left with a buffet of anomalies that

they couldn't explain. Why was Hannah's purse on the floor of her office, a place she would never leave it? Why was Hannah's body found in Mary Black's office, a place she had no reason to go? And why was Hannah's blouse tucked up under the front of her bra?

Hanukkah had arrived and Christmas was growing ever closer.

The effort to determine the manner of Hannah's death turned colder along with the weather.

Media interest in the case declined quickly, and Hannah's very public death soon became what, perhaps, it really had been all along – a private tragedy.

7

If you don't happen to be an inveterate shopper intent on milking the swollen teat of post-holiday sales – I am not – and if you aren't required to be at work – it was a Sunday, and I wasn't – the day after Christmas is a sleep-in day.

Or maybe – if the snow gods have conspired with the ski gods to dump ten powdery inches of flash-frozen Dom Perignon on the upper reaches of Beaver Creek and one of your wife's friends has generously offered two free holiday season nights at her Bachelor Gulch ski villa – the day after Christmas is most definitely a play day.

Lauren and I had packed our ski stuff and winter clothing and an immense quantity of three-year-old paraphernalia the night before and were out of bed well before dawn in an almost certainly futile attempt to beat the pre-ski traffic that seemed to always clog I-70 West into the Colorado Rockies during the winter months. She was fixing some breakfast for our still-sleeping daughter, Grace; I was loading the car. While I was on a trip into the kitchen to grab a cooler to lug to the garage, Lauren said, 'See that?'

'What?'

She pointed at the tiny kitchen TV, which was tuned to

a local channel so we could hear the ski-traffic report. Why? I wasn't sure. If the traffic was awful, we'd take I-70 into the mountains. If the traffic was light, we'd do the same thing. She said, 'That thing at the bottom of the screen.'

I assumed she meant the crawl, the strip of text that I always seemed to be reading when I should be watching the screen and that I never seemed to be reading when news about some important update was moving across the screen that I should probably be reading. From the time that crawls first appeared on TV screens, I'd decided that I was genetically incapable of reading the moving words and simultaneously attending to what was happening on the rest of the screen. I'd long ago concluded that I did not possess a twenty-first-century mind.

I lifted the heavy cooler laden with God-knows-what and took a lumbering step toward the door. 'Nope, didn't see it.'

'It said that—'

'We have breaking news from our Boulder bureau,' interrupted one of the morning anchors. With that preamble I turned my attention back toward the TV, but my eyes immediately found the crawl and I couldn't have told you which of the two anchors was speaking. 'Apparently – and details are sketchy – apparently, and this is truly hard to believe, another little girl has disappeared on Christmas night in Boulder. We have a reporter on the way to the scene right now and should have more information momentarily. June?'

June said, 'You're right: This is so hard to believe, that it's happening again. For those of our viewers who aren't familiar with Boulder, it's even the same neighborhood as last time. That was what, eight, nine years ago? We'll get those details for you and we'll be back with more right after a break.'

Lauren said, 'I'm going to check on Grace.'

'I checked her when I got up, sweets. She's fine.'

'So did I. I'm going to check on her anyway.'

She hustled toward Grace's room. I set the cooler on the floor.

Another little girl has disappeared on Christmas night in Boulder.

Lauren was breathless when she tiptoed back into the kitchen. 'Grace is fine,' she said.

'Yes.' I put my arms around her and planted my hands on her ass. Lauren and I were parents of a little girl who hadn't disappeared on Christmas night. Somewhere else in Boulder another pair of parents couldn't say the same.

'Are you catching? You're not catching, right?' I asked. One of Boulder County's prosecutors was always on call for legal emergencies that might require the presence of a representative from the DA's office. Infrequently, that meant that she was called to crime scenes. Like to the location of the disappearance of a girl.

'No, no,' she said, pulling away from my hug. 'I couldn't leave town if I was on call. You know that. Should I wake Grace?' she asked.

'Let me finish loading the car first. We'll both get much more accomplished if she stays asleep until the last possible moment.'

An hour later we were climbing through Mount Vernon Canyon on I-70 into the mountains, sharing the freeway with at least a million other vehicles. Maybe two million other vehicles. Every one of the other vehicles carried skiers or snowboarders who had, like us, crawled out of warm beds before dawn in order to beat the traffic. I searched for irony, knowing it was there somewhere.

In back, secure in her high-tech car seat, Grace was flipping through a fat cardboard book about erudite dogs and talking to herself, while next to me Lauren was flipping through radio stations trying to find the latest news about what was going on with the missing girl back in Boulder. I wasn't really listening to the radio, partly because Grace's almost incomprehensible monologue was too cute to ignore, but mostly because none of the radio reporters seemed to know much about what was happening with this year's missing girl, so they were using their airtime to talk about the other missing girl, the one who had disappeared eight Christmases before.

I'd long before decided that I despised hearing rehashes of that dreadful story.

'It's a teenager. They think she's fourteen,' Lauren summarized for me as the Denver station she was listening to faded away, its signal lost hopelessly in the mountain canyons. 'Her father went to check on her early this morning. She wasn't there. They were going to go skiing today, just like us. We did the exact same thing with Grace.'

I thought, *But at our house Grace was in her bed,* and felt a chill crawl up my spine and gooseflesh spread across my shoulders and neck. *What would it be like if she hadn't . . . ?* I tried comforting myself with the fact that it wasn't really as bad as the last time a girl went missing on Christmas night in Boulder. It wasn't.

The last time the girl they couldn't find was only six years old.

The last time a terrifying note was discovered on the stairs.

And I soothed myself with the obvious; the obvious being that six-year-olds don't often run away from home, not for real, and certainly not on Christmas night. I reminded myself that a fourteen-year-old girl might run away.

Fourteen-year-olds do run away. Maybe this girl had just run away. Probably this girl had just run away.

Numerals representing the ages of the two missing girls lined up in front of my eyes as though they were symbols spinning on a slot machine. As the numbers came to rest, I did the math. Today's fourteen-year-old missing girl was the same age – had been born the exact same year – as the tiny blonde who went missing eight years to the day before. If that other little girl had survived, the two children might be classmates, or friends, or sleep-over mates. They might go skiing on Christmas holidays with each other's families.

I felt another chill.

'Their house is only a few blocks away from – you know,' Lauren said. She meant from the other house, the one where the little beauty queen's dead body had been found by her father on the day after Christmas in an unused room in the basement, her head smashed, her neck cruelly cinctured with a homemade garrote.

'Where exactly?'

'On Twelfth, they said.'

Three blocks away. Just three blocks and eight years separated two little girls gone missing on Christmas nights in Boulder.

At that moment we were passing an overhead digital highway sign, the kind that in winter usually cautions motorists of icy and snowpacked conditions ahead. But this one had an even more sobering message – an Amber Alert. All concerned citizens were supposed to be on the lookout for a missing blonde-haired, 115-pound, five-foot-six fourteen-year-old. No name was given.

My first reaction? Selfish. I hoped I didn't know her. I hoped she wasn't the daughter of any of my friends, or any of my patients. I wanted to feel the relief of insulation. I wanted her to be a stranger.

'Amber Alert,' I said to Lauren. 'Look.'

She stared in the direction of the highway sign until we passed below it, then turned on her seat and faced our daughter. She said, 'Your parents really love you, Gracie.'

Gracie laughed.

Obliviousness, I thought, *can be a very, very good thing.*

My detective friend, Sam Purdy, told me later on that it was as though a giant warehouse had been surreptitiously constructed nearby when the other case of the missing girl had finally faded into near oblivion and that all the satellite trucks, and all the microwave trucks, and all the flimsy network pop-up tents, and a few hundred cameras and microphones had simply been secreted away so they'd be ready for the next time.

The next time had turned out to be the massacre at Columbine and the time after that had been the Kobe Bryant circus up in Eagle County. After the Kobe invasion, all the equipment had apparently been returned to the secret warehouse to await the next, next, next time the almost-tabloid media would mobilize for a full-scale assault on a Colorado town. That was the only explanation Sam could concoct for how quickly the equipment reappeared on the streets of Boulder on the day after Christmas.

I was determined to miss it all.

By noon on that Boxing Day, Grace was either enjoying or enduring her first day ever in ski school and I was busy chasing Lauren, who was a much better skier than me, and a much, much better powder skier than me, through untracked down on the forest edges of the Golden Eagle run at the top of Beaver Creek.

In Boulder, three thousand feet below us in altitude – based on what Sam would tell me later – the cameras were already in place, the high-tech satellite and microwave trucks were bouncing signals around and through the atmosphere, and producers had already begun choosing locations for the stand-ups the on-air talent would do for that night's news.

Some of the reportorial faces would be familiar from the last time Boulder had endured this invasion. Others were recognizable because of what the country had endured in the intervening years because of the tragedies that had befallen Chandra Levy, or Elizabeth Smart, or Laci Peterson. Or because of the innocent lives ended by the Beltway snipers. Or because of Kobe Bryant and whatever happened at Cordillera. Or because of whatever Michael Jackson was accused of lately. Or because of some other crime du jour.

Or.

In America, there were always plenty of candidates.

As each fresh tragedy was anointed a mega-news event, I'd quickly grown fatigued by the relentless television and newspaper and Internet and magazine coverage afforded, or foisted upon, all the previous victims and all the previous perpetrators, and upon the unsuspecting but apparently ravenous populace.

Somebody had to be watching all this coverage, right?

I suspected that I'd fatigue of this latest criminal/media extravaganza, right in my hometown, even faster. I really was determined to miss it all.

I was. Honestly.

*

Lauren and I grabbed a late lunch at Spruce Saddle, the big mid-mountain restaurant at Beaver Creek. It wasn't lost on me that I was only a couple of ridge tops away from the elegant resort where Kobe and a young woman had crossed paths, and was within shouting distance of the courthouse where that diseased melodrama had played itself out.

Lauren chose a table close to an overhead television so she would immediately know if there were any updates being broadcast about the missing girl in Boulder. I was silently trying to discern whether her acute interest in the case was an indication of parental empathy – or a counterintuitive way to stem the flow of understandable parental dread – or whether it was a more uncomplicated professional prosecutorial curiosity. I was trying to grant her the benefit of the doubt and not even consider the possibility that my wife's interest might be simply voyeuristic. Unsure, I headed for the bathroom. When I returned I spied Lauren folding up her cell phone. I took a chair that left my back to the television.

Which left me facing in the general direction of Cordillera.

'Who'd you call?' I asked.

'The office.'

'Yeah, what did you learn?' I didn't really want to know, and wasn't sure why I'd asked. Probably the same reason that I tried the door on Mary Black's office.

'This is my job. I could be involved later on. I need to . . . you know, whether . . . the girl . . .'

Not too bad, only slightly defensive. 'I know,' I said. I leaned across the table and kissed her lightly on her lips, tasting the waxy gloss of a fresh application of sunblock. 'So, what did you learn?'

I'd done it again; I'd once again asked a question that I

didn't really want to know the answer to. I convinced myself that my question was an act of marital generosity: Lauren needed to talk.

'They don't know what they have. But because of what happened last time – you can imagine – they're being extra, extra cautious. They're treating it like a crime scene, even though no one's really sure what it is exactly. The girl's family is cooperating, totally. So far the crime scene techs don't think anything's been unduly contaminated. That's all good, considering.'

She meant, of course, considering what a total mess the crime scene had been the last time. The time with the little blonde beauty queen, the one who sang and danced into our homes over and over and over again in her little sexy cowgirl getup.

'What do the police think? Was it an abduction of some kind?'

'Some of what they're seeing says yes, some says no.' She gazed around to see if anyone in the crowded cafeteria was paying attention to our conversation, and she prophylactically lowered her already hushed voice a few additional decibels. 'There hadn't been any threats, and they didn't find a note or anything like that. Nobody's called the family about ransom. There's no evidence of forced entry at the house. But there is some blood.'

'A lot?'

'More than a couple of drops. I'm just telling you what I heard from the office. It's thirdhand, or fourth.'

'Could she have run?'

'It's a possibility, apparently. The cops are trying to track down all her friends, to see what they know. Since the schools are on break, it's complicated. Some of her best friends are out of town.'

'But her family thinks it's possible?'

'I guess. Apparently, the family situation is complicated. The girl has had some emotional issues in the past. I don't have those details.'

I couldn't look my wife in the eye when I asked the next question. With the edge of my hand I moved salt that had been spilled on the table by an earlier diner into one long sodium mogul and pushed it to the side. 'And they checked all the little rooms in the basement that nobody ever goes into?'

That's where the other girl's body had been found eight years before. In a rarely used room in a dingy basement. Her tiny body had been discovered by her distraught father, who had carried it up the stairs for all to see.

'Yeah, twice at least. It's different this time. The circumstances. It sounds like it's a nice house, but it's not huge and fancy like the other one. And it only has a small basement, a partial, like ours; underneath it's mostly crawl space. They checked.'

'Twice?'

'Three times.' She smiled sadly.

'Who's on it?'

'From my office? Andy.'

'From the cops?'

'It's a big team for now. And, yes, it includes Sam and Lucy.'

'Sam won't be happy. It was one of his claims to fame that he never had a thing to do with the other one.'

'I doubt if any of them are happy,' Lauren said. 'There're so many reporters chasing everyone around that they've had to block off the street. You know that all the detectives will be under a microscope.'

Or a microphone. 'Is Jaris Slocum on it?'

She slapped my wrist to shush me. 'Babe, we're on vacation. Let's not go back there.' She held up her cell. 'I want to call and see how Grace is doing in ski school. Am I crazy?'

'You're a mother. You get special dispensation.'

She made the call. Grace, it turned out, was enjoying ski school. I wasn't surprised. As she aged and I got a chance to experience the wonder of really beginning to know her, I was learning that my daughter rolled well with the punches.

Lauren closed up the phone. I asked, 'How's your energy?' That's as close as I would get to finding a safe way to inquire about the current state of Lauren's multiple sclerosis. I knew from experience that on rare good days a couple of hours of skiing was often all that she could manage before her legs began to feel like overcooked asparagus. We'd already done a long drive up to the mountains and spent a couple of energetic hours cutting powder.

For Lauren, that was an awful lot of activity.

'Good, I'm fine. I'll wriggle out of these boots and put my feet up over lunch. That will help.'

Was I convinced? Hardly. 'We can go down the hill and eat if you want. We have all day tomorrow to ski, you know. And Tuesday morning, too. No need to press it today.'

'I'm good, Alan. I want to do the top of Bachelor's Gulch before all the powder is skied off. I love it up there.'

Arguing with her was an option. Prevailing was not. Across the room, the food-court lines were long. I stood. 'You rest, I'll go get you something to eat. What would you like for lunch?'

We drove down the hill to Boulder after a late breakfast two days later, on Tuesday.

The skiing had been a joy, Lauren's atypical stamina on the slopes was a holiday gift, and by late Monday in ski school tiny Grace had managed – for about eleven horizontal feet of a two percent grade – to comport her stubby little legs into something resembling a snow-plow. Lauren and I gladly forked over $24.95 for a DVD that proved our daughter had accomplished the dubious feat.

Midday mountain traffic wasn't bad over Vail Pass, and the Eisenhower Tunnel approach was merely aggravating, not paralyzing. On the eastern side of the Divide I kept my eyes peeled on my rearview mirror for out-of-control big-rig truckers who had already fried the air brakes on their rigs on the highest stretches of the seven percent grades.

Grace and Lauren both slept all the way from Copper Mountain to Golden.

For the forty-eight hours plus we'd been up skiing I had managed to avoid – almost completely – the media saturation coverage about the girl who had disappeared on Christmas night. Lauren had told me a few new things, but with concerted effort on my part I knew almost nothing about what had transpired while we were gone.

And I was proud of it.

But as I-70 bent to follow the final contours of the Front Range, and as the beige winter haze of the Denver metropolitan area became visible in the distance, it was clear that my brief holiday was coming to an end, and I decided, reluctantly, to reenter the real world. I killed the Otis Redding CD and tuned to KOA, a Denver AM station with enough brash watt-power to push its often dubious signal up into the crevices of the Front Range foothills. I didn't have to listen long to hear an update – 'the absolute latest on the tragedy in Boulder' – that informed me that the girl, Mallory Miller, was still missing and that the Boulder Police continued to refer to the event as a 'disappearance,' not a 'kidnapping.'

Fifteen minutes later, as I drove Highway 93 just shy of the entrance to Coal Creek Canyon, Mallory Miller's father – his first name was William – came on the air – LIVE! – with a plea for his daughter to come home, or for whoever had her to release her, or both. Whatever the problem is, he told his daughter, we can solve it.

His plea was poignant, but I didn't hear too much of it. I was distracted by something else: his name.

Gosh, I was thinking, *I once knew a guy in Boulder named Bill Miller.*

8

Details dribbled out the way they inevitably do.

I'd continued to learn a few things from my conversations with Lauren. She wasn't due back in her office until after the first of the year but was staying in touch with her colleagues daily. According to my wife the detectives working the case were apparently split into two camps during those crucial early days: those who believed that Mallory had run away and those who believed that she'd been abducted. Not surprisingly, public opinion was divided along the same fault line.

Lauren's reading of the shifting winds within law enforcement was that the runaway viewpoint was prevailing.

TV and newspapers provided background. Hour after hour of background. Given the paucity of public facts, way too much background. But apparently that was only my opinion. Four thousand reporters and camera people and producers can't be wrong.

Right?

Mallory lived in the Twelfth Street house on the Hill with her father and little brother, Reese, who was twelve years old. The Millers were separated; the children's mother had moved away from Boulder when the children were much younger. The police had been in touch with Mrs. Miller – apparently, and surprisingly, the media had not – and were confident that she could add nothing pertinent to the investigation of her daughter's disappearance.

What was known publicly about the Christmas-night events in the Miller household?

On Christmas evening Mallory had been home by herself. The Miller family had been invited to a holiday dinner at a friend's house, but Mr. Miller and Reese had gone to the celebration alone after Mallory complained about a stomachache. Mr. Miller had offered to cancel the plans, but she had insisted that they go on without her.

The physical evidence in the Miller home sounded screwy. Although a casement window near the back door was unscreened and unlocked, the family maintained that it had been that way for as long as any of them could remember. The police were not convinced that the rear window had been used to gain entry to the house, and there were no other possible indications of forced entry.

A trail of tiny blood drops ran from Mallory's second-floor bedroom down the stairs. The drops stopped abruptly a few feet from the door that led into the family room/kitchen at the rear of the house. Although DNA testing on the drops was pending, initial examination of the blood indicated that it was probably Mallory's. The upstairs bathroom that Mallory shared with Reese was a mess, and reportedly Reese had told the police that the mess was severe, 'even for her.'

Did the blood drops and the messy bathroom constitute evidence of a struggle? It depended, apparently, on whom you asked.

The record of incoming and outgoing phone calls indicated that Mallory had likely been home from the time her family left for dinner until the last time her father had called to check on her about ten minutes before nine. He had called a total of four times during the few hours that he and his son had been away from their home. Mr. Miller and Reese arrived back home at 9:20 or so.

Mallory had left a note on the kitchen counter thanking Santa Claus for a great Christmas. The note said she'd already gone to bed so that she could be fresh for their ski trip the next day.

In the note, Mallory didn't make mention of her stomach ache.

Both Mr. Miller and his son agreed that the note had been written hurriedly. Mallory, known for flowers and hearts flourishes on all her correspondence and many of her school papers, and for generous helpings of XXXs – kisskisskiss – to accompany her signature, had signed the note with a single cursive M instead of her usual florid, all lowercased 'mallory,' or her self-deprecating, ironic, all lowercased 'mall.'

Reese retired to his room, and Mr. Miller closed up the house, turned off the lights on the Christmas tree, and was in bed before ten.

The next morning, Bill Miller went into his daughter's room early – he said 4:30 – because the Millers were planning to drive all the way to Steamboat Springs the next morning and Reese had insisted that he wanted to be in line when the lifts opened to try his new Christmas snowboard in some fresh powder. But Mallory wasn't in her room. Since she hadn't actually made her bed since mounting a brief public-relations campaign to extend her curfew the previous summer, there was no easy way to know if her bed had been slept in.

Her clothes for the ski trip were neatly packed in a duffel on the floor.

Mr. Miller's initial suspicion was that his daughter had

snuck out the night before – it wouldn't be the first time – and for some reason hadn't been able to sneak back in before dawn. He guessed she had fallen asleep at a girlfriend's house, and was about to phone her closest buddy, a girl named Kara, when Reese noticed the trail of blood that seemed to start in the hallway between her bedroom and the bathroom they shared.

While Bill Miller was searching for Kara's phone number, it was Reese who called 911.

Mallory's teardrop-shaped backpack, which according to her good friends, Kara and Tammi – they were both more than willing to be interviewed by anyone with a camera – functioned more as a purse than a book-bag, wasn't in the house. Missing along with the backpack were Mallory's cell phone, her wallet, and her school planner. The school planner was important because Mallory apparently used it as an all-purpose notepad. It was where she was most likely to jot down friends' phone numbers, weekend plans, and any musings about current romantic infatuations. The girls also assured police that Mallory kept a diary – they'd both read parts of it, though not recently – but it was never located.

The absence of the school planner and the diary meant that detectives were missing a treasure trove of information about Mallory's current life. The cell phone was crucial because the memory contained the numbers of everyone Mallory considered significant.

The neighbors across the street, the Crandalls, reported that they saw a man 'loitering' on the Millers' sidewalk early that Christmas evening, before the snow had started falling. He was bundled up against the cold, they said, and walked back and forth down the block. They couldn't provide a better description.

An interesting and curious sidelight to the grand scope of media coverage of what was, at face value, nothing more than the case of a likely teenage runaway, was Mr. Miller's refusal to do interviews with any of the national media luminaries who were desperate to do a two-shot with him. He limited his on-camera time to a pair of brief appearances with a local TV reporter, Stephanie Riggs – they'd previously become acquainted on a committee that was organizing a charity run – and to occasional solo stand-ups in the front yard of his home. Each time he professed his love for his daughter and urged her to come home, or at least to call.

If someone out there has her, he'd add, please let her go. Please.

I found that I was admiring his decision not to become a media slut.

I thought he sounded like someone who thought his daughter had run away.

The lead detectives on the case were a couple of senior people that Sam liked. I didn't know either of them. A few other teams were assisting.

Jaris Slocum and Darrell Olson were assigned to interview neighbors.

Another pair of detectives was assigned to put together a detailed time line of events. That pair consisted of Sam Purdy and his partner, Lucy Tanner.

9

Diane had covered my practice while Lauren and Grace and I were up skiing.

Once I'd finished retrieving the dogs from vacation doggie-camp at our neighbor Adrienne's house, and after I'd finished unloading the car and stowing our ski gear, I phoned Diane to let her know that we were home and that I was on the clock. 'We're back from the mountains. You're free to go play. No calls, I hope,' I said.

'No calls. Your patients are always well behaved. How was it?' she asked perfunctorily.

'Perfect – great snow, terrific weather. Too short. You and Raoul have a good Christmas?'

'Yeah, you have a minute?'

'Sure,' I said. I was already wary. Diane's tone was a few degrees too serious. A few as in almost 180. I guessed that we were about to talk, once again, about Hannah, and why someone would want to kill her.

'I need a consultation,' she said.

'Like a clinical consultation?'

'Exactly.'

'Okay.'

'This isn't a casual thing. It's a formal consultation, Alan. You can't tell anyone what I'm about to tell you.'

I was standing in the kitchen and I found myself searching behind me for a stool. Something about Diane's manner screamed that this was going to be one of those why-don't-you-sit-down conversations.

'Of course.'

Yowsa, I was thinking. *What is this about?*

'It's a consultation about a consultation. In a way.'

'I'm ready, Diane.'

'Did you know that every once in a while Hannah talked to me about her cases? When she wanted an opinion about something she was a little unsure about, she'd run it by me.'

'I'm not surprised. You're good.'

'I am, but that's not the point. A few days before she died she asked me out for a glass of wine after work. No big deal, we probably did it about once a month.'

'Okay.'

'She had a specific case she wanted to discuss – a kid she'd seen the previous Friday. I didn't know the girl's name at the time, of course. Still don't, not for sure.'

What Diane was describing was far from unusual. Collegial consultations between psychotherapists are often casual, and usually conducted in a way that protects the patient's anonymity.

'Yes?'

'The strange thing – the thing that Hannah wanted my consultation about – was that this kid had come in on her own. Her parents didn't arrange the session. Kid just showed up in her office, sat in the waiting room, and wanted to talk.'

'A walk-in?' I asked. I didn't know a single private-practice psychotherapist in Boulder who saw patients without appointments.

'A walk-in.'

Diane didn't treat adolescents. Occasionally I did. I said, 'Usually a parent makes the contact, and comes to the first session. That should have been a red flag.'

Diane cleared her throat as a way of letting me know that my unfortunate propensity toward platitudes was interfering with her narrative. She added, 'I know that.' Her tone was not only scolding me for being condescending, but was also making clear that even if she didn't eat foie gras she knew what a goose was.

I tried to remember Colorado mental health law. I thought the age threshold when a child could seek treatment without a parent's consent was fifteen, but I wasn't totally certain. I'd have to check.

'How old was the kid?'

Diane answered, 'Fourteen, fifteen – I'm not a hundred percent sure. I'm pretty sure Hannah said "teenager" but . . .' I suddenly guessed where we were going. And I didn't like the road map I was seeing. At all. I feared that Diane was intimating that Hannah Grant had seen Mallory Miller for psychotherapy less than a week before Hannah died, and only two weeks before Mallory had disappeared. I said, 'You're not thinking Hannah's mystery patient was Mallory Miller, are you?'

'Everything fits.'

Other questions began making soft landings in my head like a platoon of paratroopers. Why would Mallory seek treatment without consulting her father? And why with Hannah? Had she made a second appointment? Had Hannah made a diagnosis? Was Mallory fearful? Had Hannah said anything about Mallory thinking of running away?

And the most important question: Is there any way I can avoid hearing any more about this?

But Diane had an agenda that was quite different from

insulating me from becoming more complicit, and she had a line of inquiry that I wasn't anticipating. She said, 'I can't tell anybody about this, right? That's what Hannah had wanted my consultation about. I told her that I thought she had to sit on it, had to wait and see what developed with the kid. Now, I want to hear from you if I was right.'

I hesitated while I considered the peculiar circumstances she was describing. While I pondered, Diane filled in the dead air. 'You have the craziest practice within a thousand miles of here. I figured that if you don't know what to do about something like this, then nobody does.'

I ignored the accusation, or compliment, or whatever it was. I said, 'You probably can't tell anybody anything. But it ultimately depends on what the girl told Hannah during the appointment. And on her age. For legal purposes I think you have to assume that right now you're Hannah – you have the same confidentiality responsibilities that she had when she saw the kid. Are you wondering about talking to the police? Is that it?'

'Sure, but I'm wondering about going to Mallory's father, too. I'm sure he'd love to know—'

'You probably can't talk to him. Other than the usual child-abuse exceptions to the privilege, your hands are tied. Even if you were sure it was Mallory – and it doesn't sound like you are – I don't think you could tell anyone about the girl's session.'

Because it was Diane I expected her to argue with me. She didn't. She asked, 'You want to know what she said? Why she was there?'

'To give you any useful guidance, I probably have to.' That was my way of saying, 'No, not really.'

Diane paused before she said, 'I don't really know that much. The girl was depressed about the holidays. And she misses her mom.'

10

Despite its cosmopolitan airs, Boulder is, at its core, a small town. As would likely have occurred in any other small town, it seemed that everyone knew someone who knew someone who had some connection to the missing girl. In the week between that season's Christmas and New Year's celebrations many hours were lost, probably way too many, in informal parlor sessions intended to identify the precise arcs of those degrees of separation.

My friend and neighbor Adrienne, a Boulder urologist, made it clear that one of the key players in the drama – someone connected to the Miller family, or to one of the public faces of the law enforcement team – was one of her patients. I had two biking buddies who had daughters who played on the missing girl's U-15 club soccer team. Lauren's legal assistant's teenage son's best friend used to cut the grass at the missing girl's house.

Like that.

As I'd suspected when I first heard that Mallory's father's first name was Bill, it turned out that I, too, had a tangential tie to the Miller family. It was tangential only because of the passage of time. Years before – I would have to check my records to put a precise number on the question of how many years, but I was guessing somewhere around eight or nine, maybe even ten or eleven – I'd seen the missing girl's parents for a solitary couples therapy session. Just one. Given the time lag since that session, my recall of the intervention was surprisingly clear, probably because of how disheartening my clinical appraisal was at the time.

Mr. Miller had dragged his reluctant wife in for the evaluation. It had been clear to me from the moment the introductions started that Mrs. Miller did not want to be in my office. Her demeanor had reminded me of a child who would gladly promise never, ever to eat candy again if she could only avoid the dentist's drill *this* time. All that was absent was a foot stomp.

My clinical antennae were further tuned by her appearance. Any professional who has spent enough hours with people suffering acute mental illness would have recognized that Mrs. Miller's physical appearance was just the slightest bit off. Her hair, her makeup, her clothes – everything was just a degree or two away from ordinary. My session with the Millers was on a lovely Indian summer September day, and Mrs. Miller came dressed in a wool suit, carrying a straw bag, and wearing scuffed white pumps. Over her eyes she wore big, bright Jackie O sunglasses. All the pieces, individually, were fine. Acceptable, at least. But together on a fine autumn day they totaled a sartorial sum that I guessed only Mrs. Miller could fully comprehend.

For his part, Mr. Miller was in something close to full-blown denial about the extent of the daunting challenges he faced. He appeared to have convinced himself, at least temporarily, that a few heart-to-heart sessions of some old-fashioned talking therapy would be just the trick to help lead his wife away from the middle of the field where she'd been aimlessly wandering and ease her back onto the straight and narrow marital tracks where she belonged.

Where exactly was Mrs. Miller doing her figurative wandering?

Into another man's bed? No. Drugs? Alcohol? Nothing so pedestrian.

Mrs. Miller, it turned out, attended weddings. Usually two or three ceremonies a month, but during prime nuptial season she would do more. 'Ten one month,' Mr. Miller had reported to me over the phone when he'd called for the initial appointment. 'That's her record. This past June. The truth is she'd do ten a week if she could fit them in.'

She dressed elegantly for each one of the ceremonies. Her collection of wedding outfits numbered in the dozens, and she had an enviable assortment of spring and summer hats – Mr. Miller called them hats; Mrs. Miller referred to them as 'my bonnets.' She bought nice gifts for every one of the happy couples. Many of the outfits and all of the wedding gifts were purchased from cable TV home shopping channels. She stayed away from registries – 'Who needs to be told what to buy? My Lord,' she asked aloud during our session – and apparently her gifting tendencies leaned toward ceramic figurines of animals. Puppies and kittens mostly, but occasional angels and young children.

The wedding presents were always pricey things. 'It's her only vice,' Mr. Miller had said in admirable defense of his wife's largesse. During one particular month of nuptials every newlywed couple received – after a one-hour this-is-it closeout sale on QVC – a beautiful shiny chrome home espresso machine from Italy. The piston kind. The total tab for the machines was almost two thousand dollars.

The UPS guy and the FedEx lady who drove the routes

that included the Millers' home were on a first-name basis with everyone in the household.

Other than the sheer number of weddings, and the accumulating expense, what was the problem? The problem was that Mrs. Miller had never been invited to any of the ceremonies. None. Still, she fervently believed that she was an honored guest at every one of them, and if challenged could concoct an elaborate though ultimately nonsensical explanation for her attendance.

Her typical pattern was to arrive at the church or synagogue with some breathless flair just moments before the festivities began. She'd edge herself into a prime seat for the service, usually in the second or third row right behind the family, always on the bride's side, center aisle, and she'd smile and wave at the other guests as though she knew them quite well.

She always cried during the vows.

On more than one occasion after the nuptials were complete she'd exited the church along with the bride's family and joined the wedding party for the limousine ride to the reception.

Psychotherapists are trained to ask the question, 'Why now?' Why is this man, or this woman, in my office seeking help *today*? Why didn't she come in last week, or last month, or next week, or next month? The answer to the question yields what we like to call the 'precipitating event.'

For the Millers the precipitating event for seeking psychological assistance was crystal clear. The previous weekend Mrs. Miller had, at the insistence of an irascible groom and an implacable bride, been removed from a festive wedding reception at the Hotel Boulderado by the police. The immediate precipitant for her removal was

Mrs. Miller's dubious decision to break into the celebratory dance between the newlyweds and politely, but firmly, demand her turn to waltz with the groom.

'Excuse me? I think you forgot your dance with *me*,' she'd said to him with a sad smile as she tapped the groom on the shoulder. 'You'll excuse us?' she'd added for the benefit of his befuddled bride. Then Mrs. Miller held up her silk-draped arms, waiting her turn to be swept away.

The groom, it turned out, was a Boulder sheriff's deputy. Half the guests at the wedding were Boulder sheriff's deputies. Not one of them recognized the woman in the yellow silk dress. Most importantly, the bride, who knew the detailed logistics of her wedding day as intimately as a chef knows the contents of his larder, didn't recognize the woman in the yellow silk dress.

Later that day, at the police department across town, the authorities released Mrs. Miller to Mr. Miller's custody with the strong suggestion that a mental health consultation might be in order.

Enter *moi*.

My appraisal?

Based on the brief history the Millers provided, Mrs. Miller's descent into schizophrenia had been gradual. By history, I was guessing that she'd suffered her first psychotic break at around age twenty-three – she and her husband had celebrated their own wedding when she was twenty-two – and she had begun to display more intransigent symptoms of psychosis shortly after the birth of her daughter. Mrs. Miller was twenty-four at that time. The symptoms worsened once again after the birth of her son two years later. I suspected that over the intervening years her family had consistently minimized her growing list of eccentricities, and that the reclusive behavior she demonstrated – reclusive when she wasn't attending weddings, that is – had been rationalized away one way or another. Evidence of her frank psychosis had, at times, been blatantly denied by everyone in her limited orbit.

The severe mental illness was Mrs. Miller's. The conspiracy to pretend it didn't exist, however, was most definitely a family affair. Her husband, Bill, was a nice guy. After five minutes in my office, I realized that he was a relentless cheerleader and a determined advocate for his wife. 'Whatever I can do to help, I'll do,' he said. 'Anything.'

It was my unpleasant task to suggest to Mr. and Mrs. Miller that before they focused on issues in their marital relationship – perhaps – Mrs. Miller should seek some individual treatment for the difficulties she was having distinguishing things that were real from things that were not.

'Is it that bad? Really?' Mr. Miller said in mutual self-defense after I'd asked how he felt about what was going on in his marriage. 'I love Rachel. In the grand scheme of things this is a small problem, right? I mean, we're talking weddings. It's not cancer. There are many, many times when she seems just fine.'

During my internship, while I was spending a rotation in an acute adult psychiatric inpatient unit, I had become extremely frustrated by one of my patients. He was a huge Samoan man, a schizophrenic whose communication abilities had devolved to the point where his speech consisted solely of multiple repetitions of a deeply baritone 'hoho,' sometimes singly, more often tendered in multiple repetitions. Despite his severe psychopathology and his immense size – the man outweighed me by at least 200 pounds – he was congenial and cooperative. We would sit for brief one-to-one 'psychotherapy' sessions a few times a week. Each meeting lasted five minutes, max. He would listen to me – I doubted at times that he comprehended the intended meaning of a single word I said – gesture in the air with his fat hands, and say, 'Hoho, hoho,' occasionally interrupting my otherwise useless intervention, sometimes waiting politely until I was done.

Infrequently he would smile or open his eyes wide in apparent wonder. More often his face would yield no expression at all.

My Samoan patient was already receiving enough Haldol to sedate an elephant, yet his mystifying psychotic process seemed immune to my best, though admittedly inexperienced and ultimately ineffective, attempts to be helpful.

I confessed to my supervisor, who knew the situation well, that I felt incompetent to treat the man. The supervising psychiatrist said two things that have stuck with me ever since. First, he told me that there are some people who are better at being crazy than I will ever be at being therapeutic. The Samoan, he said, was my case in point.

Second, he told me that from a psychopathology perspective, some of our patients have cancer. He was speaking metaphorically, of course, but I still recalled his caution on those days that my clinical skills seemed hopelessly inadequate to contain the sometimes incorrigible forces of my patients' mental illnesses.

I was tempted to share those pearls of wisdom with Bill Miller the day that he brought his wife into my office for evaluation. But I didn't. His hope was too inspiring to behold. His desire to lift his wife up was too gratifying to witness. He didn't want to believe that his wife had the mental health equivalent of cancer. I feared that indeed she might, but I wasn't ready to believe it either. That's how powerful his hope was.

Despite the fact that I thought I'd pulled just enough of my punches to allow Mr. Miller's hope to stay afloat, my ultimate assessment that day, and my verbalized prescription for further care, sucked all the oxygen out of the room.

Every last molecule.

In contrast to bipolar disease, which at its heart is a disorder of mood, schizophrenia is a disorder of thought, of perception. Schizophrenic thinking results in a myriad of cognitive symptoms. Hallucinations, delusions, and paranoia are the most common. In a schizophrenic's world, what most of us consider orderly thought begins to deteriorate, and cognition becomes subject to interferences from beyond the confines of usual perception. The process that results appears to an outsider to be bizarre, tangential, repetitive, or oddly referential.

An extreme example was my Samoan's baffling chorus of hohos. But in a schizophrenic's brain the variety of ways that faulty neurochemistry can cause thinking to deteriorate is large. In severe cases the outcomes are almost universally tragic.

The problem that was most apparent to me during my brief appraisal of Mrs. Miller was the extent of her delusional thinking – specifically her irrational belief that she had been a special invitee to all those weddings. Although the nature of the invitations remained her secret during our interview, that was where I focused my attention as I presented my suggestions to the Millers.

Mr. Miller seemed somewhat relieved by my prescription for additional help. For him, it represented an injection of helium that might provide enough lift to keep his airship of hope afloat. But Mrs. Miller resisted my recommendation and argued and bargained and then bargained some more. I couldn't follow her train of thought as she tried to explain the imperative she felt about attending the weddings. The truth was that her thinking more closely resembled a corral of bumper cars driven by preadolescents than anything like a metaphorical train.

She wept for a good five minutes before she ultimately relented to my suggestion and to her husband's gentle prodding. She only relented, I was certain, because of her husband's insistent kindness and his repeated promises that he'd be beside her no matter what, and because I'd managed to make it clear on that day that my resolve was a more than decent match for her thought disorder.

The fear in her eyes when she realized what was about to happen next was as poignant a thing as I had witnessed in my office in a long, long time. She rested her head on her husband's shoulder and with eyes full of fat tears she said, 'Okay, okay. Okay, okay. Okay, okay. Okay, okay.'

He said, 'I'm here. I'm here. I'm here.'

I'd been doing clinical work for too long to consider entertaining the clinical delusion that the fact that Mrs. Miller had relented for that moment meant that the road ahead would be smooth.

'No more weddings?' she'd asked me incredulously only a moment after her four pairs of *okay*s had trumped her husband's three-of-a-kind of *I'm here*. 'Oh Willy, does this mean no more weddings?'

Bill – Willy – looked at me for direction.

I said, 'Yes, I'm afraid it does.'

With a despair that I could feel all the way to my toes, she lamented, 'What will they do? Oh, what will they do?'

What I saw in her eyes wasn't concern, it was fear. She hadn't said, 'What will *I* do?' She had said, 'What will *they* do?' She was worried about 'them.'

I wondered, of course, who 'they' were. The brides and grooms with whom she hadn't yet celebrated? Or perhaps – and I knew this was more likely – the speakers of the voices that I suspected were whispering or shouting wicked nuptial imperatives into her ears.

I didn't know. Nor did I suspect that she would tell me. Not that day.

While the Millers were sitting in my office I'd already acknowledged to myself that I wasn't the best-equipped mental health professional in town to help Mrs. Miller with her individual treatment. I explained my rationale to the Millers, and with their consent I picked up the phone and called Mary Black – the same psychiatrist who was sharing offices with Hannah Grant before Hannah's death – and asked if she could do an urgent emergency assessment.

I'd chosen a psychiatrist to assist Mrs. Miller because I knew that the initial phases of Mrs. Miller's treatment, and likely the long-term progression of her care as well, would involve the shuffling and management of anti-psychotic medications, and in Colorado the provision of those pharmaceuticals was the domain of the medical profession. I'd chosen Mary Black as a psychiatrist for Mrs. Miller not only because Mary was good, but also because she was relatively new in town and she was still hungry for fresh patients. I didn't think it was advisable for the Millers to wait weeks to see a psychiatrist and begin treatment.

Mary graciously agreed to evaluate Mrs. Miller later that afternoon. Mr. Miller had driven his wife the few blocks over to Mary's office directly from mine, and I'd never seen the Millers together again.

Months later, at a summer party at a mutual friend's house, Mary Black had suggested to me – 'You know that woman you referred to me? The wedding woman?' – that Mrs. Miller's care had quickly degenerated into a carousel of poor treatment compliance, failed trials of conventional drugs and the newer atypical antipsychotic compounds, and repeated short-term, stabilizing, acute hospitalizations.

The wedding planners and pastors and ministers and rabbis in town knew all about Mrs. Miller by then. Ushers at virtually every wedding ceremony in the county carried an eight-by-ten glossy of her in full nuptial regalia, and after six months of futile mental-health treatment she was being turned away at some church or synagogue door almost every Saturday.

It was precisely the kind of outcome that I had feared.

When she was done telling me the story of what had happened to Mrs. Miller, Mary Black told me one other thing. She said, 'I don't think my husband would stand by me the way her husband has. It's inspiring. Truly inspiring. The things he's done for her . . .'

Mary's eyes told me something else: that she knew that I knew that I owed her one.

Bill Miller came back to see me a little over a year later. It was the January right after the horrid Christmas when Boulder's little blonde beauty queen had been discovered dead in the basement of her home. Bill and I met for only a few minutes, maybe fifteen. He'd asked for the time so that he could thank me for my help with Rachel. I'd told him, honestly, that I didn't think I'd done much.

Although he'd suggested that his wife's treatment with Mary Black hadn't gone particularly well – and explained that he and Rachel were temporarily separated – he didn't offer any details and I didn't ask for any. We talked briefly about the Christmas-night murder of the little girl, how hard it was for his kids, and he asked me whether I'd noticed the story in the *Camera* about the young orthodontist who'd been hit by a car and killed a few days before Christmas near Chatauqua. I said I had. He told me he'd witnessed the accident, and I wondered briefly if that traumatic experience was why he had come back in to see me.

But as I waited for Bill to irrigate that wound, he moved on. He said that he and the kids were coping, and he made a particular point of explaining how well things were going for him at work – he'd just been promoted to a post he'd always coveted – as though he wanted to emphasize for me that, despite his wife's illness and his marital problems, his family life hadn't totally fallen apart.

Although I don't really remember, it wouldn't surprise me to learn that I had ended the session with some generalized offer of future help, something like, 'Let me know if there's anything I can do.'

He'd probably said, 'Thank you,' and that had been that.

11

'The girl was anxious about the holidays? And she misses her mother? That's what the session she had with Hannah was about? That's it?' I said to Diane. 'No. No, that's not all of it,' Diane said. 'Come on, I'm doing this from memory. It was no big deal at the time. I didn't take any notes. The whole consultation lasted five minutes, maybe. God, I should write things down. I just should.'

'What do you remember?'

'The girl told Hannah that her mother has a severe mental illness and had left Boulder years ago. The girl doesn't talk to her much, misses her. Hannah was speculating about the mother having bipolar disorder or schizophrenia, but she didn't really have enough information. She was worried about the girl developing symptoms.'

I wanted to tell Diane that I already knew the details. I wanted to tell her about all the weddings that Mrs. Miller attended, about the lovely bonnets and the QVC gifts, and about the delusions, and the voices. I wanted to tell her that at the time I did my eval that I thought Hannah was right about the schizophrenia, wrong about the bipolar disorder.

Instead I said, 'You can't tell anybody, Diane. You can

only divulge the fact that this girl saw Hannah for psychotherapy if you have reason to suspect that there has been, or is likely to be, child abuse. Otherwise the privilege holds.'

'But she can't seek care without a parent's permission until she's fifteen.'

'You're sure about that?' I asked.

'Yes.'

Diane was often sure about things that turned out not to be true, but I suspected she was right about that one. 'Even if it's true, I don't know whether that would abrogate her privilege.'

'But it might.'

'You're not even sure it was really Mallory. You'd have to violate privilege even to be certain. God knows there would be lawyers involved, and once there are lawyers involved, anything can happen. Either way, the privilege won't evaporate today. If they started litigating this tomorrow you wouldn't have an answer before next year's aspen season. You know lawyers better than I do.'

'What do you mean? You're married to one, while I' – she paused for effect – 'am married to a Mediterranean god.'

I decided not to take that detour with her.

'What if she's dead?' Diane asked.

Shit. 'Diane, do you know that she's—'

'No, no, I don't. I don't. But if she were, if that was determined, I was wondering if I could—'

'No, you couldn't – confidentiality survives death. Well, actually you'd have to tell her parents if they asked, because they would probably have control of her estate, which includes all her medical records, but—'

'Why would they ask? If they didn't know she'd been in treatment, why would they ask?'

'Exactly.'

Diane and I had been partners longer than Lauren and I had been married. I wasn't surprised that we were finishing each other's thoughts. But the ping-pong nature of the conversation we were having felt awkward to me. Why? I suspected that each of us was in possession of some information that we weren't sure how to handle, information we didn't want to keep to ourselves, but information we weren't at all sure we were permitted to share.

'The girl also told Hannah—'

'Wait, I want to do this face-to-face. I have a patient late this afternoon at the office. I'll come downtown. You available?'

She sighed. 'I was just about to head out to the after-Christmas sales on the Mall. Things are going to get really picked over if I don't get down there soon.'

After-Christmas shopping on the Pearl Street Mall? I would have preferred to be strapped into a chair and serenaded by The Captain and Tennille.

'With Raoul?' That was wishful thinking on my part. The worse the party, the more grateful I was for Raoul's company. After-Christmas shopping on the Mall sounded like a very bad party.

'Shopping? With me? Are you kidding? He won't shop with me.'

There was a caution there I knew; Raoul was a wise man. I swallowed a sigh. 'Okay, where do think you're going to be? I'll meet you someplace.'

The little office building that Diane and I owned together was an architecturally pedestrian – certainly not a painted lady – early 1900s Victorian house on the west end of Walnut, a couple of blocks from the Pearl Street Mall. The odds of finding street parking in downtown Boulder during the closeout-sale-frenzied week between Christmas and New Year's were about the same as the odds of being eaten by a great white shark, so Diane was planning to stash her Saab behind our building and start her quest for bargains near Ninth and Pearl on the west end of downtown. Since I had a patient to see, I told her I'd park at our offices, too, and suggested we rendezvous outside Peppercorn at three.

Dirty snow from the Christmas-night snowstorm lingered in shady places along the herringbone brick pathways of the Mall, but despite what the calendar said, the day was pleasant in the sun. That's where I was sitting enjoying an afternoon interlude when Diane sauntered up to me at about ten after. She was carrying two huge shopping bags. I gave her a hug and a kiss on one cheek. She gave me one of the bags to carry. In many ways – mostly but not entirely good – Diane and I were like an old married couple.

We began walking, the sun low against our backs. From the heft of the bag in my hand, I surmised that she had been scouring the sales for either bricks or bullion.

'This doesn't happen to me, you know,' she said. 'This is the sort of thing that happens to you. This stuff with this mystery girl and Hannah. This murder and kidnapping and cops and criminals crap I seem to be mixed up with. It's your specialty, not mine.'

I was tempted to argue that it was debatable that Hannah had been murdered, and that it seemed more likely that Mallory was indeed a runaway and not a kidnap victim. But Diane's bigger point was close to the truth. Karma did seem to deliver mayhem to my door with disturbing regularity.

'If it's what you think it is, I'm mixed up in it, too, Diane.'

For a moment she was quiet. She either didn't quite hear me, she didn't quite believe me, or she was busy discounting my words as an unwelcome empathic gesture.

Finally, she replied, 'Sure, you were part of the Hannah thing. I know, I know. I know you were there. And well, now you're part of this other thing, but that's only because I've dragged you into it. Listen, if you'd rather I talk to someone else about this, I understand. But I really felt I needed a second opinion about what to do next, and I don't know anyone else who has as much experience with crazy therapy crap as you do.'

Crazy therapy crap? Once again I was tempted to argue her premise, but recognizing the futility, I said, 'The truth is that I was a little bit mixed up in the Mallory thing already, even before we talked.'

She heard me that time. Her voice grew conspiratorial. 'What?'

I shook my head and kept walking. 'I need to make this a consultation, too. My knowledge is clinical, just like yours.'

She'd grown tired of the forced-infantry-march nature of our pace and abruptly stopped walking. Once I realized she had stopped I did, too, and turned back to face her. Over the top of her head the sun was looming just above the highest peaks of the Front Range in the southwest sky. The light was sharp but gentle. It felt only faintly warm on my face.

'Tell me,' she said.

It was a shrink phrase, psychotherapy shorthand for 'go on' or 'don't stop there' or 'damn your resistance, spill the beans.'

'This is for real – a professional consultation – you can't tell anyone.'

'Holy moly,' she said.

I wished I had my sunglasses on my eyes instead of in my jacket pocket. I was squinting into the sun. *Holy moly?* 'Is that a yes?'

'I'm thinking. You get into the weirdest things, Alan. I'm not sure I want any part of whatever it is.'

She was playing with me. 'Sure you do,' I said.

'You're right, I do. I'm a glutton for punishment. Okay, go ahead and consult with me.' She raised her chin an inch and tilted it up to the side as though she were opening herself for a right cross. I opened my mouth to reply just as she changed her strategy. 'No, no, let me guess.' She made a face that a bad acting student might make to try to portray someone cogitating, contorted it a few times for dramatic effect, and finally said, 'Nope, I give up.'

'Years ago, I saw the Millers, Mallory's parents – those Millers – for an assessment. One session only. Turned out to be a long eval, over two hours. I saw them as a couple, immediately recognized that Mrs. Miller's individual problems were . . . significant, and referred her on to Mary Black for ongoing treatment and some serious pharmacological intervention. I never saw them again. Mary took over from there. Mr. Miller came back sometime later to thank me for my help. But I never laid eyes on the kids, don't even remember if I knew their names.'

Diane was a smart lady. She made all the appropriate connections instantly. 'That must be how Mallory knew about Hannah, right? Right? I bet the crazy mother parked Mallory in the waiting room while she had her psychotherapy sessions and her med consultations with Mary. Don't you think? If Hannah had seen a little girl alone in the waiting room she would have chatted her up. You know she would have. She would have made friends with her. Especially if she saw her sitting out there alone on a regular basis. That's the connection. That's it.'

'Yes,' I agreed. 'That's probably it.' Hannah's kindness was almost as legendary as her obsessiveness. I had no trouble manufacturing a vision of Hannah on her knees in the waiting room connecting with a lonely or frightened little girl who was waiting for her mother to finish an appointment with her psychiatrist.

Hi, sweetheart, what's your name?

I'm Mallory.

I'm Hannah. You waiting for your mom to finish her meeting?

'Holy moly,' Diane repeated.

Diane started walking down the Mall again. I tagged along behind. 'Holy moly' was a new phrase for Diane. I was already beginning to hope that – like most everything designed by Microsoft – it came equipped with built-in obsolescence.

I said, 'I'd bet mortgage money that her disease isn't stable. Rachel Miller sabotaged every last treatment that Mary Black tried years ago.'

Diane added an edge to her tone and said, 'Why do you say "disease"? Almost everyone else says "illness."'

'A lot of other people say "clients." I say "patients." Do you know why? "Patient" is from the Latin. It means "one who suffers." It fits what we do.'

She smiled, and shifted her voice into sarcasm mode. 'I bet if a new client walked into your office and had to listen to you parsing Latin all day long, she'd become one-who-suffers in no time at all. You didn't answer my question.'

'Other people say "illness"?'

'They do.'

It probably wasn't true. Diane's penchant for assuredness about this kind of thing often had scant correlation to reality. Regardless, it took me only about three steps to arrive at an answer to her question. 'Think about it. The word is *dis-ease. Dis. Ease.* It's apropos, don't you think, to what we deal with every day?'

In my peripheral vision I could tell that Diane had shaken off my explanation with the same ease with which she'd just ridiculed the tiny bit of Latin I recalled from high school. I consoled myself with the fact that she was equally dismissive as she discounted her husband Raoul's opinions about just about everything political.

Thankfully, she moved on to a fresh thought, and said, 'In case you didn't know it, she's in Las Vegas. The girl told Hannah that her mother is living in Las Vegas. She gets phone calls from her every once in a while. Her father doesn't know that they're in touch as much as they are. It's a source of conflict. The girl wasn't sure what to do.'

'Vegas?' I asked, but it was more of an 'ah-ha!' exclamation than a question. I was thinking, *Of course Rachel Miller is in Las Vegas. Where else would someone go who is addicted to weddings?*

'You don't sound that surprised, Alan. Does she gamble? Is that part of her pathology, her dis-ease?'

'No,' I said, refusing to bite. 'She goes to weddings. That's what the presenting complaint was for the couple's therapy: Rachel Miller went to lots and lots of weddings. She thought she was a special guest at all of them. It was the center of her delusional world. I suspected that she had command hallucinations but she didn't admit to hearing voices during our one interview. Her husband told me she did, that she heard voices.'

'Paranoid schizophrenia?'

'That's what I thought at the time, but a lot has changed in how we all view psychotic process, you know? I'm not sure how I'd diagnose her today.'

'Mixed thought and mood disorder? That's what you're thinking?' Diane asked.

'Something like that, yes.'

By that time Diane and I had covered all four blocks and were at the east end of the Mall. We were waiting at the light to cross Fifteenth onto the sidewalk on the still-sunny side of Pearl Street. I said, 'You want to keep going or head back?'

'I don't care. We can walk to Denver if you want, but I want to hear more about Mallory's mother and all the weddings.'

It took me a while but I explained Mrs. Miller's odd nuptial delusions to Diane, who had many questions, some psychological in nature, more having to do with wedding logistics, owning all those outfits, and buying all those gifts.

I had answers for a paltry few of the questions in any of the categories, psychological or matrimonial. After multiple prods on her part I tried to refocus her by saying, 'I only saw the Millers for that one session. That's all. Most of my energy went into trying to understand her history and then trying to prepare the two of them for a whole different kind of treatment than they'd come in the door thinking they'd get.'

'Receptions, too?' Diane asked, ignoring my pleas of ignorance.

I told her, yes, that Rachel had also attended the receptions. I shared the story about the one at the Boulderado where she'd been busted by the sheriff's deputy.

Diane had more questions. While I protested my continued ignorance about most things matrimonial, Diane chided me that it had been a very long session I'd had with the Millers, and I should know more than I was letting on.

Once Diane had – finally – exhausted her queries about

Mrs. Miller and her serial wedding attendance, I had a question of my own. It was the question that I had wanted to ask Diane since the moment she told me that Hannah had done an intake with the girl who was probably Mallory. 'Do you think it's possible that Mallory went to Vegas to see her mother? Based on what Hannah told you, would she have done that? Could that be what this is all about?'

'It's possible. Hannah stressed that the girl missed her mother. May even have said it a couple of times, so you have to wonder. Hannah focused on the mother/daughter relationship and the conflicts between the girl and her dad.'

'Might explain the Christmas Day stomachache,' I said. 'Her holiday anxiety, missing her mom.'

'Psychosomatic?'

'Why not? If she was worried enough to seek a therapist on her own, she could certainly be worried enough to develop symptoms.'

She paused after a couple more steps. We had walked all the way down to Eighteenth Street by then, almost a full ten blocks from our cars. I stopped and turned back to the west. The late December sun was just a slash of brilliance above the Divide and pedestrian traffic was thinning out on the Mall.

'What was the mother like, Alan? Could she have come and taken Mallory?' Diane asked.

'I suppose that's possible. Anything is, but—'

'The cops would check that first, right? They would have gone to Vegas and checked with Mallory's mother to see if her kid was there, to see if the mom had been in Boulder?'

'Yes,' I said. I was also thinking that the Boulder cops who went to Vegas would probably have found a truly disturbed woman.

Diane casually tapped me on the shoulder and handed me the second shopping bag. Like a fool, I took it.

We started walking back in the direction of the mountains. The western sky was much brighter than the eastern sky had been. She asked, 'So are you ready now?'

Segue or no segue, I knew exactly what she was talking about. We really had been friends a long, long time. 'Sure, as ready as I'll be. So what else did the girl tell Hannah?'

12

The moment the sun completed its descent behind the Rockies the day turned from pleasantly brisk to downright cold. What I had been considering a light breeze felt decidedly like an icy wind. Diane had seen it coming – now that I was schlepping both of her shopping bags she was able to shove her mittened hands deep into her jacket pockets for additional warmth.

My gloves were in my car and the flesh on my hands was the color of the fat on a slab of uncooked bacon.

'The kid was concerned that her dad was "up to something" or "into something." She'd left Hannah with the impression that she didn't like it, whatever it was. The girl was feeling like she had to do something about it, or else. That kind of thing.'

'"Up to something"? That's a quote?'

'Close as I can remember. It was a casual consultation – I didn't exactly memorize it. I didn't know what was about to happen.'

'"Or else"? What did that mean?'

Diane shrugged. 'I should have asked. I didn't ask. She also had some friend trouble, too, was conflicted about some guy she was seeing.'

'Boyfriend?'

'I guess.'

'It felt like typical adolescent stuff to you?'

'At the time it did.'

'And the nature of what the girl's father was up to?'

'Hannah didn't know.'

'Precipitant?'

'See, that's the thing. I asked Hannah that, too. Hannah felt there was some urgency for the girl, but couldn't get the kid to admit to anything.'

'A secret?'

'I wish I knew.'

'The holidays?'

'Hannah didn't stress that part. I suppose it's possible.'

'The police should know all this,' I said. 'Boulder's two most high-profile recent . . .'

I didn't know what to call Hannah's death and Mallory's disappearance. Diane did. 'Crimes. The word you're looking for is "crimes." "Felonies" would work fine, too.'

'Whatever. The police would want to know that there's a possible connection – a big connection – between Hannah's death and Mallory's disappearance. But nobody knows about it but you,' I said.

'And you,' she reminded me.

'Mostly you. It's too bad you can't tell the police.'

She skipped for one step. I think that's what she did, anyway – just one little schoolgirl skip. Why? Who knew? 'I bet that twerp Slocum would love to know what the two of us know, wouldn't he? He'd probably cuff me again and throw me in the slammer if he knew what I was keeping from him.'

I was thinking that not only would Detective Slocum like to know, but so would Diane Sawyer, Katie Couric,

Geraldo Rivera, and Oprah. Not to mention the *Enquirer* and the *Sun* and the *Star*.

And Bill Miller.

I was also thinking that Diane's continuing animosity toward Detective Jaris Slocum, though completely understandable, was one of the ways that she was postponing her grief about Hannah's death. That moment, however, wasn't the time to confront her with that particular reality. Years of experience with her had taught me that with Diane I had to pick my spots.

'Raoul wants me to sue Slocum. Did I tell you that?'

'For what?'

'He doesn't care. He calls him "that little fascist." "Let's sue that little fascist, baby," he tells me. He hates it when I say it, but sometimes he's such an American.'

I said, 'Raoul has too much time on his hands. He needs to go start a new company or something.' Diane's husband was a legendary Boulder entrepreneur. When he wasn't nurturing somebody else's start-up tech company, he was busy casting the bricks to create a new one of his own.

As we crossed back over Fifteenth to the herringbone pathways of the Mall, Diane asked the money question: 'So what do I do about all this?'

'Did Hannah leave any notes?'

'She named me in her will to handle the details of closing up her practice should anything happen to her. But I haven't found any notes about that session. Zip, *nada*.'

Few therapists show the foresight to make death stipulations in their wills. But Hannah had. I said, 'She knew Paul Weinman back when, didn't she?'

'Yes, she knew Paul.' Paul had been another friend of Diane's, a psychologist who'd skied into a tree at

Breckenridge years before. His sudden death, and the subsequent uncertainty about what to do with his current cases and his practice records, had caused a lot of procrastinating Boulder therapists to make plans for what would happen to their practices in case of their own death.

'Do the police have her appointment calendar?' I asked.

'Hannah just used initials, same as us. They would have to cross-reference the calendar with her billing records or her clinical files to find out who she was seeing. Cozy is handling the cops for me, and he's not going to let them see anything confidential.'

'Anything else important in Hannah's records?'

'Not really. Closing her practice has been routine. I've done a few one-time visits with her patients to check for decompensation or acute reactive problems to her . . . death. I decided to pick up a couple of her cases. Oh, and did I tell you I'm going to see the woman who was at her office that day, the day that Hannah died?'

'The woman with the hair?' *And the Cheetos.* 'You're seeing her for treatment?'

'I am. She's having a lot of trouble. I guess it's not too surprising, considering. She's coping by becoming a little Nancy Drew, trying to solve the mystery of what happened to her therapist.'

'Isn't it kind of odd seeing her? Given what happened.'

'You don't think it's a problem, do you?'

I wasn't sure. Psychologists are prohibited from treating people with whom they have another existing relationship. It means, for instance, that I couldn't treat Grace's preschool teacher, when Grace gets around to having one. But I didn't know if the fact that both parties had been present when a possible murder victim's body was discovered really constituted a preexisting relationship. The issue had never come up before in any of the ethics discussions I'd had.

I didn't want to make Diane crazy, so I immediately resolved my ambivalence by saying, 'No, I don't think so.'

'Good. Anyway, I've referred a few of Hannah's other patients to other therapists in town. Don't be hurt. I'm not ignoring your talents – they all wanted female therapists, baby. But most of them decided not to continue for now. I'm still having her office phone lines forwarded to my number. The hardest part of the whole thing has been letting people who hadn't heard what happened to her know that she is dead. And, you know, how she died.'

'I can imagine.' We took two more steps. 'Is it possible you spoke with her?'

'With whom?'

'Mallory.'

'What do you mean?'

'Is it possible she was one of the people who called who hadn't heard about Hannah's death?'

'Oh my God.'

'Well?'

'It's possible. I had a couple of difficult calls . . . a woman asked . . . she was young – I guessed a CU student – wanted "Dr. Grant." I'm not sure I ever got a name. I told her what had happened and she . . . hung up. Oh my God.'

'When was that call?' I asked.

'Last week. Maybe Monday. Oh my God, I may have talked with her.'

'Do you remember what you said?'

'I've been upset,' Diane said, her voice suddenly hollow. 'I might not have handled it well. When Hannah's patients asked me how she died, I . . .'

'Suggested the possibility she'd been murdered?'

'It's not just me, Alan. Everybody – the papers – I'm not the only one . . .'

I touched her. 'It's okay.'

'The kid was really upset. I offered to meet with her, but she hung up.'

What did it mean that Diane might have talked with Mallory a few days before she disappeared? Maybe nothing. But it was possible that Mallory walked away from the conversation believing that her therapist had been murdered.

'What about the other call? You said there were two difficult calls.'

'The other one was from a man. Wanted to know what would happen to his therapy records. I assured him I had custody of them and that they'd stay confidential. He wouldn't give me his name, either. He asked how he could get the records. I told him. He didn't want a referral. He was almost . . . belligerent.'

I didn't reply right away. Diane wanted to move on. 'Speaking of records, Hannah's attorney – the guy who drew up her will – called me a couple of days before Christmas and asked if she had left any records that would allow final bills to be prepared.'

'For her patients?'

'Yes.'

'That's rude. Who's the attorney?'

'Guy named Jerry Crandall. I don't know him. He's a general-practice guy, doesn't do much divorce work.' Diane did do a lot of divorce and custody work; she knew all the family-law attorneys in town. 'But that's what I told him, too, that it was kind of cold. He said he had a fiduciary responsibility and that Hannah's accounts receivable are an asset of her estate.'

'Fiduciary responsibility aside, I'm not sure I'd like to get a bill from my dead therapist.'

'He's a lawyer. Can I finish?' Diane didn't wait for me to say yes. 'I told him I'd take a look and get back to him. While you guys were up skiing I checked through Hannah's practice calendar and matched things up with her recent process notes, gave him a list of unbilled sessions. When I compared all her records I realized that the session with this kid wasn't in her calendar, didn't have any notes, and had never been billed. It was the only one not in her calendar.'

'No other sessions without notes?'

'None that I found. Hannah was Hannah.' Loud exhale. 'What do I do, Alan?'

'In a word, nothing. Hell, Diane, you're not even sure it was Mallory. I think the kid is entitled to confidentiality, so you can't reveal what you know from the session.'

'It was her,' Diane said.

I ignored that. 'Any hint of abuse during the consultation?'

'No.'

'You can't tell anyone then, including the police.'

'What if the police knew Mallory had been kidnapped? If the parents got a note, or a ransom demand. Would that change things?'

I thought about it for the length of time it took to try, and fail, to pass three young mothers pushing strollers wheel hub to wheel hub on the bricks of the Mall. It was the pedestrian equivalent of trying to drive past some recalcitrant semis that were rolling side-by-side on the highway.

'Sure. Then it would be a whole different ball game. By definition a kidnapped kid is a kid who's being abused, and abuse changes all the privilege rules. If you thought you knew something that could aid the investigation into her kidnapping – once the authorities decided it was a kidnapping – you would have an ethical and legal responsibility to divulge it to the police because of the child-abuse exception.'

Diane said, 'But the police say she ran. As long as that's the current theory, I can't play the I-think-she's-been-kidnapped card.'

The holiday lights that were strung on the trees on the Mall began snapping on block by block, and within seconds snakes of twinkling dots wrapped the skeletal forms that stretched out in front of us. Diane and I both watched the spectacle develop for a moment.

'That was pretty,' I said. 'Sorry, your hands are tied.'

Hers may have been figuratively tied; mine were literally going numb from the cold and the weight of the shopping bags I was carrying.

'I suppose this means that I probably shouldn't prepare a bill for the intake and send it to Mallory's father.'

Diane's last comment was intended sardonically, but I recognized some fuzzy edges at the margins; the ramifications weren't as clear as she might have expected. 'It's an interesting point, Diane.'

'What do you mean?'

'If you were looking for a way to tell her father that you know something, sending him a bill would probably be an ethically acceptable excuse for letting him get a toe inside the consultation room door.'

'And why would I want to do that?'

'I'm not sure you would. But just for the sake of argument, let's say you believed that what you learned from Hannah's consultation might help track down Mallory.'

'And if I did believe that . . .'

'The fact that no bill has gone out yet might give you

an avenue to breach confidence with her father. If you were sure the kid was Mallory. Did Hannah say anything about billing arrangements for her session with the girl?'

'Not a word. But I have to work under the assumption that the kid didn't want her parents to know about the therapy, don't I? Knowing Hannah, I bet she did the session pro bono, anyway.'

'Why? Why would you assume that the girl wouldn't want her father to know about the therapy?'

'Why? Because the kid just showed up without an appointment, and she told Hannah that he was up to something and she wasn't happy about it.'

I played devil's advocate. 'But what if he's the one who sent her to see Hannah? What if her father already knows all about whatever it was that caused her to go? Ninety-nine out of a hundred kids are in psychotherapy because somebody sends them, and the someone is usually one of the kid's parents. A kid doesn't often go on her own.'

Diane's tone grew dismissive. 'If Mallory's father sent her into treatment he'd have told the police that his daughter had seen a therapist recently, right? That would be important information to consider after her disappearance.'

'You would think.'

'And the police would have contacted that therapist, right? To try and find out what the kid was troubled about.'

I knew where she was going. 'Unless the police already knew that the therapist was dead.'

'But if they knew that Mallory was seeing Hannah and that Hannah was dead, they would have sent whoever had legal custody of her practice records – *c'est moi* – a subpoena in order to get access to the treatment notes.'

'Agreed. If the cops were thinking.'

'Well, none of that happened. None of it. Nobody from the police department has contacted me about Mallory. And I certainly haven't been subpoenaed.' As she began to connect more of the dots Diane's foot speed kept pace with her mouth speed, and I had to hustle to keep up with her. 'So I'm left thinking that Mallory sought out Hannah for treatment on her own, which would tell me that she didn't want her father to know what she was up to. Or . . . her father had sent Mallory to Hannah, which – given his subsequent silence on the matter – would tell me that for some reason he doesn't want the police to know what his daughter was up to.'

I said, 'That about covers the possibilities.'

'As a therapist, I don't especially like either theory. But I'd put my money on Mallory as the one who was trying to keep the secret.'

We arrived at the intersection with Broadway. The pedestrian signal was red and enough traffic was humming past us to rule out jaywalking. I lowered Diane's shopping bags to the bricks and lifted my hands so I could show her that my fingers were curled into hooks. I asked, 'Do you mind taking these bags back? My hands are frozen.'

She looked imposed upon.

And I realized, belatedly, why her husband refused to shop with her.

13

I had an additional tie to the Miller family, one that certainly fit any definition of tangential anyone might wish to apply, one that was marked by the requisite degree or two of separation. The link didn't come into focus for me until my solitary psychotherapy appointment late on the afternoon of the day that I played reluctant Sherpa for Diane as she trolled the Mall for Christmas bargains. The source of the connection was someone I never would have anticipated.

Bob Brandt.

Bob had been coming to me for individual psychotherapy for almost two years, and progress had been glacial. Pre-global-warming glacial. The meager speed of the treatment neither surprised nor particularly disappointed me. Diagnostically, Bob's underlying character was a caustic blend of toxic pathologies. Had he been using health insurance to pay for his treatment – he wasn't – the DSM-IV code his insurer would have required would have had as many digits as a Visa card.

The first five of those digits would have spelled out the cipher for schizoid personality disorder. In addition to having a serious schizoid character, Bob was also a chronically depressed, mildly paranoid guy. Forty-three years old, he'd been ensconced in the same dead-end clerical position in the physics department at the University of Colorado for almost two decades.

His mother and an older brother were his only living relatives. Bob had maintained contact with his mom for most of his adult life. A few years before, however, his brother had written him a letter notifying him that their mother was moving to an assisted-living facility near his house in southern Colorado. Bob had interpreted the missive as his brother's order to 'butt out,' and he hadn't spoken with either his mother or his brother since.

Where did reality lie? Sadly, I didn't know. Nor was it clear to me exactly how Bob felt about the artificial estrangement. He deflected all my inquiries about it, and resisted my occasional attempts to question his harsh appraisal of his brother's letter.

Bob had no current friends or romantic relationships and no history that I could uncover of any significant friendships since childhood, or of romantic relationships, ever. His sole social outlet was occasional attendance at local Scrabble clubs and tournaments. Mostly, though, he preferred to play his games online.

The Internet, for all its interpersonal anonymity, is a schizoid's dream.

Schizoid.

The dictionary, nonpsychological meaning of the word is the 'coexistence of disparates.' Something that is part this, part that. In mental health terms, schizoid has surprisingly little in common with either its *Webster's* definition or its similar-sounding, polysyllabic psychopathology cousin, schizophrenia. Unlike schizophrenia, schizoid personality disorder isn't a disorder of thought or perception.

Not at all. Schizoid personality disorder is a disorder of relating.

People with the malady have a history, often since early adolescence, sometimes even before that, of aloofness from relationships, emotional coldness, immunity from praise or criticism, generalized anhedonia – the inability to experience pleasure – and limited affective range.

The portrayal fit Bob like a custom-made wetsuit.

Bob was, by his own description, 'a dork, a geek, a nerd, a snarf – you pick the synonym for loser, that's me.' He had a head shaped like the bow of a boat, and I surmised that his hair had been receding from his temples since the second or third grade. Exploratory surgery would be necessary to determine if he actually possessed a chin. His eyes were tiny and at times they seemed to shake in their sockets. The effect was so disconcerting to me that early in the treatment I'd actually referred him for a neurological evaluation to have those vibrating orbs assessed.

The neurologist had a name for the condition, which he assured me was benign. As was my style, I'd managed to forget the specific medical terminology by the time I was reading that night's bedtime story to my daughter.

Bob liked cars, or, more accurately, was enamored of his own car. He had a thirty-something-year-old Camaro with a big motor that he'd bought from a guy in Longmont who'd lovingly restored it to its original ebony luster. Every time Bob mentioned the old muscle car, which seemed like at least once a session, he reminded me that its condition was 'cherry,' and every month or two he assured me that it was a 'matching numbers car.'

After two years of reminders I still didn't know what that meant.

Bob lived in a couple of rooms he rented above the

detached garage of a modest house near Nineteenth and Pine. He described his landlords as 'old people,' and maintained that he never spoke with them at all. Despite the fact that they lived less than fifty feet from his rented rooms, he mailed his rent check to them every month.

He could walk to work at the university from his flat and used the classic Camaro primarily to cruise around downtown or the Hill or other student haunts on weekend nights. In a rare flash of insight he'd once acknowledged that he drove his prize around town on pleasant evenings hoping that someone would find his ride cool, though the few times that he and his car had generated attention out in public he'd been pretty certain that the students had been taunting him.

After a lifetime feeling that he'd been born with the birthmark of a bull's-eye on his chest, Bob was familiar with being taunted and appeared immune to it. Frankly, the incidents with the university students hadn't seemed to trouble him. He was perplexed, however, that the kids didn't find his car cool.

To Bob, that was crazy.

Over the last year he had begun to visit Boulder's clubs and bars with some regularity, at least a couple of times a month. His pub-crawling wasn't designed to accommodate a drinking habit – a period of severe bingeing in his early twenties had actually caused him to swear off alcohol. Regardless, he was way too cheap to splurge on nightclub-priced drinks. And he didn't go out to the clubs to hang out in the glow of the pretty people. After a firm confrontation from me one day – 'Come on, Bob, why do you go?' – he admitted that he went out to nightspots to 'watch them.'

I guessed that he meant the girls, but I couldn't get him to admit it. So I reserved judgment, aware that Bob could just as well have been spying on the boys. In my presence, he'd never admitted to any feeling that I would categorize as either romantic or sexual toward people of either gender.

That's all he would say about his clubbing predilection, that he went to 'watch them.' I was left to wonder: If the watching wasn't some once-removed sexual thing, was it voyeuristic? Anthropological? Maybe part of some arcane sociological experiment? After almost two years of trying to understand such things about Bob I still wasn't sure, and on those Tuesday nights when I was driving home after I'd completed a session with him and found myself still musing about Bob's narrow life, the fact that there was so much I didn't know troubled me.

I suspected that the pretty objects of Bob's fascination were at least equally troubled when they looked up to discover Bob's shimmying eyes locked on to their own as they downed designer cocktails in Boulder's latest trendy nightspot.

I also had little doubt that Bob would avert his eyes the moment his prey noticed that he was staring. I knew it because in two years of sessions Bob had never held eye contact with me for more than a split second.

Other than the regular interaction he had with his boss in the physics department at the university – it was at her insistence that he'd sought therapy – the psychotherapy with me was, to my knowledge, Bob's primary ongoing human relationship that didn't include at least one cyber-buffer. Although I suspected that he trusted me more than he trusted his boss, I reminded myself that he didn't even trust her enough to allow her the responsibility of keeping the begonia on his desk watered during his infrequent holidays from work.

He certainly didn't trust me enough to accept my oft-repeated suggestions about the potential benefits of psychopharmacology. I raised the issue occasionally, but never pressed it. Although I held out hopes that the right antidepressant might dent his veneer of despair, the odds of medication impacting Bob's underlying character disorder were slim. But then – I had to admit – so were the odds that psychotherapy would ever make any profound difference in his functioning.

That didn't mean I wasn't going to try.

Bob did trust me just enough to come back to see me every Tuesday afternoon at 4:45. That was the foundation of our relationship. In two years of treatment, he'd missed only one session, and had canceled that appointment four weeks in advance. Forty-five minutes, once a week, that was our deal. Bob knew what time our appointment started. He knew when it ended. After a hundred tries, though, he still had only the most vague concept of what should happen in between.

I saw him on a sliding scale, discounting my usual fee by well more than half so that he could afford to come in. Bob would always pay me at the beginning of the last session of each month, just before I handed out my bills. His personal check to me was always placed in the same type of security envelope, was always folded the same way, and was always double sealed, once by licking the flap, and once by the addition of two long strips of Scotch tape.

Bob's handwriting was tiny and precise and rounded. The first time he gave me a check I had to use a magnifying glass to read the amount. I didn't know how the university credit union managed to clear his checks. But it did.

On occasional Tuesdays during our time together we did something that loosely resembled traditional psychotherapy. More often the sessions were an odd interchange that to an outsider probably would look more like social-skills training than anything psychotherapeutic. Not unlike someone afflicted with Asperger's syndrome, Bob had no innate sense of how human interaction should work. He would end up being insulting when his intent was to be impersonally cordial. He would often be cruel while he was merely trying to create some protective psychological space. During the first year of treatment we'd spent a half dozen autumn Tuesdays troubleshooting how Bob might respond differently when a student walked up to his desk in the physics department and said, 'Good morning,' or 'Hi.'

His previous stock reply – 'What difference does it make?' – hadn't been working too well for him.

The most surprising thing about psychotherapy with Bob? As the months passed I'd grown fond of this man who was about as easy to get close to as a porcupine. In the lingo, I had developed a positive countertransference for him. And maybe because I'd developed affection for Bob my empathy for his plight was sometimes swollen out of proportion.

I vowed to keep an eye on it.

14

Bob's connection to the Millers didn't appear to be particularly unique or interesting. He hadn't babysat Mallory, nor had he gone to high school with Mrs. Miller. He wasn't a family friend, hadn't played Santa at any Miller family holiday gatherings. In fact, his particular connection to the girl's disappearance seemed to be a relatively common affliction that he shared with many viewers of cable news TV stations. Bob, it turned out, had quickly grown obsessed by Mallory's disappearance, which, I feared, meant that for at least forty-five minutes a week I was likely to be forced to be vicariously obsessed by Mallory's disappearance, too.

I was less than thrilled by the revelation that Bob was transfixed by Mallory's plight. As he described his fascination my silent protest was a pathetic *No, please no*. At a clinical level Bob didn't need the obsession; his pathological casserole was certainly not wanting for the addition of an obsessive crust of any description. At a more selfish level, I'd already begun hoping – like the great majority of Boulderites – that the case of the disappearing girl was going to go away gently, that Sam and his like-minded police colleagues were right and that this time the case of the disappearing girl wasn't really a case of a disappearing girl at all. Like ninety-nine percent of Boulder's residents, I was hoping that Mallory Miller – despite what I'd learned about her recent history from Diane – was just a girl who'd left home for one of the many bad reasons that young teenage girls choose to leave home.

But I wasn't to be so lucky. From the first time Bob mentioned her name – 'Do you think she ran? Or do you think she was kidnapped? Mallory?' – I became concerned that Bob and I would begin to spend some unknown number of Tuesday sessions rehashing the latest news and gossip about her. Since Bob devoured the *Enquirer* and the *Star* – he didn't buy them; he scoured the student union looking for discarded copies – I was even going to be force-fed tidbits about Mallory that I wouldn't have been exposed to in the more reputable news sources.

How did I know all this?

Because Bob had been transfixed by the Kobe thing, too. And the Michael Jackson thing. Not to mention the Scott Peterson thing. That's how I knew.

I was realizing, almost even begrudgingly accepting, that it was beginning to look like I couldn't get away from Mallory Miller no matter how hard I tried.

The Tuesday session with Bob during the week between Christmas and New Year's was like dozens before it. Bob was distracted and distant, and we spent a chunk of the allotted time in silence. He surprised me by ending the appointment with a request he'd never made before: He asked if we could meet again later that week.

Could I actually be witnessing nascent signs of attachment, the therapeutic Holy Grail in the treatment of a schizoid personality? Highly unlikely, but I gladly offered him an additional session on Thursday, the penultimate day of the year.

15

The phone rang later that evening while I was giving Grace her bath. Lauren spoke for a few minutes before she joined me in the bathroom and handed me the portable and a towel for my hands. 'It's Diane,' she said, and I exchanged the delights of playtime in the bathtub for the dubious pleasures of the telephone.

It struck me as not a great deal.

'Hi,' I said as I moved out of the bathroom and walked across the master bedroom to the big windows facing the mountains. The still-snowy spots on the winter landscape seemed fluorescent in the moonlight.

'I've been thinking,' Diane said.

'Yeah.'

'About Hannah.'

I wasn't at all surprised. Diane and I had talked about Hannah a dozen or more times since her death. We'd do it a dozen more, and maybe a dozen more after that. My friend liked to process out loud, and Hannah's death continued to haunt her.

'These things take time, Diane. They just do. This time of year especially, you know. The holidays make it harder.'

She sighed. 'That's not what I mean.'

I stuffed my repertoire of grief platitudes back into storage and said, 'Okay.'

'What if this is why she died? Because she met with Mallory Miller. What if somebody killed Hannah because she met with the kid that one time?'

'I'm . . . listening.'

'Don't use that voice. I hate that voice. You think I'm crazy? Tell me this didn't cross your mind.'

'I can honestly say it didn't cross my mind.' It had – briefly – but I wasn't about to admit it and inadvertently provide monster chow for the dragons inhabiting Diane's cave of paranoia.

'Hannah might have been murdered, right? That's a possibility?' Diane's tone was hoarse, slightly conspiratorial. I couldn't figure out why.

'Are you at home?'

'Yes.'

'Why are you whispering?'

'I don't know. This is the sort of thing people whisper about, isn't it?'

'Okay, just wondering.'

'Now answer me.' She was still almost whispering. 'It's a possibility that Hannah was murdered, right?'

'Yeah.' The coroner's finding on manner of death was 'undetermined.' That conclusion didn't mean Hannah had been murdered, nor did it mean that she hadn't been murdered. We both knew Diane had her own hypothesis on the matter.

She spelled out her theory for me anyway. 'Slocum hasn't been able to identify a motive to support a conclusion of homicide, right?'

'Yeah.' I could graciously grant Diane the motive argument, fully cognizant that Slocum hadn't been able to identify means or opportunity, either. He was 0-for-3.

'Well, what if this was the motive? Something Mallory told Hannah. Something that needed to stay secret.'

I tried to imagine some possibilities. Couldn't. The time frame seemed wrong. Hannah had died over a week before Mallory disappeared.

'Like?' I asked.

'I don't know. I thought you would have . . . an idea. This is your bailiwick, not mine.'

Bailiwick? I was hoping it wasn't a new companion word to *holy moly.* Regardless, Diane was doomed to be disappointed by the sparse contents of my bailiwick. I didn't have any theory about the secret that Mallory might have shared with Hannah.

From the bathroom Lauren called out, 'Check the stove for me, sweetie. I have something cooking.'

I inhaled, and followed the tantalizing aroma of spicy hot cider all the way to the kitchen. A cinnamon stick and some cloves were floating in a steaming apple brew. Lauren had been preparing a treat for us when the phone rang. I shut off the gas to the burner but stayed close by so the steam would rise toward my face.

Diane wasn't patient about the delay. 'You still there?' she asked.

'I'm thinking.' What I was thinking about was whether I should add some good whiskey or a dollop of rum to my cup of hot cider.

'You done yet?'

I said, 'Maybe if Hannah had died after Mallory disappeared, it might make some sense to wander down this road. But Hannah died first. And that was over a week before Mallory disappeared.'

'You think I'm crazy.'

It wasn't a question. 'No crazier than I thought you were before you called.'

'Funny.'

'Based on what you told me there was nothing incendiary about the session. Nothing worth killing Hannah over.'

'She said her father was "up to something." Remember?'

'But the question is what? She may have meant that he wanted her to take up the viola, or change schools, or get braces. Who knows? Hannah didn't spell it out.'

'I expected you to be more helpful, Alan.'

No doubt because this is my bailiwick. I said, 'Sorry.'

'You don't want to do this, do you?' she asked.

Her question wasn't an accusation. Diane was belatedly recognizing my resistance to be involved with anything that had to do with Boulder's latest missing girl.

'No, I don't. But I will.'

'Is it because of Grace?'

'I'm sure that's part of it.'

'What then?'

'I'm working on that. I don't like the parallels to eight years ago. The whole thing is creepy. I'm a father now, it's . . .' I could have just admitted that I wasn't working on it very hard, but Diane wouldn't have let me off the hook. The truth was that I wanted the whole Mallory Miller thing to go away.

She softened. 'Think about it, please. See if anything jumps out at you. Can you at least do that?'

'Sure,' I said. 'I can do that.'

Grace was in fresh jammies, Lauren was swathed in soft flannel, her slender feet cushioned in sheepskin Uggs, and the mug of hot cider, with a little bourbon, was warming my hands. The three of us sat together on the couch in the living room and read bedtime stories about little girls and flowers, and dogs and friends.

Grace cackled and giggled and was delighted at the pages.

I held my daughter a little tighter than usual as Lauren's late-day gravelly voice soothed us all.

I waited until Grace was in bed and Lauren was settled into the soothing rhythms of a game of pool in what – had we possessed a table and chairs instead of a tournament-quality pool table – should have been the dining room, before I went downstairs and climbed on the road bike that I'd set up for indoor workouts in the basement. I warmed up quickly, maybe too quickly, and soon had my spin up where I wanted.

If a girl, I wondered, a fourteen-year-old girl, had shown up in my waiting room wanting an emergency appointment, what would I have done?

Mallory had probably told Hannah it was 'important,' or something similar. I didn't know a therapist, myself included, who wouldn't have listened to what she had to say. Why? 'Important' could have meant she wanted to report abuse. And if a kid wants to report abuse, it's the responsibility of adults, especially mental health professionals, to bend over backward to listen.

I also wondered whether Hannah had made the connection between the teenager in her office and the little girl she might have seen in her waiting room ten years or so before. Had Mallory said anything to remind her?

Remember me? I'm Mallory.

I tried to put myself in the same circumstances. Would I remember a kid so many years later? Would I even recognize that it was the same kid?

I didn't think I would. Miller is a common name. Sometimes my friends' kids changed so much in only a couple of years that I hardly recognized them. Adrienne's son Jonas had grown so much in the past year that he looked like a completely different child. Sam's son Simon had gone from little boy to man-child, it seemed, in weeks.

Even if Hannah had remembered the small child she had befriended in the waiting room, the memory wouldn't have given her many clues. Hannah would have no reason to know anything about the details of Mary Black's care of Rachel Miller.

But why was Mallory so vague about her concerns about her father?

That was my most troubling question: Why would a girl insist on a session with a therapist and then be vague about what was happening at home?

I made some assumptions about the session that I thought were safe.

Hannah would have asked Mallory directly about drug use, specifically about alcohol. Hannah hadn't told Diane about any concerns with substance abuse, so apparently she felt satisfied with whatever answer she'd received from Mallory.

Given that Mallory had revealed her mother's history of mental illness, I suspected that Hannah had directly or indirectly done some version of a mental status exam during the interview to see if what afflicted mother might also be afflicting her progeny. Had Mallory passed?

I didn't know that. Probably. But there were plenty of unknowns.

I listened for a moment to the sharp cracks and gentle taps that punctuated Lauren's pool playing. Returning my attention to the bike, I reminded myself that I was doing a lot of speculating.

Mallory had said her father was 'up to something.'

But what had he been up to?

Was it related to Mallory's anxiety about the holidays?

And why had Mallory chosen that day to sit in the waiting room to see Hannah? A great question. I didn't have a great answer, or even a good one.

16

Coloradans don't tolerate gray skies with any equanimity.

Other weather we endure. Gray skies, no.

On the high desert landscape where the Great Plains rise into the Front Range of the Rockies, we live through the often relentless heat of June and July with little complaint, reassuring each other that even though it's 103 degrees outside, at least it's a dry heat.

Our once-a-decade oh-my-God blizzards, or our annual winter cold snaps of day-after-day temperatures below zero and wind chills that feel arctic? Most of us write them off as the price of living in close proximity to the best skiing on the planet.

The hundred-mile-an-hour winter Chinooks blowing out of the mountains in January and February? *Hey, lean into it, it's only a little wind.*

Golf-ball-size hail? Fierce summer thunderstorms? *We live in a desert. We need the moisture.*

But the absence of sunshine?

After two consecutive overcast days the grumbling begins, everyone's temper shortens, traffic cops stop giving warnings, and people aren't quite as nice to their dogs. Add a third or, God forbid, a fourth day of concrete-colored skies, and most of the state's residents, especially the natives, begin to wonder for what it is they're being punished. A few furtively check their IDs to see if they've been magically relocated to Seattle or Cleveland or Buffalo or some other sunshine-deprived location as penance for an obviously serious transgression against humanity.

It's not that it's always sunny here. But I have to admit that it feels like it's always sunny here. The tourist board throws around statistics: We have 300-plus days of sunshine each year, we're sunnier than San Diego, much sunnier than Miami. I don't know if any of it's true. But I do know that the reality is that in Colorado I awaken every morning expecting to see the sun for a healthy chunk of the day.

One day of gray is disappointing. Two days in a row becomes a mini-crisis.

Anything more is cause for alarm.

Once the sun had set on Diane and me as we walked the Mall sharing our secrets about the Miller family, the rest of that week between Christmas and New Year's – the week after Mallory disappeared – was meteorologically bleak. Thursday brought constant flurries under steely skies. Friday taunted – the sun's silhouette was occasionally visible behind quickly passing clouds, but warming rays never reached the ground in a way that left behind even a hint of a shadow. Saturday, snow flurries fell intermittently all day long, icy winds howled from Wyoming, and by nightfall downy drifts began to cushion the bases of fences and the low sections of walls that dared to face north.

The sun had disappeared from our state – probably forever – it seemed.

A googol of reporters was camped out in Boulder, still

expecting – or, God forbid, hoping for – a garroted body to emerge from a Boulder basement.

But Mallory Miller stayed stubbornly missing.

I was getting dragged into the riddle of her absence further and further.

Everybody was cranky.

Everybody, that is, except Sam Purdy.

And Sam probably should have been cranky. He had been for all of the many years we'd been friends. A lot was going on in his life. He was on the cusp of completing his first holiday season as an unmarried man. He had just celebrated the anniversary of surviving for a year after a heart attack – he'd reminded me that it beat the alternative, hands-down – and he had just managed to complete twelve-plus months without developing a fresh gallstone.

He was still learning the ropes of single-parenting his son, Simon.

And because of Mallory Miller, he was being forced to work overtime on a high-profile holiday crime, not exactly his thing, as part of a team of many detectives, most definitely not his thing.

But Sam's mood was good. Boulder's streak of gray days was nothing compared to the winter stretches he'd endured in his family home on Minnesota's Iron Range. His health problems? He had grown philosophical about them, felt he was doing all he could – with diet and exercise – to manage them. His divorce? Despite some stumbles he thought that he and Sherry had handled it all like grown-ups. Was there enough money to go around? Of course not – as Sam had indelicately put it, 'I live in fucking Boulder. How could there be enough money?' Sam's son Simon? He was a good kid. He had some emotional bruises from what his parents' marital disruption had forced him to endure, but Sam was confident that his son would do okay.

I didn't disagree.

The Mallory Miller case? Right from the start, Sam had pitched his tent in the don't-get-too-worked-up-about-this, she's-a-runaway camp. But he was a professional cop, and until his captain told him otherwise he planned to continue to investigate the details of her disappearance as though she might have been kidnapped by some mysterious intruder.

I knew the truth about Sam's personal life. I knew that Sam's pleasant demeanor wasn't due to his positive outlook, but rather that his positive outlook was due to a girl.

Okay, a woman. Her name was Carmen Reynoso. She was a cop, another detective, a class act who lived somewhere within commuting distance of the police department in Laguna Beach, California, and she and Sam were in love. They had met a little more than a year before while on the track of a serial killer.

It was a long story in which I'd had a part, and I liked to think I'd introduced them.

Sam and Simon had tickets, or some airline's digital equivalent, to fly to John Wayne International Airport to spend the New Year's holiday with Carmen and her daughter, Jessie. Jessie, a student at UC Santa Cruz, had promised Simon a trip to Disneyland during the visit.

In Sam's world, gray skies or blue skies, all was cool.

I met Sam at the new ice rink off the Boulder Turnpike in Superior, where Simon's peewee team was playing on the Wednesday night that fell within our streak of end-of-the-year bleak weather. Simon – who, unlike his father, played offense – was doing a sleepover at a teammate's house after the game and Sam and I were going to go someplace for a beer. It had been a while since we'd had time to get together socially.

Perhaps the flyers that were posted all over the ice rink doors should have been a caution for me about how the evening might progress, but, like most people in Boulder County, I was already growing somewhat immune to them. Two types predominated. Each version was on a standard eight-and-a-half-by-eleven sheet of paper. One was on brilliant yellow stock, screamed 'MISSING!' and had a black-and-white photograph of Mallory – she was airborne, just launched from a trampoline – above a brief physical description. The other flyer was on white copy paper and was adorned with a color photograph that had been taken by a school photographer who had already taken too many pictures that particular day. Large block letters asked, 'HAVE YOU SEEN HER?'

No, was the short answer.

I hadn't seen her. But in the few days since Mallory's disappearance I'd seen, literally, thousands of the flyers. Volunteers had papered almost every vertical surface Boulder had to offer, and some horizontal ones as well, with a yellow flyer or a white one, or more often, with multiple copies of each.

Towers of Mallory.

White-and-yellow checkerboards of Mallory.

Although I was growing inured to the posters themselves, the messages weren't lost on me. MISSING! and HAVE YOU SEEN HER? ran through my mind like an ever-repeating crawl at the bottom of some cosmic TV, the messages as insistent as the lyrics of an annoying jingle.

The two photographs of Mallory – one smiling and content, the other mischievous and teasing – had a much more subtle effect on me than did the banner headlines.

The photos of the young girl lingered in my preconscious and provided fodder for unsettling dreams of the things that fathers dread. More than once I woke with a startling sense of vulnerability, a visceral awareness that I had a daughter and that it could have been she.

Sam had lost a lot of weight – I was guessing thirty-odd pounds – in the last year, but none of it in his face. He still had the face of a big, round guy. Much of the motivation for the weight loss had been medical. The past few years had confronted my friend with a minor heart attack, kidney stones, and gallstones. A new, healthy diet was one of his ways of fighting back.

He'd sworn off doughnuts and bacon and brats, and hadn't had a burger and fries in most of a year. He was learning to cook and he'd already warned me that he was going to count on me to be his running buddy while he trained to run his first 10K, the late-spring Bolder Boulder.

Health aside, most of the motivation for his self-improvement program, though he'd never admit it to me, was his recent separation and divorce, and that new girlfriend in California. Sam was a mature guy, a serious cop, and a devoted father. Still, he wanted to be buff so he could get the girls.

Prior to that night, I'd never observed Sam watching his son play in a competitive game in any sport, and anticipated that it wasn't going to be an inspiring sight, especially given the fact that the sport was hockey. Sam had a little bully in him – ask me, all effective cops do, they have to. In addition, Sam had the natural-born arrogance of Minnesotans who believe that they know more about hockey than any native – read: citizen of the United States of America – referee who might tie on skates and pull on a striped blouse in some Colorado barn. Sam granted Canadians special hockey dispensation.

I feared that it was a combustible combination of traits, and that I was about to discover that Sam was going to be one of those parents who give youth sports a rotten name. If, or when, he got too embarrassing to be with, I was more than prepared to move to a seat in the arena as far from him as possible.

Sam, as he often did, proved me wrong. Every word he screamed at the game was a word of encouragement. He knew the names of every one of Simon's teammates and lavished praise on the kids for their shots and their passing, but especially for their positioning and their defense. He even screamed out some kind words for the opposing players.

The two times he yelled out to the referees it was with a hearty, 'Hey, good call, guy. Let's keep 'em safe out there.'

Between periods I asked, 'Case driving you nuts?'

'Nah,' he said. But he knew what case I was talking about. 'If cases like that drove me nuts, I'd have been hanging out in your office a long time ago.' That thought caused him to chuckle to himself; Sam's opinion of psychotherapy wasn't particularly benevolent. Then he lowered his voice and tilted his big head toward me. 'There're still some guys who think somebody took her, a few. But it didn't come down that way. She was a kid with issues, Alan. The girl ran, plain and simple. Because of all the media and, you know – that other girl, back when, and what happened to her – the bosses have to go overboard on this, look for intruders under rugs, dot all the *t*'s and cross all the *i*'s, but everything or damn near everything says that she ran.

'Hey, a fourteen-year-old girl gone from home? It's a

sad thing. Worse around Christmastime. But it happens. This time it happened at the wrong time in the wrong town in the wrong neighborhood under the wrong circumstances, so now the whole world is watching one family's tragedy unfold. But that's all it is: one family's tragedy. I'm afraid that the real tragedy is what happened to her after she ran; that's what keeps me awake at night. Is she in a ditch somewhere? Discarded by the side of some highway? In some asshole pimp's hands? When I hear what happened to her I think it's going to break my heart. My advice? Leave it alone.'

He was probably right. But Diane's story about Hannah Grant's intake interview with Mallory was still haunting me. I wasn't able to leave it alone.

'What about the guy that the Crandalls saw, the neighbors? The one they thought was loitering on the block before the snow started?'

Sam grimaced. 'If those people were really so concerned, why didn't they call us when they saw him? He was probably just some guy out for a stroll, trying to walk off his Christmas dinner. Maybe his kids were out caroling and he was keeping an eye on them. You know what it's like after something like this. People think they've seen all kinds of things.'

'What about the blood?' I asked.

Sam looked at me sideways, as though that question had surprised him. 'Simon cut his heel on the back door last summer, on the screen. My God, did it bleed. He hopped all over the house looking for me to get him a bandage and by the time he found me, there was blood everywhere. I still don't think I got it all cleaned up. I'm not the world's best housekeeper, and I promise you that I wouldn't want the crime-scene guys checking my house for splatter. The fact that there's some blood in the

Millers' house doesn't mean any felonies came down. Hey, I bet if I walked in with some Luminol I could get your house to light up, too.'

'Well, then what about the snow thing?'

17

The snow thing.

Christmas had been on the previous Saturday. The day had been clear and cold with a high temperature in the mid-twenties. An upslope developed and snow started falling in earnest in Boulder some time around seven o'clock in the evening. At first, it had been a steady snow; three quick inches fell before the wind shifted directions around 9:30 and the snow paused for an hour. When the upslope resumed so did the snow, which fell insistently until early morning.

'All these questions? It isn't like you,' Sam said. 'You working as a stringer for the *Enquirer* in your spare time?'

'Actually, I've been trying my hardest to keep my head in the sand about this whole thing.'

'You're failing miserably.'

'I don't get the snow thing. Humor me.'

'I don't either,' Sam admitted.

Bill and Reese Miller left Mallory at home alone with her stomachache around 6:30, just before the snow started. Her cell-phone records show that Mallory made a few phone calls – all to girlfriends – in the next couple of hours, and received a few others. The first call out was at

6:39. The last call in came at 8:47. It was from her father, checking in on her from the Christmas gathering, and letting her know they'd be home soon.

Bill Miller said that his daughter answered the phone, and reported to the police that Mallory told him she was doing okay. She was all packed up for the next day's ski trip, had a heating pad on her belly, and was watching a DVD she got that morning for Christmas.

'The snow thing isn't important?' I asked Sam.

'I didn't say that. I said I don't get it. There's always something in every case that I don't get. Always.'

'Where are her footprints?'

'I said I don't know. I wasn't kidding – I really don't know.' He popped a peanut into his mouth and pointed toward the ice. 'So where do you think a place like this gets money for a Zamboni like that?'

The Zamboni that was scooting around the rink between periods grooming the ice surface looked brand-new. All shiny and painted a shade of green that was much too close to chartreuse for my comfort. It was covered with more commercial messages than the NASCAR champion stock car.

'I don't know,' I admitted.

'When I retire, I think I'd like to drive a Zamboni in a place just like this. I'd do it for free, just for the fun of it. For the kids. You know about Zambonis? How they got started?'

I admitted I didn't.

Sam did. He explained the whole history of the Zamboni as though he'd grown up with Mr. Zamboni's daughter and lived through the experience himself. I listened with some wonder, not because of any particular fascination with Zambonis but because of the extent of Sam's knowledge base. The truth was that Sam knew a lot of crap. He was the kind of guy with whom you did not want to play Trivial Pursuit.

'How come you know so much trivia?' I asked him when he'd exhausted the Zamboni tale.

'I just remember stuff. It's one of the things that makes me a good cop. And I don't consider it trivia.'

'No?'

'No. I like to think of it as information of infrequent utility.'

'It's occasionally important to know that the first Zamboni was made from an old army Jeep?'

'That's the thing. You never know what might be important. It's all just information and then, out of nowhere, something becomes useful. I just store it so it's there when I need it.'

Like the snow thing, I thought.

The Millers' home was on the eastern side of Twelfth Street, facing the mountains that rise dramatically only a dozen blocks away. How dramatically do the Rockies jut out of west Boulder? On one side of a street you're on a gentle hill. On the other side, you're on the slope of a mountain.

But that's to the west. A block to the east – in that part of the Boulder Valley 'east' means downhill – and a few doors north of their home, the Millers had a new neighbor. A neighbor they had probably never met. The new family, the Harts, had moved into their brick Tudor the previous spring and within two months of unpacking their moving vans had begun diligent work on the family passion – which involved turning the facade and entire front yard of their house into a garish, illuminated, motorized tribute to the Christmas holiday.

The number of lights involved – all of the family

members seemed to prefer to call them 'points' when they spoke to the media, which they did frequently – ran well into five figures. Six major illuminated displays – exactly half were loosely biblical in theme – ranged from three feet to nine feet in height, and eleven different motorized extravaganzas kept elves bowing, stars shooting, donkeys walking, and reindeer flying all over the front of the house and far up into the trees. An enterprising reporter with an incipient personality disorder found 116 distinct representations of Santa Claus secreted in various locations. On the wide expanse of roof beside the center gable of the house a huge arched sign of shimmering red neon announced to all that this home was indeed 'The Very HART of Christmas.'

It was something.

Families who like to make an annual trek through other people's neighborhoods in search of the best and brightest Christmas decorations seemed to adore what the Harts had done to their home. The Harts' neighbors, and the neighbors of the Harts' neighbors, all of whom had to endure the endless crawl of traffic down Thirteenth Street, were probably not quite so enamored of the family's efforts.

Boulder being Boulder, the controversy became sport, and arguments flourished about light pollution and the environmental consequences of all that electricity being used on something so, well, garish and transient. The local paper, the *Camera,* actually published a series of letters about the brouhaha, the first of which compared the Harts' extravaganza to one of Christo's installations. Follow-up missives predictably belittled the aesthetic sensibilities of anyone who could possibly think that way.

'But,' I asked Sam, 'do you think the news footage shows what everybody thinks it shows?'

'Pretty much,' Sam said. 'It shows what it shows, I guess. I don't have much argument with Fox News. Well, that's not exactly true. Let's just say I don't have much argument with what Fox News has to say about those few minutes in the Millers' neighborhood on Christmas night.'

'So?' I said. 'Explain it to me.'

'What?'

'The snow thing.'

'I can't.'

'You can't?'

He smiled. Not at me, exactly. He smiled as though he were enjoying my consternation. 'So that's it? You can't explain it?'

What he couldn't explain was the footage that had been shot by the Fox News helicopter on Christmas night. The shot was live for their 9 P.M. newscast – which had included an announcement of the three winners of Fox's best-holiday-decorated-house-in-the-metro-area contest. The Harts' home had been awarded a disappointing, to them, third place, which earned the earliest appearance of any of the winners on that night's evening news. Records revealed that the live chopper footage from Boulder was aired beginning precisely at 9:16. Viewers eager to see the ultimate champion would have to stick with the newscast until the bitter end because the helicopter would have to make a trek across the entire metro area to Aurora for a shot of the grand-prize winner.

'Snow started sticking right away, yes? Around seven?' I asked.

'At my house it did.'

'And phone records show that Mallory was still home at eight forty-seven?' That tidbit of information had been leaked to the media earlier in the week. Locally, it had been played up by one of the TV affiliates as though the scoop was as important as a cure for cancer.

Before Sam had a chance to reply the kids skated back onto the ice to warm up for the next period. 'For the sake of argument, yes, let's say there was phone activity at eight forty-seven,' Sam said. 'I don't want to talk about this during the game, so make it quick. I'm getting bored.'

After the news helicopter completed its shot of the Harts' home, it had banked away for a wide shot of the neighborhood, which included, for about three seconds – Fox timed it at 2.8614, and who was I to argue with that – the Millers' totally undecorated house on Twelfth Street. Two days after Mallory's disappearance, an astute Fox producer realized what the station might possess in the additional neighborhood footage that had been shot on Christmas night, and Fox launched a huge advertising blitz to promote its 'crucial new information in the Mallory Miller case. Tune in Tuesday. Exclusively on Fox News at Nine.'

'Mr. Miller and Reese got home around nine-twenty, right?'

'Give or take.'

'But close.'

'Close.'

'Mallory was gone by then.'

'Correct-o. We think. Nobody actually looked for her until the next morning. People forget that little detail. She had a big head start.'

'You think she was home at nine-twenty, Sam?'

'No, I think she'd already split. But I do like arguing with you. That part's kind of fun.'

Fox had done digital magic to the Christmas night footage. The resulting images of the Miller home were grainy, and the shadows were darker in a few places than was ideal, but the video was clear enough that the conclusions Fox reached really weren't controversial.

'The helicopter footage from Fox shows no footprints in the snow around the Millers' house. Not on the walk, not on the driveway, not through the yard. And no tire tracks up the driveway into the garage.' I waited for him to disagree, but he seemed to be ignoring me. Finally, I added, 'And lights were on in the house, right? Both floors.'

'So what? You know any kid who remembers to turn off lights?'

'All that's at nine-sixteen?'

The buzzer sounded. Sam said, 'It was actually nine-eighteen by then. But why quibble? We're friends.' He pointed at the fresh sheet of ice down below. 'Game's starting.'

'So are you saying you think that Mallory just happened to hustle out the door between like nine-eighteen and nine-twenty?'

Sam smiled at me pleasantly and said, 'Maybe she was watching the Christmas thing on Fox News and timed her exit perfectly to confound the helicopter. We hear she's a bright kid.'

I made a face that expressed my displeasure at his condescension.

He kneed me gently. 'Hey, Alan, so far I've just been agreeing with you about stuff you learned from somebody else. Maybe some of it's right. Maybe it isn't. But I can't tell you what I think, you know that, not if it involves what I know as a cop. But you know what else? Intruder theory, runaway theory – it doesn't make any difference. None. The lack of footprints in the snow on Christmas night is an anomaly no matter what theory you like. The kid got out of the house without leaving a trace.

How? Microclimate? I don't know. Come on, it looks like Simon's on the ice for the start of the second period. Let's give the kids some support.'

Simon was indeed on the ice, at left wing. Both teams were sloppier with the puck at the start of the second period than they had been in the first. I was about to ask Sam whether the kids might be having trouble with the fresh ice laid down by the Zamboni when he spoke first.

'Reese Miller's a hockey player. Did you know that? I've seen him play a few times. He's good.'

I hadn't seen any mention of Mallory's little brother's hobbies in the paper. But then I'd been making a concerted effort not to read about the more gossipy aspects of the case. 'No, I didn't know that.'

'He's had some trouble.'

I leaned forward so that Sam would know that I was looking at him. 'And you know this as a cop or as a parent?'

'The latter.'

'What kind of trouble?'

'God, you're nosy tonight. You heard that his dad sent him out of town for a while until the commotion dies down?'

'To visit family?' I asked. I hadn't heard.

'I shouldn't say, but yeah,' Sam said. 'I'm not sure I would have done that. Seems like a time when you'd want your kid close by.' I opened my mouth to agree, but Sam was done with the conversation. 'Let's watch the game.'

18

Bob entered my office for his additional day before New Year's Eve appointment carrying a boom box.

Mallory Miller had been missing for five days.

He and I had met almost a hundred times by then and he had never walked in the door with a boom box, or any other prop, for that matter. Without preamble, but with an almost sinister smile that underscored the fact that he seemed to lack a chin, Bob set the stereo on the table between us and pressed the 'play' button. I didn't recognize the tune at first – maybe because I'd managed to make it through the years on both sides of the recent cusp of centuries deprived of any familiarity at all with boy bands – but I realized soon enough that I was listening to a disappointing cover of Del Shannon's glorious 'Runaway.'

A run run run run runaway.

Bob's preferred, but dubious, choice of versions was a seriously overproduced adaptation of the classic featuring a harmony of voices obviously lacking in testosterone. I patiently adopted the role of audience, unsure why that day's psychotherapy required musical accompaniment, and unsure why – if we required music at all, and that song in particular – we couldn't be listening to the almost flawless original. At what appeared to be a predetermined moment Bob decided to turn the session from surreal soundtrack to painful karaoke. His voice, a strange mix of soprano and something else, added a decidedly creepy new layer to the sugary harmonies that were filling my office.

Bob had chimed into the song at the precise point that the lyrical progression had reached *And I wonder / I wa wa wa wa wonder.* But he didn't stop there. He sang, '*Why / why why why why she ran away / And I wonder where she will stay.*'

He reached forward and hit the 'stop' button.

I wondered if I was supposed to clap.

Bob could carry a tune. I had to give him that.

Once I was certain he was finished, at least for the moment, I tried to think of something intelligent to say. I failed.

Sitting back, Bob was quiet for most of a minute before he said, 'I'm writing about it.'

'You are?' I asked, trying not to reveal the true level of stupefaction I was feeling at what was happening in my office. Was Bob writing songs?

'Yes.'

Bob played board games. His favorite was Scrabble, but he'd always maintained that he was a pretty decent chess player, too, and I had no reason to doubt him. And I knew that he'd once driven all the way to Laughlin, Nevada, in his Camaro for a big Monopoly tournament at one of the casinos. Ideally, Bob's vision of ideal human interaction was that everyone should follow game protocols, that people should take turns, that everyone should know the rules, and that any and all disputes should be handled via consultation with a reference manual.

Needless to say, since most people acted as though life

had no rules and as though there were no manual to consult, in real life Bob was frustrated more often than not by the manner that people behaved.

In Bob's game-centered worldview – a perspective that he definitely applied to conversations – it was my turn to speak. His hollow yes had constituted the totality of his turn and started the clock on mine. Given the presence of the boom box on the table between us, and the revelation about the writing he was doing, that probably wasn't a good time to reiterate a salient point I'd been trying to make for most of a year about the actual parameters of human communication. I took what I hoped was a safer road. I asked, 'What kind of writing are you doing?'

'A story. I think it'll be a novel. I don't know.'

My turn again. 'What . . . are you writing about?'

I knew, of course. I was hoping that I was wrong, but I knew.

'I know some things about what happened to the girl. That's what started it but it's mostly stuff I'm making up.'

'You know some things?' I said, trying to smother the skepticism that had crept into my question.

'Things that aren't in the news. I'm thinking I might call it *My Little Runaway*.'

And thus the song.

'The girl' had to be Mallory, right? She was Bob's current obsession, wasn't she? Had to be her.

Maybe, maybe not. In psychotherapy, assumptions are termites. Let them survive unchallenged and they'll eat away at the foundation. In an effort to exterminate at least one termite, I said, 'Mallory Miller? You know some things about what happened to her?'

'Yes.' He leaned forward, his elbows on his knees, his hands clasped in front of him.

Bob leaning forward startled me. Why? Simply because

it brought him closer to me, and 'closer' wasn't one of Bob's things. 'Closer' is what schizoid personalities try to avoid the way arachnophobes try to steer clear of spiders. For a moment I considered the possibility that Bob had only leaned forward to once again turn on the boom box so that he could sing along to another song.

But he didn't touch the stereo. He had leaned closer for some other reason.

Belatedly, I realized that it was again my turn. All I could think of to say was, 'Wow.'

Bob nodded an acknowledgment that I'd caught up with the conversational progression. 'What she was thinking. You know, like that. Nobody else knows it.'

With those words I decided that Bob had indeed leaned forward to share a secret with me. From a therapeutic perspective, it was a sign of true progress. I began entertaining the possibility that he might, against all odds, be getting better, but that fantasy was short-circuited by my wish that Bob had shared a different kind of secret with me – something about sex, or petty theft, or self-medication, or violent dreams. Just about anything else.

Anything other than something about Mallory.

Bob had many personal faults. Some were born of his underlying pathology; some were more difficult to explain. He was cold. He was irritable. He was intolerant. I suspected he was a bigot. He was mistrustful. Organic vegetables were more compassionate than he was. The list could go on. And on. But as far as I knew – and after two years of Tuesdays I knew as much about him as anyone – Bob wasn't a liar.

Which meant one of two things. The first possibility was that Bob somehow did know some details about Mallory's disappearance, or at least about her state of mind prior to her disappearance.

The other option that I was considering? That Bob just thought he knew those things.

But was it likely that he could be so wrong? The natural history of schizoid personality is not that it's a precursor to schizophrenia. Although schizoids may display idiosyncratic thinking, failure in relating typically doesn't lead to psychotic failures in thinking. But, I reminded myself, the natural history of schizoid personality doesn't rule out progression to serious thought disorder either.

I forced myself to entertain the possibility that I was witnessing initial signs that Bob might be showing signs of decompensation. Usually the resolution to such therapeutic quandaries mattered little, if at all, outside the confines of the consultation room. That time? That time it might make a hell of a lot of difference. The girl in question, Mallory, was still missing, and . . . I realized that I didn't know how to finish that sentence, but also realized, belatedly, that it was my turn to finish some sentence. I said, 'You know things that the police don't know?'

He replied to my question with an apparent non sequitur. 'I rent a garage for my Camaro. I've told you that. It's why it's still so cherry.'

'Yes, we've talked about the garage.' I had to try not to sound exasperated.

'Well, the garage is right next door to Mallory Miller's house.'

He paused a long time, long enough so that I considered that it might, again, be my turn to speak. Although his news was interesting, I was getting ready to squander my move intentionally by saying something innocuous, like, 'It is? Right next door?' But Bob wasn't really done with his turn – he was the hesitant chess player who hadn't quite lifted his fingertips from the piece he'd just slid across the board.

He said, 'See, I know things. They say "write what you know." Well, I know about . . . this. At least a little.' He grimaced. Before I had a chance to respond and ask him about the reason for the grimace, he explained on his own by saying, 'But I don't want to be on TV.'

Although I'd not heard a direct answer to my earlier question – 'You know things that the police don't know?' – I was left with the impression that the answer was yes. Still, despite some concerted effort, I couldn't get Bob to say another word about Mallory that day. My intuition told me that his provocative tease about the missing girl would lose its energy if a long weekend intervened. I said, 'Let's continue this tomorrow.'

'What?'

'This seems important. Can you come back tomorrow for another session?'

'Because of her?'

'Because it seems like a good idea. To me.' What I didn't say was that scheduling three appointments with a schizoid personality in the same week was a clinical strategy that bordered on the absurd.

'I can't afford it.'

'I'll work with you on that.'

He didn't agree; he acquiesced.

His departure at the end of his session was much less dramatic than his boom box entry had been. As he did sometimes, he asked for permission to leave using the French door that led directly outside from the back of my office. The alternative route – returning down the hallway that my office shared with Diane's and then out through the waiting room – brought with it the risk for Bob of confronting another human being, an option that, on most days, he was unlikely to choose. I assented to his request, of course, and he grabbed his things and walked into the cold without a thank-you or a good-bye or a see-you-tomorrow.

I kept my eyes on him until he'd traversed the small backyard of the old house, scissored his way over the poor excuse for a fence on the south side of the property, and begun to close in on the distant sidewalk along Canyon Boulevard.

As I watched him trail away, I belatedly wondered whether I should have pressed him harder about Mallory and what he knew. But the truth was that at that moment, were I a betting man, I would have wagered that Bob's knowledge of Mallory was something that approached delusion.

The conclusion saddened me. Regardless, I'd know more soon enough.

My last clinical appointment of the year was going to be the next day, with Bob Brandt.

19

Diane didn't miss much.

'Did your schizoid man bring that boom box with him into therapy?' she asked me as we both rushed toward our office suite's only bathroom in the few moments that we were stealing between sessions.

I'd never told Diane that Bob suffered from schizoid disorder. But she was an astute diagnostician and had probably come to her own DSM conclusion about him after one or two awkward encounters while she was retrieving a patient in the waiting room.

For appearance' sake, I played coy. 'My last appointment brought a boom box with him, yeah. Actually played me a song on it. Could you hear it through the wall?'

I slowed so that Diane could make it through the door into our tiny kitchen before I did. As she crossed the space and spun into the adjacent bathroom she didn't pause to thank me for my gesture.

'What song?' she called through the closed door.

Diane was just making conversation. She didn't really care what song. I was pleased that her mood seemed improved. She hadn't enjoyed too many good days since Hannah's death.

'"Runaway."'

'Del Shannon?'

'No, some boy band.'

'Holy moly. Which one?'

To my dismay, 'Holy moly' had apparently survived the cut. 'How the hell would I know? All I listen to anymore is Raffi and The Wiggles.'

'Your boy-band days will come sooner than you'd like and you'll look back wistfully on the Raffi period. Was it about Mallory? Is that why he played the song?'

The toilet flushed loudly as I pondered the eerie accuracy of Diane's associative intuitiveness. 'Why would you guess that?'

Efficient sink sounds. The door opened. Finally.

'Because I am the psycholog-ess,' she offered, as though it somehow explained her rare perceptive skills.

'What?'

'Never mind. Could he be an Asperger? Your guy? Mr. Boom Box.'

Diane's question knocked me off balance just a little. Fortunately, I'd already given the issue some thought. I said, 'From a pure social-skills point of view, maybe. But the criteria for schizoid fit him like a glove.'

'It's trendy, you know. Diagnosing Aspies. Schizoid is so . . . sixties.'

'Yeah.' I squeezed past her into the bathroom. I didn't feel comfortable discussing Bob's diagnosis and, anyway, my bladder was screaming.

'You want coffee?' she asked.

'No thanks,' I called through the door as I fumbled with my zipper. At that moment, the thought of adding another liquid, especially a diuretic, to my system seemed masochistic.

Diane said, 'I still haven't heard from the cops about

Hannah's session with Mallory. I kind of thought I would.'

'After this much time I don't think you're going to.' The relief I'd begun to experience in the privacy of the bathroom was exquisite. Talking out loud felt like a particularly intrusive chore.

'Do you think she ran?' Diane asked.

'I do.'

'Someone should know what I learned from Hannah.'

I moved to wash my hands, but didn't reply. Wasn't sure how to reply. Eventually I said, 'It'd be great if you could say something, but you can't.'

'Too many people think they know what was going on in that family. The media does, the cops do, Mallory's father probably does, too. Truth is that it seems like a lot of people all know a little bit but nobody is talking to each other. Nobody has the whole picture.'

I dried my hands while I considered her point. I had to admit she had one. Although I could have argued that the same thing was true about almost any family anywhere, the Miller family was a special case. It seemed likely that despite the intense law enforcement and media assault on their privacy, no one had developed a complete picture of what had been going on in the Miller household prior to Christmas night.

'I've been wondering,' Diane said. 'Do you think Mary Black would talk to me?'

I opened the door. 'About what?'

Diane had one hip against the kitchen counter. She was sipping from a big pink mug of coffee. 'Mrs. Miller, Mallory's mom.'

'No, of course not. Why would she?'

She ignored my question. 'Would she talk to you, then? You referred Mrs. Miller to her.'

'Last time I checked it didn't give me lifetime access to the woman's mental-health records.' I squeezed past Diane, and began to snoop around in our little refrigerator for something with caffeine. 'What do you hope to find by talking to Mary, anyway?'

'I can't talk to her father. There has to be some way to pull all this together.'

'"All this" being the Millers' family situation?'

'Yes . . .'

She'd spoken the simple affirmation as though it constituted an incomplete sentence. I suspected that the other part of the sentence – the part she'd kept to herself – would be something about Hannah's death and Diane's ongoing lament that the cops – specifically the evil asshole, Jaris Slocum – weren't doing much to find Hannah's killer.

Diane remained certain that out there – somewhere – was Hannah's killer.

For whatever reason, she decided that it wasn't judicious to go there with me right then. I couldn't see a reason to quibble with that judgment so I spent a silent moment reflecting on some of the crazy cases I'd been involved with over the past few years, looking for lessons on how to 'pull all this together.'

All I saw were ways to repeat mistakes I'd already made; I couldn't see a single advisable choice. I said, 'Sometimes there isn't, Diane. Sometimes we end up knowing things that other people should probably know. But that's just the way it is.'

Her reply? 'This coffee's old. When did you make it?'

'Before lunch.'

She poured the contents of her mug into the sink. 'I know somebody who might talk to me. Fill in some pieces.'

'Yeah, who?' I expected a punch line.

She fumbled around in a cupboard and came out with a mint Milano. 'I never got my trip to Vegas.'

I wondered where the cookie stash was hidden; I hadn't spotted them earlier in the day. A millisecond after I absorbed her taunt I realized that she might not be joking. 'Diane, you wouldn't.'

'I wouldn't? Watch me. It's winter and it's cold here, if you haven't noticed. It's warm there. The craps tables are open twenty-four seven. Want to come?'

She'd stepped out of the kitchen and started back down the hallway to her office.

I stuck my head out the door. 'You're kidding, right? Tell me you're kidding.'

As she turned the corner toward the waiting room to retrieve her next patient she wiggled her ass in reply. Over her shoulder she called out, 'For the record, I think he's schizoid, too. Asperger, my . . .' She gave her ass one final shake to finish the sentence.

20

No boom box on New Year's Eve afternoon during Bob's additional, additional therapy time. I wasn't surprised; I actually half expected that he would behave as though our conversation about Mallory had never taken place.

Bob slipped his ancient leather-bottomed North Face backpack from his shoulder onto the floor and sat heavily across from me. He didn't bother to remove the well-worn fleece-lined denim jacket that covered one of the button-down blue oxford dress shirts he wore year round. Bob had two denim jackets. This one, with the fleece, was the winter version. The other one, unlined, was reserved for spring and fall.

He didn't say hello to me. He hadn't looked in my direction since I'd retrieved him from the waiting room and led him to my office. I thought he looked particularly tired and distant, which left me again questioning the wisdom of scheduling a third session with a man who used so much of his energy to maintain interpersonal distance.

I said, 'Hello, Bob.'

His gaze was locked on a particular spot on the wall behind me, over my left shoulder. I was tempted to turn and see what was so interesting to him, but I didn't. I knew I'd discover nothing there but paint.

If you were to examine the family histories of the last hundred patients who had sought my help, you would find quite a few who had, arguably, suffered worse childhood trauma than Bob. I don't say that to minimize what he endured when he was young, but rather to create some perspective.

As adults, none of those other patients was as psychologically damaged as Bob. To me, that meant that Bob's unfortunate childhood wasn't sufficient to explain his psychopathology.

Bob's father – the man had been emotionally abusive, and I wouldn't have been at all surprised to learn someday that he had been physically abusive as well – had abandoned the family when Bob was only four. Bob's older brother – the one who lived near his mother – was a high-school football star who'd become a college football star who'd become a successful tax attorney. Bob had more than enough insight to know that despite the fact that they had shared a house growing up, he and his brother had never really lived on the same planet.

His sister, five years older – Bob's memory of her is innocent, and his worship of her saintlike – died of leukemia a year after their father deserted them, on the very day that Bob entered kindergarten.

She'd died at home before breakfast and Bob's mother didn't permit him to miss his first day of school.

His mother was, by Bob's description, a hot-and-cold, smother-and-reject kind of caretaker whom I surmised, had she made her way into a clinician's office for a diagnostic sit-down, would probably have walked out with the dreaded 301.83 label of borderline personality disorder.

As a childhood tableau, it was an awful set piece. But sadly, I saw worse all the time.

All the time.

If a traumatic upbringing wasn't responsible for Bob's seemingly intractable character pathology, was nature to blame? Did the shuffle and deal of genetic bounty leave Bob with a particularly bad hand? Possibly.

Most likely, though, it was some combination of two powerful forces, some unpredictable interaction between Bob's genetic fabric and the bedeviled caprice of his human family.

But I didn't know for sure. The only solace I could find was that a lot of work was being done on the spectrum of disorders that covers the broad territory from autism to schizoid personality. Someday soon, maybe, we'd learn something that would allow me to be a more effective therapist for people like Bob.

Bob said, 'When Doyle sells it, I'm going to have to find a new place to garage the Camaro.'

Something I'd learned about Bob over our years of Tuesdays together was that he often started our conversations midstream, as though an important dialogue had been going on in his head and at some point in my presence – a random point possibly, but more likely not – he decided to put voice to one of the thoughts. I was left to wonder why segue, context, and transition were absent from those rhetorical equations. For the time being, until the long list of goals that comprised my treatment plan for Bob was completed, keeping up with the nature of the progression of his thinking was part of my responsibility.

That day, though, what I was most aware of was that Bob hadn't started the session talking about Mallory.

'Doyle is . . . ?' I asked.

'The guy I rent the garage from. For my Camaro.'

Bob explained the simple fact as though he was annoyed that he was being forced to repeat it for my benefit. Although Bob had mentioned the garage arrangement already that week, the truth was that I'd never heard him mention anyone named Doyle before. I was certain.

'And he's selling . . . ?' I guessed that Doyle was selling the garage.

'The house. It's been on the market for a while, since fall. When he sells it, I'm going to have to move my car, obviously.'

Bob garages his car next door to the home where Mallory Miller lives with her father and brother. And a guy named Doyle owns the house.

Interesting. Lauren hadn't mentioned that last fact to me. Nor did I think I had seen that tidbit in the paper. Not in the Boulder *Daily Camera*. Not in the Denver papers.

The house had been on the market for a while before Mallory disappeared. Had I seen that detail in the paper? I wasn't sure about that either. Maybe. I reminded myself that I wasn't exactly a student of the case.

Bob is concerned about losing the garage for his Camaro.

Check.

'Have you spoken with this guy Doyle, Bob? Do you know his plans for the . . . garage?'

With Bob, where interpersonal relationships were involved, the obvious step often wasn't obvious at all.

'He's selling the house. There's a sign up outside. What's to ask? He moved out a couple of months ago. It's a nice place. I can't afford to buy anything like that.'

Bob's reply was edgier than usual. I noticed that I was tiptoeing with him. I wasn't sure why I was doing it, but I could feel the care I was forcing into my words as I said,

'When he sells the house you'll have to look for a new place for your car?'

Bob was pulling his lower lip across the sharp surface of his front teeth. He did it three or four times before he said, 'I don't actually pay him.'

It was my turn. 'You don't pay Doyle? For the garage?'

'He, um . . . builds fountains and ponds and streams and waterfalls, you know, crap like that for rich people. That's his . . . his business. He does pretty well. I mean, to buy that house, right? It has a theater – a real theater – in the basement. It's like . . . a great place to watch movies. So cool. He has to be doing okay. I help him sometimes, on weekends mostly. He lets me use the garage for the Camaro, and lets me watch movies sometimes. The Trilogy down there? Oh, that's the deal. That is the deal. It may turn out I've been getting screwed. I don't know. I really should have done the math.'

For two years I'd known Bob and I didn't know anything about Doyle, nor did I know anything about his weekends spent building fancy water features for people self-indulgent enough to expect to have large quantities of scarce water decorating their high-desert properties. What else didn't I know about this man across from me?

Experience had taught me that with someone like Bob, the scope of my ignorance could be breathtaking.

'The Trilogy?' I asked, trying to fill in at least one blank.

'The Lord of the Rings,' he explained as though I were a dunce.

'Of course,' I said, feeling appropriately chastised. *Of course.* For Bob, what other trilogy could there have been? 'I didn't know you worked for anyone else, Bob.'

'It's just moving dirt.'

'And that means it's not important?'

'What's the big deal? We put down liners. Move rocks. Lay down some pipes, attach pumps. It's pretty easy. But people pay him a mint for this stuff. You should see his yard. Surrounded by berms and rocks. A big pond, a stream, a bridge, two waterfalls. Those fish – koi. It's pretty cool. We moved a lot of dirt for all that. I like driving the little tractor, the Bobcat? That's a trip.'

'But no more?'

'I told you, he moved. I'm watching his house now until it sells. Keeping the walks shoveled, sweeping up, checking on stuff. Timers, lights. Like that. I think I will go back and do the math. I probably got screwed in the deal.'

If he had been screwed, he didn't sound too upset about it.

Assuming that he had one, I wasn't certain precisely what emotional point Bob was trying to make. Was he aggravated at losing his garage space? Was he sad that he would no longer have a part-time job building water features? Was he going to miss whatever relationship he had with Doyle?

All of the above? I had no idea.

'Will you miss it?' I asked. The 'it' was deliberate on my part. Bob could select an object himself. Garage, job, friend. His choice.

'Miss what?' he asked, instantly abrogating the intent of my clever quiz.

Forcing myself to remain placid, I asked an obvious shrink question. I said, 'I don't know. What do you think you will miss?'

Bob sometimes did this thing with his head that was exactly half of a shake. He'd turn his head to one side – I thought exclusively toward the right, but I wasn't done testing that hypothesis – and begin a head-shaking motion, but he would interrupt the arc of the shake precisely at the moment his nose was back at the neutral position. The movement wasn't graceful; it was abrupt. His face would jerk to a stop as though it had smacked into an invisible obstacle. Typically he accompanied the motion with a verbalized, 'Sheeesh.'

Years before, I'd had another patient who possessed the same bizarre affectation. I found that curious; it was like knowing two people who each had a sixth finger growing out of his elbow.

Bob chose that moment – after I pressed him a second time on what he would miss were Doyle to sell the house – to do the half head-shake thing, and he included the exasperated 'sheeesh' for emphasis.

As I always did, I interpreted the little choreography as a sign of his impatience. With many patients I would probably have kept my interpretation to myself, but with Bob I tried to do as much as possible out in front of the curtain. Human behavior was already enough of a mystery to him.

'You didn't like my question?' I said to reveal the progression of my thoughts.

'I don't like anybody's inane questions.'

The 'anybody's' was Bob's way of cushioning the blow, of telling me not to take his 'inane' rebuke personally. I considered the fact that he was depersonalizing the insult as another sign of clinical progress. On another day I would have been patting myself on the back at the emergence of even that paltry evidence of Bob's growth in compassion.

Not that day, though. I knew it was my turn to speak, but I decided to pass. Where Bob chose to go next would tell me something.

I figured that Bob was waiting for me to take my turn

in this real-life board game of ours. After a long pause, he shifted his gaze from the fascinating blankness on the wall behind me, chanced the briefest of glances at me, and then began looking at his hands. His eyeballs began to shimmy.

As always, it gave me the creeps.

Finally, resigned that I was upsetting the world order by skipping my turn, he said, 'It's not safe yet. I'm not sure what I've gotten into. It's just too soon.'

Huh? 'What's too soon? I don't think I understand.'

'There's a lot I don't get,' Bob said.

What the hell are we talking about? 'For Doyle to sell his house?'

'I'm not sure everything is turning out, you know, the way . . . It might have been a mistake. I stumble into stuff, I do. Not very often, but, boy, when I do . . .'

'Are you talking about Mallory again, Bob?'

He did the half head-shake thing one more time and exclaimed, 'Sheeesh.'

21

I am – almost without fail – thoughtful during psychotherapy sessions. My words are measured. My mannerisms are controlled. It is unusual that I say or do anything while in a treatment session that is not considered and deliberate. That is not to say that I don't often say things that are, in retrospect, ill advised or outright stupid. Rather it is an acknowledgment that when I do, it turns out that I have made the ultimately questionable move with conscious intent.

But the next question that I asked was actually no more deliberate than had been my decision to reach across the hall and try the knob on Mary Black's office door on the day that Hannah Grant died. What I said was, 'Why don't you tell me about Doyle?'

Doyle *had* to be important. Bob, who lived his life devoid of relationships, apparently had one – however loosely defined – with this guy Doyle. In this psychotherapy, with this patient, with his problems, that was monumental news.

Was the presence of Doyle in Bob's life a sign of some drift in the continental plates of Bob's pathology? I had to suppose that it was. Could Bob really have a friend? But if

Doyle was important, why hadn't Bob mentioned him to me before that day?

Did Doyle's sudden appearance say something I couldn't afford to miss about my relationship with Bob? Or perhaps, more importantly, about Bob's perception of his relationship with me?

The context of Doyle's emergence in Bob's psychotherapy was significant, too. Bob had decided to talk about Doyle while he was discussing loss. The 'loss' in question was, at the surface, the loss of a garage for his cherished Camaro, but the fact that he raised the issue of Doyle in the context of any attachment had to be significant. Right?

Maybe. I admit that I wasn't totally certain. Part of me thought I might be making a classic psychotherapy reach.

This work I did was much more art than science.

'Doyle's just a guy,' Bob said in reply to my question.

With as much nonchalance as I could muster I said, 'But you've known him a while? I don't think you've mentioned him before.'

'I don't *know* him. I park my car at his house. And I'm *sure* I mentioned him.'

'And you work for him sometimes.'

He pondered my words for five seconds before he said, 'I work for the state of Colorado, too, but I don't know the governor.'

It was a good retort; I reminded myself that Bob was a smart guy. As an employee of a university that was suffering through an era of eroding state support, Bob wasn't terribly fond of Colorado governor Bill Owens's style of leadership. When Bob mentioned the gov during one of his not-infrequent political rants, he typically called him 'Invisi-Bill,' not 'Governor Owens.'

I chose to avoid the partisan detour. 'Before last week you hadn't mentioned Doyle.'

He backed off his earlier position. 'So you say. Unless I've been misunderstanding something, I'm here to talk about problems. Doyle hasn't been a problem. He's a guy. I do some work for him; he lets me use his garage. That's all, folks.'

The Looney Tunes allusion was an interesting addition to Bob's repertoire. I hadn't heard it before; with him, comical touches were as rare as zits on starlets. But I convinced myself to ignore it, confident it would come back around if it was important. I could've let the Doyle thing drop, too, maybe should have. But instead I chose to push a little harder. 'I find it interesting that you've never mentioned him before.'

His frustration blossomed. 'Really? You find that interesting? I haven't talked about the teller I use at the bank either. But I see her every week, too.'

Did he say 'use'? He 'uses' a teller? And who, in the age of ATMs, lays eyes on a bank teller every week? Wouldn't a schizoid guy love the age of ATMs?

I had a few choices as to where to go next, one of which was the tempting bank teller/ATM question, but I suspected that it – like Invisi-Bill and Looney Tunes – was a blind alley. I went with what looked like the no-brainer: 'By talking about him now are you suggesting that Doyle has become a problem?'

'Only if I need to find a new place to park the Camaro. When that happens, then, well . . . then I have a problem, don't I?'

'If Doyle sells the house?'

'When. Yes.'

'And your current landlord doesn't have any garage space you can rent?' I wouldn't have asked most patients that question. But Bob often missed the forest for the trees, or vice versa, and part of my job was to help him understand how the world works, especially those parts of the world that are inhabited by other people.

'He owns some big stupid supercab macho truck. There's no room in the garage.'

I leaned forward slowly, resting my elbows on my knees, slightly closing the space between us. I was almost certain that Bob felt my postural readjustment as an unwelcome intrusion. That was okay; it was my intent. 'You said it wasn't safe yet. What did you mean? Was that about Doyle?'

I was challenging Bob much more than I usually did. For many patients, perhaps most, my insistence on talking more about Doyle and the garage would not have been perceived as much of a confrontation. But Bob was feeling pressured by my persistence and he was figuratively reaching out behind him, searching for the perimeter of the corner I was edging him toward. His breathing grew more rapid and his normally pale cheeks drained even further of color.

'Yes,' he said, but it was tentative. His defenses were much more nimble than I would have predicted.

As I swallowed a silent question to myself about whether my persistence was really therapeutically indicated, I made the point I'd been leading up to for minutes, 'And I thought you were implying that you're concerned about Mallory.'

He snapped back, 'Isn't everyone?'

Another good reply. I was impressed, but perhaps I shouldn't have been. The one thing that schizoid personalities usually have mastered is distancing behavior.

Two years and counting and I was still learning things about Bob.

The banter was therapeutically enlightening, but I

wasn't about to be deterred from my quest to understand more about his surprising revelations about Doyle, and his intimations about Mallory. 'Earlier in the week – when you played the song? – shortly after you mentioned the guy you rent the garage from, you specifically expressed concern about Mallory, and talked about the writing you're doing. And today you said, "It's not safe yet."'

'So?'

'What connects Doyle's garage, your writing, and Mallory?'

Bob's mouth was open about half an inch and he'd thrust his jaw so far forward that it momentarily appeared as though he had a chin. He said, 'She's been gone a . . . while. Everyone's concerned. I bet even you are. Aren't you?'

Even me? 'Bob, this is important. Do you know if Doyle has anything to do with Mallory's disappearance?'

He shook his head. 'You never really know about people, do you? You think you know . . . but then,' he said, his voice unsteady. 'I think . . . things always turn out to be different.'

Bob's platitude was true, of course. And Bob's psychopathology probably left him more vulnerable to doubt about other people's motives than most of us. But I also knew that Bob's statement hadn't been an invitation to parse psychological principles. I asked, 'What are you thinking specifically?'

'Nothing,' he said. Then he added, with a side of sarcasm, 'My mother.'

I went back to the beginning. 'Why don't you tell me about Doyle?'

Bob stuck his tongue between his teeth. When he released it, he said, 'I know her. Mallory. I didn't think you'd . . .'

What? You didn't think I'd what?

22

I know her. Mallory.

Interesting non sequitur. Or apparent non sequitur. He hadn't answered my question about Doyle. Instead, he'd turned my attention back to Mallory. Or . . . perhaps talking about Mallory was his way of talking about Doyle.

Patience, Alan.

'You do?' I asked. 'You know her?' Despite what I'd learned about the location of the garage, and about Doyle, I wouldn't have guessed that Bob knew Mallory. Why?

Because Bob was Bob.

'We talked. While I was working at Doyle's. She'd come by sometimes. She was curious what we were doing. She liked the fish. And the waterfall. She said she could hear the water running from her bedroom window. I saw her up there sometimes. At her window. When Doyle wasn't home she'd go down and sit by the pond and watch the fish.'

Bob was having trouble stringing the short sentences together. Something was aggravating his natural wariness. Was it thoughts of Mallory?

Had to be. Or maybe Bob's admission about Mallory was diversion? Was he uncomfortable talking about Doyle and was he taking me someplace he figured I'd willingly go instead? Was Bob that cunning? I didn't think so, but I couldn't rule it out.

'We talked through the fence,' he added, not waiting his turn. 'A few different times.'

Not waiting his turn was another sign of his discomfort. The fact that he and Mallory talked through the fence? I suspected that the physical separation of the barrier made the conversation more palatable for Bob, maybe even made the conversation *possible* for Bob. Metaphorically, it was elegant.

But still . . . 'Go on,' I said.

'She's a nice girl.'

'And you spoke with her?'

'I have, yeah. A lot of times.'

Well, Bob, was it a 'few times' or 'a lot of times'?

He squinted his eyes and tightened his jaw. The grimace caused his chin to retreat. It looked for a moment as though his face just melted away half an inch below his lower lip. 'She's my . . . friend.'

As surprising as it might sound, the fact that Bob had personally met Mallory was merely a curiosity to me, another one of those 'I know someone who' anecdotes that were still swirling around Boulder about the Millers. But the fact that he'd conversed with Mallory on a personal level? And multiple times? And that he considered her a friend? That was epiphany-quality news where Bob was concerned.

From what I knew about him socially – and before that day's session had started, I thought I knew most of what there was to know – Bob didn't have repeated personal conversations with people with whom he wasn't somehow compelled to relate.

He just didn't.

'She's your friend? You talked about . . . ?'

'I told you. The waterfall, the pond. The fish. She loved the waterfall. Other things. She likes my car.'

'Other things?' I was reaching. I knew I was reaching.

'Yeah.'

'Such as . . . ?'

Another grimace. Then, again, 'My mother.'

I went to safer ground. I didn't want to. But I felt I would push him farther away if I came any closer. 'And you thought she was nice?'

Shortly after the words exited my mouth, I realized that my caution had come too late and that our rat-a-tat conversation was over. Silence descended on the room the way darkness follows a closing curtain. I waited. Bob had started breathing through his mouth. Each exhale was accompanied by a faint whistle.

Finally he spoke. He said, 'She doesn't look fourteen.'

My spleen spasmed. At least I think it was my spleen – something in there suddenly got twisted into a big, fat knot. I hadn't been aware that I didn't want to hear those specific words from Bob, but now that he'd said them I knew that I hadn't wanted to hear them.

'Time's up,' he said.

I looked at the clock.

He was right. Time was up.

Didn't matter to me. I needed some magic that would encourage Bob to stay and tell me what was haunting him. Because something was haunting him. I couldn't find any magic, so I focused on what I feared: 'You don't think she looks fourteen?'

'Do you?' he asked.

Frankly, no. In Boulder, most eleven- and twelve-year-old girls look fourteen. Fourteen-year-old girls look, well, older – sometimes a lot older. Sometimes way too much older. But I wasn't about to tell Bob that. I suspected his comment about Mallory's age had little to do with musings about the sociological implications of the increasingly early psychosexual maturity of adolescent girls.

I said, 'Bob, look at me. Please.'

He did, holding the connection for almost two entire seconds. I asked, 'Do you know something about Mallory? Where she is? How she's doing? Had she said something to you? Has Doyle?'

Way too many questions on my part. Way too many. A rational observer would have had a hard time determining who was more flustered at that moment, doctor or patient.

'Maybe you know something you should tell the police,' I added – my way of adjusting the seasoning on a therapeutic dish I was already responsible for overcooking.

Bob did the half head-shake thing again, this time minus the 'sheeesh,' before he said, 'I have to go.'

I barely heard his words. The echoes of his earlier pronouncement – *'She doesn't look fourteen'* – were gaining volume in my head. Silently quoting Diane, I thought, *Holy moly.*

'Did you talk to Mallory just before Christmas, Bob? Did you know what was going to happen?'

'I have to go.'

'I have a few extra minutes. We can go on.'

Bob didn't acknowledge my offer. He stood, grabbed his daypack, and stepped toward the French door that led outside toward the backyard, but he didn't ask me for permission to use it as he had on previous occasions. As he pulled the door open, air that was much colder than I expected flooded into the room, chilling my feet. He paused in the open doorway and turned his head back in my direction.

Our gazes failed to connect by about ten degrees. It was as though he were blind, wanted to find my gaze, but couldn't quite manage to make eye contact.

He said, 'Is something a secret if nobody knows you know it?'

My gut was still in knots. 'I don't know what you mean.'

'For something to be a secret, somebody else has to know it, right? Or . . . do they? I tell you things and you have to keep them secret. But I've never been . . .'

Been what?

I suspected that Bob's naiveté was talking, or that he was posing a trick question – a-tree-falling-in-the-forest clone – but I couldn't find the trap. Reluctantly I said, 'A secret is a secret, I guess.'

He suddenly shifted his gaze and we locked eyes for a period of time that was about the duration of a solitary flap of a humming-bird's wings. There, and then gone. He persisted. 'If nobody knows something but the person who knows it, is it really a secret? Or is it something else? What would that be?'

'What are we talking about, Bob? Is this . . . something about Mallory? Is she okay? Do you know something about where she is?'

'Other people have secrets. I didn't really know that. I mean I knew it, but I didn't . . . I don't know everything yet, but it's not as simple as I thought at first. I'm not even sure about what I know. Does that make sense?'

No, it doesn't.

I could feel him pulling away. He hadn't moved an inch farther away from me, but this prolonged connection between him and me had existed at a level of intimacy that I knew Bob couldn't tolerate for long. Now he was floating away like a helium balloon in a stiff breeze.

I tried to grab for the string that would bring him back. I said, 'But you know something? You know a secret?'

I kept thinking, *You know that she doesn't look fourteen.*

'You know secrets, too,' he replied. 'People tell you things. I do. Therapists.'

What did that mean? Was he speaking generally or was he referring to something specific that he thought I knew?

I didn't know.

He pursed his thin lips and shook his head, just a little, as though he was mildly disappointed with me. 'The story's not over. I have to figure stuff out, who to trust. I think I've already been wrong once. Doyle's not . . . the guy I thought he was.'

Trust me. Please.

'Doyle's not what? What do you mean?'

'Maybe you should read it. What I wrote.'

I opened my mouth to reply, but Bob closed the door behind him.

I was about to say, 'I'd love to.' The cold air that had rushed in wasn't the only cause of chill in the room.

I stepped outside into the frigid air. 'Bob,' I called. After two more steps across the yard he stopped and turned to face me. He didn't bother to look at me, but he faced me. I said, 'Tuesday, our regular time, okay?'

'Yeah.'

'If you'd like to meet before then I can do that. Don't worry about the money.'

He said, 'Okay,' hunched his shoulders forward, dropped his poor excuse for a chin, and paced off into the night.

23

Sam had blown some serious bucks at Runners Roost.

A year before if you had asked me what was more likely, a giant meteor destroying our planet, or Sam Purdy adorned in head-to-toe burgundy running Lycra, I would have been warning everyone to duck. But there Sam stood, right at my front door, jogging in place, his breath puffing out in little frosty clouds that stood out like flares against a sky the color of deep water.

It was 5:10 in the frigging morning on the first Monday of the year. My initial thoughts upon waking had been about my disconcerting session with Bob a few days before.

'You ready?' Sam asked. 'I say we do a couple of slow miles, then we try to bring one in around nine. What do you think? We'll work up from there.'

I tied both of my shoes before I replied. 'I think it's January, Sam, and this could really wait until March or April. The race isn't until May, for God's sake.'

The race on Sam's radar was the Bolder Boulder, the Memorial Day Weekend 10K classic, and for some reason Sam had decided that his training regimen couldn't be put off until spring. I'd volunteered to be his workout partner, and unfortunately for me his ardor for physical fitness was that of the newly converted.

'Emily coming with?'

Sam was asking about our Bouvier des Flandres. Emily was a big bear of a dog and her natural instincts spurred her more toward herding livestock than jogging on a lead alongside human beings. 'Maybe next time. Running in straight lines isn't one of her best things. She likes to roam. Let's see how it goes without her this time.'

'What about the little one? Anvil?'

'Hardly. Three miles is a marathon for a miniature poodle. At least it is for him. I'm afraid it's just you and me.' I stared out into the darkness. 'I don't even think we'll see the milkman or the paperboy at this hour.'

'Cool, let's go.'

Although it was contrary to his character to yield control, Sam wanted me to set the pace. Two reasons: From a thousand dog walks I knew the trails in the nearby hills, and since I'd run a couple of Bolder Boulders when I was younger he was granting me the status of running guru.

I knew the status assignment wouldn't endure for long. Near the end of mile one, I asked, 'What kind of trouble has Reese Miller been in?'

Sam didn't move lightly. I don't know whether it was inexperience, poor technique, just the fact that he was a big guy, or what, but the pounding beside me on the dirt trails of Spanish Hills sounded more like the *clop*, *clop* of a Clydesdale than the heel-toe patter of a jogger. I'm not much of a runner. Bicycling is my thing. But running beside Sam and his plodding strides I felt like I was floating.

'Fights.'

I didn't expect that he'd answer me at all, but his reply was too parsimonious for my taste. I considered the possibility that Sam was too winded to be more expansive, but he was in better shape than at any time since we'd met and I decided that the brevity was an indication of caution while he figured out where the hell I was coming from.

'Hockey fights?' I asked.

'Some.'

'But some not?'

'I think you're watching too much cable. It's bad for your health.'

I probably had been watching too much cable news, but I wasn't about to admit it to Sam. Blame it on Bob, and Diane. 'I don't know. I'm curious, I guess.'

'Ask me, there's already way too much curiosity about that case.'

'You brought up Reese, Sam. Not me.'

'First time, I did. And I regret it. This time you did. You still pissed at Jaris Slocum?'

I wasn't surprised that he'd changed the subject; I was surprised where he'd gone. 'What he did to Diane? Of course. He was an asshole.'

'There're reasons. Not excuses. Reasons. Cops feel pressure, too. Just like everybody else.'

'Reasons to rough up a witness who's grieving about finding her friend dead? Yeah? Like what?'

'Maybe you could cut him some slack, get over your hurt feelings. In the end it's not about what he did, it's about whatever happened to that woman.'

'That woman' was Hannah. 'I'll think about it,' I said, curious as to why Sam was suddenly so concerned about Jaris Slocum's welfare.

'You have other reasons, don't you?' he said.

'What?'

'For asking about Reese.'

The boomerang of subjects threw me. All I managed was a solitary, 'What?'

'Thought so.'

I had been trying not to sound defensive; apparently I wasn't succeeding. The truth was I wasn't that interested in Reese. Reese was a foot in the door. I wanted to hear Sam's thoughts on anything to do with the Millers, hoping to hear something that would ease my mind about my last meeting with Bob.

I said, 'No, no. What you said at Simon's hockey game got me thinking, and I've been wanting to hear what you know about Reese. Not as a cop, just as a parent.'

'Yeah? That's all you're wanting to know, what I know as a parent?'

'Exactly.'

'Pardon me if I don't believe you.' Sam's thunderous strides punctuated the silence that followed. *Boom, boom. Boom, boom.* He broke the tension by asking, 'What do you know about the Pearl Street Mile? I'm thinking it's more my distance than 10K.'

The Pearl Street Mile is a summer evening race run around the Downtown Boulder Mall. Compared to the carnival spectacle of the massive holiday weekend Bolder Boulder, the Pearl Street Mile is a relatively sedate event.

'Not much.' I told him what I knew, adding, 'You're going to pass on the Bolder Boulder?'

'No. Just trying to find the right distance for my running style.'

'And you're thinking you're built for speed, not endurance?'

My sarcasm was rarely wasted on Sam.

'You take what God gives you, you know.'

Nor his on me.

'I know.'

Sam pulled up short and put his hands on his ample hips. I stopped a couple of strides later and turned back to face him. He wasn't breathing hard but each exhale temporarily hid his round face behind a miasma of fog.

My neighborhood, Spanish Hills, is a rural enclave of mostly elegant homes – ours was one of the few exceptions – on the hillsides that comprise the eastern rise of the Boulder Valley, not far from the scenic overlook on the Boulder Turnpike. The western rim of the valley is formed by the Front Range of the Rocky Mountains, and by comparison the vanilla hills of the eastern rim are, well, wimpy.

The spot where Sam paused on our run was on the top of a rounded ridge just north and east of my house. From where I stood, Sam's right ear was totally obscuring the rock formation known as Devil's Thumb. I'd always thought that the huge natural sculpture more closely resembled an altogether different part of the devil's anatomy, but maybe that was just me.

'What?' I asked for about the tenth time that morning.

'You got something. So tell me what it is, get it off your chest. No secrets, just get it off your chest.'

Sam wasn't being a bully. He was perfectly capable of it, but at that moment he was merely making me an offer. The features on his face suddenly lit up just a little. The phenomenon was illumination, not insight. Far behind me the morning sun was breasting the almost imperceptible arc of the wide horizon of the Great Plains.

Sam and I had been here before. I knew something I'd learned in therapy that I thought he should know, but I couldn't tell him about it. With a few exceptions, the rules said I couldn't tell Sam anything a patient had told me. Life had taught me over the past few years that assiduously adhering to those rules was sometimes as dangerous as breaking them. I was confident that I would ultimately decide what to reveal based on that reality, and that with enough creativity I could find a way to tell Sam what I wanted to tell him without the rules ever knowing they'd been sullied.

Below us, the headlights of a car snaked down the dirt and gravel lane that led to my house. In the predawn shadows I couldn't identify any features of the car. The guy who delivered the morning paper? No, it wasn't him; he had a rusty, old post–World War II Dodge Power Wagon that sent its bass rumble bouncing through the hills. In its own way, the sound was as distinctive an announcement siren as the syrupy melody of the ice cream man.

I watched the car's progress until it disappeared behind the contour of an intervening hill. It was probably the nanny that Adrienne, our urologist neighbor, sometimes brought in to watch Jonas at an ungodly hour so she could keep her morning surgical schedule.

To Sam, I said, 'Do you guys know much about the house next door to the Millers? The one that's for sale?'

'Us guys?'

'The cops.'

Sam started jogging in place. The sight of the ruby fabric stretching across his thick thighs made me think of a matched pair of prosciutto di Parma.

He took off down the trail. I did, too. Over his shoulder, he said, 'There something you think we – us cops – should know about the guy next door?'

After a few strides I replied, 'Not really.'

'Not really? Or not at all?'

I didn't know enough about the Millers' neighbor to answer Sam's question, and I wasn't totally comfortable with the territory I was taking him, so I asked, 'What kind of fighting did Reese have trouble with?'

'If you've been watching all that cable then you know what those kids have been through. He's a good kid.'

He hadn't answered my question. I was forced to hustle to keep up with him; the pace he was setting for the second mile was way too fast. 'You mean been through with his mom?'

Without any hesitation, Sam said, 'What do you know about the trouble with the kids' mom?'

Startled, I realized three things. The first two? The eastern sky was brightening, and the day had begun. Number three? Maybe there hadn't been anything in the news about the difficulty that the Miller children might have had with their mom, and I'd just told Sam Purdy that I knew something he didn't think I should know.

Oops. The information wasn't particularly important. The fact that I had an avenue to know it? Sam would find that important.

24

The pace that Sam set for the last mile and a half of our run precluded chatting. Despite my usually rigorous bicycling regimen I was seriously winded by the conclusion of our morning jaunt. To my relief Sam was, too.

As soon as we'd come within sight of my house I'd started looking around for the car that had come down the lane a little earlier. It wasn't there. It wasn't in front of our house. It wasn't in front of Adrienne's either.

The hue of the sky told me that we'd arrived back where we'd started shortly before six. I invited Sam in for coffee. He declined. 'Sherry has Simon. She's bringing him back over early so she can get to class. I need to be home to feed him and get him off to school.'

Sherry was Sam's ex. She was living in Northglenn, a suburb north of Denver, and attending school at Auraria. She'd sold her flower business and was studying to be an EMT. The custody arrangement that she and Sam had negotiated was so complicated that I thought it would require single-variable calculus equations to put it on paper. But the plan worked; I'd not once heard Sam complain about the convoluted logistics.

He opened the door to his old navy Cherokee. In the thin light the dried muck on the lower third of the squat body made the car appear to have a custom paint job. Almost. 'How many miles you have on this thing?' I asked.

'Odometer broke at one-forty-seven-something. That was on the day that the Supreme Court decided who our president was going to be. So more than one-forty-seven. Plenty more than one-forty-seven.'

'How old is it?'

'It's a '90.' He climbed in. The concave driver's seat accepted his rear end the way Lauren's out-thrust hip supported our daughter's cute butt. Naturally. With just the slightest trace of a smile in his eyes – it was impish, almost ironic – he said, 'You know what? That makes this car the same exact age as Mallory Miller.'

I didn't know what to say to that.

He wasn't done. 'And the other girl, too. I'm sure you remember her. She was a 1990, too.'

The one who had been murdered in the dark hours overnight on another Christmas Day. The pretty little blonde whose one-time beauty-queen momma wanted her daughter to be a beauty queen, too. The one whose pathetic father had carried her lifeless body up the stairs from the basement like a spray of damaged flowers. Yes, I remembered that other girl. Too well.

'See you,' Sam said. 'Thanks for the run.'

The Cherokee chugged north down the lane. Before it was out of sight the rumble of the old Dodge Power Wagon signaled that the newspaper delivery guy was heading in our direction. I watched his headlights dance in the grasses before I stepped inside and started a pot of coffee. A few minutes later I was still wet from the shower when Grace announced the beginning of her day. My sleepy wife crashed into me in the doorway as we rushed toward our daughter's room.

I cherish morning in our home. I love the soft carelessness of my wife after she's slept, her flesh exposed near the unbuttoned top button or two of her pajamas. I love the fragrance at the nape of my daughter's neck after a night of sweet dreams. I love the frantic energy that the dogs bring to each and every dawn.

I adore the tang of fresh juice and the texture of bananas and the yeasty smell of toasted Great Harvest bread. I adore the first sip of hot coffee almost as much as I adore the aroma, and I relish the light that pours over the infinite plains and fills our little kitchen seconds before it jumps up and causes the crystalline formations on the Flatirons to sparkle like the facets of diamonds.

No, that day I wasn't necessarily thrilled about running around like a madman in order to make it to my office for my 7:15 appointment downtown, but it was, I figured, all part of the package.

And all in all, it was a damn good package. I felt that way almost every morning and felt great fortune that almost every day in my home started with the unspoiled promise of fresh bliss.

A year and a half earlier, Lauren had bought me a new BMW Mini as a gift. The generous gesture was intended to snap me out of a professional funk that I'd been sliding into, and her choice of cars paid homage to an old love of mine, a classic Mini Cooper named Sadie that I'd adopted in my youth. I drove the gift Mini on nice days for over a year before I sold it. I didn't sell it because I didn't like it. I sold it because every time I drove it I felt as though I was taking a holiday from responsible parenting. All the data said it was a safe car for its size. The problem, though, was its size. Compared to an elephantine Ford Expedition – and way too often on Boulder's roads that was exactly the comparison I was forced to consider – my little Mini felt like a dainty ladybug.

I'd put an ad in the paper after the previous autumn's aspen season had peaked and ended up selling the Mini to a sophomore volleyball player from CU who had apparently convinced her parents that the little car was safe enough for her.

When I pressed the button that opened the garage door the car that was waiting to take me downtown to my office was a three-year-old, four-wheel-drive Audi wagon with 27,000 miles on it. I'd bought it from Diane's next-door neighbor when she moved to Phoenix to trade the cold of Colorado's winters for the heat of Arizona's summers. The Audi was a fun car. Not as much fun as the Mini. But fun enough. It could handle all but the deepest snow, there was room in the back for both dogs, and – most important – it had more airbags than cylinders, much more sheet metal than the Mini, and, rational or not, I didn't feel like a lunatic when I strapped Grace into the backseat.

I was only two steps away from the open garage door when I spotted a fresh set of headlights snaking down our lane.

I stopped. Four cars at my house before 7 A.M.? For us, that constituted a parade.

The approaching car had a throaty rumble, not as *thumpy-thumpy* as the newspaper guy's Power Wagon, but certainly not that of a lightweight, well-mufflered, catalytic-converted Honda or Subaru either.

Despite the incipient dawn the headlights were aimed right at my eyes and they blinded me until the car was about twenty feet away. I stood still, waiting for the reveal. Finally, the driver turned the car abruptly to the left and pulled it to a stop that was short enough to cause the vehicle to slide a foot or so on the dirt and gravel.

The car was a shiny black Camaro that was much, much older than Sam's Cherokee, but still a modern automotive wonder compared to the paper guy's ancient Dodge truck.

Bob Brandt climbed out from behind the wheel. He didn't kill the engine, however, and the growl of the big motor in the Camaro continued to thunder off the hillsides. Bob didn't say 'Hi,' or 'Good morning,' or 'Sorry to intrude,' or anything else that most people might say in similar circumstances.

I didn't say some things, too. I didn't say, 'What are you doing here at this hour?' or, 'How the hell do you know where I live?'

My home phone number wasn't listed. My home address was a carefully guarded secret. I didn't encourage patients to call me after hours. I certainly didn't encourage them to drop by whenever the hell they felt like it. Whatever early-morning calm the serenity of my family in my home had afforded me evaporated like the steam from pancakes on a hot griddle.

I was feeling violated by Bob's presence in front of my garage. But at some level I also felt grateful for another opportunity to connect with Bob about Mallory Miller.

Bob spoke first. That was fine; it was definitely his turn. 'What do you think about my car?' he asked. The Camaro's motor – had he told me once, or twice, or ten times that it was a 396? – provided a percussive accompaniment that sounded like a big sub-woofer with an electrical short.

I had no intention of chatting about cars with Bob at seven o'clock in the morning only steps from my front door and my darling daughter. 'Good morning,' I said, while I told myself that Bob must have a reason – a good reason – for mounting this kind of intrusion.

Bob was dressed in his ubiquitous outfit. Chinos, long-sleeve blue dress shirt, denim jacket – the fleece-lined one. Trail runners. He appeared nervous. I'd never before seen him outside the confines of my office, though, and was more than prepared to believe that he spent much of his life appearing nervous.

'I have something . . .' He was looking at my Audi. 'That yours?'

He sounded surprised, as though he expected someone else's car to be in my garage. 'Why did you get rid of the Mini?'

He asked as though he been wondering about it for a while and thought that he deserved an explanation. I wasn't going to go there with him, either.

'You like this better?' he asked, perseverating on the car.

I counted to three. 'Bob, you said you have something . . . What? Something you wanted to tell me—'

'Something to give you. Is it the turbo? That's the turbo, isn't it?' He was still focused on the wagon. 'Fixated' might be a better word.

'I assume you came to my house because something feels urgent, Bob.' I could have just said, '*Why are you here?*'

Bob didn't get my drift. He thought about my question for a few seconds before he said, 'Should it?'

Seriously schizoid people relate the way people with sleep apnea breathe at night: in fits and starts. No organic rhythm. Just enough to maintain life. Sometimes not even that much. Nothing that should be natural and predictable about interacting with another human being is natural and predictable for them.

Allowing the realization to settle that Bob's appearance at my home at dawn was undoubtedly meaningful, I forced my discomfort that he knew where I lived away from center stage and stuffed some composure into my voice. I asked, 'What brings you to my home so early in the morning, Bob?'

What was I thinking? I was thinking *'Mallory.'*

'I have to . . .' he said. I thought he'd stopped himself before he completed the sentence. 'I wanted to give you . . . what I've been writing. We talked about it. Remember?'

You bet I remember.

He leaned into the Camaro and came back out with an old, beat-up, dark-blue box imprinted with the logo of Kinko's, the copy palace.

'Here it is. It's not done,' he said.

He held it out for me. I took it. The ream-sized carton was far from full. I guessed it held fewer than a hundred pages. I was already wondering: *Is this it? Is this really the reason he's come to my home shortly after dawn? To give me part of a novel?*

'Don't read it, yet. I'll tell you when.'

'You want me to have it, but not to read it?'

'Yes.'

I thought my question warranted a better explanation. Bob, apparently, didn't agree. 'That's it?' I said.

'I have a long way to go. I'm still trying to get it . . . I want it to be right before you read it.'

'Couldn't you have just held on to it until you decide that you would like me to read it?' *Or until you see me tomorrow?*

He chanced a glance at me. The tenor of his look was questioning whether I had suddenly become mentally challenged. As though it would explain everything, he said, 'This is a copy. It's not the original. I have one, too.'

He'd totally missed the point of my question. With Bob, that happened with some frequency.

'Okay,' I said. I was already putting together a list of things we'd have to discuss during the next day's session.

'You'll understand,' he assured me. 'When I tell you it's okay to read it, you'll understand.'

'You'll explain?'

'Yes. You like it?'

I raised the box up a couple of inches. 'I'll let you know. After you tell me when I should read it.'

'I meant the Camaro. It's cherry, don't you think?'

I gazed at the glossy black car, its pristine paint marred only by the faintest hint of Spanish Hills dust. 'Sure is,' I said. 'It sure is.'

'Yep,' he agreed.

I took a deep breath and asked, 'Bob, have you thought more about the question I asked you last week? Whether you know something about Mallory Miller that you should share with the police?'

He kicked at the dirt. 'You know the . . . that woman who was killed? Who died? On Broadway? The therapist, like you?'

Like me? I felt gooseflesh on my back. 'Hannah Grant? A few weeks ago?'

'Her. She was Mallory's . . . therapist. Mallory was afraid after she died. Really afraid. She thought . . . Mallory has this thing about Christmas. The guy that the neighbors saw? You know about that?'

Oh shit. 'Which guy? On Christmas night? Outside? That guy?'

If Bob knew anything new about Mallory and the Christmas guy it meant that he'd seen Mallory since she disappeared.

'I was watching a movie.'

'At Doyle's house? You were there?'

'Before Christmas she thought someone may have found out about . . . oh boy. And because of . . . that's why . . . she wasn't comfortable. No, not at all.'

'That's why what?' There was enough pressure in my questions to launch a rocket.

Smooth, Alan. Real smooth.

'She doesn't really like Christmas. I don't either. She was scared that she might be – Sheesh. I can't, I shouldn't . . . It happened once, it could happen . . . I have to go. I don't want you to . . .' he said. 'Anyway, I don't like to be late.'

You don't want me to what? 'I'm very interested in hearing more, Bob. It will just take another moment. You came all the way out here.'

I'm sure I sounded pathetic.

'I have to go.' He opened the door and climbed into his car. The vinyl seats were so cold that they squeaked with his weight.

'Are you scared about something, too, Bob?' I asked through the glass.

He shook his head.

'Do you know anything about where Mallory is? Anything? Please tell me.'

'I'm late.'

'I'll see you tomorrow then,' I said.

'Sure,' he said, barely loudly enough so that I could hear.

He fishtailed a little as he spun around to head out the lane. The rumble of his motor was almost enough to stifle the pounding in my ears.

She was scared. He'd said she was scared.

Was I tempted to read what Bob had written? Of course

I was, right that minute. I was also certain that my temptation was part of the challenge that Bob was positing.

Why was he setting things up to tantalize me that he might know something about Mallory Miller's fate and then keep the evidence of what he might know just out of my reach? He had taunted me already with the proposition that he knew her, was friends with her. He had just added the proposition that he knew that Mallory had seen Hannah for psychotherapy. And he'd added the tantalizing possibility that he'd been right next door in Doyle's house on Christmas night. He'd said that Mallory was scared.

I didn't know what Bob was up to with Mallory. Far from it. But trust – therapeutic trust between Bob and me – was on the table in the form of the manuscript in the Kinko's box. That much was perfectly clear.

What were the odds that Bob actually knew something crucial about Mallory?

Low, really low.

Bob's life was smoke, not fire. Heat, not light. Bob hadn't told me anything that was really new to me. I was already aware that Mallory had seen Hannah for psychotherapy. I already knew about the man who had been loitering outside, everybody did. All Bob had really added to the equation was that Mallory was scared.

And that he'd been next door watching a movie.

Hopefully, the next day I'd learn what Bob thought Mallory was frightened about. I could wait until then.

Long before the dust had settled on the lane from the Camaro's too-rapid departure, I'd flicked off the lid of the Kinko's box and looked inside. The flimsy cardboard box was less than a quarter full of $8\frac{1}{2} \times 11$ sheets. The title page was simple, the typeface minuscule.

My Little Runaway
By R.C. Brandt

In the lower right-hand corner Bob had carefully sketched the encircled *c* of the copyright symbol and beside it had typed out the word 'copyright' and beside that, the year.

I closed the box.

25

I didn't see patients most Fridays. Diane skipped most Mondays. So I wasn't at all surprised that her Saab wasn't in its usual spot in front of our wreck of a garage all day Monday while I was at the office. Anyway, she'd asked me if I would cover her practice in case she and Raoul went away for the weekend, and weekends for Diane almost always included Mondays.

But the phone call she made to me that evening caught me off guard. Dinner was done, the kitchen was clean, Lauren had Grace in the tub for a mother-daughter bubble soak. Their giggles and laughter filled the house and buoyed my spirits like a healthy dose of rock and roll.

I had the dogs at my feet. Life was good.

'Can you hear that?' Diane asked.

I heard noise but it sounded like nothing more than routine mobile-phone clutter crap. I figured Diane was in her Saab, driving behind the spine of a hogback someplace, or in the deep recesses of one of the many canyons that snake west out of Boulder into the heart of the Rockies.

'No, I don't think so. You're breaking up.'

Then I heard it – the frenetic calliope melody of a slot-machine jackpot followed by an orgasmic scream of 'I won! I won! Yes! Yes! I told you about this machine. Didn't I?' I could almost hear the cascade of dollar coins tumbling into the stainless-steel tray.

'You up in Blackhawk?'

'Nope.'

'Central City?'

'One more try.'

I could have wasted my third guess on Cripple Creek, the final member of the triad of Colorado pioneer mountain towns that the electorate had burdened with legalized gambling. Instead I went for the jackpot.

'You're in Vegas. You really went.'

'Told you.'

'How much of Raoul's money have you lost?'

'I make plenty of my own money.'

'Yeah, but you told me once that you only gamble with his.'

'I forgot I told you that. I can't believe I told you that. I'm down a grand or so.'

'Or so?'

'Maybe a little more. Single digits.'

'Single digits plus, what, three zeros?'

'My luck will change. I rescheduled my patients until Thursday. That's a lifetime in craps. Can we talk about something else? How about matrimony? You want to talk about matrimony?'

Part of me didn't want to know. But I said, 'Sure.'

'I found her. Mrs. Miller. She was hanging out at a place called the Love In Las Vegas Wedding Chapel.' Diane made sure that her pronunciation of 'love' had two syllables. 'Everybody knows her in the Vegas wedding racket; she's kind of a local legend. I only had to go to three chapels and ask a few questions.'

*

I had a picture in my mind.

A woman who had once been pretty dressed in an outfit that had once been fashionable topped by a hat that had once been fresh was sitting by herself on the bride's side of a chapel that had never, ever, really been pretty or lovely or fresh, and she was celebrating the nuptials of two people who had known each other for hours or days or months or years.

Elvis was there, too, or he wasn't.

The woman heard voices in her ears saying cruel, frightening things and one glance at her made clear that she spent many more of her waking hours tormented than she did at peace. Her face was sometimes molded into odd grimaces with tight, scared eyes, a cockeyed mouth, pursed lips, and a protruding tongue. She mumbled replies to the voices at inopportune moments and strangers in all walks of life kept their distance.

Her hygiene was lacking, her makeup was abundant and applied with idiosyncratic whimsy, and she'd resorted to wearing bad wigs to cover a tangle of hair that, during moments that approached sanity, she realized she could no longer manage.

Her teeth had begun to rot and her breath smelled like roadkill.

She lived in a homeless shelter, or worse.

She had a paper bag full of medicines but most days she hated the side effects more than she hated the voices. Although she would occasionally take a pill or two or three to quiet the rageful ranting, or to still the incipient panic, or to dull the despair that urged her closer and closer to the futility of suicide, she lugged the stained brown bag of pharmaceuticals around more as a totem than anything else.

She was a lost life who was ordered by unseen powers

to celebrate the marriages of pairs of strange people eager to believe that their own lives were full of nothing but promise. As each newlywed couple walked out the door of some tacky wedding chapel, whatever future the woman saw in them would disappear like a convention-eer's promise to his wife to behave himself in Vegas.

That was the picture I had in my mind.

'Is this going to make me sad?' I asked Diane. 'Is it going to do me any good to know?'

Lauren sometimes asked that exact question of me late in the evening when we were in bed and the late news was on TV. A story would start to air – something about murder or rape or previously unimaginable despair or desperation in a part of the world that seemed always to bring unimaginable despair and desperation. The anchorperson's eyes would be stern, his voice would be grave, and Lauren would hit the mute button and ask, 'Is it going to do me any good to know this?'

The carnival midway refrain of another jackpot, this one at a more distant location in the casino, filled my ear. Almost as if prompted by the loud celebration that followed the slot machine victory, Diane said, 'This is Vegas. You can't stay sad here long.'

She said it, I was sure, for her own benefit as much as for mine.

'Something tells me that she's managed to stay sad.'

'Mallory's mom? Yeah,' Diane admitted. 'I think she has.'

I was thinking *Reese's mom, too*, but I didn't throw his name into the mix. The refrain from the previous week's morning run with Sam was still part of the soundtrack spinning in my head.

'She's still crazy?' I asked. My question was irreverent and my choice of descriptors pejorative, but Diane knew that I was asking with a heart laden with pathos.

'You know,' she said.

I did know. It was because I knew that I was so certain that it was going to make me sad. 'Did you learn anything?' I said, but I was thinking: What could she have learned? What could Mrs. Miller know? I didn't think that Mallory had gone to Vegas to see her mom. I didn't think that Mrs. Miller would know anything that would help Diane understand the connection between Mallory and Hannah.

'It's not what you think, not what I thought. Coming here to see her? It's like poking at a hornet's nest, for some reason it gets a lot of people stirred up. It's . . . just a sec. I can't talk here – I'm going to go outside, or at least to a quieter part of the . . . It's such a trek to get out of the casino from here; if the call gets dropped I'll phone you right back. You really need to hear this.' Her next words were a simple, pleasant version of 'Yes, I'm out.' I suspected the message was intended for the croupier or whatever you call the person who handles the dice and the chips at a craps table.

Diane dropped the phone on the floor – at least that's the way it sounded – cursed, kicked it, picked it up again, and asked, 'You still there?' She laughed. 'The phone slipped out of my hand while I was trying to pick up all my chips.'

'I'm still here.'

'Good. I won five hundred or so. That's pretty good. This place is so huge.' A moment of silence. Then, 'Hi. Do you know which way's the door?'

Hi? Was she talking to me?

'Which means you're only down . . . what?' I asked.

Thud. I thought the phone must have fallen out of her hand again.

'Diane? You there?'

That's when the call died.

Diane didn't call right back.

I gave her five minutes before I tried to reach her. Her cell phone rang and rang and rang before it clicked into voice mail.

I waited half an hour, hitting redial again every ten minutes or so with the same result. I was chewing on the possibility that technology had failed somewhere, that her phone had died or that the network had burped.

Soon I started thinking that she'd simply changed her mind about talking to me right then. Maybe she'd passed an open seat at a twenty-dollar blackjack table that she was sure had her name on it in raised gilded letters, or she'd eyed a spot at a new table and thought she'd seen steam rising from those dice.

I also considered the possibility that she'd run into someone she knew – Diane knew more people than anyone I'd ever met – while making her way out of the cavernous casino, and that they had headed somewhere for a drink or a meal or . . . what?

Diane, I guessed, was staying at the Venetian, the mid-Strip gambling palace that was decked out to look like Venice, Italy; that's the hotel where she'd booked us to stay the weekend after Hannah's death. I'd never been, but she'd told me that the canals in the hotel were lined with shops and I knew from long experience with Diane that a garish SALE sign in a store window could have distracted her. Easily.

All were reasonable explanations. But none, I thought, were likely.

Had her plans changed, Diane would have called me back and told me she'd talk to me later. She certainly would have picked up my call to her cell. Were her cell not working properly she would have gone to a pay phone and called me the old-fashioned way. After tracking down the mother of a missing girl – a girl who was the patient of Diane's dead friend – and after telling me she had news I needed to hear, Diane would have done something to reach me. She wouldn't have left me hanging, waiting, wondering.

She wouldn't.

I called Raoul at home to see if he'd heard from her. He wasn't there.

I followed happy voices down the hall and found Lauren and Grace on the bed in the master bedroom, where I interrupted Lauren's dramatic rendition of *Alice in Wonderland*. She told me she thought she had Raoul's mobile number in her Palm. With monumental inefficiency, and only after pecking enough tiny faux buttons to book an entire round-trip flight to Kathmandu – including arranging for Sherpas – I tracked down Raoul's mobile number and dialed the ten digits.

'Raoul,' he answered almost immediately.

He sounded tired. The usual gorgeous timbre of his voice was disguised by the wireless ether.

'Hey, Raoul. It's Alan. Where are you?'

'San Francisco, consulting at a clueless incubator. How these people expect to make any money is beyond me. What's wrong?'

His question made perfect sense. I don't think I'd ever before called Raoul on his mobile phone. Instinctively, he knew I wasn't calling him in San Francisco to recommend a restaurant.

'It's probably nothing,' I said.

He replied, '*Mierda.*'

26

Raoul's voice, when he wanted it to, carried no echoes of his childhood in Catalonia. I'd never given much thought to whether or not the tonal charade required much of his energy or attention. I'd always assumed that he could move back and forth between the American and Catalonian accents effortlessly, the way that a skilled actor does Kerry one minute and New Jersey the next. Raoul said, 'Back up. When did all this start? When did she call you?'

I heard echoes of Barcelona, and of worry, in his perfect English. I supposed that I was hearing the Barcelona only because I was hearing the worry. The caller ID unit by the phone told me that Diane's call to me from the craps table had come in exactly forty-seven minutes earlier.

'Forty-five minutes ago,' I told Raoul.

'So she's been out of touch less than an hour?'

'Right.'

'That's not a big deal.'

I'd been doing the same comfort calisthenics. But I clearly remembered the intensity of Raoul's barely contained outrage while Jaris Slocum was holding Diane hostage in the backseat of the patrol car after Hannah

Grant's death, and I remembered how resistant he'd been to any reassurance at that time. I knew that all the fret-yoga he was doing to convince himself that the current circumstances were some version of ordinary wouldn't, ultimately, do him a bit of good. Diane being out of touch for forty-seven minutes in the current circumstances required explanation.

And when I told him what I knew, I knew he'd agree with me.

'Raoul? Do you know why Diane went to Las Vegas?'

He spent a couple of heartbeats mining the apparent innocuousness of my question for innuendo before he replied, 'She likes it there. She missed her chance last month when . . . you know.'

'Do you know why she went now?'

There it was again. The shrink's 'precipitating event' question. *Why now?*

Raoul was one of the brightest people I'd ever met. I could almost hear the gears turning in his head as he tried to make sense of the bare glimpse he was getting as he strained to see where it was that I was leading him.

'She told me that a patient's mother was there. In Vegas. Somebody she wanted to talk to about a case. That was her excuse, but she really wanted to play craps and the mountain casinos have a five-buck limit. Small bets bore her.'

'It wasn't one of *her* patients' mother she was planning to talk to, Raoul.'

'I don't follow.'

'The patient whose mother is living in Las Vegas? That patient wasn't Diane's; it was Hannah Grant's.'

I could hear his breath blow hard against the microphone. 'And you knew this? You knew that was why she was going?'

It was an accusation. His unspoken words were *'And you let her?'* I felt his finger pointing at me physically, felt it mostly in my gut. I could no more have stopped Diane from going to Las Vegas than I could prevent January from being colder than July. But that didn't matter to Raoul, not then.

'She told me she was thinking about it, about going to Vegas to talk with this woman. But I thought she was just being provocative with me. You know how she is. I didn't think she'd really go.'

'Diane always does things that other people don't think she'll do. It's who she is.'

It was another accusation. And it was right on target. 'I wish I'd listened to her. I'm sorry.'

Raoul had no time for my *mea culpas*. 'Had she talked to this person, yet? This mother?' he asked.

Before I replied I used a moment to recall the specifics of my last conversation with Diane. 'When we talked, she told me that she'd found her, tracked her down. I don't know whether or not she actually spoke with her. I think that's what she was going to tell me when she got outside. She said it was important.'

'You know what patient it is, don't you, Alan?'

My impulse was to hesitate, to cover my ass. To my credit, I didn't. I mouthed a simple 'Yes.'

'You know who the mother is, too?'

'Yes.'

'You're going to tell me.'

'You know how this works.'

Raoul was the husband of a psychotherapist. Spouses of mental-health professionals know the rules. He said, 'This is Diane we're talking about. You are the one who had better know how this works.'

I tried to deflect him, to steer him back to the current

crisis. I said, 'I don't even know where's she staying. Where do you stay when you're there?'

He took a deep breath. 'I try not to go at all if I can help it, but where faux Italian is concerned I prefer the Bellagio. The fountains are . . . something. She's at the Venetian,' he said, confirming my suspicion. 'She likes the canals. I take her to Venice, I take her to St. Petersburg, I take her to Amsterdam; it turns out the canals she likes best are inside some vapid casino in Las Vegas.'

'I'll try her room and call you back.'

'You've tried her mobile?' he asked.

'A few times.'

'Merde.' I recognized the move from Catalonian to French. The man could curse in more languages than anyone I knew. He never cursed in English, however. Not in my presence.

'It's probably nothing.' I didn't believe my own words. I said it because it was just one of those things that people say in circumstances like those.

While Raoul was still on the line, I pulled Lauren's cell from her purse and punched in Diane's mobile number. After three rings someone answered.

A female voice, not Diane's, said, 'Yeah? Who is this?'

Speaking into both phones simultaneously, I said, 'Hold on a second, Raoul. Someone's on her cell.'

'Go on,' he said. *'Allez!'*

The voice on Diane's phone demanded, 'Who's Rule?'

The lilt of the woman's voice triggered some clinical trigger in my brain. Instinctively I went into therapist mode, specifically I went into psychiatric-emergency-room therapist mode. My voice calmed, my hearing sensitized for the unexpected. Psychologically speaking, my weight was on my toes; I was prepared to change directions in a heartbeat.

'This is Dr. Gregory, may I speak to Dr. Diane Estevez, please? You answered her phone.'

'Well, she's not home.' The woman laughed. 'No one's home. That's the whole point, isn't it? Not being home? This is about as far from home as I get. So there.'

I considered the possibility that I'd dialed Diane's number incorrectly and that I was simply being confused by the lottery of errant connection. Then I heard the familiar frantic calliope riff of a slot machine jackpot and I knew that what had happened wasn't a simple wrong number. This woman was in a Las Vegas casino and she was holding Diane's phone in her hand. Why?

'The phone you're holding belongs to a friend of mine. Do you mind if I ask how you got it? Did you find it?'

'The doctor? It belongs to the doctor? Rule? Dr. Rule?'

'Yes.' I let it go. I didn't want to try to explain to this woman who Rule, or Raoul, was, or wasn't.

'Well,' she said. 'I would guess he's out playing golf.' She laughed again. Her cackle was sharp and high-pitched – the yelp of a distressed tropical bird. You wouldn't want to be sitting in the vicinity of this woman in a movie theater during the screening of a half-decent comedy.

'That's pretty funny,' I said in a voice intended to convey that, against all odds, I found her act cute. 'But I'm actually being serious. Where exactly did you find my friend's cell phone? It's important. She'll want to know when she . . . thanks you.'

'I'm playing slots. Two machines – I always play two machines. It was in the tray on the left when I sat down. Or is that the right? I get my lefts and my rights mixed up, especially when I've been drinking, and I've been drinking. Who the heck are you?'

I played the doctor card. 'I'm Dr. Gregory.'

'You out playing golf, too?' She laughed again. I had to hold the phone six inches from my ear to provide a cushion from the intensity of the din.

Diane had dropped her phone on the way out of the casino. That was the explanation for everything. That was why she hadn't kept her promise to call me back as soon as she was outside the casino. That was why she hadn't been answering my repeated calls to her cell phone.

Simple. 'You're in the casino at the Venetian?'

'You wanna bet?' She laughed. 'Or, I . . . wanna bet. I guess I'm the one who's betting.'

'What's your name?'

'Michelle. You know about Harvey Wallbangers?'

'A cocktail, right?' I reminded myself to be patient. *Corral her,* I thought, *don't lasso her.*

'Ver-y good. Nobody here knows how to make 'em. Nobody. I order one and I keep getting Tequila Sunrises. Can you imagine? I don't like the red stuff, I like the yellow stuff. In the tall bottle? You know what I'm talking about?'

'How many have you had?'

'Three, or . . . not – no, four.' She paused. 'Four. Not counting this one. Oops, this one's almost gone, too. Do you know how hard it is to make any money playing nickel slots? Well, it is. Even if you max your bets, and I do sometimes, I really, really do, it's like . . . when you win you still just get . . . well, nickels. Is that fair?'

'So you're playing nickel slots at the Venetian?'

'I am.'

'Are there any casino employees around, Michelle? Maybe right behind you? Somebody in a uniform, someone making change or . . . serving cocktails, or something? An attendant?'

'Yep, there's one right there – how'd you know? Is there

a camera on me? Am I like on one of those TV shows or something?'

'Could you please give my friend's phone to the person who works for the casino? Tell him I would like to speak with him?'

'Her.'

'Her. Fine.'

'Here,' she said to somebody, possibly the casino employee, but certainly not to me. 'Some doctor named Rule or . . . Gregory or something lost his phone while he was playing golf. Here, you take it, go on. I don't want it anymore. I need more nickels.'

A heavily accented voice – Caribbean? Jamaican? – said, 'What you need, ma'am? Change?'

And that was the end of that call.

'Raoul, you still there?'

'Of course.'

'Diane doesn't have her phone with her. Some drunk woman in the casino found it, just turned it over to a casino employee. The call died. I'll try calling back again in a minute. Diane must have lost her phone.'

'At the Venetian?'

'That's what the woman said.'

Raoul said, 'I'll call her room. Keep your line open in case she calls you.'

'Of course. Raoul, I'm sure it's okay. There will be a simple explanation for this.'

He'd already hung up.

Diane had lost her phone. Raoul would call her hotel room and find her sitting on her king-sized bed lambasting somebody from hotel security about the casino's inefficient lost-and-found procedures. That's what I was telling myself. No big thing.

In my heart that's what I didn't believe. As innocuous as the events sounded – a friend failed to keep a promise to call another friend for less than an hour – my heart told me that something sinister had occurred.

You really need to hear this, she'd said. Diane would have found a way to call.

I tried Diane's cell one more time. Without even a single ring, my call was routed to voice mail. I left a simple message, 'Hey Diane, it's Alan. Still trying to reach you in Vegas. Give me a call. I'm getting a little worried. Raoul is concerned, too. Call him.'

I surmised that the casino employee who possessed Diane's phone had killed the power and that Diane's phone was programmed to send power-off calls to voice mail.

I walked down the hall to find Grace and Lauren asleep together on our big bed. One big spoon nestled protectively around one little spoon. I adjusted the comforter so that it covered both of them, flicked off the lights, took the bedtime volumes away from the pillows, and kissed them each on the head before I retraced my steps back to the kitchen counter. I'd carry Grace from our bed into her room later on.

The phone chirped in my hand. I caught it after half a ring.

Raoul. He said, 'She's not answering. *Quin merder.*'

It was my turn to curse. I'm not multilingual; I said simply, 'Shit.'

27

'I tried her cell again,' I said. 'I think someone turned it off. The call went straight to voice mail.'

'That's enough for me. I'm going to call hotel security,' Raoul said. 'Get them on this.'

'Get them on what?' I asked, gently. 'You'll tell them you've been unable to reach your wife for an hour? So what? In Vegas terms that's an eye-blink. You know what the security people will say: She met somebody she knew, got distracted. She met somebody she didn't know, got distracted. She went to a show, went to a club, went for a walk, found a hot slot machine or a hotter craps table, went out for a meal, went out for a drink. So she's been gone for an hour? Nobody's going to care. Not for an hour, not for a day. Maybe not even for a week. Not in Las Vegas.'

'They don't know Diane. I do. You do, too. This isn't like her. If she said she was going to call, she would've found a phone. She would've called.'

'But that's the point. They don't know Diane. To them, she's just a tourist who lost her cell phone. Big deal.'

Stubbornly, Raoul said, 'I'm going to call hotel security.'

'Okay,' I said. I knew that were I in his shoes I would want to do something, too, no matter how futile.

'Write down my hotel number here.' He dictated it. 'Call it if you hear from her. I'll be on my mobile.'

I curled my tongue against the roof of my mouth and forced just enough air through the gap to cause a high-pitched, low-volume whistle to emerge. Emily, the big Bouvier, responded immediately. I could hear her lumbering in my direction from the other side of the house. The sharp tips of her nails *click-clacked* as she made the transition from carpet to hardwood. I knew that Anvil, the miniature poodle, would follow her. He'd follow not because he found my whistle alluring. He'd follow because whatever Emily found alluring, he found alluring.

In our tiny neutered dog pack, Emily was the alpha-Amazon and Anvil was the eunuch slave.

The dogs waited impatiently while I pulled on a jacket and stuffed the cordless phone from the kitchen into one pocket and Lauren's cell into the other. We all crashed together heading out the front door.

Emily ran immediately across the lane toward Adrienne's house. For her it was like visiting extended family. I stage-whispered to her that everybody was in bed; she apparently didn't care. Anvil peed copiously in the dust before he loped off in the same general direction.

Raoul's version of my predicament was simple. In his view I possessed information that might help him find his wife. Sure, he'd been married to a psychologist long enough to know that the information he wanted was privileged. Realistically, of course, he didn't care. Who in his position would?

The fact that I'd already revealed that the information

had at least a tangential tie to Hannah Grant's unfortunate demise would only aggravate his insistence that I breach confidence and tell him what he wanted to know. But what he also didn't know was that the patient of Hannah Grant's whose mother was in Las Vegas was Mallory Miller and that the reason for my anxiety over Diane's sudden vanishing wasn't only because I was concerned that it might have something to do with Hannah's death, but also because I feared it might have something to do with Mallory's disappearance.

I'd already decided that, ethical or not, as soon as I felt that Diane had been sucked into that vortex I'd tell Raoul whatever I knew. It wasn't the way the rules were written. But so be it.

Ten minutes outside with the dogs and I was getting cold. It was apparent that Emily – she didn't get cold until wind-chill numbers were in double-digit negatives – was eager to head down the lane on her usual evening jaunt, but I feared that kind of walk would yank us out of range of the cordless phone so I forced both dogs to roam the area between our house and Adrienne's. Emily found some smells that were compelling and she adapted. Anvil hung around close by. Raoul called back just as I was coaxing the reluctant dogs back inside the front door.

'Hi, Raoul?' I answered. 'You hear anything?'

'Not from Diane. Security's not going to help. I'm in a cab on the way to the airport. I'll be in Vegas in a couple of hours.'

'You're sure that's a—'

'Yes, I am. You didn't hear from her?'

Raoul's interruption shouted at me that his usual unflappable civility was developing fissures. 'No,' I said.

'Sometime tomorrow morning, if I'm not waking up

next to my wife, I'm going to want to talk to this patient's mother, Alan. Be prepared to help me find her.'

'Raoul, I—'

He hung up.

'—will do whatever's necessary.'

28

Diane's husband was wealthy. She didn't work the long hours I did. She didn't have to.

On a typical weekday before eight in the morning my car would've been the first to slide into the parking spaces beside our office building. That Tuesday should have been no different. On a typical Tuesday morning, Diane would show up at around 9:00, or 9:30. That Tuesday should have been no different.

She'd told me on the phone the evening before that she'd already canceled her appointments until Thursday. Still, given the events at the Venetian, the driveway felt empty without her Saab, the waiting room felt empty without her patients, and the offices felt empty without her laugh.

Raoul had called me near midnight the night before from the room he'd checked into at the Venetian after flying to Vegas from San Francisco. He had a suite fit for the doges overlooking the Rialto Bridge, but he didn't have any good news to report. Diane hadn't phoned him. The fact that she hadn't at least left a message on Raoul's cell was unprecedented between them. When one of them was traveling they always talked at the end of the day –

always. When they were traveling separately they always talked at the end of the day.

After a lot of cajoling, and a five-hundred-dollar incentive, Raoul had finally persuaded a housekeeping manager to agree to check Diane's room for him. The manager wouldn't give Raoul the location of her room, but reported back that there was no sign of anything out of the ordinary, nor was there any indication that she'd been there since late that afternoon. No phone calls had been placed on the hotel room phone since midafternoon. The minibar was untouched after it had been replenished midday. The housekeeper who cleaned the room reported that she'd finished the evening turndown service around 6:30. From all appearances, no one had disturbed the bed or bath linens since that time.

The casino attendant who'd been given Diane's cell phone by the drunk woman who played nickel slots and inhaled Harvey Wall-bangers had promptly turned it in to the casino's lost-and-found department.

Diane had not inquired about it.

Raoul had also begun what he anticipated would be a long, difficult process of badgering the hotel security officers to review the casino security videotapes for the time that Diane was walking across the gaming floor talking with me on her cell phone. He assumed that hotel security cameras videotaped every square inch of the casino twenty-four hours a day. Security was resisting his pleas to review that section of the tapes.

Their argument? What his wife did when she was in Las Vegas was her business, right? Not her husband's, right?

He was European, he understood. Right? They can't very well start showing videotapes of what one spouse does in their casino to another spouse, can they? Would that be fair? What happens in Vegas stays in Vegas, right?

Raoul knew that it was hard to disagree, unless you knew her.

Raoul knew her. I knew her.

Venetian security didn't know her. The identity of the person she'd run into as she walked across the casino floor? Venetian security thought that was her business.

How had she lost her cell phone? Venetian security thought that was her business.

Had she left the casino at all? Her business.

What else had Raoul accomplished by midnight Colorado time?

He'd called all the hospitals in a ten-mile radius of the Strip, searching for even the barest hint that his wife might have been treated or admitted that evening. He'd learned nothing that helped.

He'd called the Las Vegas police, seeking any indication that the local authorities had crossed paths with someone who even vaguely resembled his description of Diane. He'd learned nothing. He'd called American Express to see if he could get a list of charges she'd put on her card in the previous twenty-four hours. A supervisor would speak with him in the morning.

He'd tipped the concierge at the Venetian a hundred bucks to find a twenty-four-hour copy shop that could blow up and print a hundred copies of the photograph of Diane that he kept in his wallet.

She promised him that the prints would be waiting for him before breakfast.

'I eat early,' he'd told her, suspicious of her promise.

'I stay up late,' she'd replied with a smile.

'It's the suite,' he explained to me. 'They must have run my credit report. I think she's hoping I'm a newly calved whale.'

The midnight call from Raoul had awakened Lauren. I didn't see any advantage to be gained by alarming her into having a fitful night's sleep, so I'd explained, benignly, that Diane was in Vegas and that Raoul hadn't heard from her, that he was worried, and he'd called to see if I'd talked to her since early that evening.

Had I? My wife wanted to know. I had not, I told her, not since early evening. I kissed her, and murmured that she should go back to sleep.

Over coffee in the morning, I explained the rest of the mess to Lauren, obliquely highlighting the slippery ice of the confidentiality hazards that were out in front of me, and specifically including the fact that before we'd hung up the night before, Raoul had reminded me that he wanted to know which patient's mother Diane had spoken with the previous day. Lauren, of course, knew nothing about my patient Bob and his odd connection to the Millers' neighbor, Doyle. And she certainly didn't know that the patient's mother that Diane wanted to see in Vegas was Mallory's mother, Rachel.

'What do you think about Diane not calling?' Lauren asked me as I was kissing her and Grace good-bye before leaving for my office.

'I'm worried. It's not like her.'

'There's probably an explanation,' she offered.

'I hope you're right. But I can't think of what it might be. Diane's a stay-in-touch kind of person.'

'She's always been unpredictable.'

'About some things, yeah. Not about staying in touch. About that she's as reliable as sunrise.'

She kissed me again. 'If Raoul doesn't hear from her by midday, let me know, and I'll see if there's anything I can do. Maybe somebody knows somebody in the DA's office in Las Vegas. Okay?'

'Thanks.'

'Sam might be able to reach out, too,' she added. 'He might have cop contacts out there.'

And what, I thought, was I going to tell Sam about the Millers and Bob and Doyle and Hannah Grant that might entice him to reach out to cop colleagues in Las Vegas? 'Maybe she'll call,' I said, not quite believing that she would.

I unlocked the front door of the building, flicked on the lights in the waiting room, and started a small pot of coffee in the tiny kitchen. At 7:43 the red light that indicated that my first patient had arrived for her 7:45 appointment flashed on in my office.

It was time to go to work.

29

Raoul had my pager number. I'd told him to use it as soon as he knew anything about Diane and that I'd call him back as soon as I could.

Lunchtime came and I didn't hear from him. I tried his cell phone. My call was routed to voice mail; I left a message asking him to phone me with news immediately.

Nothing.

Midafternoon I went through the same routine with the same result. Just to be certain that my bases were covered, I left an additional message on Raoul's hotel room voice mail at the Venetian.

Nothing.

When 4:45 came around and the red light on the wall in my office flared on, I found myself becoming alarmed that almost an entire workday had passed with no news about Diane. My level of concern for her was approaching ten on a ten-scale.

I walked down the hall to get Bob. My apprehension about the session was high. I had almost convinced myself that Bob really did know something important about Mallory.

Bob wasn't sitting in the waiting room. No one was.

My first reaction? *Who flicked the switch that had turned on the red light?*

I checked my watch. Four forty-four.

I waited a minute. Four forty-five. Had Bob ever before been late for therapy? Maybe once or twice, but his absence from the waiting room was certainly an anomaly. Had he forgotten that we'd made this appointment the day before? How could he have? Given the drama in front of my house at dawn, I was sure Bob would have remembered his usual appointment time.

I flicked off the switch that illuminated the red light and returned down the hall to check my calendar and my voice mail. I was still thinking that Bob would show up any minute.

I was wrong.

Five o'clock came and went, then five fifteen, and finally five thirty, the time that Bob and I would usually be finished with his session.

The reality was that patients missed scheduled appointments all the time. If I had a busy week I could usually count on at least one no-show among my patients. Sometimes patients forgot their appointments and that was that; other times patients spaced out their appointments and the fact that they'd forgotten was ripe with therapeutic meaning. Sometimes life intervened. An injured child, a traffic accident, a late flight.

But Bob? He'd never missed a scheduled appointment. Never.

I thought about the midnight-blue box with the Kinko's logo that was sitting in the file cabinet near my desk. Bob had said, 'Don't read it yet. I'll tell you when.'

After he'd handed it to me I thought I'd said, 'I'll see you tomorrow then.'

I thought Bob had replied, 'Sure.' Was it possible that

Bob had known he wouldn't be showing up for this appointment? With most patients, I would have simply packed up my things, gone home, and not given the missed session another thought. But Bob wasn't most patients: Bob was Doyle's friend, and Bob knew Mallory.

Bob thought he knew what Mallory had been thinking. Bob had been next door the night that Mallory had disappeared. Bob had written a story about Mallory's disappearance. Bob thought Mallory was scared.

I had a copy of what he had written.

But he'd told me not to read it.

Powered by the pair of fresh batteries that I'd installed that morning, the pager on my hip vibrated with irritating insistence. The number that flashed on the screen was for Raoul's cell.

I dialed immediately. 'Raoul, it's me: Alan.'

'I'm ready to kill these people. Tell me something: Does Nevada have the death penalty? I think I'm becoming a proponent.'

'Which people?'

'Take your pick. The Las Vegas police. The fascists in Venetian security. Even the damn minister at the Love In Las Vegas Wedding Chapel. He might be first.'

'What?'

'I gave the housekeeping manager two hundred more bucks to look for Diane's calendar in her room. It wasn't there, but she let me see the notepad by the telephone. Diane was visiting wedding chapels. She wanted to talk with somebody named Rachel at a wedding chapel. She had a list of them on the notepad. I visited all three. Love In Las Vegas was the most promising.'

Without much thought, I said, 'I'm glad you found that . . .' I didn't know how to end the sentence.

Raoul did. 'On my own, you mean,' he said.

'Yes. Did you talk to this . . . Rachel?'

'Nobody at the chapel will tell me anything. But they know her, that's clear enough. The minister is a guy with a fake British accent who prances around like he's on holiday from his day job in the House of Lords. He acted really cagey when I mentioned Rachel's name. I'll find her tomorrow.'

'Diane?' I said, hopefully.

'I pray. But I'll find Rachel, and she'll help me find Diane. Despite the neon carnival and depraved World's Fair ambiance of the place, Las Vegas feels like a small town. Money is ammunition here. That works in my favor. I'm well armed.'

'The police are uninterested?'

'"Uninterested" is a generous word.'

'And Venetian security?'

'I think they went ahead and looked at the videotapes of whatever happened while Diane was walking out of the casino. When she lost her phone.'

'Did you get the impression it seemed significant to them?'

'It raised an eyebrow or two. But they won't tell me why.'

'What happens in Vegas stays in Vegas?'

'Like that. There's one woman on the security team who wants to talk with me. I flirted with her a little, and I'm going to see if I can catch up with her later on when she gets off work. Her shift ends at eight.'

I tried to imagine Raoul's frustration. His determination was apparent, but whatever he was doing to mask his frustration was admirable. I asked him, 'Why aren't you bugging me for more information about Rachel?'

'Diane wouldn't want me to. She didn't talk to me about her clients. One of the things she respects about you is how you've kept your mouth shut through all the . . . difficult situations you've been in over the years. I'm trying to respect what she respects.'

'I appreciate that. I'm in another difficult position right now. I'd really like to be more helpful, but Diane's not the only one who's . . .'

'Who's what?'

'Mixed up with Rachel's . . . problems. I've already told you more than I should.' I knew I sounded lame. If I were in Raoul's shoes, I think I'd want to string me up by my thumbs.

In a tone that was intended not only to sound calm but also to communicate his increasing desperation, he said, 'It's a reprieve, not a pardon, my friend. As soon as I run into a dead end with this Rachel person I'll be back in your face, insisting. Or worse.' At the end he managed a little laugh.

'I can't wait,' I said.

'I have to go. Before my date with this security lady later I'm going to try to see if I can find any gamblers who remember seeing Diane at the craps tables last night. I hope that some of the same people will be playing again. I'll be in touch. *Adeu*.'

'*Adeu*' is Catalonian for good-bye. Other than profanity, the only other Catalonian Raoul had taught me during the many years of our friendship was how to ask if there was a good bar nearby. At that moment, had I been on a beachfront up the coast from Barcelona, I would have been sorely tempted to try out the phrase.

I said, '*Adeu,* Raoul.' But he'd already hung up.

After only a moment's hesitation I opened the drawer to the file cabinet and withdrew the Kinko's box that Bob had given me. Almost reverentially, I lifted the lid off the box, and raised the title page in my hands.

A quick, surreptitious glance at the open box revealed that the top sheet in the pile of paper that remained in the box wasn't the beginning of Bob's story. The second page was handwritten. In his familiar, neat, incredibly cramped script, Bob had written me a note.

Dr. Gregory,

If I've told you to go ahead and read this, this is the page that I want you to throw away. You can go ahead. If I haven't given you permission, this is where you should stop. Remember, I'm trusting you. I'll tell you when.

Bob

His tiny scrawl seemed indecipherable, a missive intended for selected residents of Lilliput. I guessed that the first line was my name and the last line was Bob's, but I couldn't read the two lines in between all the way through, not at first. Only by holding the paper farther and farther from my eyes until I got it all the way out to arm's length did the script come sufficiently into focus. 'Dr. Gregory,' it read. 'If I've told you to go ahead and read this, this is the page that I want you to throw away. You can go ahead. If I haven't given you permission, this is where you should stop. Remember, I'm trusting you. I'll tell you when. Bob.'

Reluctantly, I replaced both pages – the title page and the warning page – and fit the lid back onto the box.

What could be the harm of reading the damn thing?

Bob's handwritten note had spooked me. How had he anticipated that a second caution to me about not reading his manuscript would be necessary? I decided to ask him. After checking my address book for the number, I called his home.

The phone rang and rang. No answering machine ever kicked in. As I hung up, I admitted to myself that I'd just done something that I rarely, if ever, did. I'd just tried to check in with a patient because they'd missed a session. What was my typical practice? I usually just let the issue simmer until the next scheduled appointment.

This time, that didn't sound like a judicious plan.

30

I thought she was maybe fifteen years old, but she swore she was seventeen. I didn't have to ask her age; she was apparently accustomed to protesting that she was older than she looked, and before I'd known her for a full minute she'd insisted she was seventeen, really. Her name was Jenifer Donald. The Jenifer was leavened with only one *n*, she'd pointed out – the result not of a spelling failure, but rather, I was guessing, of a momentary lapse in judgment by young parents who were intent on making sure their daughter went through life with a distinctive name.

Jenifer was from Clemson, South Carolina, and was in Boulder visiting her grandparents, who lived on the northern edge of Boulder's original downtown near the intersection of Eighteenth and Pine. 'They're so cute. They really are,' she said, referring to her grandparents. 'Some of my friends' parents are as old as my grandparents. But my grandparents are just so cute.'

'Clemson? That's where the college is?' I asked.

'The university,' she corrected. It was clear that the distinction was important to her. 'It's where I want to go. I'm hoping for a scholarship, for band. I'm a drummer. I have a good chance, I think. My PSATs were better than I expected. Much better. I take the SATs next month – I hope, I hope, I hope I do well. My parents and my grandparents want me to look at CU, too. I told them I would. That's why I'm here.' She rolled her eyes. As if *anyone* would choose the University of Colorado over Clemson.

I found myself warmed by the unfamiliar melody of her lilting voice and loving the openness with which she'd greeted me at the front door of the brick two-story home. Jenifer's pretty face was as welcoming as her manner. Her blonde hair fell in a straight shot well past her shoulders. 'What kind of doctor are y'all?' she asked. Her question wasn't at all suspicious, merely friendly.

When she'd opened the front door, I'd introduced myself as 'Dr. Gregory,' hoping the appellation would grant me some advantage with the kid who'd responded to the doorbell. I was already regretting having done it; I couldn't very well tell her I was a clinical psychologist without leaving her with the implication that Bob had a reason to be seeing one.

'So Bob's not here?' I asked, changing the subject.

'The guy upstairs in back? That's Bob? Grandpa calls him "the tenant." Don't think so.' Jenifer said 'the tenant' in a deep, gravelly voice, mimicking, I guessed, her grandfather's delivery. 'I haven't actually seen him this visit. I just got in to Boulder today – it's so cold here, how do you stand it? My grandparents have an appointment somewhere. Pill-ottos, pill-ah-tees. Those machines? We don't do that much of it in South Carolina.'

She laughed; and her laugh made me smile. She really thought her grandparents were cute and that Boulder was exotic. 'Yes, those machines,' I said.

She smiled back and shook her head. 'Would you like to come in and wait for him? I'll fix you something.'

'Thank you,' I said, stepping past her into the house. 'You're a drummer? Marching band?'

'And orchestra,' she said.

A short hallway led to the back of the house. Through a kitchen window I could see the curtained rooms above the garage. 'That's Bob's?' I asked.

Jenifer said, 'You bet.'

'Where are the stairs?'

'Other side, on the alley.'

A pile of mail was visible in a basket on the back porch.

Jenifer saw me looking. 'See that? I'm sure your friend Bob would have picked up his mail if he was home.' She lowered her voice to a whisper before she added, 'He sure gets a lot of catalogs.'

'I'm sure you're right. He must not be home.'

'Hey, I'm a pretty good cook. Y'all like grilled cheese? I make a mean Swiss on rye.'

Jenifer managed to make 'Swiss on rye' sound almost as alien as blowfish.

I said, 'I'm actually kind of worried about him. He and I were going to get together earlier today but he didn't show up, which isn't like him.'

'Are you thinking maybe he's sick?' Her voice blossomed with concern.

I shrugged my shoulders. Bob could indeed be ill; it would explain a lot. I asked, 'Is it okay for me to go knock, you think?'

She hopped past me and bounded out the door and across the back porch. 'I don't see why not. Knocking never hurt anybody, did it?'

She lifted the rubber-banded stack of mail from the basket, led me around to the alley, ran up the stairs, and knocked on Bob's door. Two sharp raps. She cooed, 'Knock, knock,' for good measure.

While we were giving Bob much too much time to make his way to the door, Jenifer seemed to be examining my face. She finally scrunched up her nose a little bit and asked, 'You really are worried, aren't you?'

I said, 'Yes, I am.'

'That's so sweet. Wait here.' In one fluid motion she jumped down the stairs, and disappeared around the corner. She returned seconds later with a fistful of keys, popped back up the stairs, unlocked the lock, turned the knob, and threw open the door.

'Go have a quick look,' she said. 'I'm sure he wouldn't mind. I'll just toss this mail in here so nobody—'

Jenifer took a half step into Bob's apartment and immediately screamed, hitting a note that – despite a volume that would have made a siren engineer envious – was so high in pitch that it almost disappeared into the range undetectable by human ears.

I hurdled up the steps three at a time, 'What—'

31

'Detective Sam Purdy, this is Jenifer Donald. She's visiting her grandparents from South Carolina.'

'Pleased to meet you,' Sam said.

I was tempted to tell Sam that Jenifer was as sweet as an August melon, and warn him that she was older than she looked, but I didn't. He'd figure it all out himself before too long.

He flipped open his badge wallet for her benefit. Jenifer hopped back from it as though it were cocked and loaded.

'So you don't actually live here, Jenifer? This isn't your house?'

'No, sir. Should I call you "officer"?'

'Detective. Dr. Gregory told me that you're here visiting your grandparents. They are due home when?'

Sam was dressed in new clothes, or at least clothes I'd never seen him wear before. Two factors were at play: One, he'd lost a lot of weight over the last year and his old stuff didn't fit. Two, he actually seemed to have started caring how he looked. The ensemble he was wearing was composed of a pair of jeans from the Gap and a striped wool v-neck sweater over a white T-shirt that hadn't even considered turning yellow. For Sam, the outfit constituted styling.

Jenifer's acute anxiety that she had done something to lure a police detective to her grandparents' door was making me nervous. She said, 'Soon. They're due back soon. Any minute I bet. But I'm not sure. They're out doing that pill . . . thing. Exercise, you know? With those machines?'

Sam sighed. He knew. Eating a healthy diet was something Sam had embraced. Exercise? That had become cool with him, too. But Pilates and yoga? For Sam, they were still on an astral plane with tats and piercings. He wasn't quite there yet. At his partner Lucy's insistence, he'd accompanied her to a solitary session of Bikram yoga – the kind that's basically done in a sauna – and was astonished, and dismayed, to learn that people were physiologically capable of sweating out of their noses.

Profusely.

And that they would pay dearly for the privilege.

I thought it would take him a while to come around to being open-minded about yoga and Pilates.

'And this guy, Bob, is your grandparents' tenant?' he asked Jenifer. 'He rents a room?'

'Two rooms. Yes, sir. And he has his own bathroom, of course. Hot plate, microwave. You know. I used to stay up there when I was visiting. It's nice. You can see the mountains real well when the leaves are off the trees. Or is it "real good"? No, no – it's real well.'

We were all standing out near the alley at the foot of the stairs that led up to Bob's rented rooms. Sam looked at me before he asked Jenifer the next question. 'And which one of you actually entered Bob's rooms?'

Jenifer swallowed and her eyes got as big and bright as table grapes. 'I did. That's when I saw – I shouldn't have done that, should I? Oh my Lord. Am I in trouble? The doctor was worried and I thought that he . . . oh my Lord!

Oh my Lord. I'm so sorry. Back home, we'd – but, oh, I really am sorry. I'll never do it again. I promise. Please don't . . .'

She couldn't even bring herself to say 'arrest me.'

'"The doctor"' – Sam glared at me – 'said you saw some blood when you were inside? And a mess?'

'I did. I'm so sorry. I don't know what I was thinking. I really don't know what I was thinking. Going into a stranger's place like that? We might do it back home, but I'm not – Y'all—' She sighed. 'I screamed. The blood, the mess. I'm so, so sorry.'

'It's nothing,' Sam said, in his best fatherly voice. 'Don't you worry; you did what you thought was best.' Sam climbed the staircase toward Bob's rooms. He stopped near the top, turned to Jenifer and me, and said, 'What I'm going to do is something that law enforcement calls a "welfare check." All that means is that I'm going to make a quick walk through his place, make certain that there isn't someone inside needing assistance, then I'm going to come right back out.' He focused his eyes on me before he continued. 'Just in case anyone's ever curious about exactly what I did in there. Understand?'

'Yes,' Jenifer replied, although it hadn't been her understanding Sam had been seeking.

He edged into the flat without touching a single surface and was back out of Bob's rented rooms in a little over a minute. Because of the way the door was situated I wasn't able to follow his progress. Once he was back on the landing at the top of the stairs, he looked at me and shook his head, 'Nobody in there. Some blood, not too much. Just what you saw near the door. And it's a mess in there, too, Jenifer, just like you said.'

'There they are. *Finally,*' Jenifer said, pointing down the driveway that led out to Pine Street.

A huge dark GMC pickup with a camper shell was pulling into the driveway. We all waited.

The second her grandparents made it out of the truck, Jenifer announced, 'The police are here about the tenant. There's blood. I looked inside. I'm so sorry. I am.'

32

'Get in,' Sam said. He pointed at his Cherokee.

I got in. The consequences of being obstreperous at that moment were too much for me to contemplate.

'There's not that much blood,' he said.

'It's relative,' I argued. 'If it was yours, I think you might consider it a reasonable quantity. Anyway, isn't that exactly what you said about Mallory's blood on the day after Christmas?'

'And it turns out I was right about Mallory's blood on the day after Christmas. Kid got nosebleeds. The splatter in the house was consistent with a sudden nosebleed.'

I could have argued the point, but it was clear that Sam was holding trump cards. 'What about the mess?'

'You really didn't go in?'

'I peeked, Sam. I was worried.'

'Being messy isn't a crime. I see teenagers' rooms that are worse all the time. There's no visible evidence that a crime was committed in the guy's flat. The kid's grandparents heard nothing. There're a few drops of blood on a wall and some bad housekeeping. Hell, he could be over at Community right now getting his finger stitched up. ER doc told me once they see people all the time who slice their hands up while they're cutting bagels. I hadn't known that. Bagels.'

'There was blood on the carpet, too,' I argued.

'You said you didn't go in.'

'You can see it from the door.'

'There wasn't that much blood on the carpet.'

'Was it fresh?'

'I didn't stop to test it.'

I opened my mouth to ask another question, but Sam stopped me. 'We have rules, Alan. Bill of Rights ring a bell? I did a welfare check. I didn't find anyone in need of assistance or see any other reason to stay in the man's home uninvited, so I left. Done.'

'You're not going to investigate, are you?'

'Investigate what?'

It was exactly the response I'd dreaded. 'He's missing. His place was tossed.'

'Tossed? So you say. You know any of this for sure?' He waited long enough to see if I was done arguing with him. 'Didn't think so.' He went on, making his case, 'Jenifer's grandparents say that they're sure Bob was home alone when? Last night?'

'Night before, actually. And they said they thought he was alone because he always is. They don't actually know he was alone.'

'Okay, they weren't sure about last night. And now it's early evening and he's not home. Big frigging deal. Where's the crime? The only crime I see is that Jenifer's grandparents are in violation of zoning codes for having a tenant and a crappy makeshift second kitchen in those rooms. But I'm going to let that one slide.'

'Big of you,' I said, trying not to sound too sarcastic. The truth was that I didn't know how to answer any of

Sam's questions without telling him things I wasn't allowed to tell him.

Sam probed the contours of my silence and came to the conclusion I figured he would get around to. 'He's one of yours, isn't he? Your . . . clients?' Sam asked, not expecting me to answer. 'And . . . let me guess, he didn't show up for his appointment with you. He's usually as reliable as milk of magnesia about showing up on time, so you're worried.' Sam didn't even bother to make these statements sound like questions.

I didn't deny anything. Didn't confirm anything.

'You want me to be worried, too,' he added.

I was relieved to be given a prompt I could actually respond to. 'That would be nice,' I said.

'Why didn't you just call nine-one-one? Why'd you call me?'

I stared at Sam for a moment. I could've told him that I called him because I trusted him and didn't call 911 because for all I knew I would end up having to introduce Jenifer, with one *n*, to Jaris Slocum. It would have suggested to Sam that I still wasn't prepared to cut Jaris Slocum any slack, and that was one argument I didn't need rewound.

I played another card instead. I suspected the card I played broke a rule, but I convinced myself that the rules were gray about whether or not I could play that particular card. 'I wonder if he has a car. That might help us find him. His car.'

Sam gave me about an eighth of a smile. 'You wonder if he has a car?' He lifted his chin half an inch and groomed the grain of his mustache off to the sides with the index finger and thumb of his right hand. 'Stay here while I go back inside and ask Bob's landlords a few more questions that I'm sure you could tell me all the answers to if you didn't suffer from such serious constipation.'

He added a comment about Jesus before he was out of earshot.

While Sam was gone, I phoned Lauren and told her I was going to be even later than I had told her I was going to be the last time I called. She wanted to know if she should hold dinner, and she wanted to tell me about the new ways that Grace was being cute, and chat about why I was tied up so late, and she wanted to know what was new with Diane and Raoul. I explained I'd fill her in on everything when I got home and told her to give Grace a kiss for me.

Sam returned after about five minutes. He settled onto the driver's seat and crossed his arms. The front of the Cherokee was pointed toward the southwest, and from the shotgun position there was a break in the trees that allowed me to see the vault of the second Flatiron outlined against the night sky. The light of the fractional moon was reflecting just right.

Sam said, 'He has an old muscle car. A Camaro. Keeps it garaged at a house over on Twelfth Street.'

I caught myself holding my breath and forced myself to inhale, exhale, act natural. 'Where exactly on Twelfth?'

'You're really going to pretend you don't already know all this? Okay, I'll play along. Mr. Donald doesn't know exactly where. But I have a suspicion you might be able to find it for me, you know, like those good ol' boys can find the exact spot you should drill your new well. What are those boys called? The ones with the forked sticks? Are they called dowsers? Ah, who cares? We're going for a little drive.'

Sam started the Jeep and made his way across downtown until he got to the Hill and turned on Twelfth Street.

We were heading south, paralleling the mountains that loomed a dozen blocks away. He pulled to a gentle stop at the curb halfway between the instantly recognizable home where Mallory Miller had disappeared and the smaller place that was next door on the north side.

Doyle's house.

'I'm guessing that's where this guy Bob keeps his muscle car,' Sam said. 'Just a suspicion. Call it cop's intuition.'

I didn't bite. Sam picked Doyle's house either because the Donalds had actually told him exactly where he could find Bob's car, or he picked it because during our morning jog I'd already mentioned the Millers' neighbor's house to him. Sam didn't misplace much information.

I was busy eyeing the real estate sign in front of the house, trying to cram the listing agent's name – *Virginia Danna, Virginia Danna* – into my memory. I asked, 'So are you going to check for a car in the garage?'

'Sure we are. Come on.'

The front yard of Doyle's house was terraced. Undulating, mortarless flagstone walls of varying heights supported a series of planting beds that radiated away from the curving center walk like the lines on a topographic map. Dried ornamental grasses were interspersed with globe evergreens and other Xeriscape-y things I didn't recognize.

I stuffed my hands into my pockets to try to ward off the January cold and followed Sam down the front walk until he moved onto a path that intersected with it and led around to the back of the house. After a few more steps, I could see the gable of a single-car garage roof toward the rear property line.

'You're not going to introduce yourself to whoever lives here?' I asked innocently.

'Place is empty. Owner moved away a couple of months ago. Guy's asking way too much is what I hear. You know, given the market and interest rates and all. But who the hell knows what's up with Boulder real estate these days? Did I tell you some agent's been dropping by begging me to sell my place? Says he already has a buyer and can get me a fortune for it. I think he's a developer and wants to scrap my shack and put up a spec. I could take the money but I'd have to move halfway to Wyoming to find someplace new to live. What's the point of that? It would mean commuting for me, and new schools for Simon.'

A casual observer might have mistaken Sam's ramblings for whining, or for the opening gambit in a friendly discussion of Boulder County property values and the moral and economic consequences of chasing the appreciated dollar. I knew better. Sam's moves were misdirection. From experience, I knew that he used misdirection the same way magicians used it.

So what was it that I was not supposed to notice?

Sam has been in Doyle's yard before.

I was sure of it. Despite the darkness he was leading me across the property as though he'd sat in on the design meetings with the landscape architect. Once we made it to the backyard, he followed a flagstone path over a little wooden bridge that spanned a curving faux streambed. When the path split, Sam chose the fork that ran toward the rear of the lot.

Only the top half of the garage was visible behind a stunning series of man-made granite – for want of a better word – cliffs. At the bottom of the natural-looking walls was a good-sized, but drained, pond that would flow into the streambed we'd crossed earlier. I had no trouble imagining the waterfall that would cascade down those rocks into that pool come spring.

'This way,' Sam said. He stopped at a garage window and shined the beam of a flashlight through the glass. The garage was clearly empty.

No cars. No cherry Camaro.

'There you go,' Sam said. 'Your guy took his car and went somewhere. Free country. Mystery solved. Nothing that requires the services of Boulder's finest.'

'You?'

'Me. This is the right house?' Sam asked. He was holding the flashlight between us down near his waist, aiming the beam straight up toward the night sky. With the up light his forest of nose hairs was illuminated with way too much clarity for my taste. His face and head took on eerie contours inside the fog of his steamy breath.

I felt like saying something in reply to his question but couldn't figure out anything that confidentiality permitted me to say.

He smiled, recognizing my conundrum. 'Thought so.'

Over his shoulder I saw movement in the Millers' home. A silhouette in the upstairs window. I tried to watch it without watching it. I said, 'I'm worried about Diane.'

'What?'

I had his attention. I repeated my concern.

'Your partner? That Diane?'

'She went to Las Vegas a couple of days ago. I was talking with her on the phone last night from one of the casinos and the call suddenly went dead. She's disappeared. Her husband flew out there a couple of hours later and he can't find a trace of her. The Vegas cops aren't interested.'

Sam moved the flashlight beam away from our faces. A second glance next door revealed the silhouette moving from the Millers' window. In an instant, it was gone.

'Your friend Diane went to Las Vegas?'

Sam knew precisely what I had told him by telling him that fact. With Sam I rarely had to say things twice. 'To talk to someone,' I said, as a way of underlining my point, just in case.

He nodded, wetting his lower lip with his tongue. 'You're looking at something behind me. Don't do it again. Look at me. Eye contact. Good, good. What is it?'

'Somebody watching us in an upstairs window.'

'Still there?'

I shook my head.

'Dad?'

'Couldn't say. Just a silhouette.'

'Which window?'

'Closest to the street.'

He nodded and ran his fingers through his hair before he stuffed his free hand into the back pocket of his jeans. 'Diane went to Las Vegas to talk with someone and then yesterday she vanished? Now you have a client you're worried about that you think may have just vanished, too? You and I are standing in the backyard of a house on Twelfth Street where said client garages his old car. Right next door a young girl happened to disappear on Christmas Day. I got it all right, so far?'

'You're doing pretty well.' *The car part is a little off,* I was thinking. *The Camaro may be old, but it's cherry.*

'Great, glad to hear it. Let me add a couple of things to the list, things I've already been a little concerned about. You know something about Mallory Miller's mother that in my book you don't have any reason to know. You probably even know she lives in Vegas. You're way too curious about Reese's aggressive tendencies for my taste. And it was not too long ago that you kind of predicted that you and I were going to knock heads about this house next door to the Millers.'

'That's three things, Sam, at least.'

'Do me a favor, ignore the arithmetic.'

'I can't confirm some of what you're saying. But I can't argue with what you're saying, either.'

'From you that's a ringing endorsement.'

I shrugged.

With gorgeous understatement, Sam said, 'Well, too many missing pieces. It all sounds too goofy for words to me.' He began walking. 'Come on. I want to hear more about Diane and what's going on with her in Las Vegas.'

He led me back out through the dormant water features of Doyle's yard. Just before we got to Sam's car at the curb I said, employing a voice that was much more measured than I was feeling at that moment, 'Diane and I were both there the day that Hannah Grant died.'

Without even a glance in my direction, he said, 'I know that. Don't you think I fucking know that?'

33

My car was across downtown outside the house where Bob rented rooms from the Donalds. After pressing me for some more details about Diane's disappearance in Las Vegas, Sam headed toward Pine Street to drop me off.

'So what do you know about the owner of the house with the water park?' I asked.

He killed the volume on the radio, squelching some country lament that I didn't really want to hear. While I waited – rating the odds at three out of ten that he'd actually answer my question about Doyle – I was thinking, and not for the first time, that most of Sam's favorite country artists could use a few sessions of psychotherapy.

'Owner's been out of the house for a while; it's vacant now, was vacant over Christmas, too, if that's what you're wondering. And yes, we've talked to him – the owner – got in touch with him right away through the real estate lady who's listing the house.'

Sam paused poignantly. Okay, provocatively. I thought he was waiting to see if my sense of self-preservation was so impaired that I would choose that moment to remind him of something he had once confessed to me about the last time – the Christmas when the little blonde beauty queen was murdered three blocks away. That time, Sam admitted one night over beers, eleven long months passed before any cop, any DA's investigator, any FBI agent – anyone in law enforcement – got around to interviewing one of the dead girl's family's nearest neighbors.

For eleven months after a child was viciously murdered, the cops had failed to interview the residents of a house with a perfect view of the crime scene.

To me, unbelievable.

But I didn't remind him. He didn't need reminding.

He went on. 'The owner gave us permission to search. No hesitation, no bullshit, totally cooperative. Agent unlocked the place and we searched it. Nothing. And all this happened in the first few hours after Mallory's father reported her missing.'

'Is the owner in town?'

Doyle. I wanted to use his name out loud, but I couldn't. I wanted to know if Doyle was in town.

'No.'

'You guys thought Mallory might have been in there after she disappeared?'

'Vacant house right next door? It's one of the first places we look.'

'But nothing?'

'Just a vacant house. Kitchen's hardly bigger than mine. Terrific yard, sure, but no place to toss a football. Definitely overpriced. Hey, what isn't in this town?'

Sam pondered the inflation of Boulder's housing stock more than I did, but taking that detour didn't seem productive to me. I asked, 'Was the Camaro in the garage when you searched the house at Christmas?'

'Now there's a good question. I don't recall that it was. If it had been, somebody would've run the tags and talked to your guy. I'm sure of that. And I don't think we've ever talked to your guy.'

I could tell that I had only about half of Sam's attention. He was considering some angle I couldn't see. His answer to my last question was probably in the vicinity of honest but he wasn't telling me all that he could. But then I wasn't telling him all that I could, either. 'Something else is spinning in that big head of yours. What is it?'

He startled a bit at my question as he pulled from Ninth onto Pine. 'I'm connecting dots, looking for a damn crime. I need a rationalization I can use.'

'What do you mean?'

He didn't answer right away, not until we were almost on the Donalds' block. My car was just ahead. The lights were still off in Bob's rooms; I would have been truly surprised if they weren't.

Sam flashed the Cherokee's headlights at a van coming at us from the other direction. The driver of the van responded by flashing to his low beams for half a second before he went right back to his brights. He beeped his horn to underline his aggravation that another motorist would deign to question his choice of headlamp settings. I couldn't see the van driver through the high-intensity glare but I would have bet he was flipping Sam off, too.

I said, 'Asshole's tugging on Superman's cape.'

'He's lucky I'm in a good mood.'

I smiled out loud.

'There's nothing here for me, Alan. Your guy's been gone, what? A day or two maybe? There's half a thimble's worth of blood near his door – and some clothes on the floor. No sign of forced entry. No witnesses. Guy's gone. His car's gone. Ergo: He split. People do it all the time without warning anybody, without telling anybody. Even their therapists. I have nothing I can give my bosses that they'll find the least bit interesting. I take this in, I know what I'm going to hear: So far this isn't a police matter. So that's what I tell you: So far this isn't a police matter.'

'Okay,' I said.

'And your friend, Diane? She's so far out of my jurisdiction it isn't funny. I put myself in the Vegas casino's shoes and I'm not going to give a crap about her welfare until another few days pass and the hotel needs her room for the next convention. I put myself in a Vegas cop's shoes, I feel basically the same way. Grown-ups do what grown-ups do. But say she's really missing? By the time people get worried enough to look for her, it will probably be way too late to do anything to help her. I pray she's okay, but just disappearing off a casino floor like that? I don't like what you're telling me. That's just the truth. I wish it were different.'

Sam pulled the Cherokee to a stop nose-to-nose with my wagon and doused the headlights. The glow from a streetlight washed into the car from the driver's side, silhouetting Sam against the glass.

'The dots I'm connecting are actually way more interesting to me,' he said. 'See, if I put on my decoder glasses I see your footprints just about everywhere I look, which shouldn't be too surprising considering your history with this kind of thing.'

I opened my mouth to disagree. Closed it. What was the point?

Sam went on. 'First? I think maybe you and your partner, Diane, have some connection to the Millers – I'm guessing Mrs. Miller, Rachel – that I don't know about. Want me to guess? Okay, I suspect it goes back a few years, maybe more. Could I guess what it is? Yes, I could.' He paused, allowing me to digest his conclusion.

'Next? I think that the Camaro man has some connection to the guy who owns the water-park house and for some reason that connection makes you much more nervous than a simple rented garage should make you. So it's something else entirely. I'd like to know exactly what that connection is, but experience tells me I'm not going to get shit from you tonight, so I'm trying not to give myself a headache about it. My assumption at the moment is that you think it has something to do with Mallory Miller. Frankly, that worries me. It worries me that you're playing detective again, and it worries me just the slightest little bit that you might be on to something that we don't know.'

The sound of Sam's stomach complaining that it hadn't seen a meal in a while filled the car. The growl made me realize that I was hungry, too. I wondered if Lauren had saved me some dinner.

'More? We already know that you and Diane were the ones who found that vic on Broadway. And—'

'Sam, you just called Hannah Grant a "vic."'

'I shouldn't have said that. She was your friend. My apologies. Habit, I'm sorry.'

'That's not what I meant. You think Hannah's a victim? You think her death was a homicide? The coroner called it "undetermined." Has that changed?'

'It's Slocum's and Olson's, not mine. I'm not the authority on that case. Manner was undetermined yesterday. Manner is undetermined today. End of story, sorry.'

In almost any other circumstance I would have pushed him. But I needed Sam to stay interested in Diane and Bob. We could get back to Hannah later. I couldn't help but wonder, though: *What do the cops have?*

'What else?' I asked. 'You were going to say something else.'

'Reese Miller,' Sam said. He'd forgotten which finger he'd used to keep track of his last point. By default, he chose his thick thumb to represent Reese Miller. 'Why are you so interested in him? Where the heck does he fit into this puzzle?' He turned his head toward me and looked right at me. 'Do you even know?'

I opened my mouth, closed it, and emitted some sound that was closer to a sigh than anything else. Reese was an unknown to me. I said, 'No, I don't really know anything about him.'

'Good,' he said. 'Listen, I have to get the babysitter home and I promised to help Simon with a poem he's writing. Did you have to write poems at his age? It's a good thing. Getting kids to write a lot. Keep me up to speed on Diane.'

I opened the Jeep's door and was freshly surprised by the bitter chill of the January night. 'Thanks, Sam.'

'Yeah,' he said. Then: 'Wait.'

I leaned back into the car. Sam looked away from me for a couple of seconds before he turned back. 'I know you expect me to find a way to help you. But I can't. There's no hook for me. There has to be something I can grab on to.'

'I don't especially want anything to do with this either, Sam. Since the day that Mallory fell off the face of the earth I've tried like hell to make this leave me alone. But it keeps tracking me down. From my point of view, you get close enough to this thing and you'll find it has as many hooks as a square foot of Velcro.'

I slammed the door shut and he drove off.

34

The clock read just shy of 8:30 when I walked in the front door of my house. Emily greeted me exuberantly, but I found my other two girls sound asleep in the master bedroom curled into the familiar big spoon/ little spoon configuration. They were surrounded by that night's bed-time books and Grace's favorite stuffed animals. Our not-so-stuffed poodle, Anvil, was curled into a tight ball at Grace's knees.

I was feeling remorse that I'd been missing out on the bedtime ritual so often.

Sound asleep at Grace's bedtime was a little early, even for Lauren, but the energy depletion that she suffered as a result of multiple sclerosis wasn't always easy to predict. If you asked her on a day when she wasn't suffering any of the acute effects of one of the disease's myriad symptoms, she'd tell you that what she hated most about the illness was that it made her days so much shorter. As each successive year took its toll, Lauren had fewer good hours, fewer strong hours, fewer waking hours, fewer hours when pain or weakness didn't drive her to bed. Ask her what she'd most like to change about having MS, and she'd tell you she wished her days were longer. She'd tell you that on most days her energy lasts about as long as daylight endures on a December day in Anchorage.

This had apparently been one of those Yukon days. That's what she called them. I'd call her from work and find her at her desk at the DA's office. I'd ask how she was doing. Too often she'd say, 'You know, babe. It's a Yukon day.'

I rearranged the comforter so that it provided some cover for both mother and daughter, kissed the tops of their heads, lifted Anvil from the sheets, and led the dogs outside to pee. Once the odd canine couple had done their thing and our little parade was safely inside the house, I checked for a message from Raoul or, even better, Diane.

Nothing.

I scrambled a couple of eggs, folded them onto some honey wheat toast, and carried my plate into the living room. I ate standing up at the big windows that faced down into Boulder, trying to spot the house where Jenifer Donald was visiting her grandparents, trying to spot the overpriced house with the water park up near the foothills on Twelfth, trying to spot the small house on Broadway where Hannah Grant had died.

Far to the west, on the other side of the vast mountains, I wondered if Raoul was on his date with the woman from Venetian security. Or was he still chatting up gamblers at the craps tables trying to find someone who remembered his wife?

And where the hell in all those lights were Bob and his cherry Camaro?

What answers, if any, were sitting in a Kinko's box in my office?

My impulse was to charge downtown and find out.

I reminded myself that what Bob had written was part of a novel.

Fiction.
Stuff he'd made up.
Stuff I was supposed to wait to read.

35

Diane, in rare moments of candid self-doubt, would express astonishment that she'd ended up with Raoul. 'Why me? Look at me. Look at him. Why on earth did he choose me?'

Raoul was an olive-skinned Spaniard with piercing eyes, a prodigious intellect, an entrepreneurial instinct for innovation, and a bloodhound's nose for money. He had a smile as sweet as honey, and his thick hair looked black until the sun hit it just so and lit it up like golden floss. He could give charm lessons to George Clooney, put on continental airs when he felt the situation demanded, or pull on faded jeans and cowboy boots and slide right into a farmhouse discussion of southern Colorado water rights as though it had been his family that had cut the first irrigation canals into the dusty San Luis Valley.

In much the same way that the progeny of Holocaust survivors have been indelibly scarred by Germany's twentieth-century embrace of the Nazis, Raoul had been bruised deeply – down to the place where tissue ends and the soul takes up corporeal space – by Spain's fifty-year flirtation with fascism. Memories of long-absent relatives, and nightmared imaginings of what had happened to them at the hands of Franco's Falangists, flowed through his blood like perpetual antibodies to authority.

The result? Raoul had wide shoulders, and a chip on them that was sometimes big enough to obscure his handsome head.

My impatience to hear an update finally compelled me to dial Raoul's cell number before I climbed into bed. He answered after three rings.

'Yeah?' he said to the accompaniment of Las Vegas background sounds. Music, traffic. Something else – hissing, muted explosions. I wasn't sure what it was.

The single word he'd spoken as he answered had carried a boatload of hope; every time his phone rang he was praying that the caller was Diane. To me, ironically, his hope meant that he hadn't found her. My own hope, which was hovering like a flat stone skipping on a smooth lake, sank instantly to the muddy bottom.

'It's me, Raoul. You didn't find her.'

He said something in Catalonian. It sounded like *'bandarras.'* From the spitting tone he employed, I guessed it had been a profanity and that it didn't really require translation, although I was always more than a little eager to add to my knowledge of the profane spectrum of his native tongue.

'Were you able to talk with that woman from hotel security?' I found myself shouting to be heard above the din.

'Marlina has a story,' he said. 'Unfortunately, it takes her a while to tell it.'

'Yeah?' I didn't get whatever he was saying.

'She's from Mexico. What's on her mind is about her brother and something that happened to him on the way from Chihuahua to Tucson. She needs to talk. With some women, it has to first be about them. She is one of those women. *Fer un solo de flauta*. Trust me, it's the only way.'

Raoul spoke about women the way he spoke about IPOs and RAM. With authority. Again, I considered asking him for a translation of the Catalonian, but I didn't.

'You haven't learned anything?' I asked.

'Not yet.'

He sounded fried – Raoul's anxiety seemed to be swelling with every conversation we had. The appearance of my voice, and not his wife's, on the line had robbed him of whatever buoyancy had been keeping him afloat. I could feel the deflation in his spirits as hope leaked away; whatever vessel he was in was taking on water and he was getting tired of bailing.

'Did you find anyone playing at the craps tables who remembered Diane?'

'I set up a half-million-dollar credit line. I assumed that would give me a little bit of latitude in the casino.'

I couldn't imagine. 'Yeah? How much were you betting?'

'Five or ten. Sometimes twenty.'

Thousand. 'You win anything?' I asked.

'I did all right,' he said. Raoul, I knew, would take no joy in a big pile of craps winnings. In his various tech businesses, he played for stakes that would make a huge pile of casino chips seem paltry by comparison. But given the events of the last twenty-four hours, Raoul would take some pleasure in the fact that he had taken the money – if it were a large enough pile – from the coffers of the Venetian.

'How good?

'I'm up eighty or so. The only luck I'm having in this town is at a craps table.'

I whistled. 'Thousand?'

'Minus four. I tipped a couple of dealers. I'm hoping they're appreciative, might let me buy them a drink.'

Two craps dealers were each a couple of grand richer than they'd been before they'd gone to work that day and met Raoul. With that kind of incentive they might be inclined to have a drink with him after their shifts were over.

I asked, 'When are they off?'

'Three hours or so. We'll see what happens. My expectations are low. I gave a woman some money to pass each of them a note that said I wanted to talk with them. She says she did it, but who knows? Their bosses may have warned them off.'

'A frustrating day?'

'They're the house. They have the cards; they have the odds. My only advantage is that I'm more motivated than they are. They don't understand that yet. One guy at the craps table slipped me his business card when he heard me ask the woman next to him about Diane. He's a VP for some shopping-center developer. They do malls.'

'A gambler?'

'In his heart, that kind of gambler. I waited until he left the table and then I called his mobile number after about twenty minutes. I told him I was the guy from the craps table. He said, "Not now." I asked, "When?" And he said, "I have your number now. I'll call you." Then he hung up.

'*Pastanaga*. I think he was playing with me.'

'He hasn't called?'

'In Vegas terms the night is young, right? Me? I'm twenty years older than I was at this time yesterday. A week more of this and I'll be ready to trade in the craps table for some pinochle.'

I could almost feel his despair. I was on the portable phone, wandering between the mostly dark kitchen and the mostly dark living room, where I stopped and found myself, once again, searching for Twelfth Street in Boulder's dark grid. Looking for the Millers' house, and for Doyle's.

The noise in my ear was Sinatra and percussion. Traffic, too. A siren.

'Are you in a club?'

'I'm at the Bellagio. Outside, watching the fountains. I like them. I know they're garish, but I like them. Have you ever seen them?'

'Only on TV.'

'Someday then.'

'Yes.' *Maybe.* 'With Diane.'

'With Diane, *sí.* Alain?'

I was a bit taken aback. He hadn't used the French pronunciation of my name for a long time.

'Yes.'

'If there were a man involved – with my wife – you would tell me?'

'What? You mean a—'

'Yes. *Un autre.* We're grown-ups here, right?'

That Raoul was susceptible to whatever affective tides the prospect of infidelity caused in other people surprised me. Where romance was concerned, Raoul lacked confidence the way Spider-Man lacks grip.

I said, 'To the best of my knowledge, this has nothing to do with another man. Nothing.'

'Thank you. I had to ask.'

'Raoul? The Rachel you're looking for? It's Mallory Miller's mother. That's who Diane went to Vegas to try to find.'

He was silent. I hadn't lost him; I could still hear the

Sinatra and the fountains and the impatience of the traffic on the Strip, but Raoul wasn't speaking. As the interlude grew longer, I immediately flashed back to the night before and Diane's abrupt disappearance from the conversation I was having with her in the casino. My heart accelerated like a teenage driver with a lead foot chasing after a pretty girl.

'Raoul? You there?'

'I'm here.'

'I was afraid I lost you.'

'You didn't lose me; I'm thinking. Diane went to see the missing girl's mother?'

'If you've followed Mallory's story in the news, you may also know that Rachel Miller suffers from mental illness. That might be important for you to know when you finally find her.'

'I don't read that kind of thing. Diane tells me, but she didn't tell me that. What kind of mental illness?'

I wasn't sure what the tabloids had reported. 'I know the answer to your question, Raoul, but I shouldn't say. It's something serious. Let's leave it at that.'

'Is she dangerous?'

'Rachel? Unlikely, highly unlikely.'

'Why did Diane want to see her?'

'I found a way to rationalize telling you who Rachel is. Giving you the why part is much harder. I'm sorry. And I'm not sure it will help you to know the answer. If I think it will, I'll tell you, I promise.'

The fact that Mallory's mother lived in Vegas, even the fact that she lived in Vegas and suffered from a severe mental illness, had been reported in the news media. I wasn't telling Raoul anything new by telling him that. If a patient tells a psychologist that the sun came up that morning, the news isn't necessarily confidential. The psychologist can share the revelation with others.

Raoul asked, 'Is Diane mixed up with whatever happened to Mallory Miller?'

'I can't' – I fumbled for a word that seemed to fit – 'address that.'

'You could if your answer was no.'

To myself, I said, *Thank you.* Raoul was absolutely right. I could tell him if the answer was no. But the answer wasn't no, and he knew exactly what that meant. 'I can't argue with your conclusion, Raoul.'

'This mess – whatever this mess is – it started with Hannah's death, didn't it?'

I thought for a moment about what I could say in reply. 'Hannah's death started a lot of balls rolling.'

He responded with, *'Si ma mare fos Espanya, jo seria un fill de puta.'* From the cadence and tone, I assumed it was profane, and from the reference to *Espanya* I guessed that a Spaniard wouldn't be thrilled to hear the phrase cross Raoul's Catalonian lips.

36

I hadn't been on the University of Colorado campus for a while. January wasn't my favorite time for a visit, and the Duane Physical Laboratories wasn't my ideal destination. But when my 11:15 appointment canceled on Thursday, I recognized that if I added the newly freed time to my midday lunch break, I had a seventy-five minute hole in my day. I decided to make the short trip from my office to the university.

The physics building is a large, angular, modern complex on the east side of the Boulder campus, segregated by roadways and by design from the cluster of lovely brick or flagstone structures that form the Mediterranean architectural core of the original university. The newer academic buildings surrounding Duane were, like Duane itself, looming, cast-concrete forms faced with just enough flagstone and roofed with just enough red tile to pay wink-wink homage to the Tuscan soul of the place.

I'd been aware of Duane for years; the tallest structure on campus, situated right across Colorado Avenue from the Muenzinger Psychology Building, it was hard to miss. But, given my arm's-length relationship with the physical sciences, or at least my arm's-length relationship with the study of the physical sciences, I'd never had reason to go inside Duane. Once I did make my way into the building looking for Bob, my initial impression was that Duane was state-university big and anonymous and that the notices on the bulletin boards were mostly about things I didn't understand and, more to the point, until that moment didn't even know that I didn't understand. A professor was looking for a research assistant to study femtosecond optical frequency combs. Another lab needed help developing microcalorimeters and bolometers based on superconducting thin-films cooled to 0.1 K.

I didn't know what any of it meant, not even close, but I was almost one hundred percent confident that I wasn't their man. The students wandering the flavorless hallways – students who likely deserved my respect because, unlike me, they might have a prayer of being able to translate the bulletin boards – seemed a bit more serious than those I was accustomed to running into in my usual haunts on campus.

A big, anonymous building full of serious students? I suspected that Bob had gravitated to the physics department by unconscious design and had ended up burrowing into an environment where he could survive – thriving for Bob wasn't really an option – for the many years he'd been putting in his time waiting for whatever would come next.

After a few false starts going to the wrong offices, I learned that Bob was actually a clerk/secretary in the office/lab where plasma physicists did their incomprehensible things. It turned out that Bob's boss, a middle-aged woman named Nora Santangelo who was shaped like a chunk of water main, was as curious as I was about Bob's whereabouts, and had a terrific intuitive sense of the parameters of Bob's peculiarities.

When I introduced myself I omitted the doctor part. I

told Ms. Santangelo – she didn't strike me as the type of supervisor that a subordinate, or a visitor like myself, should call 'Nora' – that I was a friend of Bob's and that he had missed a rendezvous we'd planned for the previous evening and wasn't answering his phone.

She responded suspiciously, 'You're his friend? I didn't know he had any.'

Point, Ms. Santangelo.

It had taken some effort on my part to refocus her on the fact that I didn't know where Bob was. 'I called here this morning. The person who answered his phone told me he was out sick. But he's not at home, either. I'm concerned.'

'Well, to be honest, I am too. I hadn't called his home – that's not the sort of thing that Bob . . . appreciates. He missed a day of work back during the spring blizzard in 2003, but that's the only other time I can remember.'

Bob's previous absence was undoubtedly excused: The infamous March 2003 blizzard had dropped almost four feet of snow on Boulder. 'He didn't call in today?'

She shook her head. 'Or yesterday. Bob usually eats lunch at his desk. Puts his nose in a book or plays games online. Scrabble. Sometimes chess. He never hangs with the rest of the staff. Never. But Monday? Around eleven in the morning he told me he was going out for lunch. Came right up to my office, walked right up to my desk, and said, "Mrs. Santangelo, I'm going out to lunch." I was so surprised – and so pleased, really – that I told him to enjoy himself, to take a whole hour.'

'Did he?'

'Sure as heck did. He never came back at all. Didn't call in. I still don't know where he is.'

'Well,' I said, while I digested the news that Bob's vanishing act had started even earlier in the week than I'd suspected.

Ms. Santangelo and I were standing in her office and I was finding myself increasingly distracted by the tubular shape of her. I would swear that her thighs, hips, waist, bosom, and shoulders were all the exact same measurement. She wasn't particularly heavy; she just looked like she'd been forced to spend her formative years hibernating in a sausage casing.

'Listen,' she said. 'Bob is . . . different. Different – different. I inherited him when I came over here from Hellems – the history department? I used to think those folks in history were peculiar, but these physicists? Don't get me started; they're something else. And Bob, he's the oddest ball in the rack. Excuse my honesty, but if you know him then you know that already. He likes to keep his distance. He can be difficult for people to deal with, people who aren't sensitive to his . . . shall we say, tendencies. But he does his job. No more, mind you, not a scintilla more. Bob does just his job. And I've finally found him a desk in a lab where everybody seems to get along with him okay. What I'm saying is that he's not on a short leash like some of the people here. I'm not going to fire Bob for whatever . . . this is.' I watched her expression as her imagination took her someplace she hadn't previously considered. 'Within reason, of course.'

'Ms. Santangelo, it sounds like you know him well. Do you have any idea where I might look for him?'

She thought for a moment and shook her head. 'Sorry,' she said, as she took a step toward the door. 'But you'll call me if you hear anything? I am concerned. Bob grows on you.'

Like a mushroom, I thought. *Or a truffle.* Something parasitic.

'Of course.' I scrawled my pager number on a Post-it

that I spotted on the desk behind me and handed it to her. 'Will you do the same?'

She said she would and I headed out the door. Before I'd cleared the threshold I stopped and turned back to her. 'Did Bob take his begonia with him? You know the one I'm talking about?'

She smiled at me. 'Of course I do. You do know him well. But I don't know the answer to your question. Why don't you and I go down to his desk and see about that darn Christmas begonia.'

As she led me down the hall toward the administrative area that included Bob's desk, I allowed myself the suspicion that Ms. Santangelo had quite a mouth on her when she was younger, but that a lot of ambition and some determined self-discipline had turned her from a damn-and-hell young woman to a darn-and-heck middle-aged one.

The Christmas begonia was sitting in what his boss said was its usual place on the corner of Bob's desk. The plant's presence told me one thing, but it told Ms. Santangelo two. She explained to me that if Bob anticipated being away from the office for an extended period – anything more than a long weekend constituted an extended period – he would carefully transport the begonia home with him. The transport was an elaborate process involving a beer-case flat and tented brown grocery bags. She also explained that if he anticipated being out of the office for a period even as long as a full day but not longer than three, he would move the plant and its pebble tray from the corner of his desk to the top of a waist-high bookshelf that sat beside a southeast facing window at the far end of the room.

'Always?' I asked.

'Always,' she confirmed, without hesitation. 'He never

puts the begonia in direct sun. And he always watered it from below, you know, from the pebble tray. He knows what he's doing with it. Bob manages to keep the thing in bloom like that from Thanksgiving until spring break some years. People always comment on it, always.'

I'd already noted that the begonia was healthy, its blossoms prodigious. I stated the obvious: 'Bob didn't expect to be gone for this long, did he?'

Ms. Santangelo reached down and caressed the petals of one of the delicate begonia flowers. 'No, he didn't. I wonder if I should move it over to the bookcase so it can get some light while he's gone. Bob would. I know he would. I just don't know if he would want me to.'

I'd followed her hands to the desktop and was scouring the surface for a clue that might tell me something about Bob's destination when he'd left work to go out to lunch on Monday. Other than the Christmas begonia, though, his desktop was devoid of anything personal. I asked, 'When Bob plays games, does he use this computer?' I was pointing at the less-than-state-of-the-art machine that filled a third of his desk.

'No, he doesn't. He has a laptop, he brings it with him to work every day. He asked me a long time ago if it's okay with me for him to hook it up to the university's network over lunch to play his games. I told him to have at it. Bob doesn't cheat. If he's unsure about a rule, he asks.'

Her response deflated me a little. 'He took his laptop with him to lunch?'

'I don't know, heck,' she said, and started rummaging in the drawers of Bob's desk. From my vantage the drawers appeared to have been arranged by a demonic closet organizer.

'Don't see it,' she said. 'He must have taken it.'

'Do you know anything at all that might help me find him?'

'I wish I did,' she said. 'I really wish to heck that I did.' She made her hands into fists and lifted them so that they came together just below her chin. 'A few of my people here are totally reliable, you know what I mean? But some of the rest? Flakes. If they were gone for the amount of time that Bob's been gone – a couple of days – I wouldn't give it a second thought. Par for the darn course is what I'd think. Par for the darn course. But Bob? He's not part of either group. He's not regular, he's not a flake. He's . . .

'You know what? I'll just say it: I don't really like Bob, but I . . . like him. Do you understand? I do hope he's okay.'

I understood.

I crammed in a quick stop at Mustard's Last Stand on Broadway, inhaled my hot dogs with only a small side of guilt over the indulgence, and made it back to my office with just a few minutes to spare before my next appointment.

37

Was the after-work plan I cobbled together a good idea? Probably not. But once my workday was done I realized that I was fresh out of good ideas, so I was left to settle for questionable ones.

I assumed that it would take me a day or so to get an appointment arranged to see the inside of Doyle's house, but I was wrong. When I phoned the listing agent asking if she could meet me for a showing, her eyes apparently began flashing dollar signs at the prospect of mining a buyer for a house for which she was already representing the seller. She asked me what time I got off work. I told her I was done at six. Without a moment's hesitation she asked if 6:15 would work for me. 'You won't believe the water features in the backyard,' she exclaimed. 'They are worth the purchase price all by themselves. Trust me, they're . . .'

I didn't tell her that I already knew.

When I called Viv, our part-time nanny, she informed me that Lauren would be late getting home, too. Viv promised me that she was happy to stay with Grace a little longer. In my head I added a small bonus to her monthly check. I also left Lauren a voice mail at her office that I would pick up some Thai takeout for dinner.

The woman I was meeting was named Virginia Danna. She pulled up in front of Doyle's house in a silver Lexus SUV, the big version, the fancy Land Cruiser clone that was all shoulders and hips. I was parked a couple of doors farther north and walked the short distance from my car in time to meet up with her near the front porch.

'Dr. Gregory?' She beamed when she spotted me coming. 'You're going to absolutely love this place. The bathrooms need a little work, but oh, oh, the potential with the . . .' She was a tall, thin – the word *svelte* actually came to mind – elegantly dressed woman with just a hint of an accent, as though she'd emigrated to the United States from someplace when she was quite young. Despite her last name, for some reason I was guessing she was from Brazil. Her wardrobe made few concessions to winter. She wore no coat and she balanced effortlessly on high heels. All in all, very not-Boulder.

'Ms. Danna?'

'Yes, yes. I'm so sorry. My manners sometimes escape me when I'm excited. And this house, it . . .' She reached out to shake my hand. 'Will you excuse me for just a moment?' She pressed a speed-dial button on her cell. 'Yes, yes. Dr. Gregory is here. We're going in now. Fine, fine. Yes, I'm sure. *Doctor* Gregory. That's right, on Twelfth. Thanks!' Ms. Danna turned back to me. 'With what's happened to some poor agents in Denver – I'm sure you heard – we're required to check into the office before all private showings. I hope you understand, it's . . .'

'Of course.'

She was in the lockbox in seconds, retrieved the front door key, and held the door open so I could precede her inside. 'I don't really like to show houses when they're unfurnished like this one is, but . . .' She sighed. 'I tried to get the owner to rent some things, you know, just for . . . The right furniture makes everything seems so much brighter and . . .'

Ms. Danna had an obvious penchant for uncompleted thoughts. Regardless, I was grateful for the opening she'd just offered about Doyle. Offhandedly I asked, 'Is the owner in town? Did he move to a larger house?'

She was easing me out of the cramped entryway into an adjacent living room with scratched red-oak floors, the original single-pane metal casement windows, and an undistinguished fireplace. 'In town? No, no. Not exactly. But we're in constant touch, constant. I promise I can get a response to an offer in a heartbeat. A day at the outside. He's motivated, he is – he's already dropped the price once. Don't get me wrong; I mean that in all the right ways. Do you live here in Boulder?'

The last question was ripe with raw hope that my answer would be yes and that I might offer her the opportunity for a real estate trifecta: a buyer who purchases a home from a listing agent and then agrees to enlist the same agent to sell his existing home. Three commissions – seller, buyer, seller – and a veritable cascade of closings.

'I do. In Spanish Hills. But I work downtown near the Mall, on Walnut, and with the traffic lately, the drive is getting . . .' I tried to find the right word before I settled on 'tiresome.'

Her excitement at my disclosure was palpable. A Spanish Hills listing? Although naming one of a few other even more precious local neighborhoods might have earned me an almost orgasmic response, in Boulder it didn't get a whole lot better for local real estate purveyors than Spanish Hills. 'Inventory' in Spanish Hills usually meant that there was a single home for sale. With my pronouncement that I lived on one of the rare parcels across the valley, I felt an instantaneous change in the electrical charge in the room.

But Ms. Danna knew that she had to sell me on the house at hand and couldn't risk my getting too sentimental about leaving my current home. She played her hand well. 'Don't I know?' she said. 'That's the beauty of living right here on the Hill. Everything is so close: Chautauqua, downtown, the greenbelt, the mountains, the turnpike, shopping. The location is so . . .'

Perfect?

I caught her staring down at my left hand and accurately predicted her next question. 'You're married?'

'Yes.'

'Children?'

'One.'

'Spanish Hills?' she mused. 'It's so pretty up there. I have clients who have waited for years to . . . the views are so . . .'

Expansive? And the houses so . . . expensive. I didn't have the heart to tell her that I lived in one of the few modest homes – modest by Boulder standards – in the whole neighborhood. She'd be so disappointed.

'Yes, it is lovely,' I said, but I was allowing my eyes to wander the recesses of the bland living room and was beginning to wonder what I'd hoped to gain by traipsing through Doyle's empty house. I moved through an opening from the living room into an equally bland dining room. Ms. Danna followed right behind me.

'Good size, don't you think?' she said. 'Plenty of room in here for a . . .'

Table? Family gathering?

The kitchen had been recently renovated and had a nice little built-in breakfast nook with a large window facing the yard. A compact laundry room was stuffed into what had probably once been a butler's pantry. The quality of the remodel wasn't congruous with the asking price for the house; the new cabinetry and appliances were the kind of warehouse stuff you might expect to find in a Boulder rental.

Ms. Danna apparently shared my impression. 'Some new countertops in here, maybe stone, or even cast concrete, and you'd need to do something with that . . .'

What? I couldn't tell. 'Yes,' I said. I was beginning to recognize her real estate dilemma. She was trying to sell a house in Boulder in winter that's main selling point was its yard. And yards don't show too well when they've been stripped of all their green, and elaborate water features don't show too well when they've been drained of all their H_20.

We made it through a quick tour of the two upstairs bedrooms and two adjacent cramped bathrooms. She had been correct in her earlier appraisal: The bathrooms were in need of a sledgehammer and a good designer. The master bath was lined with chest-high plastic tile in a color that resembled one of the fluids that Grace emitted from her nose when she had a sinus infection.

As my enthusiasm for the house failed to swell, Ms. Danna's enthusiasm about her prospects seemed to go into decline, but she tenaciously held on to some hope for the finale. 'The two highlights of this property are the media room in the basement, and that wonderful backyard. Which would you like to see first?'

She didn't wait for my reply. She hit two switches on the wall near the back door and instantly the yard lit up like a resort. My eyes were drawn to the granite waterfall that I'd seen in the dark the night before.

'That's nice,' I said.

'Nice? Imagine the water splashing over those rocks,

the sound of that stream. Fish in the pond. The birds, the flowers. In spring, I think you'll find that it's . . .'

Breathtaking?

'The basement?' I asked. 'Where are the stairs?'

The lower level wasn't the same size as the upper level. The media room was big enough – I pegged it at fifteen by twenty feet – but the whole basement wasn't even twice that size. A bland powder room, a mechanical room, and a long, narrow storage room completed the downstairs floor plan. On the top third of the storage room wall was a wide opening with a hinged lid.

'More storage?' I asked.

'Crawl space,' Ms. Danna said.

'May I?' I asked, touching the handle on the door.

'Of course.'

I opened the awning-style lid and peered into a neat crawl space about three feet high. The floor of the entire space was lined with thick-mil plastic.

'Radon?' I asked, trying to act like someone who was actually interested.

She nodded. 'Nothing to worry about. It's under control. Completely. I have all the reports. It's been mitigated to levels that the neighbors would love to have. Really, it's . . .'

Whatever. I closed the lid on the crawl space.

'Did you see that projector in the media room?' she asked. 'It's a top-of-the-line Runco. And, yes . . . yes, it's included. All the theater electronics are included. Audio, video. All of them. Denon, B&O. The furniture, too. I don't have to tell you that those chairs are all recliners, and they're not La-Z-Boys. Custom. Crème de la crème. Electronics, finishes, everything. He spared no expense down here. The owner loved his home theater, he . . .'

I didn't know what she was talking about component-wise, and I didn't really care. I was one of those people who couldn't imagine going down into the basement to watch a DVD so I could pretend I was sitting in a theater. I'd just as soon curl up with my wife and daughter and my dogs and watch a video on the old VCR in the bedroom.

'Wow,' I said, trying to sound enthusiastic.

'Oh, I forgot, the screen . . .' She took my hand and led me out to the far wall of the theater. A big white movie screen was hung within an ornately carved frame of polished wood. I was guessing mahogany. 'Now, don't you touch it – fingerprints, fingerprints. I forgot who makes it – somebody good, no, somebody great. I have it in my notes. It's the same screen that Spielberg has in his private screening room at his place in . . . The same exact one. It's like . . . the best. I promise I have the name back in the office. I'll get it for you. I will. First . . .'

Thing? 'Wow.' It looked exactly like a movie screen. Spielberg knew what he was doing.

After what I hoped was a suitable amount of time spent staring at the blank screen, I led Ms. Danna up the stairs and as we walked out the front door I gave her my appraisal of the property. 'It's a little small for us, I'm afraid.'

She was ready for that argument. 'Oh, I know, I know, but the potential? You get a good architect to find a way to cantilever the upstairs a little bit and you could expand that second story in a heartbeat. Think of the covered porch down below and the views from your new master suite upstairs. Just think! You could have a deck that faces the Flatirons! And closets? Oh, I don't have to tell you, do I? You're a man with . . .'

Vision?

The night was cold and a bitter wind was blowing down from the north with the sharp bite of Saskatchewan.

As Ms. Danna replaced the keys in the lockbox she made it clear that she was eager to show me a couple of other 'things,' though 'the price points are up a notch or two from here.' I declined, although I admit that I was curious exactly how many digits constituted a 'notch' in Boulder's hyperinflated housing market. Resigned, she gave me her card and asked for one of mine.

'I'm sorry,' I said. 'I don't have any with me.'

It was partly true. I didn't have any with me.

But I wasn't sorry.

I walked her down the serpentine front walk to her big Lexus and shook her hand, thanking her for her time. Over her left shoulder – at the upstairs window of Mallory Miller's house – I spotted what I thought was the same silhouette I'd seen the night before while I'd been trespassing in the backyard with Sam.

Ms. Danna saw me looking. 'Such a tragedy,' she said. 'That girl's father must feel . . .'

Awful.

38

'Finding reality here is like looking for condoms in a convent. There might be some around, but they're not going to be easy to locate.'

Raoul was talking to me about Las Vegas, and about how he'd spent his day. His voice was as tired as my toddler's when she was up past her bedtime. Raoul was an optimist by nature, an entrepreneur by character. Watching him treading water in a sea of despair was so unexpected that it felt surreal.

The Las Vegas cops remained uninterested in Raoul's missing wife. He had pressed them to try to ascertain at what point Diane would be considered 'missing.' One detective told him that, 'Given the circumstances, it would certainly take more than a long weekend. And so far, Mr. Estevez, that's all she's been gone. One long weekend.' The hospitals continued to have no inpatients matching Diane's name or description. As a sign of his desperation, Raoul had hired a local private investigator who was apparently chewing up money much faster than he was uncovering clues about Diane's whereabouts. All he'd learned so far was Rachel's address. When he checked for her there, no one answered.

Marlina, the woman from Venetian security, enticed

Raoul to buy her breakfast at a place near downtown that was filled mostly with locals. They spoke Spanish while they ate. Raoul learned that Marlina's brother was in INS detention in Arizona, learned how he got there – or at least Marlina's version of how he got there – and learned in excruciating detail how Marlina felt about the whole affair, but he didn't learn anything about what the casino surveillance tapes revealed.

After the frustrating breakfast, Raoul moved on to an alternative avenue of investigation: The Love In Las Vegas Wedding Chapel. As he told me about it, my impression was that relating the story of what happened there seemed to relax him.

According to Raoul's tale, the minister of the Love In Las Vegas Wedding Chapel was the Rev. Howard J. Horton. By training he was an actor who had enjoyed some success as a young man on Broadway, even once landing the role as understudy for the lead of some Tommy Tune extravaganza. After a move to California to find fortune on the Left Coast, Horton had actually defied the odds and made a living in Hollywood until his thirty-seventh birthday doing bit parts on sitcoms and lawyer and cop shows and getting occasional throwaway lines on big-budget features. In successive years in his late twenties he had been filmed making cocktails for Sean Connery, being pistol-whipped by Al Pacino, and flirting shamelessly with Sharon Stone just before being pummeled into submission by her leading man.

Raoul didn't think he had caught any of those particular movies.

The bit parts hadn't been enough to provide the foundation for Horton's hoped-for long-term career as a distinguished character actor, and as his face matured the parts he was being offered didn't. To pay the bills he'd eventually gravitated to dinner theater and later on made his way to Vegas, where he did some emceeing at shows on the Strip, fell in love with heroin, heroically managed to 'divorce the damn bitch,' and eventually ended up winning a thirty-nine percent stake in the Love In Las Vegas Wedding Chapel in a poker game with some locals that had started one cocktail hour on a Wednesday and ended late in the morning or early in the afternoon – Horton didn't quite remember; it had been that kind of game – the following day.

Horton was forty-seven years old and had been the minister of the moment at the Love In Las Vegas for almost seven years. On bad days he consoled himself that it paid the bills.

The British accent and aristocratic demeanor that Horton employed for the tourists who came to Vegas for matrimony were pure shtick, and the slick Vestimenta suit he wore in the relentless Nevada heat nothing but costume. He'd won the suit from a gay guy from Atlanta in another poker game – that table populated, with the exception of Horton, entirely by out-of-towners – and he told Raoul a hilarious story about them both stripping down to their undies to exchange clothes after the game. Howard had given up his favorite pair of cargo shorts and a well-worn Tommy Bahama silk shirt.

Raoul promised me that he'd get around to telling me the part about the protracted negotiation for the Atlanta man's thong another time.

'You promise?' I said.

'Absolutely,' Raoul assured me.

In a city where visitors were primed to expect spectacle, Horton's wedding show at the Love In Las Vegas was a whisper of sophisticated, or faux-sophisticated, understatement.

At the Love In Las Vegas, tourists who were so inclined could be married, not by an Elvis impersonator or a cross-dressing reject from Cirque, but by an ex-patriot British lord who seemed intent on bringing his interpretation of a little bit of the best of the Church of England, whatever that was, to the Nevada desert.

While Raoul waited to get a few minutes alone with the Rev. Horton so he could ask some questions about Diane and Rachel Miller, he had to choose between frying outside in the parking lot in the he-was-told unusual-for-January ninety-three-degree heat or sitting in the air-conditioned comfort of the chapel and observing the nuptials of a young couple that had driven all the way from Spraberry, Texas – that's just outside Midland and not too far from Odessa – to tie the knot in Las Vegas.

The engaged had written their own marriage vows and brought a cassette of the music they wanted played during the ceremony. Her vows ran onto three legal-sized yellow tablet pages.

His didn't.

The bride wore white – an ill-fitting empire-style dress with a long train that her second cousin had scored at the Filene's Basement annual everything-for-$299 wedding dress running-of-the-bulls in Boston. The bride was twenty-two, but didn't look it. She was as innocent as the prairie, and her face was full of the wonder that every woman's face should have before she weds for the first time.

On the final stretch of Highway 95 into Vegas she'd made a valiant attempt to memorize all the vows that she had penned onto the yellow legal pad on the haul from Spraberry to El Paso on Interstate 10, but during the actual ceremony she'd had to consult her notes every few seconds during her long recital of eternal love.

In his retelling, Raoul generously wrote it off to nerves.

Her betrothed was twenty-six years old and was dressed in a tuxedo jacket he'd borrowed from his sister's husband, a ruffled-front tux shirt sans tie, and clean – and pressed – Wranglers. His hair, greasy from all the road time, was combed into a mullet that was as sleek and shiny as the skin of an under-refrigerated fish. This was his third marriage and his second wedding in Las Vegas – he was once widowed and once divorced – and by demeanor and practice he was a love-honor-and-obey-till-death-do-us-part kind of groom. By history he apparently wasn't exactly a love-honor-and-obey-till-death-do-us-part kind of husband, but he'd promised his fiancée repeatedly – including once during the ceremony – that all that rutting was behind him.

The groom's self-written vows were an obviously plagiarized, parsed version of the popular standard. Raoul's impression was that the guy would have been better off just allowing Rev. Horton to do his almost-Anglican-cleric thing. But, Raoul noted, the bride didn't seem to be at all offended by her husband-to-be's lack of vow-writing prowess.

The wedding music, which was played over and over and over again in a toxic loop, consisted of a single upbeat song by Shania Twain with a lot of *uh, uh, oh*s in the lyrics. Raoul couldn't quite figure out the romantic relevance of the tune, but the cumulative weight of the pure repetition of the *uh, uh, oh*s eventually rendered him willing to accept the silky voiced singer's implied warning about whatever the hell it was. By the time the ceremony was over and the newlyweds had kissed and kissed again and walked hand-in-hand down the aisle toward the desert inferno that awaited them outside, Raoul knew just about all he wanted to know about the couple from

Spraberry whose wedding he had just helped celebrate, and he also knew he never wanted to hear the damn *uh, uh, oh* song again in his life.

Ever.

'He may have divorced "the bitch" but Reverend Howie still sleeps with her cousin,' Raoul said to me. 'He drinks a bit, and then he drinks a bit more. We spent most of the afternoon at the kind of saloon the Vegas Chamber of Commerce doesn't want tourists to see. That's when I heard his life story and got all that fascinating background on the happy couple from west Texas. Have to give the guy credit, though – Howie knew I was paying but he got the same crappy well-Scotch he drinks in that bar every day. He didn't ask the bartender to dust off the single malts just because I was running the tab.'

'Did you learn anything?'

It was late in Colorado – almost eleven at night – and I was exhausted. Although it was an hour earlier in Nevada, Raoul's voice told me that his long day and long story had left him every bit as tired as I was. Maybe more. But something about his day had at least temporarily softened the edge of his despair.

'He wouldn't talk to me about this Rachel woman. I could tell from his little act that he knew who she was, but he wouldn't answer any of my questions, wouldn't even admit that she hung out at his chapel. When I showed him Diane's photograph he wouldn't admit that he'd ever seen her before. I knew he was lying; wasn't sure exactly about what, or why, but I knew he was lying. I was beginning to think I was going to have to just stake out the damn wedding chapel and wait for Rachel to show up again and lead me to Diane.'

'I'm sorry.'

'No, no. That's when it hit me. I lowered my voice to a whisper, pulled a little pile of thousand-dollar chips from the Venetian out of my pocket, stacked them up in front of me, and asked Howie exactly how much he was being paid.'

'Paid for what?' I said.

'That's just what he said to me. All offended and everything. Reverend Howie's a smart guy. He's on the edge, but he has some pride. I don't think he's too dishonest. At the chapel he makes a living providing a service, as screwy as the service is. He supplements his income by taking people's money, or whatever else they might want to bet, in high-stakes poker games. But he plays those games fair. His MO? He sets people up by being a better actor than they give him credit for, and then he takes their money by being a better poker player than they give him credit for. This time? I already know he's a good enough actor, and I wouldn't think about sitting down to a hand of Texas Hold 'Em with the guy.'

'Yeah?' I had one ear focused on Raoul's Las Vegas story, the other tuned to Grace's room. She was making the kinds of nighttime noises that often precede one of those restless nights that end up with one of her parents dozing nearby on the rocker in her room until dawn. I said a silent prayer that my little daughter was merely enduring a troublesome dream.

Raoul said, 'Eventually, he told me. I had to make it clear I wasn't going away, but he finally said, "Fifty."'

'I'm sorry, Raoul. I'm too tired. I don't get it.'

'I didn't get it at first, either. See, my brainstorm was that I thought that Rachel Miller must be paying him. That that was why he let her attend all the weddings. I figured she might be slipping him five bucks, maybe ten, per ceremony. But he was trying to convince me that she was paying him fifty bucks a pop – fifty – to sit in this tacky chapel while Reverend Howie did his pretentious I-now-declare-you-husband-and-wife song and dance.' Raoul paused. 'Do you know how many people get married in Las Vegas on an average day? One hundred and fifty-three. That's what Reverend Howie told me.'

'If it's people, wouldn't it have to be a hundred and fifty-two or a hundred and fifty-four?' I asked. 'Maybe you mean couples; the number can't really be odd.'

Raoul sighed. 'Alain, your point?'

I did the math. Five weddings a week: two hundred and fifty dollars. Ten weddings a week: five hundred dollars. Five weddings a day, with one day off each week: fifteen hundred dollars. That meant that for Rachel Miller to attend weddings to her heart's content would cost somewhere between two thousand and six thousand dollars a month, or between twenty-four and seventy-plus thousand dollars a year.

Plus gifts. Holy moly. Where the hell would a schizophrenic woman living on the streets of Las Vegas get that kind of money?

I asked Raoul, 'Do you believe him?'

'At first, I thought he might be inflating the numbers to see how the negotiations would go with me, that I might be sitting in that saloon watching him drink Scotch so that I could try to outbid Rachel for some crazy reason. You know, offer him more than fifty to turn her away.'

'He's making pretty good money by allowing her to stick around for weddings.'

'That part seems clear. Tell me, how sick is Rachel? No details – I'm not asking for anything confidential – just rate it for me. Do it in a way I can understand.'

I couldn't tell him anything specific about Rachel's mental health mostly because I really didn't know anything specific about Rachel's current mental health. 'With the kind of disease that someone like Rachel has, with the kind of chronicity she's endured – she could have very visible symptoms. If you were to measure the disease of a person like that on the figurative ten-scale, say, on a bad day – a day when she's not taking appropriate medicine – she could be approaching double digits.'

'On that ten-scale?' Raoul asked.

'Yes.'

He emitted a high-pitched whistle. 'See, that's what I thought. That kind of sick is scary to people like me. Which means that Rachel is ill enough to be a serious liability at a place like the Love In Las Vegas. What bride wants somebody that disturbed camped out in the front row of her wedding?

'Reverend Howie's fee is insurance: He makes Rachel pay to attend the weddings. Who knows, he may even limit the weddings he lets her attend. Maybe he picks them himself. Makes a judgment about which ones are safe for her to be at, which ones she might create a distraction, cost him some business.'

'Raoul, if Rachel were attending all the weddings she wanted and if she were paying that much, it would cost a fortune. Where would she get that kind of money?'

Before the words were out of my mouth, I heard a prolonged whimper from Grace's room. *Damn.*

'This town?' he said. 'Too many bad ways to answer that question. Way too many.'

I shuddered at the thought of what perverse advantage some people might gain over someone as ill as Rachel Miller. 'What did Howie finally admit to you?'

'Just that she gives him money so he'll allow her to attend the ceremonies. And this is the funny part – she doesn't pay him herself – the money comes from someone else, someone who makes Reverend Howie very nervous. He wouldn't give me the person's name. He said, "You can buy me Scotch all day and all night and I'm not going to give you a name." I even pushed one of the thousand-dollar chips from the Venetian across the table and left it right in front of him. I said, "Name and phone number, Howard, and it's yours." He picked it up, flipped it, ran his fingers over the surface, and pushed it back onto my side of the table.

'I added two more and made it a nice little pile. He pushed them all right back to me. I added two more. He did the same thing.'

Howie had turned down five grand. I was thinking, *Wow.* 'So what are you going to do, Raoul?' I asked.

'I took four chips off the pile and slid the one that remained back across the table. I said, "Different question. Man or woman?"

'"Yeah?" Howie asked me. "For a grand? That's all you want to know?" I said that was the deal and he actually had to think about it. He is so wary of this person that gives him money so Rachel can attend weddings that he actually considered turning down a thousand dollars rather than reveal to me the person's *gender*. Eventually, he picked up the chip and slipped it into his shirt pocket like it was a pack of matches. He said, "It's a man. Not a man you want to fuck with."'

'That was it?' I said. 'That's all you got for a thousand dollars?'

'In business you don't always get value at the front end of a relationship. At the start you form a bond, establish platforms, ensure access. What I got for my thousand dollars is I got Howie on my payroll. And I reduced the possible suspects by half.'

'How do you find the man you're looking for?'

Raoul sighed. 'You remember a guy in Denver named Norm Clarke? Use to write for the *Rocky*.'

I remembered him. 'The gossip columnist with the patch on his eye?'

'*Sí*. Well, I know him – he did a story on me back in the tech boom times. He lives in Vegas now, knows everybody. I'm meeting him downstairs a little later for a drink. I'm hoping he can help me find the man Howie was talking about.'

Grace's unsettled whimper suddenly blossomed into a wail that was so powerful I could have sworn her lungs had been temporarily replaced by air compressors.

Raoul didn't need to be told our conversation was over. I sprinted in Grace's direction, praying that I could quiet her before Lauren's sleep was shattered.

39

After getting all of four hours' sleep I got all of four hours' warning before the next shoe dropped. I spent most of those four hours wondering whether having any warning at all was a good thing or a bad thing.

I never quite decided.

Patients, when they call my office number, are given a voice-mail instruction to call my pager directly in the case of an emergency. How often do my patients take advantage of the opportunity to reach me on my beeper? Once or twice in a bad month, infrequently enough that the mere sight of an unfamiliar phone number on my pager makes me anxious. So, on Thursday morning, while I was idling at the intersection of Broadway and Baseline on the way to work and my beeper vibrated and displayed an unfamiliar (303) 443-number, I was wary.

The 443 prefix meant the call came from a Boulder address. That's all I knew.

I returned the page as soon as I stepped into my office.

'This is Alan Gregory,' I said. 'I'm returning a page to this number.' I don't use the 'Doctor' appellation in those circumstances because I don't know if the person who called me will answer the phone or if someone else will. If it's someone else, discretion might dictate that my profession remain secret.

'Thanks for calling back so soon,' the man on the line said. 'This is Bill Miller.' And then, as if I might not know, he added, 'I'm Mallory's dad.'

What a sad thing, I mused, that he could use his daughter's unfortunate notoriety as a quick social identifier. And an even sadder thing that he would.

'Mr. Miller,' I said, buying some time while I hurriedly chewed and swallowed the ramifications of the simple fact that he had called me. 'What can I do for you?'

'Can you squeeze me in for an appointment? It's . . . important.'

'Umm,' I managed. My eloquence, given the circumstances, was profound.

'Today, if possible,' Bill Miller said.

I wondered whether he was asking me to get my tongue untied sometime 'today,' or whether he was asking for an appointment with me sometime 'today.'

If you asked me to write an ethics problem for a psychologists' licensing exam, or to dream up a delicious ethical conundrum for clinical psychology graduate students' comprehensive exams, I don't think I could have come up with something as devious as the dilemma I was facing at that moment.

'Do you have some time available?' he said, kindly pretending not to notice how flummoxed I was. 'I'll be as flexible as I need to be.'

The problem freezing my communication skills wasn't my schedule. My practice calendar that day was no more or less constricted than usual. On most days, if I was willing to give up a meal or stay late at the office, I could squeeze in an emergency.

The problem I was struggling with was that I didn't

know if I could see Bill Miller professionally at all. The issue that was complicating what should have been a simple matter of logistics was a problem of professional ethics.

My initial impulse about the ethical maze? I didn't think that I could see Bill Miller as a clinician. But I wasn't at all sure I was correct in that snap assessment. The circumstances were complex. I quickly decided that I'd never confronted another set of facts quite as complex in my entire career.

The arguments for agreeing to see Bill Miller for therapy? They were easy. He had once, albeit briefly, been my patient. His present circumstances – or at least the ones I knew about – were so public and so tragic that they might cause someone to seek professional help. Empathy and compassion both argued for me to make myself available to him.

The arguments for refusing to see Bill Miller for therapy? This is where things got messy. Psychologists are under an ethical obligation to avoid what the profession calls 'dual relationships.' At its heart, this is a conflict-of-interest clause, intended to ensure that a clinician is free to act in the best interest of his or her patient, uncomplicated by competing forces. In practice, the dictum requires that a clinician not wear two different hats in a patient's life.

In simple English, it means I shouldn't do psychotherapy with the woman who cuts my hair. I shouldn't join a book group run by one of my therapy patients.

Simple, right?

Usually, yes. But try to apply those simple guidelines to my relationship with Bill Miller. That's what I had been trying to do for the hours between his morning phone call and the midday appointment time I'd eventually offered him.

I hadn't gotten very far.

Did the fact that I was a good friend of a Boulder cop who was involved with the investigation of Bill Miller's daughter's Christmas Day disappearance qualify as a dual relationship?

I wasn't sure, but the degrees of separation seemed to be sufficient insulation.

Did the fact that my practice partner was covering the clinical work of a therapist who had died, and possibly been murdered, weeks after seeing Bill Miller's daughter for a single therapy session qualify as a dual relationship?

Once again, blank spaces seemed to separate Bill Miller's place on the board from the space that I was occupying.

Did the fact that I was seeing a patient who parked his car in the garage of the house of the man who lived right next door to the Millers qualify as a dual relationship?

Maybe, maybe not. In isolation, I would lean in the direction of 'not.' My patient had spoken with Bill Miller's daughter, considered her a friend. That was all I knew about Bob's relationship to the Millers. It wasn't much of a tie.

Did the fact that my partner and good friend had disappeared while on a trip to Las Vegas to try to arrange a meeting with Bill's estranged wife constitute a dual relationship?

I knew of absolutely nothing that tied Bill Miller to any of those events.

Did the fact that my friend and partner's husband, someone else whom I enthusiastically considered a friend, was busy looking for Bill Miller's estranged wife qualify as a dual relationship?

Probably not, for all of the same reasons.

But I wasn't totally sure. I didn't know if I should be contemplating additive effects. If *a* wasn't greater than *z*, and *b* wasn't greater than *z*, and *c* wasn't greater than *z*, did I have to be concerned whether $a + b + c$ was greater than z?

Ethical algebra hadn't been covered in graduate school.

I interrupted my obsessing over the Bill Miller conundrum to address a practical problem: Diane was still missing, and Thursday was the day she was supposed to be back in her office seeing patients. Although Diane and I shared space, our practices were separate businesses: I didn't know how many patients she was scheduled to see, nor did I know any of their names.

My problem was that I had to figure out some innocuous yet compassionate way to notify Diane's patients that their doctor would not be in the office that day. My solution was to post a note on the front door, the patient entrance to our little building. It read:

> To Anyone With An Appointment With Dr. Diane Estevez:
> Dr. Estevez is unexpectedly away from the office to deal with an urgent situation.
> She is unable to cancel her appointments personally, but will not be in today.
> She will contact each of you individually upon her return, and she appreciates your understanding, and your patience.
> Dr. Alan Gregory

At the bottom of the note, I belatedly scrawled a handwritten offer that anyone with a clinical emergency should call me, and I left my pager number.

When I'd returned Bill Miller's call, the offer for an appointment that I eventually made to him wasn't any more straightforward than was the prevaricating note I had left for Diane's patients. 'I'm not sure I can see you, Bill. I may have an ethical conflict.'

'How?' he said. 'We haven't spoken in, well, years.'

'It's complicated,' I said, lamely. 'It's not even clear to me that I actually have a conflict. I'm just concerned that I might.'

'Well, how about this,' he said. 'Let's schedule a time. In the interval between now and then you can think about your ethical problem. We'll talk, I'll run my concerns past you, and you can decide if you're able to help.'

He sounded eminently reasonable. I was reminded that even during the session with his wife so many years before, Bill Miller had seemed levelheaded and reasonable. Almost, I also reminded myself, to a fault.

'How about eleven forty-five?' I asked.

Bill Miller was close to ten minutes late for his appointment. Since I was meeting with him over the brief window in my day that would have constituted my lunch hour, I'd greedily used the free time to devour an energy bar from the emergency stash in my desk.

'Déjà vu, huh?' he said as he settled onto the chair across from me. 'It feels odd to be here without Rachel. That was one day that I will never ever forget.'

My natural human instinct was to offer condolences to Bill, to be sympathetic about whatever had happened with Mallory, to reflect on the sad outcome of the situation with Rachel. But I didn't. Instead I contemplated the fact that after so many years between visits with me his first association in my presence was to his long-estranged wife, and not to the tragedy of his recently absent daughter.

Ironically, one of the most difficult things about the psychotherapeutic relationship is the necessity for the therapist to, at times, put brakes on reflexive human kindness. Were I to presuppose to start this interaction with Bill Miller with expressions of compassion, or even overt sorrow, at his plight – or by giving him a big hug, a pat on the back, and a hearty 'hey, big guy' – I might unwittingly interfere with whatever motivation he'd had for picking up the phone.

So I waited. The truth was that most of the time, when I reached over my shoulder into my therapeutic quiver I ended up drawing out the dullest arrow, the one that was marked SHUT UP AND WAIT.

'I bet you'd like to know why I'm here,' Bill said.

'Yes,' I said evenly. 'I would. That's a good place to start.'

Bill was dressed in wool flannel trousers, good leather loafers, and a crisp blue dress shirt that was the color of his eyes. His sportcoat wasn't new, but it looked like cashmere, and hung on him with the drape of good tailoring. He wore no tie; few men in Boulder did.

'What's your ethical problem?' he asked. The question was neighborly. He could have been inquiring about a problem I said I'd been having with my gutters.

'Explaining the circumstances would lead to a whole different ethical dilemma for me. It's something I'm going to have to deal with on my own. When I reach a determination, I'll let you know.'

'But you've obviously dealt with it enough to have this meeting?'

'I'm hoping to get a better understanding about why you've come to see me. That might make my concerns moot, or it might clarify things so I'll have a clearer sense of what I should do.' That was the plan, anyway.

Bill closed his eyes for a moment, a long moment that grew into seconds. Five, then ten. Finally he opened his eyes, looked right at me, and with pain etched in his brow, he said, 'You've been at my house twice over the past two days. Why?'

40

In the same way that a boxer who has just absorbed a right uppercut has many options as he's lying on the canvas staring straight up at the klieg lights listening to a referee count 'eight, nine,' at that moment I had many options.

I could have reached back into my quiver for the safety of my SHUT UP AND WAIT arrow.

Or I could have said something classically therapeutic, and classically arrogant, like, 'This isn't about me, Bill. This is about you.'

Or, of course, I could have out-and-out lied: *'I don't know what you're talking about.'*

Instead, almost purely instinctively, I chose an alternative that I hoped might buy me a moment to think while at the same time it reinforced the separation that existed between, and needed to continue to exist between, my chair and that of my patient. What I said in reply to Bill's question about why I was at his house was, 'And that's why you're here, Bill?'

'Well, I don't think it's a coincidence.'

'Excuse me?' I was honestly perplexed by his quick reply. Bill Miller was implying that my appearance at his neighbor's house was coincident with what, exactly? I really wanted to know. 'What kind of coincidence are you talking about?'

'Why would you be at my next-door neighbor's house twice in two days with two different people?'

He apparently wasn't eager to answer my question; I was certainly not about to answer his. Discussing with Bill Miller that I'd been at his neighbor's house because I'd been concerned about the apparent disappearance of another one of my patients, and the disappearance of my partner and friend, wasn't about to happen.

'Is this meeting' – I waved my hand between us – 'a professional meeting? Did you come to see me for psychotherapy, or for something else?'

He hesitated long enough that I knew he had hesitated, which told me that he'd had to think about how to answer my question.

I said, 'The distinction is important. If we're going to work together, the distinction is important.'

'Yes, yes, of course it's professional,' he said. 'I need your help, Dr. Gregory. But I'm also concerned why you've been . . . so close to my home in the past few days.'

Was that a reasonable concern for him to have? I could have argued yes, I could have argued no. But was reasonableness the point? 'Go back three days please, Bill. Were you considering calling me for psychotherapy then?'

'What do you mean?' he stammered.

'You said that you've seen me at your neighbor's house twice in the past couple of days. I'm wondering whether that is the reason that we're talking today, or whether you had been considering asking me for help prior to that.'

Shit. By babbling on, I'd just given him a road map for how to respond.

No surprise, Bill consulted the map before he replied.

'I'd been considering it. Seeing you next door brought everything closer to the surface, a lot of old memories, unresolved, you know, feelings about . . . what's happened, so I decided to call and set something up. But I feel I deserve an explanation as to why you've been in my neighborhood so much. I do.'

Did he deserve an explanation? It was an interesting question. Were I truly interested in buying Doyle's house, that would potentially make me Bill Miller's next-door neighbor. If he and I were neighbors, the dual-relationships ethical restriction would definitely kick in: Preexisting therapeutic relationship or no preexisting therapeutic relationship, missing daughter or no missing daughter, I certainly could not provide psychotherapy to my next-door neighbor.

I decided to provide just enough of an explanation to allay his concerns.

'Bill, I can assure you that my presence at your next-door neighbor's house had nothing to do with you or your family.'

Was that really true? I actually wasn't sure.

'Are you thinking of buying that house?' Bill asked.

An easy question, finally. 'No, I'm not.'

'You were there with the woman who is listing that house.'

'I'll repeat what I said. I'm not considering buying the house.'

'Then why were you with her?'

'My presence had no direct relevance to you or your family.' Did it have indirect relevance? The question of indirect relevance had to do with Bob Brandt and the conversations he'd had with Mallory through the fence. The answer to the question of indirect relevance was either all chronicled in the pages in the Kinko's box Bob had given me, or it wasn't. My money was still riding on 'wasn't.' Barely.

I went on. 'Assuming for a moment that we each decide that we are comfortable working together . . .'

'Yes,' Bill said.

'How can I be of help?' A quick glance at the clock told me we had precious little time remaining until my twelve thirty showed up in the waiting room.

'I'm under a lot of stress.'

I can only imagine.

'I'm not sleeping. I'm losing weight; I don't have any appetite at all.'

Likely culprits for that constellation of symptoms? Depression, anxiety, post-traumatic stress. Given the circumstances of Bill's life, there were no surprises on that list. The most natural thing for me to do at that moment would have been to presuppose the source of Bill Miller's symptoms. I cautioned myself not to do it.

I pressed him, wondering aloud what he thought was going on. He responded with generalities about 'events' and 'the kids' and 'work.' I tried for some clarification. He eluded me.

Was I observing resistance – that psychotherapeutic Great Wall that separates so many patients from the issues that are most tender to them? Possibly. I decided to challenge the resistance a little. 'How was she feeling, Bill?'

'My daughter?'

Not Mallory. *My daughter.* I nodded.

'The holidays are hard for her. Always. This year, too. They haven't been fun for her since . . .'

I filled in the blanks with *her mother left.*

'Hard how?' I asked.

'She gets nervous. Withdrawn, irritable. She's definitely a teenager.'

Bill had grown anxious and withdrawn, too. As I considered the fact that the media had failed to report any details of Mallory's troubled holiday mood, and as the final moments of our appointment time dripped away, I decided not to test the flexibility of Bill's resistance any further. We made tentative plans to meet again the following Monday. I told him that I'd call him if I ultimately decided that my ethical concerns were so grave that I couldn't proceed.

Bill Miller left my office that day without having once spoken aloud his daughter's name.

Was it too painful for him?

I didn't know.

41

To my relief, my note on the door worked and none of Diane's patients camped out in the waiting room.

Until four o'clock.

At four o'clock, I walked out to retrieve my scheduled patient but was greeted not by one person eager to see me, but by two.

The unexpected person was the woman with the Cheddar-colored hair who had been so insistent on seeing her therapist on the day that Hannah Grant died. I recalled that Diane had told me that she had begun seeing the woman for psychotherapy. Was she there for her appointment?

I told the young man whom I was scheduled to see at that hour that I would be back with him in just a moment, and invited the Cheetos lady to come down the hall. We walked halfway to my office, far enough to be out of earshot of the waiting room, before I asked, 'Did you see my note on the door about Dr. Estevez? She can't be here today.'

'I saw your stupid note. I have a right to know what's going on.'

In the weeks since Hannah's death this woman had not shed any of her petulance. 'She's unfortunately away unexpectedly,' I said, stumbling over the adverbs I was stringing together.

'What does that mean?'

'She'll call you when she's back in the office.'

'That's what you said about Hannah.'

She was right. That is what I'd said about Hannah.

'I'm sorry.' I was sorry. 'I don't know what else to say. I'm sure, given what tragically happened with Ms. Grant, that this is especially difficult for you.'

I didn't know what else to say. I was also running out of big adverbs.

'How long has she been gone?'

'I'm afraid I'm not in a position to answer that question.'

'Then change your damn position.'

The top of her frizzy head reached just about to the level of my chin. Her hair had a scent that I associated with bad Indian restaurants. 'I'm available for—'

'I don't care what you're available for. Have you checked Diane's office?'

Diane, not Dr. Estevez. 'There's no need to check her office.'

'Then you know where she is. Tell me what the hell is going on.'

'I'm sorry that Dr. Estevez isn't here for your appointment. She'll call you as soon as she is free to do so. I have someone I have to see now. Please excuse me.'

I led her back toward the waiting room.

'This isn't going to stop here,' the woman said before she left.

Before I retrieved my patient, I rushed back down the hall, grabbed my keys, and opened Diane's office door. I was so relieved that it was empty.

'Jay?' I said to my four o'clock after I'd recovered my

composure and returned to the waiting room. 'Why don't you come on back? I'm sorry for the late start.'

My last appointment of the day was scheduled to begin at five o'clock. I took a deep breath, reassured myself that the finish line of my day's therapy marathon was only forty-five minutes away, and made the stroll down the hallway. Once again, though, I found two people, not one, waiting for me.

One was my five o'clock. She was a thirty-eight-year-old woman whom I'd successfully helped with depression a year before, but who was back in my care to try to stave off a recurrence of her profound melancholy after a recent diagnosis of breast cancer. She had a PIC line in her upper arm and was in the interlude between her first and second rounds of chemo. She was sitting in the waiting room with her hands folded in her lap, her eyes closed, meditating, I supposed, on some aspect of life's caprice.

At that moment my empathy for her was even more acute than usual.

The other person in my waiting room was my friend, Sam Purdy. He was dressed in his work clothes – in winter that meant a pair of aging wool trousers, a long-sleeved shirt, a tie that was loose at the collar, and a sport coat that Goodwill would have tossed into a rag pile had he tried to donate it. The jackets he wore were usually ill-fitting, but with his recent weight loss this coat was to his body what a bad slipcover was to a couch. That day, Sam's trousers were of recent vintage, as was his tie. For years Sam had owned so few neckties that I actually recognized them by their stains, but this one was new, and tasteful, and most surprising, appeared to be made of silk.

I suspected that Sam's new girlfriend had taken him shopping over New Year's. I also bet that he had a pair of silk boxers at home he didn't quite know what to do with.

Sam was reading the *New Yorker,* chuckling at a cartoon. When he looked up at me I made a querulous face at him. He shook his head just a little, flattened his mouth so that his lips disappeared under the umbrella of his mustache, and made a little 'everything's cool' gesture with his hand. The gesture closely resembled an insincere 'safe' call by a baseball umpire.

I made another querulous face.

He tapped his wristwatch.

I shrugged my shoulders and led the woman back to my office.

Forty-five minutes later my patient departed and I retraced my steps to the waiting room. Sam was asleep on his chair. A half-dozen magazines were in a heap at his feet.

'Hey, Sam,' I said.

He didn't reply.

'Sam,' I tried, a little louder.

He still didn't say anything.

An image of Hannah Grant's dead body splayed over the leather cube flashed into my mind with Technicolor brilliance. I said, 'Oh shit,' and rushed across the room.

'Got you,' he said with a sudden smile. The stubble of his beard told me it had been many hours since he'd scraped his face with a razor. He was probably as tired as I was.

'You ass,' I said. 'What are you doing here?'

'I come by sometimes just to catch up on my magazine reading. You guys have good stuff. Not like my dentist's office. You should see the crap he keeps around.'

I made a skeptical face.

He stood up. 'I'm buying you dinner,' he said. 'Come on.'

'Sam, Lauren's expecting me to—'

'No, she's not. I already cleared it with her. You have a free go-out-with-the-boys pass for the evening.'

'Yeah?' I was suspicious.

'Yeah.'

'We walking or driving?'

'We be walking.'

Although it was a cold night for a stroll, we hiked to the far side of the Pearl Street Mall toward the Sunflower Restaurant. Before Sam's heart attack I doubted that he'd ever set foot inside the organic oasis that was the Sunflower, and I was more than a little suspicious that he'd chosen it for a meal for the two of us, but I kept my apprehension to myself. Things definitely weren't what they seemed, so an out-of-the-ordinary restaurant fit right in. We spent the few-block hike catching up on kid talk. Sam was moaning that Simon was making both his parents nuts trying to juggle his hockey and snowboarding schedules, but I could tell that Sam was actually pretty happy about the logistical craziness his son's activities were precipitating.

He declined the hostess's first offer of a table, which was prime territory smack in the middle of the dining room, and instead asked for a booth in the distant corner. Once we were led to his preferred suburban outpost, he took the bench that was facing the big room; I was left with a view of a brick wall that was adorned with a large, quasi-erotic photograph of young eggplants and ripe figs. For some reason I found myself thinking of D. H. Lawrence and Alan Bates.

Then I got it: My association was to the cinematic version of *Women in Love*. I smiled at the memory, and stole another gratuitous glance at the figs. 'What is this, really?' I asked.

'Sherry has Simon. I wanted to spend some quality time with you.'

'Yeah? At the Sunflower? You really expect me to believe that?'

'I'm hurt,' he said, investing all of his energy in the menu. 'Can't even do a nice gesture for a friend. What are you hungry for? Look' – he pointed at the entrée list – 'everything here's free range and wild and shit. Has to make you happy.'

'How's Carmen?' I asked, temporarily giving up on my quest to discover the purpose of the meeting. I wasn't in a hurry; I knew we'd get there eventually. 'She buy you that tie?'

Sam looked up and flicked a quick glance at the dining room. I thought I saw him nod his head just the smallest amount.

I had to resist turning and taking a look for myself. Suddenly, Darrell Olson was at my side. Two seconds later, Jaris Slocum was standing right behind him.

42

'Hi, guys,' Sam said to the two detectives. He didn't feign surprise. I had to give him credit for that.

I glared at Sam. He made the same little hey-everything's-copacetic face and did the same hey-everything's-cool hand gesture that he'd thrown at me back in my waiting room while I was trying to figure out why he was camping out reading magazines.

'Make some room,' he said to me.

I slid over and was immediately pinned against the wall, with no chance of escape, by Darrell Olson.

Sam and Jaris Slocum – their chests and shoulders were much broader than mine and Darrell's – totally filled the space on the other side of the table. A waitress came by and took our drink order. Apparently sensing the tension at the table, she skipped any flirtation and kept her smile under wraps. We all ordered beer. Four different brands. Just another way of shouting out that we weren't a bunch of buddies sharing a pitcher.

'You guys hungry?' Sam asked.

'You bet,' Darrell said. 'I love this place.'

One mystery solved: Darrell had chosen the restaurant. I slid my menu toward him. My own appetite was wavering. While glaring at Sam, I asked, 'What's this about? You should check with my attorney if you want another interview, Detective Slocum. We shouldn't even—'

He snapped back. 'I know exactly what—'

Sam interrupted Slocum's interruption. He said, 'Call him Jaris, Alan. We're all friends here.'

What?

Slocum tried again. 'I'm perfectly aware that I need to go through your attorney to discuss . . . that other matter. I'm always eager for a chance to chat with Mr. Maitlin. But Darrell and I aren't here to talk about Hannah Grant.'

I might have been offended by the gratuitous sarcasm about Cozy if I wasn't still stuck on Sam's announcement that 'We're all friends here.' *Since when? And if we're not here to talk about Hannah, what the hell are we here to talk about?* At that moment I thought of Bob Brandt, and to no one in particular said, 'It's your move.'

'Hey, allow me,' Sam said. 'This little party was my idea.'

I thought my narrowed eyes and tight brow aptly communicated to Sam that I didn't approve of any of the choreography he'd put into his soiree so far.

'A little background to start,' he said, sticking to the charade that we were all just friends having a beer and sharing some crispy tofu triangles. 'Jaris and Darrell had a piece of the Mallory Miller investigation. Lucy and I were doing time line. They were assigned to follow up a couple of potentially promising leads: one being the empty house next door – the one that's for sale – and two being the possibility that the girl somehow ended up with her mother.'

'This is all about Mallory, then?' I asked. Despite my skepticism, I knew my question was evidence of capitulation on my part. I should have been throwing money on the table for my beer and walking full speed away from the three Boulder cops.

'A little patience, maybe?' Sam said. The drinks arrived. Sam waited until the waitress was gone again before he continued. 'I was thinking about the conversations you and I had, you know, about the guy with the car, that classic Camaro, and about the house next door to the Millers' with the waterfalls and shit, and about your friend, Dr. Estevez, and what happened to her in Las Vegas.'

Darrell said, 'Sam came to us. We heard his thoughts and started wondering whether there might be some connection, something that tied things together.'

'Some connection?' I asked, even more skeptically than before. I already feared a connection among Bob and Mallory and Diane, and I was beyond skeptical that I was hearing about this from Darrell Olson and Jaris Slocum.

'Yeah,' said Slocum.

As far as I was concerned he was nothing more than a punk with a shield. 'I'm uncomfortable with this,' I said, trying hard not to sound petulant. Sam's expression told me that I hadn't quite succeeded. I felt as though all the confidential information that I'd been trying to guard about my patients was in a balloon hovering above the table, and that each of the three detectives was dimpling the latex with the point of a saber.

The worst part? I knew I'd gotten myself into this one by trying to finesse the confidentiality rules with Sam.

'Hear us out,' Sam said.

Slocum's mug of beer was almost gone. He'd either been real thirsty, or he was real anxious. He looked toward our waitress and raised the mug and his eyebrows. He wanted a refill.

Darrell said, 'We didn't know about the guy with the

car. The one who rents the garage next door to the Millers. That was news to us. It could be an important piece of information. We should have picked up on it, but it slipped through the cracks.'

I glared at Sam. 'Slipped through the cracks, huh?'

Slocum picked up from there. 'And the fact that your friend disappeared in Las Vegas? That's curious to us, too.'

'Curious?'

'Well, worrisome, of course, but curious, too. Given the circumstances.'

'What circumstances are those?' I asked.

'Everything,' Slocum replied.

'Everything?'

'Yeah.'

I found that I liked him almost as much now that we were all friends having beers and I was calling him 'Jaris' as I had when he was ordering me around outside Hannah Grant's office and I was calling him 'Detective.' I said, 'For old times' sake, Jaris, treat me like you treated me at Hannah's office. You know, like an idiot citizen. Tell me what "everything" means.'

'Alan,' Sam said.

I remained unconvinced about the announced agenda for this impromptu meeting. 'We're not talking in code about Hannah Grant right now? You're all sure about that? If we are, my lawyer's probably not going to be too happy about it. Come to think about it, neither will my wife.' I don't know why I threw in the part about Lauren. It was petty, but then so was my state of mind.

Darrell held up a hand to shush Sam. He said, 'Let me, Sam, please.' Darrell was using the conciliator's voice that I'd heard him try on with Slocum and later with Cozy Maitlin the night that we found Hannah's body. I suspected that Darrell had been a conciliator at least as long as he'd known how to ride a two-wheeler, and that his initial mediating role had been to intervene before his argumentative parents ripped the flesh from each other's throats.

'Alan – we didn't get off to a good start with you and Dr. Estevez last month – Jaris and I didn't. Water under the bridge, right? Is that okay? Because based on what Sam's been able to tell us, it sounds like both you and her might have something to do with another situation we're working.' He lowered his voice here, and leaned closer to me. 'Yes, I'm talking about Mallory. Now, it may just all be coincidence. That's always possible. But it's also possible that everything's related.'

I couldn't resist a jab. 'If it turns out that everything's related, it sounds like you and Detective Slocum – Jaris – might have missed some important details during your initial investigations.'

Sam said, 'I'm not sure that's helpful, Alan.'

I turned on him. My tone was level. My words? Not as much. 'And you're the best judge of that, Sam? Of what's helpful? Please. He' – I pointed at Slocum – 'roughed up Diane last month for no reason other than that he'd had a bad day or his feelings were hurt or God knows what else, and now he wants to have a nice dinner with me and down a few beers and he thinks I'll just bow down and help him cover up his mistakes on the' – I caught myself and lowered my voice to a coarse whisper – 'Mallory Miller fiasco. Because what I think this is about is ass-covering.'

Slocum's face was red. He raised his glass and drained the dregs from the bottom of his first beer – a version of counting to ten to calm himself down, I thought – before he said, 'I'm guessing you need help finding her. Not to mention the guy with the old Camaro. Him, too. I don't expect you to like me – to be honest, I don't give a shit – but I'm willing to try to find these people. You want to work something out, or not? Your choice. I don't have time for your sissy-ass games.'

Sissy-ass games? I supposed that meant that Jaris and I were no longer friends. 'What can you do to help? Last time I looked, Las Vegas was in Nevada.'

Sam sighed loudly. I thought he was expressing relief that most of the cards were finally on the table.

The waitress chose that moment to return with Jaris's second beer. She dropped it off in record time and withdrew as though she'd just remembered she'd left the water running in her bathtub.

'If we reach out from here,' Darrell said as she retreated, 'the Las Vegas police maybe show a little more interest in trying to find out what happened to her. I suspect that could make a significant difference. The current situation – an out-of-state husband who can't find his wife for a couple of days – probably isn't creating a lot of investigative curiosity in Sin City.'

Of course he was right. I asked, 'And the other guy? The one with the Camaro? How are you going to help with him?'

'One phone call – and one BOLO later – every cop in the state will have an eye peeled for that car,' Jaris said.

I hadn't touched my beer. I picked it up and took a long, slow sip. 'On what pretense?' I asked.

Across the table, Slocum had already finished half of his second mug. Sam spied Jaris getting ready to jump back into the fray and decided to run interference. He said, 'That's our problem. We'll come up with one. It's not as hard as you might think. By the way, BOLO is be-on-the-look—'

'I know what a BOLO is,' I snapped, almost spitting my beer. 'So what do you want from me, Jaris?'

Sam wasn't done orchestrating. 'What do you say let's order first, okay? I don't know about the rest of you, but I'm starving here. Darrell, what's good? Think I'd like the tempeh cutlets?'

Sam's tempeh question was theater-of-the-absurd offered purely for my benefit. Tempeh was so far outside the boundaries of Sam's comfort universe that Hubble couldn't have spotted it.

Sam was thinking that he'd won, and he was pretty darn proud of himself.

43

We'd almost completed a totally silent trek from the Sunflower back up the Mall to my office when he said, 'You wouldn't have come out with me if I'd told you what I was up to.'

'Damn right,' I said.

A few more steps of silence followed. Then, without the slightest bit of animosity in his voice, Sam added, 'You should get off your high horse, see what the world looks like from down here with the rest of us.'

'And what the hell is that supposed to mean?' I wasn't as careful as Sam was about keeping the animosity out of my voice.

'Your cherished position in life – you know, psych-*o*-therapist, guardian of all the world's secrets – it's not as special as you think it is. You're just a damn guy doing a damn job. You have trusts to keep. Well, surprise, surprise, other people do, too. Other people take their responsibilities as seriously as you do.

'Me? Tonight? It turns out I saw a way to get Diane some help for whatever mess she's in. I saw a way to get some serious eyeballs out looking for the guy in the Camaro. You wanted me to find a hook for all this. Well, I found one. The way I see it, call me naive, but no blood gets spilled by my strategy. A few people have to swallow some pride – yeah, you included – but so the fuck what? You think this was an easy meeting for Jaris? The guy has his hands full; trust me on that.'

I was inclined to say that I didn't give a ferret fart whether or not it had been a pleasant meeting for Jaris, but I didn't.

Sam had his hands in his pockets and was looking down at the sidewalk as we talked. At Ninth he led us off the curb without looking for traffic in both directions. In half a second a guy heading north on a bike almost creamed him. If the man hadn't screamed a profanity in warning, I'm not sure Sam would have ever noticed.

Even with the profanity, he seemed unfazed. He muttered, 'Too cold for a bike.'

We started up Walnut toward my office. As we passed the building that was the second or third incarnation of one of Boulder's legendary breakfast houses, Sam said, 'I miss Nancy's. Those herb cheese omelettes? They were something. Lucile's is great, but I miss Nancy's.'

'Me, too.' After three or four more steps, I added, 'You're right, Sam.'

'About Nancy's? Course I am.'

I hadn't been talking about Nancy's, but he was right about that, too. 'Wonderful biscuits. Remember those biscuits? But I meant that you're right about what you said.'

'I know that, too.' He exhaled audibly. 'The fact that you admit it doesn't change anything, doesn't mean that what happens next is going to be what you want to happen next, or even that what happens next is what I want to happen next. All that's different now is that some people who care about the jobs they do are going to try to find some of these missing people.' He pulled his right hand from his pocket and yanked at the knot on his tie. 'How bad a thing can that be?'

He was right.

'I'm sorry,' I said.

'For what?'

'For being an asshole.'

'You mean a sissy-ass?'

I laughed. 'That, too.'

'Hey,' he said.

And that was that.

Almost a block later he climbed into the cradle of the driver's seat of his Cherokee. 'Carmen likes to buy me clothes,' he said.

It took me a moment to realize that Sam was revisiting the conversation we'd been having in the restaurant at the precise moment when Slocum and Olson ambushed me. I had just asked him about his tie. 'I figured,' I said.

'What do you think?'

'About the new threads?' I asked. 'Or about the fact that Carmen likes to buy them for you?'

Sam shook his head gently, and I could hear the throaty tang of a little chuckle come out of the darkness. 'See, that's the thing. I don't know one other guy who would ask me that question. Not one. And that's why I'm okay with the fact that you're an asshole sometimes.'

'Goodnight, Sam. Thanks.'

I was halfway home before I realized that I'd spaced out telling Sam about my visit to Doyle's house with the Realtor the previous night.

44

My girls were sleeping in separate beds when I got home. The dogs were squirrelly though, and I had to spend ten minutes outside with them before I could get them settled. Emily detected the scent of a critter of some kind while we were walking the lane and once we were back in the door she strolled the entire perimeter of the interior of the upstairs of the house checking to see if an unseen enemy had succeeded in breaching our defenses. Ultimately confident that all of our flanks were protected, she plopped at my feet with a satisfied sigh.

The entire house shook when she landed.

I was thinking about calling Sam to get his inevitable rage over my visit to Doyle's house out of the way, when the phone rang.

I pounced on it: Raoul.

'I'm starting to get somewhere. Couple of pieces,' Raoul said.

His tone told me that he hadn't found Diane, so I didn't ask. His words told me that he wanted to confront the practical, so I refrained from asking the question that was second on my list: *How are you doing with all this?* Instead, I said, 'What do you have?'

Raoul started with bad news, not, in my mind, a good

sign. 'Marlina's a dead end. The woman from Venetian security? One more meal with her tomorrow, and I'm done. I know exactly why the woman's been divorced twice though I still haven't figured out how she got married twice. She's playing me.'

'Okay, then what pieces do you have?'

'Two. The guy from the craps table? The shopping center developer who was playing craps at the same table as Diane? He finally called me this morning, told me he'd been drunk when I phoned him and he'd forgotten to call me back. He was cleaning out the memory on his mobile and saw my number. Anyway, he said that Diane was his luck at the craps table that night and when she cashed out, he decided to do the same. He said he was right behind her as she was walking through the casino.'

'Sounds kind of creepy.'

'*Sí*. He says as Diane's walking across the casino, two guys walk up to her, say hello. Pretty well dressed. Both of them forty to fifty. One tall, one average. One of them whispered something to her. She seemed happy to hear it and the three of them walked on together, talking. She had her phone in her hand, dropped it trying to shake hands with one of the guys. He picked it up and she stuffed it in her purse. One of the two reached around behind Diane, took the phone right back out of her bag, and tossed it on the floor by a row of slot machines. He said the guy was smooth; he picked Diane like a pro. Until the man dumped her phone, the guy from the craps table thought one of the two guys was Diane's husband, or boyfriend.'

'Fits with what I remember, Raoul.' I paused before I added, 'The guy from the craps table was going to hit on her, wasn't he? That's why he was following her?'

'Yes,' said Raoul without any animosity. He understood these things.

'So that was it? He never reported this to anyone?'

'He said that Diane didn't seem to be in any distress. The phone thing was odd, but she went with them voluntarily.'

'But he doesn't know where they went?'

'They were walking in the direction of the lobby, but he didn't follow them out of the casino. He went up to his room.'

'What are you thinking?' I asked.

'I'm thinking what he said to her had something to do with Rachel Miller. That's why she went with them – she thought she was going to get a chance to talk with Rachel.'

'That's what I'm thinking, too.' I paused for a moment. 'Somebody must have picked the phone up off the floor and put it in the tray of the slot machine where that drunk woman found it.'

'It also explains why Venetian security isn't too eager to let me see the surveillance tape. Probably looks a lot like a rendezvous to them. You know, something between . . . adults.'

'But they must have a picture of these two guys, right?'

'Right. You can't walk out of a casino without a camera seeing you. No way.'

'You said you have a couple of pieces of news. What's the other one?'

'Norm Clarke came through. I should've called him the first day I got here. I can be such a putz.'

I was surprised – no, shocked – at the Yiddish. I didn't know it was part of Raoul's language repertoire. I grabbed a beer from the kitchen so I could sit down and listen to his story about Norm Clarke.

Any good big-city daily newspaper that doesn't take itself

too seriously has one, though few are fortunate enough to have that special one that becomes a silk thread in the urban fabric. San Francisco had Herb Caen. Denver has had Bill Husted for as long as I can remember.

What's their role? Gossip columnist? Man about town? If they're good, the phrases don't do them justice. These guys, and a few gals, take the pulse on their city. They tell the rest of us what happens behind closed doors, what happens after the bars close, what's new, what's old, what's coming next. They invite us to the city's water cooler for the latest gossip on the movers and shakers, and they whisper the latest dish over the city's backyard fence. They're the ones who know what local boy has done good, and what local girl has gone bad. What famous visitor has been spotted where, doing what, with whom.

Las Vegas's version was Norm Clarke.

Norm had briefly gone head-to-head with Husted back in Colorado, scrounging the usually dull Front Range of the Rockies for paltry scoops, but years before he'd moved on to ply his trade at the *Review Journal* in the much more fertile gossip terrain of Las Vegas. By all the reports that made their way back across the Great Basin and the Rocky Mountains to Denver, Norm soon owned his adopted town.

He knew everybody in Vegas, had spies everywhere, had eaten at every now table, could get backstage at any show, and was escorted to the front of the line and past the velvet rope at any trendy club. After a few years in the desert Norm had, literally, written the book on Las Vegas, and was always busy taking notes for the next edition. His mug, and his column, graced the front page of the paper every weekend.

Celebrities weren't really in Vegas until Norm said they were in Vegas. Some begged him for ink. A few had managers and publicists call and beg him to please, please, please forget what he had seen or heard.

Back in his days at the *Rocky Mountain News,* Norm had done a feature on Raoul, and on Raoul's golden touch incubating Boulder tech companies during the heady days of the early 1990s. Raoul, who generally despised publicity, thought the piece was on the money, and he and Norm had become casual friends. They'd stayed in touch over the years even as each of their lives grew more complicated.

When Raoul called Norm asking for help in finding Diane, he was asking Norm to do something that Norm wasn't often asked to do: He was asking him to keep a secret.

Raoul's first sit-down with Norm had taken place almost twenty-four hours before in one of the many bars that dot the expansive, expensive acreage on the main floor of the Venetian. After some pleasantries Raoul had told Norm that he had a personal favor to ask, and asked Norm if he could speak off the record. Raoul proceeded to provide only the Vegas pieces of the puzzle: that Diane was in town to talk to a patient's mother, which was as good an excuse as she needed to spend some time playing a little middling-stakes craps. On Monday evening Diane had been talking to a friend on her cell while walking through the Venetian casino, and hadn't been heard from since. She'd disappeared. Hadn't returned to her hotel room. Hadn't called anyone. Nothing.

Earlier in the day she disappeared, Diane had tried to track down the patient's mother and had ended up at the Love In Las Vegas Wedding Chapel out on Las Vegas Boulevard, where she'd apparently located someone named Rachel Miller – yeah, Raoul told Norm, *that*

Rachel Miller – but Raoul hadn't been successful finding her. Raoul also told Norm about his conversation with Reverend Howie at the Love In Las Vegas and about Howie's suggestion that Rachel could possibly be tracked down through an intermediary – a man, someone who apparently made Howie shake in his Savile Row boots. Somebody scary.

Norm admitted to Raoul that he didn't have a clue about the intermediary's identity, but that he suspected the man didn't inhabit the part of Las Vegas that typically interested his column's readers.

'But . . .' Raoul had said, sensing something.

'But,' Norm had added quickly, 'I think I know somebody who might be able to help.'

The way Raoul told it to me later, he and Norm met again at almost exactly the same time that I was finishing my meal with Sam, Darrell, and my new buddy Jaris at the Sunflower in downtown Boulder.

Norm was on the clock getting ready to chronicle for his column which of-the-moment celebrities were really going to show up at some cocktail-hour charity-do at one of the trendiest of the city's many trendoid restaurants, this one high in the newest tower of the Mandalay Bay. A setup crew was bustling around the still-vacant space, frantically arranging the tiers of a gorgeous raw bar, and test-fitting the blown-glass platters that would soon be heaped with gleaming shellfish, sushi, sashimi, and maki.

Raoul joined Norm at a corner table that had a stunning view of the Strip's neon at dusk. The table in front of Norm was naked except for his ubiquitous mobile phone, a longneck Coors Light that was almost full, and a couple of paper cocktail napkins on which Norm was scribbling notes with a felt-tip pen.

Norm looked up and said, 'Raoul, hi. Any luck?'

Raoul shook his head as he sat down.

Norm asked, 'You want a drink?'

'No, thank you.'

Norm slid the beer aside and leaned forward. 'I didn't think you'd have good news. Especially given what I found out about the guy you're looking for. You ready? His name is Ulysses Paul North. That's U – P – North. Or . . . Up, North. On the street they call him Canada.'

Raoul took a second to pull it all together, then he couldn't help himself: He smiled. 'Up North? Canada? Really?'

Norm smiled, too. He held up his hand like a Boy Scout taking an oath. 'I'm good, but I couldn't make that up.' Norm's grin caused his cheekbones to levitate – just a tiny bit – and that motion caused the distinctive black, flat crescent patch that always covered his right eye to rise.

Raoul said, 'There's more, yes?'

'There's more. Canada's a facilitator, apparently. A street facilitator of some kind.' Norm sipped from his beer. 'If this place were Hollywood' – he gazed down at the flashing neon skyline of ersatz New York, and the ejaculating fountains at the Bellagio, and the distant faux icons of Egypt and Paris and Venice – 'and if Canada's people were movie stars, he'd probably be called a manager. But this is definitely not Hollywood, and Canada's clients are, well, definitely not movie stars, so there's not exactly a name I know of for exactly what he does.'

'He's not a pimp?'

'No. He probably counts some pimps and prostitutes among his . . . clients.'

'He's not muscle, protection?'

'Not in any conventional sense. But should the need arise, he has all the muscle he might want. That's what I'm told.'

'I assume he gets a percentage of—'

'He does. I was told he advises his . . . clients – I'm sorry, I keep stumbling over that word – on business matters, helps them formulate strategic plans. I swear; that's the party line. He intervenes only when necessary. Tries to keep turf fights in his territory to a minimum. Settles occasional disputes. For those services, he is paid a percentage of his clients' . . . proceeds.'

'The clients are crooks?'

Norm took a moment before he decided how to reply. 'Let's say they don't report their income to the IRS.'

'And Canada's a scary enough man to do this . . . job?'

'He is known to be ruthless when necessary. And sometimes more, when he needs to make a point.'

'Your source knows him?'

'Of him.'

Raoul sat back. 'You have contacts everywhere.' He intended it as a compliment, and as a question. Norm read it both ways.

'Everywhere I can. To do my job for the paper, I need all the eyes I can find.' He gestured over his shoulder. 'When nobody knew where Jacko was after his indictment, I found him. When Britney got married for ten minutes, I knew about it before her mother did. Roy Horn after the tiger mauled him? I knew things his nurses didn't know about how he was doing.

'Tonight? One of the busboys here is going to tell me exactly who shows up for this shindig. Sometimes it's a host who helps me, occasionally a chef. Some of my best sources are people on the fringes of the A-list. They get invited to the hot parties, then tell me who else is there. Rule number one in this business: Everybody knows somebody.'

'And one of them knows how I can find this Canada?'

‘You won’t find Canada. He doesn’t like to be found by people outside his orbit. But if you would like, the man who’s talking to me will pass the word along on the street that you would like to speak with him. That’s how it works, apparently.’ Norm shrugged, a gesture that at once apologized for the melodrama and acknowledged that the show was totally out of his control.

Raoul sat back. ‘Canada is what? Nevada’s answer to Osama? I get a canvas bag on my head and get driven out to a cave somewhere in the desert?’

Norm’s face remained impassive. ‘I’m a reporter; I don’t make this stuff up. I’d never heard of this guy before today. Odds are I’ll never hear about him again after today. This is North Vegas stuff. It’s way off my beat.’

‘But you trust your guy? Your source?’

Norm took a long pull from his Coors Light. ‘I work hard to write my column. It’s not a party. To do this right, I have to have great instincts, I have to hustle, and I have to have a good bullshit detector, or I end up becoming a joke. I don’t get them all right, Raoul, but I get almost all of them right. My gut says I have this one right.

‘I grew up in a middle-of-nowhere town in Montana. Small-world time: Turns out a guy I went to high school with is part of the North Vegas street life. I tracked him down after his photo showed up in the paper one day with a story on the homeless. He’s my source on this. He has no reason to lie to me, and it was pretty clear to me that he’s honestly afraid of this guy Canada. He would much rather have been telling me that he knew where I could get serviced by the Pope’s favorite hooker.’

Raoul pondered for a few seconds. ‘This man you know? Did he tell you anything about Rachel?’

Norm shook his head.

‘Diane?’

'No. I'm sorry.'

Norm's cell phone rang. He excused himself to Raoul. 'Sorry, I have to get this. I'm waiting for a confirmation about an item for tomorrow's column. That thing at The Palms.' He opened the phone. 'Hello.'

Raoul didn't know about the thing at The Palms, and preferred it that way. He'd read it fresh in Norm's column the next morning.

Norm listened for a moment, stood up from the table, faced the window, and said, 'Of course, yes.' He listened for a longer period, almost a full minute, before he said, 'He's with me right now.' Beat. 'Okay, you know that . . . You want me to ask him?'

Norm set the phone on the table between himself and Raoul. He nodded at it and with an extended thumb and pinky held up to his face, he mimed that the telephone conversation was continuing.

'It's one of Canada's . . . people. If you agree to leave the police out of this, totally out of this, Canada will talk with you.'

In a heartbeat Raoul said, 'Agreed. Is my wife safe? Can he tell me that? Please?'

Norm shrugged. He didn't know the answer. He picked up the phone and placed it against his ear. 'You heard?' he said. Norm listened some more, nodding, and finally added, 'It shouldn't be a problem. He'll be there.' Norm folded his phone shut.

'I'll be where?' Raoul asked.

'The tram platform at the Luxor at seven o'clock. That's only twenty minutes from now.'

'Is it far?'

'If we could get a real good running start, and if we could jump out those windows over there, we could probably land on it. But from way up here, without flying? It'll take us most of that twenty minutes to get over there.'

'You know the way?'

Norm stood up. 'Of course.'

Raoul threw twenty dollars on the table and they ran.

'We had to hustle,' Raoul said to me. 'Down the elevator, all the way across the casino, which is like the size of Luxembourg, over to the monorail station. Wait for the train, get onto the train, ride it over to the Luxor. It's a turtle. The thing moves so slowly, you wonder why they bothered to build it. My mother has a cane; she walks faster than the damn tram moves. We finally made it to the platform with only a couple of minutes to spare.'

He stopped.

'And?' I asked.

'And nothing. We stood there for half an hour. Nothing. Nobody. Trains came, trains left. Nothing.'

'Nobody met you?'

'No.'

'Now what?'

'I don't know,' Raoul said. 'I suppose I'll continue to try to reach out to Canada some other way.'

I'd grown increasingly discomfited listening to Raoul's recanting of his meeting with Norm Clarke, especially the parts about the man called Canada. I stood up and began to pace in front of the big windows that faced the mountains. My movement caused Emily to stir. She was so exhausted that it appeared as though the simple act of lifting her big head to see what I was up to required a monumental effort.

'When I got back here a little bit ago?' Raoul said.

'Yes.'

'Marlina had dropped off an envelope. A single grainy screen shot from the casino security tape. Diane with the two guys who walked her out of the casino. They're all in profile.'

'How does she look?'

'Fine.'

'Any idea who they are?'

'No.'

'It's something, right?'

'It's something.'

'Raoul, I have some news that I originally thought was good news, but may now be bad news.'

'What?'

'The Boulder police are involved. They're asking the Las Vegas police to take Diane's disappearance seriously.'

In my ear, I heard one of the familiar Catalonian profanities. Then he said, 'I'll have to call Norm, so he can tell Canada.'

45

What if this is why she died? . . . What if somebody killed Hannah because she met with Mallory that one time?

As my head hit the pillow and I tried to find the sanctuary of sleep, Diane's original conspiracy theory about Hannah Grant's death – a hypothesis I recalled I'd dismissed out of hand at the time – bounced back and forth inside my skull like the digitized ball in a game of Pong.

What if this is why she died? . . . What if somebody killed Hannah because she met with Mallory that one time?

It didn't take long for my sleep-depriving musing to move on to cover fresh ground: If Diane had been right, and Hannah had been murdered because of something she'd learned from Mallory, could Diane and Bob somehow have suffered the same fate, too?

I shuddered at the thought.

The links were there. Diane had consulted with Hannah about Mallory; Bob had talked to Mallory across the backyard fence.

It was a far-fetched stretch, but could everything – Hannah's death, Mallory's disappearance, Diane's disappearance, and Bob's disappearance – really be related? Could some immense ball have started rolling the

December afternoon that Mallory decided she just had to see Hannah Grant?

But why?

And how?

I gave up on sleeping and stumbled back out to the living room in search of a common denominator.

If Diane's theory was true, there had to be a secret in the Miller household. Something that Mallory had revealed during her single session with Hannah. Or at least something that someone thought she'd revealed.

What was it?

During that week after Christmas, the week after Mallory disappeared, Diane had said, *'She said her father was "up to something," remember?'*

So what had Bill Miller been up to?

Had he been up to something at home? At work? Planning a career change? Planning a major change in his parenting?

And why, I wondered, was Bill Miller so curious as to why I had been at Doyle's house?

Yeah, why?

During the psychotherapy session I'd had with Bill Miller earlier that day, I'd been so busy feeling guilty about being caught snooping around at Doyle's house that I'd missed the obvious: Why had Bill Miller been so damn curious about the fact that I'd been looking at the house that was for sale next door?

46

I woke Sam. He wasn't happy that I woke him. Once we managed to blunder past his unhappiness I began to explain to him why I'd interrupted his sleep. I tried to ease into it but his impatience forced me to admit earlier in the conversation than I wanted to that I had been inside Doyle's house. 'I pretended I was interested in buying the house; I got the agent to show it to me last night after work.'

'You woke me up to talk real estate?'

For a long moment he'd fooled me; I'd thought he'd sounded genuinely befuddled. 'Sam, please. That house is at the center of something. It is.'

He wasn't done poking at me. 'You liked it? I found it overpriced, personally. Kitchen's hardly bigger than mine. I don't think Lauren would go for it, anyway. She'd be fretting about Grace and all that water in the backyard. And that bridge? With a toddler? Alan, you'd never have a moment's peace.'

'Come on, Sam.'

'Okay, okay. Just remember that you're the one who woke me up. So why did you feel this compelling need to sneak into the house next door to the Millers? It's an empty friggin' house. We've been in there.'

'Given all that's happened, it seemed important to see it. I have this feeling that the Millers' neighbor is key to all this.'

'All what?'

'Everything. Mallory, Diane, the guy Bob with the Camaro. The BOLO? Why are all these people missing, Sam? Three people are missing. Don't you wonder about that? I mean, even—' I almost said, 'Even Hannah Grant,' but I caught myself. The only link I could make to Hannah in all this was through Diane, and that wasn't my privilege to abrogate.

'Three people are missing? Could be two. Could be one. Could be zero. But assuming I buy your premise that three people are missing, what does the neighbor's house have to do with Diane?' Sam asked.

Sam wasn't easily tricked. My obfuscation-by-shotgun-blast hadn't fooled him for long. I stammered, 'I don't know. That part is once removed. But there's a connection, there is. I can feel it.'

'Once removed? What the hell does that mean?'

'I can't say.'

He sighed. 'You were about to say something else. You said, "even" and you stopped. Even what?'

'Everything.' Lame, but it was the best that I could do. 'I was talking about everything.'

Sam yawned. 'You know something else, right? Don't you? Something you can't tell me?'

I didn't hesitate. I said, 'I do.'

'Fuck,' he muttered. 'What's the point in talking to you about stuff like this? It's all riddles. It's like trying to get a politician to tell you what he really thinks.' I took some solace that Sam's profanity had been mumbled and dull, and not sharply carved and poison-tipped. 'I can't start an investigation because you have some confidentiality bee in your butt, Alan. You know that. You do. We've been here before.'

'What about the snow thing?'

'Dear Lord, not the snow thing again.'

'Have you guys thought about those lines that you can string between trees and stuff? What are they called? What if they strung those between Mallory's house and Doyle's? What if they did that? What if that's how she got out of her house without leaving any footprints?'

'A patient feed you this? She slid down one of those lines? That's your latest theory? Are you nuts?'

Hearing it out loud, it sounded silly. All I was able to say was, 'No. Maybe.' Sam had no way to know I'd answered his questions in order, skipping the second one and the final one.

'Why?' Sam asked.

'Why what?'

'If she's running away, why would she care if she got out of the house without leaving any footprints? Why go to all that trouble? She didn't know when the snow was going to start and stop; she didn't know Fox was going to have a helicopter overhead. She's a kid. If she runs, she runs. Everything else is crap and you know it.'

I hadn't thought of questioning what motivation Mallory might have for trying to leave no trail behind – it was definitely an oversight in my thinking – but I found myself relieved that Sam was using the present tense to describe Mallory.

Sam wasn't done. 'Before, you said, "They"? Who's "they"?'

'The neighbor and . . .'

'Mallory? Come on? They were in this together? Now you're talking some conspiracy, right? Alan, I'll forgive you for calling. It's late. I know you're upset about your friend.'

'Sam—'

'We searched the house. We talked to the neighbor. Nothing came of it. Let it go.'

'Remember when we were in the yard and someone was watching us from the upstairs window?'

'Yeah?'

'Well, why? Why was he watching us?'

'He?'

Sam was sharper three minutes after being woken from a sound sleep than I was at the end of a long day. 'Has to be a he, right? It's only Bill and his son who live there.'

'The Millers aren't allowed to have guests? I didn't know that. Boulder and its laws? Wouldn't want to be a cop here – be arresting people for farting on the wrong side of the street.'

We'd moved from amused incredulity to aggravated sarcasm. Where Sam was concerned, that wasn't a healthy progression. With some defensiveness creeping into my voice, I said, 'I think it was a he.'

'Then what did you mean when you asked "why?" What's the big deal about somebody watching you from his own bedroom window? Maybe it was a neighborhood watch thing and Bill Miller's the block captain. Who the hell knows? It's not a crime to spy on your neighbor's yard. We'd have to arrest half the old ladies in town if it was.'

'Did you talk to the neighbor yourself, Sam? You or Lucy?'

He forced patience into his voice. It was a tight fit. 'Lucy and I were doing other things. You know that.'

'It was Slocum, wasn't it?'

'Your point?'

'Talk to the neighbor yourself, please. I don't trust Slocum.'

'I thought Jaris behaved himself tonight.'

'Barely. He was nervous. And you and Darrell were watching everything he did. I still don't trust him.'

The silence that ensued suggested to me that Sam was considering saying something else about Jaris Slocum. He didn't. He said, 'You talk about this Camaro guy as though he's a victim. You considered that he may be mixed up in all this, like criminally?'

'It doesn't fit,' I said. 'Psychologically.'

'And in your world people never act out of character?'

Sam actually asked that question with only the slightest hint of sarcasm. 'Talk to the neighbor, Sam.'

'On what pretense do I do that?' he asked.

'You're looking for that Camaro. You wanted a hook? That's your hook. Now that the BOLO is out, you want to tie up a loose end. Slocum himself said he didn't know about the Camaro during the first interview. You just have to make a call, one call, maybe go have a chat with the guy who owns the house and the garage.'

Ten minutes later I crawled into bed and sprawled on my side, facing my wife. Silently, Lauren backed toward me until I could feel the warmth from her nighttime flesh on the front of my naked thighs. I'd almost drifted off to sleep when a fresh thought forced me to snap open my eyes in the dark.

Maybe the secret has to do with Rachel Miller, not with Mallory.

Maybe this is all about Rachel.

That's why Diane disappeared.

She knew something about Rachel. Or she was about to learn something about Rachel.

I climbed back out of bed, pulled on a pair of sweats, and used the kitchen phone to warn Raoul that when he'd walked into the Love In Las Vegas Wedding Chapel and met Reverend Howie he may have inadvertently walked into something that was extremely dangerous.

But Raoul didn't answer his hotel room phone at the Venetian.

He didn't answer his cell, either.

My next thought? Sam was going to kill me when I tried to explain Canada to him.

47

All I told Bill Miller on the phone was that I had some further questions that I needed to address before I could make a commitment to see him for ongoing psychotherapy. He readily agreed to come in on Friday morning. I never quite decided how surprised I was that Bill was so accommodating about meeting with me again on such short notice. My indecision, I was sure, was a product of the fact that more than twelve hours had passed and I still hadn't been able to track down Raoul in Las Vegas.

Lauren shared my dismay about Raoul's silence. The look she'd given me that morning when I slowed her down on the way to the bathroom to let her know Raoul wasn't answering his phone was like the look I might expect after I'd told her I'd not only lost my car keys but also managed to misplace the spare set, too. 'Diane *and* Raoul?' she'd said, finally. Before shutting the bathroom door behind her, she'd added, 'Find him, honey. Today would be good.'

Bill settled into the chair across from me and without any visible indications of concern, said, 'Shoot. I'm ready. Ask your questions. I'd love to get this whole thing settled.'

In typical shrink form, my question wasn't really just a

question. 'Thanks for being so flexible,' I said. 'I'd like to know more about your current relationship with your – is it ex-wife? – Rachel.'

'Well,' he said, sitting back on the chair. 'I didn't expect that one.' He wasted a moment picking at the crease on his perfectly pressed trousers.

I, of course, grew curious about what question he had expected. But I didn't ask him that. I waited.

'Rachel and I are separated, not . . . divorced. For some reason, I thought you knew that. I feel like I don't have any secrets anymore. We never went through the whole legal process. It just never felt . . . necessary to me. Or even appropriate. Given her difficulties, I couldn't just . . . You know the circumstances back then as well as anyone.'

Actually, not as well as Mary Black, I thought. 'Are you legally separated?'

Bill struggled to find the right word before he settled on, 'Rachel is my wife.'

'And the nature of your current relationship?'

He shifted on his chair, crossing his legs, left ankle over right knee. He took a moment to make certain that his cuff was adequately shading the top of his sock. I wasn't sure he was going to answer my question at all, but he finally said, 'Rachel's in Las Vegas, still attending weddings, still delusional, still . . . psychotic. Sadly, that hasn't changed.' He paused. 'She moved there for the weddings. I'm sure you could have guessed that even if you hadn't heard about it. She still feels compelled to . . . There's no shortage of weddings in Las Vegas, that's for sure.'

Yes, I know. I know a lot about Reverend Howie and the Love In Las Vegas Wedding Chapel.

'And she's still suffering, that hasn't changed. She's still struggling with her illness, and . . . and with the medicines. She hates the medicines. She hates the new ones as much as she hated the old ones. Sometimes she takes them, more often she doesn't. They help when she takes them, but they don't solve anything. They're not a cure, not for her.' He exhaled through pursed lips. 'I hope you don't mind if I ask, but why is this important?'

I went into a matter-of-fact spiel about a psychologist's ethical burden to avoid dual relationships, and explained that it would be difficult for me, as a psychotherapist, to avoid them if I didn't even know they existed. My explanation was intentionally convoluted, but Bill seemed to buy it. I'd figured he would.

I'd counted on the fact that he would. My voice as level as a freshly plumbed door, I said, 'Bill, you still haven't told me about your current relationship with Rachel. That's the part that most concerns me.'

I thought his eyes narrowed at my use of the word 'concerns.' Maybe not. I wished I'd said 'interests.'

'Well,' he said, 'that's not exactly true, I said that . . .'

Bill's apparent predilection was to argue the point with me, but he changed his mind and seemed to decide that my statement was, in fact, accurate enough that he'd leave it alone.

'We're in touch,' he said. 'If you can call it that.'

No problem, I'll call it that. 'Go on,' I said.

'We talk about once a week. That's not true. I call Rachel once a week, but we probably only talk about twice a month.' He exhaled hard and grimaced. 'She doesn't call me . . . often. Sometimes I leave messages. And the truth is that even when I do reach her, I do most of the talking. I fill her in on what's going on here, with the family.

'She's, um . . . I still think that . . . You know, hope's not really the right word. But I have . . . I pray for . . .'

I watched fascinated as Bill's usual unshakable composure disintegrated before my eyes.

'Yes,' I said, nudging him on.

'Rachel always asks about the kids. Almost always, anyway. So often she's off in a different . . . you know. Her mind is in other places. The weddings. The brides, the grooms. Their families. It's always like she knows them, and that I know them, too. But usually she gets around to asking how the kids are doing, seems interested in what's going on with them. They don't get any older for her. They don't age. I don't know what else . . . to say.'

Although I would have preferred that Bill keep talking on his own without any prompting from me, I decided to go ahead and ask the money question – literally and figuratively. 'Do you still support her, Bill? I mean financially? How does she make ends meet? Given what you're describing right now, I can't see how she would be able to make a living, or even survive on public assistance.'

'Well . . .' he said, flustered by my latest query. 'I didn't think we were going to talk about this today. I don't see how it has much to do with your . . . ethical concerns.'

I waited. Why? I couldn't think of a thing to say.

'I pay the bills,' he said, sounding defiant. 'I pay the bills. It's something I want to do, I choose to do. I feel a . . . responsibility to her. On our wedding day, I said "till death do us part" and I meant it. My love for Rachel didn't end when she got sick. It didn't end when she decided she needed to live someplace where she could be closer to more weddings. I take my vows seriously. So, yes, I support her.'

Was there a little self-righteousness in his tone? Yes, there was. But the reality was that what Bill had been doing for his wife for almost a decade was extraordinary. Not too many men in the same circumstances would have done it. I was touched by his compassion and commitment.

'That must be a difficult burden for you,' I said.

'I don't look at it that way. Not financially, anyway. Emotionally, yes – it's hard. I miss . . . having my wife. There's been a hole in my heart since she left me. But financially? I look at it that . . . it's our money, Rachel's and mine, and that she needs some of it to live. That's all. Truth be told, I spend more of it than she does. I don't love her any less because she's ill. I tell myself that it could be worse.'

She could have cancer, I thought, ironically. *Hoho.*

Again, I waited.

'You can't tell anybody about this, right? I've never . . . admitted to anyone that I still support Rachel. I'm not sure people would understand.'

Understand? What, that you're a saint? Why is that such a secret?

'I can't divulge what you've told me, Bill. I won't tell anyone that you support Rachel.'

'Good.'

'Do the kids know?'

He hesitated before he said, 'No. They know I love their mother. That's all they need to know.'

I considered the hesitation. *What was that about?* Why would he lie about that?

I couldn't rationalize my follow-up question therapeutically. I knew I couldn't, so I didn't even try. But I asked it anyway. 'How expensive is it? To support someone in Rachel's circumstances? It must be a severe burden.'

He didn't stumble over the question. 'Of course it is. It helps a lot that she's still on my health insurance. Frankly, that's one reason why I would never – even if I felt differently – why I'd never go ahead with a divorce. If we were divorced, Rachel would have to rely on public health. That would be a . . . tragedy for her. The medicine alone . . . The occasional hospitalizations . . . The ER visits?'

Bill looked to me for an acknowledgment. I said, 'I can only imagine.'

He sighed. 'She has an apartment in Vegas, a small one, but it's a nice place in a decent neighborhood. I pay . . . a caretaker . . . to look in on her, make sure she has food, has decent clothes, is clean, you know. And I provide what she needs for . . . the weddings. Dresses, gifts. She's generous – you know that. I don't want her to be living in filth or out on the street. I want my wife to be comfortable, and to be safe.'

I almost said, 'A caretaker?' but I didn't. I was wondering if Canada was Bill's idea of a caretaker for his schizophrenic wife. Instead, I refocused on the budgetary arithmetic. I said, 'It must add up.'

'It does,' he said. I thought he was going to say something else, but he stopped.

While I waited for him to resume, I revisited the math. Supporting Rachel the way that Bill described must be costing him two, three, maybe even four thousand dollars a month, depending on housing, medical, and pharmacy costs. I figured twenty-five to fifty thousand dollars a year. A lot of money.

If I added that amount to the amount that Reverend Howie told Raoul that Canada was paying him so that Rachel could attend weddings – I figured it was probably a similar amount, actually, another twenty-five to fifty thousand dollars a year – we were talking big money. Potentially very big money, since Canada was probably keeping an additional cut for his services. My gut instinct said that the total, fifty to a hundred thousand dollars annually, had to be more than someone in Bill Miller's circumstances could afford.

Especially since we were talking after-tax dollars.

Bill tried to explain how he handled his generous allowance to his wife. 'I make a good living. The company's been good to me over the years. My career's gone well. It would be better if I could make this living in Nevada, but I can't. I consider myself fortunate. The kids and I cut some corners. We live simply. We manage. My car's a lot older than yours.'

Bill had noticed my car? That gave me a little chill.

'Rachel's not in treatment?' I asked.

'She's not interested.'

'And you don't use a home health care agency?'

'We've tried, but Rachel can be . . . difficult to deal with. Over the years, I've pieced something together, some . . . services that seem to work out. They meet her needs.' He smiled at me, just a little sheepish grin. 'Is that it? Is that all that you needed to know?'

'No,' I said. 'I have one more question. It's similar to the first one I asked.'

'Shoot.'

'What is the nature of your relationship with the man who owns the house next door to yours?'

He nodded. 'Doyle?'

I immediately knew that he'd been ready for that question; it was the one he'd been expecting from me all along. It wasn't too surprising; Bill had twice spied me loitering on Doyle's property. But I didn't want to divulge the fact that I knew the name of the house's owner, so I asked, 'He owns the house to the north of yours?'

'Yeah, that's Doyle. I barely know him.'

'Barely?'

'We were neighbors for . . . almost four years. But we weren't close. He's a loner, a single guy. He kept to himself. He'd be outside working; we'd say hi. That sort of thing. He invited me over once to look at his new waterfall, and his pond. Impressive. That's probably the most time we ever spent together. He moved away before Thanksgiving, maybe even before Halloween. The house is vacant. But you know that.'

I noted the dig, but didn't bite. 'When's the last time you spoke with him?'

'I'm having trouble understanding why that is any of your business.'

Although I knew that the reason Bill Miller was having trouble understanding why it was any of my business was because it wasn't any of my business, I reiterated my dual-relationship concerns. Not too surprisingly, Bill seemed less satisfied by my explanation than he had been the first time.

He crossed his arms over his chest. His voice grew wary. 'So you have some . . . professional relationship with Doyle? And if I'm his friend, you can't have a professional relationship with me? That's the deal?'

'I can't divulge the nature of my current professional relationships. I'm sure you respect that. You asked me for my help with something. Before I'm able to agree to that request, it's my responsibility to be certain that there aren't any impediments.'

'Impediments?'

It was a stupid word, born of my anxiety over what I was doing, the tightrope I was trying to cross. But I was stuck with it. 'Yes, impediments.'

Bill looked at me as though my subterfuge was as transparent as glass. He said, 'Last fall sometime. He told me he was going to list the house. That was the last time I talked to Doyle.'

*

A pad of graph paper. A pencil with a fresh eraser. A whole lot of conjecture.

The meeting with Bill Miller was over and I was busy trying to compute how much it would take to raise two adolescent kids in an overpriced neighborhood in an overpriced town in an overpriced world. I had one small child in a similarly overpriced neighborhood in the same overpriced town, so I could fathom a guess as to what it was costing Bill Miller to support his family in Boulder. Mortgage, property taxes, food, health insurance, car payments, some amount of recreation, teenage whims . . . hell, I hadn't even considered any additional funds that Bill might try to set aside to fund his eventual retirement.

To the sum at the bottom of my sheet of graph paper, I added the approximate costs I'd already computed that it would take to maintain a schizophrenic wife in a gambling and resort town in another state, and somehow simultaneously support her extravagant serial wedding habit.

Total all those amounts, do some rough reverse income-tax calculations, and I would have a guess, admittedly shoddy, as to exactly how many pretax dollars Bill Miller would have to earn to possibly meet all his financial commitments. My conclusion? I was guessing that Bill Miller would need to earn three hundred thousand dollars a year, minimum.

One of the things therapists do every day is listen to people talk about personal things, things like their money. Over the years, hearing various patients discuss their salary ranges for this job and that job, I'd developed a pretty good sense of what kind of living people made doing what kind of work in Boulder County.

There was no way Bill Miller made three hundred grand a year as a district manager of a chain of retail drugstores. What did I think Bill Miller was paid? Low end? Eighty to a hundred thousand dollars. High end? One fifty. One eighty, tops.

Tops.

That was not enough to provide for the two households Bill was supporting, let alone enough to have anything left over for Rachel's nuptial peculiarities, and certainly not at the rates that Reverend Howie charged.

Family money? It was possible that some trust fund somewhere or some generous recently dead relative had come to the rescue to cushion the Millers' financial burdens. But Bill hadn't alluded to anything about any family money softening his financial plight.

So where, I continued to wonder, was Bill Miller getting the money to support two households, not to mention to make all the payments to Canada and Reverend Howie, and to otherwise endow Rachel's sundry bizarre wedding imperatives?

I didn't know. But I was beginning to think that the answer was crucial.

Mallory says her dad is up to something.

I tossed my pencil onto the desk and watched it skitter across the oak and tumble to the floor.

With some sadness and a lot of resignation, I admitted to myself that I'd just crossed a serious ethical line. The meeting that I'd just completed with Bill Miller hadn't been psychotherapy. I hadn't met with him for his clinical benefit.

I'd met with him for my own purposes, whatever those really were.

48

Grace was usually all mine on Friday mornings, my day off. That morning Lauren was in a trial and Viv had a chemistry class from ten until noon. Viv had kindly agreed to watch Grace while I saw Bill Miller but I had to rush back home to pick up my daughter so Viv could get to class on time.

Grace and I often used our Friday time for outings or errands, but on cold winter mornings we sometimes tossed 'usually' out into the snow and snuggled up inside with hot cider, good dogs, and a warm fire. And books.

The temperature had dropped into the single digits overnight and snuggling seemed like a marvelous plan. But my discomfort over Diane and Bob and Rachel and Mallory wouldn't allow me that kind of leisure, so I covered my daughter in multiple layers of cotton, fleece, and Fiberfill, shuttled her out to the Audi, powered up the seat heater, and began motoring west around 9:30. Grace was a good traveler; she seemed cool with our inclement adventure.

In front of us the vertical planes of the Flatirons were draped in a thin fog, as though a designer had decided that a gauzy covering was just what the foothills needed that morning. As we angled closer to the hogbacks north of the city, tiny glistening crystals descended from the frozen mist. 'Look, Gracie, it's raining diamonds,' I said.

Gracie laughed. On Friday mornings, until she needed a nap, I was almost always funny.

I spent the next mile or so trying to explain the concept of triplets to my daughter. For a moment, I actually thought she got it. But when she started squealing, 'Three me, three me,' I was pretty sure that she was still in need of a hands-on demonstration.

I hadn't called Mary Black to tell her we were coming by, mostly because I thought she would tell me not to bother, but partly because I was ninety-nine percent certain I would find her at home and that announcing my visit in advance would give her time to get her thoughts in order, which was something that wasn't necessarily in my best interest. The reason I was so certain I would find her home was that, considering the energy it took to get one small person out of the house in near-zero January temperatures, I thought it was a safe bet that Mary would need a damn good reason to layer up her three bundles of six-week-old joy to lug them outside.

Mary, her husband Gordon, an anesthesiologist, and their triplets lived in a sprawling contemporary ranch in a tiny enclave off the Foothills Highway just south of the mouth of Lefthand Canyon. The house hadn't been built for a family with three infants, and its out-of-town, almost-in-the-mountains location wasn't the most convenient for schlepping multiple kids to pediatricians, preschool, and soccer. I wasn't at all surprised to see a FOR SALE sign out front. Babies change things. They just do.

Triplets change everything.

Before I left the car I tried to check my voice mail for word from Raoul but I couldn't get a cell signal in the mountain shadows. Yet another reason for parents of triplets to move closer to town.

I was relieved the Chinooks that the weather people had been forecasting hadn't yet started blowing. Chinooks are fierce winter downslope winds, cousins of California's fabled devil winds, the Santa Anas. Chinooks warm as they descend from the tallest peaks of the Continental Divide, the gusts compressing and accelerating as they squeeze through mountain canyons before they ultimately rupture out of the foothills onto the communities of Colorado's Front Range in fifty- to one-hundred-mile-an-hour bursts.

A wise man once said that there is definitely a place not to stand when an elephant has gas. In a similar vein, the mouth of Lefthand Canyon was one of the places not to linger in Boulder County during a serious joust with Chinooks.

It took Mary a moment to respond to the doorbell, but my guess was right – she was home.

'Alan, what a surprise.'

She looked surprised. That much was clear. Pleased? That would have been a stretch. Mary had a well-rounded son curled in each arm and the third member of the newly born trio was screaming somewhere in one of the back rooms of the house. Mary seemed inured to the wail.

'Hi, Mary, this is Grace. Gracie, this is Dr. Mary Black.'

'Hello,' Grace said.

'The babies are lovely, Mary,' I said.

Mary sighed and forced a smile. 'They are. Thanks for reminding me. Come in,' she said wistfully as she led us into a living room that had been transformed by necessity into a day nursery. The grown-up furniture – a lot of leather and stone and glass – had been shoved to one end of the long room and most of the remaining space was consumed with infant paraphernalia, including three immense boxes of Huggies from a warehouse store and two matching, side-by-side changing tables.

The memorable aroma of stale diaper pail lingered in the air.

'Let me hand these guys off to the nanny. Hold on a second. Grace? Would you like to come back with me and see all the babies?'

Grace was thrilled. She looked to me for permission – I nodded – before she took Mary's hand and followed her toward the back of the house.

'Sometimes I'm convinced that no one is ever going to come, ever,' Mary said when she returned to the living room.

'Do you know why I'm here?'

She shook her head, but I thought her expression said otherwise. Was I misreading? I thought Mary looked beat up. Her hair was ragged, her face hadn't seen makeup in a long while, and the fleece clothing she wore was spotted with some of the fluids that were either intended to go into infants or with some of the fluids that naturally and copiously came back out. Sleep? Not recently, I suspected.

'Triplets are a handful, I take it.'

'A handful? A puppy is a handful, Alan. A baby changes everything. You know that. Three? You wouldn't believe what it's like. Entire weeks pass and I don't even notice. Christmas was a blur.'

'You know why I'm here?' I asked again.

'No, not at all.'

I thought her response was wary, and just a little defensive. 'Believe it or not, I'm here for a consultation.'

She gave me a you've-got-to-be-kidding look. 'I'm really on . . . an extended leave from my practice. I was originally thinking six months, but that no longer feels like a maximum. I have no idea how long it's going to take for life to feel under control again. My consultation is that you go talk to somebody else.'

I no longer had any doubt: She was chary. I wondered for a third time if she'd somehow expected my visit and knew what was coming.

Mary and I were colleagues, not friends. We'd already exchanged condolences at Hannah's funeral, and I decided that I didn't need to squander any more time on social niceties. She hadn't exactly concurred with my desire for a consultation, but she hadn't overtly refused, either. I said, 'Mary, do you know that Hannah saw Mallory Miller for an intake session not long before she died?'

From the flash in her eyes, I knew instantly that Mary had not known. Her 'No' was absolutely superfluous. 'You're sure?' she added.

'She consulted with Diane about it right after the session. Diane didn't know who the kid was at the time, but she's put things together since. It was Mallory.'

Mary's brain was full of infants and infant things and she seemed to be struggling to shift gears to contemplate the weight of my news. 'Anything that relates to what happened to her?' she asked.

'No, not directly.'

She changed her expression. 'About what happened to Hannah?'

'Diane suspected there was. She went to Las Vegas last weekend to talk to Rachel Miller about Mallory. Diane thought that Rachel might be able to fill in some pieces.' I paused. 'You knew Rachel was living in Las Vegas?'

'Of course. Why didn't Diane just talk to Bill?'

Not 'Mallory's father.' Not 'Bill Miller.' *Bill.* 'Let's say that because of what Hannah told Diane about the session with Mallory, it wasn't an option.'

That got her attention. 'I'm not sure what you're trying to say, Alan.'

I didn't want to give Mary any more information than I had to. 'Diane disappeared on Monday evening in a casino and nobody's heard from her since.'

'What?'

'She walked out of the casino with two men and she . . . vanished.'

'Diane went to Las Vegas because of a discussion she had with Hannah about a single intake session with Mallory?'

'Within two weeks of that intake, Hannah was dead and Mallory was missing. Diane felt she had a responsibility to try to figure out what had happened. You know Diane.'

'God.' Mary turned her head as though she couldn't bear looking at me. 'What do you think I might know that would be . . . pertinent?'

'What *do* you know, Mary?'

She walked away and began folding a pile of recently laundered sleepers and impossibly small T-shirts. 'I wish it were that easy, Alan. I wish it were that easy.' She looked back at me. 'You know the rules we play by. Did Diane ever find Rachel? I wonder how she's doing sometimes. She was so resistant to treatment.'

'Diane tracked her down, yes. At a wedding chapel in Vegas, not surprisingly. Had she talked with her? I'm not sure about that.'

The triplets were quiet. Grace was singing them a Raffi song – 'Down by the Bay.' From which parent she'd inherited the ability to carry a tune wasn't at all clear. It was a recessive gene, though. Guaranteed.

'What do you want from me?' Mary asked. The question wasn't particularly provocative; Mary seemed sincerely curious.

'I'd like to know what Bill Miller was up to. His daughter told Hannah that he was up to something. I'm worried that Diane has gotten herself in the middle of whatever that was.'

'The police?'

'In Las Vegas? No help.'

'Up to?' she said. Her breathing had changed. 'What do you mean, what Bill was "up to"?'

'I'm not sure. Bill seems to have access to money he shouldn't have. He's spending a fortune to support Rachel in Las Vegas. I'd like to know where it comes from.'

She reacted physically to my words: She stepped back. 'Alan, I—'

'Do they have family money?'

'No. They don't. I shouldn't be talking to you about this.'

She was right; she shouldn't be talking with me.

It was her problem, one I didn't want to give her time to contemplate. 'What do you know about a guy named Canada?'

'Oh God,' she said. 'You know about Canada? How do you know about Canada?'

'Raoul is in Vegas looking for Diane. He found Canada.'

I wasn't about to tell Mary that I was treating Bill Miller. But I found it interesting that Mary knew about Canada, too. Was that good or bad? I couldn't decide.

Was Canada good or bad? I didn't know that either.

'What do you know about him?' I asked.

'Bill asked for some advice about him once. About trusting him. His motives. That's all I know.'

'When?'

'Years ago. Not too long after Rachel moved.'

'What did you tell him?'

'I told him that, given what he knew about the man's

background, it would be hard to predict how reliable a . . . Canada would be. Whether he could be trusted with Rachel's welfare. I told him I could argue it either way, psychologically speaking.'

'Background? What do you mean?'

'Canada grew up with a schizophrenic mother. She left him when he was young, like eleven. Took off with a guy she met in a bar. He's haunted by it.'

'Makes sense.' But in my business, hindsight almost always makes sense. Foresight is the more valuable, but much rarer, commodity. 'Which way did you end up arguing it with Bill?'

'Alan, please.'

'Help me find Diane, Mary.'

'I argued against it. I suggested that Bill use social services to help him with Rachel if he couldn't afford a home health care agency.'

I changed tactics. 'Do you know why Hannah was in your office the morning she died? Not in her own office?'

'No.'

She'd answered quickly, maybe too quickly. It's not that I didn't believe her reply; it was that I wasn't sure if I believed her reply.

'But you've wondered?'

'Of course I've wondered.'

'Is there any reason Hannah would have been in your office?'

'I didn't think she'd ever been in there without me. Ever.'

'But she had a key?'

'Yes, we each had a key to the other's office.'

Diane and I had keys to each other's office, too. 'Why would she have left her purse in the middle of her office floor?'

Mary opened her eyes wide and shook her head at that question. 'She left her purse on the floor?'

'Yes. Right in the middle of her office. That's where it was when Diane and I got there.'

'That's too strange. The police didn't tell me that. It's so not Hannah. She kept it in the back of a drawer in her file cabinet.'

'Are your records in your office? I didn't see them the day that I found Hannah.'

'What records?'

'Practice files. Specifically, your case file for Rachel Miller.'

'I have cabinets built into the back wall. They look like wainscoting.'

I'd been distracted by other things that day. The image of Hannah splayed over the leather cube, hitchhiking her way into death, continued to intrude on my thoughts with some regularity.

'Rachel's chart is there?'

'I assume it is. Why would Hannah's death have anything to do with the Millers, Alan? I still don't see the connection.'

I could have told her that I didn't see the connection either. Instead, I tried the truth. 'Hannah met with Mallory a couple of weeks before Christmas. Before too long, one of them was dead, the other one was missing.'

She pondered for a moment before she said dispassionately, 'Correlation doesn't imply causality, Alan.'

Ah yes, science.

'I think we both know it doesn't rule it out either, Mary.'

49

We agreed to take two cars into town. The nanny would watch the triplets for an hour or two. Grace would stay with me. I ended up parking in the spot behind the small building where Hannah's pristine Passat had been parked the night that Diane and I had found Hannah's body.

Mary's car, a Honda minivan with temporary plates – her new triplet-mobile, I assumed – was already in the other parking slot.

The back door of the old house was unlocked. Gracie and I found Mary standing in the hallway, her hands hanging limp by her upper thighs. The narrow passage was dimly lit and she was silhouetted by the distant front windows. I thought she seemed disoriented. As Grace and I approached she said, 'I don't like being here anymore. It's so strange. I never thought I'd feel that way. I used to love being in this space,' she said. 'Hannah and I were perfect together here. Perfect.'

'I can only imagine what it's like for you,' I said. 'Mary, I need to get Grace settled with a book or something. I'll be right back.'

I showed Grace where I'd be talking with Mary, and then led her to the waiting room where I made space on the coffee table for her books and for some paper and crayons. She chose to sit on the same location on the green velvet sofa that the Cheetos lady had chosen on the day that Hannah died. Grace settled right in, picking the crayons and paper over the books. Her cooperation didn't surprise me; I was already confident that one of my daughter's enduring skills in life would be her capacity to ride whatever wave rolled her way.

Mary had unlocked her office door and was standing a couple of feet inside. I squeezed in behind her. The leather cube was gone from the room, as was the stained dhurrie. The pine floors looked naked and ancient. The room appeared as cold as it felt.

I spotted the recessed handles for the lateral files that had been built into the rear wall. The three long file cabinets did indeed appear to be part of the beadboard wainscoting.

'I've only been back once, with the police and my attorney. The detectives wanted to know if anything was missing. I looked around and told them I didn't think so. Nothing appeared disturbed to me at the time, but I didn't do an inventory.'

I recalled how hard it had been to return to my own office years before after Diane had been attacked by a patient's husband. I touched Mary on the arm. She put her hand on my fingers.

'You know where . . . her body was, don't you? I mean, exactly?' she asked.

'Yes, I do. Do you want me to . . .'

'No. Not yet. I'll tell you if I do.' She stepped away.

'Okay,' I said. 'She was wearing a blouse that day, Mary. Button-front, collar, silk, I think. A basic thing.'

'So?'

'The front tail on the left side was tucked up underneath her bra when I found her, exposing her abdomen. I've never seen a woman do that before.'

'The police didn't tell me that. You're sure?'

'I am.'

'That's interesting. Hannah was a Type 1 diabetic – she was insulin dependent. She usually injected into her abdomen. Rather than unbuttoning her shirt, she had this habit of just tucking it up under the front of her bra to get it out of the way. Did the police find a syringe close by? Had she just taken insulin?'

'I didn't see a syringe, but I suppose it could have been beneath her body.'

'Have you seen the results of the autopsy? How was her sugar?' Mary asked.

'I assume it was within normal limits; nobody mentioned it as an anomaly.'

'If her shirt was tucked under her bra, then she was preparing to take insulin. There's no other explanation.'

'But in your office?'

'That part doesn't make any sense. She kept the insulin in back, in the kitchen. She would load the syringe back there. But she injected herself in her own office. Hannah was modest, and she was very private about her illness.'

'Always?'

'Always.'

After a poignant pause – I suspected she was still debating whether or not she really wanted to know precisely where Hannah had died – Mary stepped toward the built-ins. 'The file is in here.'

The key was secreted on the shelves above the cabinets in a ceramic jar, something small and celadon. Mary retrieved the key and unlocked the middle cabinet. She chose a pillow from the sofa and threw it on the floor before she kneeled down, slid out the top drawer, and began searching for the file. She fingered the brightly colored tabs sequentially, her middle, ring, and index fingers running after each other as though they were skipping over hurdles. After one time through the area that marked the center of the alphabet, she retraced her work.

That's when she found it.

In a calm voice she announced, 'It's here. I almost missed it, but it's here.' She pulled the dusky red folder and held it up for me to see.

My voice every bit as level as hers – we were both therapists, after all – I suggested, 'Why don't you take a few minutes and make sure that it hasn't been . . . I don't know, tampered with.'

She crossed her legs and sat on the pillow on the floor. Slowly, she made her way through the inch-and-a-half-thick pile of pages of scrawled notes and medication records and hospital admission papers and discharge summaries.

'It all seems to be here, Alan. I can't be a hundred percent sure, but everything seems to be here. It looks just the way I left it.'

I sighed involuntarily. Relief? Disappointment? I wasn't sure.

She gazed up at me. 'You thought someone stole it, didn't you? That someone was in my office that day, that Hannah heard them in here, came in to see what was going on. And that's why she was killed.'

'It was one thought. It all depended on what was in that file.'

She closed the file and stood. 'I can't tell you what's in it. You know how this works.'

'If it's a consultation you can.'

'What good will that do? You can't tell anyone what I tell you. It won't help.'

'I've been looking for Diane all week. I already know other things. Every piece helps. If I can put it all together,

I may be able to find her. I'm terrified that time is running out.'

'You won't divulge what I tell you?'

I said, 'No,' and I hoped that I wasn't lying. Was I willing to be lying if it would help Diane?

Yes. Mary had to know that.

'I wouldn't treat her the same way today. Probably wouldn't even diagnose her the same,' Mary said remorsefully, while giving Rachel's file a little shake. 'We know so much more now, don't we? Take me out for coffee, Alan. I'm dying to sit down with an adult for coffee.'

I made an apologetic face. 'Grace will be coming with us.' Grace would be thrilled to go out for coffee; she thought a petite espresso cup full of steamed milk foam with shaved chocolate on top was as good as life got.

Mary deflated, took a step, and slumped down on a nearby chair. 'I forgot. She's a sweet kid, but she's not an adult.'

'Not the last time I looked, no.'

A strong wind exploded out of Sunshine Canyon ten blocks to the west. Had the Chinooks arrived? The *whoosh* shook the house, the naked tree branches squinted together and bent to the east. Debris and dust filled the air.

I excused myself and stepped out into the waiting room to check on Grace. She seemed oblivious to the gales; in fact she was so busy coloring that she didn't notice my arrival in the room. A second blast put the first to shame – the century-old glass began to hum in the window at the front of the house. After one more selfish moment observing my daughter's concentration, I returned down the hallway to Mary's office.

She'd moved to the couch, pulled her legs up under

her, and tugged a pillow to her chest. She asked, 'Did Bill Miller ever mention to you that he'd done something he wasn't proud of? Something that was eating at him?'

'No, doesn't ring a bell. Should it?'

'I'm thinking maybe it might be important. He never really explained it all to me, but it had something to do with a traffic accident he witnessed. A young woman died. He was torn up about it.'

I surprised myself by remembering. 'She was an orthodontist,' I said.

The winds had quieted. Strange.

Mary said, 'Yes.'

50

Mary had to get back to the demands of the triplets, and the clock said it was almost time to get Grace home for some lunch and a nap. But something Mary had said convinced me to risk squeezing one more errand into our outing. I didn't even try to explain to Grace exactly what business was conducted at the office of the Boulder County coroner; all I told her was that Daddy had another short meeting.

Years before, during my brief stint as a coroner's investigator, my supervisor was a good man named Scott Truscott. I'd always liked Scott and had felt that once I wasn't working for him he'd grown fond of me, too. Grace and I tracked him down at his desk in the Justice Center on Canyon Boulevard. I introduced him to Grace and he and I spent a moment catching up before he asked, 'So what's up?'

'I'm hoping I can help you a little with the Hannah Grant thing.'

'Yeah?' He seemed interested, but just the slightest bit skeptical. 'I'd love to get that one out of the "undetermined" column.'

The words he used – genteelly chosen without overt reference to death or murder – told me that he was happy to edit his part of the conversation for Grace's tender ears.

He added, 'Why me and not the detectives handling the case?'

I could've finessed my answer, but with Scott it wasn't necessary. 'I have issues with Jaris Slocum.'

'Gotcha.' Scott wasn't surprised, obviously.

'Will you answer some questions for me, too?' I asked.

'Depends what they are.'

That was fair. I said, 'Hannah was a diabetic. Type 1. We both know that. How was her blood sugar when, you know?'

'Blood doesn't actually tell us anything about sugar level during a post; natural autolysis renders the numbers meaningless. But because we knew she was insulin dependent, the coroner checked the vitreous fluid.'

'From her eye?' I asked, a shiver shooting up my spine. I didn't know what autolysis was, natural or otherwise, but feared that asking would either tug Scott down a blind alley, or leave my daughter with nightmares.

'It's the only way to get a reliable post mortem sugar. I don't have it memorized, but she was within normal limits.' His hand reached for his computer mouse. 'You want me to check for the exact number, I can pull the labs.'

'It's okay. Did the detectives recover a syringe that night?'

'You mean with insulin in it? No. They found fresh supplies in the kitchen. Nothing already prepared for injection though, and nothing recently used.'

'Did you hear anything about an open roll of LifeSavers in her coat pocket?'

His shoulders dropped, and he frowned. 'No, nobody mentioned LifeSavers to me. It wasn't in any of the reports.'

'It was there; I saw it. The package was open, the wrapper was curlicueing out of her pocket.'

Scott appeared perplexed. 'She must have thought her sugar was low. Considering her normal levels, though, that's odd.'

'It is odd. Did you collect her . . . that night?' I skipped a word intentionally. The omitted word could have been 'body' or 'remains.'

He filled in the blank and said that he had. One of the tasks of coroner's investigators is to visit death scenes to begin collecting data, and to prepare bodies for transport to the morgue.

I said, 'Her shirttail was tucked up under the front of her bra when I found her.'

'When I got there, too. Same.'

'Ever run across that before at a death scene?'

'Never,' he said.

'A good friend of hers just told me that Hannah did that when she was preparing to do an insulin injection in her abdomen. To get her shirt up out of the way.'

Scott crossed his arms and sat back. 'I didn't consider that, but I should have. Slocum was already thinking homicide when I arrived.' He made a sound with his tongue and the roof of his mouth. 'You'll make a statement about the LifeSavers?'

'Of course; I bet the crime-scene photos will show that wrapper.'

'I'll take a look. Will her friend give a statement about the shirt tail?'

'Can't see why not. Why would a diabetic be eating sugar one minute and preparing to take insulin the next?'

'It makes no sense to me. That's one of the things I'm going to have to think about.'

We said good-bye. I bundled Grace back up. On the

way out to the car she asked, 'What are LifeSavers?'

We stopped at a convenience store on the way home and I bought her a roll. I guessed she was a Butter Rum kid.

It turned out that I guessed right.

When we finally weaved across the valley Viv was almost done cooking up a pot of macaroni and cheese. As the three of us were finishing lunch, Virginia Danna, the Realtor whom I'd tricked into showing me the interior of Doyle's house, phoned me on my cell.

After reintroducing herself she proceeded without any further niceties, her tone full of conspiracy. 'The rules have changed. They always seem to in situations like this, don't they? With Mr. Chandler dead, buyers are going to come out of the hills looking for a fire sale. Act fast and you might be able to get that house for a . . .'

Song? What house?

I walked out of the kitchen. 'Mr. Chandler is dead?' I said.

'Yes! Can you believe it? This world! Sometimes . . .' She sighed. 'A detective called me today to find out when I'd last spoken with him. You could have knocked me over with a feather when he told me Mr. Chandler was dead, maybe even murdered. Who knows what happened to him? The poor man! Murdered? It gives me gooseflesh, right up my thighs. Now, I will admit that I'm not privy to the estate situation in this particular circumstance, but sometimes people – heirs – at times like this are truly eager to settle things after a . . . especially after a . . . So if I could persuade you to make . . .'

An offer?

She went on. 'Even a lowball offer would be . . .'

Acceptable? Delectable?

I asked, 'Ms. Danna, who exactly is Mr. Chandler?'

'What? The owner of the house I showed you on Twelfth. The one with the water features and that yummy media center downstairs? I'm sorry, I thought you knew.'

'Doyle?'

'Yes, Doyle Chandler.'

'He's dead?'

She was growing impatient with me. 'Mm-hmmm,' was all she said in reply to my last question. Then she waited while I caught up.

'What detective phoned you?' I asked. I was thinking *Sam*.

'I don't recall exactly. Mr. Chandler's body was found up near Allenspark. Maybe it was an Allenspark detective.'

Allenspark is a small town in the mountains about thirty minutes from Boulder by car, not far from the eastern boundaries of Rocky Mountain National Park. When not swollen with summer tourists, Allenspark's population typically hovered – guessing – somewhere around two hundred people. The village was as likely to have its own homicide detective as it was to have its own traffic helicopter. Any investigator involved in a homicide inquiry in Allenspark would be part of the County Sheriff's department, on loan from a bigger city, like Boulder, or someone assigned from the Colorado Bureau of Investigation.

Rather than argue the point, I said, 'I'll talk it over with my wife and get back to you. The house is still a little small for us.'

'One word: cantilever. My mobile number is on the card I gave you. Call any time. When news gets out about this . . . situation, there will be other offers, certainly by close of business tomorrow. You can count on it. There have been four showings of that property this week alone and I don't have to tell you how slow the beginning of January usually is. And that screen in the basement? Remember? Of course you do. I checked. It's a Stewart Filmscreen. I told you, the best. Think hard – a house like that, a location like that, circumstances like . . .'

These.

'I understand,' I said. But, of course, I didn't.

I called Lauren. She didn't return my call until midafternoon during a break in her trial. She'd already heard through the law enforcement grapevine about the discovery of the body of an unidentified male in a shallow grave not far from a trail that meandered off Highway 7 in northern Boulder County. She said she thought the location was east of Allenspark, actually closer to Lyons and Hygiene. I asked her to get me whatever information she could and to call me right back.

'Why are you interested in this?' she asked, of course. The tone of her question made it clear she wasn't sure she wanted to hear my reply.

'It might be related to Diane,' I said.

'Two minutes,' she said.

It took her four. 'We don't have much yet. Pending a post, it appears to be a homicide. Animals had gotten to the body. ID found at the scene indicates it may be a man named—'

'Doyle Chandler.'

'How did you know? Is he one of your patients?'

I could have said, probably should have said, 'You know I can't answer that.' Instead, I said, 'No.' Were the answer yes I would have answered with stony silence. Lauren and I both knew that the silent yes would have been just as declarative as the spoken no had been.

'One of Diane's patients?'

Well, that was a thought. What if Diane had treated Doyle? I didn't think so. I said, 'No.'

'But you know him?' she asked.

'Personally, I don't. Doyle Chandler owned the house that's next door to Mallory Miller's house on the Hill. When she disappeared he'd already moved away and put the place on the market.'

'I don't think the police mentioned that this afternoon. Are you sure?'

'Yes.'

'Is this related to Mallory's disappearance?'

'I don't know. You have to wonder.'

'Diane's disappearance?'

'I don't know that either.'

'But you have reasons to be suspicious?'

'Yes.'

'Then this might be important to you: Sam's up there. He asked the sheriff for permission.'

'He's up where they found the body?'

'Yes.'

'I'll call him.'

'Have you heard from Raoul?' Lauren asked.

'No. I'm still worried.'

'Keep me informed, okay?'

After we hung up, I sent Sam a text message on his pager: 'I know about D. Call me. A.'

While I was waiting for Sam to get back to me, I took a call from Scott Truscott at the coroner's office. 'Try something on for me?' he said.

'Sure.'

'We know that Ms. Grant hit her head when she tripped that morning at Rallysport, right? On the tile floor in the locker room? That's confirmed?'

Hannah Grant, okay. I fought to change gears. 'Yes,' I said. 'The witnesses apparently agree on that much.'

'She tells the women in the locker room she's fine, and she drives straight to her office.'

'We think.'

'Okay, we think. On the way, or shortly after she gets there, though, she begins to feel that something's not quite right – maybe she has a headache, maybe she's a little confused, lightheaded – but she doesn't put two and two together, doesn't consider that she's just bumped her head and that she might have a concussion, or worse. Instead she decides that after all the exercise she'd done that her sugar's too low. She's in her car by then, she doesn't have any orange juice, so she sucks on a couple of LifeSavers. With me?'

'So far.'

'When she gets to her office she's still not herself, not feeling right. The candy didn't help – she's not feeling better yet. How do we know? Easy: She puts her purse in the middle of the floor. All her friends say she's a compulsive person, OCD, truly anal, so the purse? On the floor? That's not like her. Totally out of character. At this point I think she's feeling even worse, not better. Maybe much worse.'

'Why much worse, Scott?'

'Post showed two subdural hematomas, remember? One of those two certainly came from a blunt surface – the tile floor – at the health club, during that initial fall.'

'Yes.'

'So we know she has a subdural from that earlier trauma. My theory is she actually already has both subdurals – one from the impact with the floor, and one from something with a sharper edge, maybe the locker room bench – and she's actively bleeding into one or both of those hematomas. Ms. Grant was on aspirin therapy – you might not know that. Family history of heart disease.'

'I didn't.'

'Doesn't matter. Pressure's slowly increasing on her brain, and she's gradually getting more symptomatic. Half an hour passes, then an hour, and she's more and more confused, lethargic, maybe vertiginous. Anxious, probably. Not too surprisingly, her thinking's impaired. All she can come up with is that her diabetes is way out of whack, she has a problem with her sugar. The LifeSavers were there, Alan; in her pocket, like you said. I confirmed that with the crime-scene photos. But if she ate them, they didn't help, so she goes in the other direction, decides maybe she needs insulin.

'But her confusion is severe; she's disoriented – she can't even get her routine quite right. Instead of retrieving her kit from the kitchen to check her sugar, she tucks her shirt up under her bra the way she always does just prior to her injection.'

I saw where he was heading. 'And instead of going to the kitchen for the insulin, she's lost and she goes to the office across the hall?'

'Exactly. Maybe once she's there she begins to recognize her confusion, and she sits. Maybe not. But that's where she collapses, in that other office. Eventually, she loses consciousness. She's still bleeding into one of those subdurals. Eventually, Ms. Grant dies from the intracranial pressure.'

'Go on,' I said.

'That's where you find her. Her shirt is tucked up under her bra like she's going to do an injection, but there's no syringe around, no insulin. It's definitely possible she's eaten some candy. No weapon is ever recovered that matches the second trauma to her head. What am I missing?'

I couldn't think of a single thing left unexplained. 'Nothing, Scott. I think maybe you nailed it. No intruders, no assault, no murderer. No second blow to the head.'

'And no more "undetermined." Hannah Grant's death was accidental.'

'I can't tell you how relieved this makes me.'

'Do me a favor?'

'What?'

'Sit on this until I can run it by the coroner.'

'Of course.'

What was I thinking? I couldn't wait to give the news to Diane. She'd be so happy.

It took Sam a couple of hours to reply to my message about Doyle's body, but he did.

'How'd you hear?' Sam asked. Actually, it was more like a demand than a question.

'The real-estate lady. She thought I might spot a housing opportunity in the ashes of the tragedy that was unfolding.'

'Shit. Who'd you tell?'

'Lauren. How come you guys didn't let the DA know that Doyle Chandler lived next door to Mallory?'

'I've been busy.'

Right. 'You still near Allenspark?'

'They just wrapped things up. I'm on my way back to Boulder now.'

'How long has your guy been dead?'

'My guy?' Sam laughed, turning my question into the melodic refrain of the Mary Wells ditty. 'My guy has been dead a while. But it's frigging cold up here, so the body's been pretty well refrigerated. In the meantime, wild animals have been busy doing their wild animal thing. What they nibble on first? Let me tell you, it takes away much of my faith in the natural kingdom. ME's going to have his hands full on this one.'

'Homicide?'

'If it's a suicide, he was considerate enough to bury himself first. If it was an accident, he conveniently died by tripping and falling into a shallow grave.'

'Why'd you go up there?'

The signal faded and wavered. When it was strong enough to carry Sam's voice again, I heard, '. . . and somebody convinced me that I should be asking this Doyle Chandler about the guy who used his garage in Boulder to store a classic old Camaro. The agent thought that since he moved away from his house in Boulder, Chandler was living out this way. I'd called the sheriff to give them a heads-up that I would be chatting with him as a follow-up to the Mallory Miller thing. When the sheriff learned that some snowshoers found what appeared to be his body, they gave me a courtesy jingle.

'For what it's worth, this body shouldn't have been discovered, not during the winter anyway. Most years it would've stayed hidden till spring, at least. You'll like this – want to know how it was found? A woman on a snowshoe outing with some girlfriends had gone off by herself to answer nature's call and was finishing taking a crap when she saw part of a hand sticking out from below this log she was crouching behind. Poor crime-scene techs had to collect it as evidence.'

'Collect what?'

'Her . . . you know.'

I knew. 'What's next?'

'I got twenty minutes to get from here to pick up Simon from hockey practice.'

'You want me to get him? Meet you at your house? I'm happy to.'

'Nice of you, but I think I'm cool. I'll make it in time. Any word on Diane?'

'Nothing. Anything on the BOLO?'

'Nope. Go home, Alan. Stop playing cop.'

With that, the signal faded for good and the call dropped off into the great mobile phone ether.

I wasn't ready to stop playing cop. The day's events had shaken me and I was ready to do what I'd been thinking about doing for most of a week. I drove downtown to my office, opened the dark-blue Kinko's box, and prepared to read Bob Brandt's opus, *My Little Runaway.*

A run, run, run, run runaway.

51

The manuscript was, guessing, about a hundred pages long, but the sheets weren't numbered so I didn't have an exact count.

Bob's story started with a single provocative phrase that constituted an entire sentence, an entire paragraph, an entire page, and an entire chapter.

It moved from there into a series of short, essay-like digressions, one having to do with Del Shannon's childhood, another having to do with the mechanics of installing low-maintenance water features.

A page-turner it was not.

More than half of the sheets of paper in the box were blank.

But that solitary phrase on page one was evocative enough that the manuscript lived up to its billing in the most important area: Bob's story did indeed contain a version of what had happened to Mallory on Christmas night, and proposed a fascinating theory about how she'd managed to make it out of her house without leaving any marks in the fresh snow.

I reminded myself at least five times while I read and reread the few words on the first page that Bob had told me that the work was fiction.

Fiction. Right.

*

Once I'd completed an initial pass at the manuscript, and after I'd come up with a plan on what to do next, I had some time to kill before I made my next move. I ended up driving home after stopping on the way to buy my girls some of their favorite takeout from Chez Thuy, a little Vietnamese place that Viv – part of Boulder County's Hmong community – had turned us on to. Grace was in a terrific mood while we ate and seemed totally enamored with the way that her rice noodles stuck together.

Over sublime catfish and green onions in a sauce that had more flavors than the sky had stars, I went so far as to tell Lauren that I had some significant news that might impact the investigation of the body that had been discovered that afternoon near Allenspark. She asked for some clarifications that I couldn't provide. But she was kind enough to phone somebody in the DA's office to confirm my suspicion about what would happen next: The Boulder police had indeed already applied for a warrant to search Doyle Chandler's Twelfth Street home.

'How long will it take to get the warrant?' I asked.

'They'll have it soon,' Lauren said. 'Judge Heller has the request; I have no doubt she'll comply. This one's a no-brainer. Likely homicide? The police need to search the vic's house.'

'I'm going to have to go over there and see Sam in person. Tell him what I know.'

'You can't just call?'

'I want to help him find something at Doyle's that I think he might otherwise miss. If I don't tell him what I'm expecting to find there, and then if it turns out that I'm wrong, I won't end up having to breach privilege.'

'And you can't tell me how you know what's inside this man's house?'

'I have a hunch based on something – a story a patient . . . told me. I wish I could tell you more. If I'm right, you'll know all about it tomorrow.'

I arrived on Doyle's block around 9:30. In order to execute the search warrant the police department was out in force – I counted five law enforcement vehicles, mostly unmarked, in front of the house. Doyle's neighbors were curious about the commotion; despite the cold night they were congregated in small groups on nearby sidewalks and on front porches watching events unfold. I chose to park around the corner. If it was possible, I preferred not to be spotted by Bill Miller while running this errand.

I dialed Sam's cell phone from my car.

'I thought I told you to go home,' he said.

'Yeah, well. You get Simon on time?'

'Barely.'

'Who's watching him now?'

Impatiently, he asked, 'What's up, Alan? I'm kind of busy.'

'I have something to show you.'

'I'm working. Maybe tomorrow.'

I could tell he was trying hard to be nice, but that his decorum was on its last legs. 'I know you're working, Sam. That's why I asked who was watching Simon. I'm right outside. I have something to show you.'

'It can't wait?'

He sounded both perplexed and annoyed. I said, 'No, it can't. What I want to show you is inside Doyle's house. You'll want to see it. Trust me.'

'What? You're outside this house? That's what you meant?'

'Right around the corner.'

'I can't bring you in here.'

'Sure you can.'

'This better be good,' Sam said. We were standing in the cramped entryway of Doyle's house. With one deep inhale Sam could have filled the space by himself.

'It'll either be very good, or it won't.'

'That second possibility won't leave me feeling great about bringing you in here in front of God and everybody.' He gestured toward the interior of the house. 'Where do we go to find your treasure?'

'Basement. Where's Lucy?'

Lucy was Sam's longtime detective partner.

'Cabo San Lucas. Cancun. Ixtapa. Someplace like that. Some place I should be, but I'm not.'

I led the way down the hall and through the kitchen to the basement stairs. 'An empty house like this makes executing your warrant pretty easy, doesn't it? Don't really have to toss anything.'

'We don't "toss anything." We're careful.'

Sam had apparently forgotten that my own home had once been the target of a law enforcement search. I was in a position to make an educated argument about the actual neatness of police searches; I decided not to choose that moment to remind him.

'What did you specify on the warrant?' I asked.

Before he followed me down the stairs and into the basement storeroom he smiled wryly at my question but didn't respond. I hadn't really expected him to. I read his smile to mean, 'Nice try.'

Sam had latex gloves on his hands; I didn't. 'You have any more of those?' I asked, pointing to his gloves.

'I don't want you to be tempted to touch anything. Just keep your hands in your pockets; it's a good place for them.'

'Then open that door.' I pointed at the awning door that led from the basement to the adjacent crawl space.

'Sorry. We haven't been in there yet. I can't go in there until it's been photographed. You certainly can't.'

'My fingerprints are already on that handle. I opened it when I was here last time. You know, with the real estate agent.'

'Terrific. I'll pass that on. Let's hope your prints aren't flagged by NCIC. It'd make for a long night.'

I shrugged. 'I'll just wait until the photographers are free.'

Sam had an alternative in mind. 'Or you could simply tell me what we're looking for. I really don't have time for your games.'

'If what I think is here isn't here, I don't want to blow confidentiality. If it is here, I'll find it, and you'll know.'

He thought for a moment about my plan. 'If you're wrong about all this you're going to end up making me look like an idiot.'

'No, Sam, I'm going to end up making us both look like idiots.'

'I don't give a fuck if you look like an idiot. I do care if I look like an idiot.' With pronounced reluctance, he called upstairs and redirected a photographer from the top floor of the house into the crawl space.

He parked me on one of the recliners in the fancy theater where Doyle had allowed Bob to watch movies.

'Sit here and don't move,' Sam ordered. 'I have to go back upstairs for a while. I'll tell you when the photographer's done doing what she needs to do. Then you can go into the crawl space and uncover your amazing secret.' Sam stopped at the door. 'I mean it. Stay right here, wait for me to come back. Don't even think about going into that crawl space without me.'

I smiled at him. 'Do you mind if I put on a DVD? I hear that projector there' – I pointed – 'is a top-of-the-line Runco. And the screen is the same one that Spielberg has in his very own personal screening room. It's a Stewart, Sam. An actual Stewart Filmscreen.'

Sam gave me the finger and walked upstairs.

It took me about five minutes to get bored. I'd already played with all the levers and buttons on Doyle's fancy leather recliner. In addition to thirty-seven different reclining positions, the thing had a seat heater and a couple of recessed cup holders. All that was missing was a coin slot for a vibrator.

I checked out the vaunted Runco projector that was mounted to the ceiling near the back of the room. Since I didn't even know what I was looking at, that chore managed to use up no more than another twenty seconds.

The recessed speakers? They were only good for ten. There wasn't much to admire in a recessed speaker with the sound turned off.

Doyle's theater was actually rather spartan considering the big bucks that had been invested in its creation. No popcorn maker. No Old West saloon and mahogany bar to belly-up to on the back wall. No Xbox or souped-up Nintendo setup. The fancy Spielberg screen was all that was left for me to examine. I ambled to the front of the theater and gave it a thorough once-over. My impression of the screen was the same the second time as it had been the first: It looked suspiciously like a movie screen.

I returned to my designated recliner. *Where is the remote control?* I bet myself that Doyle had one of those fancy programmable remotes that operated everything electronic on the whole block, including his neighbors' toasters and microwave ovens. That would be an interesting find, right? That would capture my attention for at least a few minutes. Maybe there was a hockey game on TV. Sam would let me watch hockey.

I couldn't find the device. I checked the other recliners for hidden compartments and secret drawers. Didn't spot a single cubby that was spacious enough to stash a fancy remote control.

I began searching the perimeter of the room for a panel that might disguise a hidden cupboard. I used my elbow to put pressure on the wall every twelve to eighteen inches, suspecting that the room might have the kind of panel that you have to press on to free the latch.

Nothing budged. Most of the wall panels were padded and fabric-covered. Whatever was beneath them felt rock solid.

Where is the remote? What good are all these electronics without a remote control?

I was about to conclude that someone had pilfered the thing during one of the showings of Doyle's house when I guessed that the storage cabinet I'd been searching for might be secreted behind the Spielberg movie screen. I returned to the front of the room. Careful to use only my fingernails, I pulled on one side of the mahogany molding.

It didn't budge.

I moved to the other side of the screen and did the same.

That side didn't move either.

I tried the hidden latch trick and used my elbow to put pressure on the right vertical section of the frame.

The mahogany slid backward half a centimeter and clicked.

Bingo.

I released the pressure and the screen swung forward from a recessed hinge on the opposite side of the frame.

My mouth dropped open.

Well, I thought, *this part of the book isn't fiction.*

I pulled myself into the opening behind the screen, used my fingernail to flick on a light switch, and stared, trying to drink in every detail before I was banished from the house, because I knew that it was almost certain that I was about to be banished from the house.

I spent about a minute sitting there – examining, figuring, memorizing – before I hopped back down into the theater, flicked off the light switch, swung the screen back into place, and found Sam in the kitchen. He was engaged in a dialogue with a woman dressed in street clothes. I figured she was a detective or a crime-scene tech. I manufactured some fresh surprise for my voice as I interrupted them. 'Excuse me. Something to show you in the theater downstairs, Detective Purdy.'

The woman with Sam gave me a who-the-hell-are-you look. Sam glared at me, too, and seemed prepared to launch into some low-velocity attack on my character either because I'd interrupted something important or because I'd ignored his instructions to stay put downstairs.

Or both. Most likely, both.

'Now,' I said. 'It's important.'

'Give me a minute,' Sam said. He said it not to me, but to the woman in the street clothes.

52

Earlier that evening, back in my office, I had lifted a dozen or so sheets from the top of the stack inside the blue Kinko's box and placed them in my lap. I'd turned the pages one by one, lingering for a long moment over the handwritten sheet that Bob Brandt had written warning me not to read any further.

Ultimately, I turned that one, too. Considering the transgression I'd committed by arranging the fake-psychotherapy session with Bill Miller that afternoon, breaking my promise to Bob Brandt not to read his manuscript until he gave me permission seemed, by comparison, like a paltry professional sin. Right or wrong, I'd already rationalized that Bob's apparent disappearance was a sufficiently emergent circumstance to void the previous arrangement, anyway.

I was beginning to feel so adept at rationalization that I was considering running for Congress.

The next sheet in the box was the first page of actual text of Bob's book, written in that tiny font he preferred.

No one had considered the possibility of a tunnel.

Talk about starting your joke with the punch line.

A tunnel? 'No one had considered the possibility of a tunnel.'

Holy moly.

53

Doyle's excavation was a work of thoughtful engineering.

The length of the subterranean construction wasn't exactly mind-boggling; the distance between the south side of Doyle's basement and the north side of the Miller home was only about fifteen feet. And this wasn't a highway tunnel; the diameter of the mostly round bore ranged from a maximum of about thirty inches a few feet from where it began behind the Spielberg movie screen to as narrow as twenty-four inches or so near the Millers' house. Parallel tracks of angle iron were embedded in the flat floor of the tunnel all the way from one end to the other. A long string of outdoor holiday lights – white only – were stretched along the entire distance to provide illumination.

The slope of the tunnel – it ran downhill at a steeper angle than I would have expected – was curious to me, but my initial impression was that the slope was deliberate. It appeared that the floor of the tunnel dropped about six or seven feet over its short length. A husky winch was bolted to the outside of Doyle's foundation wall and a sturdy stretch of conduit connected it to the house's electrical system. The stout cable from the winch was hooked to one end of an ingenious contraption that was constructed of four sets of skateboard wheels topped with two narrow, interconnected sections of thick plywood, loosely hinged in the middle. The wheels of the makeshift sled fit perfectly into the angle iron tracks that had been set in the tunnel floor.

A flimsy remote-control unit jerry-rigged from a garage-door opener would have allowed Doyle to operate the winch from any location in the tunnel. By climbing prone onto the sled, hanging on, and pressing the remote-control button, Doyle could either slowly extend or retract the cable on the winch, which would either lower the sled farther into the tunnel toward the Millers' house or pull it back up the slope toward his own house.

Simple. Elegant.

Building the tunnel would have been tedious, no doubt. But if Doyle had managed only six inches of fresh digging a day, he could have completed the excavation in a little over a month. A foot a day and he'd have been done in a fortnight. The dirt that he'd removed from the tunnel was undoubtedly part of the weaving contours and berms of Doyle's personal backyard water park.

And the snow thing?

Mystery solved.

54

'You should close that door,' I said, after Sam had followed me back downstairs into Doyle's theater.

He hesitated, his bushy brows burdened more with aggravation than curiosity. But he complied. The chatter from the rest of the house disappeared as the door settled against soundproofing gaskets in the jamb.

I stepped across the room. Without fanfare I raised my elbow and pressed on the edge of the movie screen. The frame swung open on its long hinge, revealing Doyle's portal.

Sam stepped closer and leaned inside. He said, 'Holy shit.'

'Yeah.'

Sam did what I had done, although he pulled on fresh latex first. He lifted himself up into the opening behind the movie screen, flicked on the light switch, and stared. I watched his eyes move from the dirt cave, to the angle iron tracks, to the string of holiday lights, to the winch, to the sled.

I couldn't be sure, of course, but I thought that he was adding things up the same way I had. He didn't say a word at first; he just shook his head slowly. Admiration? Frustration? Amazement? I couldn't tell.

After a couple of minutes silently going over the specific elements and the implications of Doyle's tunnel, he hopped back down from the opening and stood next to me. 'This is what you were looking for?' Sam's voice was only a few decibels above a whisper.

'A tunnel, yeah.'

'But you thought it was in the crawl space?'

'That was my guess. I figured that was most likely. I thought we'd find the opening underneath the plastic in there.'

'You going to tell me how you knew?' he asked.

'No.'

'How did you find it?'

'Boredom. Luck.'

'Tell me how you knew about it.'

'I probably shouldn't have disclosed the tunnel to you, Sam. I absolutely can't rationalize disclosing how I know about it.'

For the time being he appeared to accept that. He put his hand on my shoulder, the act of a friend, and said, 'Come on. We need to clear out. It's hurry-up-and-wait time.'

'Why?' I didn't want to leave; if he'd let me, I was planning to stay and watch the photographers and crime-scene techs do their thing on whatever they discovered in Doyle's tunnel.

'This isn't exactly covered by the search-warrant request we made. I have to amend it and go back to Judge Heller.' He paused, filling his ample cheeks with air and exhaling loudly before he spoke again. 'And now I'm going to need a fresh warrant for the Millers' house to see how this thing looks from the other end.'

He sounded weary. 'I thought you'd be excited about this,' I said.

'You're thinking Mallory, right?' He looked back up at the opening in the theater wall. 'This is how she got out of her house that night? This is the answer to the snow puzzle?'

'Sure. You have to admit that it adds a whole new dimension.'

'I've told you before: The fact that the kid didn't leave any footprints in the snow the night she disappeared doesn't mean anything. What's important about this tunnel isn't that now we know how Mallory got out of the Miller house. That's not why the tunnel's here. What's important about this tunnel is that now we know how Doyle got into the Miller house.

'What we still don't know is why. Why did the guy living next door want this kind of access?'

Sam had a point. 'He certainly went to a lot of trouble, didn't he?'

'This is the sort of thing bank robbers used to dig to get into a vault full of cash. But if Doyle Chandler wanted to bust into the Millers' house to steal, why do all this? People bust into houses all the time. And they get away with it, neighbors even. They pick locks, break windows. But this tunnel wasn't built for some onetime burglary. This was built for long-term access. Bill Miller never reported a burglary at that house. If Doyle wasn't stealing from them, why did he want in so badly?'

'Mallory?' I said in reply to Sam's question.

'Yeah, maybe it's that simple, maybe he was a perv. Time will tell.'

'What if your underlying assumption is wrong, Sam? What if she didn't run? What if Doyle took Mallory out through the tunnel? What if that's why he wanted access to the Millers' house?'

Sam closed his eyes and his body stilled as though he

were narcoleptic and he'd suddenly started sleeping standing up. For a moment even the act of breathing wasn't apparent. Finally, he opened his eyes and said, 'Again, why? There are easier ways, and there's a lot we don't know.'

'Like?'

'Like . . . where does this thing come out in the Millers' house? Why didn't we spot it last month? That house got more attention than the new girl at a titty bar.'

'You weren't looking for a tunnel. I wouldn't have found this if I didn't suspect it was here.' I actually didn't feel like admitting to Sam that what I'd been looking for when I stumbled on the tunnel was Doyle's fancy remote control. 'Who would have guessed that somebody had dug a tunnel into his neighbor's house? Who does things like that?'

Sam eyed me suspiciously. 'You didn't go down there, did you? To the other end? Tell me you didn't mess with this evidence.'

'I went no farther in than you did.'

I waited in the vacant living room while Sam went through the house ordering all the search personnel to pack up their equipment and immediately leave Doyle Chandler's home. While he was upstairs I ambled over to the southern window in the living room and checked to see if I could spot the familiar silhouette in the front upstairs window of the Millers' house. I couldn't.

Sam was the last to clear out.

'Not a word,' he said to me as we approached the front door.

'What do you mean?'

'I don't want Bill Miller to know we're heading over there. All I've told the team is that I'm modifying the affidavit. They don't know about the tunnel yet.'

I made a zip-it motion over my lips.

Sam clarified. 'Not even Lauren.'

'She's probably asleep. I'll tell her in the morning.'

'That's fine. You can tell her in the morning. But you can't tell your source. Your patient, whatever.'

I looked at him quizzically. 'Because I know you aren't clairvoyant, I also know that somebody told you about the existence of this tunnel. It wasn't Doyle Chandler since I don't think he's done much chatting to anybody over the last few days. So it was someone else. Maybe the Camaro guy, maybe not. Doesn't matter. Keep the discovery of the tunnel to yourself.'

'I understand.'

'Wait.' He glared at me. 'You weren't seeing the kid for therapy, were you?'

'Mallory? No.'

The glare degraded into a face that was merely suspicious. 'Was Diane?'

I shook my head. I was glad I wasn't hooked up to a polygraph.

'No bullshit?'

'No bullshit.'

'And your guy's still missing, right?'

'Who?'

'The Camaro guy? You haven't talked to him.'

For the moment, I'd almost forgotten about Bob's plight. 'Yes, he's still missing, and no, I haven't talked to him.'

Sam kept his eyes on mine for a few seconds after I answered his question. He was trying, I thought, to decide whether or not he believed me.

'There's something else to wonder about, too,' he said.

'What?'

'Say the Camaro guy knew about the tunnel. What's his part in all this? You're afraid he's a victim. Not me. I'm seeing his name on our list of suspects. Everything's in play again, Alan. Everything from Christmas Day on.' He opened his eyes wide in amazement. 'And I'm right in the f-ing middle of it.'

It was at that moment that I stopped waiting for Sam to thank me for my help in discovering the tunnel. It was apparent he wasn't too happy about being right in the f-ing middle of whatever the tunnel represented.

'Sam, Mallory could be alone somewhere. If you guys have been wrong all along – if she didn't run, if she was abducted by Doyle . . . well, Doyle's dead. She could be locked in some crappy cabin up in the mountains all by herself. She may not have food or water. It's freezing outside. She may need help.'

'I know all that.'

'Did you guys find out where Doyle's been living since he moved out of here?'

Sam just shook his head. 'We have a cell number, that's all. He was pretty intent on keeping his profile low.'

'Why?' I asked.

'We don't know.'

'You don't know or you won't tell me?'

'We don't know,' Sam admitted.

'Did you find his car?'

'Truck, but no.'

Finally, he opened the front door and allowed me to walk out in front of him. 'Go home. We can do this,' he said.

I thought he was trying to convince himself, but I kept that thought to myself.

55

I took advantage of the cover provided by the cluster of crime-scene techs still huddled outside the front door of Doyle's house and immediately cut across the neighbor's front lawn toward my car. I was hoping that Bill Miller hadn't spotted me either arriving or leaving, but I didn't turn around to check for his silhouette at the window.

The night had turned cold, bitter cold, so cold that the snow on the ground squeaked beneath my feet with each step. I raised the collar on my jacket and stuffed my hands as deeply into my pockets as I could. A breeze was blowing down from the north and I lowered my face to retard the harsh chill of the Canadian air. Each fresh gust cut at my skin like a shard of glass.

'I thought that was you over there.'

Someone was leaning against the hood of my Audi wagon, bundled in a ski parka, a wool cap pulled all the way down past the ears. It took me a moment to process the available data – first, that the person was a man, and second, that the man was probably Bill Miller.

'Good evening,' I said. I thought I'd managed a pretty fair attempt at disguising my fluster.

'We need to talk,' he said.

Politely, I said, 'Well, we have a time set up, I think. I

don't have my calendar with me.' I didn't really expect my parry to work, but mounting it seemed like a necessity.

It didn't work.

'No, now. You're back in my neighborhood. And you're here with a whole shitload of police. That means we talk tonight. Is that too much to ask?'

Shitload? That wasn't a Bill Miller word.

I was starting to shiver from the cold. I was dressed to travel short distances between warm houses and cars with seat heaters. I wasn't dressed warmly enough to linger on a Boulder sidewalk in January in the face of a north wind.

'It's not appropriate for me to see you here, Bill. This isn't the place for a professional meeting.'

'You want to come over to my house?'

The tone of the question was appropriately sarcastic. When I didn't reply, he added, 'Or I could follow you over to your office. That would be fine with me, too.'

My fingers clumsy, I fumbled for the tiny button on the key that would unlock the doors on the Audi. 'Let's get out of the cold. At least tell me what's on your mind.'

Bill's ski parka was noisy. The nylon or Gore-Tex or whatever the sleek fabric was rustled and crackled as he settled into the front seat of my car. I waited patiently for the crackling to diminish, and I used the time to put the key in the ignition, start the engine, and flick on the seat heaters. Truth be told, the seat heaters were half the reason I'd bought the Audi. I never knew it before I tried seat heaters for the first time, but it turned out that if my butt was warm, I was warm.

What an epiphany.

I tried to guess what was coming next from Bill Miller. On that front, I was drawing a blank.

Bill pulled his cap back so that it sat high on the crown of his head like a kid's beanie. He stared at me. In another circumstance I would have found the portrait humorous, and might have laughed. Not that day, though. Not those circumstances.

'Yes?' I said.

Bill turned his whole body on the seat, locking his eyes on mine. His parka erupted in fresh crackles and I concluded that the fabric wasn't Gore-Tex. It would be quieter. He said, 'In Las Vegas? Where Rachel is? There's this guy named Canada.'

Holy moly, I thought. *Holy moly.*

56

I had no way knowing it, of course, and wouldn't learn about it until much later when he told me the story, but at that moment Raoul was in circumstances similar to my own.

Similar, not identical.

The weather, he told me, was warm in Las Vegas, the air in Nevada's southern desert hovering in the low seventies. Needless to say, no one was wearing a ski parka or a wool cap. And no one in his right mind was flicking on an electric seat heater.

But, like me, Raoul was thinking about Canada.

The man sitting in the driver's seat of the car in which Raoul was a passenger was wearing a cap, but Raoul wasn't totally certain what the cap was made of. Not wool. The stuff seemed to be part of the stretchy family of fabrics ideally suited to follow the curves dictated by women's swimwear. The cap hugged the contours of the man's shaved skull and was a dark enough charcoal to be mistaken for black. His shirt wasn't Gore-Tex; it was a sleeveless, well-ventilated version of the kind of shell that boogie boarders use to retard board rash. Raoul thought the random vertical ventilation slits in the garment had been fashioned with a razor blade. All the man had on his feet were fluorescent orange flip-flops with rubber soles that had been worn almost all the way through at the heels.

'You carrying?' he asked Raoul. 'I'm gonna be checking later. Tell me now be better.'

Raoul said, 'No, nothing.'

'Cell phone?'

'The cabbie who dropped me off took it. I'd love to have it back.'

'I'll look into it,' he said. They pulled to a stop at a red light. 'U.P. doesn't fuck around. You have to know that. Just go back home wherever that is, you don't know that. Don't even.'

The car was an old VW bug, similar to the first car Raoul purchased in America decades earlier after ignoring the expiration of his student visa. From dashboard clues Raoul guessed that it was a late '60s vintage, one of the models that came just before what Raoul considered to be the particularly ill-advised bumper design change in '68. The Beetle still had the original beige paint, and the original radio. From the scratchy sound of the hip-hop that was playing, the car had its original speaker, too.

Raoul liked the car. It brought back memories of uncomplicated times.

The man's ethnic background and racial makeup were a puzzle, even to Raoul, who prided himself on his ability to distinguish a Montenegran from a Serb or an Egyptian from an Iraqi across a crowded café. The driver definitely had some Asian blood – Raoul was guessing Tibet – and some African American blood as well, but something else was mixed into his DNA cocktail, too, something Raoul couldn't quite put his finger on.

'U.P. is Canada? Just want to be clear,' he asked.

The man nodded. 'Don't go talking to him that way.

People call him that, but people don't *call* him that. You dig?' He shifted through the car's four gears as though it were as natural as breathing, moving the stick with the middle finger of his right hand or with the webbing at the base of his thumb, never allowing the engine's RPMs to climb into the whining range.

'Thank you for that advice,' Raoul said. 'How would you suggest I address him?'

The man seemed honestly perplexed by the question.

'What do you call him?' Raoul asked.

'Boss.'

'That doesn't sound appropriate. How about Mr. North?'

He thought for a moment. 'That'll work.'

'What's your name?'

'Tico.'

'Thank you, Tico.'

'Hey.'

After a few days tracking his wife, Raoul knew enough about Las Vegas to know that the VW was traveling away from whatever version of civilization the Strip represented on the other side of downtown. He also knew he'd never been in that particular neighborhood before. Literally, or figuratively.

After Raoul had called Norm Clarke late on Thursday to ask him to warn Canada that the Vegas cops were going to start seriously looking for Diane, Raoul had spent some restless hours waiting to hear back. Norm had finally called Raoul and told him that another meeting was arranged with Canada, and that he should wait in a specific spot outside the meeting-room entrance of the Venetian at 11:30 that night. The man who picked him up had been an old-blond guy driving a Vegas cab that was even crappier than the typically crappy Vegas cab. The driver had what appeared to be corn silk growing out of his ears, and he smoked like a crematorium during the plague. For the short drive down the Strip the taxi was thick with a fetid Marlboro cloud.

Raoul spent much of the next twenty or so hours in a vintage – as in 'old,' not in 'classic' – sixteen-foot Airstream that had been left forlorn in one of the trailer-park slums that stain the arid fields on Tropicana Boulevard just a few blocks from the faux munificence of the Strip. The not-so-mobile villages – anachronistic oases of transiency, poverty, and despair – consumed conspicuously undesirable real estate within spitting distance of the end of the runways at McCarran International. Raoul's Airstream hovel appeared to have been in the same spot in that park so long that it looked like the rest of the place was choreographed around it.

Raoul had been alone in the trailer since he'd been dropped off. He'd killed off the long hours counting take-offs and landings, studying a couple of blackjack manuals printed in the late '60s, and watching local Vegas news for nuggets about his wife. The TV was a tiny black-and-white with rabbit ears that reached all the way to the concave ceiling of the Airstream. The view out the filthy awning window at the rear of the trailer was of the blunt end of an old Winnebago. The plates on the RV were long gone, the aluminum skin pitted, the paint faded to nothing, and the bumper stickers so sun-bleached that Raoul could only make out the one that was once a lure for Crater Lake. Raoul tried to get lost in imagining cool, deep water and high country air. Couldn't.

He was trying hard not to think about whatever was happening with Diane. Couldn't do that, either.

Before he'd assured Raoul that someone would come

soon to pick him up and take him to see Canada, the cabbie had instructed him not to wander outside the trailer.

'What about food?' Raoul asked.

'Help yourself to whatever's there,' the guy had said.

The only food in the Airstream cupboards, it turned out, was a yellow box of cornstarch, a rusty can without a label, and an old margarine tub that was half full of something that resembled ground chilis.

The water from the faucet smelled like a rat had peed in it.

Raoul had decided it was a good day to start a cleansing fast.

Despite his hunger and his impatience and a lot of apprehension, Raoul eventually got it. The last piece of Tico's heritage puzzle?

Pacific islands. Maybe even Hawaii. Raoul smiled to himself, momentarily savoring the unknowable hows and the whys of the lives that had intersected and the passions that had collided and ultimately melded together in the startling mitotic process that had eventually created this Tibetan/Pacific Islander/African American who was driving a classic old German car out into the scruffy desert beyond the urban boundaries of Las Vegas, Nevada.

But, right then, in Tico's VW bug, Raoul was – like me – thinking mostly about Diane, and about Canada.

Canada was never far from his mind.

57

'I don't understand what you're saying, Bill.'

I'd actually already made a guess. Bill was continuing the conversation we'd had earlier that day in my office, the one about all he did to support Rachel in her home away from home in Nevada.

'The caretaker for Rachel in Vegas? It's a guy. Canada's a guy. Canada – it's his name. Street name, I don't know. He's, um, kind of adopted Rachel. He looks after her. Keeps her safe. I owe him a lot for what he's done over the years. I'm . . . grateful to him.'

Kind of adopted? What does that mean?

Bill's sentences came out in a series of discrete bursts. Each succeeding sentence was tagged on as though it were a complete afterthought to what had come before. The choppy cadence was something I'd never heard before from him, which told me that he was feeling something right then that he hadn't felt before in my presence. What was that? What was he feeling?

Anxious was the best descriptor I could conjure. As an explanation though, it felt insufficient.

I said, 'Okay.' I didn't feel anything remotely resembling okay, but that's what I said.

'You know about him already?' he asked me.

'About who?' I stammered.

'Canada?'

'I don't know what you're talking about.'

It was a lie. Was it a smooth lie? Probably not. I lie like I ski. Not as well as most people I know, and my form tends to leave a lot to be desired.

'Canada's help doesn't come cheap. These things are expensive.'

These things? Was Bill telling me that he had financial issues about Rachel's care after all? I had the good sense to stay quiet while I waited to find out.

But he changed gears. He said, 'We've been together, what, three times? You haven't asked me a thing about Mallory. Do you know how weird that is after what I've been through for the last few weeks?'

I thought: *Well, Bill, we've been together, what, three times? You haven't really mentioned a thing about Mallory, either. Do you know how weird* that *is after what you've been through the last few weeks?*

I didn't say that. I said something else that was just as true, though not quite as honest. 'It's not my call. I thought you would get there when you were ready.'

'Ready? What the hell does that mean? Ready? You've got to be kidding. Hell, what's wrong with you?'

He grew quiet again. I decided to try being a therapist. I said, 'You mentioned a man – Canada? – someone you said looks after your wife. And then you obliquely referred to your daughter's situation. Is it possible that there might be a connection of some kind between the two?' I feared that I'd been way too obvious with my question.

'What are you saying?'

'I'm not saying anything. My job as a therapist is to follow closely behind you, see where you're going, look over your shoulder. Hopefully, I can point out things that you don't see or aren't prepared to see.'

'And that's what exactly? What are you implying I'm not prepared to see?'

Bill wasn't curious to hear my response, not in any sincere way. He was challenging me, provoking me, poking a finger into my chest, trying to get me to back off of . . . something.

'You also mentioned money,' I added. I added it because I guessed that money was what Bill didn't want to talk about.

'No, you're the one who mentioned money.'

'This afternoon, I did. Tonight, you did.'

'All I said is that it's expensive.'

I was too tired for verbal sparring. I wanted to go home, hug my wife, hold my daughter, play with my dogs. Eat something hot. Drink something with alcohol in it. I wanted to spend a couple of hours without anyone doing any inferring or any implying or any alluding. My impulse to flee felt selfish and cowardly, at least partly because I was certain that I was missing something that a more contemplative person would see, but I tried for an out anyway. 'Bill, these are important things for you, obviously. But I don't see any reason that they can't wait until our scheduled appointment time.'

Something about my suggestion seemed to shake him free, allow him to change track again. Not exactly what I had hoped for, but at least momentarily I felt the air between us settle.

'What was going on next door?' he asked. 'Why all the cops? Nobody will talk to me. I can't reach my lawyer.'

'I can't say. The police asked for my help with something.'

'Is it about my daughter?'

'I'm sorry. I've promised them that I wouldn't discuss it.'

'Is it?'

'Bill, I'm sorry. I can't say what it is. I can't say what it's not. I've been told not to discuss it.'

'Doyle gave them permission to go into his house?'

Doyle's dead, Bill. His giving-permission days are behind him, I thought as I replayed Bill's question in my head, tasting for disingenuousness. I was wondering if Bill already knew that Doyle was dead.

'I'm sorry.'

'This is bullshit.' Bill's voice suddenly became a hoarse whisper and the anger in it was unmistakable. 'If this is the way it's going to be, I'm not sure I can continue seeing you.'

If that was a threat, it was lame, like holding a rubber knife to my throat. 'That's certainly your choice, Bill. I'll be happy to make a referral, if you would like.'

'Yeah,' he scoffed. 'That worked out well last time.'

And what does that mean? Mary Black bent over backward to help Rachel.

'Mallory saw a therapist. Did you know that?' he asked.

I was startled. I managed a flustered, 'What?'

'The woman who died. Mallory went to see her a couple of weeks before Christmas. She didn't tell me; she left a note about it in her journal.'

I had a thousand questions. One of them was: *Have you told the police about that journal?* I chose a different one: 'Why did she see a therapist?'

'I don't know that exactly.'

'Do the police know? The therapist may have left some . . . records behind.'

He didn't answer my question. He cracked open the door of the car and prepared to climb out, but stopped. 'Do you know anything about her? Are you keeping something from me? You wouldn't do that, would you?'

Now those were tough questions. I didn't have an immediate answer for any of them.

'I'm talking father to father right now, Alan. Father to father.'

'I wish I knew something that could help you find your daughter. I'd tell you if I did.'

He considered my words, tasting them for the sweetness of truth. 'You're a father. You have a daughter, too. Imagine losing her. You have to understand the vulnerability I'm feeling.'

I swallowed. I didn't want to be reminded of that vulnerability.

Bill went on. 'A father would do anything to protect his family. Anything. You know that. The things that can happen to kids? Daughters. You wouldn't wish that on me, would you? I wouldn't wish it on you.'

I immediately began pondering the question of how truthful my answer had been. Surprisingly, I decided that, other than the existence of the tunnel, and the fact that I knew she'd seen Hannah for a single therapy session, I didn't actually know anything substantive about Mallory. I really didn't. How odd.

'You wouldn't divulge our conversations to the police, would you?'

'Of course not,' I said. I wondered how much Bill really knew about Mallory's situation. 'What do you think happened to Mallory? Did she run? Was she abducted?'

'Those are the only options?' he said.

What? Was he taunting me? 'I'm not sure what you're saying.'

'Why would she run?' Bill asked.

'Kids aren't always rational, Bill. Especially when they're distraught.'

'She was distraught. Christmas was always hard for her,' Bill said. 'Always. But I thought we were doing okay this year.'

That's what Bob had said, too – that Christmas was hard for Mallory. *Huh.* I reminded myself that Rachel had deserted her family during the holidays years before, and that it wouldn't be surprising that Mallory was suffering an anniversary reaction.

'You were doing okay, you and she?' I asked.

'What are you asking?'

'Nothing. I'm fishing.'

'Fishing?'

Bill hovered, half-in, half-out of my car for a long three-count before he stood. I sat frozen in place, still troubled by Bill's admission that he possessed a diary from his daughter that he hadn't shared with the police. 'Let's do this in the morning, Bill. At my office. Is ten okay?'

He held up his gloved right hand and extended two fingers. 'Can't do ten. I'll be there at two,' he said before he slammed the door.

The bitter air had frosted the hairs inside my nose.

But I did notice that my ass was nice and warm.

58

The same night, at almost the same time, Raoul was still thinking about Diane and Canada.

He told me later that he was surprised to see how Las Vegas bleeds out into the northern desert. There is no natural demarcation, no river, no ridge, no rail at the craps table. There is no single line in the dirt and sand where a visitor would say, well, this here is Las Vegas, and that there isn't. At some point you know you've left town, but even if someone offered you to-die-for odds, you couldn't go back and find the precise spot where it happened.

Raoul looked back over his shoulder at the profile of the distant Strip that stained the near horizon with artificial vertical interruptions and radiating flashes of neon. He guessed that he and Tico were about five miles outside of town. It could have been seven, could have been three, but he was guessing five.

Tico had yanked the VW through a lot of turns to get where they were, many more than Raoul thought should be necessary to get from point A to point B across a landscape of flat, mostly barren land. But the turns had accomplished what Tico had intended: Other than being some number of miles out in the desert north of Las Vegas, Raoul didn't know where he was.

Wide expanses of scruffy land separated the houses. In some other place, somewhere where the soil was arable, such distances between homes might make sense, but in the desert outside Vegas it seemed to Raoul that people lived as far apart as possible simply so that they could feel some separation. In Colorado's mountains, a ridge or an outcropping of rock or a thick stand of lodgepole pine was enough to leave neighbors feeling distinct from one another. Out in this endless desert, though, the geography made no natural allowances for privacy, and separation apparently meant space.

Tico doused the headlights on the VW a few hundred yards before he pulled to a stop at an expensive wrought-iron gate in an even more expensive high stucco wall. There wasn't much of a moon and the desert was dark. Raoul couldn't tell where Tico had taken him, but he was guessing the building was a residence. Tico waved casually toward a security camera mounted on the stucco wall, and seconds later the gates clanked loudly and started to swing inward.

The place wasn't much to look at. It was a sprawling, low-slung ranch with long overhanging rooflines designed to protect inhabitants from the relentless Nevada sun. Raoul dated the construction from the '60s or '70s. Somebody had once tried to do some landscaping, but the effort had been abandoned a long time before. Tall, vaguely Greek planting urns sat forlorn and empty at intervals around the property. Adjacent to the crumbling concrete driveway a swimming pool shaped like a spade was a third filled with murky water. The front of the separate pool house was almost totally obscured by junk. The shadowed symmetry of the red tile roof on the shack was interrupted by broken and absent tiles and what looked to be an abandoned array of solar panels.

Raoul said, 'That fence we went through is worth more than the house.'

'Boss isn't picky about stuff. Everything's temporary but people. That's what he says, says it all the time.'

'I take it he doesn't swim.'

'Don't go there, man.' Tico smiled. 'Don't go there. Uh, uh. No swimming jokes, you dig?'

'Yes,' Raoul said. 'Thanks. Does he live here?' He didn't expect to get an answer and was surprised when Tico decided to give him one.

'Stays here sometimes. Other places, too. A lot. He lives where he happens to be. At some point soon enough this place will get sold. They be another, and another after that. Like that. He gets 'em. Gets rid of 'em. We move on.'

'The Airstream?'

Tico smiled. 'Had that one for a while. May be gone now, too.' He killed the tiny engine on the bug. For a moment the clatter of the valves was the loudest sound in Raoul's ears.

Raoul said, 'Your boss and me have that in common. Buying and selling. I'm a bit of a speculator, too.' Initially Raoul thought Tico had been considering saying something in reply, but had thought better of it. 'You have some advice for me?'

'Advice?' Tico adjusted the fabric that clung to his shaved skull, pulling it tighter toward his ears, tight enough that a phrenologist could have done a comprehensive exam without removing the cap. 'Whatever you think is about to happen here, bro, you wrong. That's my advice for you. If you think you here 'cause you want to talk to U.P., you wrong. Want to know why you here? You here 'cause U.P. want to talk to you. No other damn reason.' He opened the door and hopped out of the car. 'I need to pat you down now. No offense.'

Raoul joined him on the driveway and lifted his arms. 'None taken. I apologize for the smell. The shower in the Airstream wasn't working.'

59

A frosty halo was framing what was visible of the moon as I turned east on Baseline toward my house. Most days, late rush-hour traffic would have dictated that I take South Boulder Road across the valley, but that night, because of the hour, I took Baseline. I was stopped at the traffic signal at the Foothills Parkway when my cell chirped in my pocket. I fished it out, managed to hit a tiny button with my almost frozen fingers, and said, 'I'll be home soon, I promise. I'm on my way. I'm sorry.'

But it wasn't Lauren. It was Sam.

'Sweet,' he said. 'Total capitulation. I find that so attractive in a man. Where are you?'

'Baseline. Across from Safeway.'

'Good, you're close. Come on over to the department. I want to show you something.'

'Now?'

'You'll want to see this.'

The signal arrow turned green. I checked my mirrors and cut across two lanes of the intersection to make one of the more illegal left turns in Boulder history, and accelerated back toward Arapahoe.

'Tell me,' I said.

He of little patience said, 'Patience.'

I arrived at the Public Safety Building on Thirty-third Street within minutes and parked on the deserted street out front. Sam was pacing in the public lobby, eating the last few bites of a Chipotle burrito that I knew had originally been almost the size of a loaf of Wonder Bread. My stomach growled at the tantalizing smell.

'Chicken?'

'Carnitas. Not too much fat. Niman Ranch pork. No hormones or shit. I get them with no sour cream, no cheese. Living in Boulder is finally starting to rub off on me.' He stuffed a final chunk of burrito into his mouth. 'Probably too much salt, though. Whatever, it's a treat. A year ago I probably would have been sucking that white shit out of the middle of a Twinkie.'

'Got any more?' I asked.

'Ha. Come on,' he said, balling up the tinfoil and dropping it into a trash can by the reception counter. He wiped his mustache with a napkin and tossed that away, too.

'You already revise your warrant?' I asked.

'Just waiting on Judge Heller and then we head back to the Hill for round two.'

I followed him down the central corridor to a detective's work area that was set up with a video monitor. The detritus of a few other investigations and the refuse of a few other recent fast-food meals littered the surface of three laminated tables that had been pushed into a clumsy U-shape.

Detectives cleaned up crimes; they apparently didn't clean up after themselves.

'Make yourself comfortable,' he said, pointing to a chair that didn't scream 'comfort.'

'I'd be more comfortable home in bed.'

'Yeah,' he said wistfully, but without any empathy whatsoever.

I sat. 'What is it you wanted me to see?'

He gestured at the AV setup. 'You tell me.'

He flicked on the monitor and used a remote control to start a VCR. After a moment's whirring the familiar logo of the local Fox news affiliate filled the screen.

'We recorded this off the air. TiVo. Somebody upstairs transferred it to tape for me to play with. VCRs I can handle, barely. TiVo? Sorry, I don't TiVo.' He chuckled at something. 'Department has frigging TiVo. When I got here we had yellow squad cars.'

I ignored the fact that the allusion made no particular sense and smiled at the memory of the banana-colored patrol cars that Boulder's cops had driven around town for a while as part of a short-lived, amusing experiment in community-friendly policing.

I expected I was about to watch tape of the local Fox affiliate's coverage of the discovery of Doyle Chandler's body near Allenspark that afternoon. Why? Sam would tell me when he was ready. Not before. But Sam surprised me, as he often did.

'Christmas night,' Sam said as the screen showed Fox's infamous Mallory Miller money shot: the helicopter footage of the Hill on Christmas night, the tape that purportedly showed no footprints or tire tracks leaving the Millers' home after the snow started falling in earnest.

'You oriented?' he asked.

'Yes.' I'd seen the footage often enough to know what was what. If you lived in Colorado in the days after Mallory's disappearance and had turned on your TV set, you had seen this film as many times as you'd seen the other little Boulder girl dancing around at beauty pageants.

Sam paused the screen, picked up a laser pointer, and let the red dot settle. 'Harts' house.'

'Got it.' The holiday lights were unmistakable.

'Millers' house and Doyle Chandler's house are over here.' He made a dot appear on the wall behind the monitor.

'Right where they've always been.'

'Fox has been kind enough to superimpose the time line on the bottom of the screen.' He started the tape again. 'Here's where the controversy starts: nine-sixteen.'

The footage was the enhanced version that Fox had promoted and promoted and promoted a few days after Christmas. It was the clip that started at 9:16 on Christmas night and stopped a couple of minutes later with the famous few seconds that showed no footprints or tire tracks leaving the Millers' home.

'I've seen this,' I said.

'Yeah, but have you *seen* it? Start with your eyes at the lower-right corner of the screen – here, Doyle Chandler's garage.' He paused the footage momentarily. The Harts' house was in the center of the screen; Doyle's house, but not the Millers' house, was visible on the lower edge.

I'd never noticed that Doyle's house showed up in the early moments of the Fox footage. Sam said, 'That's smooth snow around the garage, right?'

'Yes.'

'Fresh? You're sure.'

'Yes.'

'Well, keep your eye on the garage as the chopper moves around. With the distraction of the Christmas lights and the shadows it's kind of hard to follow, but try.'

Sam aided me with his laser pointer; he was remarkably adept at keeping the red dot targeted on the dark mass of Doyle's garage. As the angle of the shot varied with the helicopter's movement the garage would frequently shift totally out of the frame; one long absence lasted for a good half minute, another for almost as long.

I stated the obvious. 'Can't see it most of the time, Sam. It goes off the screen.'

'I know. It's important that you can't see it. The last few seconds are coming – watch carefully.'

Fox hadn't enhanced the area on the footage that included Doyle's garage – they'd focused all their technological wizardry efforts on the Millers' property – and it wasn't easy to discern much detail in other parts of the frame, especially with the startling bright lights that stayed mostly centered on the screen, lights that were emanating from the garish Christmas display at the Harts' house on the next block.

The Very Hart of Christmas.

'There,' Sam said. He paused the tape and allowed the red dot to linger on the short driveway that led from Doyle's garage to the alley. 'What do you see now?'

I stood up and moved closer to the monitor. The closer I got, the larger the pixels on the screen appeared. At first I wasn't sure what I was seeing, or even if I was seeing anything at all. Then I was.

I turned and faced Sam. 'Are those . . . tire tracks leaving Doyle's garage?' I asked. 'Those weren't there at the beginning.'

'Yeah, that's what I see, too,' Sam said. His tone was understated and self-satisfied.

Bob, I thought. Bob had pulled his Camaro out of Doyle's garage during the second extended period that the garage was out of the frame.

The tunnel. The damn tunnel.

The damn movie in the damn theater in the damn basement.

Did Bob really have something to do with Mallory's disappearance?

I was shocked. 'Did he help her leave, Sam? Or did he take her?'

I didn't have to say who 'he' was. He knew I was talking about Bob.

'You don't know where he is, do you?' Sam asked.

'No, I told you I didn't. I don't.'

'This isn't some therapist nice-nice secret-secret bullshit?'

'I don't know where he is.'

'You know where to look for him?'

I hesitated for a split second. 'No.'

Sam made a guttural noise – okay, he growled at me – and mouthed a dry 'f' sound. It didn't take much lip-reading skill to know what exactly he'd thought about saying.

'I really don't, Sam. If I did, I'd tell you. Given what already happened to Doyle, Bob could be in danger, too. I would tell you if I knew.'

He wasn't satisfied. 'You know something, don't you? You know something that could help me? Something you're not telling me?'

'Sam . . .'

'Man . . .' He stood up quickly, almost knocking his chair over.

Five minutes later Sam walked me back to my car. He seemed impervious to the cold. I bet he didn't even care that his Cherokee didn't have seat heaters.

'Chinooks tomorrow,' Sam said.

'They thought they were coming today, too. They're wrong a lot,' I replied, wondering why we were talking about the weather. 'If the Chinooks do start to blow, at least it will warm things up a little. It's too cold.'

'The media isn't going to know what to do with those winds,' Sam said. 'Should be fun.'

'What?'

'They'll be back tomorrow. You know they will. With word of the tunnel and the Doyle Chandler situation? All the trucks and all the cameras – they'll all be back outside the Millers' house doing their stupid live shots. The idiot lawyers on cable will all be saying we blew it again. Us, the Boulder cops. "It's just like Christmas eight years ago," that's what they'll say. But then the Chinooks will start blowing late morning and they'll blow the goddamn experts all the goddamn way to Denver, maybe farther. It'll be too windy to raise the antennas on their trucks. I wish I could be there; it'll be fun to watch.'

I checked his expression. He was truly sorry he was going to miss it.

'I'm going to tell Lauren about all this, Sam. The tunnel, Doyle, Bob,' I said. 'I need some advice from her.'

'Tell her to sit on it till morning. Our bases will be pretty well covered in the next couple of hours. Get some sleep for me tonight.' He stuffed his hands in his pockets. 'I don't think I'll be getting much.'

'How did you put this together?' I asked as I clicked open the wagon doors with the key remote. 'The Camaro? Why did you decide to go back and look at that tape?'

'This is far from together. The tunnel changes everything. One of the things it changes is which house we should be paying attention to. Where Mallory's disappearance is concerned, we've had our eyes on the Miller house, not on Doyle Chandler's house. On the way back here to amend the warrant app I remembered that you had asked me if there was a car in Doyle's garage when we searched the house the day after Mallory disappeared. I told you I didn't think so, but it's been something I've been meaning to ask your patient Bob about if we ever caught up with him.'

'But you decided to check the Fox footage instead? Smart, Sammy. So do you have a theory to explain all this? Does tonight – the tunnel and this video – does it change your thinking about her disappearance? You still sure she's a runaway?'

'I have a few theories,' he said. 'How many do you have?'

He waited for me to answer.

When I didn't, he added, 'Thought so. I'll show you mine if you'll show me yours.'

I left the show-and-tell right there. 'You still want to run in the morning? I'm happy to bag it if you're too busy.'

'I want to run,' he said. 'No excuses. Since it's Saturday, I'll let you sleep in. Come outside at seven-thirty – I don't want to ring the bell.'

60

I finally made it home from the police station, took the dogs out for a last time, climbed into bed, and rubbed Lauren's back until she awakened. Although I left a few names and a few details out of my story, I told her enough of what I knew that she understood the magnitude of my dilemma. I finished by asking for her advice.

Her counsel was succinct. 'Higher, on my neck. Right there.'

'That's it?'

'No, that's not it. On one hand you know a lot. On the other hand you don't know much. You need to leverage what you have. Save Diane no matter what it takes, screw the rest.'

'It's all that clear to you? I could get censured, lose my license.'

She rolled over and faced me. My eyes were adjusting to the dark and I could see the shimmer of her irises. She said, 'You'd have to sleep with a patient, kill her, and then have sacrilegious sex with her dead body before that spineless state board would yank your license, and you know it. But what if they do? You and me and Grace? We'll make it if you have to change careers. We will. Will you make it if you knew you could have done something that might have helped Diane and you didn't do it? I don't think so. You're pussyfooting around this, Alan. The rules need to be broken sometimes. This is one of those times. Break the damn rules, save your friend, suffer the consequences. You won't be able to live with any other choice, you know that.'

'Just like that?'

'Just like that.'

She reached a warm arm out from under the comforter, put her fingers on the side of my neck, and lowered her voice to a late-night whisper. 'There's some things I know about you, sweetie: You're a better cook when you're not too hungry. You're a better dad when you're not feeling too protective. And you're a better lover when you're not too horny.'

'You have a point?'

'You want this to be right too much, and it's clouding your judgment. Step back. Take off your therapist hat. Be a friend, first. You'll know what to do.'

I didn't have to think long to know that her advice was sound.

'What?' she said, sensing something.

'I'm a better lover when I'm not too horny? Really?'

She smiled and shrugged. She dropped her hand so that it slid down my bare chest. 'You want to prove otherwise?'

The truth was, I didn't. Not right then.

61

The way he told it to me later, Raoul's evening, like mine, ended with just the slightest ray of hope.

More quarry tile than he had seen in a long, long time. Big tiles – eighteen-inch squares. Brick-red, uneven surfaces, with dirty grout lines as fat as a grown man's finger. The tile extended through every doorway, down every hall. This house was apparently where the awful quarry tile from that dubious '70s design burp had gone to die.

Raoul had expected to find a posse surrounding Canada, a jury of pathetic hangers-on. He'd expected to have to weed through a motley assortment of tougher-than-shit Cristal and Courvoisier-and-Coke-drinking parasites.

Instead he found a fit, barefoot man wearing crinkled linen slacks and a faded polo shirt that was the color of the flesh of a ripe mango. The man was sitting on one of two big armchairs that shared a large, mismatched ottoman and faced floor-to-ceiling sliding glass doors in the living room. His legs were crossed at the ankles. One toenail on his left foot had turned the brown-black of just-roasted coffee beans. It was the toe next to the pinky.

Canada was alone.

'Sit,' he said to Raoul.

Tico loitered across the room near the back door where the parking lot of quarry tile started, or ended. He said, 'You cool, Boss?'

'Yeah, get yourself something to eat.'

Tico saluted with a motion of two fingers flying out from his right nipple. Raoul figured it meant, 'Yes, sir.' Or something in that vicinity. Tico spun. His flip-flops squealed once before they began a percussive *smack-smack* against the hard floor as he made his way toward the kitchen.

'I can't find her,' Canada said. 'Come on, sit.' He pointed at the chair beside him. 'You want something to drink?'

Raoul did, but it could wait. *You can't find whom?* That's what he wanted to know. That couldn't wait. He said, 'No, thank you.'

He was thinking that U.P. North was late thirties, maybe forty. The man was fair-skinned with a full head of curly jet-black hair, and he apparently went to some trouble to avoid the desert sun. He was strong. Not I-live-in-the-weight-room strong, but I've-got-a-personal-trainer and I-play-a-heck-of-a-lot-of-tennis strong.

Raoul fought an instinct that was telling him that he knew the man, or at least knew his type. Sometimes in Boulder he met the smug, self-assured, I've-got-shit-going-on-you-don't-even-know-about types at parties. At first impression, U.P. North could be one of them, just another Boulder trust-fund baby. But Raoul cautioned himself that North probably wasn't one of them. Not by a long shot.

Intimidating? Not to Raoul, not yet.

Blood? Northeast U.S., sure. Whatever that means anymore. Some French ancestry, and maybe something else. Could North have some Eastern European blood, maybe

Jewish? Raoul wasn't certain. Didn't know if he had enough clues.

Raoul sat. 'You can't find her? My wife?'

Three sets of sliding glass doors were open to the night air. The pattern meant that every other panel was glass, every other panel was screen. The prodigious sweat that Raoul had developed while doing time inside the Airstream and then compounded in the cramped front seat of Tico's bug wasn't evaporating at all. No breeze was blowing across the wide desert that night.

'I like the heat,' the man said as though he'd anticipated Raoul's thoughts. 'Hate AC.'

Raoul duly noted that his question hadn't been answered and decided not to press it. North wasn't actually talking to Raoul, he was talking to Raoul's reflection in the glass. Raoul adjusted his gaze, found the mirrored image of his host against the black hollow, and did the same. He said, 'I changed my mind. I'd love a beer, thank you.'

Canada called out, 'Tico? A brew for our guest.'

Tico came and went. He left behind a long-necked Bud that was sweating even more than Raoul. The bottle immediately left a round tattoo on the table.

'You like the desert?' Canada asked.

'I grew up on the Mediterranean,' Raoul said as a way of answering. 'Live in the mountains now.'

'I grew up on Long Island, not far from Jones Beach. I like the desert better.'

'Taste,' Raoul said. 'It's a personal thing.'

North chewed on that for a moment. 'There's some shit we do that has nothing to do with taste. It has to do with cycles. Ebb and flow. Moon and tides. Sunrise, sunset. You play golf?'

'Some. I suck,' Raoul said.

North laughed. 'Bastard game. In golf . . . in business . . . with women . . . dear Lord, with women . . . all the time, I'm big on mulligans. I . . . treasure the living that happens in the echoes. Like to think I do some of my best work in the echoes.'

'The echoes?'

'The opportunities that come back around. The do-overs. A man has to learn in life. He has to. In golf, it's not really that satisfying. It's hard to learn enough from one tee shot to the next. If you do better on your mulligan than you did on your first drive, could be dumb luck. Probably is dumb luck. In life, though, the do-overs tend to come around less often. That gives the wise man time to adjust, to be grateful for the opportunity, to make the most of the blessing of the second chance. You're a successful man. You must know about the echoes. Every successful man I've ever met knows about playing the echoes.'

Raoul drank enough of the Bud that when he pulled the bottle back down from his lips the beer leveled off at a line about two thirds of the way down the label. He said, 'If I'm understanding you right, I think maybe I do know about the echoes.'

'Rachel's one of my echoes.' Canada's eyes locked on Raoul's in the black mirror of the glass. He held Raoul's gaze like a strong man holds a handshake – a few beats too long, just to prove that he can do it. 'She's a paranoid schizophrenic. You know about that?'

Raoul decided the time was right to once again interject Diane into the conversation. 'My wife's a psychologist. I learn some things from her.'

North nodded. Raoul translated the nod to mean, 'Whatever.'

'My mother was one, too. A paranoid schiz. I watched

her do her crazy thing most of the time I was growing up. Nobody helped her out. Not really. People laughed, the ones who didn't avoid us took advantage. She ended up running away with some loser she met in a biker bar. Came home with him, grabbed some things, said she'd be back soon. I never saw her again. I still don't like to think about what happened to her next.'

Raoul felt the rhythm of the melody that was developing and decided to skip right to the chorus. 'But for Rachel, you're what happened next?'

'There's the echo. When they come back around, you get another chance. Not all the time, but sometimes. When you do, it's important to get it right. The gods count on it. They keep score.'

'You take care of her?'

'I watch out for her. Difference. Nobody can protect her from being crazy. I learned that lesson as a kid. Paranoid schizes have the kind of crazy that comes from someplace else. Someplace where the tiniest wires are jumbled, someplace you and I don't ever get to visit. All I do – all I can do – is I protect her from people who prey. That's all. I let them know if they fuck with her, they have to fuck with me. People in town have learned to leave well enough alone; people new to town need lessons. It's what I wished I could have done for my mother.'

Raoul lost the visual connection in the pane of glass as Canada shifted the range of focus from Raoul's eyes to the infinity of the desert night. From inside to out.

'That's generous of you,' Raoul said, already wondering whether his empathy was being misapplied.

'Is it?'

Raoul didn't want to argue the point. A linguistic chameleon, he adopted his host's vernacular. 'Has someone fucked with her lately?'

'People have been coming in from out of town. It's not been welcome. We've had to deal with it.'

Raoul felt the reverberation: Diane had come in from out of town. He put his cards on the table. 'My wife flew to Las Vegas looking for Rachel. She had some questions about her daughter – Rachel's missing daughter. I'm sure you know that. Before she was able to meet with Rachel, Diane disappeared off the casino floor at the Venetian. That was Monday night. I'm worried about her, very worried. I'd like to know where she is. I'm happy to tell you what I know.'

With just the slightest spice of menace added to his tone – a verbal dash of cayenne – North said, 'Doesn't make any difference to me whether or not you're happy. But you will tell me what you know. One thing, though, Raoul. May I call you Raoul?'

'Of course. What's that?'

'It's not all about your wife.'

Raoul felt some intimidation then. He shrank a little at the words, had to remind himself not to cower, and had to remind himself that Canada held all the good cards. 'Okay,' he said.

'Now, like I said, I can't find her – Rachel. You feel the echo there? Yes, me, too.' He exhaled through pursed lips. 'I'm not happy I can't find her. Are we in the same boat, Raoul? You and me? The not-happy-I-can't-find-her boat?'

'Are we?' Raoul asked.

'I think so. I think we are.'

Raoul dove so far into his host's eyes that he was almost submerged. Sensing something there, he took a last look at his cards and went all-in. 'Diane was led out of the Venetian casino on Monday evening by two men. They weren't yours?' He pulled the grainy screen shot that Marlina had given him from his pocket, unfolded it, and handed it to Canada.

'You think they were mine?' Canada asked after a quick glance at the photograph of three people walking through the casino at the Venetian.

Totally cognizant of how provocative his words were, Raoul said, 'I did.'

'If they were mine, you'd be a dead man. You feel like a dead man?'

'I admit I've felt better.'

Canada laughed. A stretch of silence consumed half a minute before he added, 'They're not mine.' He raised the photograph, grasping it between his thumb and index finger, and rotated it so that it faced Raoul. 'You don't recognize the tall guy? I'm surprised; you seem like an observant man.'

Raoul leaned over and squinted at the taller of the two men. 'Should I?'

'I hear you call him "Reverend Howie."'

'What? *Mierda*. His hair . . .'

'That's not his hair. Probably won it in a poker game.'

Raoul had participated in a thousand negotiations, some of them involving tens of millions of dollars. In every deal, instinct was his guide. He relied on that intuition and felt around in the dark for whatever direction he was going to get. 'Howie didn't take Diane for you?'

Canada hesitated before he shook his head.

'Do you recognize the other man?' Raoul asked.

Canada took another fleeting glance at the paper. 'If I admit I do, what happens then?'

Raoul jumped at the bait. 'If Diane's okay, I swear I'll—'

Canada held his left hand out. A stop sign. 'No, my friend. No . . . No. The ifs are all mine. You don't get any ifs. These two people weren't working for me. I don't know what they've done, or to whom. That means there are no ifs left over for you. We clear?'

No, Raoul thought. He said, 'Yes.'

'Good. I repeat, if I admit I do recognize him, what happens then?'

'I will be grateful for your assistance,' Raoul said.

'How grateful?'

Raoul wondered momentarily if Canada was trying to extort some money. He recalled Tico's admonition in the car – *Everything's temporary but people. That's what he says, says it all the time* – and decided that it wasn't likely that Canada was squeezing a reward from him. Raoul said, 'I will be completely grateful. So grateful you won't be playing any echoes about this.'

'Ever?'

'Ever.'

'And if you happen to run across Rachel?'

'Goes without saying. You'll know first.'

Canada poked at the photograph. 'This guy? The one with Howard? Showed up in town a day or so before your wife, went to Rachel's apartment looking for her, failed, then started asking around about how to find her. Howard alerted us that the guy came to the chapel. Howard, it now appears, was playing both ends against the middle. Well, that's a tougher game than Hold 'Em – and soon enough, if he isn't already, Howard will regret he anteed in. We started keeping an eye on the new man. Lost him for a while. Found him again. Eventually he had a traffic accident. Sad thing.'

'Serious accident?' Raoul asked.

Canada feigned a sympathetic face. 'Misjudged a curve in the mountains. His car had Colorado plates. Tico?' he called.

Tico hustled in carrying a half-eaten piece of cold pizza.

His mouth was full. Canada pointed at the photo. 'You know where?'

Tico glanced at the picture, then at Raoul, swallowed, and said, 'I could probably find it.'

'Show our friend.'

'Not sure I can do it in the dark, Boss. You tell me to try, though, I will.'

Canada tapped his manicured fingernails on the arm of the chair. 'Find Raoul a bed for the night, some clean towels, and offer him some food. You can take him out in the morning. And Raoul?'

'Yes.'

'You don't mind that I hold on to this?' He lifted the photograph. 'I'd like to show it to Howard.'

62

I was wide-eyed and body-weary long before Sam's arrival for our Saturday run, but the winter sky was too black for daybreak and the bedroom too cold to consider popping right out of bed. I waited for the growl of the paper guy's Power Wagon to come and go and for the first unmistakable illuminations of dawn before I rolled reluctantly into the day.

Even the dogs thought I was crazy. Emily sighed at me, but she didn't bother to get up to see what I had planned. Anvil, whose ears were beginning to fail him, didn't acknowledge that I'd moved.

I forced myself to drink some water and I downed a banana after mindlessly trying to peel a plantain that Lauren or Viv had stuck in the fruit bowl. The plantain wasn't ripe and wasn't at all eager to be peeled. I totally mangled the thing before I figured out that I wasn't wrestling with a mutant Chiquita.

New errand: Replace the damn plantain.

I thought I heard a car on the lane and peeked out the front door at 7:25. No Sam. I was hoping he'd spaced out the run or that he'd overslept. Jogging on a fifteen-degree morning didn't sound any more appetizing to me than had eating an under-ripe plantain.

Seven-thirty. No Sam. Out loud, I prayed, 'Give it a rest, Sammy. Take a day off.' That, of course, is when he drove up the lane. He climbed out of the Cherokee in his fancy running duds and a brand-new pair of trainers. His frosty breath was visible in long, slow rolls. Lauren's advice from the night before felt as sage to me as it had then, but I still hadn't decided exactly what I knew that I could tell Sam that might help Diane. He rescued me from my temporary paralysis by saying, 'Let's stretch a minute. I want to tell you about the tunnel search.'

The tunnel. The opening that had been excavated from Doyle's basement was cut at a steep enough angle that it actually descended all the way down below the spread footing of the foundation of the Millers' house. At that point the track-and-trolley system terminated and a vertical shaft about two feet in diameter rose straight up into the Millers' crawl space. The top of the shaft was covered by a fitted piece of one-inch-thick plywood upholstered with an ample amount of dirt that had been glued to the wood with some kind of industrial-strength adhesive.

Were someone to venture into the crawl space, any evidence of the construction project was hidden from view by the thick-milled black-plastic sheeting that stretched from foundation wall to foundation wall over the entire expanse. The plastic was installed to collect the natural radon that was common in soil in Colorado, so the gases could be vented to the outdoors and the lungs of the home's inhabitants could be protected from the toxic consequences of long-term radiation exposure.

Access from the tunnel into the Miller home was ingenious. False sills had been attached to the tops of the foundation walls in the corner closest to the tunnel shaft.

The plastic sheeting had been removed from the original sills and reattached to the false sills, where it could be easily lifted and folded back to reveal the opening of the shaft. After an intruder was ready to return to Doyle's house next door, he had only to lock the false sills back in place – which would return the plastic to its normal location – and then slide the plywood lid back over the shaft.

A cursory examination of the crawl space by someone in the Miller home would reveal no evidence of the tunnel. Once Sam was down in the crawl space, it had taken him a few minutes to figure out exactly how it all worked, despite the fact that he knew almost precisely where the tunnel should be entering the house. The only clue to the location, he said, was a slight interruption in the dust pattern on top of the plastic sheeting.

Bill Miller professed shock and ignorance at the discovery of the tunnel. Although the revised warrant that Sam delivered to Bill's door gave him no choice about the matter, he was totally cooperative with the police about access to his crawl space.

He also rapidly put two and two together and got four. 'Where is Doyle?' Bill had demanded. 'Have you guys talked to him? Is he under arrest? Somebody tell me something! Does he know where Mallory is?'

Sam made a tactical decision to allow Bill to hover close by during the search – he wanted to observe him – but he wasn't buying Bill's act. 'He knew it was there,' Sam told me. 'Might even have known Doyle was dead.'

'He knew about the tunnel? What makes you think that?'

'You interview enough people you get to know when they're lying. Meryl Streep could lie to me and get away with it, maybe Al Pacino. Definitely what's-his-face, Anthony Hopkins. But Bill Miller? He couldn't even get a bit part with the Flatirons Players. Must be the same for you, you know, in your business.'

The truth was that my patients often lied to me with absolute impunity. I rationalized my often embarrassing credulity by trying to convince myself that when my patients lied to me they were lying to themselves as well, and that was why I was so inept at spotting their mistruths.

But the simple reality is that I am gullible. In reply to Sam, I said, 'Yeah.'

He chuckled. 'Exactly what I'm talking about. Exactly.'

I asked, 'Speaking of being fooled – Jaris Slocum blew it, didn't he? His piece of the investigation.'

Sam nodded. I'd expected him to mount a defense of Slocum, but he didn't. He said, 'I'll deny this if it's ever repeated, but Slocum didn't ever lay eyes on the Millers' neighbor. After the initial search of Chandler's house was negative, Slocum did the follow-up interview by phone – by frigging phone – not in person.' Sam paused and grimaced like he had a bad tooth. 'And he never ran him.'

I was incredulous at the last bit. Sam was admitting that the Boulder Police had never put Doyle Chandler's particulars through the NCIC – National Crime Information Center – database.

'He never ran him? If he'd simply run him, you guys might have focused on Doyle a day or two after Christmas?'

'Something like that.'

'Would have changed everything. Everything. For Mallory, maybe for Diane,' I said. I'm a master of understatement.

'Woulda, coulda.'

Sam didn't seem particularly contrite about his support for Jaris Slocum. Did I want him to be? I guess I did.

It seemed to me that a whole gaggle of Sam's colleagues had been complicit in covering for Jaris. 'Well?' I asked. Sam wasn't looking at me; he was staring at his right hamstring, which was the size of a pork tenderloin.

'Jaris is meeting with the bosses now. They're trying to find a way out of this that doesn't smell too bad for the department. But no matter what, it's not going to turn out too good for Jaris.'

I considered what I'd witnessed at dinner at the Sunflower. 'Alcohol?'

'That's part of it.' Finally, he looked up from his leg.

'You knew?' I said.

'His wife left him a year ago, got his kids after a nasty custody eval. As you might expect, Jaris had developed a little animosity toward mental health professionals and lawyers after that little fiasco. He should never have been sent out to Hannah Grant's office that night, but that's hindsight – who knew that he'd be spending his evening hanging out with shrinks and lawyers?'

'Sounds like his superiors should have known enough to rein him in. You did. Darrell Olson did.'

'This all started right after Sherry left me. Despite the fact that I'd never really liked him, I had sympathy for the guy. I thought he just needed some room, some time to sort through all that was going on. We covered for him, all of us did. Could've been me, Alan. Could just as well have been me. Or you. You done chewing on him? I have other stuff I want to tell you.'

'He was still drinking the other night at dinner, Sam.'

'Couple of beers.'

'That he downed like Gatorade after a marathon.'

'And?' he said. He said it provocatively.

'And what?'

'You're doing it again, Alan.'

'I'm doing what?'

'Cops are people. Guess what? We have problems. Sometimes we handle them, sometimes we don't. Same as shrinks. Same as teachers. Everybody. Jaris Slocum screwed up. Happens. People cut him some slack. Nice people like Darrell Olson do that. Slocum hung himself with it. Happens. Get over it. Nobody knew he fudged his investigation of Doyle Chandler. And nobody guessed what was going to come of it.'

Sam offered me nothing but a stony face that was more punctuation than anything else. I read the punctuation to be a period.

I said, 'Okay, I'm done.'

'Wise. The partials we found in the search last night? One of them is Bob Brandt's right index finger.'

'Oh shit,' I said.

'Yeah,' Sam said. 'Oh shit. We have his fingerprint in the basement theater and we have his car leaving the garage of the house at the other end of the tunnel during the window when Mallory disappeared from her home. Circumstantially speaking, it doesn't look too good.'

'But nothing on the BOLO?'

'It's a rare car. It shouldn't be as hard to find as it's turning out to be. I'm thinking it's parked inside someplace. I don't think he's using it; we'd have it by now. We're going back into his place on Spruce later, this time with a warrant. We're going to test that blood.'

'Pine.'

'Pine then.'

'Say hi to Jenifer for me.'

'Jenifer?'

'The cute kid? The one who wants to go to Clemson?'

'I'll be sure to send your regards,' Sam said sarcastically.

63

Sam wasn't talkative as we ran, nor was I. My lungs were trying to recover from their shock at being forced to process enough oxygen for cardiovascular exercise in Colorado's best impression of a deep freeze. After his initial, 'Let's go,' we covered a good quarter-mile before Sam grunted anything more. He had been running on my heels, but pulled up astride me and said, 'News.'

I thought it was a question, that Sam was asking me what I'd heard about Diane. Tapping my pocket I replied, 'Nothing. Got my phone with me in case Raoul calls.'

'No, I have more news for you. About the neighbor.'

'Doyle?'

'You'll hear this soon enough: Doyle Chandler's not Doyle Chandler. It's a stolen identity. We don't know who he is. Was.'

'You're kidding.' I knew he wasn't kidding.

'The Doyle Chandler whose social security number matches that of the guy we found murdered yesterday died in a car crash with his parents, Renee and Dennis, in 1967 in Roanoke, Virginia. He was six years old at the time. The man who lived next door to the Millers filched the kid's identity. He's been using it for sixteen years.'

'So whose body was it?' I suddenly didn't even know what to call Doyle.

'We don't know, and we may not ever know. AFIS doesn't pull a match on the index print he gave for his Colorado driver's license. NCIC has bupkis.' Sam paused to allow his breathing to catch up with his talking and running. 'Animals had chewed off almost all of the fingertips and most of the face before the body was discovered. We're not going to get usable prints from what's left. We have his teeth, of course, but the guy hadn't seen a dentist in a while.'

'What about the house? There must be prints there.'

'The techs aren't hopeful – the place had been professionally cleaned after he moved out. Need to match them with something, anyway.'

'This case,' I said.

'Tell me about it,' he agreed, and fell back into position on my heels.

Five minutes later, from the ridge top above the neighborhood, I watched a sedan without headlights approach the junction of dirt lanes that leads toward our house. It wasn't a car I recognized. Light in color, GM in ancestry, its boxy shape dated it back a decade or more. Our neighbor Adrienne's latest nanny? Possibly. I kept an eye on the car as it took the turn onto our lane, but our route carried us down the other side of the ridge and I couldn't see the car's ultimate destination.

Sam passed me on the downhill and increased the pace for the final mile. I was exhausted after the run. He, too, seemed unnaturally winded. We both knew it wasn't just the jog. 'Coming in?' I asked. 'I'll make you breakfast.'

I'd already looked around for the GM sedan. It wasn't at my house or at Adrienne's.

'Have to get to work,' Sam said. 'Simon's with Sherry.'

I was perseverating on Sam's news that Doyle wasn't Doyle. But I had no easy way to digest that news, so I refocused on Sam's implication that Bob might be deeply involved in Mallory's disappearance, but couldn't get anywhere with that either. Bob was a schizoid personality. He was as schizoid as anyone I'd ever met. Bob kidnapping Mallory – or anyone else – made no more sense to me than a pedophile breaking into an old folks' home.

'You no longer consider Mallory a runaway, do you?'

Sam said, 'I go back and forth. If she is, it looks like she had help getting out of the house. If she isn't, we have a different problem. What was the neighbor's role in all this? Did he take her? Did he help her? What was Camaro Bob's? Did he have something to do with it? Looks like he did. What's what exactly, I haven't decided. I still want to know why Doyle dug that tunnel in the first place. Why did he want into the Millers' house so badly?'

The obvious was to me, well, obvious. 'He lived next door. People prey on kids, Sam. He could've become obsessed with her.'

'A voyeur? That's all you got?'

'I'm thinking worse.'

He scowled. 'Why dig a tunnel?'

'To do his thing. Access.'

'Risky as shit. Three people live in that house. He's bound to get caught wandering around in there trying to get at the girl. Doesn't work. You live next door, there're much easier ways to spy on a kid.'

'Maybe he went in at night when they were asleep.'

'There are pervs who like to watch girls sleep?' Sam asked.

After all his years as a cop, Sam's residual naiveté still ambushed me sometimes.

'There are pervs who like just about everything.'

He held up his hand. 'I don't want to hear it.'

I thought about the theater in Doyle's basement. All the top-end electronics. 'Did Doyle wire their house? Hide video cameras in Mallory's room? The bathroom? Anything like that?'

'We checked. Fixtures are all clean, attic's clean. No holes drilled where they shouldn't be drilled. There's nothing there, not a single extra cable in the Millers' house, not a single cable coming back through the tunnel to Doyle's. No transmitters. If he put surveillance in, he took it back out when he moved away.'

I thought for a moment, forcing myself to go back to basics. Psychology basics. The best predictor of someone's future behavior – maybe the only predictor – is his past behavior. I said, 'Car thieves steal cars, right? Bank robbers rob banks?'

Sam looked at me as though he'd just realized I was mentally challenged. 'Yeah, and psychologists ask stupid questions.'

'What do we really know about Doyle Chandler?'

'Not much,' Sam admitted. 'Did I tell you he was shot?'

'No, you didn't.'

'He was shot. Behind the ear, slight upward angle. Shooter wasn't real close, no burns on his skin. Slug looks like a .38. Second and third shots to his back. But they were just insurance. He was already dead with the first slug.'

'Suspects?'

'Camaro Bob's on the list.'

I didn't want to hear that. I went back to Doyle. 'You know one more thing about Doyle for sure, Sam: He steals identities,' I said.

'Yeah?'

He knew where I was going. I said, 'You were

wondering about the motive for the tunnel. There it is.'

'Doyle went into the Millers' house to build a new identity?' Sam said.

I noted – with some relief – that his question was almost entirely devoid of skepticism.

'What better place? Say Doyle went in during the daytime when Bill was at work and the kids were at school. He'd have the run of the house. Personal records, financial records, work stuff that Bill left laying around. Computer files, his e-mails, maybe even passwords. Be like Wal-Mart for an identity thief. With a tunnel he could take all the time he needed to fill in every last blank.'

'"Lying" around. Bill would leave stuff "lying" around. Not "laying" around.'

I smiled. 'Does the gratis English lesson mean you think I got the rest right?'

'Maybe,' Sam said. Even though he'd already caught his breath, he put his hands on his hips the way exhausted athletes do, stared at me, and momentarily left any parsimony behind. 'We blew it the first time. Eight years ago? We did. I don't care about the public face we tried to put on it, the damn truth is that we fucking blew it. Guess what? I don't want to be the guy who blows it this time. If you have something that'll help me find that girl, I need to hear it. Second chances don't come around too often in life. I have one. We need to redeem ourselves.'

In the years since the other little girl's death, I'd never heard Sam be so brutal in his appraisal of law enforcement's role. 'Okay, yeah,' I said.

'Yeah, you have something? Or, yeah, you understand?'

Did I have something? If I did, I wasn't sure what it looked like. I said, 'Yeah, I understand.'

He stepped toward the Cherokee. 'I don't need your understanding.'

64

I tried to stretch out my calves a little more as I pondered Sam's challenge and watched him disappear down the dusty lane. I was just about to go back inside when the square front end of an approaching car came my way. It stopped a hundred yards or so down the road, in a little turnout on the soft shoulder.

The car was the GM sedan I'd seen earlier. The sun had crested the eastern horizon and was reflecting off the windshield. From my vantage point I could tell the car was pale yellow. The hood ornament clued me in that it was a Cadillac.

I stuck my hands in my armpits to warm my fingers, and I waited.

A man climbed out of the driver's seat, stuffed his hands in his pockets, and began walking toward me.

Bob Brandt.

Even at a hundred yards I recognized the denim jacket. My thought? *Thank God you're alive.*

'Somebody's been in my house,' he said when he got within fifty feet. His voice was pressured. He didn't say hello.

So what else is new?

'I know,' I said. I'd come to the conclusion that it was

Doyle who had trashed Bob's place, but I kept the guess to myself.

'Did you read my stuff?' he asked.

That's why Bob was at my house: to chastise me for breaking his trust and spilling his secrets. That was fair – I had broken his trust and spilled his secrets. 'Hi, Bob,' I said, reframing things, at least for a moment. 'I've been worried about you.'

'Why?'

Bob's 'why' was a classic schizoid question, but perfectly sincere. His disorder left him with only the most rudimentary concept of 'concern,' at least the person-to-person variety.

'I hadn't heard from you, thought you might be in . . . danger.'

'Oh.' He played with the notion for a moment before he added, 'I went somewhere. Do you know what's going on? Who was in my place?'

'Are you okay?'

'Tired. Drove all night.'

'Are you here by yourself?'

He turned his head and looked back at the Cadillac, as though he needed to check to be sure. 'Yes. What's going on? Did you read my stuff? I told you not to. You must have seen my note.'

'Like I said, I got worried. Anyway, I think you wanted me to read it. Otherwise you wouldn't have given it to me. We can talk about it.' It was shrink talk, but it also happened to be true.

'I was just getting started. It's just a story.'

'The tunnel part is real.'

He swallowed, and his eyes started their disconcerting shimmying. He spit a solitary word: 'So?'

Bob's retort was schoolyard bravado, nothing more.

'How can I be of help right now?' I said, trying to sound therapeutic.

He seemed surprised by my offer. After a moment, he said, 'That's a good question.'

He stepped back, literally and – I feared – figuratively. Instinctively, I sought safer ground for him. 'Is that your car?'

His eyes found the Caddy and lingered there. 'It's my mother's.'

Your mother's? Was Bob being sardonic? I couldn't say. 'You like it?'

He'd returned his attention my way, but was looking past me toward the distant turnpike. Finally, he said, 'Lots of power. Good cruiser. Cushy. Only fourteen K on it.'

'Not as cherry as your Camaro,' I said.

'Close,' he said. 'Pretty close.' He made an unfamiliar popping sound with his lips. 'Maybe you can help somebody . . . I know.'

'A friend?' I asked. *Please tell me Mallory's okay.*

Emily chose that moment to erupt; she'd apparently just realized that her homeland security had been violated and that a stranger was on her doorstep. Her fierce barking – even though it came from inside the house – caused Bob to retreat a few steps.

'She's fine,' I said.

'I don't like dogs. You know that.'

I didn't think I knew that. 'She'll stay inside. Bob?' I waited until I thought I had his attention. 'The police are looking for you. They want to talk with you about Mallory. I think you should get a lawyer and go see them. I can put you in touch with someone.'

'Sheesh,' he said, and did his little half head-shake thing.

I experienced an odd sense of relief that I'd finally lit on something I could share with Sam. I said, 'You should know that whatever you decide to do, I'm going to tell the police you were here.'

He was puzzled. 'Is that some . . . rule? You have to tell?'

'No. It might even be breaking some rule. It's what I think is the right thing to do.'

He nodded. 'That's what I did, too. What I thought was the right thing.'

'You could be in danger. Doyle's dead.'

'No, he's not.'

Okay. I didn't see a point in arguing. 'The police need to talk with you.'

'I didn't do anything wrong.'

'It'll be fine then. Let me put you in touch with an attorney.'

My phone rang. I pulled it from my pocket and checked the screen: Sam. I said to Bob, 'Excuse me. This will take just a second.' I turned away, putting a dozen feet between us. 'Yes,' I whispered into the phone.

'I passed that DeVille on the way out of your neighborhood – the one we saw during our jog. Had a funny feeling, so I ran it. Expired tags, but it's registered to somebody named Verna Brandt in—'

'I know.'

'He's there?'

'Yes.'

'A deputy is on the way. I'll be right behind them.'

I turned around. Bob was almost all the way back to the Cadillac. 'Don't,' I yelled.

He jumped in the car, spun the sedan in the dirt as though he practiced the maneuver on weekends, and was gone within seconds.

A huge gust of wind whooshed from the west. I didn't

sense it coming and the blunt force of the gale almost blew me over. When I finally caught my balance I looked toward the mountains the way somebody might look to check the identity of somebody who just sucker-punched him. My conclusion? The forecast Chinooks had definitely arrived; the slopes of the Front Range were already haloed in snow that was being whipped off the glacial ice of the distant Divide.

I braced my feet and tried Sam on his cell, but didn't get an answer. I waited until the sheriff's deputy and Sam drove up, told Sam what had happened, and wished I could start the day all over again.

Lauren was planning to hang out with Grace on Saturday morning and then the two of them were going to do some clothes shopping at Flatiron. Later in the day, winds permitting, they were planning a mother-daughter 'tablecloth restaurant' visit someplace Gracie kept insisting was a big secret. I spent the morning hoping to hear from Raoul or Sam. Didn't. I filled the time writing a couple of reports that were long overdue, and did a few chores around the house before I cleaned up, hopped in my car, drove the few miles west to my office, and prepared to see Bill Miller.

I wasn't looking forward to the visit, and half hoped he would bag the session because of the Chinooks.

65

Bill was waiting for me.

His car was parked where Diane usually left her Saab, not too far from the doors that led from our offices to the backyard. He was standing between the taillights, leaning back against the trunk, his arms folded over his chest. The January sun was already low over the southwest mountains and the fierce wind gusts were blowing anything that wasn't bolted down from the west side of town to the east. Some day soon, one of these Chinook events was going to propel our rickety garage from our side of downtown to the other.

I stopped my wagon parallel to his car – but a few feet farther from the rickety garage than usual – and stepped out. I didn't like that his car was parked in back. I didn't like that he wasn't waiting for me by the front door.

He greeted me with, 'You knew.'

I chose defensiveness. Wise? Probably not. 'I'd given my word to the police, Bill. I also knew you'd find out what happened soon enough. I'm sorry I couldn't tell you. It would have made things easier for both of us.'

He nodded; he'd probably traversed that territory himself. 'What's your role in all this?' he asked. 'Why were you at Doyle's last night? And those other times?'

His voice seemed to carry better in the wind than mine did; mine felt like it was being swallowed up like spit in the ocean. 'It has to do with what was making me concerned about the dual-relationship problem I talked about.'

Bill nodded as though he understood. But I wondered how he could even hear, let alone understand. The nod must have meant something else.

'When we talked last night did you know that Doyle was dead?' he asked. I had the sense that he was methodically going down a list of questions. I also had the sense that he didn't really expect to learn anything novel in my responses.

'Same situation, Bill; I couldn't talk about it with you. I knew you would find out this morning anyway.'

He turned his head momentarily so he was gazing west toward the mountains, frankly into the wind. His hair flew back behind him like he was a character in the cartoons. 'Do you know where my daughter is?' he asked.

I half heard him, half read his lips. 'No, I don't. I wish I did,' I said.

'You're sure?'

'I am.' Almost reflexively, I asked him the same question. 'Do you know where she is, Bill?'

'No.'

'What's the third option? The other night you suggested the possibility that running and kidnapping weren't the only options.'

'Hiding.'

'Hiding? From what?'

He surprised me by taking a quick step closer to me, closer than I liked. 'Life. Yes, hiding. I have a story to tell you.'

In retrospect, that was the point when I should have stopped him. Walked away. Told him therapy was over, or that it had never really begun. Handed him my license and let him use it for a coaster. Given him the phone number of the state board that censures wayward psychologists, like me. Something.

But I didn't. I still had a scintilla of hope that Bill knew something that would help me find Diane.

'One day last spring,' he began, 'I came home from work and found Doyle Chandler inside my house, sitting at my kitchen table drinking a beer. My beer. My records – my files, my bills, my check-book, you name it – were spread out all over the table in front of him.'

'Bill, I—' I tried to interrupt him. Why? Something visceral was still telling me to get him to stop.

'I'm not done.' He raised both eyebrows and through a hissing exhale said, 'Give me this. I deserve this.' I stepped back involuntarily. He immediately closed the distance between us. 'Doyle knew everything about me. Said he'd spent almost a month going through my things. Paperwork, letters, tax returns, computer files. Passwords. Everything. He knew about Rachel, her . . . problems. He knew the kids' grades, their teachers' names. Knew I have a swollen prostate, that my LDL's too high. Everything that makes our family different from the Crandalls across the street, everything that makes us who we are, he knew.'

I had an incongruous impulse to comfort, to tell Bill the truth about Doyle Chandler, his neighbor, and the truth about Doyle Chandler, the boy who'd died in a car accident in Roanoke with his parents back in 1967. I wanted to try to placate Bill with the fact that he'd been had by a damn good con man.

A blast of wind sandblasted my skin. The impulse passed.

Bill went on. 'I was irate. I asked him what he was doing in my house. He just laughed. I demanded that he get out, that the kids were coming home any minute. He stood up and walked over to the refrigerator and pointed at our family calendar. He said, "No, they're not. Reese is at hockey practice till seven. Coach usually keeps them late, you know that. And it's Kyle's mom's turn to drive, anyway. Last time she stopped and got the kids dinner at Pizza Hut, remember? She'll probably do something like that again – Frannie's like that, such a sweetheart. And Mallory is studying at Kara's. Cute kids, Mallory and Kara. Really cute kids.'

'He knew it all. Everything. Take a minute, try to imagine it. Go ahead, try. What that would be like. He knew every secret. Every intimacy. Every dirty detail. When you think you know how bad it feels, double it. Then double that. That's what it was like.'

I tried to digest what that kind of intrusion would feel like to a father. Surreal.

A huge piece of Styrofoam jumped the fence to the west and crashed into the side of Bill's car. I ducked; he continued to seem oblivious to the fierce gales. I forced myself to observe him, to try to read what I could about his affect. I wasn't getting a clear sense of where he was at that moment. It was apparent that he had no trouble summoning the rage he felt at Doyle Chandler. But there was something else present in the mix, some other emotional component that I couldn't put a finger on.

'Doyle had already gone through every last thing I owned and decided that simply stealing my identity wasn't enough of a payoff for all his effort. He wanted money, of course,' Bill said. 'Lots of it.'

'Why didn't—'

'I go to the police? Because I have things to hide. He

knew by then that I couldn't go to the police. Same reason I couldn't turn over Mallory's diary when I found it after she disappeared.'

'Things to hide?'

'Everybody has something they don't want the world to know. Everybody. For some people, it's something embarrassing. Maybe even humiliating. For some, it's something . . . worse. To save my family, I did some desperate things years ago. I made hard choices. For me it was something worse.'

'Rachel and Canada?' I said, guessing that Bill's secret had to do with money. Instantly, I wished I hadn't guessed, at least not out loud.

'Do you know? I'm not sure . . . doesn't matter. I'll tell you.'

'Bill, it's not—'

'Shhhh. I'm not done.'

For a fleeting second, right then, I felt menace from him. The scent of peril was fleeting, like a waft of perfume as a lovely woman waltzes by. I allowed myself the luxury of believing that I'd misread him, and I somehow convinced myself that it was okay to dismiss the menace as an illusion, to allow it to be carried away on the wings of the Chinooks. In retrospect, that was a bit of a mistake.

'Rachel's illness almost buried us financially. When we came to see you way back when it was already bad, but after? That year after? Lord. The medicine, the doctors, the hospitals. Not to mention all the damn weddings. There were always more and more damn weddings, always. Rachel was better when she went to weddings, much better. The voices weren't as frequent, not as scary. So I fed the beast, paying for the outfits, the gifts, everything. I was in so far over my head. Mortgaged to the hilt, credit cards maxed out. Every month I was borrowing from a new Peter to pay an old Paul.

'I was about to declare bankruptcy. I didn't know what else to do. Then the voices began telling Rachel – demanding – that she had to move to Las Vegas or . . .' He took a moment to reflect on some ugly, ugly room in his wife's private hell. 'And that meant she would need even more money. I begged her not to go, but the voices were too frightening. I thought I was going to lose everything then. The house, the kids, Rachel.

'Then I got handed a way out. My boss had just been promoted to western regional manager – a big deal for him. His wife threw him a surprise party up at the Flagstaff House just before Christmas. Late, close to two in the morning, I was driving behind him down Baseline and . . .' Bill shook his head, disbelieving. 'He was distracted, I guess. I don't know what it was, but a pedestrian was walking from the Hill over to Chautauqua, right across Baseline. I saw her clearly from a block and a half away – she had her hands in her pockets, her head down against the cold. Walter just mowed her down.

'She must have flown a hundred feet in the air. Turned out she was a young mother, an orthodontist. He never even touched his brakes; he just plowed into her. I still see her body flying. Sometimes, I feel the impact when I'm asleep.

'He killed her, of course. She was dead at the scene.'

He paused, and I reminded him that he'd told me about the accident years before when he'd stopped by to thank me for my help with Rachel.

'I didn't tell you the next part. Walter was in shock. Kept saying, "What happened, Bill? What happened?" I saw an opportunity. I told him to shut up and listen to me.

As out-of-it as he was, he did. When the cops came, I told them what I saw. A white van was coming up Baseline in the other direction. The woman walked out from behind it. My boss couldn't have seen the woman. I told them I was right behind him and I didn't see her until she was in the air. It wasn't Walter's fault at all. That was my story.'

'You made up the van?' I asked.

'It was two in the morning. I figured I was the only witness. My boss matched his story to mine. It worked. Why wouldn't it? Turned out his blood alcohol was just a hair below the legal limit so he wasn't even arrested. He was never charged with anything. He didn't go to prison. His promotion was secure. His family . . . was safe.'

'You saved his ass?'

'I did it for me, not for him. I was saving my family. I told you I was desperate. I don't even like Walter. He's a prick.'

'I don't understand,' I said. But I did. Before I'd left her office, Mary Black had suggested enough that I could guess the rest.

'I knew Walter would be grateful.' Bill suddenly seemed out of breath.

'The promotion you got,' I said, filling in a blank for him. 'The one you told me about years ago?'

'Yes, that promotion. My salary went way up, and then it went up again. I began getting regular Christmas bonuses. That was eight years ago. I had a good job, better than I deserved. I was making enough money to make ends meet here and enough to keep Rachel safe in Vegas, barely.'

'Until Doyle Chandler showed up at your kitchen table?'

'I'd kept a record about everything that happened in case Walter ever turned on me. When Doyle started coming into my house he did it simply to steal my identity, but then . . . then he ended up finding every last thing I'd kept about Walter and the orthodontist. Newspaper clippings. Notes. Everything. Once he understood what I'd done, and how vulnerable I was, he changed his plans. Doyle wanted a cut.'

'How much?'

'He asked for ten thousand a month. We settled on five at first. But I knew I couldn't do five for long. Canada was demanding more and more money to keep doing what he was doing for Rachel in Las Vegas. As she got sicker he had to pay more people more money so that she would be . . . left alone. What choice did I have? What could I do? I was in so deep.

'When Doyle moved out in the fall and put his house on the market, I thought he might have realized that the till was empty, you know? Hell, he knew my finances as well as I did. Better, maybe. I thought – God, I was naive – I thought things might be over. But that's when Doyle went to Walter and started blackmailing him, too. Walter and I realized he'd moved away so that we couldn't find him. My boss wasn't happy. He's not a pleasant man when he's not happy.'

The sky was getting dark and, despite the warming winds, I felt winter and January all the way to my bones. It wasn't just the temperature, though; I knew that.

'Bill, would you like to come inside?' I said. 'Sit down?'

He looked around as though he'd needed to remind himself we were indeed outside, nodded, and followed me to the back door of my office. Once we were in I flicked on some lights and sat across from him as though we were doctor and patient.

Were we? Partly yes, partly no. Mostly no. All the ethical guidelines I'd always held so dear were designed to keep therapists from feeling the ambiguity of roles I was feeling right then, were designed to keep patients from suffering the conflict-of-interest vulnerabilities Bill was floating in right then. What a mess I'd made.

The thing was, I wasn't too upset about it.

Bill crossed his legs, uncrossed them, stood suddenly, and moved to the southern windows. His back was to me, and he seemed to be focused on the advancing sunset that was visible through the skeleton of the ash trees. My sense was that he wasn't sure how to resume his narrative. I could have drawn the shut-up-and-wait arrow from my quiver. I didn't. To help him find a way to restart his story I chose an option that I thought was a gimme: 'That's when you found out he'd dug a tunnel? The day Doyle showed up in your kitchen.'

'No, I had no idea that's how he'd gotten in. Learning about the tunnel last night was a complete surprise to me. A tunnel? Never crossed my mind, not for a second. I thought Doyle had a key to our house, that he'd discovered where we hid our spare, or had somehow gotten hold of one of the kids' keys. That's what he'd led me to believe. He had told me not to get an alarm, not to change the locks. Told me I'd regret doing any of those things. When he'd threaten me with what I was going to regret if I didn't cooperate, he'd always mention the kids.'

'He threatened them?'

'He tried. I threatened him right back. I told him if he came into my house when the kids were home, I'd kill him. If he so much as talked to them, I'd kill him. I think he believed me.'

She was scared. That's what Bob had said about Mallory. *She was scared.*

Was that why she was scared?

'What did Mallory know about all this?' I asked.

'Mallory,' he said in a long exhale. His breath temporarily clouded the window glass in front of his mouth. 'Mallory.'

I thought he was about to cry.

66

'She hasn't had a good Christmas since she was six.' Bill said into the glass. 'That's eight years, most of her life. She hates Christmas.'

She misses her mom. Diane had told me that Mallory missed her mom. The year that Mallory was six was the year that Rachel abandoned her family for the lure of Las Vegas weddings.

Psychotherapy 101: Christmas for Mallory was irrevocably linked to loss.

Finally, I thought I understood why Mallory had felt so compelled to see Hannah Grant for psychotherapy: Mallory hadn't had a good Christmas since she was six. She went to see Hannah because she didn't want to have another bad Christmas, another Christmas when her primary emotion involved desperately missing her mother.

'She'd get so scared,' Bill said. 'Every year, right after Thanksgiving she'd start to get scared.'

Scared? That's what Bob had said about Mallory, too. *She was scared.* Why scared?

'Scared?' I asked. I would have suspected that Mallory would show signs of anxiety or depression on the anniversary of her mother's abandonment. But fear?

Bill wiped at his eyes with his fingertips. 'She thought it was going to happen again. She couldn't be comforted. No matter what I tried to do over the years to help her deal with it, nothing worked.'

Rachel had deserted her family eight years before. Was Mallory afraid that her father was going to leave, too? Was that the vulnerability she felt? 'What, Bill? Mallory thought what was going to happen again?'

He turned back from the window. His face was pink and bright. 'What happened eight years ago on Christmas? Mallory thought she'd be next. Every year since that year, she's been afraid that she'd be next. That the same man was coming to get her.'

Oh my God, what an idiot I am. Mallory was scared because of the murder of her friend. 'They were friends? When they were little?'

'Classmates. A sleep-over or two. You know what it's like for girls when they're that age. That Christmas, Mallory was already so vulnerable because of . . . what was going on with her mom. What happened that night scared her so much. She used to cry and cry every time she saw the pictures on TV. And those pictures were everywhere.

'She was so determined to confront her fears about Christmas, to grow out of it. She desperately wanted to get past all this, to feel safe.'

'The police know all this?'

'Of course; it's why they think she ran. They think she got spooked and left to go find her mom and that something – you know – happened to her on the way.'

'Did she know about Doyle? About the blackmail?'

'She knew something was up with me, that I wasn't myself. She'd mentioned it. It's in her journal.'

'Did she know about the tunnel?'

'I know what you're thinking – that that's how she got out of the house. But how could she know about it? I didn't know about it until last night. She was terrified of the basement. A basement is where her friend's body was found eight years ago. She never went down there. Never.'

'Doyle?'

'Doyle could have shown it to her, I guess. But why? He had too much to lose if he exposed what he was doing. And I think he knew I meant that I'd kill him if he went near the kids.'

I thought, *Bob*. That's how she could know. Bob's fingerprint was in the basement. Bob was taking care of Doyle's empty house. Bob knew all about the theater – he had told me that he thought it was a great place to watch movies. And Bob certainly knew about the tunnel.

Bob and Mallory had talked.

Had Bob actually been there on Christmas night, holed up in Doyle's theater watching movies?

Mallory's friend – the other little girl, the tiny blonde beauty queen – had died eight years before as Christmas Day became the day after.

She was scared, Bob had said about Mallory.

She thought it was going to happen again, her father had said about Mallory. She feared that someone was going to come into her house and do to her what someone had done to her little friend. She feared that someone was going to bust in and leave her head crushed and her neck garroted, that someone was going to abandon her alone and dead in her grungy basement on Christmas night.

Doyle? Bob? The man loitering outside?

Who?

I'm a gullible guy. But I'm aware that I'm a gullible guy, so aware that sometimes I catch myself and pause long enough to question what I'm hearing. Right then, I stopped, and I questioned. *Do I believe what Bill is telling me?*

Yes, kind of.

Is he telling me the truth? No, probably not completely.

I replayed some of the earlier conversation I'd had with Bill Miller. '*When Doyle moved out in the fall and put his house on the market, I thought he might have realized that the till was empty, you know? He knew my finances as well as I did. Better, maybe. I thought – God, I was naive – I thought things might be over. But that's when Doyle went to Walter and started blackmailing him, too. Walter and I realized he'd moved away so that we couldn't find him. My boss wasn't happy. He's not a pleasant man when he's not happy.*'

'What,' I asked, 'did your boss do when Doyle started blackmailing him?'

'Same as me. He paid him off, bought some time. After so many years you don't expect to get caught.'

Content is the aphrodisiac of psychotherapy. For a therapist, it's so tempting to get caught on the wave of the story, to get lost in the facts and the promise and the details of the narrative. What suffers when the therapist succumbs to that seductive lure?

Process. And process – what is going on in the room – is almost always where the truth hides. I forced myself to be a therapist. I returned my attention to the process.

'Why did you decide to tell me all this, Bill?'

'I didn't know what you'd already figured out. I actually thought you might know too much. That would be a whole new problem for us.'

'Us?'

'Me and Walter.'

'I don't quite understand,' I said. But I did.

Bill's voice was almost apologetic as he said, 'I've just tied your hands, Alan. You can't tell anyone what I told you. It's confidential, now. I can't afford to have anyone know what I've done. Walter can't either. So, just in case – for some insurance – I've sealed your lips.'

Was Bill right?

In his reading of the law, and of my professional responsibilities, yes.

In his reading of me, no. He had no way to know, but I was more than ready to say 'screw it.' Was I angry? A little. Less than I would have anticipated. 'Doyle knew everything,' I said. 'He may have—'

'Doyle's dead, remember?'

'Did you—'

'Kill him? No. God, no. I would have liked to, I might even have been willing to, but . . . no.'

'Did your boss?'

'He's probably capable of it. Walter's in Vegas now trying to find Rachel. To see if Mallory's with her. We have to keep her under control. He and I are in the same boat on this one. Our families are both at risk.'

'Rachel knows about the orthodontist?'

'She's my wife; of course she knows. I don't have secrets from Rachel.'

I stated the obvious. 'You're desperate, then. You and . . . Walter?'

'Yes, we are.'

'Why did he go to Vegas?'

'One of us had to get to Rachel. I couldn't – the press might have spotted me. They're everywhere.'

I'd noticed. 'Do you think Mallory's there?'

'I hope she is.' His despair about his daughter was palpable.

'The alternatives are so horrifying that I can't even . . .'

My cell phone rang. I checked the screen: Raoul. Thank God. 'I need to get this,' I said. 'It's an emergency. There may even be some news that affects Mallory.'

'Go ahead then,' Bill said.

'Raoul?' I said. 'Any news?'

'I'm at the hospital with her. She's okay.'

Diane? 'Hold on a second; I'm with someone.' I covered the phone and turned to Bill. 'Could you please go out to the waiting room while I take this?'

Reluctantly, I thought, he walked out of my office and down the hall. I kept my hand on the phone until I heard the waiting room door open and close.

67

'She's really okay?' I said.

'She's safe. She held my hand. We talked. She had a little food. Now she's sleeping.'

'Where has she been? What happened?'

'I was sure Canada had Diane, or he could lead me to her. I had it all wrong.'

'What do you mean?'

'None of Canada's people have seen Rachel since Tuesday. Turns out Canada's had me on a leash since I got to Vegas. He's been watching me, concerned I'd be causing him more trouble with Rachel, later on hoping that I'd lead him to her.'

'I don't understand. How did you find Diane?'

That's when he took a deep breath and slowed his voice and began relaying the long story about the ratty cab and doing dead time in the Airstream and about the old VW bug and Tico, and about playing the echoes with Canada.

Before dawn on the morning after Raoul met with Canada in the walled house in the scruffy desert outside of the city, Tico fired up the VW and drove Raoul into the desolate mountains west of Las Vegas. Raoul recalled seeing a sign for Blue Diamond near their destination – so wherever that is, that wasn't too far from where they ended up. Just as it was beginning to get light Tico stopped the bug on a mountain curve, and asked Raoul if he was up for a little hike.

'This is where the accident was?' Raoul asked him, recalling Canada's story the night before.

'The guy's driving too fast,' Tico said, pointing down the road. 'Way too fast, and he comes around the curve – that one – and sees a guy standing in the road with a .45 pointed at his windshield.' He held up both hands. 'This is what I hear. The man in the road fires a shot – you know, to warn the guy – a little bit over the top of the truck. Driver doesn't handle it good. Freaks.' Tico then pantomimed a dive off a cliff before he kicked off his flip-flops and began pulling an ancient pair of orange high-top Keds onto his bare feet.

A moment later Raoul followed him down a scruffy hillside covered with nothing but scree and big boulders. They went down a hundred feet or more into a narrow wash that had been invisible from the road above. A battered, crushed, bronze Silverado with Colorado plates rested upside down on a rock that was half the size of Tico's VW. Inside was the body of a man. The stink was horrific.

Tico said, 'That's the guy, the guy in the picture with Howard, the guy who met your wife in the Venetian. You want me to check for ID?' Raoul wasn't able to come up with an answer for him, but Tico pulled on some work gloves and crawled into the overturned truck. A minute later he handed Raoul a Colorado driver's license.

The name meant nothing to Raoul. 'What's farther up the hill? Where was he going?' Raoul asked.

'A couple of old cabins. Might be important. To you, anyway.'

'But not to you?'

'This . . . accident? It happened before Rachel lost touch with the boss. We weren't too interested in what was up there. Not our business, you dig. We stay out of things that aren't our business. That's one of the boss's rules.'

'Can we look?' Raoul asked him. 'At those two cabins? Now?'

Tico said, 'I got a little time.'

The second cabin they checked, the last one on the road, was where they found Diane. Raoul went in alone and found her cuffed to an iron bed. She'd been there a long time. She was delirious, almost unconscious.

Tico used his mobile phone to call somebody down in Vegas, asked them to send help. Then he told Raoul, 'I gotta go before, you know . . . And my man? The police don't need to know about the Silverado. That'd be better for everybody.'

Raoul told him he understood and he promised to come up with a story for the police.

Fifteen minutes later people started showing up to help Raoul save his wife.

I briefly relayed to Raoul most of what I'd told Lauren the night before. I told him about the tunnel and the car that had left Doyle's garage right around the time Mallory disappeared. I told him that Doyle Chandler wasn't Doyle Chandler, and that whoever he really was, he was dead.

'Are you coming home?' I asked.

'As soon as they clear her to travel,' he said.

'Can you tell me who the guy in the Silverado was?'

'Does it make a difference?' he asked. 'I promised I'd be discreet. The cops didn't find it. It needs to stay that way.'

'I think I know.'

'Who?'

The irony didn't escape me: Raoul was protecting secrets, too. I gave him the name he already had: 'Guy named Walter.'

His voice grew tight. 'You've known about him for how long?'

'This afternoon. Just now.'

'He was a bad guy?'

'He had something important to hide. He was afraid Diane might have learned what it was from Hannah.'

'When I get back we'll have a beer, you'll tell me how you know all this.'

'I'm looking forward to that, Raoul. Listen, I'm with a . . . patient. Call me back when I can talk with Diane, okay? Please?'

We said good-bye after Raoul asked me if I had any idea how to thank someone for saving his wife's life. 'Canada?' I wondered.

'No, Norm Clarke,' he said.

I thought I'd read somewhere that Norm had a weakness for foie gras, but I promised Raoul I'd think more about it and stepped back out to the waiting room to get Bill Miller.

The front door was wide open. The coffee table was tipped over, magazines scattered on the floor.

Bill was gone. *Damn.* Immediately, I regretted leaving him alone for such a long time.

The winds seemed to have stopped.

68

Huh. What did Bill's hasty exit mean? Why the overturned table and the open door? Had something happened while I was talking with Raoul, or was Bill making a statement about his frustration with me, or about his annoyance that I'd interrupted our meeting to take a phone call?

My relief that Diane was okay was so strong at that moment that I wasn't particularly upset about whatever had prompted Bill's departure, but I was perplexed. Why had he taken off so suddenly?

I was becoming more and more convinced that Mallory's Christmas night disappearance had been accomplished with Bob's help. What had happened next? I was guessing that she'd talked Bob into driving her somewhere and I was hoping that she'd somehow made it to Vegas to visit her mother. Where were mother and daughter right then? I didn't know. Raoul's story satisfied me that Bill's boss, the by-then-dead Walter, hadn't been successful in tracking them down in Vegas.

But where was Bob? If Sam had caught up with him, I was sure he would have called and let me know.

I straightened up the waiting room, walked back to my office, and phoned Bill Miller at his home. No answer. I left a message, and asked him to call me back on my pager. Then I called home. The girls were still out on their excursion. I left Lauren a message that I was going to run a few errands and that I'd be home in time for dinner.

As cold as it can be in Colorado in January, there are always respites, warm days in the high fifties or low sixties when the sun defies its low angle in the southern sky and the blue above is just a little bluer. I was surprised when I stepped outside to discover that the Chinooks had abated and left the day so much warmer than it had been earlier. The seat heaters in the Audi seemed superfluous. I flicked them off and drove east to begin my errands.

I felt the vibration of my pager while I was waiting in line to buy some fish for dinner at Whole Foods. Had Lauren asked for ono or opah? I couldn't remember. I pulled the beeper off my belt and read Bill Miller's familiar number. My turn at the fish counter had arrived, so I mentally flipped a coin and chose a good-sized piece of opah before I meandered over to the relative quiet of the dairy department to return Bill's call.

'We need to talk,' he said.

'I went back out to the waiting room and—'

'I just got a call about Mallory.'

'From whom?'

'The Colorado State Patrol. They found a body, a girl, in a ditch near I-70 west of Grand Junction.'

'Oh my God,' I said. 'What can I do?'

'I want to talk to you before whatever happens next. I need to make sure I'm thinking straight.'

'Bill, you just admitted that you're using the therapy to shut me up. I don't think I'm the right person to—'

'Fire me tomorrow. Tonight I need some help.' He sounded genuinely frantic. I couldn't imagine his terror. I looked at my watch. 'My office. Ten minutes,' I said.

'I have to be here, at home, if they call back. I can't leave. Can you come over?'

'I'll be right there,' I said. I tossed the opah on top of a display of organic butter in the dairy case, and sprinted to my car.

69

Maybe it was the time of day, just past dusk. Or maybe, as Sam predicted, the fierce assault of the Chinook blitzkrieg had scared everyone off. But the media encampment outside the Millers' home was deserted, the street peaceful. Doyle's house was dark.

Bill met me at the front door. I didn't even have to knock.

'Thank you for coming,' he said as he ushered me inside. 'Can I get you something? Some tea? I make good hot chocolate. That's what the kids tell me, anyway.'

'No, thank you.'

His cordial greeting left me off-balance as he led me to the back of the house and a battered oak claw-foot table with some mismatched pressed-back chairs. 'Sit, please.' He pointed me to a seat that faced the service porch and the rear yard. 'Thank you,' he repeated.

'What can I do to help, Bill?' I wanted to get down to business, whatever it was. I wanted to get home. I wanted to convince myself that I hadn't made a big mistake by agreeing to this impromptu house call.

'You being here helps.'

It wasn't what I wanted to hear from him. 'Bill, I'm glad you find my presence comforting. But my advice to you is simple: Tell the police everything you know. The journal, everything. If you have new information, they need to know it. Mallory's welfare is more important than anything else.'

'I appreciate your counsel. You were absolutely right about Rachel years ago. But I'm not sure you really understand the dilemma I'm in. Calling the police isn't an option.'

'Mallory's safety is the most important thing. Your legal situation is secondary.'

'I'm her father. She needs me. Both kids do.'

'I'm sure that's true, but—'

'But nothing. If someone had your daughter, or your wife, or both, you would do anything to get them back, wouldn't you? Anything?'

Once I had. Once when a madman was trying to break into my house I'd closed my eyes and pulled a trigger to protect my pregnant wife. I'd do it again if I had to. And again after that.

Bill had continued talking through my silent reverie; I wasn't sure if I'd missed anything. When I tuned back in he was saying, 'Like right now, if you didn't know where your family was, I bet you would do anything to find them, to make sure they were safe. Right?'

'Of course.'

'Do you?'

'Do I what?'

'Do you know where your wife and daughter are right now?'

What? 'What do you mean?' I was trying to keep my voice level. I was certain I was failing.

'Your family? Do you know where they are right now?'

No, I didn't know where they were. 'Right now? What are you saying, Bill?'

'Nothing. I'm just trying to describe my situation in a way that might make sense to another father. The desperation I'm feeling. Do you understand the desperation?'

'Are you threatening my family, Bill?'

'What on earth are you talking about?'

'Have you done something to my wife or daughter?'

'See? That's exactly what I'm talking about. Right now? I think you're beginning to get it. My desperation. That's good.'

'Answer my question.' I stood up. 'Have you done something to my family?'

A creaking sound pierced through the house. The floor? A door? Had I caused that?

'Did you hear that?' Bill asked. He stood, too.

'Yes. Is someone else here?'

'No. Maybe it was nothing. Old houses, you know.'

Was he unconcerned, or merely cavalier? I couldn't tell.

Another creak disturbed the quiet.

'Then again,' Bill said. 'I'm going to check around a little. You want to call your wife and daughter, ease your mind, you go right ahead.'

Bill stood and left the kitchen. Immediately, I pulled out my cell and phoned home. No answer. I tried Lauren's cell. No answer. I placed the phone in front of me on the table. My heart was pounding. Bill came back into the room.

'See anything?'

'No.' He spotted the phone on the table. 'Don't worry, I'm sure they're fine,' he said, as though he knew I hadn't reached Lauren.

Any pretense of patience gone from my voice, I asked, 'What can I do to help, Bill? You said this was about Mallory. Tell me what's going on or I'm leaving.'

Certain sounds are as clear as photographs. Glass

breaking is one of those sounds. The stark retort of shattering glass filled the house.

'Shit,' Bill said. He stood.

I stood, too. 'Where?' I whispered.

'Sounded like the basement.'

I wasn't so sure, but it wasn't my house.

He moved toward the stairs. 'I'm going down. Probably just some neighbor's kid trying to scare me. It's been like that around here.'

'I'll call nine-one-one.'

'No, this is my home. No police. I'll handle it. Stay here.'

He flicked on a light and disappeared down the basement stairs. I spotted a rack of knives on the kitchen counter and shuffled a little closer to them.

Before I reached the counter, all the lights in the house flashed off, at once.

70

I stumbled back toward the table to grab my phone and as I reached out I managed to push it over the edge onto the floor. The phone clattered and slid away into the darkness. I dropped down to my hands and knees to try to locate it.

'Alan!' Bill stage-whispered from the basement. 'Down here, please, hurry.'

'I'm calling for help.'

'Please, it's Mallory!'

The tunnel? I scrambled to my feet and felt my way toward the basement stairs, found them, and slowly started descending. A solitary step into the basement I ran into someone. The shock of the collision took my breath away.

'It's me,' Bill whispered. I could feel his breath on my face. 'Come on.'

He took my wrist and led me across a room and through a doorway. 'This is where the glass broke, I think.'

I couldn't see broken glass. But then, I couldn't see much. 'You said it was Mallory. Where is she?'

'What are you talking about?'

What? 'Where's the tunnel?' I asked.

'In the crawl space.'

Somewhere nearby, a door closed in the house. Bill released my arm and stepped away from me, back toward the door we'd just come through.

I moved in the same direction.

'Shhh,' he said.

'Is there a phone down here?' I whispered.

'Quiet. I need to listen.'

The door at the far side of the room we were in opened slowly. A figure paused in the doorway – a black silhouette against an almost black background. Burnt food on a cast-iron skillet.

Mallory? No. Too large, too masculine.

Bob? Maybe.

I was about to call Bob's name when the person's right arm began to rise and a brilliant flash blinded me and a deafening roar blasted my ears. Before I could even process the first explosion, another one erupted. Then, I thought, another. The figure's knees began to buckle and he grasped at the door frame with both hands.

The support did him no good. A second later he heaved forward and collapsed to the floor.

My hearing temporarily gone, my eyes useless in a basement dark as a moonless night, I was most aware of the smell of the burnt powder from the gun. I was trying to figure out what had just happened. Bill touched my arm and forced a flashlight into my hand. I flicked it on and saw the gun he was holding. It was a revolver. A big thing.

'Over here,' Bill said. I pointed the light in the direction of his voice. He'd stepped away from me and was standing in front of a gray electrical panel. With the benefit of the illumination he reached up and pulled hard at the main power circuit.

Instantly the lights in the house came back on.

With great relief I realized that I didn't recognize the man in the heap at the foot of the stairs. It definitely wasn't Bob.

The butt of a pistol had come to rest two inches from the man's nose. Had the man been holding it? I didn't remember hearing it clatter to the floor. I said, 'Who is it? Do you know him?'

Bill moved closer. 'It's Doyle.'

He didn't sound surprised.

71

I was.

'Doyle's already dead, Bill.'

'That must have been somebody else they found in the mountains. That's Doyle, right there.'

I used the toe of my shoe to move the pistol away, knelt, and placed my quivering fingers on the side of the man's neck. I couldn't find a pulse. I thought of Hannah a month before, the same fingers, the same result.

'Who was it that they found near Allenspark?' I asked.

'I don't know. I don't care. Doyle's dead for sure, now. For me, that's nothing but good news.'

Bill wasn't upset.

'Why . . . did you shoot him?'

'He broke into my house. You saw that.'

'He's been in your house a dozen times. Why did you shoot him?'

'You saw what happened. A broken window. An intruder in the dark. He was going to shoot me. Us.'

He stressed the words 'intruder' and 'dark.' I thought his explanation sounded rehearsed and I immediately questioned whether Bill knew that Doyle was going to be in his house, in his basement. 'Did you know he was coming over?'

Bill didn't answer me. 'Did you? Did you know he was coming over?'

He still didn't reply. I thought, *Damn, make my day.*

You set this up, you bastard.

Car thieves steal cars. Bank robbers rob banks. For Bill, this was the white van and the orthodontist all over again.

I started up the stairs to get my phone to call 911. When I was about halfway up I heard a woman's voice. 'Willy? You down there? What was that noise?'

72

Willy?

Rachel.

'Rachel? Baby?' Bill said.

This time he sounded surprised.

73

Sam didn't arrive first – some patrol cops did – but he was there within fifteen minutes.

He wasn't happy to find me in Bill Miller's house. He wasn't happy to hear Bill Miller claiming that he and I had been having a psychotherapy session when we heard the glass break. He wasn't happy to hear me concur with Bill that what he had told me prior to the shooting had to stay confidential.

What was Sam happy about?

I think he was reasonably pleased that Rachel Miller was there, and that she was insisting that her daughter, Mallory, was fine. 'She'll be here any minute. Any minute,' Rachel kept saying. 'Don't worry, don't worry.'

Before he and I were separated by the cops, Bill readily admitted shooting the intruder in his house, whom he continued to insist was the man he knew as his next-door neighbor, Doyle Chandler.

Sam parked me in the Millers' living room. 'You okay?' he asked.

I said I was.

'Good. What about Rachel?' he said to me. 'How did she look to you? As a shrink.'

'From what little I saw, not too bad. I suspect she's on

her meds. I'd have to evaluate her to be sure, but she looks much better than I would have predicted.'

'Do you believe what she's saying about Mallory?'

'I think she believes what she's saying about Mallory. It's either delusional, or it's not. I don't know her well enough to tell you which.'

'Thank you, Dr. Freud.'

'There's a chance she's telling the truth, Sam. That's a good thing. Hope, right? Has she said how she got here?'

'"With Mallory and her friend." I'm thinking Bob, the Camaro guy.'

'You never found him this morning?'

'No.'

'Is Bill claiming the shooting was a "make my day" thing?'

Colorado has a frontier-justice 'Get Out of Jail Free' law that permits citizens to use deadly force to protect personal property. Intrude on a Coloradan's homestead – and raise enough of a ruckus while you're at it – and you had better hope that the homeowner isn't armed, because he or she has every legal right to blow you to smithereens, even if you're not threatening any imminent bodily harm. The law is popularly known as the 'Make My Day' law.

'Yeah,' Sam said. 'He is. Loudly. Was it?'

'I'm not a lawyer, but probably. Glass broke, power went out, suddenly the guy is there in the basement. Bill shot him. Three times, I think.'

'Three?'

'Yeah. I think three. He kept shooting.'

'Was the guy armed?'

'It was dark. After the lights were back on, I saw a gun next to him on the floor.'

'All sounds pretty convenient.'

'Maybe, I don't know. Bill's been through a lot.'

'The broken glass? You see it?' Sam asked.

'No.'

'Wasn't a window. Somebody put a couple of clear vases or something on the sill in the basement window well. Anyone who opened the window would have knocked them off. I find that kind of . . . suspicious.'

'People put stuff on windowsills all the time.'

'Window was unlocked,' Sam said. 'No sign it was forced.'

'A lot of people have been in and out of this house lately.'

'You sticking up for him?'

I didn't want to go there. 'Bill said the guy he shot was Doyle, Sam. Is that possible?'

'Yeah, I heard. Maybe he has a twin,' he said. 'Only thing I know for certain about this whole mess is that there are way too many Doyle Chandlers around for my taste.' He stood up. 'Tell me again, why were you here?'

I looked him in the eye and told him it was privileged, which told him almost all he needed to know.

Diane wasn't in danger anymore. I had secrets to keep.

'Figured.' He ran his fingers through his hair while he continued to stare at me. His next sentence surprised me. 'Scott Truscott says you solved the Hannah Grant thing.'

I shrugged. 'I had a thought; I shared it with him. He put it all together; I guess the coroner agreed.'

Sam's raised eyebrows mocked me more than his words did. 'A thought? You had a thought? You seem to have a lot of thoughts.' He paused. 'And a lot of sources.'

I took the comment exactly as Sam intended it – as an accusation.

A patrol cop stuck her head into the room and said, 'Detective? That Cadillac? The BOLO? We got it.'

'Where?'

'CU. Parking lot near the stadium. SWAT's responding.'

He looked at me, waiting to see if I was going to be obstinate. I surprised him, I think. I said, 'Duane Labs. Plasma physics. Fourth floor.'

Sam repeated the location into his radio as he rushed from the room, leaving me alone.

I walked to a beat-up mahogany secretaire, picked up the telephone, and called my house. Lauren and Grace were safely home from a wonderful dress-up afternoon, enjoying high tea at the Brown Palace in Denver. Turned out that Gracie loved scones and clotted cream and peppermint tea in china cups, and was absolutely over the moon for cucumber sandwiches. I gave Lauren a concise version of what was going on in Boulder and assured her I'd be fine. After we hung up I dialed a second number from memory.

'Cozy?' I said. 'Hate to ruin your Saturday, but someone I know needs a lawyer.'

74

Bob had indeed told Mallory about the tunnel.

She'd used it on Christmas night to get away from the bad guy she had convinced herself was waiting to do to her what had been done eight years before to her young friend. She'd discovered Bob watching movies in Doyle's theater, and had asked him for help in getting away.

Bob had complied.

Mallory had stayed in Bob's flat for the first few days after she'd left home. Once she'd recovered from her Christmas night fright, she ended up mostly terrified about the ruckus she'd caused by running away, and fearful of the repercussions she was sure she would face when she surfaced. She never was quite sure what to make of the fact that the therapist from whom she'd sought help had died.

Out of boredom as much as anything, she finally cajoled Bob into a road trip to see 'our mothers.'

Their first stop was Las Vegas, where they picked up Rachel. The second stop was the assisted-living facility in southern Colorado where the trio paid a brief visit to Bob's mother. That's where Bob switched the Camaro – it had developed a problem with its clutch – for his mother's pale-yellow '88 DeVille, which was almost, but not quite, as cherry as Bob's '60s muscle car.

After the real fake Doyle was killed by Bill Miller in his basement, the police didn't have too much difficulty piecing together the identity of the fake fake Doyle.

The man whose body had been discovered in the shallow grave near Allenspark turned out to be a homeless man named Eric Brewster whom Doyle had apparently hired to be an unidentifiable corpse rotting in the woods. That probably wasn't the job description he'd offered Brewster when he'd recruited him off the streets of Cheyenne, but that was the job the poor man got. Doyle was ready for the Doyle Chandler identity to die, and he'd picked Brewster carefully, choosing a man about his size and coloring. He gave Brewster some of his own clothes before he led him out into the woods and shot him in the head. Doyle planted his ID on the body, reasonably figuring that a winter and spring in the elements would destroy any clues, except DNA, as to who the dead man really was. Without a sample for matching, he knew the DNA wouldn't do law enforcement any good.

Doyle Chandler would be dead for at least the second time.

Raoul brought Diane home on a medical jet charter on Monday, the day after he rescued her. Medically she was going to be okay. Psychologically? We held our breaths; time would tell. She'd have love and support, all she needed. Would it be enough? I hoped it would. Diane was tough.

She used Scott Truscott's assessment that Hannah Grant's death was a tragic accident as a crutch to help herself get back on her feet. I wasn't too surprised that Diane was back to work within a week. The first patient she saw on her initial day back?

Fittingly, it was the Cheetos lady. We passed each other in the hall as Diane led the woman from the waiting room to her office. She smiled at me as though we were buddies.

All, apparently, was forgiven.

With Diane safe, and Bob safe, and Mallory safe, I went back to keeping secrets. I was well aware that had Raoul found Diane even half a day later, I probably would have spilled all the beans I had on Bill Miller. With my friend out of harm's way, though, I knew that revealing what I'd learned from my patients would have been nothing more than a self-destructive act of reprisal.

Still, believe me, I had considered it.

I didn't reveal what I knew about Bill and Walter and the orthodontist. I'd initially learned all those things in my role as a psychologist, and couldn't rationalize revealing them. Did I feel good about keeping those secrets? No, I didn't.

Deep down, I'm quite fond of the idea of justice. But, as fond as I am of justice, it's not the business that I'm in.

Walter's family soon reported him missing, but I kept my mouth shut about the location of his body. Raoul did, too. I wouldn't have known anything about Walter if I hadn't been treating Bill, so I considered that information privileged. Was I haunted by the fact that I had knowledge that could help end a family's fruitless search for a missing husband and father?

Yes, I was.

Nor did I ever publicly share my suspicions that Bill had enticed Doyle back to his house so he could murder him, once and for all, or that I thought he'd arranged for me to be there as his hapless witness. I couldn't prove any of it, but I believed it all to be true. I think Sam did, too. He told me that the police had some phone records that provided circumstantial support to the theory.

But Sam didn't think he could prove it either. Lauren admitted that when the DA reviewed the evidence, she'd concurred.

The Millers became a family again: Mallory was home, Reese came back from his sabbatical with out-of-state relatives, and Rachel moved back into the house. Would the familial bliss last? I had my doubts. Mary Black, still consumed with her triplets, referred Rachel to a psychiatrist in Denver who was having success treating people with symptoms like Rachel's with some innovative pharmaceutical cocktails.

Miracles happen sometimes. Rachel needed one, probably deserved one.

Bill?

As the dust was starting to settle I phoned him, and asked politely for one last session.

He declined.

I rephrased my request, turning it into something a little less polite and a little stronger than an invitation. He relented, as I knew he would, and when he came to my office to see me I didn't bother to waste any time on therapeutic niceties. I told him I wanted both of his kids in therapy, and gave him the names of the carefully chosen therapists I wanted each of them to see. I made it clear that I wasn't making a suggestion; the consequences of not heeding my advice would be harsh.

'Yeah?' he said, cocky as shit. His attitude was, 'What the hell can you do to me now?'

I had placed my walnut-framed Colorado psychologist's license upside down on the table between us.

'Yeah,' I said, failing to match his cockiness.

He crossed his arms. 'I don't think so, although I appreciate your concern.'

It was readily apparent that he didn't actually appreciate my concern. I reached down to the table and flipped the frame right-side up. In case he didn't recognize the parchment document, I said, 'That's my psychology license.'

He looked down at it. 'So?'

'I'm willing to lose it.'

He eyed me suspiciously. Disbelieving my resolve, I think.

I added, 'What are you willing to lose, Bill?'

'You wouldn't.'

I handed him a copy of a letter that I'd mailed the day before. 'Read this. All it lacks is a name. Your name, actually.'

He took a moment to read the letter.

'You release my name like this, you'll never work again.'

'Maybe. My colleagues on the state ethics board have always proven themselves to be rather lenient, even to a fault. Regardless, I'm willing to take the risk. If it does come to losing my license, I think I can find work, but something tells me it won't come to that. Why? Because I don't think you really want your role in this whole thing examined by a panel of skeptical strangers with Ph.D.s.'

Was I blackmailing him?

Yes.

Bill knew plenty about blackmail. He'd seen it from both sides.

Ultimately, he accepted my prescription about his children because he didn't have much choice. How did I know he followed through? Both therapists called and thanked me for referring the kids. I felt some consolation that Reese and Mallory were getting the best mental health care possible. Would it be enough to save them?

In truth, probably not. I wasn't even sure what saving them would look like. But I held out hope for them anyway.

75

The letter that I'd mailed the day before I met with Bill Miller?

The head of the Ethics Committee of the Colorado Psychological Association didn't know exactly what to do with it.

Psychologists don't usually turn themselves in for ethical violations.

But I did; I turned myself in for multiple violations of the ethical code of the American Psychological Association.

There's a psychological phenomenon, an ego defense if you will, called undoing, or sometimes, doing-undoing. A husband sends flowers to his wife the day after he flirts shamelessly with his secretary. A mother makes a special dessert for her daughter after she sentences the kid to death row for not putting the cap back on a tube of toothpaste. It's unconscious psychological misdirection – the substitution of an act that is acceptable to the ego for something that was not. In the world of psychological defenses, it's the great cosmic chalkboard eraser.

Turning myself in for unethical conduct was my own twisted version of doing-undoing.

What I'd prepared and submitted to the ethics board

was a detailed account of my multiple professional transgressions in the clinical care of both Bill Miller and Bob Brandt. Although I had to withhold plenty of specifics – including my patients' names – I put in sufficient evidence of misjudgment to make my myriad ethical lapses crystal clear to my colleagues.

I'd also sought written permission from both Bob and Bill to release their names to the ethics investigators, but both, not surprisingly, chose anonymity and declined to participate in the inquiry. Neither was eager to prolong public scrutiny of their behavior. Without the cooperation of the patients involved the board had little to go on other than my self-damning appraisal of my own professional conduct.

The head of the board phoned and asked me, mildly exasperated, what I thought they should do with me.

I suggested a sanction: a full year's monitored supervision of my practice by a senior, respected psychologist.

The board greedily concurred, content to have the matter behind them.

I felt a little better, but not much. As an ego balm, doing-undoing is a notoriously ineffective palliative. And when you know you're doing it – and employ it without the insulation of unconscious motivation – as I was, undoing amounts to little more than a half-hearted *mea culpa*.

76

Bob?

Our regular Tuesday at 4:15 came around slightly less than forty-eight hours after he and Mallory had been picked up by the police in the plasma physics reception area in the Duane Building at CU. Mallory was watching Bob deadhead his Christmas begonia when the first few SWAT officers burst into the room and scared the crap out of both of them.

Head down, as usual, he walked into my office for his appointment at the regular time. He plopped his backpack onto the floor and sat across from me without a word of greeting.

We'd been there, literally, a hundred times before.

Bob had spent one night stewing in police custody while Cozy Maitlin convinced the authorities that his client was guilty of nothing more than piss-poor judgment. Mallory had repeatedly denied that Bob had ever coerced her to do anything, denied that he encouraged her to run away, vigorously maintained that the road trip had been her idea, and asserted that he'd never placed a hand on her during their entire time together. Mallory's only actual complaints about Bob were that he wasn't very friendly and hardly ever said a word that wasn't about cars or board games.

Rachel Miller confirmed that Bob had been a well-behaved, if boring, companion to her and her daughter.

The police discovered no evidence to the contrary. None.

I waited only a moment for him to settle onto his chair before I said, 'Hello.'

He was staring at his hands. I supposed that Bob knew that I had arranged for Cozy to represent him. Although Bob Brandt and Cozier Maitlin were probably the oddest client-attorney pairing since Michael Jackson and anybody, I suspected that Cozy would have told Bob how lucky he was to have him for a lawyer. I doubted Bob would mention it to me, and I wondered if I should bring it up if he didn't.

'Am I going to be charged?' he said, finally breaking the silence, and interrupting my reverie long before I'd reached anything approximating a decision.

With kidnapping? Didn't look like it, but that was definitely a question that should be directed to Cozy, not to me. It was my turn, though, so I said, 'Charged for what?'

'For last week.'

Oh. 'The session you missed? No, I won't bill you for that.'

Bob acknowledged me with a nod, but he didn't thank me. Did I expect him to? No, not really.

When he finally raised his face enough so that I could see it, I spotted a cold sore the size of a lug nut on his lower lip. The rounded wound was fresh and blistered. Had to hurt. I thought, *Stress*. He didn't speak again for a while. Then, 'I almost lost my job. It was stupid.'

'What was stupid?' I could have asked. But the recent idiocy options were numerous. Too numerous. Plenty by him, plenty by me.

More by him.

I waited. The Kinko's box sat beside me on the small table next to my chair. Had Bob seen it when he walked in? I hadn't noticed him even glancing in my direction.

'She asked. I didn't kidnap her. Sheesh.'

No half head-shake, just the 'sheesh.'

Although technically it was my turn to speak, Bob said, 'I shouldn't have shown her the tunnel in the first place.'

I could have argued with him at that point, suggesting that maybe what he shouldn't have done was drive a minor who was the subject of a national manhunt across state lines, but time was on my side. An entire year of Tuesdays littered the calendar ahead. Bob and I would get there eventually.

'She was scared after that therapist died,' he said. 'I thought she should know how to get out of her house.'

His tone, I thought, was defensive, which wasn't too surprising. But was Mallory's fear really the way Bob was going to try to rationalize his decision to help her stay hidden when the whole world was frantically looking for her? I suspected not.

Why? Pulling off that argument would require that Bob convince me that he'd suddenly developed a capacity for empathy. Sadly, the events of the previous couple of weeks would no more leave Bob with empathy than they would leave Bill Miller with a well-functioning superego. 'Go on,' I said.

He sighed before he turned away, reached down, and rooted around in his rucksack. He lifted out an electronic device about the size of a paperback book and held it up for me to see.

I couldn't help but smile. It was a fancy, programmable remote control. The one from Doyle's basement, no doubt.

'Perhaps you should give that to your attorney,' I suggested.

He stuffed the remote back into the daypack and gazed out the window. The southern sky warned of dusk. He said, 'She doesn't look fourteen.'

My spleen didn't spasm. I allowed the force of gravity to press me solidly against my chair.

'Tell me,' I said.

I thought I'd try to be a therapist for a while.

Acknowledgments

As usual, I got a lot of help.

My gratitude to the kind, talented people at Dutton, especially Carole Baron and Brian Tart, and to my agent, Lynn Nesbit.

Jane Davis, Elyse Morgan, and Al Silverman continue to support me in ways that are personal as well as professional. I've said thanks. I'll say it again, knowing it's not enough. Nancy Hall, once more, brought her critical eye to the process.

If I wore one, I'd tip my hat to Virginia Danna and Darrell C. R. Olson, Sr. Call it courage, call it blind faith, but they paid good money to charity to have their names used for characters in this book. I think I'll just call it generosity. Norm Clarke, on the other hand, was a draftee. His gracious, one-of-a-kind introduction to Las Vegas and his willingness to let me give him an important role in the story were much appreciated.

Robert Greer, who does more things well than anyone I've ever met (other than perhaps his late wife, Phyllis), provided some consultation about one of his many specialties. And although I've long been indebted to them for pushing the swing, the Limericks – Jeffrey and Patricia – deserve some fresh credit for one of this book's small secrets.

Xan, Rose, and my mother, Sara White Kellas, continue not to be surprised that I'm able to do this. They believe, and what is better than that?